THE MAGICAL BEINGS' REHABILITATION CENTER: THE COMPLETE SERIES

Vampires Drink Tomato Juice, Goblins Wear Suits, and The Lost Files of the Magical Beings' Rehabilitation Center

K. M. SHEA

THE MAGICAL BEINGS' REHABILITATION CENTER: THE COMPLETE SERIES

Cover design by Myrrhlynn

www.kmshea.com

ISBN: 978-1-950635-01-6

Created with Vellum

Vampires Drink Tomato Juice

THE MAGICAL BEINGS' REHABILITATION CENTER: BOOK 1

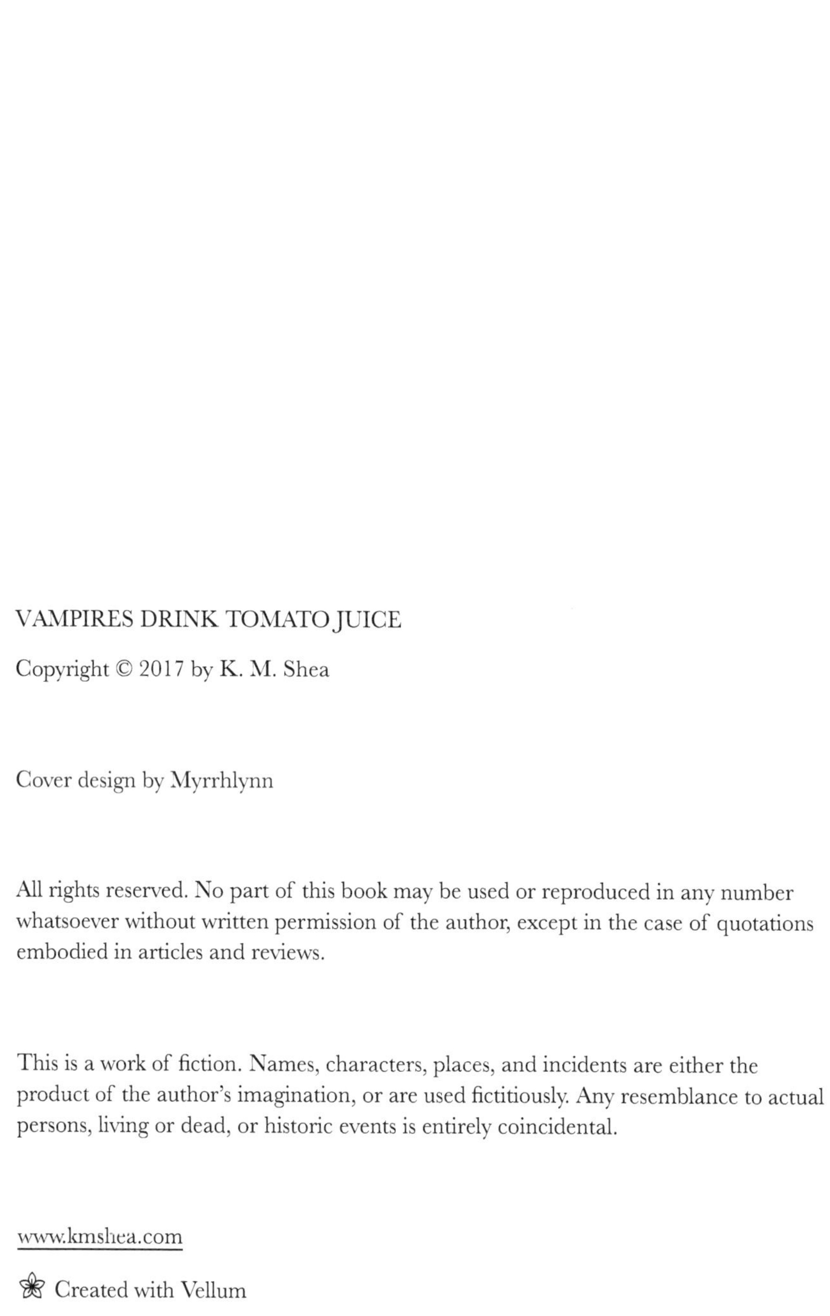

VAMPIRES DRINK TOMATO JUICE

Cover design by Myrrhlynn

www.kmshea.com

Created with Vellum

For Sara,
Who loves this series more than it deserves.

1

My Life Explodes

I have to break it to you: humans aren't the only beings on the planet. I know, I know; I sound like some kind of UFO freak or Sci Fi nerd, but you're thinking about the wrong thing. Try picturing something more…*magical*—like a character you would find in a Disney movie or in one of those paranormal books.

Yeah, that's right. Magical beings live among us.

This is your fault, Dave. I wouldn't sound like a lunatic if I hadn't met you, you disappointing vampire.

I'm not a psycho. I used to be normal. I hung out with my best friend, Fran. I went to school, but my afternoons were *free*!

And then I met Dave.

Now, instead of watching my favorite shows or hanging out with my friends, I rush to Chicago to put flea collars on werewolves. I tutor elves, shove tomato juice down the throats of vampires, argue with a stubborn Pooka, do paperwork for cyclops, and more.

Did I mention that THIS IS YOUR FAULT, DAVE?

Welcome to the MBRC, the **M**agical **B**eings' **R**ehabilitation **C**enter.

My name is Morgan L. Fae. (Yeah, it's close to the legendary

Morgan le Fay. Even at my birth, the universe was already playing cosmic jokes on me.)

I'm from a relatively normal family, and I was your typical teenage girl—until I hit age 16 and my Spanish teacher left the week after homecoming on maternity leave.

That was how I met Dave, the stupid and chubby vampire.

"Class, this is Mr. Smith," Vice Principal Russ announced as I flipped through my Spanish workbook. "He will be your substitute teacher until Mrs. Allen returns from her maternity leave."

I looked up from my homework, wondering what kind of person would be standing in for my strict Spanish teacher.

Mr. Smith was short and had a shock of red hair that drew attention to his pasty, pale skin. He looked like he was in his 40s. His hairline was creeping towards the back of his head, and his beer belly drooped over his pants.

He was an average guy as far as substitute teachers go.

"Sí!" Mr. Smith beamed. "Gracias, Señor Russ! I am very excited to be here in first-year Spanish!"

"Second-year Spanish," Mr. Russ said.

"Exactly! Second-year Spanish!"

"I expect you all to be on your best behavior. That means *you*, Mr. Wilkins," Mr. Russ said, eyeing a junior on the other side of the room.

The junior protested that he was always good, and Mr. Russ left with a disbelieving snort.

"Right…Hóla?" Mr. Smith said, tipping his head. "We should start with a vocabulary review of the chapter."

The class stared at him before Toni and Dani, two girls from the school's popular clique, blew him off and started swapping homecoming pictures. Scott, the Mr. Wilkins Mr. Russ had warned, threw jelly beans at a poor girl named Stephanie. Meanwhile, Mr. Smith tried to bumble through the lesson.

"Okay class, so el menu is the menu and…el…el cocinero is the cook. What is la mesa?"

One girl, Rosaline, the best Spanish student in our class, raised her hand with an air of superiority. "The table," she said.

"Right you are, mortal," Mr. Smith said, paging through the book.

Those of us who were listening swapped shrugs. We had been taught by weirder people before.

"Who can tell me what la m-mesera means?" our temporary teacher asked, ignored by half of the class.

I'm not sure who was more relieved, us or him, when the bell rang. My classmates scrambled to gather their books and hurried off to their new destinations. I was one of the last to leave, finding it difficult to shove my Spanish book in my bag. Fran, my best friend since elementary school, is the secretary for the sophomore student council. She uses my backpack as a billboard or storage unit for whatever event the student council has scheduled next. This time it was leftover homecoming parade flyers.

As I turned to go, I noticed Mr. Smith hefting a bottle of tomato juice onto his desk. He stared at it, his face scrunching up with dislike, uncapped it, and drank a mouthful.

"Blech," he said as I left the room.

He was undeniably odd.

Any thought of Mr. Smith's weirdness disappeared the next day. "Class, I would like to introduce you to a new student, Frey Christenson," Mr. Smith beamed.

The class stared.

Frey Christenson was a tall, lean guy with a track star's build. His skin was pale, not the paper shade of the sub's skin, but more like the white-blue shades of snow. His hair was silver. It was a nearly colorless shade of blonde that can only be achieved with the help of dye, but it glinted in the school's fluorescent light.

"Hey," Frey smiled, dazzling us with his vibrant, forest-green eyes.

"Please take a seat, Frey. Th-Gracias," Mr. Smith said, waving the teenager away.

Frey walked across the room with ease, totally aware of all the female eyeballs glued to him, and chose a spot on my side of the room. He sat near the front of the classroom, spaced between two of my friends—Samantha and Emily. It looked like I would be getting the scoop about Frey at lunch.

Toni and Dani frowned. No doubt they wanted the new kid to sit near them (there was an empty seat behind Toni because the duo had chased away a geeky guy named Rob the first week of class) and felt slighted that he chose to be closer to the front of the room.

I winced sympathetically. Frey had just committed social suicide. But he was so gorgeous, he might, eventually, be forgiven.

"Okay, time to learn more Spanish tenses. But first, let's review the months!" Mr. Smith said.

Throughout the lesson, Mr. Smith occasionally glanced at Frey, as though he were searching for some kind of approval. The new boy stared at him, his long body neatly folded in his desk. I didn't think about it—not because I'm not observant or something. I just had more important things to attend to. Like Brent Patterson—the guy I've had a crush on since sixth grade. He was in my American Government class later that day.

Class progressed, Mr. Smith sweated, and the lunch bell rang. I gathered up my things and left with my classmates. I stopped at my locker to stow my stuff so I wouldn't have to lug it with me to lunch.

"Hey, Morgan. Did you ask your sub about taking down the homecoming flyers and putting up the penny drive posters?" Fran asked, nearly tackling me into my locker.

"I knew I forgot something. There was this new kid who is absolutely *gorgeous*! But never mind, I'll tell you at lunch if Samantha and Emily don't. Save me a spot at the table," I said, turning back in the direction of my classroom, some of Fran's flyers in my hands.

"Where are you going?" Fran shouted.

"To ask Mr. Smith," I said, hurrying up the hallways. By the time I reached the Spanish classrooms again, the bell rang, announcing the next class period had started. Thankfully, I knew Mr. Smith had lunch break now, so I wouldn't be interrupting him.

"Hey, Mr. Smith, I have a question," I called as I opened the door before freezing like a frightened deer.

"You have to drink it, Dave," Frey, the hot new student, snarled, practically force-feeding the Spanish sub a bottle of tomato juice.

"No, no, no! I'm sick of it! I can't stand it. You try sipping that stuff for a decade. I want blood! The real stuff," Mr. Smith complained, fighting his student. He managed to push the teenager away from him.

Then he hissed at Frey.

No joke.

He literally bared his teeth at him—his canines were a little over-pronounced—and *hissed.* Like a cat.

"I'm here as your handler to make your rehabilitation easier, Dave," Frey said, not at all fazed by the hiss. "You will listen to me. Don't make me get stern, Dave."

"Werewolves suck," Mr. Smith, AKA Dave, announced.

"I warned you, Dave," Frey said, crouching down.

I'm still not exactly sure what happened next. One moment, Frey stood in the classroom, and I blinked. When I opened my eyes, there was a white, arctic wolf snapping at Mr. Smith with some serious teeth.

"Holy crap!" I said, staring wide-eyed at the pair.

Mr. Smith and the white wolf swung around and stared at me. It was then that my brain concluded that Frey was, in fact, a werewolf. And Mr. Smith? A vampire.

All I can say is that the *Twilight* books *lied.*

2

The Truth about Vampires (and Werewolves!)

I stared at my teacher and the new student, who was still a dog. They stared back. I backed out of the room, closing the door in front of me. I studied the door for a second before shuffling away, Fran's flyers still clutched in my hands.

Within seconds Mr. Smith, the vampire, and the new kid descended on me.

"Hey, hey, hey! Where are you going?" Frey the werewolf asked, once again in a human body.

"To get my head checked," I said, wandering in the general direction of the nurse's office.

I'm not stupid. *Harry Potter*, *Twilight*...I know those books aren't real. They're fiction, okay? Fiction. Make believe. I might like reading them, but the idea of actually sharing the world with vampires and werewolves did **not** give me a warm, tingly feeling.

Not to mention that if there WERE such a thing as vampires, they would not be overweight, middle-aged men whose hair seemed to be eating itself.

Therefore, there was only one option: there was something severely wrong with me. Maybe I would have to see a specialist.

"If she tells anyone what she saw..." Frey the werewolf growled.

"Yeah, yeah," the vampire said before grabbing me by the elbow. "Why don't you come back to the Spanish room with us and sit down miss…um…"

"She's your *student,* and you don't even know her name?" Frey appropriately howled.

"Well, *sooorry*! It's my second day," Mr. Smith whined.

"Two days in, and you've blown your cover. That has to be a record."

"It's Morgan, Mr. Smith. My name is Morgan."

"Right, Miss Morgan, come along. And I insist you call me Dave," Dave the chubby vampire said, turning me around and guiding me back to the Spanish room with a helping hand on my elbow.

As he and Frey escorted me into the Spanish room, a part of me reasoned that if they really were a vampire and werewolf, I (most likely their food of choice) should not walk into a room with them, alone. I mercilessly shut that part of me up and reminded myself that vampires and werewolves were fictitious creatures the entertainment industry was cashing in on.

"Miss Morgan, about what you saw," Dave nervously laughed.

"Forget it. She saw the whole thing," Frey shrugged, dropping his slender track star body into Dave's chair. "I'll take her to the MBRC to get her memory wiped."

"What?" I asked.

Dave frowned. "Is that really necessary? Maybe they can hypnotize her."

Frey shook his head, ruffling his silver hair. "The best hypnotizer we have is a siren who just left to help rehabilitate a flock of phoenixes two days ago. Plus, hypnotizing doesn't have the same memory-free guarantee, and it might not stick. She'll have to be wiped."

"But that always makes mortals loony. They're never the same after," Dave argued.

"Um, I am personally in favor of hypnotizing," I said

"See!" Dave triumphantly folded his arms.

"As far as we're concerned, you don't get a choice," Frey said to me before turning to Dave. "I'll take her to the MBRC right now. Cover for me while I'm gone?"

"How?" Dave asked.

"You're a teacher. Say I had to be sent home or something. Just. Don't. Screw. Up. While. I'm. Gone," Frey said, emphasizing his speech by poking Dave the vampire in the chest with every word. "Okay, let's go," Frey said, grabbing me by the arm before sweeping me out of the room.

Before I knew it, we were blowing out of the front doors of the school, heading for the train station several blocks down.

"Um, we need to sign out in order to leave school grounds during lunch hours," I said.

"Ahhh, Morgan. So human. So tiny. I have bigger worries than getting approved permission to leave," Frey sighed, still yanking me along with his iron grip.

"Where are we going?" I asked, playing with the idea of making a break for it. I still had Fran's flyers. Maybe I could throw them at him? If I was lucky, I would give him a paper cut on his pretty face.

"To the MBRC: the Magical Beings' Rehabilitation Center," Frey replied.

"What?"

"Try not to think too hard about it. You won't remember any of this in an hour," Frey said.

Within minutes, Frey forcibly escorted me up to the train platform, kindly purchased round-way tickets for both of us, and held me rooted to his side as we waited for the train to Chicago to arrive. (He made me throw out Fran's flyers while we were there.)

Oakdale, the suburban city where I live, is just a fifteen-minute express train ride away from Chicago.

As I stood on the platform, the easily excitable part of me—which I was beginning to suspect was the idealistic, childish, romantic part of me—wondered if we were going to walk through a pillar like Harry Potter, or if we were waiting for a train to go flying past us like in the Chronicles of Narnia.

It was neither.

The train to Chicago came; Frey pulled me onto it, and we settled down in a seat, Frey sandwiching me against the window.

The conductor came around to punch our tickets. It was an older gentleman with hair as silvery as Frey's. He eyed Frey and me beneath bushy eyebrows. "Shouldn't you kids be in school?" he suggested.

Frey looked bored and tossed his arm across my shoulders. "We're doing just that. We're college students, sir. Man, do I really look that young, Morgan? We get asked that question practically every other *day*," Frey said, his voice hitching like a whining dog.

The conductor shook his head and moved on. I doubt he believed us. I wouldn't believe us. Ignoring the fact that we looked too young for college, *we weren't carrying backpacks or books.*

"Sorry about this," Frey apologized, removing his arm the second the conductor entered the next car. "Thank you for cooperating. I was surprised you didn't scream when you saw us fighting."

"Why would I scream? There's no such thing as vampires or werewolves," I firmly said.

Frey snorted. "So you're one of those."

"What?"

"One of the deniers. There are two types of people in this world, Morgan. The deniers and the screamers. Well, three types if you count the fainters, but I lob that bunch in with the screamers."

"Huh?"

"When people see something otherworldly like Dave or me, they will either deny its existence even though the proof is smacking them in the face, or they will scream and/or faint."

"I see."

"Yeah."

We were silent the rest of the train ride. We piled out of the car with all of the other passengers at Chicago's Union Station. Frey led me through the station, navigating our way past other trains. I followed him until we reached a set of stairs that would lead up to the surface of the station. I automatically tried to go up, but Frey continued on our path.

We separated for a second before Frey's grip on my arm snapped us back together like a bungee cord.

"Aren't we going up?" I asked.

"Nope. This way," Frey said, tipping his head.

I followed him past several food vendors and information desks, heading for a darkened wall I had never really noticed.

Frey walked up to a door that was marked "employees only" and pushed it open, dragging me after him.

At this point, I was beginning to wonder if I was about to be murdered.

We walked through some kind of boiler room, went down several sets of stairs, passed through two more employees-only doors, and halted outside a giant iron door where this *huge* guy was seated.

"What are you doing here, Frey? I thought your case student is working in Oakdale?" the big guy said. His voice was low and so loud I swear I could feel the ground rumble beneath my feet. (Did I mention he was *big*?)

"Hey, Tiny. We had a security leak," Frey said, cocking his head in my direction. "We're here to get her memory wiped."

"Hi," I said, waving weakly.

The giant—no, he couldn't be a *real* giant—sympathetically smiled at me. "Sorry about this. We appreciate your cooperation. Let me take down the barrier," Tiny said before turning around and fumbling with some gears.

A bell tolled, and the giant iron doors faded, leaving behind an equally giant wooden door, which the huge guy opened for us.

"Enjoy your stay," he cheerfully said.

"Thank you," I said. "What was that?" I asked as Frey and I entered the doors and walked down a dimly lit hallway.

"This place is guarded by a magical barrier. We can't have outsiders getting in here. Tiny is one of the guards."

"And what place are you referring to?" I asked, seeing a light at the end of the hallway. (Here I *really* started to worry that I was going to die.)

"This place. Morgan, welcome to the Magical Beings' Rehabilitation Center," Frey announced as we left the hallway.

My mind broke.

The dark hallway opened up into an auditorium-sized room that had to be several stories tall. Rooms and hallways branched off in every direction. The floor was tiled marble, and the architecture was beautiful, mirroring Union Station, but what was remarkable about it was the beings that swarmed it. Elves, fairies, nymphs, dryads, fauns, werewolves, vampires, chimeras, brownies, enchanters, shapeshifters, dragons—*any* kind of magical creature you can imagine, and then some—strolled through the rehabilitation center. At that time, I didn't even know the names of all the animals, beings, and creatures that slithered, walked, and flew around me.

A woolly mammoth ambled past, smacking its baby with its trunk when it stopped to stare at me.

A herd of white unicorns followed it, gossiping and twittering to each other like elderly women.

"What did that mammoth stop for?"

"I'm not sure."

"Probably that human over there."

"The country bumpkins must have never seen one before."

"Be nice, Pink Sky! Not everyone has received the education we have."

The unicorns simpered to each other as they moved on.

Nearby, a giant nearly trod on a pair of hobgoblins, getting a stir out of them, "Hey, buddy! Watch where you're going! We're walking here!"

In the center of the room was a hexagon-shaped information desk. In it sat a chatty, three-foot-tall hobgoblin who answered about six phones while sending out a dozen emails, a large lizard/gator creature who patiently leaned over the desk and explained to a family of dwarves that mining in the rehabilitation center was strictly prohibited, a regal-looking centaur, a tiny fairy, and a baby dragon that chased after the fairy.

"Come on. This way," Frey said, dragging me in the direction of the desk. "Hey Toby, is Dr. Creamintin in?"

The hobgoblin, who was rail thin and an interesting shade between gray and pale green, didn't look up as he cranked out a hundred emails per minute.

"Just one second Hold please If you'll wait I'll find out for you It will be one moment," the hobgoblin said without taking a breath.

Frey leaned against the desk. "Toby, I thought as part of your rehabilitation program, you're supposed to stop drinking coffee."

I stared at the tiny fairy, which was probably the height of my hand. He whistled at me, suggestively wriggled his eyebrows, and cat-called. Because he was sidetracked by me, the baby dragon snatched him out of the air.

"I'm not being rehabilitated am I no sir-ee I'm working **in** the rehabilitation center There's a big difference you know because that means I'm not being rehabilitated Yes Dr. Creamintin is in and he is available Shall I message him that you're coming?"

"Yeah, thanks. See you guys," Frey said, waving farewell.

"Goodbye, Frey," the centaur bowed.

"Doggy! Spit Gristles out this instant! You have no idea where he's been," the gator/lizard creature lectured the baby dragon as we left.

Frey led me through the main chamber, barely yanking me into a hallway in time to avoid being run over by a huge dinosaur.

"I thought dinosaurs were extinct," I whispered to Frey, staring over my shoulder as I followed him down the hallway.

"No way," Frey snorted. "They were tired of the racism, or in their case speciesism, so they decided to go underground with the woolly mammoths, chimeras, and pegasus. The Fairy Council ruled that the dragons should hide with them, but those greedy guts fought the proclamation until the knights started hunting them down in the medieval era."

"So, the whole asteroid thing?" I asked.

"A sham. And here we are," Frey said, pausing outside an ordinary-looking door. "Dr. Creamintin is one of the doctors who help magical beings rehabilitate into normal, mortal society. Either he or one of his staff members can easily wipe your memory for us," Frey said before opening the door.

A ruffled-looking owl the size of a barn cat was fluttering in the air, shouting at a wincing faun. "I told you to keep your glamour on at *all times*, you stupid goat!"

"You didn't mention Dr. Creamintin was an owl," I observed.

"Oh, that's his assistant, Aristotle. Dr. Creamintin is a sorcerer," Frey said, herding me farther into the doctor's office as the shouting owl followed the faun into a back room.

"How many times do I have to tell you, boy? I'm an enchanter —not a sorcerer," an old voice warbled.

"Dr. Creamintin, I'm so glad you could see us on such short notice," Frey smiled, reaching out to shake hands with an old man. He had shaggy white hair, a long, well-trimmed beard, and a craggy nose. Dr. Creamintin looked like a stereotypical illustration of Merlin, King Arthur's legendary wizard, except he wore a lab coat instead of wizard robes.

"No problem, no problem at all. Sorry, but all of my examination rooms are full at the moment. We'll have to talk here. What is this trip about, my boy?"

I looked around, calmly taking in the strange sights. (I was handling this all very nicely.)

The receptionist was a mermaid, I kid you not. She sat in a tub of water behind the desk, a headset strapped to her head. She typed away on her computer, occasionally stopping to adjust the straps on her shell bikini.

There were shrieks and snorts of laughter coming from the examination rooms behind her. The doors were closed, so I wasn't sure what was back there. Besides Frey and me, there were three other patients seated in padded chairs in the waiting area.

One patient was a nervous-looking pixie who kept rolling a gold coin across her tiny knuckles. The second patient was what I would eventually learn to call a gnome. Don't be fooled by those ridiculous lawn statues; gnomes actually look a lot like short monks.

Finally, there was a young dryad, a tree spirit, who was standing in front of a large mirror, fussing with her clothes. The poor thing looked like she was *trying* to be a human but had failed pitifully.

She was wearing a pair of bootcut jeans and a green, long-sleeved t-shirt. Perched on her head was a garland of oak leaves. Some of the leaves were entwined in her red hair. She wore no shoes, and her green shirt seemed to emphasize her fair skin and make it look a little green, like she was a large plant.

"We have a problem," Frey told Dr. Creamintin. "Dave and I accidentally revealed ourselves to one of his students."

"Why am I not surprised?" Dr. Creamintin said. "Everything that vampire starts ends in disaster."

I stared at the dryad some more before speaking. "Are you trying to look human?" I nosily inquired. (Hey, if my memory was going to be wiped, I might as well be rude and obnoxious while I had the chance.)

The dryad was startled and turned to face me. "Yes," she said in a whispery, soft voice. "I am scheduled to start high school in three days."

"You'll want to ditch the leaves," I suggested.

"Why?" the dryad asked, fingering the greenery tucked in her hair.

"It's way too bold, even if you're trying to make a fashion statement. Everyone will think you're either doing drugs or need drugs. You'll want some shoes, too."

"Shoes?" she asked.

"Shoes," I said, pointing to my feet.

"We need her memory wiped. She handled it well and didn't draw any attention to us. There's no additional clean up," Frey said, continuing his conversation with Dr. Creamintin.

"If it's just one girl, why don't you try hypnosis?" Dr. Creamintin said.

"But Aisis left for a two-week assignment," Frey reminded the doctor.

"Why do you humans wear shoes?" the dryad inquired, removing the oak garland from her hair and combing out the extra leaves.

"Our feet aren't tough. We need them, or we would scrape them up every day. Plus, they're loads of fun to accessorize with," I said as I eyed the dryad's feet. Her soles looked as thick and hard as tree bark. "Your jeans are nice, but I think you should change your shirt."

"What's wrong with my shirt?" the dryad asked.

"Come now, Frey; it's just one girl. If you wipe her mind, there's no telling what kind of dolt she'll turn into," Dr. Creamintin scolded.

"Maybe you didn't hear me," Frey said. "She *saw* us. She saw me as a wolf, and she saw Dave looking vampiric."

"Truly, I suspect more damage was done by bringing her here," Dr. Creamintin said, sounding amused. "If you had let her be, the situation would have smoothed itself over. Humans think themselves to be rational creatures. Eventually, she would have talked herself out of what she saw. I know Dave is not your first assignment, Frey, but there is no need to be *this* cautious."

I considered the dryad's clothes. "Nothing, strictly speaking. But you'll want to dress it up and put on earrings or something. It makes you look a little plain. Do you have a jacket or something?"

"Earrings?" The dryad said, her eyes brightening.

"Yeah. Like these," I said, pointing to my ear lobes. I was wearing sterling silver earrings shaped in a Celtic knot.

"They never mentioned earrings," the dryad smiled.

"I know what I'm doing, Dr. Creamintin," Frey bossily asserted.

"Fine, fine. I'll take her in back in a moment; just give me a minute. Now Nyla, please. I'm *telling you* normal humans *do not* wear leaves in their hair," Dr. Creamintin said, turning to the dryad I was chatting with. "Hm?" he said, blinking when he set his sights on her leafless head.

"I need to go shopping again," the dryad, Nyla, informed the good doctor. "For shoes and earrings!" she said, smiling in my direction.

I nodded in approval. "Very good. And remember to vary your wardrobe colors. The girls will criticize you if you stick to green shades. Try browns and golds. Or some blues," I suggested.

"Right!" Nyla smiled. "I'll see you later, Dr. Creamintin!" she called over her shoulder before hurrying out of the office.

Dr. Creamintin watched her go. "I have tried convincing that dryad for two months that humans don't don greenery. What on earth did you tell her?"

"I said people would think she did drugs," I truthfully shrugged. "Can I go home yet?"

Dr. Creamintin narrowed his eyes. "No," he said before whipping around to face Frey. "I refuse to wipe her memory."

"What?"

"It's foolish to wipe her memory and potentially harm her brain. No, we'll wait until Aisis returns. In the meantime, I want you to bring her with you when you report in after school."

"Why?" Frey complained.

"I think she could assist me with one of my more difficult patients," Dr. Creamintin said.

There was a roar from one of the back rooms. "And we're very busy now, so I must go. Good day, Frey."

"But, Doctor!"

"No buts, Frey. You made the mistake. It is your duty to resolve it in a civilized manner. If you're so worried she'll blab our secrets, you can keep a close eye on her," the doctor paused to turn around and scrutinize me. "But something tells me she'll be fine. Good day, Frey," he said before disappearing into a back room.

"Great," Frey muttered.

Apparently I was the newest short-term volunteer of the Magical Beings' Rehabilitation Center, whatever that was. "I'm not sure my parents will let me get a job," I listlessly said. "Probably only if I can keep my grades up."

Frey hustled me out of the MBRC and had me back on the train ASAP.

"So," I said, noisily sipping on the Jamba Juice he had bought in Union Station to shut me up when I started complaining about missing lunch. "What now?"

"I don't know," Frey said, covering his eyes. "What is Dr. Creamintin *thinking*? If anyone from the security department finds out, we're all going to get hauled in for questioning, and I'll be held accountable!"

"It's not like I'm going to tell anyone," I said, fully occupied with my Mango-a-go-go-flavored juice.

"Really?" Frey drawled, obviously not believing me.

"Yeah. This is freaky business. My parents would haul me off to some sort of shrink if I started talking about it. Why don't we just leave well enough alone? You and Dave-the-chubby-vampire leave me be, and I'll forget all about what happened," I proposed.

Frey stared me down with his green eyes. "And you couldn't have said this before I hauled you down to the MBRC?"

"I was in shock," I informed him. "Besides, it's not like you gave me a chance to talk. I wasn't sure if you guys were even friendly. For all I knew, you might try and kill me so Dave could drink my blood."

"And what changed your mind?" Frey asked, quirking a silver eyebrow.

"Buying me Jamba Juice. And seeing the MBRC. But mostly the Jamba Juice," I considered, sipping at my delightfully fruity smoothie. "Besides, I might be hallucinating. I'm about ninety-eight percent sure I have a concussion."

Frey looked like he wanted to slam his head into a wall. "I can't leave you alone. Not now. Dr. Creamintin requested that you return with me, and I have to follow his orders."

"Why?"

"Because he's the doctor I report to."

"For what?"

Frey sighed. "I guess there's no getting around it. The MBRC is all about rehabilitating magical beings into mortal society. While the MBRC is our main headquarters, we've got agents and handlers—magical entities who have successfully rehabilitated into mortal society—across the world. We handlers help other magical beings make the move from hiding underground to successfully integrating with humans."

"So, when were you rehabilitated?" I asked, noisily reaching the bottom of my Jamba Juice.

"I wasn't. My siblings and I were some of the first werewolves to be born into human society," Frey proudly said. "I'm in the first generation of the magical beings that grew up with humans."

"I see," I said, popping off the lid of my drink.

"You know you're taking this all rather calmly."

"Why wouldn't I? Now I *know* I have to be dreaming," I said, sadly observing that I had finished my Mango-a-go-go.

"Why do you say that?" Frey asked.

"Because none of this," I said, waving my hand through the air. "Is like the stories. Everything is far too dorky. I mean really, the MBRC? What is this, Sesame Street-the magical edition?"

"Dorky?" Frey scoffed, mildly offended.

"Yeah, dorky. Where are the hot vampires, the magical wardrobes, the beautiful elves, and the daemon companions?"

"Only a fraction of Americans are as beautiful as Hollywood portrays them to be," Frey said.

"Oh. That's true," I said, thinking it over. Generally speaking, stories are written only about good looking people. Why wouldn't that same rule apply to magical creatures? But that didn't mean I had to like it.

"Well...I still think I'm having a nightmare," I decided.

"I thought you said you had a concussion."

"You are a jerk," I grumbled.

"No, I'm a werewolf," Frey corrected.

Ten minutes later, Frey and I wandered back to school. We had spent so much time at the MBRC, we only had one class left, which would begin in approximately 15 minutes.

"I'm not going back to the MBRC today," Frey whispered as we stealthily kicked up our heels outside the school building, waiting until the bell rang so we could slip in the school while students moved to their final class. "But tomorrow is Friday. After his work day ends, Dave has classes to attend, and I have to give my weekly report. You will come with me."

"Yeah. Sure. Right," I said to the brick wall, leaning against the cold surface.

The bell rang, and Frey straightened up. "I'll see you in Spanish tomorrow before finding you after school."

"Yeah," I said, pushing off the wall, following the silver-haired werewolf into the building. "See you."

Frey disappeared in the stampede of students that swarmed the hallway, leaving me wondering if I was utterly mad.

I was practically a zombie when I got home that afternoon. Right after dinner, I collapsed in bed and slept like the dead until my alarm clock went off in the morning. I tried to convince myself it was a terrible dream, but even with that hope, I was somewhat surprised when I strolled into Spanish class the following morning.

Frey sat in his front seat and ignored me. Toni and Dani were standing in front of him, asking him questions that he answered with an easy smile. When I entered the room, he didn't even glance at me.

Jerk.

Neither did Dave the vampire. He awkwardly stood at the front of the room and bumbled through the lesson, still unable to remember my name and face along with everyone else's.

"I guess it really was a dream," I grumbled, leaning on the locker next to Fran's after school.

"What are you talking about? You've been acting weird ever since you skipped lunch yesterday," Fran said, most of her body disappearing into her messy locker.

"Nothing. What are we doing today?" I asked, shifting my backpack.

"I thought you usually tried to 'accidentally' run into Brett on Fridays after school?" Fran asked, her voice echoing in her locker.

"He told me during American government that he was leaving early today. He's got a dentist appointment."

"I should have known," Fran snorted.

"Are you ready to go?"

I shrieked and jumped two feet into the air, startling Fran inside her locker.

I swung around to stare at the silver-haired guy that had popped up next to me. "Frey," I said, placing a hand over my thumping heart.

"Morgan," Frey said.

Fran popped upright. "You didn't tell me you were doing something with the transfer kid," Fran hissed in my ear before smiling. "Hi, Frey." (As the sophomore student council secretary, she was on the welcoming team for Frey. Apparently I missed that explanation yesterday when I skipped lunch.)

"I didn't think I was," I hissed back before turning to Frey. "Are you sure about this?"

Frey raised a silvery eyebrow. "I told you about it yesterday. We don't have a choice."

"What's going on?" Fran asked, hip bumping me.

"Morgan and I have the same after-school job," Frey smiled, shifting into a friendly persona. "We work for a doctor near Union Station."

"You didn't tell me you got a job either," Fran scolded.

"It's…uhhh…a very sudden opportunity. Just came up yesterday," I said.

"Right, so let's go," Frey said, slinging his backpack over his shoulder before reaching out and yanking me along by my wrist.

"Bye, Fran," I called over my shoulder. Frey continued to yank me down the hallway without waiting for her reply.

"Can I at least put my coat on?" I grumbled when we moved down the main staircase, my heavy backpack hanging from my fingers.

"Fine," Frey sighed, pausing just outside the school doors. He took my backpack from me, allowing me to shrug on my lightweight, fall jacket. "Come on," he said, practically throwing my backpack at me when I finished adjusting my collar.

I grumbled and shouldered the bag as we left the school building. Dave was waiting outside.

"Is it time? I'm so excited, I can hardly wait. I hope you give me a good grade," Dave grinned, holding a black umbrella over his head as the sun shone down on the parking lot.

"He's coming with?" I asked. Great. Being seen after class, *outside* of school, with a substitute teacher? Yeah, my social life was officially dead.

"Yes. Dr. Creamintin and I review his progress and behavior for the week. We don't grade you, Dave," Frey said before starting down the sidewalk, moving in the direction of the train station.

"So, Dave. Will vampires really die if they're exposed to direct sunlight?" I asked, eyeing Dave's dorky umbrella.

"No, not at all," Dave said. "I only experience an allergic reaction."

"A what?" I asked. Once again popular culture fails me. Thank you, every vampire novel known to mankind.

"If Dave is in the sunlight too long, he burns like an albino blonde cheerleader rubbed in baby oil, sitting on the beach," Frey narrated from the front of our little line.

"Is that just Dave or all vampires?" I asked, inspecting Dave's pasty pale complexion.

"I would have to say most of us vampires burn easily," Dave supposed. "I mean, come on. Once you die, you're going to lose your skin pigmentation. Of course, my case is worst than most. Usually it takes a few decades for the burning issue to kick in," he said as he twirled his umbrella over his head.

"Right. Logically." I said, walking closer to Frey and hoping this experience would soon be over.

3

The Shy Unicorn

The train ride seemed to take forever. Dave had to face the same direction as the train was moving, or he got motion sick. Dave also couldn't sit near any smokers, or he hacked like a sick Chihuahua. (We had to move cars twice because of this.) Dave also had to sit as far away from Frey as possible. "I'm allergic to dog dander," he said after nearly sneezing his eyeballs out. (No seriously, they almost popped out of his eye sockets. It was gross.)

It stretched on and on. By the time we finally reached Union Station, I had to wonder why the MBRC hadn't eliminated him yet.

We were late, so Frey hustled us through the station, past Tiny the guard giant, through the main chamber of the MBRC, and down to Dr. Creamintin's office.

"Frey, so good to see you again. Ah, and you've brought back the beautiful Morgan. Excellent," Dr. Creamintin beamed before turning to Dave. "Dave, how are you? Enjoying your first week in mortal society?"

"Oh, yes! It was wonderful!" Dave beamed. (Again, the entertainment industry LIES to us. Dave beams about five times per second. He is not emo, nor is he angst-ridden.)

"Don't stretch it. You were only out there for three days," Frey pessimistically added.

"I have one harpy and a dwarf before you two, so you're going to have to wait for Aristotle to check in with you," Dr. Creamintin said, reaching past his mermaid secretary to check his files.

"Great, we'll take a seat," Frey said, moving for the open chairs.

"Morgan, dear, I have a task for you," Dr. Creamintin called after me as I moved to follow Dave and Frey.

"Yes, Dr. Creamintin?" I asked.

"Felisha, Westfall is here, correct?" Dr. Creamintin asked, scratching his scalp.

"Yes, he is, Dr. Creamintin," the mermaid acknowledged.

"Excellent. Morgan, Westfall is a young male unicorn who is going to be sent out to an MBRC equestrian therapy barn. He will live with roughly a dozen other magical equines under the supervision of three elves that run the stable. Mortal, nonmagical folk visit the barn during the day for therapy riding sessions. Westfall, as I said before, is young. He needs more exposure to humans before he leaves us. Would you mind chatting with him?" Dr. Creamintin smiled.

"Sure. Although, I've never ridden or interacted with a horse besides pony rides at the zoo," I said. "I'm not sure what I'll be able to tell him."

"You don't have to tell him anything. If you can get him used to normal humans, that will be plenty," Dr. Creamintin snorted. "Dave and Frey will be at least an hour or two. After checking in with me, Dave must pick up his weekly supply of tomato juice."

Behind Dr. Creamintin, Dave scrunched up his face.

"Don't complain, Dave," Dr. Creamintin said without looking over his shoulder at the sour vampire. "We already give you enough blood to supply two rehabilitated vampires. You aren't going to get anymore, you greedy guts."

"Where do you get the blood?" I asked, fascinated.

"We have agents in the hospitals that take nearly expired blood before it is tossed and smuggle it to us," Dr. Creamintin said, making a note on a clipboard.

"Blood expires?" I wondered.

"After 35 days," Dr. Creamintin nodded. "Unless it's frozen, that is."

"Doctor, the patients are waiting," the mermaid, Felisha, reminded him.

"Thank you, Felisha. This way, Morgan," Dr. Creamintin said, sweeping me away before I had a chance to wave goodbye to Frey and Dave.

He herded me past the examination rooms, around a corner and up a hallway. "We keep our larger patients back here. Here he is. Westfall, I have someone I would like you to meet," Dr. Creamintin announced as we turned another corner and the little hallway opened up into a stable.

I was expecting a white unicorn with a pearly horn. Again, I was let down.

Westfall was a delicate, smaller-sized unicorn. He closely resembled those Arabian horses from the desert. He was not white at all. He had a black mane and tail and brown fur with just the slightest hint of red to it. (Later, Westfall would teach me that his coloring was "bay.") His horn was not pearly, but a shiny gold color.

Westfall was munching on a bit of hay when the good doctor and I found him. He looked up as Dr. Creamintin called him, and when he caught sight of me his eyes bulged. He shot backwards, cracking himself on the rump when he hit the wood fence behind him. He scrambled away from us, clearly terrified of…*me.*

"Chat with him, huh," I said as the horse fled to his stall, which was nothing but a few wooden fences thrown together.

Dr. Creamintin sheepishly laughed. "I did say it would be plenty if you could get him used to you," he said before turning his attention to the skittish horse. "Westfall, that is no way to behave. Stop being a sissy, and get out here to introduce yourself."

I folded my arms across my chest. "I thought unicorns were white?"

"Not all of them, my dear. Only certain lines—mostly the British ones. Westfall, there's no use hiding behind the hay pile.

Your scared, little rear hangs out behind it," Dr. Creamintin shouted to the unicorn. Dr. Creamintin glanced at his watch and sighed. "I have patients waiting, Westfall, so I have to leave. I trust Morgan. I know I'm leaving you in capable hands. Do try and say *something* to her, lad," Dr. Creamintin tisked before turning to me. "Just stand here and talk. If he ever comes out from behind the hay pile, you are progressing marvelously," he said before striding off, disappearing down the hallway with a swish of his lab coat.

"Right," I awkwardly said, clapping my hand's together. Westfall's back end, the only visible part of him behind the stack of hay bales, flinched at the sound. "Okay. I'm just going to…go sit over here," I said, spotting a metal crate several feet away, leaning against another stall.

As I sat down, I cast my eyes around the makeshift stable. It had six stalls that varied in size. The smallest looked like it was suited to house a miniature pony. The largest was big enough that Westfall could roll around in it and still have plenty of room. I remembered the baby dragon from the front desk and darkly contemplated what animals usually stood in it.

I scraped my shoes on the ground, which was covered in wood shavings. The barn smelled soft and woodsy, and oddly, it had *skylights*. I was considering how on earth Dr. Creamintin had gotten *skylights* when he was beneath Union Station, when I noticed the skittish unicorn had rotated his body and was peering out at me behind the hay.

"Hello," I smiled.

I must of have shocked him because he shrieked like a little girl and disappeared behind the hay again. I nearly fell off my crate in surprise because I didn't think he could talk, much less scream.

"Something tells me that working here is going to be disappointing and educational," I muttered as Westfall shook. "So long, childhood fairy tales!"

After a couple minutes of various strangled shouts leaking out of the delicate unicorn, I recalled Dr. Creamintin's orders to talk.

"I am going to sound like such an idiot," I grumbled before

changing my voice into a friendly, inviting tone. "I'm Morgan. A human. Obviously. Um…I know Frey Christenson, if that is his real name, and Dave the vampire. Dave is my teacher. I found out about the MBRC because I walked in on a fight between him and Frey," I rambled.

Westfall continued to hide.

"Right. Well, let's see. I have three brothers; the oldest one is Michael. He's named after the arc angel. Then there's me, then Odie, and finally Peter. Odie's real name is Odin. He and I have the same godparents. They named us. My dad is a math professor, and our godparents are his best friends who teach at the same college as him. Roman, my godfather, is a history professor. Karen is a mythology professor. That's how Odie and I got mythological names."

I thought about it before laughing. "All in all, Morgan isn't a bad name. My best friend, Fran? She's named after this sitcom from the '90s. A show about a *nanny*," I broke off into laughter before quieting in the awkwardness of the moment.

"Yeah. Funny," I said.

I talked and talked and talked until I was blue in the face. It didn't do any good. The frightened unicorn stayed in his horrible hiding spot.

After half an hour of monologuing like a Shakespearian play, I was running out of things to talk about.

"So. A therapy barn huh. Sounds pretty cool," I said, turning over conversation topics in my head.

Westfall quivered behind the hay.

"I haven't been to a barn. I've only ridden the ponies at the zoo as a kid," I volunteered. "That's pretty cool that you're going to live in a therapy barn though. It means you'll be helping humanity. That's neat. I can't imagine why you would want to do that. I mean, humans don't believe in unicorns anymore; plus if you're in a riding therapy barn, wouldn't that mean you have to let humans ride you?" I questioned.

I nearly jumped three feet into the air when the unicorn unexpectedly answered me.

"I want to."

My head snapped up, and I stared at the chocolate-eyed equine that was peeking behind his hale bales, watching me with a terrified but resolved expression.

Realizing I was making it more difficult by staring at him, I shifted my eyes back to my feet. "Why?"

"I'm a unicorn. I can heal," he proudly said. "Riding me will make them far better than riding any normal horse. I'll use my magic to help them."

"Wow, that's pretty cool. Do you know what other kinds of horses will be staying there?" I asked.

Westfall was silent.

I looked up, his bravery failed him, and he retreated back behind his hay bale, his butt poking out.

Another half hour of talking yielded no further results.

When Dr. Creamintin came to collect me, I told him of my failure.

"That's not a failure, girl," he laughed while handing me a candy drop to soothe my scratchy throat. (Talking for an hour solid does that to you.) "The fact that he acknowledged your presence and spoke to you is a major breakthrough!"

"I still don't understand why he's going to live in a therapy barn if he's so terrified of humans," I muttered.

"He wants to get over his fear. Unicorns are healing creatures. They are eager to help people. Westfall just has to conquer his fear first," Dr. Creamintin sagely said before turning me over to Frey as the werewolf entered the room.

"That will be all for today, Miss Fae. I do look forward to seeing you next week, if you're free" he smiled. "Thank you for your assistance."

"No problem," I said, waving goodbye. I plopped down in a seat and wondered how long this arrangement would last. Not like I wanted to be paid or anything. It was interesting to be able to see all of the magical beings…but sooner or later, I suspected my social life would take a blow because of this.

"Is Dave done?" I asked.

"He's finishing up some paperwork with Aristotle. We have to pick up his tomato juice dosage, and then we can leave," Frey said, shifting in his seat.

"Great," I slumped in my chair. "Why does he need tomato juice anyway?"

"It's used to repress his desire for blood," Frey described. "The MBRC has found that you cannot wean a vampire completely off blood. You can, however, greatly inhibit their hunger for it by supplementing it with tomato juice."

"Icky," I said

"I am very grateful that as a werewolf, I have no limitations on my diet."

Dave was rather lachrymose when he finished meeting with the talking owl. He picked up his gigantic jugs of tomato juice (which Frey carried like they were little cans of tuna) and shuffled out of the MBRC without a complaint, although he did a fair amount of sniffling.

The train ride home was merciful. Dave was too wrapped up in his sadness that he apparently hadn't done very well (DUH! I mean, HELLO, I was trailing after him like a dog on a leash, why do you think that was?), so he didn't cause a big fuss when a smoker sat down near us.

My weekend was normal. I hung out with Fran Friday evening, caught a few Saturday morning cartoons with my youngest brother before leaving for the mall with Fran, returned home for the essential "family dinner" my parents insisted on having, and went to the movies with a few friends of mine. On Sunday, I was dragged to church by my parents, did my homework, and surfed the internet.

I had almost forgotten that my pleasant, nonmagical world wasn't so ordinary by the time I returned to school on Monday.

Frey ignored me like usual; Dave was unable to name me as usual, and the day progressed finely.

I finished an English paper, admired Brent Patterson in American government, and practically skipped to my next class. "Today is such a wonderful day," I announced, popping down in my seat for math class.

Hunter, a classmate of mine who is a borderline friend, looked up from the book he was reading, *10 Secrets to Better Leadership*. (Hunter was always reading strategy and leadership books. I assumed it was because he wanted to be some sort of political leader when he grew up. Hah!) "You seem to be in a better mood today. I was worried when you skipped class last week. It is not like you," he said, a small smile twitching across his lips as he flicked his sunglasses off his face. (That's the other thing about Hunter. He wears sunglasses *all* the time. He *claimed* it was because his eyes were sensitive to sunlight. Again, Hah!)

"Yeah, let's just say I love life and its mediocrity," I hummed, shifting in my seat.

"Yes, of course," Hunter politely agreed. "What are you doing after school?" he asked.

"Fran and I were thinking about hanging around the park," I said. "She doesn't have student council activities for once. Thanks, by the way, for helping out with decorating for homecoming. She really appreciated it. And I'm so sorry she still can't remember your name. It's really rude of her, but she doesn't mean it," I said.

Fran went nearly insane homecoming week with all of the decorating, float building, window painting, and contests. The sophomores were responsible for decorating a portion of the school, and Fran couldn't find anyone to do it, so I asked Hunter to help me.

He did, but Fran was never quite able to grasp his name the whole day.

Hunter shrugged. "I don't take it personally. I'm just one of those people who are hard to remember."

I stared at Hunter. "Yes, of course," I said, mimicking his earlier comment. Hunter was *not* easy to forget, and it wasn't just because of the sunglasses. The guy was quite hot if you could get him to put down his leadership books.

"So, what are you doing after school today?" I asked.

"The usual. I have to return home to work," Hunter said, sliding his book into his backpack.

"Where do you work again?" I asked.

Hunter paused, his eyebrows puckering. He opened his mouth to reply when our math teacher stepped into the room.

"Good afternoon, class. Please get your homework out and pass it forward," he said.

Hunter and I ruffled through our notebooks, and I completely forgot about my question.

At the end of the school day, I happily closed my locker door and frowned when I realized Frey was standing behind it. "What?" I asked as I shrugged my coat on.

"Time to go. We're going to miss the express train if you don't hurry," he said.

"You're kidding, right? I thought I only had to go on Fridays," I frowned.

"Oh, no. Thursdays are the only days you don't have to go," Frey said. "That's the only day Dave doesn't have to take supplementary classes."

"What?"

"Supplementary classes. The MBRC hosts classes that teach patients about normal, human life. Right now Dave is in Introduction to Human Society," Frey prodded before turning up the hallway.

I grumbled as I followed him, digging out my cell phone. Frey held the door open for me when we left the school, and I growled a word of acknowledgement at Dave as we walked towards the train station, my fingers tapping out a text message to Fran so she would know I had left.

"You know," I said to Frey's backside. "It's going to be really suspicious if you keep ignoring me in class but everyone always sees us leaving together."

"Doesn't the presence of a teacher make it seem less weird?"

Frey countered.

I glanced over my shoulder, Dave's sunny disposition returned over the weekend. He was some distance behind us, twirling his umbrella and hopping like a frog to avoid cracks in the sidewalk.

"No. He probably makes it worse, actually. As it is, he's not following close enough to look like he's with us," I disagreed.

"True. I'll think about it," Frey remarked.

"THINK about it? My gosh! Are you a jerk or what!" I said, stopping on the sidewalk.

"What?" Frey asked, turning around.

"You have to actually *think* about acknowledging my presence when I've been an *angel* about this whole mess? I should go blab your secret to the world!"

"No one will believe you. You said so yourself," Frey smirked.

I stared at the smirking canine. He was supposed to be SWEET! What was WRONG WITH HIM!? Hadn't he ever read *Twilight*? *Harry Potter*? At the very least, he was supposed to be misunderstood! "That's it. I'm not going. You can explain the situation to Dr. Creamintin yourself," I decided.

The smirk fell off Frey's lips really fast.

"What?" he asked.

"I'm not going. You can't make me go. I'll scream that you're a girl abuser. I'll shout that you fathered my kid and won't accept responsibility," I flatly said.

"You don't have a kid," Frey said, his eyes growing wide.

"They don't know that," I said, motioning to the general public that strolled, biked, jogged, and walked past us.

Dave finally caught up to us, panting from the exertion of hopping. "Mable, what's the problem?"

"It's Morgan," I darkly corrected.

"Morgan," Dave said. "Let's go talk things over with Dr. Creamintin. He'll be able to make you understand. Frey has this alpha-male dominance issue. It's because he's a werewolf. He's probably just ticked that Dr. Creamintin is treating you special."

"What?"

"That is not true!" Frey bristled.

"You shut up, or you'll forever be labeled a pervert!" I snarled while stalking past him, stomping towards the train station.

Dave trailed after me, humming a little ditty, while Frey remained shell-shocked.

He caught up with us at the train station and bought our tickets while reproachfully glaring at me.

During the train ride, I sat next to Dave and refused to look at Frey, who also refused to look at me. Dave seemed unaware of the tense atmosphere and spent most of the train ride remarking about the beautiful scenery.

Frey and I stormed through Union Station before moving down the stairs and passageways that led to the MBRC.

"Wonderful day, isn't it?" Dave smiled at Tiny, who was able to read the dark situation between Frey and me.

"Um, sure," Tiny said as he fumbled with the locks. The iron doors faded, and the giant flinched when Frey and I, still locked in silence, stormed through.

When we reached the main chamber of the MBRC, I dodged a Chinese dragon before heading in the direction of Dr. Creamintin's office.

"Where are you going?" Frey asked, catching my shoulder.

"To Dr. Creamintin's," I replied, shrugging his hand off.

"We have to take Dave to his classes first," Frey said.

"Maybe you do, but I report directly to Dr. Creamintin," I said before storming off, barely avoiding a large troll.

I reached Dr. Creamintin's office and threw open the door. "I'm here," I announced. "What do you want me to do?"

Dr. Creamintin poked his head out of an examination room and correctly read my mood. "Ah, Morgan. You're looking powerful today. I would like you to continue talking to Westfall. There's a kelpie—a water horse—with him in the stables. If he's not too hostile, you can brush him while you talk to Westfall."

"Brush the horse. Got it," I said as I stomped past the doctor, moving down the small hallway.

There were two horses in the barn today besides Westfall. One was a white creature with a foaming gray mane and blue eyes. I couldn't say I was a big fan of his eyes; they were a little creepy.

The other horse was big, beautiful, and black. He was far bigger than Westfall and looked more powerful. He reminded me of Zorro's horse, or a knight's horse. The only odd thing about him was his eyes. They were the pale yellow color of the moon on water.

Westfall looked hopeful when I first arrived and was clearly trying to work up his courage.

"Good afternoon," he said, his voice trembling.

All of my anger from Frey disappeared as the bright-eyed unicorn looked triumphant and impressed with himself. He was just so *cute*!

"Good afternoon, Westfall," I said as he retreated to his hay pile. I turned on my heels to flick my eyes back and forth between the horses. "And which one of you is the kelpie I'm supposed to brush?" I asked.

The white horse sniffed contemptuously, but the black horse released a friendly nicker.

"You then?" I asked the dark horse. He arched his neck prettily. "Great, let me find brushes. Brushes, brushes, where are you? Ah, there we go," I said, spotting them near the silver crate I sat on during my last visit. "I don't even know what a kelpie is. Dr. Creamintin said something about a water horse. Do you know what they are, Westfall?" I called over my shoulder as I grabbed the bucket of brushes and carried it over to the black horse's stall.

"Um," Westfall bashfully said. "That's not, he's not a..."

I turned around to smile invitingly at the unicorn. "Yes?" I asked. Someone must have worked with the little guy over the weekend; he was way better than last Friday.

The unicorn hesitated, trying to decide what to say, until he lost his bashful look and looked absolutely petrified.

I quirked an eyebrow as I felt something *dark* hang over me. I turned around. The black horse innocently swished his tail.

I looked back at Westfall. He was quivering like a jello block behind his hay. "Nothing," he squeaked.

I picked up one of the brushes and started at it. "Ugh, Frey is such a *jerk*! He's acting like a brat. He refuses to say *hi* to me in class even though he's dragging me here to the MBRC after school. He claims he has bigger things to worry about than mortal society, but I think he wants to score a date with either Dani or Toni, which is why he doesn't want to admit that he knows me," I said.

The black horse side-stepped me and stuck his head in my brush bucket. When he removed his head, he was holding a black rubber brush, the hand-strap clenched between his teeth.

"This brush first?" I asked.

The big horse nodded.

I tossed my original brush back in the bucket and attacked the horse's fur with the rubber brush. "Magical animals are so much more intelligent than regular, domestic animals. Don't get me wrong; horses are pretty smart. But they would never be able to interact like this," I said, rubbing the kelpie's neck.

He nickered and twisted so he could brush his velvet muzzle against my cheek.

"So, Westfall, how long until you move to a therapy barn?" I called.

The only noise the unicorn made was a whining sound similar to air leaking out of a balloon.

I sighed. Looks like the bay hadn't gotten *that* much better. "Conversation topic," I muttered, brushing the black horse. "Hmm. So my best friend Fran tells me the school is going to be throwing a Halloween dance," I announced.

Again I monologued for an hour, brushing the black horse as I went. Westfall occasionally made squeaking noises, which, I suppose, was an improvement over the awkward silence of Friday.

"You are a beauty," I told the black kelpie, gently stroking his cheek when I finished brushing him.

The equine breathed into the palm of my hand before resting his large head on my shoulder and ruffling my hair with his lips. He gently tugged on my hair with his teeth, pulling just hard enough to let me know he had a grip on me.

I laughed and pulled my hair out of his mouth. "If I get more split ends because of you, I will trim your magnificent mane," I threatened.

The kelpie shook his head and affectionately lipped my shoulder.

I patted his muscled neck before leaving him in his stall and turning to Westfall.

"It was great seeing you again, Westfall," I smiled. The golden-horned unicorn was mostly out from behind his hay bale, but I had a suspicion that if I walked toward him, he would quickly back up. "I'll see you tomorrow," I said, checking my watch.

"Hummm," Westfall said, anxiously weaving and glancing at the newly brushed kelpie.

"Bye, guys," I called over my shoulder as I walked out of the stable.

I moved down the little hallway and popped into Dr. Creamintin's office. The good doctor was talking with Frey while leaning against his front desk.

"Equine shock therapy completed, Dr. Creamintin," I announced, walking up to his side, icing out Frey. "I don't think Westfall's poor nerves could handle me much longer."

"And how was the kelpie?" Dr. Creamintin asked, setting his clipboard on Felisha's desk.

"Excellent. He is very beautiful," I said as the mermaid secretary loaded files onto Dr. Creamintin's clipboard.

"In a savage way, I guess he is," Dr. Creamintin supposed.

I was about to ask what he meant when I felt Frey lean in on me and *sniff*.

I'm not kidding. He was tipped in my direction, hovering about a foot above me, and sniffing at my neck. He was like Kitty, my family's cat, when he smells another cat on me and gives me that accusing look that says I've been cheating on him.

"WHAT are you doing?" I asked, taking several large steps back.

"There is a very funny scent on you," Frey said, inhaling several times to clear his nasal passages. "Very…earthy."

"I was in a barn. What do you expect?"

"Thank you, Felisha. Right, then. I must be along. Dave should be finished with his class soon. Have a safe journey home, and I'll see you two tomorrow," Dr. Creamintin said before picking up his clipboard and motioning for a tiny fairy to follow him across the room where they disappeared into an examination room.

As I watched them leave, Frey muttered behind me. "Very earthy. Very strange."

4

The Perverted Pooka

Tuesday wasn't all that different from Monday. Frey ignored me; Dave bumbled through class (although he got my name right for once), and at the end of school, Frey popped up by my locker and escorted Dave and me to the MBRC.

I sat next to Dave on the train, texting Fran and acknowledging the occasional comment from cheerful Dave. Frey scowled at us.

Once we got past Tiny and into the main chamber of the MBRC, I flounced away, leaving Frey to guide Dave to his classroom.

"Good afternoon, Dr—oh, he's not here," I said, throwing open the door to Dr. Creamintin's office.

"Good afternoon, Morgan," Felisha greeted, smiling at me. She waved with a flip of her green fish tail.

"Good afternoon, Felisha," I greeted, strolling across the empty waiting area.

"Dr. Creamintin is with a patient. He requested that you again talk to Westfall and brush the kelpie," the mermaid said, typing away on her computer.

"Excellent. Thank you, Felisha. I shall do just that," I said, pushing away from the desk. I walked down the hallway, humming under my breath as I entered the stable.

"Good afternoon, Westfall, kelpie, crabby white horse," I greeted the three equines that were still housed in the stable.

"Good afternoon," Westfall bravely replied. He was standing in the aisle, his legs locked. It was only sheer will that kept him from retreating to his hay bale, I think. The little guy really did want to get over his fear of humans.

The black kelpie nickered a greeting as I picked up the brush bucket and joined him in his stall.

When I glanced over my shoulder, Westfall was still standing in the aisle. "So, Westfall, do you have to take any classes before going to live in this therapy barn?"

"No. I work with a team of specialists who teach me how to act," Westfall said as I started brushing the kelpie.

"Really? That sounds interesting," I said, giggling when the black equine lowered his head to smell my jeans.

"It is very ed-ed-educational," the little unicorn said, eyeing the kelpie with fear.

"What kind of things do you have to learn?" I asked.

"I cannot talk. No matter what. That is the number one rule," Westfall replied, his eyes still glued to the big horse that I brushed. "Even if the humans greet me, I cannot greet them back."

"Wouldn't it be more difficult to not talk back if they insulted you?" I asked, frowning.

"No. My mother raised me to have very good manners," Westfall said.

I laughed as the kelpie wedged his muzzle against my neck.

"Um," Westfall said.

"Yes?" I asked, turning to face him.

He scrambled, his legs sliding underneath him, back to his hay pile. "Nothing!" he squeaked.

I sighed. Apparently he wasn't ready to face me yet. Again I felt something leer over my shoulder. I spun around.

The black kelpie was innocently arching his neck, although the white horse flared his nostrils at me and pinned his ears back.

"Weird," I said before I attacked the kelpie's mane.

After my hours of chatting with Westfall (who occasionally surprised me with softly spoken questions), I returned to the office and followed the pattern of the day before.

Dr. Creamintin thanked me; Frey sniffed me, and I swept out of the office, pushing the muttering werewolf away from me.

The pattern continued Wednesday. Westfall got the courage to stand in the aisle for a full half hour and ask me, in his quivering voice, questions about humans. The kelpie affectionately nudged me, nibbled on my hair, and breathed on my neck. I left the stable; Frey not so discreetly sniffed me and said I smelled; I threw Dr. Creamintin's clipboard at him and stormed out.

Thursday was blessedly Frey-free, and instead I hung out with Fran.

"I'm freeee," I sang, waltzing around the student council room. (I suspect it was originally supposed to be a supply closet, the room is that small.)

"Your after-school job makes you that unhappy? I would have thought spending so much time with Frey would be a dream come true," Fran said, making a checkmark on her list of things to do. "The boy is *hot.*"

"Please," I scoffed. "I'm not that shallow. Yet. Besides, there's Brett to think of."

"What about me?"

Speaking of my crush, in strolled Brett Patterson, his boyish smile stretching across his lips.

"Hey, Brett," I smiled.

"Hi, Morgan. Hey, Fran," he said, turning to smile at my friend. "What are you two up to?"

"Meh," Fran said, waving a hand in a shooing motion at Brett. I took the liberty of answering for her.

"I'm keeping Fran company and enjoying my day off work. Fran's got student council stuff to iron out," I smiled.

"That's Fran—always busy," Brett said, fondly smiling.

"Hmn," Fran said, her forehead wrinkling as she stared at her list.

"What are you doing?" I asked Brett.

He shrugged. "I was bored, so I figured I would pop down here and see if Fran was doing anything interesting."

"I'm not," Fran said, setting the list down before picking up a new sheet. "I'm going over the penny war figures. Terribly boring. You should leave, or you'll be just as bored," Fran said. "And take Morgan with you."

I could see that she was making an opportunity for me, but I would never take it. Not when I hadn't had a chance to talk with her since Sunday night. "No, Fran, that wouldn't be right. How about we go out for ice cream? The three of us? I'll drive! Michael isn't finished with football practice yet."

"Sounds great," Brett said.

"Alright. Let me post the results on the school website, and then we can go," Fran caved.

On Friday, I was not only looking forward to the weekend but also to visiting Westfall again. Perhaps the day off had given the little unicorn more courage.

I sat with Dave on the train ride over. (Frey still ignored me in class.) We chatted a little, Dave telling me the pros and cons about being a vampire.

"Well, you'll never age anymore…right?" I asked.

"Yes, but I cannot see my reflection in a mirror," Dave mourned.

"So? You can't visit a fun house at a fair?" I asked, trying to see the downside of such a side effect.

"No, I can't style my hair!" Dave wailed, self-consciously patting his forever-in-limbo shock of red hair.

"Oooh," I said, enlightened to his dilemma.

"I can't tell if I ever have something on my face, or if my nose is broken, but most importantly, I can't see my hair! I'll be trying to style my hair without a mirror until Jesus comes back!"

"Uh, don't you mean for all eternity?" I corrected.

"Oh, no! I know an Egyptian vampire who met the guy. He's totally coming back!"

"Uh-huh. So, were you a Civil War vet or something?" I asked. All American vampires were Civil War veterans, or at least from the Civil War era.

"No. I was made a vampire out of pure spite in the '20s," Dave shrugged.

"Oh? How?" I asked.

"I annoyed a vampire so much he bit me to shut me up. Didn't work very well because then I followed him around and complained for five years straight that he has trapped me in a flabby, balding body," Dave said as the train slowly halted in Union Station.

"How did you annoy a vampire?" I wondered.

"I'm not sure. All I know is that one minute I was walking up the road, singing, and the next minute one of my neighbors is biting me on the neck and shouting at me to shut up," Dave shrugged as we exited the train, Frey shuffling behind us.

We walked to the MBRC, cheerfully greeting Tiny before parting in the central area of the MBRC. Dave had to ask one of his teachers a question before reporting to Dr. Creamintin for the weekly check in.

I easily found my way to Dr. Creamintin's. "Hello, Felisha," I greeted as I swept into the room, moving past a pair of startled nymphs.

"Hello, Morgan. Dr. Creamintin said he wants to check in with you before you leave today," Felisha said.

"Got it," I called over my shoulder before taking the winding hallway back to the stable.

"Good afternoon, boys," I called, tossing my backpack and jacket in the corner.

"Good afternoon, M-Morgan," Westfall greeted, standing by the brush bucket.

"How are you today, Westfall?" I asked, slowly and cautiously approaching him.

"Very f-fine, thank you," Westfall said. "And you?" he asked, his voice climbing in pitch as I drew closer to him.

I bent over and slowly picked up the brush bucket. "I am wonderful."

"Could you, maybe, a-after you're done brushing, well, Him," Westfall said, quickly glancing in the direction of the nickering kelpie, "perhaps, try brushing…me?" Westfall squeaked.

I beamed. "Why Westfall, you've come very far in a week. I will be glad to," I said before walking over to the black kelpie.

The white horse flattened his ears and snarled, lunging at me as I passed his stall.

This made the black kelpie trumpet and rear, planting his hooves on the ground with a crack.

The white horse retreated to the back corner of his stall and glared at me.

"Shhh, shhh," I said, approaching the black kelpie. "He's just bad tempered. Ignore him."

The black horse affectionately pressed his head, which was the length of my upper body, into my chest.

I smiled and stroked his cheek bone before retrieving a brush. I kissed him on his muzzle before starting my work.

"Westfall," I called over my shoulder, "are your teachers pleased with your progress?"

"Indeed," Westfall nodded. He scooted back in the direction of his hay pile. "They were the ones who suggested I ask you to brush me."

"Cool."

"Morgan, are you alright?" Dr. Creamintin called from the hallway, his voice getting louder as he drew closer, "I heard horses."

"Yeah, I'm fine Dr. Creamintin," I called, moving to the front of the stall, a brush hanging from my hands. "The white horse got cranky, so the kelpie corrected him," I smiled as Dr. Creamintin—with Frey in tow—entered the stable.

"White horse? What the—," Dr. Creamintin skidded to a stop once he set his eyes on me.

Frey stiffened. I could see his hackles rising, even though he wasn't currently a dog.

Dr. Creamintin groaned as the black kelpie lipped my shoulder behind me. "Devin! You cursed Pooka!"

"...What?" I asked, confused by Dr. Creamintin and Frey, who was *growling*.

What really distracted me, however, were the human arms that abruptly snaked around me and pulled me against a distinctly *male* chest.

"You can't say I didn't do it right under your nose, old man," the chest rumbled as a rich voice right behind me said.

I blinked once and turned my neck. The black kelpie was gone. Instead a tall, sleek but muscled young man who was probably in his early twenties held me. He wore solid black, and his hair was a beautiful, luxurious black shade with body in it most girls would kill for. His skin was fair, but his eyes were a luminous mixture of white and yellow—the same full-moon shade as the black kelpie's eyes.

"Who are you?" I calmly asked—impressive considering how freaked out I was at this new development.

"I'm your kelpie," the stranger said with a gorgeous smile before moving to nuzzle my neck.

Frey started towards us, but he didn't need to. In a split second, I pushed the strange newcomer far away, snatched up a hoof pick, and held it threateningly close to his throat.

"What?" I asked my voice dangerous and low.

"Now, now, Morgan. Granted, Devin has severely wronged you, but he meant no harm. He is the Pooka. Mischievous jokes are his forte," Dr. Creamintin soothed. "Why don't you come out of that stall, and we'll get this mess straightened out."

"I have been REALLY GOOD about accepting all of this," I said, my voice hitching as I backed away from the horse-guy, gesturing with the hoof pick. "REALLY good. But you mean to tell me that this whole week, I've been brushing, hugging, and touching a horse who was really *this guy*?" I shrieked, pointing with the hoof pick at the yellow-eyed stranger.

Dr. Creamintin stared wide-eyed at me as Frey sniffed the air. "Ummm…" the good doctor said.

"I HATE YOU ALL!" I screamed, sitting down with a huff as tears of humiliation and embarrassment leaked out of the corners of my eyes.

"Darling," the horse guy said, holding his arms out as he chuckled in a rich voice that sounded a lot like his nicker.

"GO AWAY," I shouted, throwing the hoof pick at him. It bopped him in the head and made him pause.

"Well done, Devin," Dr. Creamintin said. "That is yet another human you have psychologically scarred. This is *not* good for your record young man, even if you are a council member."

"Hey, I was nice to her," horse boy protested, rubbing the spot where the hoof pick had cracked him.

"Nice to her? What on earth were you *doing* to her? She was practically soaked with your scent every day," Frey accused.

"Quiet mongrel," horse guy coldly said. "This is far beyond the likes of *you*."

"Why you—," Frey snarled.

I sat in a heap on the stall ground, pretty much forgotten as I bawled my eyes out. This really was the final straw. I could accept the fact that my weird teacher was a vampire. I could put up with Frey's moodiness. I was even happy to help Dr. Creamintin with his patients, but hugging a horse, kissing its muzzle, innocently thinking it was *just* a horse and then TA DAH, it's a GUY. Well, I just couldn't take it.

I was shocked out of my crying when I heard Westfall. "Morgan?" he asked.

I pulled my head out of the huddle of my arms, my mascara probably horribly smeared. The little unicorn had dared to enter the stall and lowered his head so it was mere inches away from mine.

His doe eyes were shadowed with concern for me, and he adorably tipped his head.

I sniffed before breaking into sobs and stumbling to my feet, throwing myself against Westfall.

I threw my arms around his neck and cried into his black mane. "Westfall! It's not fair," I wailed.

The little unicorn stiffened for a moment before warmly draping his head over my shoulder.

"Frey is so mean, and then pretty horses that I like suddenly turn into hot guys. I-I—," I broke off into sobs.

After several minutes, I finished crying and stepped back from Westfall, rubbing under my eyes to try and remove any dripping mascara.

"Feel any better?" Horse Guy asked me, still in the stall with us.

I scowled and spun on my feet, bending over to pick up the brush bucket. "You shut up! I never want to see you AGAIN!" I shouted, throwing the entire brush bucket at him.

"Ow!" he yelped as the various brushes, picks, and horsey items rained down on him.

I stalked out of the stall and stomped over to the hay bales Westfall usually hid behind.

I threw myself at the base of the stack and folded my arms, stewing as Westfall hesitantly joined me.

I was going to scalp that black-haired boy if I ever saw him again. Little did I know "Devin the Pooka" was going to become a big part of my life.

Frey was sent to escort me home, which he did only relatively unwillingly. Before I left, Dr. Creamintin said that Westfall had undergone a significant breakthrough by comforting me in my hysteria.

Being home over the weekend was a nice reprieve. Fran and I hung out with our friends, watched movies and even did our nails.

Monday went by fairly well. I talked to Brett a lot during class, and Hunter tried cheering me up in math class by offering to "visit" whoever was making me so unhappy.

I probably would have been unwilling to return to the rehabilitation center if it wasn't for Frey. The werewolf surprised me silly in Spanish class.

I was wrestling with my backpack, digging out my Spanish textbook, when Frey entered the classroom.

He tossed his head, making his fluffy hair flop for a moment.

"Hey, Frey!" Dani and Toni chorused across the room.

Frey did not respond to them.

Instead, his lips formed a dazzling smile while he shifted his gaze to me. "Hi, Morgan."

"Hi," I growled an automatic reply as I finally managed to dig my book out. I thoughtlessly set my book on my desk. It was then that it sunk in: he had acknowledged my presence.

I froze as Frey walked past me and stared at the moody werewolf, wondering what he was up to. (I would be hard-pressed to admit his greeting made my toes curl in my shoes.)

Dani and Toni were frowning at him. He had probably committed social suicide again by ignoring them, but not for long. Frey was tricky. He would get back into their good graces.

What really shocked me dead was when Dave announced we were going to do partner work. Usually, I worked in a group of three with Samantha and Emily. They sit on either side of Frey, so I started gathering my stuff up to move in their direction.

Before I slid out of my seat, there was the heavy tap of books being dropped on the desk next to me.

It was Frey.

The werewolf hefted himself into the desk and smiled.

"You know," I blinked at him, "if this is all out of pity or a way to goad me into returning to the MBRC, it isn't going to work," I informed him, even though I knew that wasn't entirely true.

"Well…we're friends, right?" Frey awkwardly asked. "Plus, I don't know Spanish."

"…If you don't know Spanish, why are you in here?"

"I have to keep an eye on Dave, and he doesn't teach any first-year classes."

"Right, of course," I sighed, looking at the worksheet Dave had given us. Apparently, I would be doing it without any help.

I glanced up at Dave and blinked. He was pointing to his nose and then me before making disdainful expressions.

Deciding that he was weird, even for a vampire, I wrote his actions off. If I had sat down to think about them, I probably could have stopped a lot of future drama.

I am ashamed to say that I allowed Dave and Frey to drag me to the MBRC without much resistance. Acknowledging my presence had raised Frey in my esteem. And yeah, a part of me wanted to return to the interesting center.

"Today, I think I would like for you to work at the main information desk in the center chamber," Dr. Creamintin said, scratching at his beard with a capped pen.

"Is this just pointless busy work because you don't have anything for me to do?" I asked.

"No," Dr. Creamintin insisted. "You will be an asset to their work. The front desk is often forced to research topics on humanity that you will instinctively know. You'll be saving them a great amount of time."

I sighed. I didn't have much of a choice. Frey and Dave had already left for their check in with other management, and Frey had my round trip train ticket. (Cheeky canine probably took it for that exact purpose!)

"Okay," I agreed.

"Excellent. Aristotle will introduce you to the employees at the desk," Dr. Creamintin beamed.

"What what? I shall do no such thing!" the fluffy little owl argued.

"Cease your complaining, Aristotle. Until Dave and Frey return, you haven't any work to do. Now go introduce the poor girl," Dr. Creamintin ordered.

"Nevah, I say, nevah!" the owl decided, shaking his little butt.

"Too bad, I say, too bad," Dr. Creamintin mocked before snatching the little bird off his stand on Felisha's desk and throwing him out of the office.

"Blackguard!" Aristotle called as Dr. Creamintin helped me out of the office as well.

"Beak brain!" Dr. Creamintin said before slamming his office door shut.

Aristotle scoffed mid-flight, his little wings flapping to keep his chubby body aloft. "Very well, then. This way, child. This way. Step quickly!" he said before flying off down the hallway.

I nearly lost the owl when we flew into the main chamber, and he disappeared behind a flying pegasus. In the end, I wandered up to the information desk, alone, and was surprised when Aristotle swooped down and landed on my shoulder.

"Ahem! Attention, attention," Aristotle called to the magical beings behind the large, pentagon-shaped desk.

The same beings were positioned there as the ones I saw on my first excursion to the MBRC. There was a caffeine-high hobgoblin, a polite lizard/gator creature, a regal centaur, the perverted fairy, and a baby dragon that was slightly bigger than a housecat.

"What's wrong, Aristotle?" the lizard creature asked, holding the squirming baby dragon in her webbed paws.

"This is a human. Dr. Creamintin has decided to lend her to you for the day. She is perfectly average and perfectly normal," Aristotle announced.

I wondered why everyone's eyes lit up during Aristotle's proclamation.

"You are to treat her kindly and with the respect that is due to any possession that belongs to Dr. Creamintin," Aristotle continued.

"Excuse me?" I sputtered.

"That is all. Good day," Aristotle finished, taking flight.

"What's your name, honey?" the lizard asked.

"Morgan," I supplied.

"Morgan," the lizard smiled, which was actually a more soothing gesture than you would think. "I'm Corona. This is Doggy," she said, holding the baby dragon up a little higher. "The little fairy is Gristles. Keep an eye on him. He's a little...mischievous. The hobgoblin is Toby, and this is Orion," Corona said, motioning to the centaur.

"It's very nice to meet you all," I hesitated, searching my brain for the right words. "What can I do to help?"

"I think it would be the most helpful if you worked with Toby. Don't you agree, Orion?" Corona asked, waiting for his regal nod before turning back to me. "Toby handles a lot of questions about human society. He'll refer some of them to you," Corona explained, welcoming me to duck behind the desk.

"Yo," Toby waved before he started scribbling down a note with enough fervor to break the pencil.

"I'm afraid I don't understand. How can I help *you*?" I asked, glancing around the desk.

A sunny-looking dryad danced up to the desk. Orion shifted to help her, his black horse body moving beneath him.

"We don't know much about average humans," Corona said. "At least not nearly as much as you do. We get asked all sorts of questions about humans, and we're expected to find the answers. Please, take a seat," she said, motioning to an empty chair next to Toby's chugging computer.

As I reluctantly sat, Corona dropped the baby dragon and turned away, moving to speak to a harpy that was waiting in line.

"Patients, beings who want to be rehabilitated, send me questions See? I answer them real fast, 1 2 3 done Like so You get?" Toby said, his pale green fingers clattering across the keyboard.

"I think so," I said, shifting in my chair.

"Okay here we go First question: I just moved to a new city and there's a school next door All the kids, every last student, wear the same clothes Are they all related Is this one of those mafia families I need to be careful around You know the answer?" Toby asked, swiveling to face me.

"Perhaps," I said after thinking for a moment. It took a second to distinguish when the question ended and when Toby's remarks started.

"You sure, I can check real quick 1 2 3 I check that fast," Toby said, his words zooming out of his mouth while the Google search engine page abruptly popped up on his computer screen.

"You use Google to answer questions?"

"If Wikipedia doesn't have the answer," Toby said.

"Wow. Well, the answer to the patron's question is school uniforms. The kids most likely go to a private school that requires school uniforms. Males and females have an assigned uniform. It's like a dress code for work, only it's for students," I answered.

"Dress code got it that was fast!" Toby said, sounding impressed.

"Thanks," I said, glancing at my feet. That was when I noticed the baby dragon was sitting underneath Corona's chair, curled up like a cat, staring at me.

I smiled and waved at it.

Toby moved onto the next email. "Next question Dear MBRC my next door neighbors have started attacking pumpkins with knives and etched demented faces in the vegetables' surfaces what is going on sounds like they're cannibals we can say they're cannibals," Toby said, his long fingers already typing out a reply.

"They aren't cannibals," I said. "That would require the humans to be pumpkins and then eat the pumpkins. They're decorating for Halloween, which is October 31. They're carving Jack-o-lanterns," I said, fluttering my fingers, trying to coax the dragon towards me.

"Wikipedia say Jack O' Lantern is a carved pumpkin with insides scooped out you humans are scary freaky," Toby said, typing out the reply.

"It's a holiday," I said, smiling as the baby dragon stood and stretched before ambling in my direction.

"Holly day is Christmas not no Hallolatern," Toby paused.

"Holiday is what we call days we celebrate. Christmas is a holiday, so is Hallo*ween*. For Hallo*ween,* we make Jack O' Lanterns," I corrected, sad when the little dragon paused a foot away from me before scurrying back to Corona.

"Right next question."

The sheer volume of questions *astounded* me. Toby was thrilled that we averaged one question per 25 seconds. His previous average was 35 seconds. Of course, I think the answers he was sending out with me around were probably more complete and truthful than his Wikipedia and Google answers.

"Look, Toby, I *promise you*, poodles don't get the fancy hair cuts because humans sell their fur. It's just for *show*. Originally, they were hunting dogs so they were cut funny to warm their joints. Google it!" I said, leaning back in my chair.

"Then what do humans do with the fur hmmm I think it goes to black market 1 2 3 and it gone made into coat just like 101 Dalmatians."

"That was a *movie*," I groaned. I was pleasantly surprised when there was a sudden weight on my lap.

The blue baby dragon had hopped up on my lap and was holding its chin out, clearly wanting something. I hesitantly offered my hand, which he started rubbing his head on.

His scales were stiff, but slightly flexible. The scales were all approximately the size of my finger nails, and they curled up, placed over each other in a protective coat.

Doggy's chest rumbled in an adorable purr.

"Google say you right I think it lie but we answer and we done," Toby huffed, pausing to take a drink of his fourth cup of coffee.

"Uh-huh. Whatever you say, Toby," I said, tickling the blue, baby dragon under its cheeks.

"Toby, it's your time to go on break," Corona announced.

"You got it," Toby said, zipping out of his chair and hopping over the desk in seconds.

"I see you've made a new friend," Corona smiled as the baby dragon flipped on his back so I could rub his tummy. The scales there were softer and yielded under my touch. Doggy cooed in satisfaction as I rubbed him.

"Yes, he's adorable," I smiled.

"Isn't he? His mom works here as an instructor for dragons. I was friends with her long before the MBRC started up, so I offered to watch him for her while she works. He's no trouble anyway,"

Corona said, opening a drawer of the desk. She dug out what looked like a circular dog biscuit and held it out.

Doggy bolted upright on my lap and balanced on his hind legs, eagerly holding out his paws. Corona gave him the biscuit, and the baby dragon clutched the cookie between his paws before rolling back on his spine.

He nibbled at it and, noticing my gaze, held the cookie up.

"No, thank you. It's your cookie," I said.

Doggy opened and closed his mouth in a happy snap before chomping on his biscuit.

"Has Toby been giving you any problems?" Corona asked.

"No, not really. Besides that last question about poodles, we've been doing pretty well. He can be a little hard to understand, though. He speaks so quickly, it's like his sentences have no punctuation and flow into each other," I laughed.

"Tell me about it. Someone needs to put that hobgoblin in rehab for caffeine. Oops, looks like I'm needed. You can take a break. Toby should be back in ten minutes," Corona called, shuffling back to her seat. She smiled across the counter at a willowy elf.

I tickled Doggy while he continued to munch on his cookie but froze when I heard a deep, rich voice.

"So this is where they stashed you. How amusing!"

I looked up and bristled.

It was him.

The fake kelpie.

Horse Guy.

5

Walking a Werewolf

"Fake Horse Guy," I said, hugging Doggy to my chest.

"Devin, actually," he corrected. "The Pooka if you want to be politically correct." His smile was white and sharp.

"Beat it," I snarled.

He gave me a falsified look of injury. "What, is it because I'm not soft and fluffy that you don't want to hug me anymore?"

My face *burned* with humiliation and fury. I'm pretty sure I could have fried a piece of bacon on my cheeks at that moment.

Doggy, picking up on my mood, barked and snarled at him. I pat the baby dragon once before setting him down and scooting out of the desk. The other MBRC employees were busy helping people, but Corona saw me go.

"Look here, *buddy*," I said when I reached the black-haired guy. "I mean it. *Go away*. I never want to see you *again*," I said, prodding him in the chest with the edge of my decently long fingernails.

He chuckled and looked down at me, his yellow eyes glowing with amusement. "You could hardly make me leave, even if you wanted to, sweetheart."

I narrowed my eyes. "Watch me."

Fake Horse Guy spread his arms out, telling me to go ahead.

When I deeply inhaled, he said, "That's what I thought," and took a step towards me. Which was exactly what I wanted.

"NOOOO!" I screamed, my shrill voice piercing the hustle and bustle of the main chamber. "PERVERT! DON'T TOUCH ME THERE!" I shrieked as I fell backwards, landing on my butt. The palms of my hands stung, but the guy's stupefied expression made the whole act totally worth it.

"Wha—," he started, but a *gigantic* griffin stalked up behind him, flanked by a stout dwarf and a slender nymph.

"You there, what did you do to the mademoiselle?" the griffin demanded. His voice was fascinating to listen to. It was sharp and golden.

"I recognize him," the nymph spat. "That's Devin. The Pooka. He went after one of my river sisters."

Both the griffin and the dwarfs' eyes widened. "You're the *Pooka*?" the griffin demanded.

"Oh, tha's rich! No small wonder yer feelin' up the lady," the dwarf spat, giving me a sympathetic look as I stumbled to my feet and did a reasonable impression of blubbering.

"Gentlemen, and lady," the fake horse guy said, scrambling to get a hold on the situation. "Clearly there has been a mistake."

"There's no mistake. Especially when the Pooka is involved," the griffin said, his words were crisp and pronounced.

"Come along. Leave the lady alone," the dwarf said, prodding Fake Horse Guy in the gut with the tip of his axe.

"I never—" the handsome guy started.

"You did. And I won't let you do it again," the nymph argued, the blue hues of her skin catching in the light.

My rescuers escorted the objecting shape-shifter away.

I couldn't help the smirk that twitched across my lips as I slipped back behind the desk. Doggy rubbed up against my legs as I plopped back down in my chair. Ahhh, the sweet, sweet taste of a win.

That was when I noticed the cyclops.

It threw me for a minute. (Not like anything about the MBRC

didn't.) In all of the plays and stories, cyclopes are stupid, clumsy creatures that are gigantic and wear animal skins for clothes.

Not this one.

He was dressed in an Armani suit, gold cuff links sparkling, tie properly tightened…I imagined even his shoes were shiny. He had perfectly trimmed, perfectly combed brown hair, and his face was quite fine looking…except for the whole one eye thing.

He was tall, but not over 6'6, and after some of the giants I had seen, that seemed pretty small. He was leaning over the counter, blinking down at a single form, a fancy pen clenched in his right hand.

At first I scoffed. *Twilight* had failed me (thank you Dave), why not the classics? Epic fail, *Odyssey*. Epic fail.

It was then that I realized the cyclops appeared to be having some sort of trouble.

He kept blinking at the form, occasionally tilting his head forward or backward to try and get a better look at the papers.

"Can I help you?" I asked.

The cyclops looked up and hesitatingly smiled. "It's nothing. I'm just—I'm supposed to fill out this form," he said. "And I'm having a hard time making it out."

I blinked. The font on the form was straight up Times New Roman. It was printed in an easily readable size, too.

The cyclops must have sensed my confusion and continued. "I'm a cyclops, you see? We have terrible depth perception, and most of us are far-sighted," he sighed. "Sadly, human contacts and eyeglasses don't fit us."

He spoke in a pronounced, yet friendly tone. Not at all like the man-eating cyclopes from *The Odyssey*.

"Would it help if I were to fill out the form for you? My… coworker is currently on break, so I'm free to help until he gets back," I offered.

"That would be magnificent. Thank you ever so much," the cyclops professed.

Behind me Corona and Orion stirred.

"Do you think we should tell her?" Corona whispered.

"Let her discover it for herself," Orion said, his voice old like a forest but as rich as a chocolate truffle.

Wondering about their conversation, I still continued. "I'm Morgan, by the way," I smiled as I took the paper and the fancy pen from the cyclops.

"I'm Nick," he said, which had to be the most anti-cyclops name on the planet.

"Alright, Nick, have you ever been…arrested and/or do you possess a criminal record?" I prompted, reading the first question.

"No," Nick said.

Within five minutes, Nick was on his way, paperwork finished and properly filed. As I sat back down in my chair, immensely pleased with myself, Corona called out to me.

"What on earth did *the Pooka* want with you, Morgan? That was a neat trick you used to get rid of him," she said as Doggy hopped on my lap.

I cuddled the baby dragon, gentle with him in spite of the sour glare that took over my face. "He tricked me."

"Oh, goodness. Please don't say he offered to take you on a wild ride?" Corona said, covering her reptilian mouth with a webbed paw.

"What? No!" I said, horrified. "I was working in Dr. Creamintin's office with a unicorn. I was supposed to be brushing a kelpie, and I mistakenly thought that *guy*, Devin, was the kelpie. I mean, he was a big, black horse, and he responded when I asked who I was supposed to brush."

"So…he tricked you into brushing him?" Corona asked, leaning back against the desk. Orion joined us at this point, his black hooves clopping on the marble floor.

"Yeah. It doesn't sound very bad, but I brushed him like three times. He was friendly as a horse, plus he looked like a horse, so I was…affectionate with him."

"Oh," Corona said, exchanging understanding glances with Orion.

"I mean, I thought he was a *horse*! I don't mind if a horse lips my shoulder or nuzzles my neck, but a *guy* doing that? No way!"

"It's odd. Generally, he uses his male shape to lure in helpless girls, not the other way around," Corona murmured.

"What *is* he anyway, a shape-shifter?" I asked, shifting in my chair.

"No," Orion said, speaking directly to me for the first time. "He is *the Pooka*."

"Alright, then, what's a Pooka?" I said.

"Not a Pooka, *the* Pooka," Orion corrected.

"Devin is the only one of his kind. The idea is that he is both a normal human male and yet one of the fairies because he can take on several traditional animal shapes associated with the Pooka. Most commonly, he uses the form of a horse, but he can also take on the shape of a dog," Corona said. "The Pooka is known for being a mischievous sprite. He, it is always a he, plagues travelers or people who may stumble upon him in the dark. Generally as a horse, he lures them onto his back. The second they mount up, he bolts and takes them on a wild ride before dumping them in the nearest swamp or river. Some of the old Pookas were so rough, they would kill their riders. As a dog, he chases people through the moors."

"You mentioned there were other Pookas, but I thought you said he was the only one?" I asked.

It was Orion, this time, who replied. "The title of the Pooka is passed through the males of Devin's line. His father was the previous Pooka and his grandfather before him. When the current Pooka dies, his son becomes the next one."

"So…there aren't any girl Pookas?" I asked.

Corona could see where I was going with this. "No," she replied. "As I mentioned before, only males can be the Pooka, and there is only one at a time. The Pooka will marry a regular human—sometimes she knows what he is; most times she doesn't—and from their children, a single male offspring will be born with the ability to shape-shift. Additionally, there are easily identifiable personality traits that are passed along. Like Devin's penchant for mischief," Corona dryly said. "He's not malicious. He is a practical jokester and something of a womanizer, but he's completely harmless."

"I'm not so sure about that," I glowered as Orion turned to help a fire elf.

Corona laughed, her dark eyes dancing with amusement. "You have nothing to fear from him, Morgan. Soon the Fairy Council will catch up with him and drag him back to Britain for work purposes. Besides, I doubt Frey will allow him to get much closer to you. Pack dynamics would drive him to stop it."

"What?" I blinked.

Corona didn't answer and picked up a ringing telephone. "Good afternoon. This is the MBRC's main information desk, Corona speaking. How can I help you?"

I settled back into my chair, intending to wait for Toby, but I spun around when I heard someone speaking across the desk. "Um, excuse me. Are you, by any chance, Morgan?"

I turned around and smiled. A young, female cyclops was hopefully blinking at me. Again, shattering the cyclops-literature-norms, she wore an adorable black skirt, a white tailored shirt, and stood probably a few inches over six feet. She had a black clutch in one hand and fussed with a simple silver necklace that hung from her neck with the other hand. Her single eye was fastened on me.

"I am," I acknowledged. "Can I help you?"

She looked immensely relieved, and the death grip she had on her purse slackened. "Thank goodness! Nick said you might be able to help," she said, digging in her clutch to unearth two rolled up sheets of paperwork. "I've been trying to fill this out for days, but I'm afraid I just can't make out the font. The MBRC refused to give me a PDF copy so I couldn't enlarge it as usual on my computer," she said, looking hopefully at me.

I glanced over the sheets. It was the same, basic form I helped Nick with. "I would be glad to help you. Let's start with your name, shall we?"

By the time Toby popped back behind the desk four minutes later, I had finished helping the female cyclops and sent her on her way.

"Youreadytoanswermorequestions?" Toby breathed.

Apparently he had more coffee while on his break.

"Sure," I agreed.

"Herewego123," he said, his fingers flashing across the keyboard. "DearMBRCwhatisadoggybag?"

The second question/answer session with Toby was much more intense. I resolved to switch his coffee with something decaffeinated if I ever had to work with him again.

When Frey strolled up to the desk, I was so relieved to see him I could have hugged him.

"Time to head home, Morgan," he announced as I snatched up my backpack and things.

"Excellent. Good night, guys! It was fun working with you!" I said, lunging out of the desk before Toby spit out another question. I barely dodged Gristles, the pervo fairy, who was sitting on the desk. "See you later!"

"Tomorrow actually. Morgan will be returning here tomorrow," Frey smiled at everyone behind the desk before he turned on his heels and strolled out. "How was your afternoon?" he asked in a conversational tone as we walked down the hallway.

"Interesting. Really interesting. And I mean that on a multitude of levels," I said, glancing over at him before bulging my eyes.

He was once again sniffing in my direction, although this time, he was much more discreet. He noticed my gaze and gave up all pretenses of being courteous. He stopped and leaned over to sniff my neck. He pulled back, the tip of his nose twitching.

"You saw Devin."

It wasn't a question.

"Yep."

"He left you alone?"

"After some encouragement, yes," I carefully phrased.

Frey looked disgruntled for a moment before he started charging forward. We popped out by Tiny. Dave was waiting there for us. We waved goodbye to the giant before wandering through Union Station.

I was most suspicious when Frey paused for a moment. "I'll be right back," he said before disappearing up the stairs.

"So. Morgan. How was the front desk?" Dave asked before twirling on the tips of his toes.

"Good. I helped answer questions with Toby," I replied.

"*Oh.* You were working with *that* little carefully caffeine-cultivated creature?" Dave asked.

"Yes. I saw Devin, too," I said, spitting out the name.

"Oh, my," Dave said, nearly falling over mid-twirl, his beer belly jingling. "I meant to talk to you about that, Morgan. Frey may begin acting…oddly."

"What?" I asked, my forehead wrinkling.

"Here you go," Frey said, hopping down the last three steps with athletic ease. (That, at least, was something the books didn't lie about.) As he breezed past me, he shoved a Mango-a-go-go flavored Jamba Juice in my hands. "Your favorite flavor, right?" he asked, peering over his shoulder to check.

"Y-yes," I stammered, unused to Frey's kindness.

"Good. Come on, we don't want to miss the train," Frey beckoned.

On the way home, Frey sat next to me, his arm casually thrown across the back of our seat. Occasionally, he let it slide down to bump me in the neck before returning it to its previous position.

We didn't talk, and Frey alternated between peering past me to look out the window and watching the other passengers.

Across from us, Dave mouthed, "See? Oddly!"

I could only wish I knew why Frey was being so…kind. It was making me paranoid.

Tuesday followed Monday's pattern. Frey actually *stopped* by my locker to chit chat with me once between classes, and again we were partners during Spanish. (I didn't exactly appreciate that part. I had to wade through Spanish verbs without any partner or teacher assistance—Dave knew even less Spanish than Frey did, which was a pathetic excuse. He had been alive far longer than either of us and had a long life ahead of him.)

I probably would have continued to be pleasantly surprised by Frey's sudden personality swap, but the events that took place during my lunch hour made me question the safety of my heart.

I was eating with Fran, Emily, Samantha, and a few other friends when Frey tapped me on the shoulder.

"Frey, hey. What's up?" I asked, discreetly wiping my mouth with a napkin after greeting the werewolf.

"Hey Morgan. Can I talk to you for a bit?" Frey asked tipping his head away from the lunch table.

Emily giggled, and Fran outright smirked as I said, "Sure," before I slid off the bench.

"What's up?" I repeated as Frey led me out of the cafeteria and towards the front doors.

"I need to ask you to do a big, big favor for me," Frey said, turning to face me.

"What is it?" I asked.

"I need you to take me for a walk," Frey said, holding out a forest green collar and leash.

"*What*?!"

Frey reached out and clamped his free hand across my mouth. "Not so loud," he whispered, glancing at the secretary seated behind the front desk. He exhaled when she did not look up.

"What do you mean, *a walk*?" I shrilly asked when he removed his hand.

"I'm going to change, so I need you to walk around with me, holding my leash," Frey said.

"Whatever for?" I tightly asked. Every particle of my being said this whole idea was *wrong*. Why did he want to go on a walk?!

"Look, Dave refused to drink his tomato juice again, and he got away from me in the hallways. I saw him run outside, and the fastest way to track him would be to transform into a wolf and sniff him out. But I can't run around like a stray pet. I *must* be on a leash."

"Can't I just put the collar on you once you've transformed and leave it as that?" I begged.

Frey shook his head so emphatically I swear I could hear his brains rattle. "No. No way. That's not enough."

"What do you mean?"

"I used to do that whenever I needed to transform—wear a collar that had my family's address on it. I would even curl my tail like a husky so I looked less fierce. But whether it's because I'm an actual wolf, or because I'm so large when I transform, the last time I did that, someone called animal control. I was shot with a tranquilizer and taken to the humane society. My parents had to come with a wizard to bust me out. It was horrible," Frey said, shivering at the memory. When he looked up, I'm pretty sure he could tell I was starting to break. "Please, Morgan? I really need your help," he said, the green depths of his eyes turning soulful.

A warm feeling bubbled up in my stomach, and I squashed it down with the strength of a troll. *Think of Brett; think of Brett*! I told myself. (I didn't need a wizard to tell me a magical guy was nothing but trouble. I would NOT fall for Frey or anyone from the MBRC!)

I sighed. "Fine. Let's go. I want to get back early enough to finish eating lunch."

Frey's face transformed into a toothy smile. "Thanks, Morgan, come on. Let's go outside. Here, you can use my jacket," he said, handing me his black jacket to throw over my shoulders as we exited the building.

Together, we walked around the building, heading for the parking lot.

"Here's good," Frey said, stopping behind the first row of cars.

I took the leash and collar from Frey and awkwardly turned around. "Right so… what now?"

I heard Frey's shoes shuffle on the cement, and seconds later, a wet nose pressed against my hand.

I looked down, and there was Frey. He was *huge* and unmistakably wolfish, even with the curled tail.

"Um, so I put the collar on, right?" I asked, crouching down next to canine Frey.

He nodded and stretched his neck out very nicely so I could loosely buckle the collar on. With a lot of resignation, I clipped the leash to the collar.

"I want to go on the record of saying this is so wrong. It feels wrong; it looks wrong; it's just *wrong*. What kind of werewolf needs to be walked on a leash?" I complained as Frey started off, his tail wagging as he padded along.

Frey led me around the back of the building, his nose to the ground as we passed the field house, soccer field, and track and football field.

I was jittery. Walking Frey on a leash felt like I was pulling wings off fairies—although I was grateful for Frey's jacket, which served as a very nice windbreaker.

I was finally settling into the idea of the transformed and trotting Frey being on a leash when we walked across the teacher parking lot and saw a teacher.

"Oh, my gosh! That's Miss Grebki, my English teacher!" I hissed. "If she see's us, we're toast!" I said, throwing myself behind a car.

Frey peered around the corner of the car and sniffed the air. He turned back to me and cutely waved his tail in a circle above his head like a husky before trotting off, heading straight for my teacher.

"Wait, Frey, no—wait!" I hissed before the canine dragged me out from behind the car.

"Morgan, what are you doing out here? With a dog?" Miss Grebkei added after a moment's hesitation.

"I, um, you see," I stammered, glancing down at the white wolf.

Frey did nothing to help me and instead sat down, cocking his head at me.

"This is... Dave's—I mean Señor Smith's dog. He asked me to watch him for a few seconds, but it's been ten minutes, and I can't find him anymore. We're looking for him," I said.

"Really?" Miss Grebki said, shifting her weight to one side as she fixed me with an evil eye.

"Absolutely," I nodded.

"Morgan!"

I looked up with intense relief, spotting Fran standing on the edge of the peace garden. She was with Brett Patterson, shielding her eyes against the sun as she stared at me.

"There's Fran. She must have found Señor Smith. Bye, Miss Grebki," I said, setting off at a jog. Frey loped at my side, flinging his tail around like a carefree dog.

"Fran, I am so glad to see you. You too, Brett. You guys just saved me," I said, drawing closer to them. "What are you doing out here?"

"I have study hall, and I wanted to talk to Fran," Brett grinned.

"I came looking for you. Someone said they saw you leave the building with Frey. What's up with the dog?" Fran asked, staring down at Frey, who once again had his nose to the ground.

"This is Señor Smith's dog. I'm watching him for a few minutes," I said, the lie coming to me a little easier this time.

"What's her name?" Fran asked, crouching down to look at him. "She's gorgeous."

"It's…um…Whitey," I supplied. "He's a boy," I added, feeling embarrassed for Frey's sake, although the wolf didn't appear bothered by the gender mix up.

"He's huge! Woah, look at his *teeth*!" Brett whistled when Frey looked up with an opened-mouthed dog smile.

"Well, if he poops in the Peace Garden, make sure Señor Smith cleans it up," Fran said, straightening up.

"Fran!" I yelped, horrified as I clutched Frey's leash to my chest. I checked to see if he felt offended.

He didn't even look up. He was busy sniffing the air, his tail curled on his back.

"What?" Fran asked, brushing her arms for warmth. "It's a legitimate point."

I shut my eyes to try and delete Fran's horribly insensitive words from my mind. I opened them again when Frey barked—a deep, rumbling noise.

I could see Dave running across the Peace Garden, heading for the school doors.

Frey tugged once on the leash, which I dropped. He barked again and broke into a sprint, full-out pursuing Dave.

He caught him at the edge of the garden, barking as he

launched himself into the air and landed on Dave, tackling the vampire to the ground.

"Aww, look. He's so happy to see his master," Fran said as Frey grabbed the neck material of Dave's shirt and shook his head, snapping the vampire like a rag doll.

"Um, sure," I agreed. "Okay, so, Whitey has been reunited with his owner. Let's go back inside and eat."

"All right. But what happened to Frey? You've got his jacket," Fran said as we turned to head back into the school building.

"Oh, he was the one who asked me to watch Whitey for Señor Smith because he had to step out for a minute. He'll be back later for his jacket," I evasively said as we passed Dave and Frey.

The vampire was choking on the collar of his shirt as Frey tugged him backwards towards the gardens.

Ten minutes later, Frey dropped by my lunch table for his jacket as a severely disgruntled Dave—who now sported several magnificent looking bruises—headed to the staircase that led to the foreign language rooms.

"Thanks for the help, Morgan," Frey whispered into my ear as he reclaimed his jacket.

"No problem," I said, blushing in spite of myself as he grinned at me.

No, no, no! Think of Brett! Think of Brett!

Later that afternoon, Frey, Dave, and I piled on the train after school and started our journey to the MBRC, which gave me some time to ask Frey a few questions that were bothering me.

"When am I going to get hypnotized? It's been a while. Isn't that siren back yet?" I asked, slipping my cell phone in a pocket after reading a text from Fran.

"She's returning tomorrow, but it will take her all day Thursday to catch up with her paperwork. I've asked Dr. Creamintin to schedule an appointment with her on Friday," Frey said, tossing his arm across the back of our seat.

I nodded but was a little surprised. I thought Dr. Creamintin might refuse to hypnotize me because I was such an asset. Internally, I supposed I couldn't be that much help; I was just one teenage girl. Besides, I knew the office would have to wade through so much red tape in order to keep me, it wouldn't be the logical choice.

I was surprised when Dave spoke on my behalf. "That's unexpected," he said, giving his thermos of V8 a dirty look before taking a swig of it. "I would have thought Dr. Creamintin wouldn't let her go."

Frey made a noise in the back of his throat, and Dave gave me a meaningful look.

I didn't know how to interpret it, and shrugged back at the vampire as Frey's arm bumped my neck.

Little did I know that Dr. Creamintin actually *had* been making noises about meddling with my memories—he was quite against it. (It wasn't often he had a willing subject on hand to help out.) In reality, it was *Frey* who was pushing the process along.

"Today, I'm working with Toby again, right?" I asked, tugging on a lock of my hair.

"Yes, I believe so," Frey nodded.

"Great. Can we stop at a Starbucks or McDonalds or something? I want to pick up a cup of coffee for him," I said.

Frey froze. "Let me get this straight. You want to give Toby, *Toby*—the hobgoblin who has caffeine instead of blood pulsating through his body—that Toby, more coffee?"

"Not quite," I grinned at him. "I want to give him *de*caffeinated coffee and let him think it's regular."

"Oh. That might not be such a bad idea," Frey considered.

"If I'm there long enough, I'll try to start swapping his pots of regular coffee with decaffeinated. Although I suppose it's probably not worth the trouble if I'm only here until Friday," I said, biting my lip.

The smile actually went out of Dave at the thought, and Frey stared out the window. We were somberly silent until we reached the station.

After we picked up Toby's decaffeinated coffee at Starbucks, Frey dropped me off at the information desk.

"Just shout for me if you need anything. I mean that literally. I'll be within hearing distance of you today. Even over this racket, I'll be able to hear you," Frey seriously promised. "So if that *guy* comes again…"

I smiled and leaned against the desk. "He won't," I promised.

"Right, so…," he trailed off, making a motion with his hands. I entertained the thought that he wanted to hug me but thought better of it. He was clearly at a loss for how we were supposed to part. "Right," he repeated before abruptly turning on his heels and walking away.

I sighed and slipped behind the desk.

"Don't think too deeply about it, dear," Corona suggested as Doggy twined about my legs and barked at me, flapping his little dragon wings with delight. "He's only acting that way out of instinct. Probably. Although I suppose…Frey is rather brisk, but even he could fall for someone."

"What?" I asked, squatting down to pet the blue dragon.

"The affection, the worry, his desire to keep touching you. It's all a natural part of being a werewolf, not because he's a hormonal teenager," Corona told me, shaking a webbed paw at me before turning to a client.

"Someone had better explain this to me soon," I muttered to Doggy before standing and approaching Toby.

"Hey, Toby," I called to the hobgoblin. He only muttered a greeting, his fingers flying across the keyboard. "I brought you some coffee," I added.

He whirled around, facing me with one of his nicest smiles. "For me?" he asked, tapping his long fingers together.

"Uh-huh. It's a thank you for being so…nice," I lamely said, offering him the disposable coffee cup.

Toby took the cup and slurped half of it down in one gulp. He smacked his lips and looked reflective after swallowing it. "Tastes different," he observed.

"It's Starbucks," I smiled.

Toby's eyes lit up, and he beamed. He did not thank me, but this was the first time the hobgoblin truly grinned.

"I hope you know what you're doing," Orion said while walking past, flicking his black horsetail.

"It's better than it looks," I assured him in a whisper before taking my seat beside Toby.

Toby worked at the same fast and furious pace as he had the day before. He chugged down the coffee within twenty minutes and didn't seem to be perturbed that no caffeine rush followed the actions. In fact, I had so ingratiated myself with him by bringing the coffee that he did not mind the interruptions to our Q&A time, and they were numerous.

A cyclops, a harried-looking mother towing two children behind her, showed up fifteen minutes into my shift.

"Is Morgan here?" she asked, looking absolutely desolate as her children stood behind her, sticking their tongues out at each other.

"Morgan?" Corona asked, turning to me. I was already standing, having heard my name.

"I'm Morgan. How can I help you?" I asked, striding over to her, flicking Gristles the pervo fairy when he landed on my shoulder. (He was probably trying to look down my shirt.)

A sigh of relief rushed out of the cyclops. "I need your help. I have to fill this out by 4:40, and I can't read it," she said, sounding utterly frustrated while tossing a packet of papers onto the desk.

"And they won't send it to you as a PDF file?" I guessed.

The cyclops shook her head.

I nodded as I nosed through the packet. "This is just a simple change-of-classes request forum? It doesn't look too difficult. We can get it done with plenty of time," I smiled reassuringly at the mother.

"Thank you, thank you!" she repeated.

"You're welcome. Could you give me your name—spelling, too—please?"

Eleven minutes later, the cyclops was on her way, her children trailing after her.

"Dear, you have no idea what you have gotten yourself into," Corona commented behind me.

"What do you mean?" I asked, turning around to face the talking reptile.

"The cyclopes are a nice race," Corona factually said. "But they're horrible readers and will exploit anyone who is willing to help them."

"What do you mean?" I said as I plopped down in a chair next to Toby, who was talking on the phone.

"I mean you'll be getting dozens and dozens of requests to help fill out forms. The first cyclops you helped spread the word. They'll all be flocking here now. Don't feel bad; it's happened to all of us at some point. Eventually, you will have to tell them no; there's not enough time to help them all," Corona said before turning to a pair of tourist fairies who fluttered in front of the desk.

As Toby started yelling at the poor creature on the other end of the phone call, I leaned back in my chair and wondered. Would I really have to turn them away? If all of the employees at the information desk had been plagued with this sort of problem at one point or another, it was obviously a serious issue. The MBRC wasn't correctly providing for one of the races they professed to be rehabilitating.

"Okay you ready to go 123?" Toby prompted after hanging up on his customer.

"Sure," I replied.

"Alright next question: I saw someone walking a guinea pig on a leash down Main Street of the town I live in Is this normal behavior I should copy?"

"Oh, gosh. No. Tell them NO!"

Corona was right. By the time Toby finally took his break at approximately 5:15, only about ten minutes before Frey would drop by to pick me up, I had helped at least half a dozen cyclopes.

They were easy to assist. Generally it only took five to ten minutes, and Toby was in a fairly good mood and didn't mind that I got up every few minutes to aid the newest cyclops client.

"I'm going to run to the bathroom really quick; I won't be long," I told Corona before slipping out of the many-sided desk.

"Sounds great. Frey will be by soon to pick you up," she reminded me.

"Right," I acknowledged before plunging into the hustle and bustle of the main chamber, moving in the direction of a small inlet Corona had pointed out to me the day before: the bathrooms.

I dodged a sorceress and her five students, walked beneath a beautiful phoenix, and skirted around a white, hairy creature that looked suspiciously like a yeti before reaching the bathrooms. They were a little weird as the stalls were built for a variety of beings, but they were probably the cleanest, prettiest bathrooms I had ever set foot in.

As I left the bathrooms I was still marveling over the differences, so I was totally caught off guard when a male arm was thrown across my shoulders and spun me around.

It was Devin.

6

The Formation of the Cyclops Union

"Hello, Morgan!" he beamed down at me, his yellow-moon eyes glittering. Without warning, he hugged me tight and nosed my neck. He moved so fast my brain wasn't able to keep up, which was a good thing for him.

Before I reacted with violence, Devin deeply inhaled and abruptly jerked back. He glared at my neck and sneezed three times. "That mutt's been hanging around you again, hasn't he?" he sneered, his upper lip curling with distaste.

"Yes," I said without apology.

Devin cringed and rubbed his nose. "He smells like dirt. Dirt rubbed on a wet dog."

"What does that have to do with me?" I asked, taking a step away from the shape-shifting fairy.

"He rubbed his scent all over you," the handsome boy grimaced before showering me with his dashing smile. "But it's no matter. It only makes the whole thing more amusing. How are you, lass?" he asked, suddenly grabbing me by the shoulder before pulling me close.

"I was fine until you showed up," I said as I tried to squirm out of his grasp. This time, however, he did not move into any intimate/inappropriate contact. Instead, he pulled his black shirt sleeve over his hand and scrubbed at my neck. "What on earth are you doing? Do you want a repeat performance of the last time we met?"

"*I* am driving that mongrel mad," Devin said, moving to forcefully scrub the front of my neck. I gurgled in protest. "And really, Morgan, you cheated."

"Stop that!" I said, slapping his hands away when I managed to break out of his arm hold.

"It is going to be delightful to see his reaction," Devin smirked.

"I don't get it. Why would it make him freak out?" I asked, brushing myself off.

"Frey is a werewolf. He's got some baggage and abilities and crap that normal humans never have. One of them is his supreme sense of smell. He naturally *hates* me; I'm far higher up the hierarchy of power than he is—the dope—so of course he would *hate* it if I snagged you right out from underneath him," Devin said, surveying the crowd.

"So you're saying that's why he's been so cautious about me seeing you?" I asked.

"Yep."

"It's not that you tricked me, and I've probably been mentally scarred for life, and he's actually concerned for me?"

"Well, maybe a small sliver of his humanity feels that way, but I guarantee his werewolf part just *burns* when he smells me on you—a person he considers to be a pack member."

"But I'm not a werewolf. How could I be a pack member?" I argued.

"You don't have to be a werewolf to be pack," Devin shrugged. "Dave is one of his pack members; most likely any little siblings he has are, too. Frey is a part of his family's pack, and then he has his own. Anybody he sees as being underneath him or below him, or anyone who needs him and his protection is part of his pack. If I really got to you, I would not only whisk you right out of his pack, but plop you up higher on the power scale than him. Of course, that would only be if I was serious about you," Devin supposed.

While Devin talked, my blood boiled.

I was not shocked about the casual way Devin talked about taking and dropping me. Corona said he was a womanizer. Based on the way the nymph reacted to him yesterday and even from my own experience, I could confidently say Devin was probably the number one enemy of women across the globe.

But Frey?

I had actually thought he was warming up to me. I thought we were becoming friends.

Talking to me instead of Dani and Toni, being my Spanish partner, stopping by my locker, buying me Jamba Juice, it was all an *act*. He was just trying to control me! I remembered how easily he would let his arm fall to bump my neck; he was probably trying to rub his scent on me the same way Devin just had.

"You can't completely blame him," Devin continued, interrupting my boiling anger. "It's a natural instinct for him. He thinks he's protecting you. Actually…he sort of is. It doesn't help he's an ignorant male. I'm sure he's aware to some extent that he is flirting with you, but he isn't doing it to be cruel," Devin said, sensing my hot rage. "All the same, though, this is going to be fun," he gleefully added.

Devin's speech did not drain the anger from me, but he did have a point. If Frey was acting based on instinct, I couldn't completely blame him. We were different races. When I was twelve, a foreign exchange student from Poland stayed with my family for a year. She was a nice girl, but it was a lot harder to try and understand the differences between our cultures than I would have originally thought. And she was human! The differences between werewolf culture and human culture had to be like night and day.

But still. Frey had played with my feelings, intentional or not.

I scowled as I considered my options. I could either scream at Frey, or I could play the game, perfectly aware of what Frey was doing, and perhaps wheedle a few more Jamba Juices out of him before my memory was tampered with on Friday.

Devin made the decision for me. "There he is, over by the desk! Come on!"

There was a flash of yellow, and when I turned to face Devin, he wasn't there. In his place was a handsome, black dog that was built like a German Shepherd.

"Your dog shape?" I guessed.

A pink tongue rolled out of the dog's mouth, and he leaned forward to lick my hands.

I smiled and squatted down, sinking my fingers into Devin's soft, black fur.

Devin managed to lick my chin before I remembered that he was actually a human. I placed one leg on his doggy chest and kicked, sending him skidding away.

He smacked into a wall as two fairy godmothers floated past me, tisking.

"Did that young lady just kick that poor, poor dog?" the first fairy godmother asked.

"She did. She must be a wicked step-sister," the second fairy godmother said.

"No licking, nudging, touching, nosing, rubbing, *or* patting me," I warned Devin before I stood and stalked off into the crowd.

Devin pitifully whined behind me, but I ignored him.

"Hey, Frey, is it time to go?" I asked him as I walked up to the desk.

"Oh, hey. Yeah, you ready?"

"Yep, just let me grab my stuff," I said, ducking behind the desk to grab my light jacket and backpack. "It was great working with you guys today," I told Corona and company, pausing to pet Doggy before I slipped out of the desk. "Tell Toby I'm sorry I missed saying goodbye to him," I said, walking up to Frey before setting my backpack down. As I hunkered down to dig through the pockets of my bag, I spotted Devin weaving through legs and appendages. He was watching Frey with open anticipation flashing on his canine face.

I stood up when I found what I was looking for, a hair tie.

"I'll be sure to do that. Thank you for your help today, Morgan," Corona smiled, hefting Doggy in her arms as Frey shifted closer to me to pick up my jacket for me.

I grinned and started to collect my hair up in a messy bun,

leaving my neck uncovered. "Oh, no prob! It was fun—," I started before Frey deeply inhaled while standing up from his crouch, his arm brushing mine as he stood. When he reached full height, he froze and inhaled again.

"Morgan, you saw Devin again," Frey growled.

"Yeah," I said, putting on a long-suffering face. "He accosted me when I was trying to find the bathroom."

I was pretty sure dog Devin flinched somewhere behind me.

"What did he do? You didn't fall for whatever romantic drabble he spouted, did you?" Frey asked, his eyes flickering over my body as though waiting for me to break out in hives. "You didn't let him, like, touch you, right?" Frey continued reaching towards me with both hands. Now that I understood the situation, I could clearly see he was dying to try and wipe Devin's scent off me but had enough restraint not to.

I was hurt.

I had hoped that maybe he was concerned for me, but no. Frey didn't ask if Devin had done anything to hurt me—although I had been the violent one ever since Devin had taken on his human shape—the only thing he was concerned with was my standing level with Devin and the fact that I smelled like the fairy horse.

"It's fine," I sighed. "He hugged me. That was all."

Frey leaned a little closer to get a better whiff of me and shook his head. "He more than hugged—,"

"You know it's too bad that his personality is so rotten," I said, taking my coat from Frey before slipping it on. "He's really cute," I shared before stooping over to pick up my backpack. I shouldered it and waved once at the crew behind the desk.

Corona looked faintly amused. "We'll have to talk tomorrow, Morgan," she said.

"Right, bye!" I chirped before walking off. "Frey, you coming?" I called.

My call broke Frey out of his shell-shocked stupor, and he hurried after me. "Devin is only good-looking because he's a fairy. You need to be careful, Morgan. He's a total player; he's not serious about you," Frey lectured as we scooted around a pair of glowing lizards.

"I know that."

Frey released an unconvinced huff and spent the entire train ride home discreetly trying to bump my neck with his arm while pulling me into some of the most amusing idle chit chat in my life.

By the end of school on Wednesday, I was no longer amused and back to anger. Frey was not desperately clawing to keep me in his grasp, but the more I mused on it, the more I could see it was his werewolf nature driving him to befriend me.

It was in the way he would talk to me, the superior tone he took on, like he was an alpha male of a pack. It was the way he herded and bumped me to the train station—it wasn't a protective motion, it was a you're-so-stupid-you-can't-get-to-the-train-station-without-my-help sort of motion. He would ask me questions about my life, but only while leaning back, making it absolutely clear he was doing me a real honor.

The sad thing was I probably would have fallen for it, hook line and sinker, if Devin hadn't have said something earlier. That was what really infuriated me.

I was so grateful when we arrived at the MBRC, I practically ran to the information desk, Toby's decaffeinated coffee in hand. I skidded to a stop when I trotted into the main MBRC chamber.

Through the mass motion of magical bodies, I could see ten or twelve cyclopes, lined up by the information desk, waiting.

Frey and Dave caught up with me and followed the line of my gaze.

Dave whistled. "Got yourself saddled with quite the project, didn't you missy?" he asked before plunging into the busy MBRC, getting swept along with the crowd.

"You've been helping the cyclopes?" Frey asked, watching the one-eyed beings.

"Yeah. They have trouble reading their paperwork," I said, a little stunned at the line.

Frey nodded. "That's a good thing, you know," he said with probably the first speck of sincerity he had uttered since I met him. "No one is willing to help them, even though cyclopes are some of the wealthiest creatures in the MBRC. The center is oddly impatient with them. Someone needs to help them," Frey shook his head, knocking himself out of his musings. "Good luck," he smiled, placing a warm hand on my back before sliding it across my shoulders.

Before, I would have interpreted it as a romantic gesture. Now, even though I melted a little, I reminded myself it was just an excuse to wipe his scent on me.

I gave Frey a strained smile. He didn't notice the difference and stepped into the chamber, trailing after Dave.

I slowly wove my way to the information desk, dodging dragons and wizards left and right before ducking behind the desk, smiling at the waiting cyclopes.

"I told you, dear," Corona clicked at me. "We haven't the time to help them all."

I slipped off my backpack and jacket and thoughtfully stared at the group. "I'm not sure," I replied before handing a joyful Toby his coffee. "Toby, I'm going to be busy for a little while. Give me…oh… twenty minutes, and I'll be back. I promise we'll beat yesterday's record," I said while scratching the top of Doggy's head before backing out of the desk again.

Orion, who was in the process of aiding a family of fauns, stopped to watch me with an interested cock of his head as I approached the swarm of cyclopes.

"Hi guys, I'm Morgan, and this is just a wild guess, but I'm thinking you all need help with paperwork," I ventured, my voice friendly as I did my best tour guide impersonation.

The cyclopes sheepishly glanced among themselves and nodded while I studied the group.

If I had to hazard a guess, I would say they were all white collar workers with impeccable fashion taste. The least dressy male was sporting slacks and a polo shirt. The females wore suits or skirts, Gucci bags and Prada shoes on all of them. Their paychecks had to be big enough to support their wardrobe, which was an interesting thought.

"Oh, Odysseus. What a far cry these creatures are from the stupid sheep-herding barbarian you blinded," I murmured before addressing them. "I am quite willing to help you; however, I have a few questions of my own," I said, meeting their one-eyed gazes. "Why on earth don't you wear contacts or glasses?"

A collective slump of shoulders followed.

Two of the cyclopes, a classy looking female who wore a black Chanel suit and a male who looked fabulous—one eye and all—in a delectable Ralph Lauren suit, stepped forward.

"Human contacts and spectacles don't fit us," the female said, a genuine smile flitting across her lips. "The whole one-big-eye in the middle of our head thing makes it difficult to find glasses with the right shape and contacts that are big enough," she added, pointing out to me that while their eye(s) were quite pretty, coming in a wild array of colors that humans didn't possess (hers was periwinkle blue), they were also larger than a normal human's.

"So?" I shrugged, continuing to chatter like a bubbly tour guide. "Who says you have to use human eyewear?"

The Ralph Lauren suit guy cleared his throat before speaking in a pleasant, tenor voice. "Our visual aid needs are a very low priority for the MBRC. Daily glamours need to be cast on fairies. Vampires must be supplied with tomato juice. Dragons must be fed, and unicorns must undergo surgical changes. Coming up with a cyclops contact is hardly important."

"What's a glamour?" I asked, momentarily distracted.

"Fairy magic. It's like an illusion we wrap ourselves in to hide our magical characteristics and make us look human," the female Cyclops with the periwinkle eye explained before the Ralph Lauren guy launched into his lecture again.

"We can function in the real world through the use of a head glamour, which gives us the appearance of having two eyes. All of us here have at least one assistant beneath us who can read memos and notes to us. We use our computers, increasing the font sizes when we can. We get by. We need the MBRC's help to survive."

I folded my arms and narrowed my eyes, leaning back to gaze at the expensive designer clothes my cyclopes were wearing. "Does the MBRC charge you?" I asked.

"No, not really. The MBRC runs largely on monetary gifts and donations," the periwinkle-eyed female slowly said. "They charge for some basic care, but most instruction and assistance is free; we're simply encouraged to give donations."

"However," a cyclops from the back piped up. "We cyclopes make up a hefty amount of the donators. With the exception of our eyes, we fit in with humans and have minds that are naturally gifted for business. Additionally, we live longer than the average human, so we have more time to gather knowledge, learn additional languages, accumulate wealth, etcetera, etcetera," he added.

"So the MBRC is unwilling to help you guys, some of its top donators, see better?" I flatly asked.

The cyclopes glanced at each other, clearly never having seen it that way, if you'll pardon the horrible pun.

"It does sound terrible when you say it like that," the periwinkle female volunteered.

"Right. We're going to take care of this. Does the MBRC have some kind of eye doctor?" I asked.

"Yes, ophthalmological research." one of them replied.

"Excellent. Would someone please lead the way?" I said.

They stared back at me.

"To the ophthalmological branch?" I clarified.

The cyclopes exchanged puzzled looks but shrugged their shoulders and started out.

We marched into the ophthalmological branch, the female cyclops with the periwinkle eye leading me and my one-eyed army. (On our way there, she took the time to introduce herself to me. Her name was Sandra, another anti-cyclops name.) When we reached the front desk, a glasses-wearing human (sorceress most likely, even though she didn't dress it) was seated there.

"Can I help you?" the receptionist asked very carefully.

"Yes. Hello. I'm looking to make an appointment with someone in charge of research or medical improvements in this branch," I smiled, painfully aware I looked like a school girl next to my designer-label wearing compatriots.

The receptionist raised an unbelieving eyebrow.

"You see, my friends and I are very interested in improvements in the area of eye glasses and contacts, specifically ones designed to fit cyclopes. I'm quite certain they would be willing to make a generous donation to fund your research," I said, turning around to make sure my guess wasn't off base.

Behind me the cyclopes furiously nodded.

"I'll be frank, young lady, we're swamped," the secretary said. "We have colorblind werewolves who drive trucks for a living and are apparently incapable of memorizing the order of lights at a stop light. We have miniscule, elderly fairies that need petite glasses in order to properly function. We have blind dragons—which I don't need to tell you is a highly dangerous situation—and a horrible eye fungus has recently swept through the dryads. We don't have time to research eyewear for cyclopes. Sorry," she said apologetically to the cyclopes behind me. "They can function. They've been functioning. All they have is a problem reading things up close. It's easy to get around," she said before looking back at her files and notes.

I turned around and leaned against the desk, propping my elbows up as I considered my options. Listening to that lady talk reminded me ever so much of my older brother, Michael. Michael was unfortunately named after Michael the arc angel, and as such, he fancied himself God's greatest gift to the world. When manipulating Michael, it was best to be open and blunt and tell him what he had to lose.

I resolved to use the same method on this maddening woman.

"Well, there you have it guys. I told you they were too stubborn and pigheaded to care, but it's the MBRC—what do you expect? This is why I wanted to open that clinic in Japan. Not only do they have better technology, but we could focus on you guys and your needs. I mean come on; with your funds, it'll be a snap. And the second the other cyclopes see what we're doing, they'll surely withdraw their funds from here and follow us to Japan. Come on. I know an elf from Glamourizing who's in contact with a unicorn herd in Hokkaido. They can hook us up," I said, pushing away from the counter while I prayed none of them would ask me what on earth I was talking about.

The receptionist rolled her eyes. "I know what you're trying to do. Idle threats will not work on me," she frowned.

I turned around and cocked my head. "Who said they're idle?"

"The MBRC is one of a kind. Magical beings need its help to survive. No one is an island unto themselves," she said in a snarky receptionist way.

I reached out and grabbed the Ralph Lauren suit guy. "His suit could pay for my first year in college. Let us talk to the research guys to see if this is even feasible, please. Or would you rather try to explain to your bosses why some of the biggest donators in the MBRC are all in Japan?"

The receptionist scowled. "Just how big of a donation would you give us?" she suspiciously asked.

"How many digits guys, four?" I ventured.

"How about six?" someone suggested.

"If we all chip in a little, we can get a seven figure sum without much difficulty," Mr. Ralph Lauren suit man acknowledged. I dropped his arm and my jaw.

The receptionist's eyeglasses slid off her nose.

"Well," she blustered. "If you're going to make it worth it…"

Turned out she wasn't the receptionist, but the director of ophthalmological research. Yeah, Sha-ZAM! Knowing that my cyclopes were very willing to hand over a seven-figure sum, she was quite happy to arrange an appointment for the following day.

The cyclopes were beyond ecstatic and enthusiastically back-slapped me the entire way back to the information desk. They also pleaded with me to attend the meeting with them, which I agreed to. (Visions of me taking over the MBRC with leadership help from

Fran and Hunter—Hunter had to know something useful after reading all those books—danced through my brain. I could make a cyclops UNION!)

When I got back to the information desk, I told the whole story to an amused Corona and an interested Orion, Corona chuckled at me about the whole Japan thing. "An elf in 'glamourizing'?"

"Hey, give me a break! Besides this room, the only thing I've seen of the MBRC is Dr. Creamintin's office," I said.

"The frog in the well does not know the greatness of the sea," Orion said.

"Ahem," Toby coughed, clearing his throat. He drank his coffee in my absence and was starting to lose patience with me since my supposed gift of caffeine was consumed.

"Right, Toby, I'm coming," I said, bending over to pick up Doggy before making my way to the hobgoblin's side. I winked at Orion and Corona as I plopped down in my chair, my attention once more on Toby.

"Thank you lets go 123," Toby started, banging on the keyboard with his long, green fingers.

Eighteen phone calls and countless emails later, I collapsed in my chair as Toby said his goodbyes before he puttered off to his break. Frey and Dave would arrive any minute, but I was mentally spent.

Our question-answering average for today was 21 seconds. Toby was a slave driver!

I was leaning back, massaging my head, when a velveteen voice interrupted my thoughts.

"So you think I'm attractive?"

I removed my hands from my eyes and twisted around. Devin was leaning on the desk, a deliciously devious smile curling across his lips as he propped his chin up on his hand.

"What?" I asked, my voice cross.

"Yesterday, when talking to that mongrel of yours, you said you thought I was quite handsome," Devin smirked.

I crinkled my nose. "I don't ever recall calling you handsome," I countered. "I said you were cute. You know, like a pony?"

Devin straightened, tipping his head like a posing model. "I am merely interpreting what you meant to say. I am not cute. No part of me is cute. I am what you would call dangerously handsome."

"Right. And I'm a mermaid," I said standing up.

Devin rolled his eyes. "If you choose to be blind, that is your own choice, hapless human."

"You are so full of yourself," I said, slipping on my jacket before shouldering my backpack and exiting the desk.

"I would rather be full of myself than full of crap," Devin shrugged before jumping into a new topic. "So what are you going to do about Frey?"

"What do you mean, what am I going to do?"

"You know, his whole canine-instincts thing, getting up in your space, pretending to like you in order to woo you away from me—any of this ringing a bell?"

"There's nothing to do. I'm getting hypnotized on Friday. Come next Monday, I might not even remember Frey's name,"

Devin hesitated. "You're what?"

"I'm getting hypnotized. Dr. Creamintin is arranging it for me. Frey was all for removing my memories, but Dr. Creamintin and Dave insisted hypnotizing was a safer route."

"You mean you're not staying on?" Devin asked, sounding shocked.

"Uh, no."

"Why not? You could be a consultant or something. Heaven knows we need more instructors around here with actual experience in the human culture."

"No. I am a regular high school girl. I want my social life back," I said, doing my best to ignore the resistant voices in the back of my head that shouted I really wanted to keep working.

"You're in HIGH SCHOOL?" Devin groaned, lifting a hand up to his forehead. "Good Lord, I should have known. That flea bitten Frey is in high school as well," his yellow eyes landed on me and he looked oddly flustered.

"What, did you think I was in middle school?" I asked.

The fairy horse muttered something like, "Almost robbing the cradle, and I didn't even know it," before straightening back into his model-like poses and smiles. "I was under the impression you were in college," he ruefully smiled.

"Nope. Sophomore in high school," I said, working hard to keep a pleased smile off my lips. I always love being mistaken for a college student.

Devin frowned. "But you can't leave," he said, reaching out to take my hand.

"Why not? And let go," I ordered, tugging on my hand.

"Because—," Devin started.

"Morgan," said a stormy voice.

Frey, his green wolf eyes narrowed, his stance stiff and wide, some of the muscles on his face twitching with anger, had found us.

"Frey, hello," I said, painfully aware that Devin was still holding my hand. "So, it's time to go?"

Frey clenched his jaw, clearly trying to control his fury. "Why are you with the Pooka?" he asked, his eyes were fastened on the space between Devin and me. It was like he was so angry, he couldn't look at either of us.

I rolled my eyes, not at all impressed. "Come on, Frey. We were just talking," I said before yanking my hand out of Devin's grasp. I adjusted the straps of my backpack and strolled over to the angry werewolf.

Frey finally raised his eyes to stare at my face. "*Talking*?" he spat.

"What is your problem?" I asked.

"No girl just *talks* with Devin," Frey snarled.

"Your concern is noted. But I hardly think I'm in danger of being ensnared by him. I'm being hypnotized on Friday. Remember?" I asked.

"About that. Why are you letting her go, mutt?" Devin asked, leaning past my shoulder to peer at Frey's face. "If she were mine—,"

"But she's not! Leave, outsider," Frey demanded, his shouts causing some stir among the magical beings around us.

"Lay off him, Frey. He hasn't done anything to you," I said.

Devin flashed me a charming smile before smirking at Frey. "Why, thank you, Morgan," he started before I cut it off.

"Devin, shut your mouth and *leave*. I don't need you rubbing it in his face," I ordered.

"Rubbing what in my face?" Frey asked, his voice tightening with something that sounded a lot like…well…*fear*. "You haven't—you can't stop her hypnotizing, *Pooka*."

"What are you talking about?" I asked before waving it off. "Never mind. Look Frey, I know about your whole 'instinct' thing," I said, making quotation marks in the air with my fingers. "Devin told me all about your pack mentality and how offending it would be if Devin dated me or something equally as ridiculous."

"Yeah," the fairy horse shot over my shoulder.

"Shut *up*, Devin," Frey and I snarled.

Devin meekly backed down.

"I don't know what you're talking about," Frey stubbornly said.

I lifted my hands as though to strangle him. "GRRR-AGH! You blockhead! Do you have fur in your ears or something? I said I KNOW ALL ABOUT IT!" I shouted the last line with such force and feeling that a purple genie that was floating by stopped to stare at us.

I continued my tirade. "I know you don't care for me personally, but you feel responsible for me, so the thought of Devin whisking me away is unbearable!"

"That is not it!" Frey shot back.

"Oh, really? Then why do you get so upset whenever I'm with him, or whenever I express some admiration of him?"

Frey sputtered for a moment before glaring at the gleeful Devin. "This is your fault," he snarled at the black-haired fairy. "If you had just kept your stupid horse muzzle to yourself—No! If you just stayed with the Fairy Council like you're supposed to and stop skulking around the MBRC, this wouldn't have happened!"

Devin shrugged. "Your petty jealousy is hardly noteworthy. It stimulates only a mild interest. If you hadn't reacted so hilariously, I might have left her alone."

"Stop trying to pawn off the blame, Frey," I snarled. "I knew from the moment Devin switched out of his horse form that he was a conniving, backstabbing, womanizing flirt."

"Hey!" Devin objected.

"But you," I shook my head at Frey. "I thought we were friends! And it turns out you're just as bad, just as territorial and self-centered as him!" I said, jerking my thumb behind me to point at Devin.

The Pooka was slightly put out. "That's harsh," he complained.

"You know what? Fine! If you're so happy with him, why don't you go home with *Devin*?" Frey hissed.

"Fine!" I said, snapping my head up and down.

"Fine!" Frey returned.

"Fine!" I said as he turned around and headed in the direction of Dr. Creamintin's office.

Frey stopped and turned around to shout at me. "I'm *GLAD* you're getting hypnotized! I can't wait until you're not around anymore!"

"Yeah? Well, I can't wait to forget YOU!" I shouted, a fairy godmother scuttled past us and shot me a concerned glance. A T-Rex moved between us, his predator eyes raised, staring at the ceiling as he probably wished he were somewhere else.

Between the dinosaur's legs, I could see Frey growl at me before stalking off for Dr. Creamintin's.

7

I Negotiate with the Magically Inclined

I glowered at his backside and headed for the MBRC exit.

It wasn't until I reached Tiny that I realized Devin had followed me.

"Hello, sir," Tiny respectfully said, saluting Devin.

"Hello—Tiny, isn't it? Good work, today," Devin said, ambling after me as I stalked ahead with quick, jerky steps.

When we rejoined the population of Chicago, I glanced up and caught Devin's yellow eyes. "Bye," I said before heading for a ticket window.

"No, you don't," Devin said, reaching out to snag me.

"I need a ticket," I said, sullen and not caring. "Frey has my round-trip ticket."

"Fine, fine. Go off on your warpath. I'll just follow the wreckage like it's a yellow brick road," Devin said, whimsically fanning his hand while looking off to the side. I stomped off before he realized I had left. "Hey!" he said, moving into a normal-paced walk to keep sight of me.

He waited just past the ticket counter, his arms folded across his broad chest, while I purchased my ticket home.

"What do you want?" I demanded.

"You liked that mongrel, didn't you?" Devin asked, following me as I stomped towards my appropriate platform.

"No, I didn't," I said, purposely reminding myself that I was head-over-heels for Brett Patterson. There wasn't a *chance* I liked Frey, not when I had a major crush on Brett!

"Then why are you so mad? You were perfectly pleasant before he snarled at you. Even after all I told you, you still nursed some hope didn't you?" Devin drearily sighed.

I turned on my heels to glare at him. "Is this fun for you? Do you like intentionally hurting people and rubbing things in their faces? Yeah. Maybe I did hope against all hope that Frey wasn't completely overrun by 'instincts,' whatever that means. Maybe I hoped he would apologize. So what? You want a cookie for guessing my feelings?" I snarled before storming off.

I was more than mildly surprised when Devin materialized at my shoulder as I found the platform.

He didn't say a word. Even when we climbed on an express train, and I wrathfully plopped down in a seat. He sat next to me, people-watching and winking at cute girls while I stared out the widow. It was a long but quiet train ride.

Devin flashed me a smile when I stood up to leave at my Oakdale stop, but it wasn't his charming, flashy smile. It was more… empathetic. I knew I had to look pretty miserable if the self-absorbed playboy Pooka felt even remotely bad for me.

That night, for probably the first time in my high school career, I played video games with Odie and Peter, the bloodiest, most violent video games they had. Engaging in computer-animated fist fights oddly soothed the turmoil that raged inside of me.

When I went to bed, I stared up at my white ceiling for a while, wondering what I was going to do tomorrow. It was Thursday, so Dr. Creamintin would not be expecting me—especially after I blew up at Frey like that—but I told the cyclopes I would be there for them.

"They wanted me there. Plus, I like helping them," I reasoned, refusing to allow my mind to paint a picture of a furious Frey. "I'm going. I don't care about Frey. The cyclopes asked *me* for help."

Thursday afternoon, I looked up and down the hallways of my high school before hastily leaving the school grounds. The final bell had just rung, and students swarmed the hallway.

I hurried down the sidewalk, setting my course for the Oakdale train station. I wasn't terribly worried about running into Frey. He said he didn't have to go to the MBRC on Thursdays. Technically, I should be safe.

All the same, I glanced up and down the platform after buying my ticket to Chicago, feeling like a spy on a dangerous mission.

The train ride to Union Station was uneventful, but finding the MBRC was a little more difficult than I expected. I went in the wrong door first (I pushed open an employees-only door and got a face full of pipes), and when I finally found the right entrance, the trail seemed to last much longer than I remembered.

After fifteen minutes of walking, I finally stumbled upon Tiny. "Hello, Morgan. Why are you here without Frey?" he asked.

"I promised the cyclopes I would come to their meeting with ophthalmological research today," I explained, shifting my backpack.

Tiny's bushy eyebrows rose. "So *you're* the one organizing the cyclops union?"

"What?" I blankly asked, briefly recalling my visions of world domination with the business-minded cyclopes surrounding me.

"It's been the talk of the MBRC. The cyclopes have been organized under some figurehead who is an elf in underground glamourizing and owns a unicorn herd in China," Tiny reported.

I stared at the giant before laughing. "Oh man, rumors can get so blown out of proportion," I giggled while Tiny uncomfortably shifted.

"Well," Tiny started. "If you really are here on request of the cyclopes, it's a good thing I lowered the Confounding Charm for you."

"The confounding charm?" I asked with interest.

"It's a low-level glamour spread in the hallway. It puzzles and confuses regular humans who try to come this way. I could feel you wandering around in it, so I lowered it for you. You're *supposed* to have a magical escort you know," Tiny said, shaking a finger that was the length of a football in my direction. "But I'll let it slide. Just this once. Here, I'll open the door for you," Tiny winked.

"Thanks, Tiny," I smiled as Tiny worked on some cranks and the image of metal doors faded.

"No problem," he said, pushing open the door for me. "My mom's cousin's daughter married a cyclops. They're good folk; they deserve the help. Good luck!" Tiny wished before the doors swung shut behind me.

I walked down the dark hallway, feeling a little apprehensive before I popped up in the central chamber. I skirted around a pair of yetis, squeezed between groups of wood elves, and headed for the information desk.

My intent was to talk to Corona, but instead I ran into Nick—the first cyclops I had aided.

"Morgan! Great, I found you. Come on, the other *cyclopes* asked me to get you for the meeting. We were horrified when we realized we had no way of contacting you," Nick said, grabbing my arm before leading me through the swarming masses.

"You got here right on time," Nick said as we ran underneath the belly of an Ice dragon from Antarctica. "The director of ophthalmological research decided to start the meeting a little early."

"What? That's unprofessional," I complained.

"Not really. One of the MBRC board members and an administrative assistant to the MBRC Administrator are sitting in on the meeting. Starting it early was the only way the board member could attend," Nick said, pausing to straighten his Armani suit outside the glass doors of the ophthalmological office.

"The MBRC Administrator?" I asked.

"He runs the center. The board makes the rules and laws. It's up to the administrator to keep the organization running smoothly."

I self-consciously smoothed my hair. In an attempt to look more professional, I had worn khaki pants, a camisole, and a white sweater. Now I almost wished I had worn a skirt of some kind.

"Here we go," Nick said before pushing open the door for me.

Sandra, the female cyclops with the periwinkle-colored eye, was waiting for us.

"Hey, Sandy," I smiled. "You look great!"

"Thank you, Morgan, but we need to hurry. Come on, let's go," she urged.

The three of us hustled up a hallway before abruptly stopping by an oak door, which Nick smoothly opened.

The ophthalmological director—the sorceress I had mistakenly thought to be a secretary at our previous meeting—was seated at a table with four other people. One was the cyclops who had previously worn a Ralph Lauren suit. His name was—get this—Ralph. Sitting to the director's right was a scientist in a white lab coat; I guess he was a wizard in training—even though he didn't have a beard like Dr. Creamintin, he had that magical aura to him. At the head of the table was an elf—the board member probably. (He was disappointing. He was handsome in a very subtle, snobby way, but he certainly wasn't a *Lord of the Rings* elf.) Between the elf and the director was a beautiful girl who was holding a glass of water.

"Careful," Nick muttered in my ear. "She's a selkie."

At the time, I had no idea what a selkie was, so I didn't know what to be careful of. Selkies are Irish/Icelandic/Scottish mythological characters. They are essentially seal people. They have two forms, a seal form which they use to play and live in the ocean, and a human form. To take on their human form, they have to shed their skin. (Yeah, it sounds gross.) If they want to return to their seal form, they just put the pelt back on. Lore talks about how, after turning human and then returning to the sea, selkies can't become human again for seven years. This is a bunch of hooey storytellers made up in order to make legends more tragic.

Anyway, selkies, males especially, are rather…gifted in the arts of seduction, or in our case persuasion.

"Board trustee Elros Gloriath, administrative assistant Bryna Kerrigan, allow me to introduce you to Nickolas Vontreba and

Sandra Koplin. The human, Morgan Fae, is their negotiator," the ophthalmological director said.

Bryna, the selkie, smiled sweetly and dipped her head at us. The elf merely blinked, casting jealousy through my system when I noticed how long and perfect his eyelashes were. (Okay, so maybe he wasn't completely substandard.)

"Um, hello," I greeted, taking a seat between Nick and Sandy.

"Trustee Gloriath, assistant Kerrigan, it's a pleasure to meet you," Nick said in a perfectly polite, business tone.

"Right, so let's cut to the chase. The cyclopes are willing to invest in eye research if we work with them to develop contact lenses or glasses," the eye director said, shuffling papers before looking up. "They have indicated they are willing to donate a seven-figure sum," she finished.

I could practically see the dollar signs in her eyes. Her wizard-y assistant almost drooled.

"How difficult would it be to create glasses or contacts? Which one would take more time?" Bryna asked, picking up a pencil with her free hand, to take notes. (She still held her glass of water.)

The director tapped her fingers on the table surface for a moment. "Technically, the eyeglasses would be the most simple to create, but in terms of mass production, the contacts would be the easiest route. In contacts, the only thing to change would be the prescription. With glasses, each set would have to be customized to fit their owner. Additionally, a glamour would have to be applied in order for the cyclopes to wear them in public."

"We already have some rough sketches for cyclops spectacles and contacts. The ophthalmological research department has been approached with this request before," the side-kick eye doctor chimed in, placing a manila folder on the table before removing sketches from it and passing them out.

"And why was the project abandoned?" Elros asked, his forehead wrinkling as he studied the sketches.

"It was deemed to be of low importance," the assistant said, uncomfortably shifting in his chair before glancing at the cyclopes and me. "Although the project itself is relatively simple and would be easy to complete."

"We are a busy department, even if you ignore the freak outbreaks like the dryads' eye fungus," the director admitted, "not to mention we're low on funding the way it is."

Elros dropped a sketch of contact lenses and looked bored. Bryna looked up from her note-taking and smiled before exchanging glances with Elros.

"The lack of funds is significant," Elros admitted, staring down at the drawing before looking at Nick and the other cyclopes. "How is this proposition?" he started. "You donate the seven-figure sum to the ophthalmological research branch for the purpose of general research. The research department will devote time and research to your problem when they deem it fit."

I didn't wait for the cyclopes to respond. "Absolutely not," I declared without a moment of hesitation. I could feel Nick and Sandy freezing up on either side of me. I wasn't sure if it was because that stupid elf had the GALL to suggest the cyclopes fork over cash with no guarantee of help, or if it was because they were having a panic attack since I disagreed with a *board member*. Whatever that was.

The eye doctor and her assistant were staring at Bryna and Elros as if they had lost their heads, which made me suspect this was the elf and selkie's private idea.

"Excuse me?" Elros asked, one of his eyebrows forming a perfect, elliptical and irritated arch. "And why do *you* feel your opinion matters, Miss Fae?"

"It's not a matter of opinion," I said, leaning forward. "It's a matter of being remotely intelligent. You're telling them to hawk up over a million dollars with no guarantee of being aided."

"The MBRC is significantly behind its budget, Morgan," Bryna said in a silky, sunny voice. "We need help to meet our expenditures. You can help us," she earnestly said.

Her pretty voice might have distracted me if I were not so enraged. "If you guys are over one million behind in EYE

RESEARCH, you need to hire a new accountant and make a smaller budget," I flatly replied.

"Morgan," Sandy hesitated. "Maybe we should take the deal—."

"No way," I said, shaking my head as I turned to face her. "You don't see them shaking down leprechauns for their gold or selling fairy dust on the black market. The bottom line is they want your money, but they don't feel like helping you."

"We never said that," Elros insisted, his musical voice growing tight.

"You said the research people will devote time to the issue when they deem it *fit*! Mrs. Director just finished talking about how busy they are—they'll *never* deem it fit," I said.

Sandy looked worried and cast her periwinkle eye around the table, but Nick took a stand.

"Morgan is right. We fund the MBRC through *donations*. We do not have to contribute this money to eye research, and we certainly aren't going to if we don't receive a guarantee that we will be helped," he firmly said, taking the lead.

I nodded smartly in agreement.

Bryna and Elros exchanged glances again. "We don't want to upset you," Bryna sweetly started.

"No, you just want to take our money," Ralph chuckled. It wasn't a light chuckle, it was dark, like Bryna and Elros were silly children spouting outlandish ideas.

"We aren't opposed to aiding the cyclopes. As I mentioned before, the project would be relatively simple. Perhaps a little time-consuming, but certainly not challenging," the director said.

"Friends," Bryna smiled, although her eyes didn't glitter so prettily anymore, and she set her glass of water down. "Let's try to discuss this."

In the end, I didn't say much more. Nick and Ralph did all the talking, and Mrs. Director practically shut out Elros and Bryna when it became apparent that she was in danger of losing her much-needed funding.

The cyclopes agreed to donate $500,000 immediately. $250,000 of that would be devoted to research for cyclops contacts; the rest would be a sign of "goodwill" on the cyclopes behalf, which would be used for any funding the ophthalmological research department needed. (Apparently that eye fungus from the dryads was really sucking up the funds, and a lot of the infected dryads lived like hippies and didn't have money to donate.)

When the contacts went through for testing, the cyclopes would gift the department an additional $250,000 for researching glasses. Once the prototypes for glasses were finished and in circulation, the cyclopes would donate a minimum of $500,000 in appreciation.

I had a feeling the numbers might grow larger as the cyclopes grew more thankful, but I didn't say this.

When the meeting was over, Elros gave me a dirty look, as though I were an overgrown cockroach or something. Bryna, however, seemed to lose her overly sweet edge and smiled at me.

"It was great to meet you, Morgan. The lightwood fairies have been gossiping about you like mad," Bryna grinned.

"About what?" I asked as we left the conference room.

"About you and the Pooka, of course. He's a member of the Fairy Council," Bryna said as we left the cyclopes behind. (They were busy talking with the eye doctors.)

"If he's a Fairy Council Member, why does he wander around like a hobo?"

Bryna giggled. "I'm sorry. Devin is something of a celebrity in our circle, and he hasn't had a fling in the past two years that's lasted longer than a few days."

I pushed my eyebrows up my forehead. "Really? I don't think I've known him for even two weeks yet," I recalled.

"It helps that you're one of the only humans to find out about us that hasn't had their memory instantly altered," Bryna confided.

"Well, the rumors will die down soon," I said as we left the ophthalmological office complex. "I'm getting hypnotized tomorrow."

"Really? Why?" Bryna asked, her eyes widening. "I would have thought with all the work you've been doing, you wouldn't want to leave. You were really passionate back there," Bryna said, gesturing to the office.

I shrugged. "You're right. I can't say I *want* to forget everything. Even though initially the whole magic and fairies thing really freaked me out and I hated it, and even though sometimes Frey and Dave drive me up the wall, I really do find this place interesting. But I don't have much of a choice. Frey told me I had to be hypnotized or have my memories removed."

"I'm sorry," Bryna said as we entered the main chamber of the MBRC.

I waved her off. "There's nothing either of us can do about it. It was great meeting you, Bryna. Good luck with the future."

"Thank you," Bryna smiled. "Hopefully we'll be able to get contacts for the cyclopes made and an antifungal for that eye fungus. Goodbye, Morgan."

"Bye!" I waved before moving through the MBRC main chamber.

It was here that I unwittingly set off a string of events that greatly morphed my future.

I did not see Frey, which was my main worry of the day. I was so concerned about running into him—even though it was his day off—I didn't notice that I caught anyone's attention, or that I caused any problems.

I didn't notice that I scared the poop out of a minotaur who had never before seen a human, so he stopped abruptly when he saw me. This caused a centaur behind him to run into him.

The centaur was traveling with a very large sphinx, who also stopped to make sure his friend was okay. Now, the sphinx was very tall, and his stop was sudden, so a flying gargoyle collided with his head and fell down, landing on top of a siren.

The siren—gifted with her beautiful voice—screamed bloody murder and made pretty much everyone in the room stop whatever they were doing and cover their ears.

I had made it to the exit/entrance hallway by this point, so all I did was wince and skip away.

The entire mess captured the attention of two High Elf brothers, Aysel and Asahi.

"That's the little human that's causing the stir in the lower ranks," Aysel stated, watching me disappear from sight.

"She looked happy," Asahi, ever the sweetie, noted.

Aysel did not react. "I heard she's getting hypnotized tomorrow. Good riddance."

"Really? I think having a human tutor would be fun," Asahi said, glancing at the hallway I had disappeared into.

"Mmm," Aysel said.

That short little interchange would change my life forever.

8

My Memories to Be Modified

Friday morning came all too quickly. I woke up early and stared at the ceiling of my room, considering writing notes about the MBRC so I could read them at a later date and remember…but my heart ached with thoughts of Frey, so in the end, I decided I was better off forgetting.

I got up and dragged myself to school like normal. Fran picked up on my morose mood, but we didn't have much time to talk. In fact, the day proceeded like any other Friday until I reached Spanish class.

"And so, after you finish this word search, complete page 23 through 25 in your workbook. I will be out, briefly, making copies of your homework for tomorrow. Miss Morgan, would you come with me to lend me your aid with the copy machine? Thank you," Dave said, exiting the room before I could refuse.

I slid out of my seat, glancing at my fellow classmates. Depending on their grades and social standing, they either started working on their homework or turned in their seats to chat with friends. No one reacted as though anything were out of the ordinary.

No one except Frey, that is.

As I walked towards the door, he practically branded my back with his green eyes. The way his silver hair fell down over his forehead, shadowing his face, made him look wolfish. (Well…more like a starved wolf. That boy is beyond skinny.)

I shivered and exited the Spanish classroom. Dave closed the door behind us and walked across the hall to lean on a locker. He slowly slid to the ground, looking funny in his rumpled suit as he sat on the floor. He patted the spot next to him in an open invitation.

"I thought we were going to make copies?" I asked, folding my arms across my chest.

"I deceived you," Dave cheerfully said, shooting me a smile that had no business being on the face of a vampire. "Sit," he ordered, patting the ground again.

I muttered before stalking across the hallway and sitting down, pulling my knees tight against my chest.

Dave ignored my sulk and reached into his pocket and pulled out a small thermos. After popping the cap off, he took a sniff of his tomato juice and gagged. "This stuff is unfit for human consumption," he complained.

"Yes," I agreed. "But you aren't human."

Dave shot me a wounded look, his flaming eyebrows crawling down his face, which only emphasized his retreating hairline. "Morgan, I called you out here to see if you were okay."

I laughed. "Of course I'm okay. Why wouldn't I be okay? Today, I get to leave all of this stupid drama behind me."

Dave took a sip of his tomato and scrunched his face up. "Nasty stuff," he muttered before turning back towards me. "Look here, young lady. I know that miserable werewolf hurt you, but if you don't want to give this up, you need to put your pride aside for a minute and tell me that."

"Why? I didn't think it mattered whether I wanted to be hypnotized or not," I said, playing with a pre-ripped hole in my jeans.

"It does," Dave insisted. "The MBRC isn't full of horrid despots, little mortal. If you wanted to stay on, I'm sure Dr. Creamintin could appeal your case."

I took a deep breath and mindlessly stared at the door to the

Spanish classroom. Not get hypnotized? I hadn't thought much of it…to remember the cyclopes, and Doggy, and Corona, even Aristotle, Devin, and Dave!

And then I remembered Frey's nasty scowl as I left the room with Dave. "No," I firmly decided. "I want to forget."

"I hope you aren't biting off your nose just to spite your face," Dave observed. "I'm very sorry for what Frey did, but I can't help but think that you are being just as petty as he."

I was, but I would never admit it. To me, at that moment, Frey had hurt me enough that I wanted to forget about the dragons, fairies, and magic.

"So, you didn't have anything you wanted me to make copies of?" I asked, pushing myself into a standing position.

Dave waved his hand in a negative before taking another sip of tomato juice and grimacing. "That was all, Miss Morgan."

"Right," I said, walking towards the door.

"I'm afraid I won't be seeing you again before you are hypnotized."

I stopped by the door.

"It was a very fun experience, having you at the MBRC," Dave kindly smiled, his pale skin creasing with the gesture. "I shall miss you on our train rides."

"Thanks," I awkwardly said, reaching out to grab the doorknob.

"And, Morgan," Dave paused before speaking again. "I do hope, for your sake, that the hypnotizing helps."

"It will," I said, my voice as hard as rock. I opened the door and strolled back inside, leaving Dave alone with his tomato juice thermos propped up on his belly.

At the end of the day, Frey was waiting for me at my locker.

"Let's go," he barked.

"No. I'm putting my books away first. Then we can go," I said, spinning the dial on the lock.

Everything about getting to the MBRC was awkward. Walking

to the train station was awkward. (Frey walked about ten feet in front of me, and neither of us made any attempt at conversation.) Waiting for the train was awkward. (I stood as far away from him as I could while still standing on the right platform.) The train ride was awkward. (Frey and I sat in separate seats, staring out our windows.) Arriving at the MBRC was awkward. (Tiny started to greet Frey and me before catching on to our arctic moods.)

In fact, my back was tight with agitation by the time we reached Dr. Creamintin's office.

Dr. Creamintin, who was talking with the mermaid secretary, looked up when we entered. "Morgan, Frey, is today the day already?" Dr. Creamintin inquired.

"Yep," I said, forcing a smile across my lips.

"Yes," Frey said, a smug smile etched in his face. I wanted to snap his lanky body in half right then and there.

Dr. Creamintin's cloud-like eyebrows rose at the differences in our response before checking his schedule. "Aisis is waiting in the second room."

"Aren't you coming with?" I asked, pausing by the desk as Frey started out for our assigned room.

Dr. Creamintin shook his head. "I don't do hypnotizing. I would only get in the way. Thank you, Morgan, for all you've done here," Dr. Creamintin said, offering me a hand.

I took it, and he squeezed the living daylights out of my hand. "No, thank you. I don't think I've done that much at all," I said.

Dr. Creamintin shook his head. "That's wrong, but I guess we'll never be able to convince you," he said with a rueful smile.

"Morgan," Frey called.

"I'm COMING," I snapped at the werewolf. I gave one more pleasant smile to Dr. Creamintin and Felisha. "Thank you. For everything," I said before walking after Frey.

Frey opened the door to the examination room and followed me inside.

Aisis, my hypnotizer—who also happened to be a siren—was seated in a chair, going over notes.

I was all prepared to meet a bird babe decked out in a leather bikini or something equally as gaudy. Aisis, just like Dave the chubby vampire, Nick the handsome cyclops, and Frey the not sweet and not buff werewolf, put legends to shame.

She wore a white lab coat that swaddled her frame like a baggy bathrobe and square-framed glasses that were just *wrong* for her. Her gorgeous red hair was pulled back in a bun so tight it pulled her eyebrows up, and her smile was sweet, not at all seductive.

The only hints I had that Aisis was a siren were her nails, which were quite long and claw-like, and the wings nestled on her back. But they weren't even hawk wings; they were pigeon wings. I am not kidding. Pigeon wings that, when tucked up and folded, were nearly as big as Aisis herself.

I *burned* to pull her hair out of the bun and break her glasses. She could be so pretty if she just *tried*!

"Good afternoon, Frey. And you must be Miss Morgan L. Fae," Aisis smiled before half-scolding Frey. "Frey, you gave me a heart attack when I saw her name. I thought for sure you were making me hypnotize one of King Arthur's relatives!"

I rolled my eyes—I was dealt Morgan La Fae witch jokes enough in real life to know what she was alluding to. "My godmother is a professor, and she got a real kick out of naming me Morgan," I explained.

"Well, Morgan, it's very nice to meet you—although I wish it was under different circumstances. I'm Dr. Aisis Ligeia. I will be handling your hypnotizing today. Do you have any questions before we start?" Aisis asked, pushing her horrid square lenses (they really didn't work with her face shape) up her button nose.

"Am I going to remember any of my normal life from the last two weeks? Will I recognize Dave?" I asked.

"Those are good questions. No, you will not remember Dave, or Frey for that matter. However, you will remember all of your normal life from the past few days. The only things I will tamper with are your memories of the MBRC and anything magical. The details of the last two weeks will feel hazy, but you will be completely relaxed and at rest. Nothing will strike you as being odd. In fact, you won't be able to even tell that we've modified your memories. Hypnotizing is not an upsetting process," Aisis smiled.

"How does it work?" I inquired.

"First, I will lull you into a state of relaxation with my voice. I'm a siren, so singing is the most powerful tool I have," Aisis smiled, self consciously brushing off her white lab coat with her clawed hands. (This motion made me realize she had a few red feathers at the bottom of her hairline on her neck.)

"Then, I will discuss your memories with you and begin covering them up. Hypnotizing doesn't remove the memories; it pastes over them, like putting wallpaper over an old coat of paint," Aisis explained. "I do this all using my voice. Frey is concerned you may break through the memories, so today I'll herd your brain into a continuous loop, which will make it easier to cover your memories."

I nodded and wiped my sweaty palms off on my jeans as I leaned back against the wall, completely ignoring Frey, who was in the corner a few feet away from me.

"Do you have any more questions?" Aisis asked.

I exhaled and swallowed before cheerfully replying, "Nope!"

"Great. Hop up on the bed, and we'll begin," Aisis said as she dug into the pockets of her lab coat.

I uneasily seated myself on the examination bed, my legs hanging over the edge.

I fiercely scrubbed at my jeans with my palms, trying not to think about what was going to happen. No matter how much I wanted to forget everything, the idea that someone was going to mess with my mind was not reassuring.

"Morgan," Frey started.

I looked up and met his green eyes.

He opened and closed his mouth several times, clearly searching for words.

"Frey? Here, you'll need these earplugs so you don't hear my song," Aisis said, passing the werewolf a set of wax earplugs.

Frey took them in his hands and stared at them for a moment

before finally speaking to me again. "Bye," he mumbled before placing the earplugs in his ear.

"Are you comfortable, Morgan?" Aisis asked, standing in front of me, her hands clasped.

I wiggled on the examination table. "Yeah."

"Good," Aisis nodded before turning to Frey. She flicked her thumbs up. Frey returned the gesture. "Okay, let's get started. Now, Morgan, I want you to listen to my singing, please. Don't worry; this will all be over in a few minutes," Aisis said before launching into a song.

It didn't have any words, the song that is, but it was *beautiful*. It was unearthly. I suspect only angels would be able to outperform Aisis. Her voice was haunting and alluring. I didn't want her to stop singing, ever! Her pitch rolled and tolled, stretching high and low. I found myself relaxing, and when she changed songs, I was a goner.

Beautiful singing, sounds like a lullaby.

"Morgan, listen to the sound of my voice."

"…forget it all…"

"….MBRC…..forget"

The voice came in and out of focus, like a radio station.

"Have no memories of magic."

No memories…

"You will never, ever, remember meeting Dave Smith or Frey Christenson…."

Dave? Frey? Who were they?

"Morgan," someone said, shaking me.

"Mm," I muttered.

"Morgan, come on! I want to go home."

Ugh. It was Michael.

"MORGAN!" my brother shouted, savagely pulling my hair.

"I'm awake!" I snarled, shooting out of the desk I was folded in. I blinked, wiping the sleep away from my eyes before yawning.

"Come on. Football practice is over. I want to get home so I can shower and go out tonight, and we're late," Michael said, already halfway across the Spanish room.

I rubbed at the crick in my neck and gazed around the room.

"I couldn't find you anywhere, and you weren't answering your cell phone! I probably wouldn't have found you, but I ran into some guy who said you were napping in the Spanish classroom. What were you doing in here anyway?"

I thoughtfully gazed at the ceiling as I followed my older brother out of the Spanish classroom, dragging my backpack behind me. What *was* I doing in the Spanish room? Maybe I fell asleep while helping Fran with student council duties, and she left me for dead again.

"Do you think you could walk a little faster?" Michael called, a ways down the hallway and irritated. I could almost see the veins throbbing in his forehead. "I'm pretty sure Odie's dead turtle can move faster than you."

"I'm coming, I'm coming," I yawned, lazily shouldering my backpack before trailing after Michael. Man, I was tired.

The weekend was nice. I finished my homework right away so I could go out with Fran on Saturday and Sunday. We laughed and joked and watched a ton of chick flicks. Fran insisted on watching *Eclipse*, which shouldn't be a surprise because she's a big fan of those books. But oddly, as we watched it, I felt myself growing frustrated…as though I had been misinformed or wrongfully guided about something.

I returned to school on Monday with much hesitation. I live for weekends. School days are so boring. Everything proceeded like normal until I went to Spanish.

This chubby guy with a suicidal hairline waltzed into our class instead of Mrs. Allen. "Good afternoon class!" he sang, which was oddly disturbing. He was so white, if I placed a marshmallow on his skin, I probably wouldn't be able to find it again.

I stared at him, my eyebrows furrowing. "Something wrong,

Morgan?" one of my friends, Samantha, asked as she headed for her seat.

"Who is that guy?" I asked, staring at the weird, singing dude.

Samantha looked at me like I was crazy. "Um, Mr. Smith? Or *Señor* Smith, I suppose. Our sub for Mrs. Allen?"

I stared at her, and she shook her head at me.

"Where have you been for the last two weeks, Morgan, out to lunch?" my other friend, Emily, asked.

As I observed the pale-skinned teacher while he fumbled madly with notes, I wondered what my friend meant about two weeks.

I started to look back down at my desk when movement out of the corner of my eye caught my attention. It was a guy. A tall, lean guy with a track star's build. His skin was pale—not the paper shade of the sub's skin, but more like the white-blue shades of snow. His hair was silver. It was a nearly colorless shade of blonde that can only be achieved with the help of dye, but it glinted in the school's fluorescent light. His eyes were a vibrant, forest-green color.

I hadn't seen him before in my life.

Oddly, people weren't really reacting to him. Dani and Toni, the popular girls in our class, didn't even flutter an eyelash at him. (Which was twisted. Usually they would be all over someone like him in seconds.)

The silver-haired guy glanced at me and *smiled*. I actually twisted in my seat to look if there was anyone behind me. There wasn't.

The guy plopped down in a seat between Emily and Samantha, as if that was his spot. My friends didn't react out of the ordinary. They smiled at him and said good morning, acting like they knew him. Or like they were familiar with him.

I was weirded out.

But it got worse. During class, we had a partner activity. I headed for Emily and Samantha, because I always work with them. "Hey guys," I greeted, snagging an empty desk near one of them.

"Hey, Morgan. You aren't working with Frey today?" Emily asked, her eyes darting to the silver-haired boy.

"Who?" I asked. Talk about a weird name.

"...Frey?" Samantha said, pointing at the silver-haired guy.

I was about to ask why on earth I would work with him when the guy, Frey, interrupted. "Nah, we're going to mix it up a little," he winked. "I'll work with you today, Samantha."

"Fine with me!" Samantha said, pleased to be working with the random hot guy.

The rest of the class proceeded normally, and when the bell rang, I stormed the halls with my classmates. As soon as I lost sight of the pudgy sub, and the silver-haired guy, my head buzzed.

"*You will never, ever, remember meeting Dave Smith or Frey Christenson....*"

Well, that was weird.

Monday was dreadfully boring and dull. I didn't even get to hang out with Fran, who shooed me off after saying she felt sorry for me that I no longer had my after-school job. (What job??)

I expected slightly better of Tuesday because face it, Monday, the first day back at work or school, sucks.

It didn't *exactly* disappoint me.

When Michael and I got out in the student parking lot, we had to walk along the school Peace Garden. Normally, this place is abandoned until lunch time, when some of the skaters and goths come outside to eat lunch. But this morning, there was a guy standing at the edge of the garden. A *hot* guy.

He was definitely older than Michael. He was probably in college, most likely some senior girl's boyfriend or someone's older brother. He was dressed too cool to be a student teacher. His hair was a beautiful, luxurious black color with body in it most girls would kill for.

In spite of his hotness, my hand just *itched* to smack him, which was weird because I am not a violent person. He glanced at Michael and me, and when our eyes met, he smiled, holding my gaze. His eyes were a hypnotic mixture of yellow and gold, like a pale moon.

He nodded at me as my brother and I walked past him, and I actually stopped for a moment. (He was that hot!)

"Morgan, come on," Michael growled. "You said you had a dictionary in your locker, right? I want to borrow it. So can we *please* get to your locker *before* the bell rings?" he said in his snotty, superior older brother voice.

"I'm coming," I said, rolling my eyes before I hurried after him.

Tuesday grew even more special because Brett Patterson, my crush since sixth grade, walked with me from my first-hour class to my second-hour class.

"Did you get the homework done for American Government?" Brett asked, shaking a lock of his mussed hair out of his face.

"Um, no," I said, giving him my brightest smile. "I always finish those worksheets right before lunch."

"I know, right? They're so easy," Brett laughed. "So, how's Fran?"

"She's good. She's getting ready for the Halloween dance. I think someday her student council responsibilities are going to drive her over the edge."

"Yeah. Sometimes it's hard to think that Fran, the same Fran who ate peanut butter and pickle sandwiches in second grade, is our student council secretary," Brett said.

"Especially considering our class size. When we were in elementary school, there were only thirty of us. Now there's like…four hundred?" I said, tucking a strand of my hair behind my ear.

I was so wrapped up in my conversation with Brett that I almost missed someone calling my name.

"Hey, Morgan."

The speaker was a boy. A tall, lean guy with a track star's build. His hair was silver. It was a nearly colorless shade of blonde that can only be achieved with the help of dye, but it glinted in the school's fluorescent light. His eyes were a vibrant, forest-green color.

He was walking in the opposite direction of Brett and me, but he waved and smiled at me, as though he knew me.

I had never seen him before. (Believe me, *that* cute of a guy I would remember meeting.)

"Hi," I lamely said, staring at the guy as he walked past me.

"Who was that?" Brett asked as I twisted around to peer at the cute guy.

"I have no idea. I don't think I've met him before," I said.

I didn't think I said this very loud, but the silver/blonde-haired guy froze and whipped around. His green eyes were wide, and he stared at me as though I had slapped him.

Embarrassed, I quickly turned back around. "Okay, I gotta run, Brett."

"Alright. See you in American Government."

"Yeah, bye," I said before hurrying away, anxious to leave the cute stranger behind. I waved to Brett and turned down a different hallway as my head buzzed like a bee hive.

"*You will never, ever, remember meeting Dave Smith or Frey Christenson....*"

I stopped in the middle of the hallway, a little lost in my mind. Why was I hurrying? And why on earth did I leave Brett behind? I just blew one of my very few chances to talk to my crush!

9

Never Remember Who?

My frustration only increased when I got to Spanish class. I was having serious problems remembering the last chapter of Spanish. I knew that Mrs. Allen was gone on maternity leave, but I couldn't remember anything beyond that. Did we even have a sub?

"Hello, Morgan!"

I looked up from my Spanish textbook and stared. Some strange old guy was talking to me. I was a little weirded out by the fact that a perfect stranger was greeting me, but most of my attention was spent trying to not stare at his shock of red hair—which appeared to be cannibalistic and was slowly eating itself. As he laughed, his pudgy beer belly jiggled.

"Ready for another day of Spanish?" Weird Man asked.

"Umm," I said, scooting back in my chair. Was this one of those creepy school invaders the principal was forever warning us about? Or was he just someone's dad whose face I had obviously forgotten? I mean, the guy knew my name!

"I'm sorry, who are you?" I carefully asked.

Weird Man's cheerful smile abruptly fell off his face. His skin went from pasty pale to ghost white, and without saying anything else he retreated to the doorframe and exchanged hissed words with someone in the hallway.

My friends, Samantha and Emily, edged through what little part of the door Weird Man didn't occupy.

"Wonder what's got Señor Smith so frazzled? Hi, Morgan," Samantha said, stopping near my desk.

"Hey guys. Who?" I asked.

"Who who?" Emily asked, dropping her backpack on the ground.

"Who is Señor Smith?" I asked, glancing at Weird Man again.

"Señor Smith? Our sub," Emily slowly and carefully said, pointing to Weird Man.

I frowned. "Since when?"

Samantha rolled her eyes. "Okay, it was weird when you pulled this memory fog thing yesterday, Morgan. But now it's just bizarre."

"What?" I asked again.

"Class, please be seated," Señor Smith tightly said as he bustled back into the room and headed for the teacher's desk.

Samantha and Emily shrugged and waved to me before going to their seats.

"Señor Smith, where's Frey? We saw him in the hallway," Samantha said, plopping down in her seat.

Who was Frey?

"He had some urgent business to take care of. Please open your books," Señor Smith said, his eyes fastened on his teacher's guide.

Spanish was a little tense. Señor Smith seemed to be worried about something. At least there was no homework. But when I left the Spanish classroom, my ears rang for a minute, forcing me to stop and lean against the hallway wall.

"*You will never, ever, remember meeting Dave Smith or Frey Christenson….*"

"Hey, Morgan, you okay?" Fran asked, finding me seconds later.

"…Yeah," I said, wrinkling my forehead.

"What's wrong?" Fran said, placing a hand on my shoulder.

"…I think I fell asleep during Spanish. I don't remember much of class," I said.

Fran patted me before hauling me off to my locker. "It happens to the best of us. Come on. Tell me how your day was?"

"Not too bad. Oh my gawsh, there was this really hot guy standing in the Peace Garden today, AND I got to walk with Brett to my second class!" I squealed.

"You saw him, too? The hot guy I mean, not Brett," Fran said. "He was sitting on a bench in the Peace Garden when I came in early for a student council meeting this morning. He reminded me of a Greek god communing with nature or something," Fran dreamily sighed.

"Really? I don't think he was that hot," I said, remembering my urge to slap him.

"Whatever. Your hotness detector is broken. I don't know why you moon over Brett when Frey is hanging around you."

"Who?"

"Oh, that's right. Emily said you two aren't talking. So, what are you doing this weekend?"

Wednesday morning the hot guy was not in the Peace Garden, an observation I made with a little sadness.

School proceeded like normal, until I went to my Spanish class. Our substitute teacher was this weird guy, Señor Smith, and we had a new (and very cute) student, Frey. When I asked some of my classmates who they were, they gave me really weird looks.

I dunno. Maybe they were introduced yesterday when I slept through class? But the weirdness was multiplied when class ended. I was leaving with the rest of my classmates when I remembered I had a question about the previous day's homework assignment. Rather than elbow my way through the stream of students coming *out* of the classroom, I decided to wait just outside the door.

When the last kid left, I poked my head back through the door.

The new student was still there, sitting on a desk, talking to Señor Smith.

"So, she won't remember meeting us? Ever?" Señor Smith said, rubbing some of his red hair.

"Nope. Every time she meets us, every time she sees us, she's going to forget it as soon as we're out of sight. Aisis reviewed her hypnotism notes and realized she messed up in the wording that directed Morgan to forget us," Frey said.

"Excuse me?" I said, stepping into the room. The words were out of my mouth before I could stop them.

"Ah, Miss Morgan!" Señor Smith said, his eyes widening as he plastered a large smile on his face.

"Relax. She's going to forget this conversation as soon as she leaves the room," Frey gloomily said. "We can say whatever we want in front of her."

"Are they going to bring her in to fix it?" Señor Smith asked, turning away from me to properly address Frey.

"Um, you guys are talking about me, right?" I asked, standing right by the door. (This whole conversation was going south really quickly, so it was best to stand by the nearest exit for strategic purposes.)

"No, they aren't going to do anything about it. Dr. Creamintin and Aisis decided this can probably be lived with if we take certain precautions," Frey said, staring at his shoes.

"Like what?"

"I need to avoid all contact with her, and you need to announce that you are a sub every time you enter the room. They say our positions only need to last about a month. Then the teacher you're replacing will return from maternity leave."

"Ohh, that is totally easy to follow and everything will be OK. NOT!" Señor Smith shouted before pulling at his already thinning hair.

"Hey, could you like, stop ignoring me?" I asked, still refusing to leave my post by the door.

"So *that* is a permanent state then?" Señor Smith asked, pointing at me with an accusing finger.

The new student waited for a few moments before replying. "Yeah. It is," he said, his green eyes trained on me.

Señor Smith seemed to deflate. "How sad," he said, his shoulders slumping.

"Hello? You guys can hear me, right?" I asked.

Frey sighed, a sound from deep in his chest, and slid off the desk. He walked towards me, the saunter of his gait reminding me of something…*canine*. I started taking steps backwards as he drew closer and kept moving until I was in the hallway.

Frey stopped at the doorframe and leaned against it. "I'm sorry, Morgan," he said, very quietly. I had to strain my ears to hear him. "I thought it would be different if they erased your memories. If you didn't remember Devin maybe…," he trailed off and ran a hand through his silver hair. He looked up again and sadly smiled at me. "Goodbye, Morgan," he said before closing the door.

I was totally confused. What the heck was he talking about? Why was my head suddenly—

"*You will never, ever, remember meeting Dave Smith or Frey Christenson….*"

…Why was I staring at the closed door of my Spanish room? I shrugged my shoulders before moving down the hallway. "Lunch time!" I cheered.

Yeah, Wednesday was a normal day.

Thursday was pretty normal too. I was looking forward to Halloween next week, and everyone was pretty happy. School passed by in a total blur; I couldn't even really remember attending my Spanish class!

Brett seemed a little distracted in American Government class—well, to be truthful, he seemed sad. But I didn't have time to take a lot of notice (yeah, yeah. I suck at paying attention to my crush) because I seemed to have lost my cell phone and assignment notebook right before American Government.

"Is something wrong, Morgan?" Hunter asked, putting down his newest leadership book to watch me shake the contents of my backpack out on the floor.

"I can't find my cell phone. Or my assignment notebook," I said, digging through the trash that fell out.

"I wasn't under the impression that you used your assignment notebook. Ever," Hunter said, blinking in the sunlight.

Today he wasn't wearing his sunglasses—a momentous occasion. "I don't, but I have lots of phone numbers and addresses in it. By the way, you shouldn't wear your sunglasses so often. They hide your pretty eyes," I said.

Hunter's eyes were the sparkling color of amber and topaz.

Hunter chuckled and skated his finger across the screen of his smart phone. "Would you like me to get you a new phone?"

"What? Oh, no. It'll pop up eventually. Is that what your family business is? A cell phone company?" I asked. (I was forever teasing Hunter because a driver in a *suit* comes to picked him up every day. He said it was part of the family business, whatever that meant.)

"Perhaps," Hunter shrugged.

"You know..." I said, shoving my arm in my backpack to fish around. (My cell phone had to be crammed somewhere in there.) "Everyone is seriously going to believe those ridiculous rumors that you're part of the mob if you don't own up soon. What, is it an embarrassing business? I won't laugh."

Hunter grinned at me with perfect, straight white teeth. "It's not embarrassing; it's just difficult to explain," he persisted. "I told you before: my family does a lot of importing and exporting."

"Yeah, yeah," I grumbled. "Go ahead and don't share with your only friend," I dramatized before growling. "Seriously, where is my cell phone?" I complained.

"I can have a phone to you by the end of the school day," Hunter tempted.

I narrowed my eyes. "Your family must have money, how else could you just throw around funds like that? Are you dentists?" I asked. I had entertained that thought before—Hunter did have a stunning smile.

Hunter looked amused and picked up his book again. "It's a trade secret."

"Bully," I declared. "That's it. I'm not working with you for our next math partner project."

"Really? Are you sure about that? Usually I have to explain the chapter to you," Hunter said behind his book.

"Ah! And now you're insulting my intelligence! Friend abuser," I complained before tossing my backpack aside. "This sucks."

"Do you want me to try calling you? You haven't changed your phone number since we did our biology project together, have you?"

"No, I haven't. And that's okay. Fran already tried that for me," I gloomily said, staring at my backpack.

"Don't worry; it will turn up," Hunter assured me.

"I hope so," I muttered as our math teacher turned on the overhead projector, starting class and ending our conversation.

Hunter was right. Both my cell phone and assignment notebook popped back up in my backpack right before my last class.

But on an interesting note, the hot guy from the peace garden was there after school.

I saw him because I was headed for the public library to do some research for an American Government paper. (Yeah, I admit, early in the morning Brett told me he was going to swing by the library after school to pick up a book, so I was going there in hopes of running into him. Fran was going to meet me there after she finished up with some student council stuff.)

So, I left school through the front doors, and will wonders never cease, the hot Garden Guy was there. Although it was pretty cold outside, he wore only a light jacket, which wasn't even completely zipped up. I could only see his profile. He was actually inside the garden this time, sitting on a bench.

As I approached the garden, he checked his watch, sighed, and got up, walking towards the sidewalk I was on.

His pace was perfectly set so he ended up walking almost directly next to me.

I glanced sideways and studied his face for a few moments before he looked up from checking his watch and caught me staring at him.

He gave me one of the dreamiest smiles I've ever seen.

I jerked my head forward and began blushing red. My heart was pounding in my chest, but there was also a sincere wish to punch him.

"Going to the library?" Hot Garden Guy asked.

"Yeah," I squeaked, nodding my head. "You too?" I asked after an awkward pause.

"Yeah," he grinned before glancing behind him. "I was waiting for someone, but I don't think they're going to show."

Internally I wanted to lecture whatever person (a girl most likely) had stood him up. Looks like his shouldn't be wasted! Unless my theory that he was someone's older brother was correct?

We walked to the library in silence. Garden Guy didn't do much besides tuck his hands in the pockets of his jacket and stroll along near me.

I waltzed into the library in a daze. (I wasn't used to such attractive guys walking so close to me. I mean, Brett is cute in a "boy next door" kind of way. But Garden Guy could be a *model.*) Sadly Garden Guy disappeared shortly after reaching the library, and Brett never came.

Fran and I went out for ice cream afterwards, and I told her about my silent walk with Hot Garden Guy. We proceeded to theorize about his attachment to whoever went to our school before laughing ourselves silly.

Friday is always, without a doubt, my favorite day of the week. This Friday though…things got strange.

First of all, the day started *badly*. Michael's girlfriend wanted to go to McDonald's for breakfast, so we had to get up really early. And of course Michael didn't want his kid sister tagging along on his date, so he dropped me off at school.

Did he drive up to the front and drop me off at the building? *Noooo*! He dropped me off at the beginning of our school drive, which is several blocks long. I normally don't care about walking, but it was freezing outside, and the sun hadn't risen up high enough to shine over the hill that's in front of our school.

It was a long, cold, and lonely walk.

I stalked the whole way there, muttering under my breath and looking like a wild woman, I'm sure. And there to witness it all from a bench in the Peace Garden was Garden Guy.

I didn't notice him until I was nearly past him, grumbling and stomping angrily in my winter fashion boots. I stopped when I saw that he was watching me with a lazy grin.

"Hey," he drawled.

"…Hey," I said, staring at him.

At that moment, the first rays of the sun peaked over the hill, bathing Garden Guy in golden light.

I blinked a few times at the sight before realizing I was staring and that he obviously wasn't going to say anything else. So, I started walking again, wondering what on earth he was doing on school property at this ungodly hour.

I stopped and turned around to stare at Garden Guy again.

He wasn't even wearing a jacket today.

"Aren't you cold?" I blurted out. Somehow I couldn't be anything but blunt around this guy.

"No," he said, shaking his head, which made his gorgeous mane flip. "I don't get cold while I wait for this person. I could wait for them for a thousand years and never grow cold."

"That's a stupid thing to say," I said before clasping my hands over my mouth.

Garden Guy got off his bench and ambled towards me, his pale yellow eyes glowing. "What gives you that impression?" he asked with his glittering smile.

"Because you won't live for a thousand years in the first place," I said, removing my hands from my mouth. "And obviously they stood you up yesterday after school. Why are you here so early, anyway? Hoping they'll see you as they go in?" I asked, internally changing theories. One of the girls attending our school had to be his ex. There was no other reason a guy would go through such work.

"I can't complain; she's looking at me right now," Garden Guy said, leaning slightly over me.

I admit it, I got majorly creeped out. Garden Guy may be hot, but if my brother Michael has done anything for me, he has taught me to run away from all dudes who seem to be the extreme type, like this guy.

"Umm, I think I need to go now," I said, backing up.

Garden Guy blinked twice before he abruptly dropped out of his romantic mode.

"Are you serious?" he asked, his black eyebrows snapping together while his eyes grew darker. "I'm out here at *sunrise*. SUNRISE, MORGAN! I don't normally get out of bed until **noon**. I time everything perfectly, the flippin' sun even hits me like I'm some kind of crappy Romeo, and you don't remember?! I HAVE BEEN HANGING AROUND A HIGH SCHOOL FOR YOU! THE LEAST YOU COULD DO IS SLAP ME!" he shouted, stalking into the Peace Garden before turning and coming back towards me, creating a pacing circuit.

I took a tiny step backwards. Was he some sort of sadist?

"I even hired a dew fairy to steal your cell phone and stupid logbook so I knew where you were going after school! I do not enjoy being a stalker, Morgan! I enjoy being followed, not vice versa. Why won't you REMEMBER, you stupid, little human?" Garden Guy ranted. "I had to make a *special request* to try and get your memories back. I made a deal with Aysel. *AYSEL*, Morgan, *AYSEL*. I am a Fairy Council Member. I shouldn't have to make deals with spoiled elves!"

He whirled around, anger dancing in his yellow irises. He stared at me for a moment before his face morphed into a look of pained torture. "Morgan," he whispered, his eyebrows slanting up, his eyes crinkling down. "Why won't you remember me?"

I couldn't answer him.

So he left, disappearing down the sidewalk.

He wasn't in the garden after school either. (Not that I looked or anything.)

I didn't tell anyone about this encounter, not even Fran. It seemed too odd, too unreal. His emotions were so *raw*—as though I was someone special to him. Was I really that special to anyone?

Friday was cool. I think I fell asleep again in Spanish—I can never seem to remember anything that happens in that class. I get the feeling that my grade is going to suffer because of that.

Fran and I hung out for most of Saturday. We went to her house and played around there. She's got a karaoke machine, so some of our friends came over and we really belted out some songs. Sunday was typical. I went to church, did some homework, and watched a movie with my brothers.

I dunno. The weekend seemed somehow cheapened by that guy's display of loyalty and emotion.

Wait, what am I saying?! He's clearly a nutcase!

Anyway, I approached school with Michael on Monday morning with a great deal of reservation. I had mixed emotions when I walked by the garden and didn't see hot/psychopathic Garden Guy.

School was…school. I fawned over Brett, talked with Hunter, and Fran kept me back after our last class let out to form an impromptu study group. She's really bad at political classes, and I happen to study American Government like a fiend so I can answer any question Brett Patterson asks. (Lame, I know.)

Anyway, she had a test coming up, so Fran wanted to review with me for an hour.

When I finally left—Fran was still in the school computer lab, skimming internet study guides when I took my leave—the front entrance of the school was pretty much abandoned.

Our athletic fields are behind the school grounds, and any club that was still meeting met inside the building, so it was just me. I knew I had a while before Michael would be done with football practice, but I had a sketching assignment to finish for my art class, so I figured the Peace Garden would be the perfect nature scene to copy.

I found a spot, settled down, and dug out my sketchpad.

But after several seconds of sketching I heard…a horse neigh.

Now, I'm no farm girl, but I know horses aren't supposed to be in the school garden. So, I set my sketchpad on my lap and twisted around, looking for the practical jokester that was trying to pull one over on me.

No one was around.

When I untwisted my spine I *swear* I saw a horse through the bushes straight ahead of me.

"Whoa," I said, rocketing to my feet, sending my sketchpad flying.

The horse (It was reddish brown with a black mane and tail) disappeared.

I blinked a few times and rubbed my eyes to make sure I wasn't delusional. I did a 360 degree inspection of the area before slinking off in the direction the horse had disappeared in, plunging straight into a sea of bushes.

"This is ridiculous," I said, shoving my way between two fat bushes. "Seeing a horse in the middle of the city? I have finally lost my mind, ack!" I said when I got a branch in the face.

I made it through the wall of bushes and spit out a leaf. "I should have just taken the path around," I muttered darkly.

There was a large hedge in front of me, but I could hear voices.

"Did she see you?" someone asked.

"I, I think so," a timid voice replied.

A horse whinnied.

"I mean she did! She did!" the timid voice shrieked.

Carefully, I stalked towards the hedge before walking along side it. (This time, I would follow it around. Even I couldn't throw myself through three solid feet of branches and leaves.)

I was all prepared to peer around the corner like a sneaky snake, but when my eyeballs saw the sight, my whole body jerked out from behind the hedge.

Standing in the middle of the peace garden was a chubby guy with red hair who was steadily growing bald, a cute, petite, bay-colored horse, and one giant, beautiful, black horse that had yellow eyes like the moon.

I didn't hesitate.

There was never a question in my mind who that black horse was. After all, he broke my brain the first time I found out who he was. And as soon as I saw him, I knew what he had done for me.

"DEVIN!" I shouted, running across the lawn.

He reminded me about the MBRC.

10

A Pervert Becomes My Hero

Devin tossed his horse form aside in a blur and sprinted towards me. I threw myself at him, giving him a strangling hug when we met in the middle.

We were laughing, hugging, maybe I was even crying a little bit. Devin's hands stayed around my waist, which is a real accomplishment for that pervert.

"I was going to kidnap you if this didn't work," Devin said into my hair.

I laughed. "You should have just been your perverted self. I would have smacked you and remembered your tricks!" I said, releasing my choke hold on him and getting off my tippy toes. (He was practically holding me in the air.)

"Why did this work anyway? I thought Aisis made me forget all about you?" I asked as Devin released me but tugged on my hair.

"She did, in a way. She told you to forget all about me, but she never told you to forget about my horse form."

"She didn't know you met him in any of his alternate forms."

I looked up at the speaker and finally recognized Dave the chubby vampire.

"Dave," I grinned, jogging the few feet to give him a side hug.

"Do you remember me, Morgan?" a timid voice asked.

I turned to face the last being in the Peace Garden: Westfall.

"Westfall!" I gushed, walking the few steps before throwing my arms around him. "I'm sorry this is probably making you uncomfortable, but it's so *good* to see you," I said, squeezing his horsey neck as I buried my face in his thick, black mane.

Westfall lowered his head and rested it on my shoulder. "I'm very glad you're back, Morgan. I never got to say goodbye."

The little unicorn sounded so sad, this time I really did cry.

"I'm sorry," I whispered, squeezing him tight one more time before stepping back to look him in the eyes. "I'm so sorry," I said, stroking his cheek after rubbing tears out of my eyes. My hand froze as I realized something was different about the mystical equine. "Westfall, your horn! Where is it? What happened?"

"It got sawed off," Westfall said with a proud little snort. "It will grow back over time, but it needed to be removed for my stay at the therapy barn."

"You mean you're ready?" I asked, my eyes widening.

"Almost. I have been brushed and petted by lots of humans this week, but there's one last step. Morgan, would you be the first human to ride me?" Westfall asked. He backed up slightly, tucking his head against his neck, steeling himself for a no.

I reached out and placed a hand on Westfall's neck, unable to keep an idiotic smile off my face. "I would love to," I said.

Devin laughed, materializing at my side. "Welcome back, Morgan," he said, throwing an arm over my shoulder.

"Do I get to keep my memories this time?" I asked. I was too happy to be bothered by Devin's touchy-feely character.

"Yep. It was part of the deal," Devin confirmed before carefully studying Westfall. "And now we have to figure out how to smuggle this little coward back *out* of the school grounds. He had two meltdowns on the way in here."

"What deal?" I asked, my eyebrows furrowing.

"Morgan?"

After a week of utter cluelessness, I finally recognized this voice. It was Frey.

I turned around—Devin, that grabby Pooka, moving with me so he could keep his arm on me—to face Frey.

He was standing by the hedge, in the exact same spot I stood when I got my first glimpse of horse-Devin. He didn't look angry. In fact, the way he sadly looked at me with his big green eyes and his hands shoved in his pockets reminded me of an abandoned puppy.

"Hey, Frey," I said, walking forward. (Devin's arm slid off me like a dead fish.) I stopped a few feet short of the silver-haired werewolf.

"So, you got your memories back," he said, lowering his eyes. He nodded his head a few times while awkwardly hunching his shoulders.

"Yep," I said, biting my lip. I paused before saying, "Look, Frey," at the exact same time Frey said—

"Morgan, I'm—."

We both broke off our sentences and blinked at each other.

I did my best to smile. "I'm sorry," I said. "I really was being a first-class nag at the end. I was really stubborn and bratty. Sorry. I shouldn't have held your nature against you."

Frey shook his head and looked at the ground. "It's my fault. I shouldn't let Devin get to me like he does."

Behind us, Devin snorted.

I whipped around to glare at him, but Frey continued.

"I was born in human society. I should know better. I should have been more sensitive to you; I was just so focused on using you," he said.

I was surprised by this admission. I didn't think I would ever hear such an emotionally intelligent apology uttered from a boy's lips.

"So, let's forget about it," I suggested. "We were both being stupid. Sounds good?"

Frey nodded a few times before cracking a smile. "Yeah. Sounds great!"

"Wonderful. Thank you for that Hallmark Channel reunion," Devin said, rolling his eyes as he walked forward to ruffle my hair.

"Devin!" I objected, slapping his hands away. "Don't even start!"

"What? I, for one, think it's a good thing you two have made up. You're probably going to be seeing each other outside of class a lot anyway," Devin said with a kingly shrug of his shoulders.

"What are you talking about?" I asked, furrowing my eyebrows.

"Not much. Come to the MBRC tomorrow, 'kay?" Devin asked, his head lolling to the side.

"Um…sure," I agreed.

"If you ask Dr. Creamintin, he can direct you to my class center," Westfall said. "I'll see you tomorrow?"

"Wouldn't miss it for the world, cutie," I said, walking over to Westfall and hugging him.

"We had best return to the MBRC. Ahhh, my instructors are going to lower my grade because I missed my lessons today," Dave mourned.

"So?" Frey asked, one silver eyebrow arching. "You're already the lowest in your class. Do you not remember why Morgan knows about us in the first place?" Frey asked, his familiar bossiness returning.

"Technically, that was your fault," Dave said, emphatically pointing at the werewolf.

"If you just drank your tomato juice—,"

"That drink is poison!"

"Oi, could you two stop the student and teacher bit for once and get Westfall back to the MBRC?" Devin asked, crossing his arms over his chest.

Frey frowned, but Dave grabbed the werewolf's arm. "Let's do him this one favor. I'll explain the situation," Dave said in a lowered tone. "Come, Westfall. Let's find my umbrella. If I don't get some shade soon, I'm going to closely resemble a lobster," Dave said before setting off through the bushes.

"You're sneakier than usual today. Have you been sneaking sips of A+ blood again?" Frey suspiciously asked as he followed Dave, Westfall trailing after them.

"So. What deal?" I asked, turning to face Devin.

Devin sighed and rubbed his forehead. "You are almost as stubborn as that mangy mutt."

"Devin," I said, tapping my foot.

"Yeah, yeah. Come here," he gruffly said before reaching out and pulling me into another hug. This one was tight. I was pressed uncomfortably close to his chest, and he rested his lips on the top of my head.

"Hey, Devin," I said, growing cross when I noticed the way my heart was erratically beating. This was Devin. Playboy, perverted Devin. He might be hot, but I think he's had more groupies than any boy band.

Think about Brett. Think about Brett. The familiar mantra popped back into my head, and I clung to it with relief.

"You had better be worth it," Devin grumbled into my hair, squeezing me tighter still as I wriggled in his grasp. "Not only will I be the laughing stock for robbing the cradle, but it was *Aysel*! You have no idea how much that pains me," he sulked as he continued to hold me, poking my spine for good measure.

"Um, what?"

"Just say thanks."

"Thank you, Devin."

"You're welcome, Morgan."

"..."

"..."

"...Could you let me go now?" I asked.

"*Oh. My. Gosh.* Would it kill you to be quiet for thirty seconds?" Devin growled.

I didn't reply and instead fell silent, my face pressed painfully against the zipper of Devin's jacket.

After a while, he released me, ruffling my hair, and stepped back. "See you, Morgan," he said.

"Yeah, yeah," I muttered, brushing off my jacket with the utmost concentration to hide my blushing face.

When I looked up, he was gone.

I didn't think much of the incident, and inside I mostly rejoiced, utterly excited to remember every part of my life again.

Perhaps if I hadn't been so self-absorbed, I would have remembered that Devin normally just fondles me; he never clings as he did that afternoon.

If I hadn't been so self-absorbed, maybe I would have been able to tell him just how grateful I was.

This time, Tuesday afternoon, when I shut my locker door, I was prepared to see Frey there. "I'm ready!" I declared, my jacket already on, backpack hefted over my shoulder.

Frey only nodded, but a lopsided smile broke across his lips as he watched me.

"So, you two are talking again?" Fran asked, standing up next to me before she reached out and pinched my cheek. "How cute! You're just like a couple of elementary students."

"Owie," I muttered as Fran yanked my face up and down by my cheek skin.

"If you're ready, Morgan, we should head out. Work's waiting," Frey said, slowly edging backwards.

I grabbed Fran's hand and pulled it away from my face before rubbing my red cheek. "Yeah, I'll second that. See you tomorrow, Fran."

"Uh-huh. Bu-bye," Fran said, smirking at me and wriggling her fingers in a suggestive wave.

After we left the building and picked up a singing, umbrella-toting Dave on the edge of the school grounds, Frey filled me in. "So, I talked with Dr. Creamintin, and he told me that from today on, you're going to be a privately employed worker at the MBRC," Frey said as we walked towards the train station.

"That sounds a lot like an unwilling volunteer or conscripted slave," I said, wrinkles puckering on my forehead.

"No, you'll be paid," Frey said. "But because you'll be going there five days out of the week (maybe more based on your clients), you'll be getting a monthly train pass, compliments of the MBRC. You'll get the passes through me. Your employer decided it would be easier to have me dole out monthly passes rather than send them to you."

"Wait, I have a specific employer?" I asked, starting to feel irked. Unless it was my cyclops union, I wasn't sure I *wanted* to work for the bureaucratic MBRC. And I don't even know what bureaucratic means!

Frey uncomfortably scratched the base of his skull. "I *really* don't want to get in the middle of this," he muttered.

"Devin made all the arrangements for you," big-mouthed Dave blabbed.

"He what?" I darkly said.

"It's better if Dr. Creamintin explains it to you," Frey said, shooting Dave a warning look.

I'll admit, I was pretty psyched when I got the monthly train pass. I have this thing for punch cards and tickets. Don't ask. Because of my already good mood, getting to the MBRC was an even better experience than usual.

"Morgan! You're back!" Tiny greeted me, his face beet red with cheer.

"Hey there, Tiny! How have you been?" I asked as he turned cranks and gears so we could get through the door.

"I'm great. It's good to hear you're back with us. Now, don't forget me when you meet your posh new clients," he winked.

The smile fell off my face. "My what?"

Frey coughed and hacked like Dave when he's near a smoker before making an X with his hands at Tiny. As if I didn't notice. "Right then, let's go. You don't want to keep Westfall waiting, do you, Morgan?"

Properly distracted, I followed Frey through the door while waving goodbye to Tiny. "Wait, I'm riding Westfall today?" I asked, looking down at my American Eagle jeans. I wasn't exactly in riding clothes.

"I thought you were?" Frey frowned as we popped into the central chamber of the MBRC. "Look, Dave and I have to get to class. Go to Dr. Creamintin's. He'll be able to straighten everything out. Okay?"

"Yeah, okay," I agreed, watching the magical inhabitants of the MBRC stroll, fly, and glide by.

Man, I had missed this place.

"Goodbye, Morgan," Dave called as Frey yanked him away.

I stood with a sappy smile and watched a pegasus prance past me before I snapped out of it. "Right, Dr. Creamintin," I said, blinking at a girl that walked past me, carrying a goose and a golden egg.

I entered the bustling flow and headed for Dr. Creamintin's office when I saw a familiar face.

It was Devin.

A black duffle bag was thrown across his shoulder, and he walked with a confident saunter, speaking to two men in black who scurried after him like cockroaches and scribbled notes down in little notebooks. The suits looked almost human, but what really caught my attention was the fact that Devin did not have a female entourage (unusual), nor was he eyeing up any of the girls in the vicinity (a downright rarity!).

I changed directions and headed for the mischievous Pooka, intending to chew him out for contracting me out to people like I was a minion.

When I popped up in his sight, I spoke, "Devin!"

He didn't pause. He looked straight through me and kept talking. "So, contact Benson and tell him he can shove it. I'm not budging an inch on the seven-league boots issue," Devin said as he blew past me.

"Devin!" I repeated in a louder, angrier tone.

The little rat didn't respond; he didn't even look over his shoulder.

"Um, sir, the girl?" one of his followers said, glancing back at me.

"She is unimportant," Devin told the suit. He didn't even meet my gaze; he acted as if I were a ghost. It was like I didn't exist.

All the anger fizzled out of me, and I was left with something that felt suspiciously like hurt.

Devin kept talking as he and the suits disappeared in with the crowd, his voice dropping out of my hearing. "And tell Ruseo to have my rooms ready when I arrive. The council is meeting tonight; I won't have time to drop by before..."

I stared in the direction Devin had sauntered, even after he was long gone. His personality had obviously undergone a complete transformation overnight. I mean, *something* had to have happened.

Devin hugged me so happily yesterday. Why the sudden change?

▭

"Devin is such a *jerk*!" I fumed to Westfall as I stood next to him.

"You've mentioned that once or twice," Westfall said with a nod, jingling his bridle.

I managed to contain my irritation by the time Dr. Creamintin took me to the MBRC riding arena, where I would be the first human to ride Westfall. Speaking of the doctor, he was standing back with the rest of Westfall's teachers, watching us from the far side of the sandy ring.

I kicked sand, getting dust on my borrowed boots before my ill-fitting helmet slid on my head and hit the ridge of my nose.

"...Are you ready to get on?" Westfall ventured after observing my temper tantrum.

I was trying to delay the inevitable. "Westfall, are you sure about this?" I asked as the bay unicorn walked away from me and towards the mounting block, the saddle stirrups swinging against his belly.

"Sure about what?" he asked, carefully lining up next to the mini step ladder.

"About being ridden. I thought no one was supposed to ride a unicorn," I said as I trudged after him, eyeing the English saddle that was perched on his back. (I wished it had a horn.)

The idea of riding a unicorn felt about ten times more awkward than leading werewolf Frey on a leash. And that's saying something.

"Oh, that's only the prissy British ones," Westfall said, shaking his head.

"Are you sure? This feels pretty sacrilegious," I said, glancing at his teachers. They were lined up, whispering amongst themselves as they watched us.

"There's no rule that unicorns can't be ridden. We just don't usually choose to be mounts," Westfall said, widening his nostrils before blinking his warm eyes at me.

I pushed the helmet up so I could gaze suspiciously at the bay-colored unicorn. "Then is it because I'm still a…*you know*. Is that why I can ride you?" I asked, squirming uncomfortably.

"Because you're a what?" Westfall patiently asked.

"You know, because I haven't really dated much, and I'm still a vir—," I paused, Westfall still looked completely lost. "You know, if you don't know what I'm talking about, then we're not even going to go there," I said, looking down at the stepping stool.

"We haven't all day, Miss Morgan!" one of Westfall's teachers obnoxiously called from the far end of the ring.

I scowled at them before my helmet slid forward again.

"It's okay, Morgan. You can trust me," Westfall said, getting my attention. "I won't let you fall. I won't let anything happen to you," he said with a stubbornness I didn't know he possessed.

I blew hair out of my face. "Alright, Westfall," I said, climbing the mounting block. "How do I get on?"

"Grip my mane with your left hand and the saddle with your right hand. Put your *left* foot in the stirrup, push off the mounting block, and swing your right leg over my back," Westfall calmly instructed.

"Right," I grimly said, following his orders. I paused before pushing off. "…Are you sure—,"

"I'm positive, Morgan."

"Okay," I said before swinging my leg up and over, throwing myself in a jumble on top of the saddle.

Westfall, to his credit, didn't wince, even when I launched myself onto his neck.

"Oh, my gosh. You are *so* much taller than I thought," I said into Westfall's mane.

"You can sit up, Morgan. I won't move until you're comfortable," Westfall kindly said.

It took me a few seconds before I sat up, squeezing the daylights out of Westfall's gut with my knees while I tangled my hands into his mane.

"Is your right foot in the stirrup? Good. Now take up the reins," Westfall started.

"No," I stubbornly said.

"Morgan, I'm not going to bolt. You can remove your hands from my hair," the bay said, sounding a little hurt.

"It's not that," I quickly amended. "I know I can trust you. It's me and my balance that I don't trust. Besides, that's not the point. What I mean is that I'll ride you and break pretty much every fairy tale rule I know, but there's no way I'm going to direct you with those rein things. Not a flippin' chance."

Halfway down the arena, Dr. Creamintin laughed.

"This isn't funny!" I shouted.

"I'm going to start walking, Morgan," Westfall announced.

"Okay," I said, holding my breath for the first few steps the skinny unicorn took. Westfall's stride was a tippy, rocking motion. I'm sure for people who *like* to ride, it would have been very comfortable, but I was pretty certain I was going to fall straight off his side.

Dr. Creamintin was still laughing by the time we reached the far end of the arena. Westfall's other instructors were in various stages of trying not to laugh.

"You're doing quite well, Westfall," said a *giant* guy—I suspect he's part ogre—who was pointedly staring at Westfall and ignoring me.

Dr. Creamintin, however, was not so kind. "You look like a white asparagus, Morgan," he belly laughed.

"You!" I hissed as Westfall sedately walked past.

"What, aren't you fulfilling a childhood dream?" Dr. Creamintin grinned.

I considered his words as Westfall made another circuit around the arena. When we reached the far end, another one of Westfall's instructors spoke. "Westfall, do you think you're ready to trot with the human?"

"What's a trot?" I asked, finally gaining enough confidence to untangle my left hand from Westfall's mane so I could scratch an itch on my side.

"Oh, it's like a jog," Dr. Creamintin said with a sagely nod.

"You mean we have to go faster!?" I wailed.

This time, all of the instructors laughed.

"I'm sorry that, as the first person to ride you, I was such an uncoordinated dope, Westfall," I apologized, patting the saddle-free unicorn.

"Don't be," Westfall said with a horsey smile. "Most children I aid won't be used to riding. Besides, you helped me get over my fear of humans. Perhaps I could help you become a better rider?" Westfall shyly suggested.

He was just too cute!

"That would be nice," I said, hobbling along. "But please, not for a while? My legs are *killing* me."

"It's a deal," Westfall said, bobbing his head. "I have to go back to my teachers, but thank you, Morgan."

"No, thank you, Westfall," I smiled, waving good bye as the petite equine returned to his teachers in the riding arena.

"Don't you get a sense of satisfaction from that? I knew you would be a good fit for your new employer," Dr. Creamintin said, folding his arms as he stood next to me.

"About that. Please explain. Frey said something about Devin auctioning me off," I said, my eyes turning into slits.

"Oh, dear," Dr. Creamintin sighed. "All right. In order to receive permission from MBRC management to reverse your hypnosis, Devin had to pull a few strings," Dr Creamintin said as we left the arena.

"He has that kind of power?" I asked with disbelief before plopping down on a stool to switch to my school shoes. "Am I really that big of a deal?"

"The MBRC has a tight lid on those who know about us," Dr. Creamintin nodded. "It's virtually unheard of that a regular human, much less a teenage girl without any connections to magic would be allowed to know of us. Devin had to go pretty high up to get the clearance needed to reinstate you. He also had to make a few promises, one of them involves you."

"Oh?" I asked, feeling a little more reasonable. I mean, if Devin did it for my sake…

"Yes. It was requested that you would become a private tutor for a certain MBRC member," Dr. Creamintin said as I stood. "You will work at the MBRC, but you won't be employed by it. You are a private consultant. That's a very rare position, you know," he insisted.

"So, who am I tutoring? And what can *I* possibly teach them?" I asked.

Dr. Creamintin laughed. "Ahahah, that's where it gets a little complicated. Your pupil is a nice lad named Asahi."

"What is he? A werewolf?"

"No. A High Elf."

I couldn't have been more shocked if Dr. Creamintin told me I was going to be schooling the MBRC Administrator himself. High Elves are like the celebrities of elves. Even with my limited exposure to magical culture, I knew they were something special. (After all, wasn't the MBRC Administrator a High Elf?)

Much of what Dr. Creamintin told me after that didn't sink in. So, he wrote down the room I would need to report to the following day and sent me home. I spent most of the evening as a mindless lump in front of the TV before completing my homework.

For the greater part of Wednesday, I formulated ideas of what my pupil would look like. I pictured Legolas, the stereotypical elf, before musing on all of the magical beings I had met on the MBRC. There was Dave the fat vampire, Frey the skinny/not muscled werewolf, and Westfall the delicate, bay-colored unicorn.

"He's probably going to be butt ugly and really short," I said, propping my head on my chin.

"Who?" Fran asked after drinking her milk.

"No one," I said, shaking myself out of my reverie.

"So, now that you're talking to Frey again, are you over Brett Patterson?" Fran asked with a coy grin.

"Psh, never," I snorted.

"Personally, I find myself pining after the mysterious and hot Garden Guy. I wonder what happened to him," Fran sighed.

I wisely kept my mouth shut and concentrated on my burger.

Frey and Dave escorted me to the MBRC, leaving me by the information desk. "Orion or Corona will be able to direct you to the right room. Just show them the note Dr. Creamintin gave you," Frey said, somewhat distracted by Dave, who was staring at a cartload of blood packages. "Dave. Dave, stop looking. If you're that hungry, drink some tomato juice. DAVE! You're drooling! Man up!"

I smiled and waved goodbye to the frazzled werewolf and salivating vampire before skipping off to the information desk.

I was about halfway there when Corona looked up and saw me, a smile breaking across her reptilian features. "Morgan!"

"Corona, how are you?" I grinned before Doggy popped out from behind the desk and launched himself at me. He hit my chest like a ton of bricks. "And Doggy! How are you, boy?" I cooed, cradling the little dragon.

Doggy offered me a biscuit which he clutched in the talons of his back left foot.

"Why thank you, how kind. But why don't you eat it?" I suggested.

Doggy insistently passed the cookie from his back foot to his front paw and offered it up as I held him like a baby. I tickled his tummy to distract him. (I wasn't sure what was in those dragon treats, and I wasn't that gung-ho on finding out.)

"So, you have returned to us," Orion said, swishing his horse tail.

"You work with me again 1 2 3 we answer questions?" Toby asked, talking as fast as ever.

"No, I actually have a new assignment," I said as Doggy snuggled into my arms. "I'm hoping you guys can tell me how to get to the room I'm supposed to go to."

"You not here to help?" Toby asked, pushing his bushy eyebrows up before he took a sip of coffee.

"No, sorry."

The hobgoblin grunted and answered a ringing telephone.

"Don't let him get you down," Corona whispered. "He was devastated last week when you were gone. His average to answer a question was 84 seconds."

I blinked at the hobgoblin, who chattered away on the phone while his long fingers tapped out words on the keyboard.

"Morgan, which room do you seek?" Orion asked.

"Oh," I said, digging Dr. Creamintin's note out of my jacket pocket. "Here. Dr. Creamintin gave my room assignment to me yesterday, but I was a little out of it," I blushed as I shifted Doggy so he was perched against my left hip, getting biscuit crumbs on my shirt as he ate.

Corona and Orion peered across the counter to look at my note. Corona let out what I *think* was supposed to be an impressed hiss, and Orion's eyebrows crawled up his forehead.

"*You're* Asahi's private tutor?" Corona asked, sounding awed.

"Is he a High Elf?" I asked, scratching Doggy beneath his chin while I looked for the lewd little male fairy that usually scampered around the desk. "Hey, where's that tiny pervert fairy?" I added.

"Gristles is gone on break. You're teaching *Asahi*?" Corona repeated.

"Um, I dunno. I'm teaching a High Elf," I said, brushing Doggy's crumbs off me.

"Truly, the stars have aligned if a human is tutoring a High Elf," Orion said with the appropriate amount of mystery afforded to centaurs.

"Look, who is this guy?" I asked.

"Asahi is, as you said, a High Elf. You'll be able to recognize him on sight," Corona nodded.

"How?"

"Asahi is Japanese for morning sun. His mother rather appropriately named him because, frankly, he's pretty…*golden*," Corona said.

"Asahi is the light that shines in the morning," Orion added. This information wasn't new; he was just being a centaur I guess.

"So I'm looking for someone gold?" I said as I pressed my lips together.

"You'll be able to tell it's him. I promise," Corona assured me as Orion moved away to help another MBRC member. "But finding the room you will be using might be a little difficult. It's on the indigo wing, which means it's the third floor. See that indigo-colored band up there?" Corona asked, pointing to the third level of the room.

"Uh-huh," I said, squinting to see better.

"Okay, then it's down kitsune hallway. That will be pretty easy to spot, just go up the stairs to the third level and take a right. Keep walking around the perimeter of the main chamber until you see a hallway that branches off and is decorated in foxes. It will have a Japanese feeling to it. If you get to the banshee hallway—you'll hear that one a mile away before you see it—you've gone too far," Corona continued. "Follow the kitsune hallway until it intersects with the Chinese dragon hallway. That's a pretty obvious hallway too. When you reach the intersection, take a left. It will be the fourth room on the right. The door will have a large, red dragon painted on it."

I was pretty sure I didn't stand a chance of finding the room. "Okay," I said, my eyebrows furrowing.

Corona took notice and stood up straight. "Why don't you take Doggy with you? He knows the MBRC like one of his claws. He'll get you there."

"Will he be able to find his way back here?" I asked.

"Of course. He knows he'll get the leash if he doesn't," Corona said, waving a webbed paw in the air.

"...The leash?" I asked.

"Look at the time! Honey, you got to get going! Asahi won't mind waiting on you, but if *Aysel* finds out, he'll chew you out for sure. Good luck!" Corona said before her attention was claimed by a hovering fairy.

I dubiously looked down at Doggy, who had long ago finished his cookie and was now mostly occupied with chewing the shoulder strap of my backpack.

This little guy was supposed to help me through the maze and get me to my room? I would be lucky if I didn't accidentally wander into a man-eating unicorn section.

"So, Doggy, Corona says we're going to the red Chinese dragon room. Can you get us there?" I asked, carefully picking my way through the magical crowd.

Doggy sneezed on my collar bone.

"That's what I thought," I wryly replied.

To his credit, Doggy did quite well. (Although I was a little out of breath after hauling myself *and* the little dragon up two sets of stairs.) I started walking around the perimeter of the room and would have walked right past the kitsune hallway if Doggy hadn't dragon-barked at me and nearly thrown himself out of my arms.

(I had to wonder how I missed the hallway; the walls were covered with foxes that were jumping, sleeping, eating, playing, etc.)

But even I knew when we reached the intersection with the Chinese dragon hallway. A sculpture of a Chinese dragon (which is really long and doesn't have wings, unlike European dragons) hung in the hallway, and up and down the dragon corridor were paintings of Chinese dragons that *literally* slithered across the walls.

"I'm supposed to take a left...I think," I said before Doggy yipped, agreeing with me.

I stared at the doors on the right, but there none of them were decorated with red dragons. "Did Corona send me down the wrong hallway?" I wondered, turning around.

"Can I help you?" someone asked.

I turned around, again, and couldn't but smile given that Corona had been absolutely right. "You're Asahi?" I guessed.

11

I Tutor the Morning Light

Asahi's hair is the richest gold color I've ever seen. His eyes are gold as well, the reflective color of *real* gold. Like someone had melted gold bars and fashioned eyes for him. His skin was not pale, but bronze, like he was a surfer or something. Asahi's smile was too big and too white for him to look like Legolas. But he had that mystical air everyone thinks elves have, even though he was far more personable.

Plus, his clothes were pretty weird. They looked more like something a prince from Arabian Nights would wear than an elf. On his upper half, he wore nothing but a shimmering gold vest that was encrusted with jewels. Earrings dripped from his tapered ears, and a gold circlet with an amber drop circled his head.

His pants were cream colored and kind of poufy. They were tucked into gold boots, but they also had gold embroidery on them as well as other glittering jewels and gems.

Asahi was so much like the stereotypical, beautiful elves, and yet he was not. He glittered like the morning sun, and he had that haunting beauty with the high cheek bones and long, pretty hair that everyone pictures elves as having.... Still, when I was picturing

High Elf, I hadn't exactly been thinking of a prince waltzing out of Aladdin.

I'd have to apologize to Corona for doubting her one-word description.

"I am Asahi," the elf acknowledged. (I was slightly disappointed; his voice didn't sound very melodic or elf-like, but it was warm like his name.) "And you are?" he asked. His earrings clinked as he tipped his head to the side.

"I'm sorry, I'm Morgan Fae," I said, glancing down as Doggy jumped off me, hovering in the air for a few seconds by beating his little wings before he fell to the ground.

The little dragon snorted before setting off down the hallway, hopefully going back to the main desk.

"Oh, Morgan!" the warmth in Asahi's voice increased by ten degrees Fahrenheit. "You're going to be my tutor."

"Uh-huh. I'm sorry, but I think I might be a little late. I was having a hard time finding the room," I nervously said, rubbing my sweaty palms together.

"There's no need to apologize," Asahi laughed. "It's this door right up here," he said, gesturing up the hallway before leading away.

I could tell I was going to need my mantra if this guy was my student.

Think of Brett. Think of Brett.

He was too good-looking and sweet for his own good.

"Um, so exactly what am I supposed to teach you?" I asked, still smiling like a dope as I trailed after the sparkling high elf.

"Whatever you like. I am very interested in humans. I've never met one that's under the age of forty," Asahi said, twisting his neck so he could smile at me.

He had a nice smile. It was like sunning yourself on the beach.

"Okay," I said as we stopped just outside a door on the *left* side that had a red dragon on it. (So Corona had gotten her directions wrong! Hah!)

Asahi opened the door for me, and I stepped into the already lit room.

I immediately felt dwarfed.

The room was *huge*. It was fan shaped with a white board in the front where I would presumably stand. The rest was filled with desks for students. It reminded me of a college lecture room, with the exception that all the lights were burning phoenix feathers, and the ceiling (which was quite high) was decorated in stars that not only glittered, but also moved if you stared at them long enough.

"Wow," I said as Asahi entered the room after me, heading towards a desk in the front row as the door slowly swung shut.

"Wait!" someone screamed before there was a crunching noise.

A girl, who was probably a year or two younger than I was, was pinched between the door frame and the door. She gurgled, waving her arm frantically in her pinched position while her mop of white-blonde hair fell over her face.

I lurched forward, hurrying to push the door open so she could fall inside the room.

She fell in an ungraceful heap on the ground, her shouts muffled on the wooden ground.

"Are you okay?" I asked, letting the door click shut before I crouched by her side. Asahi joined me, helping the girl sit up.

She reminded me of a Victorian doll. Her skin was pale like porcelain, her hair fine and curled in perfect ringlets. She wore a frilly, black, floor-length dress that had white accents and lace.

She looked up at me, blinking large, inky black eyes. She was quite beautiful until a goofy smile broke across her lips. "Hello."

"Hi. Um. Who are you?" I asked, leaning away.

"Oh!" she said, rocketing to her feet. "I'm Madeline, and you're Morgan," she said, keeping her black eyes on me. When her smile widened, I could see her canines were ever so slightly more pronounced than her other teeth.

"Are you, by chance—," I started.

"A vampire? Yep," Madeline said, brushing off her dress as Asahi and I stood. "I'm here under the Pooka's orders," she said before leaning towards me and whispering, "He asked me to keep an eye on you when you teach the elf."

Devin told her to come?

I was a little confused by that. When I saw him yesterday, he made it pretty clear he didn't care a lick about me. Maybe she was senile? But she seemed sincere…

"So, you're going to be tutored, too?" Asahi asked with his warm smile.

Madeline wasn't affected by him and spared him a nod and a half smile before turning back to me.

Oddly, Madeline somewhat comforted me. She seemed a little young for how I pictured *Twilight* vampires and everything, but she was quite pretty and pale, more fitting to be a vampire than Dave.

At least that was what I first thought.

Madeline twirled me to the front of the room before making a beeline for a desk.

Asahi seemed to accept the vampire's intrusion quite easily. He adjusted his Arabian Nights vest before joining her, the gold beads in his hair clicking as he seated himself.

"Ready," Madeline said, folding her hands on her desk.

The elf and vampire stared at me for a few very awkward moments.

"Sorry," I nervously laughed, folding my arms across my chest as I stood there. "I don't really know where to start."

"Introduction!" Madeline cheered.

"Um, I'm Morgan Fae. I'm sixteen, and I'm currently attending high school. I'm here to teach you about…humans, I guess?"

Asahi blinded me with another brilliant smile.

"So…How experienced are you two when it comes to humans?" I asked.

"I was human. Once," Madeline said quite proudly. She wilted for a moment. "Although, that was in the women's suffrage era, so I suspect things have changed quite drastically."

"I have been in human society less than half a dozen times. As I mentioned before, all the humans I know are over 40 and are scientists and enchanters here at the MBRC," Asahi said.

"Why don't you have more experience with humans?" I asked, leaning against a podium. "I imagine we're difficult to avoid."

"We stick to the magical places in the world," Asahi clarified.

"Places like the MBRC, the Redwood forest of California, the less-populated parts of New Zealand and America and Japan, Disney World, and Atlantis," Madeline listed, ticking the places off on her fingers.

"Wait, Disney World?" I interrupted.

"The most magical place on Earth," Madeline said.

"Magical beings, in this age, remain isolated. We have for centuries," Asahi explained.

I tapped my chin. "So, do you know anything about humans?"

"Of course. Many of us aspire to live in human society, and, at a minimum, to peacefully coexist," Asahi nodded. "We take classes. I have even completed advanced human psychology," he smiled.

"I like dresses," Madeline said.

"Hm," I said, digesting the information. "Is there a topic you're particularly interested in, Asahi?" I asked. Asahi was my employer, so I may as well try to address his needs first.

"Would teenagers and high school be acceptable?" Asahi suggested. "I only know what the centaurs have told me, and I suspect they might be biased."

"The emo equines? Yeah, they're biased," Madeline nodded.

"For instance, what does emo even mean?" Asahi asked, acknowledging Madeline's comment with a smile.

I dropped my backpack on the ground before I dug out a notebook and a pen. "Okay, so topics of discussion: the meaning of emo," I said, scribbling notes in my notebook.

"Isn't being emo mean being goth?" Madeline asked.

"Not necessarily," I corrected. "How about we look at the different subcultures of high school? Sometimes it's pretty hard to understand, but it should be *hilarious*."

"Going over normal, everyday life would be helpful, too. What do humans do in their free time?" Asahi queried, his gold eyes burning with interest.

I continued to scribble topics in my notebook. "A fair warning: the information I present is totally going to be biased from my opinion. What my friends and I do with our time is going to be different from the jocks, and even more different depending on the parts of the world you go to. Plus, my view on high school subcultures is going to be from my own subculture's reference."

"What subculture are you?" Madeline asked with wide eyes.

"Hmm," I said, tapping the pen on my lower lip. "Normal?"

"You are probably a part of your own subculture, but you don't necessarily realize it," Asahi brilliantly informed me.

"I guess I'm probably a prep," I considered.

"What's a prep?" Madeline asked.

"Oh, gosh. We're going to need Wikipedia. Can we get a computer in here and a projector?" I asked.

"Sure. I'll just ask my brother," Asahi said.

"Perfect."

"What's a computer?" Madeline asked. "Is it that box thing humans spend most of their time watching?"

I spent the better part of an hour trying to correct Madeline's ideas of computers as well as Asahi's misconceptions. Apparently, a professor had told him computers were how humans did magic.

I was enjoying myself, feeling oddly vindicated by the pair's external beauty. Storytellers hadn't gotten *everything* wrong after all.

My smugness was blown to smithereens halfway through the class.

"Remember: TVs are what display television. That's what we watch movies on… although you can watch DVDs on computers, too," I trailed off as I realized how confusing human technology was.

Madeline and Asahi gave me clueless smiles.

"Here, let me draw you a diagram," I hastily said, flipping a page in my notebook. "Ouch," I muttered when a sheet of paper sliced a pad of my finger. "Paper cut," I said, holding my finger out in front of me.

A single drop of blood oozed out of the fresh cut. I froze, remembering I was with a vampire. I looked up, expecting Madeline to transform into some kind of salivating, starving beast.

Her eyes were fastened on my bleeding finger, but rather than looking hungry, she looked *ill*. She grew pale, even though she kept her smile in place, and a second later, she tipped out of her chair, hitting the ground like a load of bricks.

The vampire had fainted.

I am not kidding.

"Madeline?" I said wiping the blood off on a sheet of paper before hurrying to her side. "Are you okay?" I asked as she started coming around.

"Oh, my, I can still smell it," Madeline moaned, bringing up a hand to pinch her nose shut as she hunched her shoulders.

"I'm sorry, Madeline, you must be hungry or something. Do you have any tomato juice on you?" I asked as Asahi crouched down next to me.

"Oh, it's not that," Madeline said, plastering her other hand over her eyes as she slowly sat up. "I've got hemophobia."

"...What?" I asked, leaning back.

"I'm afraid of blood," Madeline said, turning in my direction. Her voice was pinched thanks to the hand over her nose. "It makes me sick. Thankfully, this time I only swooned. Sometimes I cannot hold onto my lunch," she confessed.

"You are a vampire...who is afraid of blood," I said.

"Yes."

I stood up and walked away. "I take it back. This place trashes all fairy tales known to mankind," I muttered.

"Drinking blood is the worst experience. I can get by on tomato juice, but my doctors insist I drink a blood cocktail once a month, otherwise I have the tendency to get woozy. But I would rather be woozy than drink blood," Madeline complained, blindly fumbling to her desk.

Curse you, Dave the chubby vampire. If I hadn't met you, I wouldn't have known what a big fat lie all my favorite childhood stories were.

At 5:30, Asahi and Madeline escorted me down to the information desk so I could catch the train home. Madeline promised to meet me at the desk the next day to take me up to our classroom.

Frey sent me a text message that he and Dave were going to have to take a later train. Apparently Dave was staying behind for remedial lessons because he skipped Monday to help me recover my memories.

I was just leaving the main chamber of the MBRC, purring over my new monthly train pass, when I heard someone call my name.

"Morgan!"

I turned around and grinned when I spotted Sandy and Ralph, my cyclops pals, cutting through a crowd of nymphs as they hurried in my direction.

"Sandy, Ralph! How are you guys?" I smiled when they drew close enough to me that we could talk without shouting.

"We're wonderful—but Morgan, why didn't you tell us?" Sandy asked, clutching her blue purse—which matched her adorable skirt —after giving me a hug.

"Tell you what?" I asked, distracted when I realized Ralph was wearing a pair of glasses. "Oh wow! They've got glasses out already? Those doctors moved *fast*!"

"Not yet, actually. The researchers are having a hard time creating a pair of glasses that work well with a glamour. This pair is actually one of three styles they're testing out. They asked me to try them on for the day," Ralph beamed before Sandy smashed him in the arm with her purse. "I mean why didn't you tell us, Morgan?" Ralph echoed his facial expression shifting from glee to hurt.

"Tell you what?" I repeated.

"That you were getting your memory modified!" Sandy said, planting her heels and frowning down at me. She was quite tall to begin with—well over six feet—but her stiletto heels really put her up there.

"I didn't think it was important," I said.

"You didn't think it was important?" Sandy squealed, her jaw dropping.

"What Sandra means, Morgan, is how could you think that?" Ralph said. "Because of you, we cyclopes are receiving visual aid!

We owe so much to you! It was rather alarming to search for you at the information desk only to be told you had been hypnotized and would no longer be knowledgeable about the MBRC."

"Welcome back, by the way," Sandy beamed, reaching out to hug me again. "I usually can't stand it when Fairy Council Members throw their weight around, but I'm glad Devin did this time."

"I'm sorry guys. I should have told you," I agreed, deciding to ignore the reference to Devin. "I was just being a teenage drama queen," I sighed.

"The important thing is that you're back, and you remember," Sandy nodded.

"What are you up to these days? Corona told us you were no longer working at the information desk," Ralph said, brandishing a folded newspaper at the desk that was halfway across the room.

"She's right. I'm tutoring a High Elf named Asahi," I said.

Sandy's eyebrow flew up her forehead. "Wow. You really are an earth-shaker, aren't you?"

"Unbelievably so," Ralph nodded, tapping the newspaper in his hand. "I'm half surprised there's not an article about you in the MBRC Daily Sentinel."

"The what?" I asked.

"It's the daily newspaper that's published by the MBRC," Ralph said, unfolding his newspaper to pass it across to me. "It's a useful tool that relays news to everyone in the MBRC, much the same way a local, daily newspaper does for cities and towns."

I stared at the day's issue of the MBRC Daily Sentinel.

The front page was splashed with the headline of: "MBRC Board to Approve Goblin Imports Contract."

Whatever that meant.

"Cool," I said, lacking any other relevant words.

"Listen, Morgan. We would love to talk, but we were right about to report to the eye doctors we're working with, and we really need to keep that appointment. I'm sorry," Ralph said, checking his watch after he took the newspaper back.

"Oh no, I completely understand. In fact, I need to go, too. I'm going to miss my express train. It was great seeing you guys," I said, waving the pair off.

"It was great to see *you.* Thank you, Morgan. But next time you're in a mess, won't you let us know?" Sandy asked.

"I will," I nodded. "Good luck with your appointment. Bye, guys!" I said before heading down the hallway, breaking away from the pair.

On the train ride home, I scratched out a list of definitions to give Madeline and Asahi while reminiscing over my cyclops union and mentally musing over the confounding puzzle of a hemophobia-stricken vampire.

"Fran, it's cool to be nerdy, but not geeky, right? Or is it the other way around?" I asked, staring at my notebook with frustration.

"What, are you working on a paper for English or something?" Fran asked me as she stapled a packet of papers.

Michael and I always got to school with thirty minutes to spare, so Fran and I usually hung out in a computer lab or the student council room and finished school work before classes started.

"Sorta. I'm trying to define the difference between nerd and geek for an assignment," I said, rubbing my eyes.

"Nerds are the super academics—the ones who are going to invent super computers and cures for cancer. They're the ones you want to marry! Geeks are the extreme Star Wars and *Lord of the Rings* fans," Fran flippantly replied.

"So, it's cool to be nerdy, right?"

"Cha."

"Thanks," I said, scrawling her explanation in the margin of my notes.

"Hey, Morgan. Hi, Fran!"

My eyes shot up from the notebook, and I smiled up at Brett Patterson. "Hey, Brett! Come on in; no one else is here."

"Hey, Brett," Fran said, beckoning with a hand after I elbowed her.

I did my best to give Brett an inviting grin as he entered the tiny student council room.

"So, what are you two up to?" Brett asked, smiling as he plopped himself down on the table, sitting across from Fran.

"Homework," I smiled.

"Student Council work," Fran said. She didn't even spare him a glance as she efficiently stapled another stack of papers.

"That's right. The Halloween dance is this weekend, isn't it? Are you student council guys making posters for it?" Brett said, poking a finger beneath Fran's various packets so he could study one.

"Yep. It is our responsibility to advertise it," Fran briskly said, pounding the stapler again.

"Ah," Brett said, watching her.

I don't know why, but Fran always seems to channel an old business lady whenever Brett was around. She gets really blunt and borderline rude.

"So, what's new with you, Brett?" I asked.

"Not much. Cassie has the car tonight, so I don't have wheels." Brett launched into a rant about his older sisters (whom we knew from elementary school) when I saw movement behind him.

Frey—unmistakable with his silver hair—walked past the open door. A few seconds later, he reappeared, walking backwards. He caught my eye and smiled.

I beamed at Brett before glaring at Frey and shaking my head.

A Jack O' Lantern smile spread across Frey's face, and his green eyes gleamed as he nodded.

I violently shook my head again and slid my pointer finger across my throat in a slitting motion.

Frey beamed angelically.

Our silent exchange caught Fran's attention. She welcomed Frey into the room with something that sounded like *relief*. "Frey, why are you standing out there? Come, talk with us. Are we still celebrating that you and Morgan have kissed and made up?"

"We did not kiss or make up. I'm just…talking to him again," I hissed at Fran while Frey trotted into the room and plopped down next to me.

"Hi, Honey," Frey said, grinning at me before leaning close. (I could practically *see* his figurative doggy tail waving in a 360° loop. Whatever he was planning, it wasn't good.)

"Get away," I hissed, shoving him away from me.

Brett blinked at us. "So, are you two dating or something?" he asked.

"NO!" I shouted, slapping my hands on the table. "Not at all. We're coworkers. We have the same after-school job."

Frey gave Brett his best wolf-like smirk. "That's what she says anyway."

I turned to stare at him, trying very hard to control my anger. I whipped back around to address Fran—who was openly laughing—and Brett. "One second, please," I said before spinning back to face Frey, scooting my chair away from my childhood friends. "*What do you think you're doing*?" I hissed to Frey.

Frey was chuckling. "Hooo, man. Devin's gonna be *pissed* when he finds out!" he hooted.

"Finds out what?" I snarled, glancing backwards to make sure Fran and Brett weren't listening.

They weren't. Fran was busy stapling, and Brett continued to complain to her about his sisters.

"Finds out that after everything he's done, you're still sweet on some dopey human," Frey grinned. I swear to you, his canine fangs were poking out, making him look like a mischievous wolf.

My mouth dropped open, and I gaped at him.

"But I am hurt," Frey said with a falsified sniff. "How can you be so enamored with such a boring, normal guy when *I'm* around?"

"H-how, how did you figure it out?" I hissed, grabbing Frey by the collar of his t-shirt.

"It was pretty obvious during that week you were constantly forgetting about me. I saw you in the hallway, and you were batting your eyelashes like a woodland creature in the Bambi movies," Frey scoffed.

This was from the emotionally constipated werewolf that couldn't figure out why I was so upset with him for buttering up to me when he had an ulterior motive.

"Why can't you be emotionally sensitive when it *matters*?" I yowled, hitting him.

"Hey, that's animal abuse!" Frey shot back.

"See, they even have their own little inside jokes and pet names. Cute, huh?" Fran said.

I finally tuned into my friends and realized Fran had actually been chatting to Brett about me and Frey. I shot Fran a horrified look. She *knew* I had it bad for Brett! What was she doing?!

Fran caught my look and pushed her eyebrows up while looking down at her papers. "Like I said, broken hotness meter," she whispered to me. "I'm still cheering for that one," she added, tilting her head past me, towards Frey.

I groaned and pounded my head on the table.

Frey laughed and mussed my hair.

"You two are pretty close," Brett observed, to my horror.

WHY did knowing about the MBRC turn my life completely upside down?

12

My Class Size Increases

"Morgan, this is my very close vampire pal, Esmeralda," Madeline said, giving me two thumbs up.

"How many times have I told you? We're not friends," Madeline's supposed pal said, flipping her hair over her shoulder.

If Madeline was pretty, Esmeralda was beautiful. She had curly raven black hair, flawless, olive skin, and deep, brown eyes. She didn't look anything like a vampire. She was too…vibrant.

"She's just saying that," Madeline stage-whispered to me.

Esmeralda scowled. "I am not. I hate vampires. All vampires. Especially the old, clueless ones like you," she said before turning to me. She stared at me, slowly inspecting me from head to toe. "I think I'll like you. You seem normal, which is a rarity in this nuthouse. The name's Esmeralda. Been a vamp for five years now," she nodded.

"I'm Morgan. Nice to meet you," I smiled. "We should probably head to the room," I suggested, wondering if Asahi was going to be okay with adding another unregistered, non-paying student. If I knew anything about the sunny elf, he would probably welcome the dark beauty into the class with a smile.

"You see, this is my plan to combat Asahi's blinding personality,"

Madeline said as we moved towards the stairs, narrowly avoiding getting run over by a minotaur.

"Your plan to what?" I asked.

"Before he left, the Pooka gave me detailed care instructions for you. He said I wasn't supposed to allow Asahi, or any of his relations, to be alone with you. He said your weak, feeble humanity would be crushed beneath Asahi's aura, and you would be sucked in and fall helplessly in love with him whether the High Elf meant to be friendly or not," Madeline said.

I wouldn't have believed that Devin gave her the orders, but the bit about being sucked in sounded like him.

"I see," I said, climbing the stairs.

"High Elves are famous for their good looks. It's probably just as well they've got the looks in elf races. Can you imagine if the Beer Brothers looked like them?" Esmeralda snorted, folding her hands behind her head as she effortlessly trotted up the stairs.

I paused, mid step. "Wait, before he left?"

"Hm?" Madeline asked, skipping up one more step.

"You said Devin left?" I asked, leaning against the stair banister.

"Yes. He went back to Britain. That's where the Fairy Council is being held this decade," Madeline nodded.

"So…he's gone?" I asked.

"Yeah. For a couple of months at least," Esmeralda said. "The Pooka is notorious for leaking out of council duties, so when they manage to get him in the council, they hold onto him for as long as possible."

"So…he's gone?" I repeated, staring blankly at the wall. I couldn't help the pokes of sadness that prodded my heart.

"…Morgan?" Madeline asked, standing a few steps below me so she could peer up at my face.

"Sorry. Let's go," I said, starting back up the steps while I tried to silence my traitorous heart.

We wove around the hallways for a while before Esmeralda finally found the right room.

"Asahi!" I said, entering the room.

The bright sunshine boy was there, wearing another Arabian

Nights costume. "Morgan!" he said, his face breaking into a dazzling, sincere smile. "I'm so glad to see you," he said without any trace of embarrassment.

"Hooo, you got a computer in here. Sweet. I didn't think the MBRC owned any that were lent out for classes. I've only seen them used in office work," Esmeralda said, her eyes drawn to the front of the room where a giant, bulky computer was stationed.

"My gosh. How old is it?" I asked, drawn towards it like a car accident.

"I dunno. Pre-flat screen monitors, that's for sure," Esmeralda said.

"What's a flat screen?" Madeline asked, peering over my shoulder.

"Ew, try turning it on," Esmeralda suggested as I stood in front of the computer.

"We got a pretty good one," Asahi said, sliding out of his desk to approach the mammoth computer. "Don't tell, but Aysel stole it from accounting," he grinned.

The computer hummed as it turned on. The screen flashed, and my mouth dropped open.

"You've got to be kidding," I said.

"Woah," Esmeralda laughed.

My throat tightened, and my voice grew higher. "Is this Windows '*98*?" I said, staring at the start up screen. The old fashioned Windows icon winked at me.

"I know. It's great, right?" Asahi laughed. "They're still using Windows '94 in the psych department!"

"Can this thing even run PowerPoint?" I asked, poking the computer tower. "Furthermore, does it have a USB port for my jump drive?"

"No wonder the MBRC has such bad human relationships. They're like twenty years behind the technology curve," Esmeralda said.

I looked up and nearly flung myself at Asahi. He looked like a kitten that dragged a frog home in hopes of praise and was rewarded with screams instead.

"I can ask Aysel for a better one," he said.

I couldn't help myself. "That's okay, Asahi," I said, my stupid, sappy smile resurfacing. "This is a good computer. It's a good room. You did well!"

I was rewarded with a sunny Asahi smile before Madeline flung her arms around me and leaned against me.

"She's my friend first," Madeline said.

"Okay," Asahi agreed, smiling at her.

"Right, so let's start," I said, clearing my throat.

Asahi returned to his desk, and Esmeralda followed him, but for some odd reason Madeline was still glued to me.

"Hi," she smiled when I looked down at her.

"...Is there a reason you aren't letting go?" I asked the petite blonde.

"Not really."

"Then would you go sit down?" I asked.

Madeline paused and thought about it for a moment. "Okay," she said, taking a seat between Esmeralda and Asahi.

"Right, so before I dive into the high school social structure, I figured I would explain the clique that I'm a part of," I said, leaning away from the computer. "I'm what you would call an academic, perhaps a borderline prep."

"So, you're smart?" Madeline ventured.

I shrugged. "More like I make an effort to finish my school work. My friends and I are slightly more ambitious than your regular student. We all see ourselves as going to college, and we get fairly good grades. We're all involved in school clubs in order to round out ourselves for college applications, and we're pretty clean cut. An exaggeration of our clique are the preps. Preps taken to extremes are generally kids who plan to go to Ivy League schools, wear lots of polo shirts and cardigans, and like to monogram as many of their things as possible."

"But you're not a nerd?" Madeline asked.

Esmeralda laughed.

"No, my friends and I are smart, but we aren't brilliant enough to be nerds," I answered.

"I learned about nerds in my human psychology class," Asahi brightened.

Until 5:30 rolled around, I spent most of my time trying to teach Madeline and Asahi (Esmeralda already understood) about the delicate high school hierarchy and the various cliques that supported it.

As would become custom, when class was over, Madeline and Asahi escorted me downstairs. Today, Frey and Dave were waiting for me.

"Hey, Morgan. How's the tutoring going?" Frey greeted, squinting past me as I waved goodbye to my students. "Is that Madeline?" he added.

"Yeah. She claims Devin sent her to keep an eye on me. How do you know her?" I asked, adjusting the position of my backpack before smiling at Dave.

Dave jutted his lower lip out and sulked. Judging by his mood, he probably got a bad report back from his teachers again.

"I've just seen her around a lot. She's a pretty active member of the MBRC, even though she isn't in an administrative position. She's one of the older vamps who stays permanently in the area," Frey said, turning to lead the way out of the MBRC.

"Really? I didn't think she was much older than a century. She said she was from Britain's Women's' Suffrage Era," I said, following.

Dave trailed after us, pouting into his thermos of tomato juice.

"Yeah, that's not very old if you meet some of the ruling vamps," Frey agreed. "But it's generally only the vampires that are less than a hundred years old who involve themselves with the MBRC. Bye, Tiny," he said when we passed the guard.

"See you tomorrow, Tiny," I said.

"Bye," Tiny rumbled, waving a meaty hand in farewell.

"I'm not surprised she's glued to you. She's probably one of the few females the Pooka associates himself with that *doesn't* have a massive crush on him. It would make sense to send her after you. She wouldn't get jealous. In fact, she'll probably end up liking you more than him, which is probably what he planned for," Frey frowned.

I snorted. "You give him too much credit. I have no idea how Madeline found out about me, but I doubt Devin sent her. He doesn't care about me."

As we joined the sea of humans in Union Station, Frey eyed me. "You're joking, right? After all the strings he pulled to get you back?"

"I saw him the other day before he left the MBRC—which he didn't tell me he was doing—and he completely blew me off," I said, stubbornly lifting my chin into the air. I would not cry. I would not cry! I blinked back the stinging sensation in my eyes as Dave dragged himself from his sulk and spoke.

"Perhaps, my dear, you should try judging the Pooka based on his longer-term actions towards you, not just a one-time encounter. Although the Pooka appears to be human, you must remember that he *is* a fairy. He probably has a difficult time understanding you as well," Dave said as he innocently scooted towards a trash bin.

Frey intercepted the vampire and plucked the thermos from Dave's hands before hitting him over the head with it.

"Ouch!"

"What Dave is saying is that you are waaaaay too sensitive," Frey said, wiggling the thermos at me.

I frowned. "Somehow I doubt that."

Frey, however, had already removed his attention from me and started lecturing Dave. "You need to stop wasting this! If I have to ask the MBRC supply elves for another box of thermoses, they're going to report me to waste management. Also, you need to stop sighing over blood like a love-sick school girl," Frey said, punctuating some of his sentences with smacks to Dave's head.

"Ow!" Dave whined, rubbing his stinging cranium.

Perhaps the books didn't *completely* lie. Werewolves and vampires fight alright…just not the way everyone assumes they do.

On Friday, I stopped by the MBRC information booth to say hello to Corona and company before heading up to my classroom.

"So, how's the tutoring?" Corona asked, flicking Gristles away.

"Okay. I've really only taught them for one day so far," I considered, adjusting my winter coat. (I was starting to get hot.)

"Them?"

"Yeah, these two vampires, Madeline and Esmeralda, popped up and played around in the room yesterday," I nodded.

Corona looked thoughtful, but any reply she was going to give me was eclipsed by a honey sweet, southern accent.

"I know I have another class soon, but I just *had* to drop by and see how my baby is doing," a female voice drawled.

I looked over and up, and found myself staring at a flamingo pink, female dragon. She wasn't quite as *big* as some of the other dragons I had seen in the chamber, but she was still the size of a small bus. (A *pink* bus.)

"Miss Bea, how are you?" Corona called to the dragon.

"I'm fine, sugar. Thanks for asking. Is my baby—oh, there he is," the dragon, Miss Bea apparently, said before reaching behind the desk and scooping up Doggy with one large claw.

Doggy barked happily at her, his little tail thumping against her claw as he leaned into her.

"Aww, my little Sweetie!" Miss Bea cooed.

"Miss Bea, this is Morgan. She's the human I was telling you about the other day," Corona said, leaning against the desk before flashing a serpentine smile at me.

"Hello, Morgan," Miss Bea said, dragging the "o" of my name out with her southern accent. "Aren't you just the cutest thing! Corona tells me Doggy is just infatuated with you!"

I smiled brightly. "Doggy is adorable," I said, glancing at the little dragon. "How old is he?"

"Oh, I think he's about a year and a half now, isn't he Miss Bea?" Corona approximated.

"Yes, yes he is. My little boy is growing up!" Miss Bea gushed, carefully scratching under Doggy's chin with the point of one of her claws.

"So when will Doggy learn to talk?" I asked, hoping I wasn't asking a rude question.

Miss Bea blinked at me before laughing. "Oh my, Corona, you didn't explain it to her, did you? Doggy is never going to learn how to talk. In fact, he probably won't grow much bigger than he is now. He's a Miniature Doodle," Miss Bea said.

I blinked. "A Miniature Doodle?" I asked.

"Doggy is to Miss Bea what your family cat or dog would be to you," Corona explained.

My brain tried to reject this information. A dragon keeping another dragon as a pet? "But I thought he was your baby," I blinked, feeling very lost.

"You poor thing. You must be as confused as a crocodile in a swimming pool," Miss Bea sympathetically clicked.

"A Miniature Doodle," I repeated.

"Yes," Miss Bea said, the corners of her mouth twisting upwards in a dragon smile. "It's like dragon and poodle put together."

My brain pretty much flat-lined there.

I mean, come on. I had heard of Labradoodles, Lhasapoos, Yorkipoos, and dozens of other bizarre poodle breeds…but I <u>never</u> thought I would hear someone refer to a dragon-poodle hybrid.

Corona must have sensed that I was completely lost and hastily stepped in. "Doggy is one hundred percent dragon, but his dragon breed is more like a toy dog. Miss Bea is a genuine full-blooded Western Pike Dragon: an intelligent, advanced breed."

I found myself nodding even though I still didn't get it. "Of course," I agreed. "I think I need to go teach an elf…," I said before wandering off in the direction of the staircase.

"Goodbye, Sweet Pea! It was nice to meet you!" Miss Bea called in her southern drawl, Doggy adding his own howl.

I raised a hand in a farewell wave before plunging into the crowd.

By now I knew where my classroom was…sort of…so it only took a few minutes before I found my room.

I opened the door, noting that the painted red dragon on the door distinctly *preened* as I stepped inside the room.

Asahi was the only one there, wearing another one of his over-the-top genie outfits.

My mind was distracted off the thought of dragon poodle as I considered Asahi's clothes. Did *all* High Elves dress like Asahi? I didn't think so. The elf I met with my Cyclops union seemed to be a normal dresser. Then again, he wasn't a High Elf.

"Morgan, hello!" Asahi smiled, scattering my thoughts to the wind.

"Hi, Asahi. Madeline hasn't popped in yet?" I asked, shedding my jacket and backpack as I headed for my podium, distastefully turning on the computer as I swept past it.

"No, not yet," Asahi shook his head. "But I expect she'll be along any moment."

The door slammed open as Esmeralda confidently stepped in, ignoring the dragon door decoration that hissed at her. "Feel free to cheer, for I am here," she said, taking two steps inside before hooking onto the door with one of her feet and kicking it shut.

"Hey, Esmeralda," I said, Asahi smiled and waved behind me.

"Wassup' my studlies?" Esmeralda grinned.

"Did you just call me a studly?" I asked.

"Sorry. I got carried away. You're the first person I have met since I entered this pixie-powdered hell hole that understands slang," Esmeralda shrugged.

"Good point. You're forgiven," I benevolently said.

"Good afternoon, everyone! I've brought another friend," Madeline shouted through the door before pushing it open.

Madeline and her friend—a medium-height, scruffy-looking teenage guy—tried to enter the classroom at the same time. They locked shoulders and collided with the doorframe, their feet sliding out from underneath them. They crashed to the floor, yelping when they hit the ground.

"Are you two okay?" I asked, crossing the room as Madeline's friend hopped up. (Madeline took a few seconds longer to react.)

"Yeah," Madeline said, straightening up before brushing off her frilly doll dress. "Morgan, this is Frank. Frank, this is Morgan, our human teacher," she said dusting her hands off. "Frank's a werewolf," she added for my benefit.

It was a good thing she did, too. I never would have guessed it otherwise. Frank was the direct opposite of Frey in werewolf class. No, he wasn't big and muscular; he was actually even scrawnier than Frey, but at least Frey had pretty eyes and cool hair. Frank's hair was the shade of mutt-brown dog fur, and he didn't have Frey's confidence or grace. If anything, he reminded me of a coyote trying to pose as a dog: nervous and a little shaky. However, in spite of his mangy look, he appeared to be quite sweet.

"Hello, Morgan," Frank said, rapidly blinking several times before offering me an unsure smile.

"Hi, Frank," I said, giving him my standard nice-to-meet-you smile.

Madeline slapped him on the back with a crack, which didn't even draw a wince from the scruffy werewolf. (Perhaps he was stronger than he looked?) "Frank has never been in human society. So, I thought this class would be good for him."

I folded my arms across my chest. "You are aware this isn't a class, right? It's supposed to be Asahi's tutoring session."

"I don't mind," Asahi said, waving his hand with a careless grace while Esmeralda plopped down a few seats away from him.

I frowned at Madeline.

Madeline smiled and reached out to latch onto my arm. "Come on Morgan, the more the merrier! Plus, the more people we have, the more his light will be diffused," Madeline said, pointing at Asahi.

"Right, whatever. Go sit down," I rubbed my forehead.

"What is today's topic?" Asahi asked, a fountain pen appearing in his hand. He held it poised above a piece of expensive-looking parchment.

"Geeks. And how they're different from nerds."

"You want to marry a nerd!" Madeline cheered as she plopped down in a seat, successfully reviewing the chant I had taught yesterday.

"Exactly," I acknowledged, making the light-haired vampire squeal.

I walked over to the old computer and grimaced as I leaned up against it. "Now a geek is someone who is an extreme fan, generally of something fantasy or science fiction related. It has to be something unreal, not like…soccer or sports or something. They can be male or female, like girls obsessing over sappy vampire stories or fairies or something, and guys obsessing over aliens."

Asahi raised his hand.

"Yes, Asahi?"

"Why would a geek be someone interested in fantasy? It's not like we aren't real," he said, reminding me of my audience.

I coughed. "Uh. Yeah, the thing is, humans don't know that."

Frank scratched his scalp, and Madeline yawned while Esmeralda did a crossword puzzle.

"Hmm," Asahi said, pursing his gorgeous lips. (Yes, it is possible for someone to have gorgeous lips.)

I took the moment to continue with my lecture. "Okay! So, this is what a stereotypical geek looks like!"

I was so happy when I got home that night. Since it was Friday, it meant I didn't have to teach for two whole days! I mean, Asahi and everyone were pretty cool, but it was really *hard* trying to figure out ways to describe the way people act. Esmeralda was a help, but sometimes I would forget who they were, which created a few awkward moments—like the whole geek-fantasy thing.

Saturday night was the Halloween Dance I had to attend thanks to Fran's demands. It was actually pretty cool. I got to talk with Brett, and decorating was a real blast since Hunter decided to help for a while early Saturday morning.

By the time Sunday night rolled around, I was getting ready for class again.

"Maybe I could hit up goth, emo, and punk all in one session?" I murmured, tapping my pencil on my notebook.

"Okay," Fran said, plopping down in our booth, carefully setting her refill of her Mountain Dew soda down on the table. "We've exhausted lots of topics and juicy gossip. Should we dissect each and every little thing Frey has said to you, revealing his intentionally hidden flirting?"

I rolled my eyes. "Fran, you're totally barking up the wrong tree…or maybe Frey is?" I paused, considering my word choice. "It doesn't matter. I'm not interested in him. Why are you so against me liking Brett?"

Fran quickly back-peddled. "It's not that I don't want you to like Brett. I just don't get how you can have a hottie like Frey hanging at your heels and go for our old school chum," she said, studying her nails with a frown. "Can you tell my nail polish is chipping?"

I glanced at her fingers. "Yeah. You're wearing electric orange. It's obvious that it's peeling. But you're not going to side-track me. Frey and I aren't like that. He's, he's just a friend. He's watching out for me," I said.

Fran raised her gaze and continued to frown, this time fixing her eyes on me. "Maybe, but there's something different about you. You're acting way weird. And yeah, you still like Brett, but you don't talk about him as much," Fran dropped her eyes so she could stir her soda with a straw. "I just thought you were moving on or something."

She was right: I didn't have the time to worry about clubs or school crushes when I was tutoring a *High Elf* and trying to survive the MBRC. But it wasn't like I could tell her that.

"Well…we've been busy," I lamely defended myself.

"So, you still like Brett. Okay, I'm on board," Fran said, smiling warmly at me. "Are you sure you aren't part dog? You're *awfully* loyal."

"Thanks, Fran," I said, rolling my eyes.

"So, being sent to the principal's office is a lot like being sent to the

MBRC Administrator's office? He's the highest pack member around here," Frank asked, raising his hand.

"Yep. The principal is the guy who doles out student punishments," I explained, leaning against my dry erase board. Today's lecture was centered on the structure of the high school punishment system.

"I still think it's all bogus," Esmeralda said, rolling her eyes. "Blue slips, pink slips, detentions—none of them actually mean *anything*."

"That's not true. Blue slips stand for discipline problems whereas pink slips are for tardy students," Asahi objected, glancing at his notes before smiling at Esmeralda.

"No, what I mean is nothing actually *happens* if you get a blue slip or pink slip. Yeah, you sometimes get a detention, but it's just a mind game," Esmeralda said, shaking her magnificent hair.

"I specialize in mind games," a fairy, one of two that Madeline invited in for today's class, volunteered.

"I'm sure you do," Esmeralda quietly breathed out between clenched teeth.

"Mind games?" Frank asked, clearly perplexed. If he had dog ears, they would be flattened.

"Let's not drag high school politics into the system, Esmeralda. I don't think they'll follow it," I strolled down the front row of desks.

"Sounds great!" Madeline said, smiling brightly at me.

"You are still not allowed to talk. Bringing four additional students with you today has put you out of my good graces," I told the fair-haired vampire, raising a finger at her.

Madeline pulled a sad face and looked as innocent as a doll. I don't know what possessed her to do it, but once again, Madeline had dragged in more "friends" for today's class, proudly introducing them to me like a cat presenting a dead mouse.

Not that she brought anyone bad with her. I actually liked the sphinx—whom I had thought for sure would be a know-it-all. She, the sphinx, sat quietly on the ground, listening to every word like a star pupil.

The half giant/troll/ogre dude worried me a little bit, but he was quiet for the most part. I only found him alarming when he shifted in his chair—which would make his desk squeal in protest.

The fairies though…

They were a little stuck up, which I could have dealt with if I didn't feel so horridly let down by their appearance. Going off Asahi's dazzling looks, I was expecting sparkles, willowy limbs, high-pitched voices, butterfly wings, and big eyes.

To be fair, they were slender and petite, but their wings looked like they bought them from Wal-mart during Halloween. One wore bright purple and blue eye makeup and horribly mismatched lip stick. The other favored pink and green makeup and smeared what appeared to be glitter across her cheeks. Everything about them looked *cheap*!

Mentally unable to call them fairies, I referred to them as the Pastels.

"What if you don't turn in your homework on time?" Frank asked, scratching at his hair. (I was seriously concerned he was accidentally going to rip a tuff straight off his skull one of these days.)

"It varies from teacher to teacher," I said, stopping next to the sphinx. "Some will let you get away with it as long as you hand it in that day. Other teachers will dock your grade on the assignment, and some of them will simply give you no points—which can be a major drag to your grade."

"Ouch," Frank winced in sympathy.

The troll/giant guy nodded in agreement, the legs of his chair buckling.

"Amateurs," one of the fairies huffed. (The blue and purple one I think.) "I bet we could inflict more damage than that."

"Of course you could," Esmeralda scoffed. "Just reveal yourself to a group of elementary girls, and you'll instantly crush all their hopes and dreams about pretty fairies."

"Take that back, blood sucker!" the green and pink fairy demanded.

"GUYS! This isn't a debate or open discussion. This is me teaching Asahi. You can just *leave* if you don't like it," I declared.

"That's right, Morgan. Put your foot down," Madeline agreed.

I turned around, intending to stalk over to the doll-like vampire and strangle her with my bare hands, when Frank posed another question to me.

"So, who has more punishing power: the principal because he's the highest authority, or the teacher because they can threaten to use the principal, and they control your grade?" Frank asked, itching his side.

At times like this, I really liked Frank. He was no Asahi, but he did have the same sweet sincerity that came with wanting to learn—even if his hygiene left something to be desired.

"That's a good question. Most students will never be sent to the principal's office for disciplinary measures, so naturally, the teachers seem to be a bigger threat," I replied.

"Is it possible for us to see pictures of your elusive principal?" Madeline asked.

"No," I bluntly said. "The computer doesn't have a port for my jump drive, and we don't have a projector," I said before digging my cell phone out of my pocket and glancing at it. "That's all for today. Goodbye," I decided, walking back to my podium so I could shut down the computer. (Honestly, I don't know why I bothered to turn it on in the first place.)

Esmeralda yawned and folded her arms behind her head while standing up. "See ya tomorrow, Morgan," she said before sweeping out of the room, almost bowling over the fairies, who glared at her back before following her out.

The sphinx stood and regally bowed at me, a gesture that the giant/troll/ogre dude tried to copy before stumbling after the sphinx, leaving the room ungracefully.

"Good class, Morgan," Madeline said, hugging my arm.

"Thanks. Although I really wish you wouldn't bring so many *friends* with you," I groaned, rubbing my eyes with my free hand. I will admit it. Madeline was starting to grow on me. If Asahi's a puppy; she's a kitten. You can't not like her for very long.

"T-thank you for teaching us, Morgan," Frank said with all the formality he could muster. His efforts were slightly wasted by his incessant scratching.

"No problem. I'm happy to help you, Frank," I said, smiling at the scruffy werewolf.

"I'll see you three back here tomorrow?" Asahi asked, tilting his head, making his amber earrings jingle.

"Yep," I agreed.

Asahi nodded. "I swear to you, I shall have Aysel find us a better computer. You cannot show pictures as a result of my failure," he said, his eyes looking forlorn.

I reached out and patted his shoulder. "It's fine, Asahi. Who cares if we can't see photos?"

"Really? I think it would greatly further the educational experience," Madeline said, opening her big, fat mouth, making Asahi look even more shamed as he hunched his shoulders.

"*Quiet*, Madeline," I growled, elbowing her in the gut before turning back to Asahi. "It's fine, Asahi. Really, it is. I'll see you tomorrow," I assured the gold elf as I dragged Madeline with me towards the door, Frank following in our wake.

"Okay. Goodbye," Asahi waved before Frank shut the door.

"Aww, he's so sweet," I sighed, releasing Madeline—who still clung to my arm.

Madeline frowned. "Yeah," she agreed. "But he kind of has to be like that in order to balance out Aysel," she said before turning to wave to Frank. "Bye, Frank. I shall see you tomorrow."

"Yeah, bye," Frank said, scratching his head again.

This time I was close enough to him that I *swear* I could see little black bugs hopping around him. "Frank, do you have fleas?" I blurted before clasping my free hand across my mouth.

Frank yawned like a dog, snapping his jaw shut with a click. "Hmm? Yeah. I get them sometimes when I change and romp in state parks and stuff. I probably should have taken a bath Friday to get rid of them. And the ticks," he said, thoughtfully itching his abs. "Thanks again, Morgan. I'll be in class tomorrow."

I felt my jaw drop open.

Frank. Had fleas.

He was going to infect the whole class!

Wait, scratch that. He was going to infect *me*! Oh, my gosh, I had been around him today! Did they jump onto me?! What about Madeline? She hung out with him! Did the fleas hop onto her?

My internal balance was so upset that I didn't notice when Frank left, and Madeline started towing me to the MBRC lobby.

"Frank has fleas," I said when I finally found my voice.

"Yes. Loads of werewolves do. The shifters are a little better about it, but I think it's because they're more sensitive," Madeline said.

"Frank has fleas. I could have gotten fleas from him," I repeated as we went down the stairs.

"Hmm? Oh, maybe? I forgot about that. Vampires don't get fleas. The whole being dead aspect tends to make bugs stay away from you. Well, a few days after you change, that is. I remember a hoard of flies *swamped* me the day after I changed. That's when you still smell like a normal dead thing. After that, our magic flavors our scent so much that bugs stay away. Either that or maybe the tomato juice permeates our skin and insects don't like that smell? But yeah, I think the bugs followed me until a week after I became a vampire," Madeline reasoned.

"We have to do something! Give him a flea wash, a spray, something! He could give the *sphinx* fleas! Her fur is too gorgeous to ruin!" I gaped, stopping at the base of the staircase.

"Well, what can you do? Frank isn't domesticated or house broken. Werewolves like him don't see fleas as being something horrible," Madeline asked.

"I'll think of something," I promised before I started pushing my way through the sea of magical creatures. "I'll see you tomorrow, Madeline."

"Right. Goodbye, Morgan!"

13

De-fleaing a Werewolf

"So. Why are we in the dog aisle again? I don't have a family pet, and you've only got a cat," Fran asked, watching me stare at a wall of tick, flea, and bug dog repellants inside the Furry Friend's Pet Shop.

"Because I've got this friend who needs some of this stuff *really* bad," I said, staring at a bottle of flea guard shampoo. "You can *see* the bugs on the animal."

"Man, what did their dog do? Roll in something dead?" Fran asked, wrinkling her nose.

I hadn't thought of that. After Fran said it, I wished she hadn't mentioned it either. "My gosh, I hope not," I weakly moaned.

"Don't tell me you're doing this for Whitey or whatever his face is. You know, Señor Smith's dog?" Fran said, flicking a finger at a tick spray.

"What? *No!*" I squeaked, absolutely horrified on Frey's behalf. "No, no, no. Whitey would *never* get fleas!" Frey was way too health conscious for that…right?

"Fran? Morgan?"

Even in my state of flea-induced panic I recognized that voice.

"Hey, Brett," I smiled, snapping out of it to address my longtime crush.

"Hey. What are you guys doing here? Are you getting a dog?" Brett asked, smiling at us.

"Hardly. Morgan's friend has a dog with flea troubles," Fran said, once again adopting her cooler temperament around Brett. Maybe she didn't like him? The idea was odd. We had been classmates since elementary school.

"What about you?" I asked.

"Oh, I'm here to pick up a flea collar for my sister's dog. She's got one of those scrawny little purse dogs," Brett said, reaching past me to pluck a box off the shelf.

"A flea collar?" I asked, growing interested. Maybe I wouldn't have to tell Frank any product I gave him was a flea killer if it was just a collar!

"Yeah. The collars last a few months, which suits my cheap sister just fine. Although it does make the dog's fur sorta greasy," Brett said.

As I stared at the flea collars, a maniac smile spread across my lips. "That is the perfect idea! But...would one collar be strong enough?" I muttered.

"How big is this dog?" Brett asked, watching me study a box for a flea collar that had a photo of a Saint Bernard on it.

"Huge," I said, picking up two of the largest flea collars available. I stared at it, narrowing my eyes. Maybe I could tell Frank they were bracelets?

"I always wanted a big dog," Brett said, looking at Fran. "They're so much cooler. You don't have to worry about killing them if you accidentally sit on them or something."

Fran shrugged. "I hate pets," she said before glancing at me. "Except for Morgan's cat."

"Hmmm," I said. Even though Brett was there, I found myself occupied with a problem: how would I con Frank into wearing one of these? I looked up, about to ask Brett how obvious the flea collar was, when I saw Hunter walk past the far end of the aisle.

"Hunter," I called.

Hunter stopped and turned towards us, momentarily flicking up his expensive looking sunglasses. "Morgan. Hey," he said when I waved at him.

Brett and Fran twisted to look at him and stared for a few moments before reacting.

"Oh, that's right! Hunter, you're in our class aren't you?" Brett grinned.

"Really? I thought you were a junior," Fran said, smiling at our quiet classmate.

"Nope, he's a sophomore," I nodded as Hunter walked up to us. "What are you here for?" I asked, gesturing at the aisles around us.

"We have a tank of saltwater fish at home. We're about out of food for our sea horses," Hunter said, his dark sunglasses hiding his glittering eyes. "And you?" he asked, offering me a smile.

"Flea-bitten dog," I sighed, looking back down at the flea collar I held in my hands before amending my statement. "Not mine, though! It's a friend's.... How can I convince him that he shouldn't take it off?" I said, trailing off into another mutter.

Hunter, oddly, looked amused.

"Sir," someone called.

All of us shifted our gazes to a bald man wearing sunglasses and a black suit who was standing at the end of the aisle. He looked sort of like an FBI agent, but his complexion was *really* waxy and almost purple-hued. I'm not kidding. He looked like the dead bodies you see on the CSI shows.

"Right. Good luck with the fleas, Morgan. I'll see you guys in school," Hunter said before tucking his hands into the pockets of his designer jeans and strolling towards the suit guy.

When he disappeared down an aisle, Brett released a low whistle. "Man, I guess the rumors *are* right. His family must be involved in the mob!"

Fran rolled her eyes. "For someone who didn't recognize him ten seconds ago, you seem to be quite educated about his family history," she snorted. "Not to mention that the idea is ridiculous. Besides, he lives in *Oakdale*, also known as 'The-City-Where-Nothing-Happens.'"

"Hey, we're just a train ride from Chicago! Morgan, back me up," Brett pleaded.

I nearly did agree with him, just for the sake of being on the same side as Brett, but my honor won out in the end. "I'm going to go with Fran on this one."

"But didn't you see his bodyguard? The sunglasses and suit?" Brett protested.

"Keep it down. He's going to hear you," Fran ordered before turning to me. "Are you set?"

"Yeah, I think so. We'll start with one, and if he keeps it on maybe I'll come back for a second one in a few weeks," I decided, putting the second box back on the shelf.

"Right. Whose dog is this again?"

"A friend from work," I inventively replied.

"Uh-huh. Well you tell this friend you aren't his errand boy, and he can come get his stupid dog's flea products *himself* next time."

"Of course, Fran."

"So, now that I have it, how do I give it to Frank?" I wondered, patting the pocket of my coat where I had neatly arranged the flea collar in a nice, white box. (I mean come on, it's not like I could hand it to him in the wrapping I bought it in! There was no way I was telling him this was a flea collar.) "I better not be next to him when he puts the collar on. Those fleas and ticks will be abandoning ship!" I muttered to myself.

"Moooor—gan!" Madeline sang, popping up next to me. "How are you?" she asked in a sing-song voice.

"Hey. I'm good. But hopefully in a few minutes I'll be excellent," I said as we pushed our way through the MBRC lobby.

"Really? Why?" Madeline asked.

"I think I have a solution to Frank's fleas. What's going on?" I asked, nodding towards a group of oddly dressed, humanoid-looking people. (I knew the MBRC well enough to know that just because they *looked* human didn't mean they *were* human.) They were dressed in dark, somber-colored cloaks—wine red, black, midnight blue, maroon, and dark purple. They perfectly fit the description of a wizard from Harry Potter.

"Oh, it's a vampire coven," Madeline said, standing on tip toe to have a look. "Some old, foggy, ruling vampire—we call them Elders—must be visiting the MBRC. They always have trails of followers. I'm not exactly sure why. They just stick to them like flypaper. See, that greasy, cripple-looking guy in the center is the Elder," Madeline explained, pointing out the male vampire in the center of the group. He had greasy hair, a pinched expression, and he looked quite unhealthy. "Come on, we can push through just in front of them if we're quick," she said, pointing to the gap some distance in front of them before scurrying off.

I followed her, sniffing the air as we moved. The MBRC never smelled normal per say. There was always a faint whiff of singed hair from the fire elves, flowers from the dryads, dirt from the dwarves, and brimstone from the dragons. But today, the lobby just *reeked*.

And I don't mean it smelled like Michael's dirty gym socks when he hasn't cleaned them for three weeks, I mean it *really reeked*! Like, like rotten eggs left out in the sun smeared over the carcass of an animal that had been soaking in formaldehyde.

"Oh, my gosh," I gagged, covering my nose and mouth with one hand as we hurried through the open gap. "What is that horrible SMELL?"

Everyone in a twenty-yard radius of me froze, including the vampire coven.

Perhaps I said it a little louder than I meant to.

Okay, yeah, I definitely said it *a lot* louder than I meant to. But I didn't think it would stop everyone dead in their tracks, Madeline included.

The vampire groupies stared at me, their mouths open in shock. In the midst of them, I could see the vampire Elder guy glowering at me.

Madeline abruptly swung on her heels and started bowing at the shell-shocked clan. "I'm sorry. Excuse my friend. She's just a human, and she didn't know what she was saying! Excuse us. We apologize. Sorry," she groveled before grabbing my hand and backing away, bowing as we backed out of the rock-still area and immersed ourselves back with traffic.

The Elder kept up his glare as we disappeared from sight, one of his eyebrows twitching with anger.

When Madeline twisted so we faced forward, she took off running, dragging me with her. I have never seen her run up so many stairs so quickly before. We didn't stop running until we darted up the dragon hall.

"Oh. My. Word," Madeline said, her breath coming in great gasps. "I have never before been so close to decapitation in my *life*!"

"I don't get it. What happened?" I asked, sucking in air.

"You insulted an ELDER, that's what happened," Madeline laughed, leaning against a wall before collapsing on the ground. "I can't believe you! You're even more incredible than Devin said you were!"

"…What?"

"Hahah!" Madeline freakishly giggled, apparently she was on some kind of adrenaline high.

"How did I insult that Elder guy? I didn't even talk to him!" I complained, rubbing my wrist.

"You complained about the smell," Madeline said, arranging her skirt around her while she chuckled.

"Yeah, well, I think it was pretty founded. The lobby smelled horrible!" I complained.

"You don't get it," Madeline said through a snicker while shaking her head. "That smell was the Elder!"

"…Huh?"

"Vampire Elders are the leaders of vampire covens. They're very, very old. Naturally, your body is going to start to smell when you're dead but still walking around for several hundred years. The magic we have keeps our bodies from decomposing, which would keep us from reeking like a rotting carcass for the first few centuries, but we haven't figured out a way to get rid of the smell for good, and it generally flares up around the fourth or fifth century after changing."

I gaped at her. She couldn't be serious!

"Since the Elders can't get rid of the smell, no matter how much perfume they use, it became an unwritten rule that you simply *don't* mention the reek. Ever. Whether you're vampire, fairy, or animal," Madeline said, slowly standing up on shaking legs. "Go figure we forgot about ignorant humans," she said before erupting in laughter.

I frowned. "I don't know what is so funny about this. I find it downright creepy. Your bodies would rot? Although…I suppose that's logical…you being dead and all. Man. Hollywood really has *everything* wrong," I said, shrugging in my hot jacket.

Madeline leaned up against the wall again and kept laughing.

"Right. Well, I'm going inside. Feel free to join us when you've regained your composure," I said before walking to our room and opening the door. Madeline was still laughing when I shut it behind me.

Asahi was already seated, pouring over yesterday's notes (although he looked up and greeted me when he heard me come in). But, of course, he was not alone.

The giant/ogre guy was there, too. He was talking, very quietly, with Esmeralda. The fairies multiplied over night. There were now three others who sat separate, away from the Pastels. These three were dumpy looking, all dressed in browns and greens with pale skin, dark hair, and dark eyes. They didn't give off that snotty feeling the other fairies did. They were more like scared baby bunnies. Sitting with them was the drabbest looking elf I could ever expect to see in my life.

The sphinx was sitting on the ground again, this time chatting with a dryad who sat next to her.

The group was finished off with Frank, who was shivering in his seat like a nervous coyote.

I smiled as I set my sights on him. "Frank," I said before dumping my backpack on the ground. "Just the werewolf I was looking for."

Frank's eyes widened. "D-did I do something wrong?" he asked, shrinking in his seat as I approached him.

"Not at all," I said, shaking my head as I dug out the white box that held his flea collar from my pocket. "I just wanted to give you something," I said, holding the box out. "I was out shopping yesterday with my best friend. When I saw it I totally thought of you. It *so* matches your style," I said with my most convincing sales smile.

"What is it?" Frank asked, staring at the box.

"Open it up," I said, placing the box on his desk.

Frank carefully lifted the lid off the box—very aware that the Pastels were watching him. "It's a…a…" Frank trailed off.

"It's a necklace!" I happily chirped, mentally congratulating myself. "I got black because I thought it would totally match *everything* you wear," I added.

"So, this goes around my neck?" Frank asked as he unbuckled the collar. He didn't sound put out. If anything, he appeared to be pleased; he was no longer shivering like a wet dog in January.

"Yep! Here, do you want me to put it on you?" I asked.

"Yeah," Frank eagerly nodded.

"Okay, you put it around your neck like this, and this strap slides through the buckle," I said, quickly slipping it around his neck.

"Wow, thanks Morgan! This is so cool!" Frank beamed.

"Uh-huh. No problem," I said before backing away, shrugging off my jacket, joining Madeline by the computer. I hoped the dollish girl wouldn't make a fuss that I gave Frank a present and not her—she entered the room just in time to watch me put the flea collar on Frank.

Madeline frowned as she stared at the werewolf. "What is Frank wearing around his neck?"

"Don't ask," I said between clenched teeth.

"Really? I think it looks cool. Can I get one?"

"NO."

"So, why is it so important not to mess with humans?" the pink Pastel fairy sneered as I finished my lecture on cheerleaders. "I think it's *hilarious*."

"What do you mean?" I asked, placing my hands on the podium as I frowned.

"Everyone constantly talks about how we need to integrate with human society. Why do we have to? Why can't we just bother humans like we've done for centuries?" she continued.

I tapped my fingers on the podium. "This sounds more like an ethics issue rather than something I can teach," I said.

"What she means, *fairy*, is shut up," Esmeralda translated, drawing the Pastels' scorn.

"But it's not fair. Why do *we* have to hide? Shouldn't it be the humans hiding from us?" the blue fairy demanded.

"Why should we?" I shrugged. "Obviously we're the dominant culture. You wouldn't have hidden yourselves away in places like the MBRC if you thought you stood a chance against us."

The fairies gasped, but Asahi backed me up. "Morgan is right. Humans are advancing while magical societies remain stuck in the past. Our medical care is atrocious compared to theirs, and that's with elves and fairies who can heal at abnormally fast rates. Their methods of communication are far better than ours ever were. It used to take a year to assemble the Fairy Council. Now, you can send them all an email, and they'll turn up in minutes," Asahi argued. "It is our fault that we were driven underground. Magical society can learn a lot from humans; that's why we need to integrate with them."

"Plus screwing with their brains—like I *know* you do, Melony—is just plain rude. How would you like it if they ripped your wings off you like you were a fly?" Esmeralda snorted.

The Pastels had grown tight-faced with Asahi's gentle defense, but when Esmeralda spoke, they grew downright hostile, their sloppily bedazzled faces turning red as their Halloween-special wings flapped and buzzed with agitation.

"It's not like it does any permanent damage," pink Pastel snarled.

Madeline daintily laughed, sounding quite evil even though she looked like a Victorian doll. "Goodness gracious. I can't believe you're saying that when the MBRC has the Cuckoo Ward."

"The what?" I asked, coming out from behind the podium.

"The Cuckoo Ward," the sphinx said. Her voice was gravely and deep but warm. "A hospital wing in which the MBRC keeps human patients who have been mentally or physically damaged as a result of overexposure to our society," she recited.

I whistled. "I didn't know about that," I said, thanking my lucky stars Frey hadn't insisted I enter *that* kind of place when Dave blew their cover.

"Teacher, why don't we take a field trip there?" Madeline asked, raising her hand.

Next to her, Frank looked nervous. But then again he usually does.

"Can we really *visit* it? It can't be open to the public," I logically pointed out.

"Oh, sure it is," Madeline chirped. "The advanced classes go there all the time to observe the humans."

"I can ask for permission," Asahi volunteered with his unflappable smile.

"Seconded!" Esmeralda said. "All in favor?"

"Aye," a chorus of voices cheered.

"This isn't a democracy," I argued. "Just because you guys vote to go on a field trip doesn't mean I'll allow it!"

"Please, Morgan?" Madeline begged. Frank nodded with her.

"Yeah, come on Mo-Mo. I think you'll find it interesting," Esmeralda promised.

"Mo-Mo?" I asked, my eyebrows crawling up my forehead.

"I'm trying to give you a nickname."

"Really? Why don't I have a nickname?" Madeline asked.

"Because you're not cool enough."

"Waah! So mean!"

"Morgan," Asahi called, getting my attention. "Please?" he asked, performing the finishing blow to my educational uncertainty with his sweet eyes.

"Alright," I caved. "Let's schedule it for this Friday. Does that give you enough time to get permission, Asahi?" I asked.

"Yep, plenty of time."

"Fine. Class is dismissed for the day."

On Wednesday, I entered the MBRC with Dave and Frey and immediately headed for the help desk. I wanted to get as much information on the Cuckoo Ward as possible, and I figured Corona, Toby, and Orion would be the people (?) to talk to.

"Corona, Orion, how are you guys? Where's Toby?" I asked, sliding up to the desk.

"Morgan! We're doing fine. How are you? Toby's probably crawling the walls of his cave. He flipped out on a MBRC Board Member when they made a pot of decaf coffee, so our boss has put him on one-week leave to detoxify and get the caffeine out of his system. I doubt it will work," Corona said.

"Morgan," Orion acknowledged with a mysterious and elegant tip of his head.

"Can we help you with something?" Corona asked.

"Yeah. My class and I are going to Cuckoo Ward on Friday. I was wondering if you could give me some information on it. I'm trying to prepare myself."

"Of course," Corona said, grabbing a few pamphlets as she started her impromptu lesson. "The Cuckoo Ward—named after the bird that lays its eggs in the nest of other birds—was designed to house and comfort humans who have been *damaged* as a result of those in our magical society," Corona explained.

"Someone told me the damage could be physical or mental. What the heck does that mean?" I asked, planting my elbows on the countertop.

"To damage the body does not mean you have damaged the mind," Orion said with his obligatory amount of mystique.

Honestly. Centaurs.

"Sometimes some of the more malicious fairies will play pranks on humans. Pranks that can't be undone," Corona carefully said. "For instance, one of the patients is...well...*blue*."

"You mean they feel blue?"

"No. I mean their hair and skin are shades of *blue*. Now, a fairy glamour will cover up some oddities, but using fairy magic on humans is always risky. Plus, the glamour would have to be applied twenty four hours a day, which is quite a feat. So the MBRC took custody of the human."

"Uh-huh," I nodded. "And mentally damaged?"

"Some creatures will push humans beyond what their brains will tolerate. As a result, their mind isn't quite the same. You'll see lots of mentally damaged patients—it's the more common ailment," Corona said.

"Wow. That's...sad," I concluded, feeling uncomfortable about our upcoming field trip. This wasn't going to be educational. It was going to be awkward and heartbreaking.

As though reading my mind, Orion said, "In order to create better understanding and to bridge the gap between our societies, one must first reach out and make the impact."

"..." I said.

"Right. Well, many of the Cuckoo Ward patients are there only temporarily until our doctors and healers are able to properly rehabilitate them. This process sometimes takes months. Does that answer your questions?" Corona asked.

"Yeah, it's certainly a start," I agreed as several magical entities walked past the help desk. "Thank you."

"Here are some more pamphlets that should help prepare you. I can assure you, the Cuckoo Ward patients live in absolute comfort. The MBRC takes full responsibility for its mistakes," Corona promised me.

I smiled, about to reply, when a young centaur joined me at the desk. He was my age, certainly a teenager, but what drew my attention to him was that he was *nothing* like Orion.

He was bay-colored, like Westfall. His horse body had brownish fur, and his tail and hair on his head were ink black. At least, I think they were. The young centaur had dyed streaks of blue through the black strands. His hair was styled with some kind of sculpting gel, and he plastered it over one of his eyes, making him look like an off-center Cyclops who wore too much eyeliner. Unlike Orion, he wore a shirt and…well…his butt was *branded*. I'm not kidding: he had two butt brands on either cheek like some kind of ranch horse!

He also had an iPod strapped to his upper arm, and I recognized the messenger bag that rested against his human torso as a laptop bag.

To sum it up, if this teenage centaur didn't have the horse body trailing after him, I would have thought *for sure* that he was a customer from Hot Topic!

"Dad. I want to go out with my friends tonight. Mom says I need your permission," the centaur said in a sulking voice.

My eyes practically popped out of my head. This technology-toting, emo-posing colt was *Orion's* offspring? Orion the mystical pony man? Orion the "look at the stars and the message will be clear" *Orion*?

Orion frowned and addressed the younger centaur. "Tonight you have your celestial-gazing class."

"Not interested. My friends and I are going to listen to music and write gothic poetry," Orion's brat said, shaking his head. (His hair didn't move an inch.)

"Is that..?" I whispered to Corona.

She nodded and glanced at the father and son. "Orion's son, Perseus? Yes."

Orion's frown intensified. "You have fallen behind in your studies, Perseus. You need to concentrate for the sake of your future."

"You don't understand me!" Perseus hotly complained.

I gawked at the mini family squabble with an open mouth. "I can't believe he looks like that."

"Believe it. All the centaur teenagers are going through that dark phase. Dr. Creamintin told Orion that the young ones are just trying to create a separate identity as centaurs, and that went over like a fat pixie. Orion—all parent centaurs for that matter—is a traditionalist," Corona said, placing her paws on the desk as she watched Orion.

"You must look to the sky, Perseus," Orion said, folding his arms across his chest.

"Why? To see a roof?" Perseus snorted.

"You are young. You do not understand the ways of this world."

"But I do know that life is unfair!"

"…I don't get what they're arguing about anymore," I hissed to Corona.

She sighed, "Neither do they. Perseus, I would like to introduce you to Morgan. She's the human that tutors Asahi," Corona said to the centaur colt.

Perseus turned to look at me and stared.

"Hi," I waved.

"You're human?"

"Yeah."

"True-blue human?"

"Yep."

"Do you go to high school and eat lunch in the school cafeteria?" he suspiciously asked.

"…Yes?" I replied, wondering where he was going with this.

"Do you listen to music and use computers?"

"Yeah."

"Most importantly, do you have a cell phone?" he asked, leaning back and smirking at me like this was some test I was sure to fail.

I frowned and pulled my phone out of my pocket and held it out.

Perseus' eyes widened. "Wow. You really are a human," he said, sounding surprised.

"Of course," I frowned deeper, pocketing my cell phone and scooting away from him.

"Rock on. You're teaching a class, right? I'll come with," Perseus said, turning entirely away from his dad.

"Um, nobody uses 'rock on' anymore, and I didn't really invite you—" I trailed off when I saw Orion nodding violently behind him (or at least nodding as enthusiastically as Orion could manage while looking dignified and centaur-like). "But… of course you're free to join us?" I offered with much hesitation.

Orion gave me a closed-lip smile—the most approval I had seen from him. Ever.

Suddenly, arms closed around my waist and a mini explosion hit my back.

"WHOA!" I yelped.

"Surprise!" Madeline said. "Come on, Morgan, we've got to get going," she whined, letting my waist go only to drag me away by the arm.

"Thanks, Corona!" I called over my shoulder before Morgan bodily dragged me away, Perseus trailing after us.

"So, how are you? Asahi says he might have a better computer for us. What are we going over today?" Madeline chattered before glancing over her shoulder at me when we hit the staircase. "We have an Emo Equine tagalong. Someone you know?"

"Yeah, I worked at the information desk with his dad. I guess he's joining the class," I said, glancing at Perseus, who was following us like a black, branded shadow. He appeared to have no problem climbing up the stairs. Interesting.

The trip to the classroom was normal. Madeline talked and yanked on my hand, and Perseus clip-clopped behind us. But once we reached the room, things got interesting.

"I think we need to take a fieldtrip to the Chicago Zoo," Madeline announced as we swept inside the classroom.

"Why?" I asked, baffled.

"Because I've never been to a zoo before," Madeline said, fluttering her eyelashes.

I rolled my eyes. "Right, that should be our motivation for a fieldtrip," I scoffed before falling silent when I realized just how *quiet* the room was.

The reason for the silence was sitting next to a beaming Asahi in the front row.

"Hi, Morgan," the cheerful Arabian Night elf prince greeted me. "This is my brother, Aysel."

14

Aysel, the Moon Flood

Aysel.

It was a name I had heard many times before but had never actually understood. I remembered Devin complaining about him, Corona commenting on him, and Madeline squirming over him.

Now I understood why.

If cheerful, brilliant, uniquely dressed Asahi was the opposite of how I pictured a High Elf, Aysel fulfilled my every stereotype.

His hair was long, silky, and black as night. His eyes were piercing silver. He was willowy, fair skinned, and he dressed like the costume designer for *Lord of the Rings* was his personal tailor. He was wearing some kind of…robe-ish-draped cloak thing. The most elvish thing about him, however, was the pointed look of snobbish beauty he wore on his face like a mask.

Aysel looked up and pinned me to the floor with his silver eyes. "Morgan," he breathed, his voice quiet and cold. "I would like to speak to you. *Outside.*"

"Okay," I squeaked.

Perseus squeezed through the door behind me, and plopped down next to the sphinx as Aysel stood.

"Morgan, I'll come with you," Madeline said, her eyebrows drawing together in a frown.

"No. I'll be fine. Wait in here for me," I said, patting her shoulder.

Madeline looked unconvinced. "Devin warned me about Asahi, but he *threatened* me when it comes to Aysel," she whispered.

"It's fine. What's the worst he could do to me with a room full of witnesses just next door? Go sit down," I hissed as the elf drew near.

Madeline hesitated before she nodded and stepped aside.

Aysel swept out of the room, obviously expecting me to follow. When I did, he closed the classroom door.

"Miss Morgan, I was under the impression Dr. Creamintin made things clear to you," he said, his voice sharp.

"Made what clear to me?" I asked, taking a step backwards when he fixated his searing eyes on me.

"You have been hired as my little brother's tutor. I am *not* paying you to teach a room full of MBRC misfits. I am paying you to educate my little brother about human society."

"Technically, you haven't paid me at all yet," I said, the words spilling out of my mouth. Internally, I wailed and wanted to rip my own tongue out. WHAT WAS I SAYING?! I had no idea what made Aysel so powerful, but even *I* could tell he wore that power like a cloak!

Aysel's eyes narrowed into little slits before his face smoothed over like a fresh snow fall. "Additionally, you have failed to present any information of actual relevance and instead focus on interesting but useless human school psychology."

"No one told me what I was supposed to cover, so I was doing what I know best. If you have a curriculum, give it to me. I'll totally follow it. But you can't stick me with twentieth-century technology, no lesson plan, and then complain about it like an—" I quipped before slapping a hand over my mouth to cut off my sentence. I *knew* I was about to call Aysel an unschooled brat. What was wrong with me that I couldn't filter my words?

Both of Aysel's dark eyebrows crawled up his forehead in a

gesture of disdainful snobbery. "Twentieth-century technology?" he asked, his voice frighteningly calm as I slowly lowered my hand.

"Yeah. Windows 98 is older than I am. If that's the best technology you guys have, it's no wonder you can't understand humans," I laughed before clamping my hands over my mouth again. Seriously, what was wrong with me?!

Aysel frowned, his silver eyes glittering as he studied me. "You may continue teaching your class of buffoons," Aysel said, apparently choosing to ignore my pointed remarks—*thankfully!* "But you will tutor Asahi and Asahi *alone* for one hour every day. Do we have an understanding?" he asked, his voice as cold as stone.

I nodded, not trusting myself to remove my hands from my willful mouth.

Aysel smirked and swept away in his elf robes, leaving me standing alone in the corridor. When he was gone, I peeled my sweating palms away from my mouth and collapsed against the wall. What on Earth just happened?

I pushed off the wall and rolled my shoulders back, clearing my throat before opening the door to the classroom and bowling over Madeline—who was pressed her ear against the door for the whole conversation.

"Aha-hah, hi," she sheepishly laughed, picking herself off the ground.

I frowned at the blonde vampire but sucked in air like a man freed from prison. Aysel's presence was…intimidating.

"Yeah. Just like Asahi, Aysel's name is very appropriate for him," Madeline volunteered as she watched me flex my shoulders.

"What do you mean?" I asked.

"As she did with Asahi, Aysel's mother named him after seeing him. Aysel is Turkish for moon flood." Madeline said, standing up.

"Moon flood?" I muttered. How appropriate. Yes, Aysel's searing eyes reminded me of the silver moon hanging in the sky. The cold way which he held himself and his jet black hair only added to the picture.

"Of course Aysel is a girl name, but no one brings it up. He wears it like a male name, plus I'm pretty sure he would kill anyone who mentions that," Madeline blithely continued.

My mouth dropped open. "What?" I yelped. I was about to cross-examine Madeline when Asahi distracted me.

"Morgan, did Aysel tell you?"

I felt myself growing weary. "Tell me what?" I cautiously asked, drawing closer to the sunny elf, feeling his brilliant disposition warm my heart where his brother had frozen me.

"About the computer? He lifted a computer with Windows XP and brought it here so you can show your PowerPoint presentations now," Asahi grinned.

I felt myself automatically returning his smile, but I was really happy to hear that. XP wasn't Windows 8, but at least it wasn't Windows Vista or Windows 98.

Maybe Aysel wasn't so bad?

….what was I saying? He was *worse* than bad!

So Aysel's little talk upset me more than I should have let it. I let class out early and tutored Asahi for a full hour, alone. (Madeline was there, snoozing in the back corner, but otherwise the classroom was empty. Hah! Take that Aysel.) I wandered back to Union Station and actually was so distracted about my lack of control when it came to talking with Aysel that I actually forgot about Frey and Dave and left on the first express train that came.

I texted Fran on my way home, ate dinner with my family, finished my homework, talked to Emily and Samantha for a while, and went to bed.

I woke up sometime around three a.m. and snuggled deeper into my blankets before flipping over.

It was then that I noticed the shadowy figure leaning against my dresser. I opened my mouth to utter an ear-piercing shriek, but the figure *leaped* across my room and slapped a hand over my mouth.

"Don't scream! It's just me," a male voice whispered.

I squinted in the darkness as the blue hues from my digital clock lit up silver hair. "Frey?" I mumbled against his hand.

Frey nodded and backed up as I reached across to my bed stand to flick on a lamp.

"Oh, my gosh, Frey! What *possibly* made you think visiting my room in the middle of the night was a good idea?" I hissed when my cheerful lamp lit up the room.

Don't be fooled by the books ladies. It is *NOT* romantic to wake up and find someone *staring* at you while you sleep in the pitch-black darkness of your house! It did NOT feel like a dream. I wasn't even *tempted* to sleepily mutter to him when he was just a black shape in my room. I was more prepared to scream "*stalker*" and look for my can of mace. It felt *creepy*. Not only had Frey somehow managed to get in my house without anyone knowing, he was also in my room—which was pretty messy—watching me snore and drool! (Plus, my drawer full of unmentionables was open and spilling across the floor, and I had pretty much abandoned my clothes last night in the middle of my room.)

Creeptastic, that was the only way to describe it. My fellow females, NEVER think that some guy popping up in your room, uninvited, in the middle of the night is anything but disturbing.

"You left the MBRC without Dave and me, and this couldn't wait until tomorrow," Frey protested, quietly returning to his post by my dresser.

"I have a *cell phone*, Frey! That's why humans invented them: so we can be contacted in emergencies!" I snarled, pulling my blankets closer in a defensive gesture.

There was no way I was going to let Frey see me in my pajamas.

"Sorry," Frey muttered, looking a little put out.

I was tempted to throw my pillow at him. How dare he sulk when he was the one who was creeping through my house! "What is it?" I growled, my voice hoarse with sleep.

"I heard Aysel visited you. I wanted to make sure you were okay," Frey said.

I muffled a yawn and nodded. "I'm fine. He didn't really rip into me or anything. He got huffy and left. Although he is sort of scary," I admitted.

"Be careful with him, Morgan. Aysel is very powerful. He's being groomed for a position of leadership," Frey warned me.

"What do you mean?" I asked.

Frey shook his head and wouldn't respond.

Perfect. He got me up in the middle of the night to sprinkle me with cryptic warnings like a centaur. Just perfect.

"I was wondering…do you know of any magical creatures besides Dave and me at school?" Frey asked.

I stared. "No. Definitely not. Why?"

"Just wondering," Frey shrugged. "Sometimes I can smell brushes of magic on you."

"Frey, I work in the MBRC," I reminded him.

Frey shook his head. "No, not that kind of magic. It's…*darker*. More like oil, but it only leaves the barest traces."

More cryptic warnings. How touching.

"Was there anything else, Frey?" I asked, flopping down into the comfort of my mattress.

"Nope. I'll see you tomorrow in school," Frey said, standing straight before padding across my room to push aside the curtains of one of my windows.

"No more night visits, Frey," I warned him, sitting upright.

"Yeah, yeah," Frey said, rolling his eyes before opening the window, letting the *freakin' cold* night air into my bedroom. "You'll need to close the window behind me," he warned before hopping out of the second-story window. He landed on the roof of the porch that's directly below my room before disappearing, probably dropping off the side.

I grumbled and scooted out of my bed to close the window, scowling at Frey's moonlit back that retreated across my backyard. "I think it's time to invest in window locks," I muttered.

Viewing it in the light of Frey's little nighttime visit, I wasn't all that surprised to see him in my tutoring classroom the following day. What *did* surprise me was that he had brought a cheerful, chipper Dave along, and somehow the duo had gotten to the MBRC and my classroom before me *and* without alerting me they were even coming to the MBRC today.

"Hey, Morgan," Frey said, lazily waving at me.

"Miss Morgan, I must say I am looking forward to listening to your lecture," Dave said, his pot belly jiggling with delight.

"What are you guys doing here?" I asked, watching Dave deflate.

"Dave isn't doing so hot in his classes, and one of his professors heard about your sessions through another vamp. He recommended Dave attend your lessons on Thursdays since he has no regular classes scheduled. Naturally, as his handler, I had to come with," Frey said with a benevolent bow of his head.

"I see," I said, gazing at my sea of pupils. This week had so rapidly expanded my class size that I couldn't even recognize everyone on a daily basis. There were at least three other vampires besides Madeline and Esmeralda attending, maybe more.

As I wondered why my class was growing so large even though I wasn't really a teacher, I walked up to the desktop computer and turned it on while digging my jump drive out.

I paused when I noticed a white envelope taped to the computer that had my name written on it. I peeled it off and peaked inside. There was a check written out to me from a Vincent Moonspell. Must be Asahi's and Aysel's father.

"Helllooo," I purred before putting the check into my backpack. Apparently when scoffed at, Aysel reacts speedily.

I glanced at the computer screen, waiting for the familiar Windows XP greeting while I shrugged my jacket off. Instead the words "Windows ME" flashed.

"No!" I gasped. "He didn't!"

"Hello, Morgan! Aysel got us a different computer. The techies told us Windows ME was a rare operating system, even though it's older than Windows XP, so we decided to go with it," Asahi said, popping up next to me with his brilliant grin.

Even Asahi's sunshine smile couldn't clear away my horror. "No, this can't be! I've never even *heard* of Windows ME! Aysel must have done it on purpose!" I hissed under my breath.

"Windows ME isn't as good as Windows XP?" Asahi asked, catching on to my revulsion.

"Yeah," I agreed, regarding the computer with absolute dislike. "Windows XP is perfect. It's amazing. It might be old, but at least it *works*!" I moaned.

"Oh, I'm sorry," Asahi said in his kicked puppy voice.

I grimaced and forced a smile on my lips before turning to the dejected elf. "Don't worry about it, Asahi," I said through gritted teeth. "It's fine. Why don't you go take a seat, and we'll start class, okay?"

Asahi nodded and retreated to his desk, leaving me to stew in my bitterness.

That stupid High Elf! I *knew* yesterday's words couldn't have gone unpunished! Stupid, mean Aysel!

Fieldtrip Friday was a little stressful, mostly because I felt like I was babysitting a class of five year olds. I arrived with Frey and Dave—I probably don't want to know how and why they got permission for Dave to skip classes so he could come with us—late and a little rushed.

A quick snoop around the room confirmed that my main students were there. (Frank was still wearing his flea collar, I was grateful to see.) I tracked down Asahi to get more information about the Cuckoo Ward.

"Asahi! Do we have permission to visit the ward today?" I asked, noting Madeline skipping towards me, her frilly skirt flopping in the air.

"Of course. My father called them Wednesday evening to let them know we would be dropping by," Asahi said with his dazzling smile.

"Hi, Morgan!" Madeline sang, giving me a side hug.

"Hey. So do either of you know how to get to the Cuckoo Ward?" I asked, wondering if I would have to backtrack downstairs to ask Corona for help.

"I know the way. I've been there loads of times," Frey said with his wolfish confidence as he walked into the conversation.

"Really?" I asked, my voice mildly flavored with disbelief as I rolled my eyes up to glance at him.

"Yep. It'll be tricky because we have to leave Union Station, but I can see we've got a couple of strong glamour users in the group. We shouldn't have a problem. We can always tell people they're extras for a movie," Frey said, waving at the sphinx, who flicked her tail as she walked past us.

"...You're kidding," I said, nearly dropping the stack of Cuckoo Ward pamphlets I held in my hands.

"Oh no. I've used that excuse before. Works every time," Frey assured me.

"So, when you say we have to leave Union Station, do you mean we go above ground?" I inquired.

"Yeah. There's a Panda Express just up Clinton Street. The entrance to the Cuckoo Ward is there," Frey said, scratching the base of his neck.

I couldn't have heard him right. "A *Panda Express*?" I asked.

"Uh-huh. If we move fast enough, maybe I can grab something to take into the ward. I'm *starving*," Frey said.

Madeline looked mournful, and Asahi beamed. "Shall I begin to organize everyone into glamour groups?" he suggested.

"Yes, please. Thanks, Asahi," I smiled, still wondering if Frey was pulling my leg. I mean really, a Panda Express? Come on! At the very least it should be a nightclub!

So...he wasn't lying.

When we finally found the Panda Express, which was no mean feat thanks to my less-than-stellar students, I stood outside gaping at it like a stupid tourist.

I think I was pretty justified in being surprised. To start off, on the way over, the sphinx was almost run over by a car; Dave got his umbrella broken by one of the Pastels; and Madeline swooned when the frumpy elf that hung out with the drab fairies tripped and fell, skinning his knee.

But none of that could compare with the shock of finding out that the entrance to a fairly high-security hospital ward that was funded and founded by magical beings was located in the supply closet of a Panda Express.

"Morgan, are you coming?" Asahi asked, pausing at the door of the restaurant. "Everyone is almost through the entrance."

The line for the magical beings to get into the supply closet had stretched out of the restaurant and onto the street. Apparently, while I gaped at the building, the line had dwindled.

"Yeah, sure," I said, following Asahi inside. I was tempted to duck in the back kitchen and see who—or what—worked there, but Frey hustled me away, toting a carry-out carton.

"What did you get?" I asked, letting him herd me away from the food and through an employees-only door.

"Sweet and Sour Chicken."

"Are you sharing?"

"Not in your life. Here we go. Just step right into the closet. Thank you, Asahi," Frey respectfully said as Asahi opened a dank closet that was filled with mops.

"Come on in," Madeline invited, already inside. "Everyone else is through."

"Right," Frey said, practically shoving me into the closet before he and Asahi joined us.

Asahi closed the door, closeting us in complete darkness.

"Um, so what now?" I asked, shifting away from a mop bucket that was poking my shin.

"One sec," Frey impatiently growled. "Ouch!" he hissed, smacking into a wall.

"You're a werewolf. I thought you were supposed to have good night vision," I mildly said.

"Shut up!" Frey snapped before the closet was dimly illuminated by a faint green light. Frey crouched over the dim light source. I heard him press several buttons before something clicked.

An engine turned on, and the closet swiveled before dropping down like a too-fast-for-my-comfort elevator.

About twenty seconds later, the closet halted, and the engine turned off. Asahi fumbled with the door knob before successfully opening it. Madeline tumbled out, and I wasn't far behind her.

We staggered into a completely white hallway. It reminded me of something from a boy band music video. Everything was white, plastic, and seemed to stretch on for miles.

By the time I straightened up and pulled my sweater down, Frey was digging into his chicken, and Asahi was closing the closet door.

"That way," Frey said, pointing down the hallway with his chopsticks before leading the way.

"I see our classmates. They must be waiting for us," Asahi said, nodding at the crowd ahead of us.

My students were stopped at a large desk where a faun wearing white scrubs sat with a clipboard. Behind her desk was a set of frosted glass doors.

"Excuse me. We're the group Vincent Moonspell called about," Asahi said, magically popping in the front of my motley crew.

"Is there a Morgan L. Fae with you?" the faun asked, tapping a pen on her desk.

"Yes, that's me," I said, squeezing between the two Pastels to join Asahi in the front.

"Great. Divide your class into groups of five or less. Each group will need an informational pamphlet. It will explain the patients' illnesses," the faun said, opening a drawer of her desk to grab a huge stack of pamphlets.

"I thought this was a hospital. Why does it feel more like a sterilized zoo?" I hissed to Asahi. (I mean really, informational pamphlets?!)

Asahi shook his head. "They provide the patients with the utmost care, but the facility also focuses on teaching MBRC members, so they're used to tours. Seeing this will help persuade younger generations that humans are not to be tortured," Asahi smiled. "Besides, this is the low-level security wing—the only one available for viewing. All the others are shut down tight."

"I see," I said as the faun stood and walked to the doors.

"Some of the patients will be wandering around the facility. Don't be alarmed when you see them. We like to provide them with as much freedom as possible. When dealing with the humans, please speak simply and don't expect a lucid reply. If *any* of you do *anything* to a patient there will be *extremely* unpleasant consequences," the faun said, placing hands on her hips while her goat ears twitched. After giving my students the evil eye, she turned around and opened the door—with magic I suspect.

When the lock clicked open, she twisted and nodded at me. I took this as a cue to organize my group.

"Okay guys, you heard her. Groups of five or less. Grab a pamphlet before you go in. We'll meet back here, in this hallway, in an hour and a half," I said, glancing at my watch.

The moment everyone started negotiating groups, Madeline clamped down on me like a boa constrictor. "I'm in your group," she announced.

"Yes, okay, let go of my neck—ack!" I hacked, tearing the blonde vampire off me.

"Can I join you?" Asahi asked with his bright smile.

"Of course," I said.

"And Dave and I make five. We're set," Frey said, jerking his thumb in Dave's direction.

The middle-aged vampire was still clutching his broken umbrella, looking quite morose.

"Sure, invite yourself in," I said, hauling my eyes to stare up at the ceiling. "We've got to wait, though. I want to make sure everyone has a group."

"You're such a good teacher, Morgan," Madeline beamed.

"A very kind individual," Asahi agreed.

Frey looked nauseated at their praise, but Dave's morale began to improve.

"Thanks, guys," I said, watching Esmeralda's group of the large giant/ogre boy, Perseus (speaking of which, why was he with us?), flea-less Frank, and the sphinx hustle through the doors.

Slowly, groups trickled through the doors under the faun's supervision until only my group remained.

"Great, let's go," I said, grabbing two pamphlets. I kept one for myself and handed the other to Asahi as we approached the doors. "Thank you, by the way," I said to the nurse faun as she opened one of the frosted doors.

"You're welcome. I hope it is an educational experience for your class," she said before closing the doors behind us.

The doors opened up into a large, white chamber that was excessively well lit. The ceiling was quite high, and everything was coated in the same white plastic as the hallway.

The room was peppered with pieces of furniture, mostly couches and desks with the occasional TV set, and the patients' rooms broke off from the chamber like a complex honey comb.

"Okay, this is **very** much like a zoo," I scowled as I eyed the first set of rooms on our left and unfolded my pamphlet.

Most of the doors to the patients' rooms were locked, if the red lights directly above them were anything to go on. (Although a few of them were green.) However, their rooms were built like a habitat for a zoo animal.

According to the pamphlet, each patient had three parts to their "quarters." They got a large sitting room that was decorated to reflect their tastes and choices of entertainment. BUT, the front wall of the sitting room was thick glass, which allowed for observation.

Their sitting rooms split off into a private bedroom and bathroom, which were not available for viewing. I guess they gave the patients some semblance of privacy. If they wanted to, they could stay in the backrooms all day long and never been seen by anyone except for their attendants...but the whole thing still smelled fishy to me.

"See, this is why you need to take me to a zoo. I'll understand what you mean, and then I'll be outraged too," Madeline said.

"Should we start our tour on the left? I believe most of the class is starting with the rooms on the right, so it is more spacious over here," Asahi indicated.

"Sounds good. Come on," Frey said, leading the way as usual.

I growled in the back of my throat but followed my friends over to the first exhibit/patient's room.

Asahi dutifully unrolled his pamphlet and glanced at the room number before finding its corresponding explanation. "This patient was hiking and accidentally stumbled on a dragon clutch. The parents dropped him off a cliff, and he received a lot of injuries as a result."

I stared through the window at the guy, who was practically clothed in a body cast. "Um, yeah. More like he shattered every breakable bone."

"Doctors expect to be able to release him in two months. They will remove his memories of the ward and instead use suggestive hypnosis to make him believe he was hit by a car and has been in a coma," Asahi continued, unperturbed with my grumbling.

"Poor guy," I sympathized.

"At least he's going to be released. Some patients are here permanently," Madeline pointed out as we strolled up to the next room.

"Hmm, I don't see anyone. They must be in their bedroom," Madeline said, peering through the glass.

"No, there's someone there. See? They've got that blanket thrown over their head," Frey said, pointing out a mass of blankets that were precariously perched on a couch.

"What happened to him?" Dave asked, scratching the bald part of his head.

"Oh, hobgoblin attack on Halloween," Frey winced, reading the pamphlet over my shoulder. "No wonder he's hiding like that."

"Ouch," Madeline winced.

Asahi looked very mournful.

"Hobgoblin attack?" I asked, staring at the shivering blankets.

"Hobgoblins are usually quite pleasant workers. They're very responsible and respectful. But on Halloween, they have the tendency to…party," Asahi explained. "They celebrate Halloween much the same way humans in their 20s celebrate Saint Patrick's Day," Asahi said, smiling at me. He was very proud he could make the comparison.

"So, they went to a bar?" I ventured.

"Yes. And after they were completely inebriated, they stumbled outside and dropped their glamour. That guy proceeded to mock them for being little and green. They retaliated," Frey said, still reading over my shoulder.

"Do you want this?" I frowned, offering him the pamphlet.

"Oh no. It's much more fun to annoy you like this," Frey said before Madeline firmly wedged herself between the werewolf and me.

"So, he's frightened because the hobgoblins scared him?" Madeline asked, pointing at the blankets.

"Yes," Asahi said, his gold eyes trained on his copy of the pamphlet. "They hope they will be able to rehabilitate him with humanity, but for now they have to wait for his mind to settle down. To adjust his memories when he's in this state would be very risky."

"Poor chap," Dave said.

"Come on, next room," Frey urged.

This room was occupied by a teenage guy. He was sitting on the couch, watching TV. He didn't appear to care that we gaped at him like he was a chimp.

"I thought I was a rarity, being a teenager that knows about the MBRC and everything," I complained, blinking at the guy—who was pretty boring compared to the previous two rooms.

"Oh, you are," Frey assured me.

"This patient is a permanent resident of the Cuckoo Ward, and he doesn't know about the MBRC. He has sustained mental delusions and damages that our doctors cannot fix or remove," Asahi read.

"Really? What kind of delusions?" I asked, glancing down at my pamphlet as well.

When I looked up again, the patient-guy was no longer watching TV and was staring at us. He abruptly stood and walked towards the door to the chamber we were standing in, confirming my suspicions that doors with green lights above them were unlocked.

"You," the patient said, scurrying through the door. He hurried towards us and skid to a stop directly in front of me. "You're like me, aren't you," he asked, smiling at me.

"Ummm," I said, glancing sideways at Frey and Asahi—hoping they would help me.

"Maybe you're not," the teenager said, narrowing his eyes while staring at me. "I *am* very special. Perhaps you can hear them?"

"How touching. He's reaching out to you, Morgan," Dave clucked somewhere behind me.

"Either that or he's hitting on her," Frey snorted.

I shot Frey a dirty glare, which made the patient yelp. "You *can* hear them. That's great!"

"What are you talking about?" I carefully asked, reminding myself this guy wasn't mentally stable.

The boy leaned forward and whispered, "I see dead people."

I froze for a moment. Was he serious?

"The unhappy ghosts are pale like death and are very cold," he continued, motioning at Madeline and Frey. "The brighter ones, well, they're friendly," he added, nodding towards Asahi.

"Wow," I said, more to my friends than the teenage patient. "How did this happen? I didn't think the MBRC had ghosts," I said, flipping through my pamphlet.

Frey plucked it out of my hands and flipped it to the right page. "We don't. Don't be ridiculous, Morgan. Everyone knows there's no such thing as ghosts."

"Apparently a group of fairies plagued him for months, dropping their glamour in front of him and scaring him at night. No one knew about it, so by the time someone from the MBRC found him, he was convinced he has the ability to interact with ghosts. So far doctors have been unable to convince him otherwise," Asahi read.

"So *that's* what Esmeralda meant when she scolded the fairies," I said, recalling the very conversation that got me roped into this fieldtrip.

"Hey, I'm ready to communicate with you now!" the patient said, interrupting us all.

I narrowed my eyes. "He probably watched *The Sixth Sense* too many times as a kid."

"Now, now, Morgan. Be nice to the human!" Dave lectured.

"Come on. If we move on maybe he'll leave you alone," Madeline suggested.

He didn't.

He followed us halfway around our loop, whining to me about happy ghosts, angry ghosts, annoying ghosts, doctor ghosts—it sort of reminded me of a Dr. Seuss book. I did feel more sympathy with him the longer he stayed with us. He latched onto my group and ignored pretty much everyone except me. He was obviously able to identify me as a human. Plus, it wasn't like he *asked* for this.

My patience did take a chip in it, though, when we picked up our next patient. Everyone—with the exception of ghost boy, he was still rattling my ear off—was standing in front of a room that housed a human girl who had been cursed by a vengeful fairy godmother so her head was *backwards* on her body. It was pretty creepy to see, so when someone said "Hey" and put a hand on my shoulder, I yipped and jumped in the air.

I spun around and stared at a human girl who was holding what appeared to be a series of large, cardboard cutouts under one arm. In her other hand, she toted a cardboard cutout of a housecat.

"Oh, wow, so you really are human! Cool, and you're with all these guys, so you must not be delusional like him," the girl said with a scornful toss of her head at ghost boy.

Ghost boy glared back, but the girl continued, "Man, it's been ages since I've see another lucid teenager. Although, you don't have a dæmon," she frowned.

"…a what?" I asked.

"A dæmon," the girl loudly pronounced, as though I were stupid. "You know! An animal form, shape-shifting manifestation of your soul. Mine's a cat right now," she said, holding out the cardboard cutout. "It's too bad you haven't found yours yet. That must really suck."

"I think I saw a movie based on that. Man, this place makes a good case against human entertainment," Frey muttered directly behind me.

"Ignore Hanna. She's whacked. She can't figure out that her 'dæmon' is cardboard," Ghost boy said, rolling his eyes.

Wow, the pot calling the kettle black.

The girl, Hanna, rolled her eyes. "Yeah, right. Are you still seeing dead people, Markus?" she sneered before turning to me. "He doesn't get that vampires and fairies exist. I mean yeah, it shocked me, too, but if there are dæmons in the world, why not fairies?"

"I'm sorry, Hanna, what is your room number?" Frey asked with a charming smile as he started flipping through the pamphlet.

"Room 114," she blushed before swapping her house cat picture for a husky.

"Subliminal messaging," Madeline whispered to me under her breath.

"Ah-hah," Frey said, finding Hanna's room in the tour pamphlet. "Oh. Well. That explains a lot," he said, passing me the paper, pointing to Hanna's patient profile once I held it in my hands.

"*Patient of room 114*," it read, "*suffers from delusions of grandeur after being hypnotized by a malicious harpy. Doctors hope they will be able to crack through the hypnosis, but the patient has been in MBRC custody for approximately half a year.*"

"That does explain it," I said as we started shuffling on to the next room. I knew firsthand how convincing hypnosis was.

Hanna and Ghost boy/Markus trailed after us, arguing about who was crazier.

"You whine and complain about ghosts all day, and you call *me* whacked?" Hanna said.

"Oh right, like carrying pictures of animals and pretending they're a manifestation of your soul is normal," Markus sneered.

"We should try and get away while we can," Frey suggested as Dave watched the arguing patients with great interest.

"Yeah. Madeline, Asahi?" I whispered.

"Righto, captain," Madeline saluted.

"Okay," Asahi nodded. He very kindly turned and tugged on the sleeve of Dave's shirt before increasing his pace.

The rest of us followed his example, leaving the arguing, delusional teenagers in our wake.

"Weirdo!"

"Nut job!"

"Stupid moron!"

"Space Case!"

"They are quite a lively pair," Dave laughed, glancing over his shoulder as the patients fell out of hearing range.

"That's one way of describing it," I muttered, waving to Esmeralda as she and her group sauntered past us, going the other way.

That was pretty much the end of the peace during the fieldtrip. Soon afterwards, Perseus got in an argument with one of the patients, claiming she wasn't really human because she didn't have a cell phone. Plus, one of the patients recognized the Pastels as snobby fairies and *launched* herself at the pair. (I was one of the ones cheering.) The girl actually managed to tear a sizeable chunk of hair out of the pink/green fairy's scalp before some nurses ripped her off the fairies.

After that, the nurse faun "suggested" it would probably be best if we left.

No one argued.

15

I Stupidly Volunteer

The weekend was a welcome reprieve for me. Compared to the stress of a too-vibrant-for-his-own-good High Elf and his brother, semi-dangerous fieldtrips, and mental hospitals in Panda Expresses, homework and tests were a breath of fresh air.

Best yet, Sunday afternoon Fran called to see if I wanted to do some (super) early Christmas shopping with her. (She's a Christmas fanatic. Always wants to get the best gifts for everyone.) I agreed, and we decided to meet up at the closest small strip mall.

Fran was there before I was—I could see her green bean hat/scarf/gloves combo a mile away. Someone male was with her. When I drew closer, I realized it was none other than Brett Patterson!

"Hi, Fran! Brett, what are you doing here?" I asked, sweeping onto the scene with a winning smile. (A copy of Asahi's. Hanging out with the brilliant elf did have its perks.) I knocked shoulders with Fran and winked at her.

"Hey, Morgan," Fran wanly smiled at me. "Brett was just going," she said, making a shooing motion at Brett.

My long time crush shifted his weight, his eyebrows low against his eyes. His shoulders were slumped, and he had his hands shoved into his pockets. He looked halfway between upset and miserable, the poor guy.

"You okay, Brett?" I asked.

"Yeah, I'm fine," Brett sighed before looking up at Fran and me. "Morgan, I know you—," he broke off when Fran *glared* at him.

And I don't mean she just narrowed her eyes at him, I mean I have never seen Fran so furious. And that includes the times her brothers ripped the stuffing out of her favorite stuffed animal elephant.

"Goodbye, Brett," Fran said. Her teeth clenched so hard I think I heard her jaw crack.

"Yeah, bye," Brett said, abruptly turning and leaving.

"...What was that about?" I asked, rather mournfully watching Brett leave.

"Nothing," Fran said before tossing an arm over my shoulder. "You mean a lot to me, Morgan. You know that, right?"

"Of course," I chirped. "I am your most important, number one priority, best friend," I impertinently grinned, expecting to be swatted at.

"Yes, you are," Fran heavily agreed.

I was silent for a few seconds before deciding to break the moment with humor. "Although I'm not sure I believe that anymore. Who would let their best friend sit out here in the cold?" I asked with a fake sob.

"Hey, you were the one who was late," Fran lectured as I threw a matching arm across her shoulder, and we turned around to stumble towards the stores with giggles. "Next time, get here on time! Ack! Don't trip, you'll take me with!"

"What do you think of Aysel?" Asahi unexpectedly prompted me late Monday afternoon during his tutoring session.

I froze. I couldn't have been more shocked if Asahi told me flea-less Frank had a thing for Esmeralda.

"Pardon?" I asked.

"What do you think of Aysel?" Asahi repeated.

I glanced up at Madeline. Normally, she would sweep in during a situation like this and accuse Asahi of using his elvish powers to manipulate me. Instead, the doll-like vampire was sleeping in an uncomfortable position on a desk in the back corner of the room, her soft snores barely audible.

"That, Asahi, is a loaded question," I said.

"You aren't instantly attracted to him?" Asahi asked, resting his chin on his hand as he stared down at his notes.

"*What*?" I asked, my voice gaining in decibels. "Aysel inspires a lot of things, Asahi, fear and dislike being the foremost. I assure you, attraction isn't one of them!" I scoffed before realizing I had just deeply insulted my student's brother. "I mean…he's very stately and royal," I lamely amended, but Asahi had already latched onto my previous statement.

"So, you didn't instantly like him when you saw him?" he asked, perking up.

"No!" I enthusiastically assured him.

"Maybe, then, I *could* introduce her," Asahi mumbled, dropping his eyes back to his elegant handwriting.

"What's this about, Asahi?" I asked, propping my elbows on the desk I had turned directly in front of his.

The faintest trace of a blush decorated Asahi's cheeks, and an adorable, shy smile spread across his lips. "A girl," he admitted.

"Ooh!" I said, leaning forward before pushing aside my printed diagrams and photos. Who needs to learn when there are secrets to be told? "Care to share? Is she a High Elf? Is she pretty?"

"She's a High Elf," Asahi admitted. "And I find her to be quite beautiful. She's very bright. In fact, you remind me a little bit of her."

"Hn," I said.

"She aims to be the first Human/High Elf Ambassador, which means she wants to be the first High Elf from the MBRC to successfully integrate with humans. She's studying to be a doctor," Asahi chattered, his light blush growing darker.

"So, she's very interested in the nonmagical?" I asked.

"Yes," Asahi nodded. "To be honest, she's what got me interested in humans.

"Asahi, I am beginning to doubt your scholarly motives," I teased. "So, what's the problem?" I asked. After all, this girl—High Elf or not—couldn't possibly resist Asahi's charms. She had to be half in love with him after seeing him smile. The only thing that kept me from becoming an Asahi fangirl was my crush on Brett!

"I want to introduce her to my family," Asahi shifted.

"You think they would object to her?" I asked.

"No," Asahi said, shaking his head. "My parents know of her. We've been friends for many years. It's my brother I'm worried about."

"Ahhh," I said in absolute understanding. His brother the nag. Of course no one would be good enough for Asahi, not with Aysel hanging over him like a messenger of death.

"I mean, Aysel can't help that everyone finds him so attractive. However, I don't want Kadri to fall for him," Asahi gloomily said.

"...wait, *what*?" I asked, shaking my head.

"Aysel. Women fall at his feet," he gloomily said, running a finger across the surface of his desk.

"....*why*?" I asked, flabbergasted. Sure, Aysel was handsome beyond what is normally anatomically possible, but he is *such* a jerk! Who could possibly fall for him?! If anything, I would think it is Asahi who would have problems like that!

"It's his charisma. His looks. He can't help it," Asahi shrugged. "But I'm afraid Kadri will be just like everyone else," he confessed.

I was trying hard to keep the horror out of my face. After all, Asahi was really pouring his heart out here. I needed to be here for him.

But *AYSEL* is popular with the females of the MBRC?!

"It's good, though, to hear that you are able to resist him," Asahi said, smiling at me. "If you can, maybe Kadri can as well."

"I'm sure she can, Asahi," I said, internally deciding if this girl chose the older brother over the younger, I would scalp her myself. "I have an idea. Why don't you have her come to our classes and then ask Aysel to drop by," I suggested.

Asahi brightened. Like, literally. He went from glittering to absolutely radiant. "That's a great idea!" he said. "I wanted to invite Kadri to our class, but she is far more advanced than our study sessions," he said before drooping. "…So why would she agree to come when my learning level is much lower than hers?" he muttered.

"How about a fieldtrip this Friday?" I proposed before nearly strangling myself. I couldn't *believe* I just said that.

Asahi straightened up. "A fieldtrip is a great idea! We could go somewhere in human society for observation or a taste of your culture!" he said, rapidly warming to the idea.

"Not the whole class though!" I quickly amended. "Just a small selection! No more than…twelve," I said, wondering if I could keep track of twelve human-hyper magical beings. Hmm…Perhaps Frey would be willing to come with?

"Great!" Asahi chirped. "I'm sure Kadri would love to come. And Aysel would, too."

That's right. The Prick would be coming with us. "Umm, are you sure your brother would want to hang out with us?" I nervously asked.

"Oh, of course! He loves you guys."

I knew Asahi was blissfully innocent, but was he really under the impression that Aysel actually *liked* anyone?

Madeline suddenly appeared at my side like a dark, murderous shadow. "Who loves whom?" she asked in a deep voice.

"No one. Aysel hates everyone!" I croaked.

"We're going on a fieldtrip again!" Asahi said.

"Great! Where?" Madeline asked with a smile.

"Um…the Chicago Field Museum," I decided, trying to pick a public place where I wouldn't see *anyone* I knew. After all, knowing Madeline, she was going to carry on like one of the patients from the Cuckoo Ward.

"Marvelous! Who's coming?"

"Yes, we should probably work out whom to invite ahead of time. It will be like an advanced-placement study course!" Asahi smiled.

"Yeah, of course," I said before shaking my pen at the High Elf. "Just make sure Kadri and Aysel can both come!" I said. There was no way I was going to submit myself to this torture if they weren't going to show.

"Of course." Aysel promised.

"Then, it's set! We're going on a fieldtrip!" Madeline squealed. "I'm going to see my first human museum!"

On Tuesday, I arrived at my classroom before anyone else, Asahi included. This was a rare occasion. I had never seen the room empty before! So, I strolled up to my wretched Windows ME computer—Aysel still hadn't switched it back—and flicked it on.

Seconds later, the classroom door opened. "Hey, I was wondering where everyone—," I said as I turned around before abruptly cutting myself off. "Nick!" He was standing in the doorway in one of his many expensive suits, a cheerful smile on his mouth. I beamed back, truly delighted to see the well-dressed/well-groomed cyclops whom I fondly thought of as the first cyclops in my Cyclops Union.

"Morgan," he smiled as I trotted up to him. "I am glad that you are doing as well as Sandra boasted you were. You certainly are a globe shaker," he teased, motioning at my classroom.

"Huh?" I cluelessly asked, scratching the base of my neck.

"Teaching a class, teaching *Asahi* no less," Nick said, shaking his head. (I vaguely wondered if Asahi and his family were royalty or something. It was always weird how everyone seemed to fawn over the fact that I was his teacher.) "But, I digress."

"How's the eyewear research going?" I asked, folding my arms across my stomach.

Nick grinned. "I'm wearing one of the prototype contacts," he said. "All cyclopes now have access to contacts. The eyeglasses are being prepped for full production."

"So, the research has been pretty quick," I observed.

"Absolutely. And with our funding, the ophthalmological research branch has also found a cure to the dryad eye fungus."

"That's great!"

"Yes."

I smiled in the somewhat awkward silence before asking, "So, what brings you to the MBRC today? Are you cyclopes being discriminated against in other ways now?" I said, already feeling the fires of justice starting to burn in me at the thought.

"No, not at all," Nick assured me. "I'm actually here to call on you. We were all very surprised, you know, when we arrived at the information desk to ask for you the day after our meeting and were informed that you had your *memory erased*."

"Oh. Yeah. Sandy mentioned that," I said, nervously scratching at my elbow.

"We were very hurt! How could you not tell us?" Nick tisked, sounding like a disappointed parent.

"I'm sorry. I didn't really think it would matter," I said.

"Morgan," Nick firmly said. "How could it not? You have done so much for us. You are the first person to come alongside us and try to help, not to mention the kindness and patience you displayed, most of all to me, with our wretched paperwork. We cyclopes in Chicago care very much for you!"

"Aww," I muttered, blushing deep red before forcing my eyes to the ground, choosing to stare at Nick's unblemished dress shoes.

"We would have done everything in our power to keep you from being unwillingly hypnotized," Nick lectured. I wonder who told him I was unwilling. "In fact, if you ever need anything again, do not hesitate to call any of us," Nick said, opening his expensive suit coat to remove a business card from an inner pocket. "Okay?" he asked, holding out the card.

"Okay," I agreed, raising my eyes to smile at Nick again. "Thanks, Nick. It means a lot to me," I admitted, taking the card.

"You are very welcome, Morgan. But, you deserve it. I don't think my kind and I will ever be able to repay what you've done for us," Nick said before checking his wrist watch. "I apologize, but I must go."

"Business meeting?"

"No. In the spirit of the kindness you have shown us, Sandra and I have decided to become activists for Shoe Elves. You know, to pass on your legacy," Nick said.

"Shoe Elves?" I double checked.

"Yes, the ones that build shoes for cobblers. Did you know they don't have healthcare or workers' comp? Horribly unorganized, that lot," Nick said, shaking his head before giving me another pleasant smile. "Take care, Morgan. Next time you're in trouble, you'll let us know?" he sternly asked.

I laughed. "I will. Thanks, Nick. Good luck with the Shoe Elves!"

"I will do my best. If Sandra and I have problems, may we call on you for advice?"

"It would be my honor," I truthfully said. "Although I'm not sure I could be much of a help." After all, what could a teenage girl tell those two business gurus?

Nick rolled his eye. "Take care, Morgan."

"You, too, Nick!"

I was more than mildly worried when Asahi didn't show for class. I decided to go through with the lesson, mostly because by the time I realized he wasn't coming, I had a full room of expectant students. I figured I would go look for him or have Madeline track him down for me after I released everyone.

It turned out I didn't have to do anything.

I let class out and poked my head outside the door as the last of my students cleared the room.

Asahi was in the hallway, bouncing up and down on the balls of his feet—making his earrings jingle. *Aysel* stood there with him, looking like an accurately carved statue.

I froze, stuck halfway between relief that Asahi was there and horror that he brought Aysel with.

"Morgan!" Asahi waved before popping over to me. "I'm here

for my lesson. Sorry I wasn't in class, but Aysel asked if he could come with me, and he wasn't free until a few minutes ago," Asahi explained, entering the room before he made his way to his usual seat.

Aysel shadowed him inside the room, moving with elegance that males shouldn't possess. He stopped in front of me.

"Hello, Aysel," I greeted, gulping as I hoped that this time I would be able to better handle myself rather than spewing every little thing I thought.

"Asahi says you wish to go on another fieldtrip. Why?" Aysel said, ignoring my greeting as he narrowed his moon eyes at me.

Immediately, in spite of my intentions, I started to blurt out, "Because Asahi wants to bring—," the words froze in my mouth when I caught Asahi's gaze.

His gold eyes were wide, and he violently shook his head as his normally tan skin grew white.

"Because," I repeated before choking. It was as if the words were triggering my gag reflex, demanding to get out of my throat. I gripped my throat with my hands and gurgled. "Because."

Aysel's expression grew pinched, his expression as hard as ice.

I coughed and spat, "There's more than one reason for it. Madeline has been begging to go see a human museum for a while—not like that would truly motivate me but hey, it's a reason. Plus, the magical beings who are coming with will find the trip educational on a variety of levels. Your brother has a particular reason for wanting the fieldtrip, too, but you should ask him rather than bullying me into telling you," I said before clamping my hands over my mouth.

"I don't think you're telling the whole truth," Aysel sneered.

"And I don't care what you think," I said, the words barely muffled behind my hand. (I could have died on the spot.)

Aysel drew back, his forehead smoothing as he studied me. He looked at me the same way my biology teacher peers at the innards of a dissected frog.

"You just went on an 'educational' fieldtrip. Why take another one so soon?" Aysel asked.

Rather than answer his question, I removed my hands from my mouth and scoffed. "I thought you said I was his tutor? Why won't you let me tutor him my way? Unless you happen to know humans better than *I* do? I want to expose Asahi to human society. I can't do much with your crappy technology, so of course the easiest way is to take him outside. *I* think he and my other advanced students are more than mature enough to handle being out in human society. Do *you* doubt him?"

"Of course not," Aysel bristled.

"Then what's the problem?"

Aysel tightly pressed his lips together and went mute.

I arched an eyebrow at him, and Aysel finally spat out. "I will be attending with him. If *one* thing goes wrong, if one *single*, insignificant thing goes wrong, there will be hell to pay," he vowed before practically stabbing me with a packet of papers and a pen. "Sign this," he barked.

"What is it?" I asked, taking the offered items.

"It's a fieldtrip release form since you're going off campus. *Sign it*," Aysel hissed.

I scribbled my signature on the dotted line mostly out of fear. Aysel swiped the papers up and swept out of the room without so much as a farewell.

I watched him go with a gaping mouth.

"Wow," Madeline said. "He sure is crabby."

"The goblin imports contract has been weighing on his mind," Asahi sighed.

"Oh," Madeline said, nodding. "That's really been dragging on hasn't it? Well, I guess his behavior is partially excusable. Goblins are notoriously difficult to negotiate with."

"...What?" I asked.

"Nothing. You should probably start Asahi's lesson," Madeline said with a flicking motion.

"You just want to take another nap," I said.

"Oh-ho-ho! You know me so well!" Madeline laughed.

On Wednesday, I pretty much had a meltdown because of stupid Windows ME.

"I *hate* this computer!" I snarled.

"Wow, Morgan, you are *such* a good example to your students," Frey mocked, splayed out in a chair. (He said it was more fun to attend my class than tag along with Dave.)

"This *thing*! This stupid *thing* just erased everything on my jump drive!" I squeaked.

"You lost your class notes for the day?" Frey asked.

"I lost my American Government ESSAY! It was five pages long!" I moaned.

Frey flinched in sympathy and actually got up to join me as I peered at the screen. "Did you tell it to?"

"WHY WOULD I TELL IT TO DELETE MY ESSAY?"

"I don't know! But computers don't do things unless you tell them to."

"You know, for being born in human society, you're pretty computer stupid," I snorted. "Computers are worse than cars when it comes to being fussy! And I'm stuck with one from the turn of the millennium!"

"Hey, what's the problem?" Perseus asked, appearing behind my shoulder like a cloud of doom.

"I'm using deficient technology, that's the problem," I muttered, on the verge of tears.

"Whoa, Windows ME? Talk about last-century technology," Perseus said.

Frey and I whipped around to stare at the teenage centaur. "You understand the concept of technology?"

"Totally! I have a MacBook, an iphone, an ipad—,"

"Holy cow, he has money," I muttered.

"Yeah. Loads of it," Frey agreed.

"An ipod. I had to get a computer with Windows on it because of all my computer games, but at least it is state of the art."

I uttered a little, pathetic sigh. "I don't understand how you can be so computer literate but everyone else in this building thinks I'm crazy when I talk about Windows 8."

"Don't worry about it. I'll hook you up," Perseus promised.

I managed a weak smile for him but was completely distracted when Frey said, "Morgan, I got your files back!"

"Really? Where?"

"Here we go! Quick, unplug the jump drive! I bet this crappy computer has a virus!"

"Yes! You're the *best* Frey!'

"I know."

With that, I forgot Perseus' promise of better technology.

…until the next day anyway.

I was going over my list of students attending the fieldtrip Thursday morning while Fran sorted through her locker.

There was an assortment of folded notes crammed into her locker, and she ruthlessly ripped every single one and tossed them in the trash without reading them.

"Fran! What's with the notes? And why aren't you reading them? One of them might be from me," I said as I set my list aside.

"They aren't from you. You text me unless we're in class together."

"That's true. But still! Why do you throw them out without reading them?" I asked.

"Because they're filled with useless drabble!" Fran savagely said, slamming a book deep into her locker.

I slowly crouched down next to Fran and put a hand on her shoulder. "Are you okay?" I quietly asked.

I could feel Fran shaking beneath my hand. "Yeah," she said, her voice watery.

Rather than berate her for obviously lying, I nodded. "And you can tell me anything."

"I know," she said, her voice horribly small. Whatever it was that was shrinking Fran—the most boisterous, vibrant girl I know—it had to be heart wrenching.

"And pestering you about it isn't going to help, is it?" I asked.

"Nope."

I sighed and sat back on my heels, trying to imagine what bit of relief I could pass on. "I have to go to work after school, but do you want to go get some ice cream together later tonight? Isn't Dairy Queen open late?"

"Just the two of us?"

"Yep."

"That sounds nice," Fran wistfully sighed.

"Great. We'll do it then. I'll text you on the train ride home."

"Okay. Thanks, Morgan."

"Hey, you're my best friend! It's what we do."

When I walked into my tutoring classroom later that day, I actually backed out and double checked I had opened the right door.

Sitting on the desk where that stupid Windows ME computer used to be was a flat screen monitor, speakers, a desktop tower that was glowing *red*, a laser mouse, and a wireless keyboard.

I almost fell to my knees at the beautiful sight.

"Hey, Morgan!" Perseus chirped, tossing his head. (His hair still didn't move.) He was standing beneath a newly installed projector, holding a remote. "I got you set up. Some of my friends helped me," he said, motioning to the three centaurs, two boys and a girl, who were camped out behind him.

All three were dressed similarly to Perseus, wearing Hot Topic clothes with severely gelled hair and branded butt cheeks. The girl was the most remarkable looking with a blue roan horse body and black hair that had strips of purple dyed into it. Her purple lipstick sadly clashed horribly with her fair skin tone. One of the centaur boys accompanying Perseus had a black horse body. The other was buckskin, which means his horsy legs had black socks on them; his tail and hair was black, but the horse fur on his body was a golden tan color, making him look pretty ridiculous because of his Hot Topic clothes.

"Perseus…thank you!" I uttered. I am not kidding, I could feel tears welling up in my eyes. I hurried over to the computer and touched the mouse with great reverence. "Is this really it?" I asked, staring at the screen.

"Yep, Windows 8. I wanted to get you a Mac, but Hercules insisted on a PC," Perseus said, rolling his single visible eye.

Behind him, the black-colored centaur snorted.

"Thank you guys, really, thank you, thank you, THANK YOU!" I said, clasping my hands in front of my chest. "The frustration, having to soothe Asahi—this means it's all *over*," I groaned.

"See, told you she would appreciate it," Perseus smugly told his friends.

"Aw, it even has Word and Power Point on it," I said as I navigated my way through the programs list.

Perseus clopped down the last few steps before moving to stand next to me, his horsey tail swishing. "We've got it connected to the projector, too," he said, pressing a button on the remote. Behind me, the wall lit up with a perfect illustration of my beautiful computer screen. "So you can show pictures 'n stuff."

"This is wonderful! It's beyond wonderful. You four are amazing!" I said, plugging my jump drive into the computer with no small amount of affection. Orion might be worried about his son, but after this, I was pretty sure the kid was going to turn out OK.

Behind Perseus, I was aware that the black and buckskin centaurs were elbowing each other. "You ask her," the buckskin hissed.

"No, you!"

"No way! You!"

"What Hercules and Hermes are trying to ask, is could we join your class on the next fieldtrip? We know you're going to the Field Museum tomorrow, but we can't make it. We have astronomy class," the girl centaur said, joining Perseus in standing at my side as she snorted with disgust at her night class. "But next time, could we?"

"Absolutely," I said with a benevolent smile, internally grateful I had asked Perseus if he wanted to come to the museum with my advanced placement group. "Just ask Perseus, and he'll let you know what we're up to."

"Actually, we were hoping we could swap phone numbers," the black centaur nervously said, standing in front of my computer with his buckskin pal.

"Oh, sure," I blinked, dropping my backpack and peeling off my jacket before digging my cell phone out of my jeans pocket. "But first, could I get your names?" I asked, scrolling into my contacts list.

"He's Hercules; he's Hermes," the girl centaur said, pointing to the black first before thrusting a finger in the buckskin's direction. "I'm Athena, and you're Morgan Fae."

"Yep," I acknowledged. "Okay, Hercules first. Do you have a cell phone?"

"Yes!" Hercules said, nodding eagerly.

Swapping numbers was a quick process, especially because I didn't know anyone else named Athena or Hermes. Perseus got in on the phone action too, so I was pretty confused when the four centaurs stared at their cell phones with satisfaction.

"Yes! We have a legit human contact!" Hermes smiled, scrolling the screens of his smart phone.

"Morgan, how many contacts do you have in your address book?" Perseus asked.

"Uhh…I think like a hundred?"

The centaurs stared at me with gaping jaws.

"Erm, my best friend has over two hundred contacts, but she's the secretary of our student council, so it's pretty necessary for her," I offered, wondering if they were dismayed that I had so few phone numbers.

"I only have nine," Hercules said in a small voice.

"Oh…," I said. "But, I mean, isn't that natural? I didn't get the opinion that many beings in the MBRC have cell phones."

"They don't," Athena agreed. "Unless you're with upper management. And I think some handlers are given cell phones to use in emergencies."

"Yeah," I agreed. "Frey has a cell phone. He's a texting fiend."

"You text, too?" Hermes asked, his eyes growing wide.

"Of course she does! She's human!" Perseus scoffed.

At that moment, Asahi entered the room, a singing Madeline on his heels.

"Mooorgan! I want an oooorgan! And maybe some pudding!"

"Pudding doesn't rhyme with Morgan or organ," I dryly burst her bubble.

"Oh! Did you get a new computer?" Madeline asked.

"It looks very…sleek," Asahi said.

Oh crud. I forgot about Asahi's computer complex. Time to do some damage control. "Yeah, Perseus, Hercules, Hermes and Athena got it for me. It's going to be great! I can show some video clips with this puppy," I said, noting that I had perfect-strength Wi Fi. Apparently there *was* some magic in the MBRC.

"Video?" Asahi asked, perking up.

"Yes, that old computer you got me, Asahi, was really wonderful. But this computer is more compatible with my stuff," I loosely explained before turning back to the centaurs. "Guys, I can't thank you enough," I said in a lowered voice.

Athena smiled and brushed a purple bang out of her eyes. "I'm glad we could help. Come on Hercules, Hermes. We have to get to class," she sighed, eyeing Perseus with jealousy. "Have fun, Perseus."

"I will," he assured her. "Ow!" he uttered when the feisty female centaur kicked him in his gut.

"Bye, Morgan," Hermes said, following Athena out of the room.

"We'll text you," Hercules promised before chasing after his friends.

"Thanks again, Perseus," I whispered before ducking away from the desk and waltzing over to Asahi. It was time to assure him that his computer really was "great," even if it was a boldfaced lie.

16

The Truth about Brett Patterson

I was fairly nervous Friday morning. I mean, I was taking a group of *magical beings* to a museum. A public museum. And yeah, it was a group of twelve nice kids, (NOT the Pastels), but one of the party members previously had *fleas*, which everyone thought was *normal.*

So, naturally I was starting to question my sanity. I resolved to find Fran and wail to her about my upset stomach just so I could complain about something to someone. The problem was that I couldn't find her.

Last night, she seemed to cheer up when I bought her an ice cream. By the time I dropped her off at her house, her forehead was no longer creased with stress and— it sounds overly dramatic to say it—despair. Something was off with my friend, but I was confident she would tell me when she was good and ready to tell me, not before then.

But even if she was feeling off…I could *always* find Fran. So, after checking the student council room, her locker, our hangout cafeteria table where the rest of our friends were, and her first-hour classroom, I decided to try the student council room again.

"Where are you, Fran?" I muttered as I tried calling her on her cell phone, again. My call immediately went to voicemail.

I hurried up the hallway, noting with faint surprise that raised voices were echoing out of the student council room/closet. It was a guy and a girl, and they seemed to be fighting. As I drew closer, I was able to identify Fran's voice and, to my surprise, Brett Patterson.

"No, Brett, I've told you a dozen times! No, no, NO!" Fran shouted. Her voice was tight with ire. "My answer is not going to change!"

"Why not?" Brett asked, frustration curling in his voice.

I slowed down, leaning against the lockers near the open door of the student council room. I peered inside. Fran was standing there, her knees locked, legs planted as she folded her arms across her chest. Brett stood in front of her, his profile visible to me. His eyes were drawn together, and he looked sad—and perhaps annoyed—rather than matching Fran's anger.

"You KNOW why, Brett!" Fran said, her voice cracking like a whip. "I would never betray Morgan!"

...What?

"You wouldn't be betraying her!" Brett groaned.

"I don't know where you get that! Dating the guy she likes is betrayal, Brett," Fran said, her jaw clenched.

My heart actually froze in my chest. I lost all coherent thoughts.

Fran and Brett?

Brett liked Fran?

I swallowed thickly, vaguely aware of the flat taste filling my mouth.

"But, Fran," Brett quietly said, "I like you. A lot."

"Sorry, but I don't feel the same way," Fran said, sounding very cold. I'm pretty sure Brett didn't hear what I heard: the tears clogging the back of Fran's throat.

She liked him.

Fran liked Brett. That much I was sure of.

"Fran, maybe if I tell Morgan that I don't like her—," Brett feebly started before Fran interrupted him.

"Don't you *dare*. I will not have you breaking her heart," Fran snarled. "In fact, if you don't learn to accept that I refuse to date you, I'm sorry, but I'm going to have to cut all ties with you."

"You're being ridiculous."

"No, I am not! I treasure Morgan's friendship more than anything. So no, I will not go out with you. No, I don't like you. Now leave, *please*!" Fran begged.

"I won't," Brett stubbornly said.

"If you won't, then I will," Fran said. She moved so fast, I didn't have time to straighten up from my leaning position on the lockers.

Fran froze when she realized I was there. Her eyes widened, and the tears she had been holding back started falling. "Morgan," she whispered as I stared at her.

I straightened up, my head still trying to catch up with the conversation I had just heard.

Brett liked Fran.

"Fran," Brett said from inside the room. "Fran, what's—oh," he said, freezing in the doorframe when he saw me.

I ignored my crush and instead took a deep breath.

"Morgan, I—I," Fran stammered.

"Let's take a walk, Fran," I suggested, twisting around. I couldn't face Brett. Not like this.

Brett liked Fran.

It suddenly all made sense. The random notes, the way Brett always seemed to pop up whenever Fran was around. Fran must have been treating him so coldly and rudely to try and rebuff him.

I was aware that Fran joined me, walking down the hallway at my side. She was shaking, and her tears were falling faster now. Her mascara was getting smeary.

"Why didn't you tell me?" I asked.

Fran flinched. "I didn't want to hurt you," she said, brushing her tears aside.

I nodded. "How long?"

"Since this summer," she said.

Ah—then this was long before I joined the MBRC.

Brett liked Fran. That single thought kept barraging my mind, making me feel like a broken record.

"He knows I like him?" I asked.

Fran clenched her eyes shut for a moment before opening them again as we walked down the mostly abandoned hallway. "I accidentally told him when he asked me to homecoming," she whispered.

I paused and turned to stare at my long-time best friend. The girl looked like someone had kicked her puppy. She was nervously wringing her hands and biting her lip.

Brett liked Fran.

And Fran had kept this fact from me for months.

"You like him," I said. It wasn't a question; it was a statement.

"No, I wouldn't do that. No, Morgan," Fran protested.

This also explained why Fran had been so gung ho about Frey and me. If I liked a different guy.... "This explains a lot," I considered before my eyes were drawn back to my long-time friend.

Fran looked crushed. The weeks of trying to hide her feelings and being forced to lie had finally caught up with her. The poor thing; it must have been torture.

I sighed. "I'm sorry, Fran. I've been a rotten friend."

Fran froze, her shoulders hunching around her ears. This was not what she expected to hear. "What?"

"You like him. You like Brett, and he likes you. Man, I must have been blind not to notice this," I groaned, tempted to pinch the bridge of my nose in a very Devin-like gesture. Fran uneasily shifted, and I smiled and reached out to hug her. "So, I'm very sorry."

Fran returned the hug with the strength of a baby. "You're not mad?" she whispered.

"No, why would I be mad?" I asked, my forehead wrinkling as I backed out of the hug.

"Because you like Brett. You've liked him for *years*, and I—," Fran started before I waved her into silence.

"That's the past, Fran. What kind of friend would I be if I were to hold you back? Like I said: you like Brett—don't you dare try to deny it—and he likes you. You should go out with him," I said. The words came out pretty easily even though they tasted like dirt in my mouth.

Don't get me wrong, my heart was totally cracking here. The guy I had liked for ages had a major crush on my best friend. Talk about a painful, one-sided love. But that was my problem, not Fran's. I wasn't going to push my emotional baggage onto her.

"But, Morgan…that…. You can't mean it," Fran insisted.

"I do," I nodded. "What, don't you believe me?"

"Well, at the beginning of the year…Ashley and Caitlin," Fran reminded me.

Ah, that was it. At the beginning of the year, two of our very good friends had stopped talking to each other—and still weren't to my knowledge—because the guy Caitlin liked had a crush on Ashley.

"Fran," I laughed. "Please give me more credit than that. You are my best friend. You've been there during all my weird spells. If I let a *guy* get between us, I would be a horrible person."

"But friends always fight over guys," Fran said.

"Maybe other teenage girls do, but we're different," I said. If my studies with my MBRC students had taught me anything, it was that teenagers needed to have the maturity that all the magical beings have. We need to have the courage to step out of the roles, stereotypes, and clichés we always push ourselves into. "I choose you, Fran. Our friendship means more to me than any dating relationship. So go ahead, date Brett. I freely give you my blessing. Although I do wish you had told me about this sooner."

"Really?" Fran asked.

"Really. Now go," I said, playfully pushing her back down the hallway, towards the student council room. "And Fran," I called.

Fran turned around, her eyes regaining some of their former mischievousness.

"Tell Brett if he ever makes you cry, I'm going to set Whitey loose to maul him," I said. I had a feeling Frey would totally get a kick out of chasing Brett in his canine form. He never liked him much anyway.

Fran beamed from ear to ear. "Thanks, Morgan," she said.

"You're welcome."

The school day wasn't much fun.

I mean, it's pretty hard to secretly nurse a broken heart when your best friend is walking on cloud nine over the same guy. But Fran did make it as easy on me as she could. Even though she was officially going out with Brett, she forbid him to get within a thirty foot radius of her and me. (She had the boy totally whipped, and they hadn't even been going out for a full day yet. That's my girl!)

American Government was *beyond* awkward since I sit next to Brett. We exchanged uncomfortable hellos and then pretty much ignored each other for the rest of the hour until the bell rang.

I was gathering up my stuff, incredibly aware that Brett was standing by my desk, scratching his neck. "Hey, Morgan," he started. "I just wanted to say, um, thanks. Fran told me what you said, and I don't think she ever would have gone out with me otherwise," he said.

"Yeah, no problem," I said, shoving my pencil bag in my backpack. I would not look up at him. I would *not* look up at him!

"So, um, sorry about—," he started, but he was interrupted by one of the most unexpected forms of help: Frey.

"Hi, Honey," Frey said, poking his head into the classroom before stepping inside, his canine eyes fastened on me. "I'm walking you to your next class," he said, firmly stepping between Brett and myself.

I have never been so utterly grateful for that jerkish furball as I was that moment. "Great, glad to see I have a vote in the matter," I grinned.

"You don't have rights," Frey snorted as I stood. He grabbed my backpack for me and herded me out of the room. "Alphas always rule the pack," he said as he joined the hallway traffic flow.

I breathed out and let the alpha comment slide as I took my backpack from the werewolf. "Thanks."

"No prob."

"How did you find out?" There was no question in my mind that Frey didn't know about the Brett-Fran-Morgan love triangle.

"Fran."

"Ah, I should have known."

"She worries about you."

"And she should. I'm going to get acid indigestion from today's fieldtrip."

"Hey, I'm coming with. You'll have no problem," Frey promised.

I chuckled before musing on the sentence. In a way, Frey was right, but not the way he meant it. Ever since I had regained my memories, I had really come to see Frey as a true friend. Thankfully, I had abandoned my girlish crush on him—after all I had Brett—no.

I actually froze in the middle of the hallway. "No," I breathed. "ohno, ohno, oh no."

"Morgan?" Frey asked, nudging me out of the way of oncoming traffic before dragging me to an empty staircase. "What's wrong?"

"Oh no," I groaned, shutting my eyes. My life was about to blow up in my face. The reason I was able to resist Asahi's brilliance, scoff at Aysel's otherworldly beauty (you know, besides the fact that he was a jerk), reject Frey's obvious hotness, and *survive* in an organization that had some of the best-looking males I had ever seen was because of the excessively loyal crush I had on Brett.

Now, because I had to give up my stupid one-sided love—much like a tragic, rejected heroine in one of those romance books Fran was forever reading— I was going to be a sitting duck.

"I must be strong," I said, gritting my teeth. I couldn't allow those magical pretty boys to get to me. I wouldn't! I mean, I couldn't be that shallow, right? (A sinking part of me whispered that yes, I probably was.) "This is going to make life far more difficult," I tersely said.

"Uh, Morgan, don't worry. I promise the fieldtrip won't be that hard," Frey said, sounding worried.

"What?" I asked.

"What?" he returned.

"Nothing," I said, shaking my head, pushing my sudden realization to the back of my brain. I would have to be on my guard. There was no way I could nurse my crush over Brett because he dated my best friend, but there was also no way I was going to let myself become some romantic sop just because High Elves, werewolves, and the Pooka happened to be hot.

Wait, scratch that last one. He wasn't even here!

"Let's go," I said, mustering my courage.

"Are you sure you're okay?" Frey asked.

"Yeah," I said as Frey escorted me to my next class. "I am peachy keen."

"...What does that even mean?"

"Shut up, Frey."

"I can't tell you how much your kindness means to me," Frey said with a fake sniffle before dropping me outside my classroom door. "Right, so see you after school. Dave is really excited about this fieldtrip."

"What tipped you off? His Chicago Field Museum T-shirt, or the fact that all our Spanish conversations today were based on visiting museums?" I dryly asked.

Frey rolled his eyes. "Goodbye, Morgan."

"Bye," I said, gliding into my classroom. I pretty much threw myself at my desk, narrowly avoiding plowing over Hunter. After dropping my stuff on the ground, I thumped my head on my desk several times for good measure.

I would not be stupid! I would not be swayed by a handsome face!

"Rough day?" Hunter asked.

I paused the self-abuse and turned to look at my classmate.

Hunter was pretty hot. I mean, he wasn't one of those guys every girl falls for, but he had a subtle handsomeness to him. Plus, he was pretty kind, all things considered. Maybe I could force myself to crush on him?

What was I thinking? I mentally waved the thought away and smiled. "Yeah. Unbearably so."

"I'm sorry," Hunter said with true regret. At least it sounded like true regret. I couldn't see his eyes because he was wearing his sunglasses inside again. "Anything I can do to help?"

"I doubt it," I said, dropping my chin to my desk again. "I'm just going to have to prepare myself. Mentally speaking. Like a samurai before a match," I decided.

"Are we talking about a test here or a fencing match?" Hunter asked.

"Neither. We're talking about love and war," I sighed.

"Oh," Hunter said, his voice edged with the horror all males hold for the topic of love. "Well, if you needed me to, I guess I could have your love-and-war problem eliminated," Hunter mildly suggested, as though we were discussing the day's lunch menu.

I laughed. "Don't worry about it. I'm just being dramatic. The problem is me. I have to face my weaknesses. Besides, their rotten personalities should save me," I reasoned.

Hunter's eyebrows pulled together in a questioning v. "If you say so."

"I do," I said, picking myself off my desk. "We didn't have any homework, did we?"

"We did. You finished it in class yesterday before we left."

"I did? Man, that is great to hear."

"Glad I could be the bearer of good news."

17

Fairies in the Field Museum

"I am so *stupid.* I am so *stupid.* I am so *stupid,*" I sang under my breath as I massaged my temple.

The fieldtrip hadn't even started, and I was already regretting that I had proposed this disaster waiting to happen.

My group and I were meeting in Union Station before we ventured on the bus that would take us to the museum. Almost all my students were there (in fact, everyone was with the exception of Asahi, his would-be girlfriend, and Aysel), but most of them were causing me to experience varying degrees of panic.

Madeline had done her best to "blend in," which meant she was wearing pink sunglasses, had a pink umbrella, a white babydoll shirt, a pink jacket, and pink jeans. I was pretty impressed she was wearing pants, but I still wondered what on earth made her wear pink. Not only did she look borderline ridiculous, but rather than blending in, her cotton-candy outfit attracted attention with its blinding color.

Perseus had swiped a glamour charm from a pal of his, which basically covered him like a cloak and got rid of his horse body...but the charm made him into a girl. He wasn't taking the sex change very well and kept fiddling with it. I could see his horsey rump twitch in and out of sight as he unhappily twisted the charm necklace. (Might I add, though, that he made a *very* fetching girl.)

Flea-less Frank was probably doing the best next to Esmeralda. The pair was talking with the Sphinx, who also had a fairy glamour that made her look like an exotic, Egyptian girl.

The two dumpy fairies and their plain elf friend were doing… okay…ish. The fairies used their magic to dump their fairy wings, but they had neglected to get different shoes. (Theirs were made of bark.) The only thing the elf did to change his appearance was to wear sweat pants and a hoodie. He had combed his wavy hair straight so it sort of/not really hid the tips of his tapered ears, but he compensated for this by pulling the hood of his hoodie up. He looked like he was drowning in his clothes.

"Extras in a movie, Morgan. I'm telling you, it works every time," Frey said, scratching his elbow through his jacket as he watched Dave sashay past.

The only reply I made was a pained moan.

"Look on the bright side. At least this got us out of our last class," Frey offered. Because of the tight schedule we were running on due to the museum's hours, Frey had Dave write us passes so we could skip our last class and catch an early express train to Union Station.

"Morgan! Sorry we're late!" Asahi called as he and a very pretty girl (probably his High Elf crush) hurried towards us.

Asahi looked a little odd to my eyes because, for once, he wasn't dressed like a stereotypical Arabian prince. He was wearing khaki pants that were just a touch too short for him, a polo shirt, and a black winter jacket. His ears looked bare without all of his earrings and gems—not to mention he was probably wearing a glamour. His ears looked perfectly normal and not at all elvish.

His elf friend looked almost completely normal, too. She wore jeans and a blue sweater that she fussed with before twisting into her white jacket. She, too, had normal-looking ears, but she still didn't look ordinary. If Asahi's hair was gold, hers was copper. The bright, shiny copper of a new penny. I'm pretty sure it was so glossy, it reflected light. Her eyes were also a hazel mixture of brown and green, but both colors were deep and vibrant. They were shades that humans can't obtain without colored contacts.

So, even though Asahi and his girl looked human, their interesting hair color and eye color set them remarkably apart. Just like Madeline's clothes.

"Hello, you must be Morgan. I'm Kadri," the elf girl said, offering her hand to me.

I shook it, smiling at her. "Nice to meet you. I'm glad you could come with us today, Kadri," I said.

"No, I should be the one thanking you. I can't go out into human public without a guardian around. This is a great opportunity for me! Thank you so much," she gushed as I wondered exactly what I had signed away in Aysel's paperwork.

"You're welcome," I said, deciding I liked her. She was enthusiastic like Asahi, and she seemed to be genuinely sweet. (I had been steeling myself for a High Elf version of the Pastels.) "Hello, Asahi. Nice clothes. Where's Aysel?" I asked, turning to my student.

"He was right behind us, ah. There he is," Asahi said, twisting around to point through the crowd.

Nothing could have prepared me for an incognito Aysel. Nothing.

Aysel made the transition from High Elf to human *perfectly*. He looked and dressed like a model, wearing jeans, a long-sleeved black shirt, and a black leather jacket.

His shiny black hair was pulled back into a low ponytail at the nape of his neck, and although his ears were human shaped, he sported a small silver hoop in one of them.

After I realized I was mentally drooling, I straightened up and grew significantly irritated with Aysel for looking so hot as a human and with myself for falling for it so easily.

"Alright, the class is here. Let's go," I barked, barely acknowledging Aysel. "Everyone has human money for the entrance fee, right?" I asked. (Yesterday we held an extensive meeting to discuss the museum entrance fee, as well as disguising the magical beings in order to appear in public.)

After hearing the chorus of yeses, I started out. "This way, guys.

Frey and I have already bought your bus passes for the afternoon. Come on," I called.

We grabbed CTA bus #1 to State Street, and there we switched to bus #146. Normally, I would have made everyone walk to State Street because it's not that far away, and Perseus really sucked at getting on busses (just because I couldn't see his horse body didn't mean he didn't have to haul it up the bus steps and down the bus aisle), but the Field Museum closes at 5:00, and I wanted to get there so we had at *least* an hour and a half, and walking was likely to take forever the way my group gawked at humans.

"This is it guys, off the bus," I said when we pulled up to the Field Museum. I popped off first and did a head count as the magical beings followed me. "Great," I said, shivering in the wind when the bus puttered off. "Let's get inside. I've already ordered our tickets online, so they'll be waiting for us," I said, leading the way.

For various reasons, I hauled my group all the way around the museum so we entered through the east entrance. We passed by two other entrances to do this, and almost everyone froze in their light clothes. Why did I do this? Because when we entered the museum, Madeline proceeded to ooh and ahh at everything as loud as a yodeler, and she was not alone. I chose the east entrance as our starting point because it was abandoned.

I left Frey to babysit the group and collect money while I ran up to the desk to claim our basic fare tickets ($12.00 per being with the student discount). I had purchased the tickets the previous night using my gas credit card provided by my parents (Hah-hah. I was going to have to intercept THAT bill before they got it), so issuing our tickets took very little time.

I grabbed a fistful of maps as the nice museum lady ran down a few of the highlights before I retreated to my group.

"Here are your tickets. Now go through in an *ordinary* fashion," I said, taking the cash from Frey before divvying out tickets and maps. "We'll be going everywhere together, so keep close to the group," I said as Madeline went through the ticket line, a nervous, flea-less Frank stepping on her heels.

"What exhibits do you think we should check out?" I asked Frey, watching our group pass through the line.

"I prefer the ancient Egypt exhibit, but you're going to want to limit us. There's no way we'll have time for everything," Frey warned.

I nodded. "Since we're starting on the lowest floor, we could swing through ancient Egypt and then head immediately upstairs," I offered.

"Sounds like a plan," Frey grinned.

"I find your lack of pre-planning appalling," Aysel said behind us.

"I told you before, Aysel. I don't care what you think," I carelessly said as I stared at the map. I winced when I realized what words came out of my mouth and sneaked a peek behind me to see how angry the High Elf was.

He looked cross, but not angry. His lips were definitely twisted into a scowl, but that might be because Asahi and Kadri were laughing like great pals behind him.

When everyone finally made it through, I had to kick them out of the white, marbled entrance area because they kept staring at the museum employees like kids at a zoo.

I guided the group through the belly of ground level like a border collie with a herd of sheep.

Madeline and Frank nearly got away from me at the ancient Egypt entrance. Madeline kept walking forward to the Man-eater of Mfuwe exhibit, which featured a man-eating lion, rather than taking the left turn.

"No, no, no. We're going this way," I said, grabbing the girl's arm before hauling her back to the group.

"Talk about a rip off. That's just a stuffed lion," Madeline complained. "And a shabby one, too! The saber-toothed tigers at the MBRC are *way* bigger than that!"

"Come along, Madeline, we're going to this exhibit now," I said before pushing the whiny vamp into the Egyptian room.

Most of the group had already ventured inside. Esmeralda and the Sphinx were camped out in the doorway. The Sphinx looking absolutely horrified as she stared at parts of the exhibit.

"They're white. White Egyptians," she said in a very accusatory fashion as she stared at the various cut outs/displays that held what even I had to admit were very *pale*-looking ancient Egyptians.

"But they do have a lot of historically accurate information. Come on, this is obviously a kid-targeted area. Let's go look at the sarcophagi," Esmeralda said, patting the Sphinx's back.

I heaved a mini-sigh and returned my gaze to the map as I stood near the exhibit exit. As a resident of Oakdale, I had taken enough fieldtrips to the Chicago museums to last me a lifetime. It was better to use this time to plan my next move.

"Humans are horrible chroniclers of the past," Aysel announced next to me, his head tilted with arrogance.

"You can hardly blame them. They don't know the whole story," Kadri pointed out. (I had a feeling she was going to become my personal hero.) "Besides, even though they have their inaccuracies, they are vastly ahead of us in technology. One can see it being used in their displays," she said, motioning at the various interactive exhibits. "We do not have the ability to recreate such technology, and we have magic at our disposal."

Aysel narrowed his eyes. "I find that I don't like you."

"That doesn't much bother me," Kadri shrugged.

I snickered under my breath and decided I would have to have a girl talk with her about Asahi. Asahi *needed* to date this girl! If he was incapable of picking up on/responding to his brother's malice, he should at least date someone who could handle it for him!

"Do you like her?" Asahi whispered on my other side before gently tugging me away from his arguing friend and brother.

"I *love* her. And I barely even know her!" I promised the bright elf as we stared at a recreation of an ancient Egyptian boat.

"Good," Asahi said, relaxing. "I was hoping you would," he said, twisting around to smile at the still arguing High Elves.

"So, you introduced her to Aysel before you came? How did that go?" I asked, leaning against the railing to take a photo with my camera phone.

"Quite well. Kadri does not appear to be remarkably affected by Aysel," Asahi said.

"Yep. That's for sure," I agreed. "Are you going to ask her out?"

Aysel's face flushed up in that adorable blush of his. "If you mean will I try to court her, I believe the answer is yes."

"Aww, good luck!" I said, reaching out to ruffle his hair. "I'm sure she'll say yes."

"Really?"

"Yeah," I said, turning around to join Asahi in observing his sibling and love interest.

Kadri had, by now, realized we were gone and was watching us with a questioning look. Her eyebrows were slightly drawn together as she narrowed in on me, probably trying to gauge whether I was competition or not.

I decided to answer her question and bodily pushed Asahi towards her. "Go get her, tiger," I drawled.

Asahi laughed and glided towards his date, causing her to give me a blinding smile.

Yep. We were going to be friends for sure.

"Morgan," Frey said, popping up next to me. "Madeline is getting nauseous because Esmeralda has got her cornered in the mummy section where they talk about removing the brains 'n stuff. Would you come get her? I don't want her barfing in here."

"Coming," I sighed.

A teacher's work was never done.

After I hustled Madeline into a blood-and-guts-free zone, the rest of the ancient Egypt tour went well. When everyone was finished, I ushered them upstairs to the main level.

I let everyone gawk at the stuffed elephants and Sue—the T-rex skeleton—while I planned our next move and tried to ignore Aysel, who seemed keen on following me and making disparaging remarks about everything.

"Imbeciles," Aysel said, scoffing at the drab fairies and elf, who were staring at a young mother pushing a stroller.

I ignored the remark and instead wondered if I should just take the group upstairs and work our way down, or remain on the main floor for the rest of fieldtrip. Frey's voice interrupted my musings.

"Dave, you're *drooling*. You *have* to drink some tomato juice," Frey said, his voice growing in volume.

I looked up to see Dave wipe his mouth off on his sleeve.

"I won't drink it. I'm fine!" the balding vampire insisted.

"Oh, look, someone's bleeding," Frey said, pointing over his shoulder.

"Where?" Dave demanded, whirling around.

"SEE! You aren't fine!" Frey shot.

"That was unfair," Dave protested.

"When was the last time you had tomato juice?"

"I'm not telling!"

"Dave, you have to drink it to satisfy the vamp in you."

"No, no, no! I don't!" Dave insisted, pouting.

The argument was starting to draw stares.

"Yes, you do, Dave," Frey growled.

"Make me!" Dave challenged.

"Okay, intervention," I said, shoving my museum map into Aysel's hands. "Hold this," I added before walking up to the arguing vampire and werewolf, remembering how I saw Frey as a transformed werewolf right after a conversation very much like this one.

"You've got his thermos?" I asked Frey, stopping short of the pair.

"Yeah," Frey said, holding it up. I took it and unscrewed the lid, wrinkling my nose at the foul smell. (I couldn't blame Dave for not wanting to drink this stuff. It smelled horrible.) I passed Frey the cap and approached Dave with the open thermos and a smile.

Dave eyed the thermos and wiped sweat off his large forehead. "What are you doing?" he asked.

"Being a teacher," I said with an angelic smile before I sprang. I grabbed Dave by the nose, pinching it shut for him, and tilted the thermos into his open mouth. "Drink it," I hissed. "Or you're going to get us thrown out."

Dave gargled and gagged for a second before swallowing. He took several swigs before I released him and stepped backwards.

"That was awesome," Frey laughed as I handed him the thermos and wiped my germy Dave-nose hand off on my jeans.

"Na-uh. That was mean," Dave complained after coughing and choking on the thick taste.

"It was necessary," I said, still scrubbing my hand on my jeans as Frey handed the balding vampire a mint. "I'll take my map back now, thank you very much," I said, tugging my map out of Aysel's hands.

The High Elf was staring at me like a dissected animal again, so I decided it was time to collect the gawkers and head upstairs.

My exhibit of choice was Plants of the World. It was a safe gamble: it involved no blood, no Egyptians, and no historical inaccuracies. All in all, no one could complain. Well, no one except for Aysel.

"These are made of glass and wax," Aysel said with distaste as he glanced among the displays.

"Um, yeah. They're models," I said, staring at a beautiful orchid.

"Why don't they have real ones?" the snob scoffed.

"Because real ones would turn brown, dry up, and disintegrate," I said. (I still wasn't able to rid myself of the habit of being rudely blunt with Aysel.) "Humans don't have magic, *remember*?"

"Hn," Aysel said.

"Um, Morgan?" the drab, hoodie-wearing elf asked as he slunk up to Aysel and me.

"Yes, what's wrong?" I asked with a smile.

"Perseus is, uh, cornered," the elf said, pointing behind us.

I turned around to see that girl Perseus was indeed stuck. He was plastered to a glass case, a bench directly behind him, and a group of rambunctious elementary schoolers on either side.

Again might I remind you that even though I—nor anyone else

for that matter—couldn't see Perseus' horsey body, it was still there. And that was what had him stuck. He was penned in like livestock.

"Okay, I'm coming," I said rolling my shoulders before heading over to the centaur. "Perseus, you don't need to be so frightened of kids," I said, wading through the children who scattered like playful puppies.

"But I could step on one of them," was Perseus' surprisingly non-emo, thoughtful reply. (Perhaps the female disguise was wearing off on him?)

"Pft, they're kids. They push each other down for fun," I said, sneaking around him to wade through the kids on his other side, effectively spreading the pack.

Female Perseus' button nose wrinkled in disbelief. "I don't really—,"

"It's fine. You can even butt slam them. Just make sure not to be too mean in front of their parents," I assured him, patting his shoulder before moving on.

"This is great," Kadri said with enthusiasm, watching the elementary kids. "I have never been able to observe human education before."

"Um, I think the point here is the museum," Esmeralda said before turning to grin at me. "Thanks, Morgan for bringing us. This is the first museum I've been to since I turned vamp."

"No problem. I'm glad everyone is enjoying themselves," I smiled.

"Humans are quite imaginative and creative," Asahi said, looking at a flower. "I mean, we magical beings have a wide array of talents, but we tend to stick to our strong points."

"What do you mean?" I asked.

"Magical beings excel in history and past arts, but we aren't very innovative. Dwarves will always be forgers; shoe-elves will always be cobblers," Kadri nodded. "There isn't a kind of magical being that excels in technology or imagining the future."

I was vaguely aware that Aysel ghosted between Asahi and me as I considered my reply. "I'm not sure that's true. Maybe older generations were like that, but you guys aren't. Perseus got me a computer fitted with the newest technology. And Kadri, isn't your desire to work and observe humans part of imagining the future? I mean sure, races will always have specializations. Unicorns will always be the best healers, and sirens will always have fantastic voices. But I think everyone at the MBRC is working towards a new future, together," I said, staring thoughtfully at the flower in the case as I contemplated Westfall, Perseus' friends, and the cyclopes.

When everyone was silent, I jerked my eyes away from the model. "What?" I asked my friends who were staring at me.

"That was very profound," Asahi said.

"Wow. Morgan, you are right!" Kadri smiled.

"That's why you're the teacher," Esmeralda winked.

Even Aysel couldn't find anything rude to say.

The smile on my face fractured when I heard Madeline say, "Oh, my gosh! Hey, guys, they have dinosaurs!"

I paled. "I forgot the Evolving Earth exhibit and the Elizabeth Morse Genius Dinosaur Hall are attached to Plants of the World," I muttered through stiff lips as Asahi, Kadri, and Esmeralda ambled towards Madeline at the far end of the hallway.

"Why would that matter?" Aysel asked, staying by me.

"Because if they complained about the discrepancies in the ancient Egypt display, I don't want to even *think* about what they'll have to say about the dinosaurs!" I moaned before hurrying after my eager students and friends.

"Oh, my. They're dead wrong on everything!" Madeline announced in an embarrassingly loud octave.

"Madeline! Quiet!" I hissed as I stalked into the exhibit.

"But Morgan, get this! They think dinosaurs died out 'millions of years ago.' How ridiculous is that?" Madeline laughed before I managed to get a hand around her mouth to quiet her. But it was too late; her disbelief had already spread through the other MBRC members.

"These guys are speciesist," one of the fairies declared. "They only showcase big dinosaurs! What about all the small ones? The smaller dinosaurs are more populous!"

"Not to mention they're horribly wrong about their history.

They say here humans never lived with dinosaurs. That's hogwash. Why do they think the dinosaurs decided to go underground in the first place?" Kadri snorted.

"Why do they have fossils? Fossils are boring. Besides, the real thing is still crawling around under Union Station," Perseus said, jabbing his (her?) finger at a display case.

The hoodie elf avoided looking at the dinosaur bones and murmured, "How disrespectful, to disturb the bones of the dead!"

I moaned and released Madeline as the mothers around us gave me the evil eye and herded their children far, far away. "Guys, be quiet!" I begged. "Come on, don't you want to see, um, the Chinese exhibit? Or how about a nature walk, or Eskimos?"

"But Morgan," Frey said, passing me as he clicked his tongue. "This wouldn't be a proper, educational fieldtrip if we did not see both the ignorance of humans in addition to their brilliance."

We unfortunately spent a lot more time in the dinosaur area than I wanted to, but eventually I did manage to herd them over to see the China exhibit—which they were quite impressed with.

I had to practically *drag* everyone out of the museum at 5:00 p.m. We caught the buses back to Union Station—which again was a tricky practice, this time because everyone was so excited about the various humans they saw they just bubbled with information. (The fairies talked about a teenage boyfriend/girlfriend couple they saw for both bus rides. I had seen the couple they were talking about, and nothing about them struck me as being odd or even interesting, but the fairies talked about it like it was the greatest thing since the iPod.) On CTA bus #1, Madeline accidentally gave herself a paper cut with her museum map, and I had to grab her as she swooned. Thankfully, I've moved to keeping a stash of Band-Aids in the butt pocket of my jeans ever since befriending the hemophobia-stricken vampire, so I slapped one on her cut before she was able to get a good look at it.

By the time we reached Union Station, I was exhausted.

"That was amazing! We need to do it again," Madeline exclaimed, twirling in a circle.

"No. No, we don't," I said, shaking my head as I passed her.

"I think we should," Perseus said with a snort, tossing his head. (The gesture looked fairly funny with his girl glamour still spread on him.)

"We could go to Shedd's Aquarium," the Sphinx suggested, leading the way to the MBRC.

"No," I said, intending to nip this idea in the bud.

"Really? But we could get a discount," Kadri said.

"Huh?" I replied.

"The aquarium is run by the Lake Michigan mermaid clan—by the way, don't *ever* mention Asian carp to them—so we could totally get in for cheap and go behind the scenes and stuff," Kadri explained.

Hmm. I always did like the aquarium, and going behind the scenes did sound appealing.... "I'll think about it," I promised.

"Great!" Asahi said, swapping grins with Kadri while the rest of our group members squealed and/or cheered.

"Okay, we're here. I'll see you all in class next week Monday," I said, stopping just outside the employees-only door that would lead to the MBRC.

"Yes, teacher!" Madeline said with a mock salute.

"Thank you again for taking us," Asahi said.

"Yeah, it was fantastic. Thank you so much," Kadri added.

"You're welcome. If we do make another fieldtrip in the future, I hope you can come, Kadri," I said, winking at Asahi.

"Thanks! I can't wait to go to the aquarium!" Kadri chirped.

"Ah—but I didn't say we would for sure go there—" I started, but Frey cut me off.

"Come on, Morgan. You're a big softie. We all know you'll cave, so just admit it and get it over with. Dave and I still have to report to his teachers, so you'll be riding the train home alone. Is that okay?" the werewolf asked.

I rolled my eyes, waving goodbye to the fairies and elf who moved through the employees-only door with Asahi and Kadri. "I'm a big girl, Frey. I can take care of myself."

Frey looked unconvinced.

"Are you joking? I'll be riding a train! It's not like someone will kidnap me," I complained.

"Bye, Morgan," Esmeralda and the sphinx called.

"Bye guys. Goodbye, Perseus," I said. The female impersonator waved before diving through the open door, ripping his glamour necklace off as he went.

"Oh, Esmeralda—" Madeline said, hurrying after the dark-haired beauty, also disappearing into the magical hallway.

"Right, well…don't talk to strangers. Or anyone who smells suspicious," Frey warned.

I rolled my eyes. "Of course, Frey."

"Come on, Dave. I wonder what your instructor will have to say about that little temper tantrum you threw in the museum," Frey said, turning to the balding vampire.

"Do we have to tell him?" Dave whined, wringing his hands.

"Uh, yeah! He's hilarious when he yells at you. Bye, Morgan. See you Monday," Frey called over his shoulder before disappearing through the door with Dave.

"Thank you for inviting me along. It was really interesting," Frank said, itching at his flea collar. (I was grateful to see he was still wearing it! Thank goodness those things last longer than a month.)

"You're welcome, Frank. I'll see you Monday?"

The nervous boy nodded before casting an anxious glance at Aysel and slinking through the door, leaving me alone with Mr. Snobbypants himself.

I decided Aysel intended to lecture me about something. Why else would he hang back when his beloved brother had already skipped off with his soon-to-be girlfriend? "Yes, Aysel?" I asked, turning to face the incredibly handsome High Elf.

"Your classroom technology needs have been met?" Aysel asked, a look of cold superiority settling over his face.

"Yes. Some centaurs got me hooked up," I nodded.

"You will be taking the…advanced-placement group on another extracurricular activity?" Aysel questioned.

"Probably," I sighed. "But not for a few weeks. Maybe over

Christmas break," I pondered. "Don't tell me you want to come with?"

One of Aysel's dark eyebrows arched up. "Hardly," he said. "I merely want to make sure you remember that you should be focusing on my *brother's* education, not these parasites."

"With the exception of Dave, Madeline, and Esmeralda, you can't call them parasites. And I am, too, focusing on Asahi—but his desire for education might not be as pure-hearted as I thought," I frowned before remembering who I was talking to. "What I mean is, shouldn't I help as many MBRC members as possible?"

"You are being paid to tutor my brother. You are not an actual MBRC employee; therefore, MBRC members do not concern you," Aysel said, moving so he could lean against the station wall. (It was unfair that he could be so elegant and still so masculine.)

"That's just plain mean, not to mention selfish," I blurted out. Rather than clamping my mouth over my hand like I usually do, I decided to go ahead and spill my guts. He hadn't fired me yet, so I was probably okay. (Besides, something told me that Asahi's affection for me neutralized any desire Aysel had to get rid of me.) "How can you claim to be a part of a society that integrates magical beings with humans when you won't even let them integrate with each other?"

Aysel narrowed his beautiful moon eyes. "I am only following the thoughts of our leadership. The MBRC Administrator also believes that we should concentrate on the beings that show the most promise."

"Yeah, well your administrator is a real ass," I snorted, watching several pasty guys in suits pass us. (A vampire coven maybe?)

Aysel grew absolutely *livid*. "DON'T insult him," he hissed, rocketing off the wall to leer over me like a wolf on a sheep. "A mere human like you could not possibly understand the thousands of issues our administration deals with. If the Lake Michigan mermaids aren't fighting amongst each other, the goblins are demanding more import rights, and the wind fairies are dabbling with airport traffic."

I sensed this wasn't just about tutoring Asahi anymore. "Hey, I didn't insult the MBRC itself—I think it's doing a lot of good. Dave has been getting a lot better at playing human after just a few weeks. I just think the whole survival-of-the-fittest thing is a sucky attitude that you guys obviously don't closely follow. I mean, hello, you've met Madeline right?"

"You don't know what you're talking about," Aysel hotly promised.

"You're right. I don't. I'm an outsider who sees issues—like the millionaire cyclopes whose needs are being ignored—and I fix it. I start a class and loads of magical beings attend it because they don't have a clue what it means to be human," I sneered, standing on my tip toes to try and shorten the distance between us. (Oh dear, even I knew I was getting catty.)

"You insolent ingrate!"

"Condescending prat!"

"Ill-bred dolt!"

"Stuck up brat!"

"Excuse me."

"WHAT?" Aysel and I growled together, turning on our interrupter.

It was one of the waxy-looking guys in the suit. He was wearing sunglasses, was bald, and would have been a shoe in for the FBI or something if it weren't for his purplish complexion. "Sorry to interrupt, but we're running on a tight schedule. We *were* waiting for you to leave, Miss, but it doesn't appear that your argument will be ending anytime soon, so I'm sorry, but we're going to have to take you with," the suit guy said to me as several other suit guys gathered behind him.

"Huh?" I said.

"Run!" Aysel hissed.

"Too late," suit guy said, throwing what looked like a fist full of glitter in my face. I felt my body go limp, and I crashed to the ground in a heap before my eyes closed, and I abruptly and inexplicably fell asleep.

Magic, was my last coherent thought before I slipped off.

18

In Which I am kidnapped

When I woke up, I was splayed out over a couch. It was a really nice couch with cushy pillows. I actually forgot why I was asleep in the first place and snuggled deeper into the fleece blanket that was tucked around me.

Someone shifted nearby, and I rocketed upright, my hair sticking out at funny angles as I wrenched my neck to get a good look at my surroundings.

I was in what appeared to be a warehouse. It smelled faintly of motor oil and was decorated mostly in cement and metal. There were a few grimy windows, but I couldn't hear cars or any sounds of industry and traffic. I say appeared, though, because the ceiling wasn't very high, and the place was *heated.*

Aysel was sitting on a couch not far from mine. A blanket was neatly folded on the cushion next to him, and there were two bottles of water and an unopened sandwich by his feet. He was writing in a notebook, his fancy black pen moving a mile a minute. He flicked his eyes up and noticed I was awake.

"Feel free to eat," he said, motioning at my couch with the hand that held the pen. "They haven't poisoned it or anything," he said as

I peered over the edge of my couch to see that I too had a sandwich, water, and—oddly enough—a Twinkie.

"What happened?" I asked, combing my hair with my hands. That was when I noticed the tether. A metal, silk-lined bracelet was fastened around my wrist, and some sort of leather leash was attached to it, looping over the top of my couch. I lurched forward on my knees to peer over the back of my cushy furniture, following the leather line. It was tied around a metal support beam directly behind my couch, but the leash had enough length in it that I could probably go sit by Aysel if I wanted to.

"We have been kidnapped," Aysel announced in a clipped voice before he began writing in his notebook again.

"We? WE?" I shouted. "It's YOU! YOU got yourself kidnapped and me along with you!" I groaned. There was never any question in my mind that someone would kidnap Aysel. The bratty elf probably had it coming—I bet he insulted a fairy politician to his face or something. The question was why did *I* get dragged into it?

Rather than deny my accusation, Aysel nodded. "That is correct."

I scratched my head and arranged my fleece blanket around me, smugly noticing that Aysel had a tether too, and his was much shorter than mine. It was right about then that the situation hit me.

I had been kidnapped.

I didn't know why. I didn't know by whom, although it was probably safe to assume it was the work of magical beings. I didn't know how or when I would get home, or even if I would ever be able to leave.

I had been kidnapped.

I could feel the hysteria setting in as tears started to pool in my eyes. Why me? What about school? What would my parents think? And Fran! But what were these people going to do to me? Would they hurt me? I heaved a dry sob before hugging myself.

"Calm yourself, Morgan," Aysel dryly decreed from his couch. (I wanted to pinch him hard when he said that.) "There is no need to panic."

"WHAT? I have just been kidnapped, and you don't want me to

panic? This situation doesn't just call for panic. It calls for mass hysteria, hyperventilating, and lots and lots of tears!"

Aysel impatiently sighed and put his notebook aside. "Listen to me, human. We are perfectly safe. I expect we will be released in approximately forty-eight hours, not at all worse for the wear. Eat your dinner and go back to sleep if you insist on being hysteric. I have no desire to hear your whimpering sobs."

My mouth dropped open. "We've been *kidnapped,* and you want me to sleep?"

Even I couldn't believe Aysel had the gall to say that.

A door opened, and one of the purple-y, fake FBI agents entered the heated warehouse. "You're awake," he rumbled, adjusting his sunglasses in the florescent lighting. "Do you need anything? An extra blanket? Some chips?" he said, smiling at me with very white teeth.

My mouth remained open as I stared at him. It occurred to me that we might have been kidnapped by some freaky group of High Elf worshipers.

"I'm sorry, we can't let you go," fake FBI agent guy said. "But we have contacted the MBRC Administrator, and the negotiations are underway, so you can expect to be released by tomorrow or Sunday."

"What?" I squeaked. We were hostages? They were making a case against the MBRC Administrator?!

"I require the latest Magic Journal Sentinel," Aysel said, returning to scribbling notes on his notebook.

"Very well," our kidnapper said before turning back to me, hunkering down in front of my couch. "And you, Miss? Is there nothing you want?"

I licked my dry lips. "Why are you negotiating with the MBRC Administrator?" I croaked.

Pasty man tilted his head. "Who else would we talk to? Administrator Moonspell is the one holding up our imports contract."

"Huh?" I said.

"She's human. She hasn't got a clue about current events," Aysel said, infuriating even when being held hostage.

Pasty man frowned. "We knew she was human. We have to tell our King about her…eventually."

"King?" I parroted. "Imports contract?"

"They're goblins," Aysel loftily said, as though I were stupid for not noticing. "They've been wading through paperwork for months to try and get a contract that will allow them to import pixie powder and sell it for cosmetic and glamour purposes to MBRC members. They finally got it passed by the board, but the MBRC Administrator needs to sign off on it, and he's been dragging his feet."

"Yes," Pasty Man, aka a goblin, acknowledged. "You are our reminder to the Administrator that he needs to sign it."

"You're no goblin!" I accused. "You look perfectly human! Well, except for your waxy complexion."

"I am too a goblin!" Pasty Man said, outraged.

"Are not! You might be bald, but you have nice teeth, and you aren't at all disfigured! Plus, you don't look gnarly!"

"We have a good dental plan, and why would I look disfigured?"

Aysel rolled his eyes.

I shook my head. No way. No way could goblins look so… human! He had to be lying. Maybe he was only half goblin and didn't want to admit it. "Why would the MBRC Administrator care if you kidnapped a High Elf and a random human girl anyway?" I demanded, folding my arms.

"Because," Aysel dryly said, "he's my father."

I froze. "He's WHAT?"

For the second time that day, everything started clicking.

That's why everyone at the MBRC raved over the fact that I was teaching Asahi. I always thought they adored the sunny elf, but of *course* they would know about him if he was their leader's kid!

That also explained why Devin had to cut a deal with Aysel to get me back. As the son of the MBRC Administrator, he could ask his dad, and BAM, it was done.

Perhaps that was also why Aysel was so obsessed with his brother's education. Maybe he and Asahi were both aiming to be future leaders of the MBRC?

And finally…this was probably why Aysel is such a brat. How

could you be the son of a highly-esteemed administrator/politician and *not* be spoiled? (Asahi is the exception!)

I made a mouse noise in the back of my throat as I sank into the cushions of my couch.

"Miss, are you okay?" Pasty Man asked, anxiously leaning forward.

Just outside the warehouse someone roared, "**YOU DID WHAT?!**"

The warehouse door violently banged open, almost as though it were blown off its hinges.

"Oh," Pasty Man said, standing up. "The Goblin King. Someone must have told him we grabbed you as well."

I was still collapsed in my couch, on the verge of laughing my guts out because of the absurdity of the whole situation. I didn't notice the Goblin King until he was twenty feet away and storming closer.

Again I rocketed upright. "*Hunter?*"

My classmate froze, as though I had shot him. "*Morgan?*" he said, his amber-topaz eyes widening.

Aysel actually *tossed* his notebook aside. "You know each other?" he asked, his voice thunderous.

"Yeah, we're classmates," I said before turning on Hunter. I stood up and stalked the remaining few feet towards him. "*Goblin King,* Hunter? Really? Not a chance. I could see you being magical, but you're no goblin."

Hunter closed his eyes and rested two fingers on his temple. "This is what I hate about Fairy Tales. They're so stereotyped, people have a hard time accepting the truth."

"But you look human! You're not oddly colored, or short and scary looking! None of your guys have pig tusks or animal parts either!" I argued.

"Those are *European* Goblins you're thinking of," Hunter said, dropping his hand to look me in the eyes. "Those worthless gits were concerned about keeping the goblin lineage pure, so they did a lot of intermarrying and inbreeding. Didn't turn out so well for the bloodline. Because of *them,* everyone is convinced

Goblins are fat, ugly creatures," he said, disdain rolling off his words.

"But you're not even bald like the rest of your goblin guards," I protested.

Hunter rolled his eyes. "My men shave their heads because in our culture it is a symbol of fierceness. My hair is too gorgeous to be sheared off."

"Hunter," I said, reaching out to grasp the sleeve of his trench coat. "What is going on?"

Hunter sighed and twisted his wrist so he gently clasped my hand. His skin was soft but very cold. He squeezed my hand once and let me go. "Get that leash off her, *now*," Hunter said, his voice icy as he turned to address his men. "She's coming upstairs with us."

Aysel stirred behind us. "She will not leave my sight," he said.

Hunter and I turned around to stare at him.

Aysel was frowning, his eyes narrowing. "Morgan L. Fae is under the protection of my family. I will not allow you to take her without me."

Hunter rolled his eyes, unimpressed with Aysel's show of possession. "Very well, bring the elf with," he gestured as his men snapped my cuff off like they were breaking a pretzel.

I gaped at the show of strength before Hunter called. "Come along, Morgan. You haven't eaten dinner yet, right? Aren't you hungry?" he tempted, walking away from me.

I hurried to follow him as some of his cohorts released Aysel, who gathered up his notebook. The High Elf trailed behind at a more sedate pace, escorted by four goblins.

Hunter led me to a staircase, which I paused before going up. It occurred to me that I should try and run since I was free…even though it was *Hunter* who accidentally had me kidnapped, I still trusted him. He was still my friend. He wouldn't do anything to harm me. Plus, Aysel wasn't at all worried. He wasn't any crabbier than usual. So, I had a feeling things were okay, if not a little confusing.

"I'm serious, Hunter. What the hell is going on?" I cranked, climbing the stairs.

"I thought Logan explained the situation to you? I had Aysel kidnapped to remind his father that he needed to sign our contract," Hunter said, reaching the top of the stairs.

"Yeah, so Pasty Man mentioned. But did you really have to go to such an extreme?" I panted, hopping up the last step.

Hunter wrinkled his forehead in a display of royal confusion. "It is common practice," he said.

"Huh?"

"I believe this is the fourth time we have kidnapped Aysel, correct, Logan?" Hunter asked Pasty Man.

"It is, sir," Pasty Man/Logan confirmed.

"He's kidnapped all the time. We are hardly the only organization to use the Administrator's children as collateral. Let's see, the Chicago Banshee Confederation took him once or twice; so did the South End Satyrs. The Blood Fang vampire coven has taken him several times. I think the Chicago Cathedral Gnomes took him once. He told us last time he was here that we are his preferred kidnappers—which we should be. We let him do MBRC work and use our high-speed internet," Hunter said, watching Aysel's progression up the stairs.

Aysel, hearing us refer to him, glared up at Hunter with his beautiful moon eyes. "Ah, but his brother is kidnapped even more frequently. Isn't that right, Aysel?" Hunter called down to the High Elf.

"Who?" I blinked.

"His twin brother. Sunny guy, he's got a million-watt smile and dresses like a genie. We've never kidnapped him, but he's always in the MBRC Daily Sentinel," Hunter shrugged.

"*Asahi*!" I said. "People kidnap *Asahi*?" I wondered how they managed to do that. They probably didn't have hearts. "Wait, Asahi is your *twin*?" I gaped as Aysel and his guards joined us.

"Asahi, yes, that's the younger twin's name. It's insane how often he's kidnapped. I have to wonder if he's very smart. Not like I've met him though—*we* have never kidnapped him," Hunter said, strolling over to an elevator, pressing the up button.

"And who is *we*?" I asked, planting my hands on my hips.

"The Chicago goblins. Officially we're called Weller Goblin Enterprises, the Chicago branch," Hunter explained as the elevator opened with a chime.

Hunter got on, motioning for me to join him. I did, and so did Aysel and two of the goblin guards.

"Hunter, you can't seriously be the Goblin King. You're not even sixteen yet! I had to give you a ride to the store after school in September when we were getting supplies for Homecoming decorations!" I accused as Hunter selected a floor.

"You're right. I'm not the Goblin King of America. That's technically my father. However, I am the leader of the Goblins in Chicago. Everyone simply refers to me as the Goblin King because I run our organization's Chicago branch. So, as far as the employees here are concerned, I am the king. One of my older brothers runs Las Vegas, the other Los Angeles. My older sister has Boston."

"What about New York?" I dryly asked.

"Oh, that's my Father's base. Mother is fond of Times Square," he shrugged.

"You can't be part of the goblin mob!" I said, folding my arms across my chest. "You sit next to me in school. We did a biology project together last year. This has got to be a joke! Frey should have picked up on you being magical."

"Ah, the werewolf," Hunter smiled handsomely. "Yes. I did have a difficult time hiding it from him. In the end, all it took was a little extra persuasion, and the problem was solved," he shrugged as the elevator dinged and the doors opened. "We goblins are some of the most persuasive beings on the planet," Hunter told me before exiting the elevator.

I followed him. "You're good at debating?" I asked as Aysel and his guards followed me.

Hunter chuckled and smiled fondly at me. "Not that kind of persuasion, Morgan. Just as fairies have glamour, goblins have persuasion. Using our eyes and voices, we can influence anyone—

people and magical beings alike. We also have a rudimentary form of magic," he said, leading the way down a hallway. It looked pretty nice, almost how you would picture the hallway of a ritzy hotel. It didn't resemble the parking garage at all.

I stopped next to Hunter, who paused in front of an ornate-looking door. "Wait, is that why no one clearly remembers you?"

Hunter nodded and opened the door. "Yes. In order to remain undercover, I use my power of persuasion to persuade people not to notice me, or even not to befriend me."

"Why would you do that?" I asked. (That explained why Hunter was always alone, even though he was good-looking and decent—well, besides the whole goblin mob thing.)

Hunter shrugged. "I go to a human school because it was a requirement Mother set when Father gave me the Chicago branch. As it is unwise to stick out in a human environment, I try to cloak myself," he said before sweeping into the room.

"I bet that persuasion stuff comes in handy. No wonder teachers *never* call on you," I complained, hushing when I entered the room.

It had to be Hunter's office. It was carpeted with plush, red carpet and expensive-looking rugs. The room was lined with ornate bookshelves that held rows upon rows of books and magical items. There was a gas fireplace, a flat screen TV with a surround sound system, a black leather couch, and three laptops. There was a *huge*, ornate desk positioned directly in front of the window—which took up most of the back wall. A black desktop computer, a cell phone, and an office phone were meticulously placed on the desk. "Whoa, sweet room," I said, turning around.

Hunter didn't acknowledge my comment and instead spoke to his men. "I don't want that elf in here. Put him in the conference room across from us. Fasten him to the wall again and make sure he's fed. And remove that wretched truth-spell necklace he keeps on him. I don't want a repeat of the last time we kidnapped him. That will be all," Hunter said, dismissing them.

"If you harm her, you will pay," Aysel warned, his eyes flickering to my face.

Hunter looked amused. "You needn't worry, Moonspell. I know

her far better than you do. Good night," he said before closing his office door in Aysel's face.

I found the situation somewhat amusing—Aysel being put in his place was something I had never seen before—but unlike those stupid twits that are the usual heroines of paranormal fiction, I was street smart. It did *not* amuse me that I was alone in a room with a goblin who could pretty much persuade me to do whatever he wanted. It was actually a little frightening. Even though I knew Hunter, finding out about his powers was a little disconcerting.

Hunter strode across the room and plopped down in a chair behind his desk.

"What were you talking about with Aysel and a repeat of last time?" I asked, nonchalantly wandering closer to the door as I glanced out the window. The sky was black; it was probably late in the evening.

"Aysel is his father's son. Being a true politician, he wears a truth necklace. It bespells anyone he talks to so they can only tell truths," Hunter dryly said, texting someone with his smart phone. "During one of his previous stays with my organization, one of my men ended up spilling the story of his love life. It was quite embarrassing."

A *truth necklace*? No wonder I couldn't keep my mouth shut and play nice whenever I was around that brat! I was being spelled to tell the truth! "That *jerk*," I hissed.

"Morgan. I have very patiently answered your every question. I would like you to do the same for me. Tell me how you know Aysel Moonspell and how you came to be aware of magical beings," Hunter said, folding his hands on his lap.

I didn't think Hunter was persuading me to tell him. I didn't feel compelled to explain everything to him…but a part of me yearned to dump about the MBRC and explain it to an outside person.

So, I leaned against a bookshelf and spilled my guts. "It started with Frey and my substitute Spanish teacher…"

About fifteen minutes into my story—right when I was telling Hunter about the cyclopes—a goblin entered the room, pushing a silver cart that held a steaming plate of shrimp alfredo.

"Eat," Hunter said as the goblin set the plate before me.

I paused my story and suspiciously poked at the food with my fork and knife. Hunter rolled his eyes with noble grace and plucked the fork from my fingers, scooped up some of the pasta, and ate it himself.

"See; it's fine. Now continue. You were championing the cyclopes?" Hunter said, once again folding his hands across his lap.

My story went on for a full hour. I told Hunter about everything: Frey, teaching Asahi, the Cuckoo Ward, the museum fieldtrip, anything at all magical.

When I finished, Hunter thoughtfully nodded. "I am disappointed in myself," he announced.

"Why?" I asked.

"Because I knew the werewolf was at our school, and I knew you were friends with him, but I never guessed he had blown his cover. I also knew the Pooka briefly visited our school and that a human was teaching Asahi, but I never made the connection," he sighed.

"So, what now?" I asked after several minutes of silence. "You're going to release me, right?"

"Yes. But unfortunately, I can't right now. Not while I'm negotiating with Administrator Moonspell," Hunter said with a handsome smile.

I did not smile back. "What do you mean?"

"I simply can't, Morgan. If you leave, Aysel will flip out—not to mention the administrator will complain that we've released you and not his son," Hunter said, his voice as sweet as honey.

"That's a load of crap, Hunter," I said.

"See, that's why we're friends. Because it is impossible for me to persuade you," Hunter chuckled.

I was momentarily surprised. "What?"

"I was serious when I said I persuade everyone at school to see through me, to ignore me. You were the only one I could never persuade. It's not completely unheard of. Generally, humans are the easiest for us to use our powers on, but there is the occasional person that is immune," Hunter shrugged.

"I don't care. I want to go home, Hunter," I said, my voice cracking.

"Morgan, I *can't*. Okay? I really do see you as my friend. You're my *only* friend. Your stay here will not be unpleasant, so can't you just wait?" Hunter asked. Although his face was open and sweet, his eyes glittered like a tiger's.

I had to remind myself that Hunter wasn't just my friend and classmate now. He was also a leader who had an agenda. But perhaps it was wrong to judge him on these facts alone? I remembered all the projects we completed together, all the times we talked in class.

"Two days," I said. "I *will* be back in school by Monday. So, I'll give you two days," I said.

Hunter looked amused, and I realized it was probably ridiculous. I was his captive, and I was the one making the demands.

"Thank you, Morgan," Hunter said with what sounded like sincerity. "I'm sure I'll have things cleared up with the administrator by then. Do you need to call your parents? You could tell them you're staying at a friend's house. It wouldn't be completely untrue."

"No," I said with certainty. "I'm sure Frey has already come up with a cover story. He's obsessive with details like that. If I call them now, I'm sure I'll just blow the whole thing to bits," I paused. "Can I have my purse back though?"

"Of course. It will be in your room. I have already made sleeping arrangements for you, unless you wanted to be with Aysel?" Hunter asked.

"Fat chance," I snorted, standing up. "But I want to see him before I go to bed. Can I go?"

"Of course. You have free run of the place. Logan is guarding Aysel's door. If you need anything or would like to be shown to your room, ask him."

"Right. Thanks and good night," I said, exiting his office. Sure enough, Logan the Pasty Man was standing outside a closed door that was kitty corner from Hunter's office. "Hello," I greeted him, feeling a little guilty that I had just eaten and talked for an hour without thinking of Aysel and his wellbeing.

Then, I opened the door and instantly stopped feeling bad for him.

Aysel was set up on the conference room table, a laptop propped open and sitting on the table in front of him. He had shed his human/model clothes and was back in his elf-like robe attire. He also had several open newspapers scattered around him and a plate of pasta. (Apparently goblins liked Italian food?)

Clearly, he was comfortable.

"You have no sense of urgency, do you?" I complained, collapsing in one of the chairs circling the conference table.

"What I have is a lot of time on my hands and a lot of work to be done," Aysel said, typing away on his borrowed computer.

The tether was back around his hand. It was tied to the wall with a long length in it, but I suspected Aysel wasn't planning on leaving anyway. There was a red leather couch that had several fluffy blankets piled on it—most likely meant to be his bed for the night.

"Aysel, how serious is this?" I asked, setting my hands flat on the table before resting my head on top of them. "How worried and concerned do I need to be?"

Aysel actually stopped typing. He hesitated and set his computer aside before fixing all of his attention on me. "I don't know," he admitted. "Normally, the situation is not at all dangerous. It is bothersome, but not entirely unwarranted. My father can be rude and ill-mannered by purposely ignoring contracts that need to be signed, so these types of situations are expected for me.... But I'm not sure about now," he carefully said, keeping his voice low. "No one has ever before been kidnapped with me, and the fact that you personally know Hunter Weller is troubling. I would say based on the past history that there is nothing to worry about, and we will be released shortly."

"But?" I asked, hearing the hesitation in his voice.

"My father once told me none of the Wellers have friends. They have only themselves and their employees. The fact that Hunter calls you a friend is...unheard of," Aysel shifted and muttered. "Perhaps I am being overly sensitive."

"Asahi would be so proud," I grinned.

Aysel frowned but did not look very crabby.

"I think I'm going to sleep. What time is it?"

"A little after midnight. You were out of it for a while after the goblins grabbed you," Aysel said, returning to his computer as I stood and made my way over to the door.

"Okay, thanks. 'Night, Aysel," I said, placing my hand on the doorknob.

"You're leaving?" Aysel asked, his voice incredulous.

"Um, yeah," I said, turning around. "Hunter said I get my own room."

"But…you should stay here," Aysel said, at a loss for words. "I'm the one they need. You should remain with me. Besides, if anyone tries to harm you, I will be able to protect you."

I snorted. "What could you do? You're tied to a wall! Besides, there's no bed in here, and I'm not going to lose a night of sleep just because your father is arrogant. Good night," I said, exiting the room.

Now, I know almost every teenage girl reading this right now is yelling at me on Aysel's behalf because he was being sweet and asking me to stay, but let's get real, ladies. When you're kidnapped, it's not time to be romantic; it's time to be practical. Plus, based on my previous interactions with the elf, I was willing to bet it wasn't really that he wanted me to stay with him so much as it was some stupid elf pride thing. (Let's not forgot how he told Hunter that I was under his protection. Whatever that meant.)

I was *not* going to make the mistake I made with Frey and get all sappy, even if I didn't have Brett Patterson to obsess about.

"That's one good thing about today," I said as Logan showed me to my room.

"And what is that, Miss?" Logan asked.

"I totally forgot that my best friend is dating my crush."

19

The Goblin Mob

I pretty much collapsed in bed as soon as Logan got me to my room. (Well, I did check my cell phone, but the battery was dead, so that did zippo for me.) I was *exhausted*, probably from the whirlwind of emotions I had experienced that day.

I woke up the following morning, noted that my room was almost as spectacularly decorated as Hunter's office, and whined and complained to the goblin outside my door until he showed me to a bathroom.

After freshening up—I won't tell you how badly I wanted a shower—I decided I would grace Aysel with my presence and eat breakfast with him.

When I swept into his cell, he was—surprise, surprise—working on the laptop.

I cast an accusing eye to the red couch where the blankets were still neatly folded. "Don't tell me you stayed up working the whole night!" I said, plopping down in a chair.

"I didn't," Aysel stiffly said.

"Right. Logan, what's for breakfast?" I asked when the goblin pushed a silver cart into the room. (As you can tell, I woke up feeling quite a bit more refreshed and confident than I felt going to bed the previous night.)

"Waffles and bacon, Miss Morgan," Logan said, setting a plate in front of me before uncovering it.

"Wow, I love your chef," I said, staring at my magnificently golden waffles. They were topped with whipped cream and chopped nuts. A little bowl of fresh strawberries was nestled into the side. They smelled liked melted butter and cinnamon.

"I will be sure to pass on your compliments, Miss Morgan," Logan said, handing Aysel a similarly beautiful plate of waffles.

I popped a piece of bacon in my mouth and purred. I made a mental note to invite myself over to Hunter's place for dinner if I got out of this mess with our friendship still intact.

"Aysel, you have to eat this. It's like heaven on a platter," I said, munching on another piece of bacon.

"You exaggerate everything," Aysel said as he set his computer aside.

"I do not. You're just stuffy and unappreciative."

Aysel raised his eyebrows before he delicately cut into his waffle. "Openly insulting me even when I'm not wearing my truth necklace? How very daring of you!"

"I wanted to talk to you about that. A truth necklace is cheating. I nearly spilled a secret of Asahi's because of that stupid thing," I said, jabbing my knife in the High Elf's direction.

"What, that Asahi is a flaming buffoon for Kadri? Please, I already knew that," Aysel scoffed.

"Even if you did, Asahi didn't want me to tell you. I nearly choked myself while trying to keep from telling you—oh, MAN, these waffles are perfection!"

"Hn," Aysel said, eating his food. "Will you continue to tutor my brother when you return to the MBRC?"

"Yeah. Why wouldn't I?" I asked, deeply engrossed with my precious waffles.

"I was afraid this experience might have something of a dampening effect on your desire to be involved with the MBRC."

"Truthfully? No. I like the MBRC, and I love all the friends I've made there. That's not to say I'm going to be involved with it forever…but right now I'm happy. Does that make sense?" I asked, looking up from my food.

Aysel was smiling. It was the barest twitch of his lips, but the way the corners of his moon eyes crinkled, and the way his entire manner seemed to soften actually froze me. I nearly choked on a piece of waffle that I was in the process of swallowing. He was just so…*beautiful.*

"Yes, I understand," Aysel said in what could be mistaken as gentle voice.

I curled my toes in my shoes and felt a warm feeling in my stomach before abruptly pushing my waffles aside and slamming my head into the table. "OW," I declared after my forehead hit the surface with a resounding crack.

"….Are you well?" Aysel asked.

"Yeah, I'm fine," I said, rubbing my stinging forehead before pulling my plate back in front of me. "I was just reminding myself of something," I grumbled.

I would *not* fall for a magical being. *I would not!* No matter how handsome they might be when they smile! I wouldn't!

"I worry for your mental stability," Aysel said.

"Me, too," I agreed. "Are you going to eat your strawberries?"

"Yes."

"Stingy."

After eating, Aysel returned to his work, leaving me bored out of my skull, so I wandered to Hunter's office. The goblin leader was also working on his computer, but his flat screen was fitted with the newest Xbox system. I'm not really a gamer, but he had one of those dancing games, so I amused myself with the video game system for a while. I stopped for lunch—which was pizza that I swear to you was the best I have ever tasted in my life—and hijacked one of Hunter's computers to check my email.

Unfortunately, I had never bothered to get Frey's email, and I didn't know any of my students' emails either, so in the end, I mostly ended up watching stupid YouTube clips until I upgraded and commandeered his TV.

"How are the negotiations coming?" I asked Hunter, my feet propped up on his coffee table as I stared at the TV. (He had Netflix, so I was taking advantage of it and catching up on some TV shows.)

"Agreeably, you could say. I expect everything will be settled by noon tomorrow," Hunter said.

"If it's so agreeable, why not now?" I asked, turning around so I could peer at my classmate over the couch.

"Because Administrator Moonspell has agreed to sign the document, but he wants to lower the amount of pixie powder we can import, which is not happening," Hunter smiled at me.

"Hm," I said, resting my chin on the back of the couch.

"Don't worry about it. Enjoy your time playing. Besides, you didn't have any homework this weekend, did you?" Hunter asked, leaning back in his chair.

"I did," I confessed. "But it's in my backpack, which I left behind at the information desk in the MBRC. I hope Corona holds onto it for me," I frowned.

"No matter. When we go to school, I can go to your teachers with you and persuade them they need to give you extra time," Hunter shrugged.

I was aghast. "No way. That's cheating, not to mention unfair to all my classmates!"

Hunter smiled at me the way I smile at my family cat when he does something stupid or clumsy. "You have an irregularly straight moral compass, Morgan."

"What, you don't want to be friends with such a morally correct person?" I asked, draping myself on his wonderful couch, resting my head on the armrest.

"No," Hunter fondly said, standing up. "Quite the opposite actually," he said, moving around his desk. He stopped right behind the couch and propped his hands on the edge. "I find your integrity amusing."

"You make me sound like I'm your adorably chubby pet guinea pig," I said, my eyes fastened on the TV.

"I bet you'd make a cute guinea pig," Hunter considered.

"You aren't going to find out!" I shot, twisting on the couch so I could stare up at the goblin leader.

He leaned over the back of the couch, grinning. "What, you don't want to drink water from a bottle and eat guinea pig pellets?"

"I would get out of my cage and poop *everywhere*, just to tick you off," I promised. Hunter stared down at me before he broke into a laugh—which was a rich, melodious sound. I joined him as soon as I realized how ridiculous the conversation was.

Hunter chuckled. "How did we get on this topic again?"

"Not a clue," I sighed.

We were silent for a few moments, and my attention started to wander back to the TV until Hunter spoke again. "Whatever had you so upset on Friday?"

"Huh?" I asked, jerking my eyes back to him.

"In class on Friday, you seemed…troubled," Hunter described.

"Oh," I said, remembering my epiphany about the MBRC boys and that I could **not** fall for them. "It was nothing. It was just a rough day."

"That best friend of yours, Fran, I think her name is? She's dating someone now isn't she?" Hunter asked.

"Yeah, how did you know?" I asked, my heart squeezing a little.

"It was pretty hard to miss. She has him completely whipped. She was looking for you after school and refused to let him be within eyesight of her in case she found you. Do you have a restraining order out against him?" Hunter asked.

I laughed. "No. It's…well…it's complicated."

"Ah," Hunter said, pausing. "So, was he the one I was briefly considering eradicating when you showed up to class looking so troubled?"

He wasn't, well, not completely. I mean, it was because of him that I really had to watch my step around so… "Yeah, sort of," I said, deciding to come clean. "I used to have a massive crush on him."

"*Oh,*" Hunter said, his voice going awkward. (Ladies, the best way to get a guy off a topic is to start talking about your feelings. Remember that.) "Um, your friend is a—," he started.

"I told her to date him. It's fine. The whole thing was absolutely ridiculous. I'm happy for her, for them. It just made my life considerably more complicated," I said, trying to think of a way to change topics. "So, who is your chef?"

"Logan told me you find your meals delicious," Hunter grinned. "There are two chefs, actually. A goblin and a cookie elf. They're married."

"A *cookie elf?*" I asked, disbelief coloring my voice as I scrunched my face.

"Yeah. You know the Keebler cookies, the one with the little elf guy with the green jacket? The cookie elves were the inspiration for that company," Hunter explained.

"A cookie elf," I repeated.

"Yep."

"...You are *so* spoiled."

"But don't you want to come visit me now?" Hunter kindly offered with a smile that was too charming.

"Yeah, but you'll have to get a new house," I informed him. "I feel I would associate this place with the bad memory of being kidnapped."

"I didn't know playing Xbox and watching TV was so mentally scarring," Hunter chided.

"It is when one is not in the comforts of her own home," I said with a sage nod.

Hunter chuckled and leaned farther over the couch, until our faces were probably only a foot apart. "Fine, I'll buy a new house. But only if you promise to come over. Having to shuffle my staff back and forth between my branch office and the house will be quite bothersome."

"Only if the cookie elf and goblin chef come with."

"Of course," Hunter said, reaching out to gently flick one of my bangs out of my face.

At that moment, one of his goblin men opened the door and

froze when he spotted us. Instantly, I slid down the couch and away from Hunter, grabbing my heart as I realized I had been flirting with my *captor*. WHAT WAS WRONG WITH ME?!

Hunter sighed and stood up straight, coldly frowning at the intruding goblin, who looked like he was trying to decide if he should back out and pretend he never came in or throw himself on the ground and grovel.

"What is it?" Hunter said, not bothering to mask the irritation in his voice.

"I have the newest negotiation from Administrator Moonspell," the goblin said in a surprisingly high, nervous voice as he held out the sheet of paper.

Hunter took it from him and started reading over the contract. "He's starting to break. He's no longer demanding that we only fly it in from—,"

CRACK!

"OW!" I declared, rubbing my stinging forehead, which I had just slammed against the coffee table—yes, on purpose.

"Miss Morgan, are you alright?" the goblin guard asked, alarmed.

"What did you do?" Hunter asked, his eyebrows rising up in arches as he turned his glittering eyes on me.

"Just reminding myself of something," I said through gritted teeth. "I'm going to go now. Yes. Goodbye," I said, my teeth still clenched as I rolled off the couch and stood up, unsteadily walking out of the room.

Internally, I was seething. How could I be so *stupid*? What was wrong with me? First, I was thinking that the cold, arrogant Aysel was sweet and gentle, and now I was sort of flirting with Hunter—who might be my friend, but let's not forget that he still is my *kidnapper*.

"I need to get out of here," I hissed, throwing open the door to my room. "I *have* to get back to normal society!"

After an exquisite luncheon on Sunday, I was ready to go. And I don't just mean mentally; I mean physically, too. I had my jacket and purse in a pile by the door of Hunter's office. I had said goodbye to all the goblin staff, and I pretty much hovered in the hallway between Aysel's conference room and Hunter's office. (I figured it was also the safest spot for me and my delicate sense of balance around those two.)

I was absolutely elated when Aysel was taken into Hunter's office around 2:00 p.m.

"Great news, Moonspell. Your father is signing the contract as we speak. My men are preparing a car to drop you off at Union Station," Hunter said, his hands clasped behind his back as he strolled towards Aysel and me.

Aysel's stance relaxed, and he nodded.

"Thank you for being our *guest*. I hope we don't have to run into each other for a long time," Hunter said.

"Yes! I can finally go home," I said, my eyes shutting with relief as I raised my hands over my head.

"Not quite," Hunter said.

"What?" I asked, dropping my arms while snapping my eyes open.

"Releasing you wasn't part of the agreement," Hunter smiled.

"***WHAT***?" I hissed, the hair on the back of my neck prickling.

Aysel tensed next to me.

"Administrator Moonspell agreed to sign the contract if we released his son. He never stipulated anything about the human," Hunter shrugged.

"You didn't tell him about her, did you?" Aysel growled. "I should have known better than to trust that you goblins had any sense of honor."

"That's the thing. I did tell your dear daddy about Morgan. I believe your sunny twin made a big deal about it. But Administrator Moonspell never mentioned her in our talks. Indeed, he doesn't seem to care what we do with her," Hunter said with what looked like a harmless smile. "So, I've decided to keep her."

I felt sucker-punched in the stomach. How could he say such a cruel thing while *smiling* at me? "Hunter, I'm not a pet."

"I know," Hunter carelessly shrugged. "But having you around is interesting."

"Are you INSANE? I'm a person, Hunter! I have a family—I have a life! I'm not your plaything!" I shouted.

Hunter's smile did not leave his face, and he watched me with his glittering tiger eyes.

"Hunter, you're joking, right? You have to let me go! You said you would!" I said.

"See, that's the thing, Morgan. My morals are not as high as yours. I may honor all business deals I make, but I hardly extend those kinds of scruples to my personal life."

"You were LYING?" I yelled.

I was enraged and frightened. I felt like the carpet had been pulled out from underneath my feet. Breathing was a struggle.

This was *Hunter*. I considered him a friend!

"I'll never forgive you!" I promised. "I'm going to hate you for the rest of my life!" I said as angry tears leaked out of the corners of my eyes.

"I'm not leaving without her," Aysel declared.

I swallowed my despair and actually turned to look at the High Elf. His shoulders were drawn back, and he had taken a step forward so he was slightly in front of me, as though he could shield me from Hunter. His chin was raised, and I could feel power radiate from him.

"Get off your high horse, Moonspell. If your father didn't claim her, there's no way you can say she's under your family's protection, even if she tutors your baby brother."

"I. Don't. Care," Aysel said, his silver eyes were spitting sparks. "If my family does not claim her, then I will. I am *not* leaving her with you."

There was something behind his words that I couldn't quite understand.

Hunter seemed to. He raised his eyes and tilted his head to the side, trying to gauge the High Elf. "I don't believe it," he said. "Aysel Moonspell is defending someone, and not out of personal or political gain. Will wonders never cease?" he said, not at all affected by the elf's rage.

"I will not leave this facility without Morgan Fae," Aysel vowed.

Hunter smirked. "You are not in a position to make that decision, Moonspell," he said before turning his attention to the goblins stationed behind us. "Take the elf to his room. In ten minutes, you may take him to the parking garage—Donovan will be there with a car—then take him to Union Station."

"And what about Miss Morgan?" one of the goblins asked.

Hunter hesitated, I could see a pin-prick of indecision in his eyes.

"Please, Hunter," I begged.

Hunter shook his head. "Take her to her room. I will drop by to speak to her after the elf has been taken care of."

"NO! Let go of me!" I screamed, stamping on a guard goblin's foot when he reached for my wrist.

I don't know how he managed to do it, but the goblin gently toted me to my room, even though I was scratching at him and kicking him every step of the way.

Aysel oddly returned to his room without a fuss, looking absolutely thunderous as his single guard led him to his room.

"Aysel!" I shouted before I was forced into my room. The door was shut behind me, but I didn't hear a lock click into place. That meant the guard was standing there.

I let myself scream and cry with fury, covering my eyes with my hands.

After a moment, I seized the first thing I could find that I couldn't possibly use in the future for my escape—because I would escape from here—which was a porcelain horse figurine. (I know. Why a goblin decorated with a horse figurine, I'll never know.) I flung it against the door where it shattered with a satisfying crunch.

I resolved to find an item that was bigger and even more breakable when something rumbled—like food left in the running microwave for too long—and the ground shook beneath my feet.

"What the heck was that?" I shivered, picking my way around the broken figurine to open my door and peer outside.

Down the hallway, I could see goblin guards surrounding Aysel's door…which was on fire and smoldering. I'm not kidding. One of the goblins was splayed out in front of it, completely unconscious.

"He got Yulan after he removed the tether! Check to make sure he's still breathing and prepare for a fight. The elf has locked himself in the room and is using his magic!" Logan shouted.

"Stay inside," the guard outside my door ordered before pushing the door shut on me.

This time, there was the tell-tale click of the lock sliding into place, but I tried twisting the doorknob anyway. Nothing.

Aysel was fighting. If he could last against the guards, I was sure he would come for me. I needed to be prepared. "Maybe I could find a weapon…or something to throw at the guards," I said, starting to rummage around my room.

I came up pretty much empty handed. The only stuff in my room was heavy furniture, an alarm clock, and the room decorations—none of which were porcelain, but were big and made of brass. They would be like a brick weight!

I sucked air in through my teeth. "Come on, *think*! There has to be something here I could use!" I said, tapping my foot on the thick carpeting.

Shortly after that, five explosions went off from different ends of the building. They were loud—much louder than Aysel's little display of magic—and they rocked the ground, sending me sprawling.

"That wasn't Aysel," I said before an alarm pierced the air, wailing continuously.

I could hear running outside and lots of shouting. I hefted myself to my feet and pounded my fist on the door.

"What's going on? Someone let me out!" I shouted, my hand turning red. "Anybody? Help me!" I shouted through the door.

It was about five minutes before anyone opened my door, and when it finally did pop open, I was very surprised to see it was Hunter who opened it.

His face was white, his forehead wrinkled. "Morgan, come with me. We—,"

"Fat chance!" I snarled, pushing him away from me. He stumbled one step backwards, but still reached out and clasped my hand. I tried to yank it back. "I'm not going anywhere with you!"

"You don't understand. We're under attack. I have to get you out of here!" Hunter said, hauling me down the hallway.

I dug my heels into the carpeting so Hunter had to drag me, but I stumbled and fell when another explosion rocked the ground. That was when I heard the distinct sound of guns shooting.

"You weren't lying," I said through numb lips as Hunter helped me stand.

"Yes, come on!" Hunter agreed, pulling me after him.

I could still hear the guns as Hunter ducked into an enclosed staircase and led me down. His grip on my hand was uncomfortably tight, and his face was like a carved rock.

"What's going on Hunter. Who did you tick off?" I asked.

"I'm not entirely sure," Hunter admitted as we hurried down the endless stairs. "My brothers occasionally send a task force to make a raid just to make sure I don't get soft, but I don't think this is them. Guns aren't a goblin's style," Hunter considered. He didn't flinch when there was another explosion and the lights briefly flickered. (I did.)

"But it doesn't matter who it is," Hunter said. "I will take care of it. Logan is waiting for you; he'll take you home."

"You're letting me go?" I said, hope welling up inside of me as I jumped to clear the last step.

"Yes."

"Just like that?" I double checked as we left the staircase and popped out at the far end of the warehouse/parking garage.

"I may want to monopolize you, Morgan, but that is only because I genuinely like you. I would rather send you home than see you injured in my fight," Hunter said, somewhat distracted as he looked up and down the empty lot. "Where is Logan?" he muttered.

"Wait! What about Aysel? Did you let him go, too?" I cried,

remembering that the High Elf had championed me for a brief moment.

Hunter rolled his eyes. "He'll be fine, I assure you. Anyone who tries to hurt him probably has a death wish. Come on," Hunter said, starting for the far end of the room.

"I'm not leaving without him," I stubbornly said, causing Hunter to stop and turn around to stare at me.

"What is *up* with you two? Do you get separation anxiety?" he snarled before starting off again.

I tripped after him. "No, we just have straight moral compasses," I snidely said. "Hunter, you can't just leave him up there!"

"I assure you, Aysel Moonspell can take care of himself. Besides, in a situation like this, I don't care what happens to him. Getting you out is my first priority," Hunter grunted and stopped by a large keypad implanted in the wall.

He dropped my hand and started typing in passwords and codes while I nervously sniffed the air, which smelled like smoke and gunpowder.

I wandered a few steps away so I could start pacing back and forth.

The MBRC had really turned my life upside down.

When I started my sophomore year, if someone had told me I would be involved in a goblin mob raid, I would have recommended a good psychiatrist. But now? All I could do was pace and rely on Hunter to get me out.

I didn't like feeling so helpless.

I went from feeling helpless to feeling absolutely terrified when a hole was blasted into the wall of the warehouse/parking garage.

"Hunter," I uneasily said, standing up from the crouch I had dropped into as chunks of cement rolled across the ground.

Two people stepped through the large hole, the dust swirling around them like fog. They were both tall and muscled. They both wore fatigues, and they both held handguns.

One of them—a female—held a walkie talkie to her mouth. "The Princess is spotted. We're on the lower level garage. The

Goblin King is with her, out," she said before sliding the machine into her pocket.

Her companion, a giant hulking male, slid his guns into holsters.

"Hunter," I whimpered, taking a stumbling step backwards.

The two soldiers crouched on the ground before leaping forward.

I gasped and grabbed my throat when both of them transformed before my eyes as they dashed towards us.

The man changed into a lion, a huge lion. Bigger than any one I had seen at a zoo! The female became a black leopard, as sleek and fast as lightning.

They were charging towards *me*.

I screamed and braced myself for impact, but Hunter stepped in front of me, his fists glowing green. He slammed his hands on the floor, and the ground in front of us exploded into a sea of bright green flames.

Rudimentary magic, huh?

"Morgan, the door to your left is open. Exit through it, and get out of here. You're in Chicago—look for the Sear's Tower and head for it. That should get you close to Union Station," Hunter hissed.

"Hunter—" I started. I never got the chance to finish.

The two soldier-cats burst through the flames together, moving like a matched team.

Hunter shouted, brandishing his flaming fists at the cats, but to our surprise, the cats dove around him, one going to his left one going to his right.

At that moment, they transformed again, landing next to me as humans. Before I knew it, the girl was crouched in front of me, facing Hunter, aiming her handguns at him. lion guy scooped me up in his arms, smashing my face into his brick-like chest.

"The Princess has been recovered. I repeat, the Princess has been recovered. Over," the girl shouted into her walkie talkie as lion guy stood, easily lifting me like I was a doll.

Hunter swung around to stare at me, looking horrified as lion guy and panther girl made a break for it, tearing back towards the hole they had blown in the wall.

"HUNTER!" I shouted.

"Morgan!"

"Take care of him," lion guy ordered.

"Got it," panther girl said, reaching into her pocket before tossing what looked like a *grenade* at Hunter.

Whatever it was, it exploded in a shower of sparkles, burning white hot.

20

My Rescuers

I screamed as loud as I could when the cat team hopped through the hole in the wall, popping out in a hallway. "I was just kidnapped! I will not be kidnapped again!" I vowed, pounding my fists on lion guy's head. "I will go home! This can't be happening!"

"Calm down—Ow!—Miss Fae, calm down! We're not kidnapping you!" lion guy winced as he carried me down the hallway.

"Oh, yeah? Then what are you doing?" I shot, viciously ripping at his hair.

"OW! We're here to rescue you!"

I paused, considering the possibility as leopard girl ran next to us. "No way! Liars! I'm so sick of being lied to by you magical beings!" I said before pounding my fists on him.

"Miss Fae, the cyclopes sent us," leopard girl said. "We spoke with their representative, Nickolas Vontreba."

I paused. "Nick?" I asked.

"Yes!" lion guy said, desperation lining his voice as he winced.

I hesitated. My involvement with the cyclopes wasn't really publicized. Most people knew me as Asahi's tutor. There was a high probability they were telling the truth.

"Oh. Okay," I said, nearly biting my tongue when lion guy jarred me as he jumped over an unconscious goblin.

I screamed when someone dropped from the ceiling directly above us, swooping down in the shape of a bat before transforming mid-air into a human.

He performed a flip and hit the ground running, keeping pace with us.

"This is the Princess?" bat boy asked.

"It is," leopard girl acknowledged. "Where are the others?"

"Gathering in the foyer. Another group of assorted magical beings has broken into the building. Kit Fox is assessing whether they're friend or foe," bat boy said.

"Great. That will be our retreat point," leopard girl said.

"The Goblin King?" bat boy asked.

"Subdued," the hulky guy carrying me said.

"For now," leopard girl frowned. "I doubt he really went down that easily," she said as we rounded a corner.

A large mountain cat was waiting there, sitting on its haunches in front of a closed door. He stood and transformed into a human, a guy, as we drew close. "Ah, yes, the rescued princess!" he said, grinning at me.

"She's not rescued yet. We still have to get out of here," lion guy said. He gave no sign of fatigue even though he had just carried me for several minutes while jogging. (He wasn't even breathing heavily!)

"Stay focused; we're going in," leopard girl said, digging her guns out of their holsters.

"Why does everyone keep calling me princess?" I asked, tightening my grip around lion guy's neck.

"It's your code name. We picked it out because we're being paid a princess' ransom to get you home," the guy who was previously a mountain lion winked as the doors opened.

Inside was mass chaos.

More of the military soldier people were inside, shooting at goblins if they weren't involved in hand-to-hand combat. However, rather than spraying the goblin guards with bullets, they appeared to be hitting them with paintball pellets. A soldier would shoot, and a goblin would yelp and be spattered with a thick, colorful spray.

"...What are you shooting them with?" I asked, watching one of the goblins get nailed with a cloud of pink paint. The goblin sneezed and fell to the ground, his eyes tearing up.

"A charmed mixture of paint and pepper spray. It's a bugger to get off," mountain lion guy grinned.

"Nice," I admired.

"Gather up in a cross A type formation," lion guy said, shifting me in his arms. "We need to make sure the Princess is properly guarded."

"We really shouldn't be bringing her in here," leopard girl frowned as she and the other two males arranged themselves around lion guy and me, forming a wall.

My mouth dropped as a white wolf loped past us. "FREY?" I shouted.

The wolf froze before swinging around, turning into a silver-haired boy as he stood. Yes, indeed, it was Frey.

"FREY!" I shouted, squirming in lion guy's arms.

"Morgan! You're alright!" he grinned. His eyes bugged out of his skull when he noticed my entourage. "The Shadows are here for *you*?" he said before getting distracted with a goblin.

As Frey knocked the goblin down, my eyes swept past him. On the far side of the room, I could see more of my friends and students. Esmeralda was there, holding a goblin in a headlock. The Sphinx was there as well, standing on top of a fallen goblin as she spoke to Esmeralda and a tiny little fox that had absolutely gigantic ears.

There was a small, spindly looking canine that looked like a coyote pretending to be a wolf—that *had* to be Frank. Even though he looked nervous and had his tail clamped between his legs, Frank leaped at a Goblin, knocking him to the ground.

I could see the drab fairies and their elf friend. They appeared to be doing some sort of magic that was rendering the goblins' powers of persuasion useless.

Perseus and his pony pals were there, swinging and kicking at any goblin that came near them. Westfall was with them, sending goblins flying as he bashed into them. (I had a hard time believing sweet Westfall could be so violent!)

I hardly noticed as my shape-shifting guards waded through the onslaught, heading towards my friends.

"Sunglasses, boys," leopard girl reminded her comrades before flicking a pair of shades over her eyes. The men followed her example (lion guy had to shuffle me around to find his), and I noticed that the rims of their glasses glowed briefly after they slipped them on.

A group of four goblins hurried towards us, their suits still neatly pressed although they had ditched their sunglasses. Their eyes were brilliant shades of colors that were wrong for human eyes: venom green, electric orange, and blood red.

"Great job retrieving the girl," the goblin in front said, his eyes starting to glow. "You should pass her off to us. We'll take her to safety," he tempted. Clearly, this was goblin persuasion at work.

I tightened my grip on lion guy's neck.

The guy who was once a mountain lion actually chuckled. "Of course…NOT!" he shouted, flipping a handgun from a holster before shooting two of the goblins with the pepper spray paintballs.

Leopard girl nailed the remaining two.

Bat boy swore. "They have Viper cornered, and he's lost his sunglasses," he said, motioning to the far side of the room where I could see a man in fatigues slumped over, his eyes going glassy.

"DON'T break formation," leopard girl snarled.

"But—," bat boy protested.

"Protecting the girl is our first order of business," lion man rumbled.

I frowned as I watched one of the goblins reach for the mentally captive soldier. "FREY!" I shouted. "FREY!"

"Yeah, what do you want?" Frey snarled, abruptly appearing by my rescuers.

"Help that guy," I said, pointing to the soldier.

Frey rolled his eyes. "Of course you would make demands and

shout orders while being rescued. I don't know why I thought you would be any different than normal."

"Frey!"

"Yeah, yeah. I'm on it. HEY, FRANK! COME ON!" Frey said before dropping to his wolf body and uttering an eerie howl.

Frank appeared at his side, and together the duo snuck through the crowd, their hackles raised before they jumped together in perfect synchronization, tackling the soldiers surrounding my rescuer's comrade.

I struggled in lion man's arms until I was propped up a little higher, better able to observe the struggle splayed out before me.

I blinked hard when I noticed a girl with white blond hair wearing a track suit. "…Madeline?"

The vampire dispatched a goblin with astounding speed. Her method, however, was quite interesting. Rather than bodily fight anyone—because even I knew the petite, breakable Madeline wouldn't stand a chance that way—she approached a target, tugged on their shirt sleeve to get their attention, and when they turned to face her, she would smash them in the face with a frying pan.

I wasn't quite sure where she got the pan from, but I didn't think I wanted to know.

When she heard me call her name, she spun around. She looked pretty funny because she had one of those swimmer nose plugs rammed up her nose, and a white, gauze headband was tied around her forehead.

"Morgan! You're okay!" she chirped, stepping over her fallen foe.

"Madeline, what are you doing here?" I said, absolutely aghast.

"Saving you," Madeline said.

"But the blood!" I said, shaking my hand.

True, the bullets were more like paint pellets, but goblins, shifters, and my friends alike were all bleeding. No one was dripping with gory wounds or anything, but for Madeline, a *paper cut* was enough to send her into a swoon.

"Oh, that's why I have these," Madeline said, motioning to her nose plugs and gauzy headband.

"What could those possibly do?" I asked.

"They block it from sight—ah, see," Madeline said, turning slightly green when a goblin with a cat scratch stumbled past her before being cracked unconscious with a head butt from *Dave* of all people.

In response to the sight of blood, Madeline yanked the gauze over her eyes. "See? I can't see it or smell it."

"Yeah, but now you can't see at all," I pointed out.

"That's not true. I can sort of see through this. Hey guys!" she said, turning around to shout to our friends. "Morgan is fine! The Shadows got her—WHOOP!" she yelped, tripping over a fallen goblin.

"Oh, sure, you can totally see," I agreed.

"Hey, Morgan!" Esmeralda called as she and the Sphinx double-teamed a goblin. "So, they did get you, awesome!" she said as the large-eared fox she and the sphinx had been speaking with transformed into a surprisingly tall and buff woman.

"These magical beings are friends of the Princess," the buff woman said, speaking to leopard girl and lion man. "I believe the perimeter is secured."

"Cool," Esmeralda said. "So, like, shouldn't we be leaving? I mean, we have Morgan," the bronze beauty pointed out.

Leopard girl gave a decisive nod and dug out her walkie talkie. "Shadows, we're pulling out. Disengage in combat and prepare to leave," she said before frowning at Esmeralda, the sphinx, and Madeline as the blonde popped back up on her feet after pushing the blindfold out of her eyes. "How will you notify your companions that we are leaving the premises?"

"The old fashioned way," Madeline said before turning on her heels and shouting at the top of her lungs, "HEY GUYS! WE'RE LEAVING!" she said as Frank and Frey took down a pair of goblins.

Leopard girl did not groan, but her face went completely blank. (Madeline has that effect on most people.)

"It's about time!" Perseus and his pony pals complained, galloping past. "Let's go!"

"Shadows, this is Gold Leader. We're pulling out," leopard girl said into her walkie talkie before she jogged through the room. (The number of standing goblins had greatly dwindled, so there were only a handful or so left. They were *that* good.)

As everyone started piling out through the gaping holes in the walls—which made the place resemble a block of Swiss cheese—I peered over lion guy's massive shoulder.

What I saw behind me made me tighten my grip on the soldier.

It was Hunter. He was standing at the back entrance of the room, his hands tucked behind his back as he listened to some of his men speak. When he caught my gaze he smiled and tilted his head.

I'm allowing you to leave.

He clearly communicated that to me with the quirk of his lips.

I swallowed and thankfully noted that some of the shape-shifting soldiers had noticed the goblin leader as well.

"He's letting us go," leopard girl snarled, backing out of the room with several other soldiers.

"That may be, but we've got Miss Fae. It doesn't matter how or why," lion man pointed out.

"I don't like that kid," leopard girl growled.

"Hackles down, buddy. Let's deliver Princess to the client," mountain lion guy said.

We poured into the street like a massive costume party.

Sure enough, as Hunter had said, we were in Chicago. I could see the Sears Tower (Well, really the Willis Tower now) on the horizon. We started weaving through the city streets. My friends were intermingling with the soldiers, calling out to me in various degrees of relief.

"Morgan, girl, you are *such* a riot! I love hanging out with you!" Esmeralda laughed.

"I don't believe this qualifies as 'hanging out,'" the sphinx elegantly said before smiling at me. "I am glad you are unharmed, teacher."

"We totally hacked into your cell phone to find you!" Perseus said, he and his friends pranced along in front of us. "It was so easy," he boasted.

"Best fieldtrip EVER!" Hercules laughed.

"I don't believe this qualifies as a fieldtrip either," the sphinx corrected.

Madeline flounced along next to lion man, intent on filling me in, "We were so worried about you, Morgan! I mean, when I went back to get you, I couldn't find you anywhere, and Corona said you hadn't come back for your backpack. Frey said you were probably crabby and just went home, but I didn't believe him one bit! And then Administrator Moonspell got the call from the goblins, and Asahi heard you were with Aysel, so he told Frey, and Frey told me, and I told Esmeralda who told everyone else! We knew that mean, old administrator wasn't going to worry about you; Asahi told us as much. So, we decided to organize a rescue party for you! It took us a whole day to get organized and prepared. Frey said it was a mad idea, but I think it turned out rather well," she said, chattering away like a happy bird.

"So, who are you guys?" I asked my soldier rescuers when Madeline paused for a breath.

They hesitated a moment before lion guy spoke. "We're called the Shadow Shifters. We're a high specialized mercenary team. All of our members are shape shifters and are extensively trained in rescue and sting operations."

"They're like the marines for magical beings," Esmeralda said. "Only they can be hired out. Sweet, right? You got saved by heroic mercenaries!"

Mountain lion guy laughed. "I think this is going to be one of my favorite missions."

"Keep your head screwed on; we haven't delivered Princess yet," leopard girl snapped as we turned a corner.

"Morgan, I am glad you are okay," flea-less Frank shyly said before being jostled aside by Frey.

"This is, of course, if we ignore the fact that you were stupid and went and got yourself kidnapped in the first place!" Frey said

I ignored the pushy wolf and kept sifting through the crowd, looking for my friends.

I didn't see Asahi, but because he was the MBRC Administrator's son, I can't say I was surprised. I mean, it would be foolhardy for him to wander into the very complex where his brother was being kept.

Wait.

Brother.

"OH, MY GOSH! WE FORGOT AYSEL!" I shouted.

"No, we didn't," Frey snorted. "That guy can totally take care of himself."

"Rescuing Aysel Moonspell was not part of our contract," the buff lady agreed.

"I bet he'll be at the MBRC before us," Esmeralda agreed. "The goblins have to be eager to get rid of him."

"Yep!" Madeline nodded.

I felt unconvinced and struggled to try and pry myself out of lion man's grasp. "Okay, we've left the building pretty far behind. I can walk now," I said.

"It isn't safe. They may yet pursue us, and we need to be able to send you away quickly," leopard girl said.

"Yeah. I doubt you can run as fast as me," lion man grinned.

I scrunched my face up, about to argue, when Westfall appeared next to my shifter guards.

"Perhaps it would be best if Morgan were to ride me," Westfall offered.

"Aw, thanks Westfall!" I said, reaching out to hug the unicorn's head. A stubby knob of his re-growing horn pricked me, but I didn't care. Riding a unicorn still violated many of my childhood beliefs, but being held bridal-style by a guy I didn't know was getting just plain weird.

"The unicorn would be able to flee faster than any of us here," the buff lady considered.

Lion man swapped glances with leopard girl, who nodded. "Alright, then," lion man said, stopping to set me down on the ground.

Madeline took advantage of my moment of freedom to tackle-hug me. Esmeralda joined her, pulling Frank and Frey into the hug as well.

Soon, I was surrounded by a mass of bodies, and I laughed,

unable to identify them all. It was touching, the fact that my magical friends were willing to go through such lengths for me.

"Okay, okay, we need to keep moving," Lion guy said before tossing me onto Westfall's back.

"Whoa!" I squeaked, clamping my legs around the unicorn's belly before throwing my arms around his neck. "There's no saddle this time," I said, getting Westfall's brown fur all over my clothes.

"Don't worry, Morgan. I'll be careful. You won't fall," Westfall promised.

"Okay," I shakily said, releasing the death grip I had on his neck. I forced myself to sit up straight but kept my hands buried in his mane.

Westfall's walk was a comfortable, rocking motion, but it still took a while for me to grow relaxed enough that I was able to look up, which was when I noticed we were leaving the goblin district and entering a more heavily populated area. What does this mean?

People.

Lots of people. And the Shadow Shifters dressed in their fatigues were the least of my worries. After all, we had centaurs and a sphinx in our ranks! This spelled disaster.

People were staring at us, whispering as they gawked.

Leopard girl gave the mountain lion guy a meaningful look, and he nodded before threading his arms behind his head. "Man, I *love* filming battle scenes! Especially when we get props! But clean up is such a pain in the butt!"

"Yeah, not to mention actresses can be such divas," bat boy grouched.

"I just hope we can finally get that shot the director wants with this next take," Frey said. "I think wardrobe is going to have a heart attack when they see our clothes. We only have two clean sets left!"

I was about to hiss at them and tell them how ridiculous they sounded, trying to pass off a mangled bunch of soldiers and creatures as actors, but I paused when I heard some of our gawkers speak.

"Oh, it's a movie!"

"Yeah, that makes sense. Don't you see the shotty craftsmanship of those centaurs? You can so totally tell their horse body is mechanic."

"I heard they were going to be filming a movie downtown. Didn't you?"

"Oh, yeah. Of course."

"Those fantasy movies, I never much liked them. They always look so gaudy and fictitious."

"Is that girl on the horse the main heroine?"

"Could be. They must be a pretty low budget film if she is."

I felt deeply offended but also shocked beyond all belief. The movie thing actually *worked.*

"Told you," Frey laughed under his breath as more onlookers scoffed.

"I bet it's going to go straight to DVD."

No one let me get off Westfall until we were inside the MBRC. More specifically, the shifters wouldn't let me slide off the sweet unicorn until we entered the main chamber, which was unusually abandoned.

Everyone from the help desk was there with Asahi, who was standing by a bunch of people in stuffy looking clothes. But, most importantly, my cyclopes friends were there.

"Morgan L. Fae, sir," lion man said, carefully steering me forward.

"Nick, Sandy!" I shouted, making a beeline for my one-eyed friends. I threw myself on Sandy, who caught me and stumbled back into Nick to keep her balance.

I hugged them both, squeezing my eyes as tight as I could to keep the tears from leaking out of my eyes.

"Thank you," I whispered.

"For what?" Sandy asked, sounding amused as she patted my back.

"For sending someone to get me," I said.

"It was the *least* we could do, Morgan," Nick said, sounding shamed. "We cyclopes talked it over and considered going to get you ourselves, but while we are excellent businessmen, we are not very athletically talented. We decided it was best to hire someone to go in our place."

"I'm sorry we weren't strong enough," Sandy gently said.

"No! You were! It just—I, thank you," I stammered, searching for the right words. "It means a lot to me, to know that you care enough. I felt so helpless," I confessed.

Sandy smiled. "You're safe now. I'm glad we could bring you home."

I grinned back at her and took a step back before moving to exchange greetings with Ralph and the other cyclopes that were present. That was when I noticed the two briefcases.

"What are those?"

"Oh, yes, that's right. Shadow Shifters, your payment," Nick said, snapping his fingers before gathering up the briefcases and carrying them to the mercenaries. "The agreed payment was $210,000, wasn't it?"

My mouth gaped open. "WHAT?" I squeaked.

"Yes, amazing isn't it? They gave us a great discount since the Chicago goblins are not the violent type," Sandy smiled.

I gaped at the group with a dropped jaw.

"Welcome home, dear," Ralph said, patting my hand.

"Morgan! Morgan," Corona called, walking across the empty chamber in her serpentine gait. "I'm so glad you're back! Everyone was so worried! I sent your backpack home with Frey. He took it to your house. Oh, Morgan!" Corona said before reaching out to hug me.

Her scaly skin felt oddly textured. "Hi, Corona. It's good to see you."

When she released me, Orion spoke as Doggy flung himself at me. "I see the clouds have cleared from your skies."

"Dad, would you please be *quiet*!" Perseus moaned. "You're so embarrassing!"

I laughed at the teenager and smiled at Orion. "Thanks, Orion."

"Welcome home, Morgan," he said, offering his hand. I took it, and we shook before a wilted Asahi appeared at my side.

"Morgan? Are you okay?" he said, his golden eyes larger than usual as he hunched his shoulders around his neck.

I smiled, melting a little, and threw an arm across the High Elf's shoulders. "I'm fine, Asahi," I assured him.

"Really?" he asked.

"Yes."

"I'm sorry—it's my fault you got kidnapped. If you weren't my tutor—" he started before I interrupted him.

"No, Asahi, it wasn't your fault at all. It was stupid Hunter who made the decision to kidnap me. Not you. Besides, if my life is a little more interesting just because I'm your teacher, I'm okay with that," I said, surprising myself when I realized it was true.

"Really?" Asahi asked, perking up.

"Yep," I nodded.

Asahi hugged me. "Thanks, Morgan," he said before abruptly releasing me. "Oh, Aysel is back!"

My jaw dropped. "Already?"

"Yes. He got here about five minutes before you," he said, motioning to the circle of what I assumed to be MBRC administration staff members.

As though on cue, an irritated-looking Aysel stepped out of the hodge-podge of bodies, brushing himself off as a crease in his forehead deepened with irritation. He looked up and met my gaze, and the forehead creases and wrinkles disappeared.

I slowly walked across the chamber, stopping a few feet away from him.

"I'm sorry we didn't bring you with," I said in a small voice.

"It is just as well you didn't. Besides, I hear you didn't have much of a choice," Aysel wryly said, his lips twitching as he stared at me.

I nodded and licked my lips. "I'm glad you got back."

Aysel hesitated. "And I am glad you are safe."

My stomach was twisting oddly, and I found it difficult to swallow. "Oh, screw it," I muttered before reaching out to hug the stuffy High Elf.

I was pretty surprised (and horrified) with my own actions, but Aysel shocked me to my core when his arms closed around me. His hug was warm and pretty gentle. He actually placed a hand on the back of my head.

At that exact moment, there was a thump followed by a crack. I removed my face from Aysel's robes and stared at the source of the sound.

It was *Devin*, coming out of the entrance hallway of the MBRC, his teeth clenched in anger with four guys trailing behind him. Hanging off his arms were two gorgeous fairies with pouty lips and thick hair.

In front of him was a black, leather brief case that was splayed out and popped open, almost like he had thrown it in anger.

"WHAT THE HELL!?" he shouted. "I finish the Seelie-Unseelie court parley early, amend the Antarctic Dragon agreement, call for an emergency release of the Fairy Council and rush here on a plane only to find you in the arms of AYSEL MOONSPELL?"

"Devin?" I asked, stepping away from Aysel. "What are you doing here?"

"MADELINE!" Devin shouted, ignoring me while shaking off his groupies. "I told you to keep her on a leash around those two brats!" he said, motioning at Aysel and Asahi.

"I did!" Madeline complained. "I can't help it if she bonded with Aysel in captivity! Besides, I decided she's too precious to be your friend. I'm divorcing you from her on her behalf."

"You backstabbing blood sucker!" Devin declared.

"Womanizing pervert!" Madeline shot back. "You actually dared to bring other women with you when you came to see her?"

"It was supposed to make her jealous!" Devin shouted before kicking the briefcase across the room.

It slid to a stop a few feet away from me, which allowed me to see its contents.

It was stuffed to the brim with informational readouts about the

Chicago goblins and my kidnapping. Most of the papers had hand-scrawled notes on it, and many of them were crumpled. There were also handwritten notes that nastily ripped on Devin for daring to call a recess in the Fairy Council for the sake of one of his girlfriends.

I looked up at the Pooka, who was still bellowing in Madeline's face. "If you hate men so much, why didn't you keep her from them?"

"And risk being unfriended by Morgan? Never!" Madeline scoffed.

"Drop out!" Devin scoffed. I noticed that in spite of the fire in his words, he had dark circles under his eyes, and his clothes were rumpled beyond all recognition.

He really had rushed here.

"And now because of the whole kidnapping thing, everyone in the council knows that I fancy her!" Devin groaned.

"I thought that would have been obvious the way you allowed Administrator Moonspell to hustle you out of here in exchange for allowing Morgan to regain her memories," Madeline dryly said.

"NO! It wasn't! I managed to fool them all and con them into thinking she was just a stupid girl to me, and then SHE GETS KIDNAPPED!" Devin shouted.

"He didn't take the news well," one of the guys behind him attested. "Councilmember Windstorm threatened to put a stick of soap in his mouth."

I walked up to Devin, whose back was to me as he argued with Madeline.

"Did you even help her at all, you useless vampire?" Devin growled.

"A lot more than you did," Madeline snorted.

"Devin," I said.

"WHAT?!" the Pooka shouted, spinning around to face me.

I took a deep breath and stood on my tip toes to hug him. I linked my hands around his neck and squeezed. "Thanks," I said.

Devin went rock-still for a moment before he moved. He picked me up so I was propped against his shoulder and my feet hung in the air. "You should have called or something," he complained.

"My battery was dead. Besides, I didn't know you had a cell phone."

Devin was stubbornly silent before speaking. "You only need me, no one else."

I rolled my eyes. "That's a lie if I ever heard one," I snorted. You see, unlike most girls, I am not deceived by pretty words. (For the most part.) And I still hadn't forgotten how Devin had strolled in here with a gorgeous fairy on either arm. (I suppose I should thank him: I might have been in possible danger if he wasn't such a notorious playboy.)

"Just be quiet, and let me have this moment!" Devin complained.

I obliged and allowed Devin a few seconds of silence. "That's better," he said, setting me down.

I let him go and spun around when I heard Madeline gasp. "Of all the nerve!"

Strolling out of the crowd of administrator staff was Hunter with two bodyguard goblins. He carried a scroll—his signed contract most likely—and looked rather satisfied as he led his men through the chamber.

"Hello, Morgan. I'm glad you're alright. I'll see you in school tomorrow?" he said with a friendly smile.

I narrowed my eyes at the handsome goblin. "I haven't forgotten that you were going to keep me against my will, Hunter."

"Of course not. But I'll still see you tomorrow. We sit next to each other in math," he reminded me, ignoring Devin's growls and Aysel's glares with a pleasant smile.

"Hunter," I said as Devin tensed next to me. "If you want to remain friends, you had better not try anything funny."

"Or else?" Hunter asked.

"Or else I'm going to tell Fran you want to be on student council. And no one on that committee can remain invisible very long, even if they want to," I threatened.

Rather than frown at me, Hunter grinned. "That sounds like a match point. Very well, Morgan, no funny business. I look forward to seeing you tomorrow. Logan left your things with the sunshine elf over there during your touching reunion with his brother," he said before sailing out of the room, his goblins shuffling behind him.

"I *really* don't like that guy," Frey said.

"Really? I think he's cute," Esmeralda said.

Madeline starred at her friend with horror. "You must be joking."

"No. I'm just shallow," the bronze vampire shrugged.

"Can I go home now?" I asked, feeling weary to the bone.

"Absolutely," Asahi nodded, handing me my purse and jacket. "My father sends his apologies for this terrible experience."

"He's not here?" I asked, peering around the room. I had assumed he would be here to observe the recovery of his son.

"No," Asahi said, shaking his head.

"Oh," I blinked, feeling bad for the Moonspell twins.

"Come on, doll," Devin said, tossing an arm over my shoulders. "I'll buy your train ticket home."

"That sounds wonderful," I agreed.

21

The End?

In the end, Frey, Dave, Madeline, and Devin escorted me home. Frey and Dave went their separate ways at the train station, but Madeline and Devin took me to my house.

"Here we are," I said, sighing with pure pleasure as I stared at my family home. It had never before looked so picturesque and beautiful to my eyes.

"Now, remember," Madeline said, shivering in her coat as the setting sun cast red hues on her light-colored hair. "Frey said your family was hypnotized to think you were off visiting a relative, so all you need to do is say that you enjoyed your stay, and life will proceed normally."

"I remember," I nodded. My eyes were drooping, and my stomach was growling. All I wanted to do was eat dinner and take a bath. "Good night, guys," I said, starting up the sidewalk.

"Morgan, wait," Devin said. He shoved his hands into the pockets of his jacket and growled. "Here," he said, thrusting a slim, white cell phone at me.

I blinked. "What is it?"

"It's an MM phone. Take it," he barked.

I took the contraption in my hands and flipped it over. The phone was designed like a smart phone. But instead of having a keypad or screen, the only thing that adorned its surface was a mirror. "It's a…phone?" I asked.

"MM stands for Magic Mirror. You can make calls by telling the phone who you want to call. The mirror closest to the individual will pop up with your image, allowing you to see them and them to see you. It's magic-powered, so the battery won't die. Use it to call me—or for emergencies," Devin gruffly said.

I stared at the odd-looking phone. "I didn't know magical beings had such advanced technology," I said.

"We don't. Only Fairy Council members are supposed to have these. I had a techy friend of mine whip one up Friday night while I was still in the negotiation meetings," Devin said.

"Thanks, Devin, I don't know what to say," I said, staring at the phone.

Devin placed a hand on my head and pressed my forehead into his shoulder. "This is fine," he said.

Behind him Madeline snorted, "Player."

Behind her someone asked, "…Morgan?"

I peered around Devin and Madeline to see a stricken Fran standing on the sidewalk wearing a winter coat, hat, and gloves. Her eyes were red and swollen, and her face was puffy. She had obviously been crying.

"Hey, Fran," I said, mustering a smile. "What's up?"

"I, I," she paused, her gaze flickering back and forth between myself, Devin, and Madeline. Her eyes showed a faint trace of recognition when she saw Devin, but she looked hurt when she saw Madeline. "You really are mad at me, aren't you?" she whispered.

"I'm sorry, what?" I asked, feeling stupid.

"About dating Brett. I promise I'll break up with him, Morgan! I shouldn't have gone out with him. I'm such a bad friend, doing that even though I knew you liked him! I looked for you everywhere after school, but you left early, and then I figured I would drop by when you were finished with work so we could hang out and talk about it, but your parents told me you were visiting your Aunt Erma in Toledo, but you *hate* your Aunt Erma, so I knew it had to be a lie, and now I see that you have new friends and—," she abruptly cut off, sniffing as she blinked back tears. "I'll go," she croaked.

"Fran, wait," I called after her. "I want you to meet these guys. They're my friends from work. Madeline, Devin, this is Fran: my best friend in the whole world," I said, strolling up to Fran so I could give her a side hug.

Madeline reacted beautifully. "Hello, Fran. Morgan has told me so much about you. I've wanted to meet you," she said.

Of course she had. The idea of meeting a member of my school's student council mesmerized the blonde vampire.

"So, you're the one that's been with my little doll at school. Thank you for watching her," Devin said with his most dazzling smile.

"Pompous playboy," Madeline muttered, looking off in the horizon.

"I'm going to ignore that, wretched twit," Devin smiled.

"You're not mad at me?" Fran whispered as Devin and Madeline glared at each other.

"Not at all. I've just been visiting Aunt Erma, and my cell phone died, so I am *really* tired," I promised. It was close enough. Staying with the goblins was more fun than a weekend with Aunt Erma, but the wreckage was about the same.

"So, you're the hot garden boy," Fran said, her eyes inspecting Devin from head to toe before she shook her head. "He's no good, Morgan. You can tell the guy is a total player."

"I beg your pardon?" Devin sputtered.

"HAH-HAH! I knew I would like you, Fran!" Madeline crowed.

I had to smile as I watched my best friend interact with my new friends. It felt oddly right, to watch the magical parts of my life interact with the normal parts of my life.

I hadn't yet achieved a balance between the two, and the trouble with Hunter was still weighing on my mind. But for now, this was good.

But, I still can't totally forgive Dave for blowing my world apart. DO YOU HEAR THAT, DAVE?!

THE END

Goblins Wear Suits

THE MAGICAL BEINGS
REHABILITATION CENTER: BOOK 2

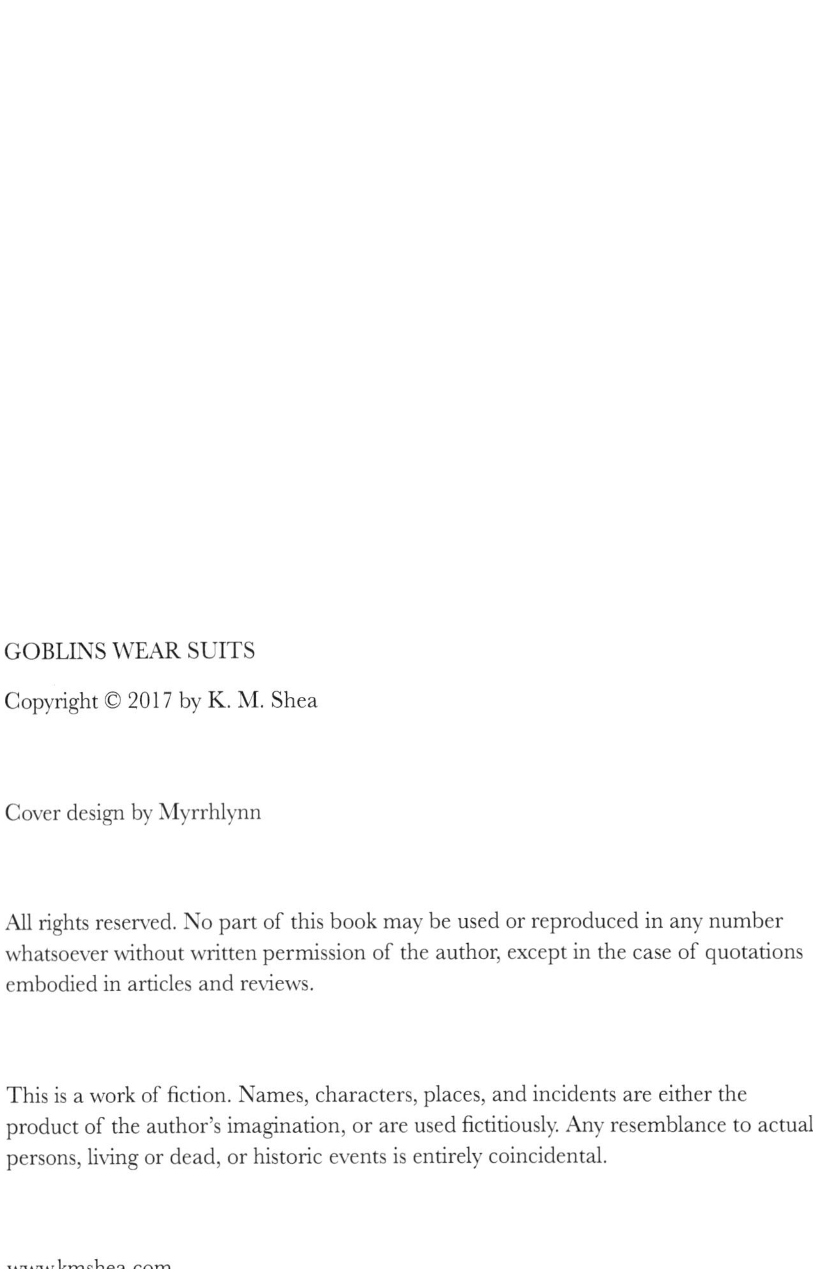

GOBLINS WEAR SUITS

Cover design by Myrrhlynn

www.kmshea.com

Created with Vellum

For the readers who never gave up asking for a sequel,
Thank you and enjoy.

1

Work Fun

When I arrived at the Best Buy parking lot, it was almost midnight. All the store lights in the area were dimmed, but the parking lot lamps were still on. They cast an eerie glow on the lone figure in the lot: A tall, boney man who appeared to be in his 40s.

I parked the borrowed car a little ways from him and got out. "Hey, Vlad," I said, circling the car to climb into the passenger's seat.

"Good evening, Miss Morgan," Vlad said, tipping forward in a shallow bow.

"You ready for this?"

"I have prepared to the best of my abilities."

"Uh, okay. Get in."

Vlad eased himself into the driver's seat and buckled up.

"Left pedal is the brake. The right one is the gas," I said, fiddling with the heat vents. January in the Chicago area is no picnic —it's *freezing*.

"This circular wheel is what one uses instead of reins, yes?"

Oh gosh. He wasn't kidding when he said he'd never driven a

car. "Yeah," I said, double checking my seatbelt. "Twist the key and start 'er up."

Vlad was able to do all of that and shift from the park to drive without any mishaps. I was beginning to think my worry about tonight was unfounded. Vlad moved slowly with uncertain movements. Even if he didn't know how to drive we would be fine if he was this cautious.

Hah-hah. Yeah, what a joke.

"Good. Now ease your foot off the break—GAAAAAH!" I squealed, like the car, when Vlad stomped his foot on the gas.

The car shot forward, tires squealing on the dusting of snow that covered the parking lot.

"Don't push down so hard," I said, clutching the door for reassurance.

"I don't understand?" Vlad said as we picked up speed.

"You don't have to floor it!" I said, my voice getting louder as he hurtled towards a lamppost.

"Floor it? I beg your pardon?" Vlad said.

"*Get your foot off the pedal*!" I screamed, my heart buzzing like a hummingbird.

When he stare blankly at me—instead of looking at our incoming doom—I shouted, "BRAKE!" and yanked on the steering wheel to avoid the lamp.

Vlad used his other foot and slammed on the break. The car made some really angry noises, but after I pounded Vlad's leg he got my drift and removed his foot from the gas pedal.

We sat there for a few moments while I shook with adrenaline. "Okay. Yeah. Let's review," I said, launching into a rundown of pedal usage—emphasizing that only ONE FOOT is used when driving—even though I had already schooled him on this yesterday at our prep-meeting.

The car idled, recovering—like me—in the few minutes of respite.

Lack of heat was no longer a problem for me. My heart was going a million miles per minute. I was so high on adrenaline my nose no longer registered Vlad's distinct old people/moth ball smell.

(Thankfully he wasn't so old that his body was in the reeking stage, or the tight quarters would be a lot more unpleasant.)

"Remember, this is not an all or nothing thing. *Ease* down on the gas pedal. Now…Let's try again," I said, shoving the words out of my mouth with great reluctance. (Luka so owed me for this.)

"Yes, Miss Morgan," Vlad obediently said.

I braced myself, but, thankfully, this time Vlad was slower to start. He eased forward on the pedal until we rolled along at a steady five miles per hour.

"This is good. It's great, even," I said, breathing again.

"I thank you for the compliment," Vlad said.

"Okay, great job. Now we're heading towards a light. It's a ways off so we're good, but you'll want to start turning soon so we don't hit it. Cars don't have the best turn radius so you want to start turning before you have to turn. Turn the wheel in the direction you want to go. In this case let's take a right," I suggested.

"As you wish, Miss Morgan," Vlad said. As he started to turn the wheel he stomped on the gas pedal. Vlad then yanked on the wheel and, with our increased speed, we started going around and around in a tight circle, like a hamster running in its wheel.

Several curses tumbled from my lips before I managed to shout, "Stop, *stop*!"

Vlad frowned. "This vehicle appears to be broken. It remains on this circular path."

"Straighten the wheel and use the brake!" I shouted, plastered against the window thanks to the hefty centrifugal force we had going on. (I guess I did learn something in physics.)

Vlad—who apparently never does anything halfway—yanked the wheel straight and slammed on the brakes.

I was thrown forward against my seatbelt—which cut into my chest and stopped my air supply. I wheezed for a little bit before I managed to say, "Why?"

"I'm sorry. Why is being applied to…?"

"*WHY* did you speed up?" I asked, irately turning to face the older man after putting the car in park.

Vlad stared at me as if I had lost my mind. "It is common

knowledge that horses slow down in corners and turns. One must always hasten them if one hopes to keep the same speed."

"Vlad, I told you driving *cars* has nothing to do with driving and riding horses," I said, clasping my shaking hands together to keep myself from strangling Vlad—he was a powerful being, after all.

"I am beginning to sense the truth in your words," Vlad said.

I breathed deeply to keep from planting my palm on my face in exasperation. "Yes," I calmly said. "At this learning stage, what's most vital is that you know how to use the brake pedal, and that you *do not* extensively use the gas pedal. If the car is getting slower as you turn, just *leave it*. You need to understand the basic mechanics before you attempt to do this at higher speeds."

"Yes, Miss Morgan," Vlad said, momentarily cowed.

I shut my eyes and tilted my head back for a few moments, mustering my strength before saying, "Take the car out of park, and let's try this again."

I clung to the door as Vlad moved his foot. Instead of switching gears the engine roared as Vlad pressed harder and harder on the gas pedal. "It will not move," he frowned as I cursed more.

"That's because you're pressing the *gas* pedal, which is the WRONG PEDAL!" I said after expressing myself with enough swear words to get me grounded if I were at home.

"Oh, my apologies. I momentarily forgot the pedal order," Vlad said, switching to the brake and changing gears. "Also what does this 'crap' mean that you are incessantly whispering?" he asked, his pronounced canine fangs flashing in the dim light.

"It means my life is doomed," I groaned.

When I saw Baobab—my MBRC appointed and paid for administrative assistant—the following day, she raised her eyebrows. "You look terrible, Miss Fae."

"Don't even start," I said, striding through my office with great anger. "Please make a note that anytime a MBRC board member asks me to teach a vampire that's two centuries old to drive a car, it is an *automatic refusal*," I hissed, turning to face my assistant—who also happened to be a fairy.

Baobab was brawny for a fairy. She was tall and thick, and her skin was a beautiful coffee color. Her hair was dark chocolate with swirls of green, and her wings—iridescent and rarely used for flying—were shaped like dragon fly wings.

"I believe several of your colleagues warned you that teaching Mr. Vladimeer might not be as simple as you were told it would be," Baobab said.

"Yeah, well I didn't think it would be so life threatening. We are going to take Luka to the cleaners for this—MBRC board member or not," I said, plopping down into my chair. "What is this?" I asked, looking at my desk, which was shrouded in papers.

"Your mail," Baobab said. "Everyone wishes to tell you what to do with the rest of your life."

"Here too? I get enough junk mail from colleges and technical schools at home," I groaned, flipping through the mail. Granted at home it was pamphlets that depicted clear faced 20-something-year-olds holding the obligatory armload of books and posed in various places on green college campuses.

My MBRC mail, keeping in step with the place, was also mostly pamphlets. However, these pamphlets were for services and companies somewhat similar to the MBRC—mostly working in the realm of magic rehabilitation—that were also, according to the handwritten notes scrawled on the pamphlets, conveniently located near random human colleges.

Because balancing my normal life with the magical community over the past two years hadn't been difficult enough. No, No. I totally should continue with the fun into my adult life.

Perhaps I should explain.

I'm Morgan L. Fae. Once upon a time I was a normal high school student. But then, through the actions of one balding, fat vampire, and a tall, skinny werewolf, my life collided with the magical.

Fairies, elves, shifters, goblins, dwarves, vampires, all of them are real.

However, even with the existence of all these magical beings, they don't go prancing around in the streets with normal people like you and me. Oh no. They went into hiding centuries ago, fleeing to places like the underwater city of Atlantis (it totally exists. One of my students went on vacation there and brought back pictures) the uninhabited parts of Asia, the North Pole (the Santa Claus rumor started somewhere) and so on and so forth.

Some of the creatures have been hiding longer than others—just ask any dinosaur and they can vouch for me.

After watching humans dominate the globe for so long, the magical beings decided that as we haven't gotten ourselves all killed off yet, we're probably here to stay. So now they want to rejoin the modern world. Thing is, after being out of touch with current events for anywhere from several centuries to several thousand years, magical beings know squat about everyday human life.

Things like toy dogs, malls, and ice makers totally freak them out. About eighty percent of them think the internet and computers are human magic, and most of the software and technology they use is about a decade or two behind the current trends.

So, in order to rejoin human society, a rehabilitation process is needed. Because of that need, the MBRC, or the **M**agical **B**eings' **R**ehabilitation **C**enter was founded by Administrator Vincent Moonspell. It is supposed to meet the needs of the magical so they can be taught how to function in the human world. It does everything. Seriously. The MBRC provides contacts and glasses to near sighted cyclopes, holds human sociology and psychology classes, and has an in-house hospital. You name it, they do it.

As illegal as my entry to the secret world of the magical was, I was allowed to keep my memories instead of having them wiped—as is protocol—because of my acceptance of the magical, and my knowledge as a normal high schooler—which is invaluable to the Center.

As a sophomore in high school I was a private tutor for a high elf named Asahi, who also happens to be one of Administrator Moonspell's kids.

Now, an eighteen-year-old high school senior, I am an MBRC

consultant. I teach an advanced placement course—which consists of Asahi and some of the students I started with as a sophomore—and technically a course called Introduction to the American Education System. I also hold at least one seminar a month, and I usually do personal favors for MBRC board members and personnel.

My little driving crash-course with Vlad was a deal I made with the vampire representative for the MBRC board. He was going to pay through the nose for putting me through that terrifying hour.

"I'll deal with this later," I said, shoving the mail pile into an empty garbage can. "What do you have for me?"

"Your presence is requested Saturday evening for the MBRC board meeting with the Chicago branch of Weller Goblin Enterprises. Dr. Creamintin sent you an invitation to a party—it is Aristotle's birthday next week. Nickolas Vontreba and Sandra Koplin asked that you would take a look at a new contract they drew up with the MBRC regarding cyclopes' donations. The field trip for your advanced placement course was approved, and Asahi requests your presence in Introduction to the American Education System tonight,"

You see, even though I'm listed as the professor for Introduction to the American Education, Asahi is really the one teaching it. He's my registered teaching assistant. I speak to the class about once or twice a week when Asahi is feeling anxious about a topic. I don't know why he gets so nervous. He can define high school cliques and explain the nuances of dodge ball better than any normal human.

"Did Madeline drop by?"

"Yes."

"Did she have anything important to say?"

"She spoke of the Pooka for a few minutes before she ripped a cuticle and knocked herself out with the sight of her own blood."

"She is so weird, even for a vampire," I said.

"Perhaps, Miss Fae."

"What did she say about Devin? He isn't at the MBRC, is he?" I nervously asked.

Devin, or the Pooka as most magical beings referred to him, was a powerful guy who served as a member of the Fairy Council—the highest governing body the magical community has. He was also a close friend of mine who is unfortunately gifted in flirting and raising my heartbeat.

"Madeline did not mention it. However, as the Fairy Council does not adjourn for another month, I should think he is still in Britain," Baobab said.

"That's awesome," I said, sighing in relief. "Alright. I need to track down Asahi and see what he wants help with. I have my Magic Mirror and cell phone on me if you need me," I said exiting my office space.

I almost slammed the door into a tall, waxy looking man who stood outside my office.

"Sorry," I said, before going on my way.

The MBRC is a maze of tunnels and chambers that lies next to and beneath Chicago's Union station. My office is located in the magic mouse hallway where most teachers have their offices. My schoolroom was located three flights down in the pegasus wing, and it took quite a bit of walking to get to it.

When I finally reached the room I was thrilled to find my target. "Asahi, what did you need?" I shouted into the vast room.

The classroom was the size of a small high school auditorium, and it was fitted with the best technology in the center thanks to my friendship with a handful of young centaurs that have a passion for human tech.

"Morgan, good afternoon," Asahi said, popping out from behind a projector. "I'll be with you in one moment," he said before speaking to a young faun who clattered along behind him.

"Morgaaaan!"

I was nearly tackled to the floor by a pile of frilly skirts and blonde hair.

Madeline had found me.

"Get off. I can't breathe," I gasped, rolling the petite vampire off me.

"I talked to Baobab this morning, but she wouldn't tell me when you were arriving today," Madeline said as she stood and fixed her skirts.

"Was there something you needed me for?"

"Not really. Everything has become so dull, so I thought I would visit you."

"Baobab said you stormed and raged about Devin."

"Naturally. Devin is always doing something worth raging over," Madeline scoffed.

Madeline wasn't exactly a man-hater, but as she was turned into a vampire around the time of the women's suffrage movement—and by a male vampire no less—she was generally distrustful of the gender and acted as my self-proclaimed white knight, working to keep as many males away from me as possible.

"He's trying to get out of the council early, you know," Madeline said.

"He's always trying to get out of the council," I said.

Madeline hesitated. "Yes."

"But?"

"Pardon?"

"You think there is more to the story?" I asked.

Madeline flicked a lock of her hair over her shoulder. "I do. I think he's worried about the political arguments taking place over here."

"Ah," I said.

Magical Beings are about as politically savvy and underhanded as the most cunning US Congressman. In the MBRC alone there were warring political factions. They typically limited themselves to insulting each other. Occasionally, though, there were outside political forces—like Weller Goblin Enterprises. Weller Goblin Enterprises wouldn't hesitate to kidnap a person, or two, to blackmail a MBRC politician.

"Are Weller Goblin Enterprises causing trouble again? They have a meeting with the MBRC board this weekend," I said.

Madeline shook her head. "No. Haven't you seen it in the Magic Journal Sentinel? There's an anti-human group raising a ruckus over the sudden popularity of centers like ours."

"An anti-human group?"

"Yeah," Madeline said, squirming with discomfort. "Not everyone in the magical community thinks we should rejoin human society."

"Oh."

"The majority thinks we should," Madeline was quick to add. "It's just a few power hungry nuts here and there. You know, politics."

"Yeah," I agreed, happily distracted when Asahi bound up to us. "What did you need, Asahi?" I asked.

"I was wondering if you wouldn't mind starting off today's lecture with a question session. The students came up with some excellent questions yesterday that are beyond my knowledge," Asahi said, his various earrings and bracelets jingling.

Although Asahi is a high elf, he persists in dressing like a genie. He usually wears a colored vest with gold embroidery and a few gaudy jewels, puffy pants, and these funny looking, pointy shoes. Kinda weird, right? He pretty much shines in a crowd thanks to all the bling he wears. But it suits Asahi, oddly enough.

"Sure," I agreed.

"Also, Aysel wants to speak to you. He said he would be waiting outside after you finish with the class," Asahi said.

"Sure," I said with a lot less enthusiasm.

Madeline patted my shoulder in sympathy. "If you're lucky it will be over swiftly," she said.

"Thanks," I said, stifling a groan as Asahi hurried to the podium at the front of the room to arrange his notes.

"You're welcome."

"No, reading levels don't indicate higher or lower status in the classroom. It's a tool educators use to gauge what level of books their students should be reading. A child that starts the school year with a low reading level may finish the school year with the highest reading level. There are no side-effects to this change besides the level of book the kid can read," I said, comfortably leaning against the podium.

This was my second semester of "teaching" Introduction to the American Education System, and after teaching my advance placement class for two full years I was pretty comfortable standing in front of a room packed with strangers, explaining human stuff. A nice side-effect of this comfort was my grade in my senior speech class. My teacher kept trying to recruit me for the debate team and the forensics team because I was such a good speaker.

"Yes, the dryad in the back corner," I said, pointing to a student who had his hand raised.

"Professor Fae, when is 'show and tell' no longer a part of classroom activities?"

I tilted my head back as I thought. "It varies from school to school, but it is acknowledged as an elementary school activity. I would say the final grade that you might see the occasional show and tell session is fifth grade. Generally it's found in kindergarten through second grade."

"Does show and tell impact a student, psychologically speaking?"

"In some ways, yes. Show and tell is all about kids bringing something they find interesting into class. If they manage to dazzle everyone their popularity will increase for a few days," I said.

"What is something worthy of a popularity increase? Ancient artifacts? Gold?" the dryad's companion, a leprechaun, asked.

"No. Kids do not bring valuable items to show and tell," I said. I folded my arms as I strained my memory. "When I was in first grade a kid brought in his Labrador puppy. He was the class favorite for a week."

"Animals? Children can bring animals to show and tell?" the dryad asked with interest.

It seemed I had unintentionally started a heated topic. I winced and glanced at the clock. "Occasionally, with parental and school permission. I apologize, students, but that is all the time we have today."

"Thank you Professor Fae," the class of fifty-something students chorused. (I always felt like a poser whenever they called me professor, but in spite of my best intensions they seemed stuck on the title.)

I winced as I stepped away from the dais.

"Thank you, Morgan," Asahi said.

"No problem. I'll see you in class in…an hour?" I asked.

Asahi nodded. "Until then."

"Yep," I said making my swift exit. I slipped outside the door to find Aysel waiting in the mostly abandoned hallway. He looked magnificent as usual—the stark opposite of his twin brother in looks and temperament. While Asahi had brilliant blonde hair and gold eyes, Aysel had dark hair matched with silver eyes. He dressed more like a stereotypical elf from a Lord of the Rings movie, and he was about as warm as an ice storm.

"Aysel, hey," I said, bracing myself.

"Morgan," Aysel said, one eyebrow arching in ire. "We need to talk."

I groaned. "Do we have to?"

"I have no wish to spend time in your presence either, but there are events you need to be informed of," he said, looking up and down the hallway.

Besides us the only being in the area was a tall, waxy guy leaning against the wall about forty feet away.

Aysel frowned at the man. "Let's step into my office," he said, turning to go back to the MBRC government wing.

While Asahi was interested in humans and teaching his fellow magical beings about them, Aysel was more business minded and was following in his father's administrative footsteps. I'd be surprised if, by the end of the decade, he wasn't an MBRC board member. He was already an assistant or secretary or something for his dad. (I swear his title changes on a weekly basis so I haven't bothered learning it for a while.)

"Alright, what do you want?" I said when we entered his lavish office.

"You need to be made aware of certain…issues," Aysel said.

"Issues?"

"Recently an isolationist group called Fidem has made several threatening statements directed at the MBRC," Aysel said.

"An isolationist group?"

"Magical beings organized and united under the belief that we should remain in isolationism, and cut ourselves off from the outside world."

"Oh, yeah. Madeline and I talked about it right before class. They're also anti-humans, right?"

"Yes," Aysel said, his usual scowl deepening. "Due to the size and depth of Fidem's power, the MBRC is following protocol and informing all human employees of the potential risk."

"Oh, so you've told the human enchanters and magic users too?" I asked.

Aysel nodded. "I am aware of your…private security. However, it is MBRC law to inform all employees after receiving a threat."

"What did these Fidem guys say?"

"Nothing of worth." Aysel said. The impatient tap of his fingers showed how little he was worried about the situation.

"But what were the threatening statements?"

"The usual empty promises of financial and physical attacks against the Center if we do not begin reducing human contact."

"The usual?" I asked.

"We received threats before you were hired. This is hardly new behavior."

"Yeah, but 'usual behavior' has seen both of us kidnapped," I said.

"It is unlikely Fidem will take any action. Isolationists are to magical beings what rednecks and conspiracy theorists are to humans. They are of lower intelligence and possess fewer numbers. There is nothing to fear."

"Uh-huh. Well. Thanks for telling me."

Aysel sourly shrugged. "It is protocol."

"Right. Can I go now?"

"Yes."

"You look really crabby. Do you know that?"

"*Goodbye*, Morgan."

2

Considering My Future

The following day I met Fran—my best friend since elementary school who knows nothing about my unusual job—for coffee at McDonalds before school.

"Why do we do this?" I asked, grouchy and unhappy with the early hour. Between the MBRC, school work, and my pathetic excuse of a social life, I can't say I get the recommended eight hours of sleep.

"Because it's the only time we see each other outside of school and we can't meet after because of my extracurricular activities and your work schedule," Fran said, stirring her java chip frappe. (I have no idea how she can consume an iced coffee when it's snowing.)

"We're crazy," I said, propping my head up with my hand.

"Possibly," Fran agreed. "What are you doing this Saturday?"

"I'm available in the morning, but I'll be working in the afternoon and evening."

"Can't you switch hours?"

"Nope. It's a meeting I'm required to attend," I said, looking at the customers around us. There was a cute, old couple eating breakfast together, and a guy with a purplish complexion sat at the table next to us, but otherwise most of the McDonald's customers came in for their orders and marched right back out.

"I don't understand how a doctor—even if he is a research doctor—can have so many meetings," Fran said. Since my MBRC adventure started in our sophomore year, she's been told I work for a doctor. Thankfully she isn't terribly interested in my part time job.

"It comes with the territory," I said, swirling my cup of hot chocolate. "How about Sunday?"

Fran bit her lip. "I have a date. But I could always cancel—,"

"Don't you dare," I said, smacking my hand on the McDonald's table before I realized it was covered with sticky residue. "It's with that Ethan kid you met a few weeks ago at Starbucks, right? Go on the date. He's the first guy to lure you out since—"

"*Do not utter his name*," Fran growled.

"Don't mention whose name?" a silver haired boy with a track star's build asked, plopping down on the booth seat next to me.

"Hey, Frey," I said. One would never guess it by looking at his build, but Frey was a werewolf. (He was the same werewolf that introduced me to the MBRC after his assignment, Dave-the-fat-vampire, blew their cover. Dave was now a fulltime teacher at our school, which is why Frey was still my classmate.) "We were just talking about…" I trailed off.

"Brett Patterson, right?" Frey said.

Fran sat ramrod straight, her eyes transformed into narrowed slits. Her plastic cup crackled in her hand as she clenched it.

"Try not to say his name," I muttered to Frey.

"Sorry," Frey said.

"I still don't get why you two haven't dated each other, yet," Fran said, brightening with the topic change.

"What do you mean?" I asked as Frey shook his head in distaste.

"You have the same part time job, you're always whispering to each other and acting all secretive, and you've been great friends since Frey transferred here. You're a perfect couple."

Yeah, all because Frey's werewolf instincts labeled me as a pack member, or in less convoluted terms: family.

"You're reading us wrong, Fran. We're more like…siblings," I said.

"Yeah. Or a dog and its owner," Frey said.

"I had better not be the dog," I said.

"Plus try to imagine us *actually dating*," Frey said.

Fran sipped her java chip frappe. "You would kill each other by the end of the week," she said.

"Yeah," I agreed. "Frey is a loner type."

"Being tied down isn't my style," Frey said with a wolfish grin.

"I have a theory that you just don't know how to romantically treat a girl," I said. "I mean, would you wag your tail at her?" I said under my breath so Fran couldn't hear.

Frey scowled.

"That's true. There appears to be no passion between you two," Fran said. "You have your little inside jokes, and you tease each other, but you have no physical chemistry. I could see you two punching each other out, but I can't imagine you kissing."

"Gross," Frey said.

I smacked the werewolf. "It sounds way awkward," I admitted.

"I guess you're right—it wouldn't work out between you two. You really do fight like siblings—with all the name calling and childishness I mean," Fran said.

"Hey now, I am not childish!" I said.

"Plus Frey is too much of a toothpick for you. You need a guy who at least has some muscle on him," Fran said.

"I have muscles," Frey said.

"You're so skinny you could fall down a storm sewer," I said.

"What? That is so not true!" Frey said.

"Yep, you can do better, Morgan."

"Thanks, Fran."

"Girls! And you wonder why I don't date," Frey grunted. "But you are missing an important detail. There's no way I would date Morgan. Too many guys at work have a thing for her," Frey said.

"What?" Fran asked, leaning forward in interest.

"He's lying," I hastily said.

"No I'm not."

"Yes, he is," I said, kicking Frey under the table.

"I'll keep the coworkers in mind," Fran said.

"Please don't," I said.

"We're going to rectify this lack of a boyfriend, Morgan," Fran said, leaning back in her chair. "This is our senior year. We have only a few months of high school left. You should live it up."

"I'm uninterested in guys our age," I said. "I find them immature and big-mouthed," I said, eyeing Frey.

"So it must be Devin that you're after, then?" Frey said before I elbowed him in the gut.

"Devin?" Fran said. "That's Hot Garden Guy, right? You've brought him around a few times, but I thought you said he's in a college program in the UK."

"He is," I said. "Frey is just being a rumor-monger. I don't have anyone I like, Fran. I don't have the time."

"I guess that's true," Fran sighed.

"Besides, it's not like I'm worth less because I don't have a boyfriend."

"Of course not," Fran said, sitting up straight again. "Did someone tell you otherwise? They're wrong, you know. I think it's really impressive how you're going out into the world, making connections, and networking for the sake of your future."

"You're giving me too much credit," I said. "I don't have a clue what I want to do after high school."

"Did you look at the websites I sent to you for the college in Florida?" Fran eagerly asked.

"No. I'm so sick of looking at colleges I could puke. I don't even know what I want to major in," I said.

"Florida? Didn't the—I thought our place of work offered to give you a scholarship if you attended a local college?" Frey said.

In other words the MBRC would help pay for college if I stayed local so I could continue teaching. Tempting, but I wasn't sure I wanted to work such a time consuming job for the duration of my college career, as I was positive Administrator Moonspell would contractually obligate me to do.

"Yeah, but I don't know if I want to stay in the area," I said.

"You better make your mind up soon," Fran said. "You need to get your college applications in."

"I know," I grumbled.

"You already know where you want to go, Fran?" Frey asked.

"My first choice is a college in Florida, but I have two back up schools in Illinois incase financial aid falls through," Fran said. "What about you?"

Frey shook his head. "Trade school. My Dad is an electrician and owns his own company. I want to inherit it—eventually."

"Wow. That's cool," Fran said.

I took another slug of my hot chocolate. "I didn't picture you as the family-business type."

Frey shrugged. "I'm going to keep my job with the, er, doctor. I want to take some business management classes, so I'm still going to enroll in college after I learn my trade. I have a few years of school ahead of me, and I enjoy my job. It's fewer hours for me anyway," Frey said.

True, as Dave's handler he did less and less with the chubby vampire. Dave was (slowly) getting better at fitting in with humanity.

"That's weird. I swear Morgan has more hours than ever," Fran frowned.

"Frey does a different type of work than I do. I help with the research. Frey is more…application-task orientated," I said, scrambling for an explanation.

"Yeah," Frey said, quick to agree.

"Oh. Well, I need more napkins. I'll be right back," Frey said, sliding out of her bench.

"That was close," I said.

"Yeah. But you seriously haven't made up your mind about what you want to do?" Frey asked.

I shrugged. "There are so many options. I don't know if I should just shoot for the normal and mundane, or try to keep working at a rehabilitation facility. I've gotten job offers from just about every start-up rehabilitation facility in the states and the UK," I said. "Everyone seems to be taking it for granted that I will attend college."

"It's become something of the social norm," Frey agreed.

"It seems to be the only thing people can *think* of," I scowled.

"You'll figure it out. Good luck with your decision. I imagine you have a lot of outside pressure? Beyond your parents, I mean."

"Yes."

Frey shook his head. "Good luck," he repeated.

"Thanks. I need it."

When I opened the door to my MBRC office a young man in his early twenties stood just inside. He had a white smile, black hair with body in it most women would kill for, and eyes that were the yellow color of a full moon.

He smiled, flashing dangerous dimples at me. "Morgan, how I have missed you—"

I slammed the door shut, cutting off his words. I stared at the office door for a few moments before I shook my head and started down the hallway.

The door snapped open behind me. "That was terrible. I took a red-eye flight so I could get here in time for your work hours. You could have at least listened to me call you beautiful or something."

"Go away, Devin," I said, walking past a tall, waxy looking guy leaning up against a wall in the hallway.

"Why are you so harsh?" Devin asked, catching up with me. He threw an arm over my shoulder and leaned so close his lips brushed my ear when he said, "You'll never get rid of me with cruel words. I find them endearing."

"Cut that out," I said, shrugged his arm off and pushing him away from me.

"Crabby today, are you? What rubbed your fur wrong?"

"Nothing rubbed me wrong. I was perfectly fine until you showed up," I said.

"What? What could *I* possibly have done to offend you?" Devin asked, his throaty, velvet voice laced with falsified pain.

I stopped walking and stared at him. "Are you seriously asking that?"

"Perhaps."

"Fine. Let's start with your greeting."

"What is wrong with the way I greeted you?"

"You spoke in a fawning, cooing voice."

"I haven't seen you for months. Perhaps I wanted to fawn and coo over you," Devin said, his voice colored with amusement. "Would you rather I call you my sweet darling?"

"That's what I'm talking about. Cut that sweet-talk out or I swear to Administrator Moonspell, I will accuse you of being a pervert in front of the MBRC board and get you banned from here. Again."

"I don't understand why my language upsets you so," Devin said, his voice losing its sappy edge.

"It upsets me because it's fake."

"No it's not."

"Yes it is! Devin, whenever you called me from Britain you had a pack of female voices in the background, giggling at everything you said. You have the loyalty of a stray tom cat."

"So what kind of loyalty are you looking for?"

"It's not the loyalty it's just—Gah! If you treated me like a normal person I wouldn't be so angry with you all the time," I called over my shoulder as I started walking again.

Devin caught up with me, his sweet talk gone. "Did you look at the program pamphlets I sent you?"

"The UK exchange student programs? Yes. I'm not going to study abroad."

"Why not? It will be a magnificent experience for you."

"Let me rephrase that: I'm not going to study abroad for all four years of college, and I'm certainly not going to study abroad my freshman year."

"Why not study in Britain all four years? You won't get another chance to do this."

"First of all, it would get way too expensive."

"The Fairy Council would give you an internship, if not

straight-out hire you. They have only a few human liaisons, and several of them are so old they are going to croak any day. They would welcome your presence," Devin said.

"I don't know if I want anything to do with the magical community while I go to college," I said.

"What?"

"It's not that I am no longer interested in magical beings, and I wouldn't rule out a career with you all…but…I missed out on a lot of high school norms because of my work here."

Devin raised an eyebrow. "Like?"

"Well, I didn't get to hang out with my friends as much."

"What friends? I recall you seem to have an absurd amount of friends among the members of the MBRC."

"My high school friends. I mean, I still get to hang out with Fran a few times a week, and all my other friends I see during school, but it's not the same."

Devin stopped walking. "You mean to tell me that fifty years from now you will regret that you worked in the MBRC for your high school career, shaping the *future* of the magical community, because you will be sad you did not spend more time on friendships that very likely won't last after you graduate high school?"

"I know it sounds stupid."

"Sounds stupid? It most assuredly *is* stupid."

"What do you want me to say? I don't know what I want to do. I don't know where I want to go to college, and I don't know what I want to do with my life! But four years away from everyone I know and love is definitely not it."

"I would be there," Devin said.

"Yeah, with your fawning fan-girls. Don't be ridiculous, Devin. The moment you're back in the UK you will forget I exist."

"I never forget you," Devin said.

I stopped walking again and waited until Devin looked me in the eye. "Then there's something going on that I don't understand. I don't know if it's fairy politics or what. I'm telling you, Devin, I don't get it. And there's no way I'm going to put up with it."

Devin sighed and ran a hand through his luxurious hair. "What are you doing this weekend?"

"Saturday morning I'm hanging out with Fran. In the evening the MBRC board has a meeting with the Chicago branch of Weller Goblin Enterprises."

"I'll take you out to dinner after the meeting," Devin said, turning and walking in the opposite direction.

"But—Devin!" I called after his retreating figure. He ignored me and kept walking. "GRRRR. That Pooka!"

"Finally our field trip to the Museum of Science and Industry has been okayed by MBRC administration," I said, clicking the remote so a picture of the museum flashed onto the overhead screen.

My students clapped and released various noises of approval.

"It's been too long since we've gone on a field trip," Madeline said.

"That's probably because the last one ended in disaster—no thanks to you," Frey said.

"It wasn't my fault that child lost its tooth when it did," Madeline objected.

"Yeah, but you didn't have to scream like someone shot you and faint," Perseus—one of the young centaurs who acted as my private technical support team—snorted.

"We didn't even get to go inside. It would have been our first amusement park visitation," said one of several drabby fairies in my class with a great deal of wistfulness.

"It was my fault. I should have known it was too early to take you all to Six Flags," I said. "Perhaps in another year. Or two. Anyway! This field trip has been approved for next week Saturday. Bring your human money and disguises or you will have to remain behind."

"Yes, Morgan."

"That's it. You're dismissed," I said. As my students dispersed I grabbed a small box from my podium and approached one of my students, a shy werewolf named Frank.

Frank was busy itching his collarbone as I approached.

"Hi Frank, I have another necklace for you," I said, opening the box to reveal a black band with a buckle.

Frank stopped itching long enough to smile. "Thank you, Morgan. My last one busted when I transformed into a wolf. I'm sorry," he said, hanging his head.

"I'm just glad you like wearing them. It," I said, handing the "necklace" to Frank.

"Yeah, it's become something of my trademark in my pack. They're all jealous," he said before itching his scalp.

"I'm glad, let me know when you need another," I said, edging away from Frank as he strapped the necklace around his neck.

"Okay, thanks again."

"You're welcome," I said, retreating to the far side of the room. What Frank didn't know was that his "necklace" was actually a flea collar. Frank belonged to a wild, rambunctious pack, and as a result he often went frolicking in state and national parks—getting himself infested with fleas, ticks, and other parasites.

Perhaps it was cruel of me to hide the truth from him, but at least my class wasn't going to break out with fleas.

I was packing my jump-drive in my backpack when I was grabbed from behind in a bear-hug and hauled into the air. "Morgan! How you doing, Chicka?"

"Hi, Esmeralda," I said, greeting one of my former students.

Esmeralda was a vampire, like Madeline, but she had been turned into one in the past decade and had a good handle on being human. She attended my classes more as a way to meet other magical beings. Since growing more comfortable with her new companions, she spent the past year or so traveling. (She was the student who went to Atlantis.) She was a beautiful teenager with olive colored skin and a fiery temper.

"You're back from…?"

"New Zealand. They've got loads of elf clans out there. I have lots of pictures and some video footage. Do you wanna see them sometime?" Esmeralda asked.

"I would love to," I said. "What kind of elf clans?"

Esmeralda made a funny face. "Just about everything. There's some high elves, and a fire elf clan since there's lots of hot-springs and inactive volcanoes and stuff. I also ran into this totally weird, hippy elf clan. I don't know what kind of elf they were, but they were bizzaro. Like, the Madeline version of elves."

"I resent that implication," Madeline said, latching on to my arm.

"I think it was a good explanation," I said as we started for the door. "I've got to drop some stuff off at my office. Do you want to come with, Esmeralda?"

"What? You don't ask me? I'm hurt," Madeline said as we left the classroom and started down the hallway.

"I assumed you were coming with whether I invited you or not."

"You could still invite me to avoid hurting my feelings."

"Yeah, I would love to come with. Is Baobab still your assistant?"

"Yep. I'm not giving her up until MBRC wrenches her from me," I said.

"Awesome, I want to catch up with her. Where was Asahi tonight, anyway? I didn't see him among your students."

"He left a few minutes early. I hope he remembers to tell Kadri about the field trip," I said.

"He's still dating her?"

"Yeah."

"I'm surprised they're not married yet," Madeline said.

"No kidding. It's been two years since they started that elvish courting thing," Esmeralda said.

"They're still young. They can't be older than, what, 23 or 24-years-old?" I asked.

Madeline hooted. "Are you serious? No way. Asahi is in his 40s."

"...he what?"

"Elves live longer than humans, remember? High elves in particular. In human years I suppose Asahi would be about 21—but that's typically when elves choose their spouse anyway," Madeline said.

"Yeah. I wonder what the holdup is," Esmeralda said, glancing over her shoulder as we climbed a flight of stairs.

"Devin is back in town," I said.

Madeline puffed up like an angry cat. "He *what*?"

"Yep. I saw him right before class—he was waiting for me in my office."

"It's a wonder Baobab didn't take a stapler to his head," Esmeralda said. "The Pooka dated one of her sisters for, like, two weeks. It didn't end well."

"What did he want?" Madeline asked.

"Nothing in particular. He gave out the usual sappy story and wondered why he wasn't in my good graces," I said.

Esmeralda glanced over her shoulder again. "Um, guys, I hate to be a party pooper—"

"A party *what*?" Madeline asked, crinkling her button nose.

"But I think we're being followed," Esmeralda finished.

"By whom?" I asked.

Esmeralda discreetly tipped her head backwards. "Purple-y looking guy back there. Looks like he's in his early thirties, and is wearing a suit," she whispered.

I looked back at the guy trailing about thirty feet behind us. "Oh, no. It's not what you think. That's just Krusher. Sorry, I forgot you left before he started coming around here."

"It's Harrison, Miss Fae," the man—who was in all actuality a goblin—called.

"Harrison?" Esmeralda blinked.

"Yeah. Hunter assigned him to me about three months ago. He's my bodyguard. He trails me all day long," I said before gesturing at Harrison to come closer.

"This is one of my former students, Esmeralda. Esmeralda, this is Krusher," I said, making the introductions.

"It's Harrison," Harrison said after nodding to Esmeralda.

"Why do you call him Krusher?" Esmeralda asked as the goblin retreated to his customary post—which was about thirty feet behind me.

"Because Harrison is totally a terrible goblin name," I said.

"No it's not. All the goblins I've met have been similarly named," Madeline said. "They customarily have elegant and refined names."

"Yeah, but I mean by fairy tale standards it's a terrible name. I mean, I could call him Harry for short. But then he's like Prince Harry. A goblin is supposed to be fierce and frightening to behold not a…" I turned around to narrow my eyes at Harrison. "Handsome, sophisticated, James Bond type."

I didn't know much about Harrison, and not for lack of trying but because he's *dead boring*. He conversed about as well as a stick. And he—just like every other American Goblin—was a terrible fairy tale let down. The only thing otherworldly about him was his somewhat purplish, waxy complexion and his unnaturally white teeth. Before meeting modern day goblins, I thought they were supposed to be gnarly creatures with pig tusks and grotesque faces.

I am telling you, historical literature and poems have totally failed us in accurately describing mythical creatures and beings.

"It's nice being friends with a Goblin King, huh?" Madeline said.

"In what way?" I sourly asked.

"He's pretty hot," Esmeralda said, drawing an eye roll from Madeline.

"I like Hunter. I could do without the baggage he brings with him, though," I said, starting for my office again.

The reason why the MBRC board dragged me into every meeting that involved goblins was because I was on great, if not complicated, terms with the Goblin King of Chicago: Hunter Weller.

Hunter was my classmate from school, and a good friend. Our relationship had occasional strains—he once kidnapped me for a weekend, and in a strike of retaliation I signed him up for the yearbook committee our junior year—but in general my presence was enough to assure better behavior from him.

Plus I'm totally immune to the goblin power of persuasion, their main magical strength.

"Does the Pooka know about Harrison?" Esmeralda asked, twisting around to waggle her fingers at Harrison.

"I think so," I said. "I'm pretty sure he would have said something earlier today if he didn't."

Esmeralda shook her head. "Your life is so weird. You know that, right?"

"Thanks for the ego boost."

"Welcome!"

3

Warnings Issued

The Saturday meeting was boring. I sat in a chair at a desk with a special plaque that read *Human Liaison*. The MBRC board was seated around a horseshoe shaped table. Hunter stood at a podium placed in the opening of the horseshoe. A goblin advisor and a pack of bodyguards loomed behind Hunter, motionless and silent.

The board members listened carefully to Hunter's presentation —a request to give a pixie powder license to a special, goblin funded, magical being only nightclub. (Pixie powder is a legal ingredient used by magical beings to supplement glamours and disguises, but the MBRC has a tight limit on how much can be imported into Chicago, and who can distribute it.)

As the discussion took a turn from boring (the necessity of pixie powder sellers) to dangerously mind-numbing, I leaned back in my chair and yawned.

"—assure you, there is great need of another pixie powder vender. According to our studies only two other sellers are open during the hours our nightclub operates. Both are situated far away from *Firefly*," Hunter said, referring to his nightclub. "Clearly there is a need and a market."

"Mr. Weller. We do not care about supply, product demand, profits, and economics as much as we are concerned with responsible vendors," Luka Farka—the vampire representative board member who owed me big time for that nightmare of a driving lesson—said. His s's were soft hisses.

Hunter gave Luka his business smile—flashing his white teeth. He hadn't worn sunglasses to the meeting, so his eyes glittered like polished topaz gems. "If that is the case, Weller Goblin Enterprises is the perfect vendor. Most of the pixie powder available in Chicago is imported by us. You already trust us to be importers, why not vendors?" he said. His voice was coaxing and warm.

Luka did not look impressed, but the fairy and dryad representatives were enthralled.

"Mr. Weller does have a valid point," the fairy board member said.

"I agree," the dryad said.

Elros Gloriath—one of two elf representatives on the board—scowled. "Get your head out of the clouds. He's using his magic on you."

The wizard representative straightened up in his chair. "He is?" he said, his voice shaded with a touch of panic. He had a blindfold tied around his head so he couldn't see Hunter's eyes. (Apparently Hunter's persuasion magic had terribly affected him in previous meetings, before I came along.)

I stood, accidentally thumping my knee on my desk, and strolled towards Hunter and his cronies. No one seemed to notice or care when one of Hunter's bodyguards—Logan, I knew him quite well from the weekend I was kidnapped—stepped aside so I could take his place behind Hunter.

"Don't be a twit, Dante. He can't affect you as long as your eyes are covered," Luka said.

"Perhaps," Hunter said in his velvety voice.

The wizard squeaked and huddled in his chair.

Ranulf, the werewolf of the board, rubbed his eyes. "What I wouldn't give to have Blood here," he said, referring to the Blood

Binder, the dragon board member who was the acting representative for all magical creatures.

Blood Binder was a calming presence on the board, but he was gone for the week—making a special report to the Fairy Council with the second elf board member.

"You all are making a big deal over nothing," the dryad trustee said.

"Indeed!" said the fairy board member. "I make a motion to grant *Firefly* a license.

The wizard panicked. "I can't tell if I'm being enthralled to vote or not!"

"You're fine, Dante," Ranulf said. "Apricot, Privet. Pull yourselves together," he snapped, slamming his meaty fist on the table.

"There's nothing wrong with us. We simply see the logic in Mr. Weller's argument," the fairy insisted.

"We never should have approved a dryad representative. One vapid fairy is enough," Luka said.

"What do you mean by that, trustee Farka?" the dryad said, leaning across the table to glare at the vampire.

"Only that a board member must be responsible, cunning, and knowledgeable—something neither dryads nor fairies are particularly known for. A second vampire would have been a better choice."

"Luka," Ranulf growled.

"WHAT?" the fairy and dryad shrieked.

Hunter chuckled.

"Stop it. This is exactly what he wants," the wizard said, his voice tight.

The rest of the board members ignored him.

"If you believe the vampires deserve *two* representatives, you are sadly mistake, trustee Farka," Elros said, his narrowed eyes framed by gorgeous eyelashes.

"What sad reason can you cite for such a refusal? The elves have two representatives *and* the Administrator is a high elf," Luka said.

"Elves *founded* the MBRC. Naturally we have a bigger say in it," Elros said.

"Or a monopoly," the fairy representative said.

"I beg your pardon?" Elros said.

Before the conversation could continue, I leaned forward to address Hunter. "If you don't stop whatever you're doing, I'm going to kick you."

Hunter twisted so he could smirk at me. "I'm trembling in my custom-made shoes."

"Hunter," I said.

"Fine, fine," he grumbled. "Ladies and gentlemen, I'm sure we can come to an agreement," Hunter said, his voice projecting above the argument.

The fairy and dryad board members—who were under Hunter's powers of persuasion—blinked when he released them.

"What?" the fairy said.

"You seem to have forgotten why we are here," Hunter said. "Allow me to remind you: I want a powder license for *Firefly*. I am not here to ratify or make changes to MBRC board dynamics."

Elros glared at Hunter, as if he could skewer him. "The board is prepared to offer you a Type C powder license."

Hunter frowned. "Type C is the lowest license which will allow only a small amount of powder to be distributed each day."

Ranulf caught sight of me standing behind Hunter. He nodded in my direction, acknowledging my supposed action in the situation. In reality the board gives me too much credit. Hunter is totally a business freak. He wouldn't let their argument get too out of hand, or they would never give him a license.

"*Firefly* has limited business hours, and we would still like to encourage magical beings to make their powder purchases during the day from an MBRC certified seller. A Type C license is the only license we are prepared to grant you at this time," Elros said.

Hunter sighed, as if aggravated. "Fine," he said, turning his back to the board. The barely-there smile on his lips told me he got exactly what he was hoping for.

"All in favor of granting *Firefly* of Weller Goblin Enterprises a Type C powder license say aye," Elros said.

The board was a chorus of ayes.

"Opposed?" Elros asked.

No one spoke.

"The license has been granted. This meeting is adjourned," Elros said.

The board members scattered, eager to get away from Hunter and each other.

"I am sorry they pulled you in here," Hunter said, following me back to my desk.

"No you aren't," I said.

"You're right, I'm not. I'm glad someone else had to listen to them squabble and argue too," Hunter said.

"For someone who got exactly what you wanted, you sound pretty pouty," I said, gathering my purse.

Hunter shrugged. "It's nothing. What are you doing now?"

"I'm—"

"Going out to dinner with me. Hello, Morgan," Devin said, sliding in to my personal space and the conversation with a natural ease. He placed his arm around me and tried to nuzzle my hair. "Did the meeting go well?"

"It went fine, thanks," I said, squirming out of his grasp.

"Councilman, you're back in the States, I see," Hunter said.

"Yes," Devin said.

"Even though the Council hasn't released for its break yet."

"Of course."

"I should have expected as much."

"I'm hurt that you didn't."

Devin and Hunter nodded to each other during the weird exchange. They got along surprisingly well, which is a real challenge for them with their *special* personalities.

"Councilman, it's a pleasure to see you here. Good evening," Ranulf, the werewolf, said, offering his hand.

Devin shook it. "Thank you, Ranulf. It is good to be home."

"How are things with the Fairy Council?"

"Well enough. Councilmembers Windstorm and Featherlight are digging in their hooves about centaur herd preservation," Devin said, wearing charm and power like a shirt.

Hunter heaved his eyes at the older man. "It was good to see you, Morgan," he said.

"Yeah, it was good to see you. What book are you going to use for your British Literature paper?"

"I'll probably do something involving Shakespeare," Hunter said. "You?"

"I was thinking *Pride and Prejudice*."

"What, not Dracula?" Hunter teased.

"Hah-hah, very funny."

"I thought it was. The first draft isn't due for two weeks. You know that, right?"

"Yep. But with all my hours at the MBRC, homework tends to get pushed to the last minute. It'll go easier if I start thinking about it now."

"True. Which reminds me, I brought you something," Hunter said, placing a briefcase on my desk. He removed a bag of cookies from the interior and passed them off to me. "From Cinna," he said.

"Oh my gosh, thank you," I said hugging the cookies to my chest. Anything cooked by Cinna was to be treasured. He was one of two chefs that worked for Hunter. The best thing about him was that he was a cookie elf. Cinna can bake heaven into a pie. I'm not even joking. And don't get me started on his donuts.

Hunter looked amused. "You're welcome. I'll see you Monday?"

"Yeah," I said, totally absorbed with my cookies. "Bye."

Hunter chuckled and left the room with his men. Er, goblins.

When Devin finished talking to the board members—Ranulf wasn't the only one to pay his respects, Devin might be a flirt but he was a darn good councilman—he turned to me. "Ready?"

"Yeah," I said, finishing my third cookie.

"What is that?"

"A red velvet cake cookie. They're fantastic."

"And where did you get them?"

"Hunter's chef made them for me."

Devin raised an eyebrow. "You accept food from him?"

"What? It's not like he's going to poison it," I scoffed, securing the remaining cookies in my purse.

"I suppose so," Devin said. "You don't go accepting food from every random being that offers it to you, do you?"

"No!" I said, outraged. "I'm not that stupid."

"Good. Come on. I had to pull strings to get reservations tonight. I don't want to lose our table," Devin said, heading for the door.

"This place better not be fancy," I said. "I'm in jeans, and I don't have a change of clothes with me."

"You'll be fine. Besides, we match," Devin said, indicating his dark toned jeans.

"Right," I said, rolling my eyes.

Dinner was a new experience. The restaurant entrance was a sewer, which wound deeper and deeper underground before pitching us into a long, narrow tunnel.

"You had to get reservations for this place?" I said, tripping in the dim light.

"You'll understand when you see it. You like international food, right?"

"Yep."

"Good. Here we go," Devin said when we reached the end of the tunnel. "Two under the Pooka," Devin said to a thick, trollish guy who guarded the door.

The troll listened to someone talk on the other side of his headset before he stepped aside and nodded us in.

Once we were inside I felt suitably more impressed.

The tunnel pitched us out past the shores of Lake Michigan, and the restaurant was built underwater. The ceiling and most of the walls were glass, letting customers look up into the sky hazed by several feet of water, and peer into the depths of the lake. What really wowed me were the tables. Each dining table was set on top of a rug. Customers would eat sitting down on the rug, which floated, like Aladdin's carpet. Like, seriously, they moved around the room. The rugs—which weren't driven by anyone I could see—seemed to have some sort of magic intellect that kept them from running into each other. The restaurant was quite big, so there was a lot of space to float around and up and down in.

"Wow," I said.

A small fairy the size of a water bottle fluttered up to us. "The Pooka, party of two? Right this way. Your carpet is ready for departure," she said, zipping through the crowd.

Devin and I hurried after her, stepping onto an indigo and gold patterned Turkish rug.

"Please remain seated at all times while onboard your dinner rug," the fairy said. "Your food and drinks will be brought to you while you are in the air. If, for any reason, you need to return to the ground, please inform one of our employees. My name is Mayberry, and I will be your server tonight. Please enjoy your flight, I will return once you are airborne to take your drink orders," our small waitress said as Devin and I sat on the plush rug.

"This is awesome," I said when the rug lifted an inch off the ground, gradually rising higher.

Sitting on a floating rug is a lot like sitting on a water bed that moves up and down like a reaaaalllyyy slow kiddie ride at a county fair. It felt a little eerie to be floating twenty feet off the ground, but it was smooth and gentle, even if the rug surface rippled like water.

"Strictly speaking this is a chain restaurant—similar to your Olive Patch," Devin said.

"Olive Garden," I corrected.

" However, Chicago is a no-fly zone for magic carpets and most methods of flying. So it has become unusually popular here," Devin explained. "Also, because the MBRC attracts a lot of international magical beings—who find it difficult to blend in with human society to eat—its menu has become increasingly more popular as well."

"Either way, it's incredible," I said as we floated along a wall, lazily passing Lake Michigan fish on the other side of the glass.

I caught Devin's thoughtful expression in our dim reflection cast on the glass walls. "Okay, Devin. What's up?"

"What is up?" Devin repeated, amused.

"Why did you bring me here?"

"I thought you would enjoy it."

"No way. At least, that wasn't your primary motivation," I said.

"I'm hurt by your accusations."

"*Devin.*"

The Pooka was rescued by our fairy waitress wielding a tiny pad of paper. "What would you folks like to drink?"

"Water, please," I said.

"I'll have a Pan's Pint. She'll take a Honeydew Bubble Tea," Devin said.

"A what?" I asked.

"Great, I'll be back with your orders in a few minutes," the fairy said, fluttering off.

I stared at Devin.

"It's a sweet tea drink from Taiwan. With your passion for Jamba Juice there's not a chance you won't love it," Devin said.

"That's not what I want to know."

Devin looked around the restaurant and held up one long finger, asking me to wait.

A few minutes later our drinks arrived—Devin's in an icy mug, mine in a clear, plastic cup. My drink was light green with a fat straw and black bead things at the bottom of the cup.

"Are you ready to order?" our waitress asked after our drink deliverer—a small dragon the size of a large dog—flew away.

"Morgan, do you trust me to order, or do you want to see a menu?" Devin asked.

I was inclined to ask for a menu, but a sip of my drink changed my mind. "You can order," I said before sucking down my bubble tea. It had a creamy, melon flavor and the black beads had the consistency of unflavored gummy bears. The drink was weird, but it was totally delicious.

Preoccupied with my drink as I was, I missed what Devin ordered before the waitress flew away.

"Now. Why have I brought you here?"

"Yeah," I said.

"You won't believe me if I tell you it's only because I want to spoil you?"

I chewed on one of the jelly beads and stared at Devin.

"Two reasons," Devin said, holding up two fingers. "First I wanted to confirm the MBRC has warned you of Fidem."

"Yes. Aysel told me. He said it was nothing to worry about."

Devin raised his eyebrows. "He's trying to sugarcoat it, is he?"

"Huh?"

"What did Aysel tell you about Fidem?"

"That it's an isolationist, anti-human political group. They're the magical beings version of rednecks."

"Rednecks? Hardly," Devin said. "Fidem is a *military* group. They haven't been destroyed because they are too big for any one group to take down. If the seelie and unseelie courts united with the Fairy Council it could be done. But it is more likely that Madeline will learn to enjoy blood before that happens."

"A *military group* has threatened the MBRC?" I exclaimed, my melon bubble tea sitting wrong in my stomach.

"Not quite. A member of Fidem personally issued the threats. His name is Krad Temero. He is a very dangerous dark elf and is responsible for a branch of Fidem's military power," Devin said, tapping the table with long fingers.

"So he's got a personal vendetta?"

"It is more that as a captain of Fidem he sees it as his responsibility to eradicate rehabilitation centers," Devin said. "Most authorities hope it is a personal threat, and that he does not seek to involve his underlings from Fidem in the battle."

"How strong is he?"

"Magically speaking? Quite. There have been several attempts against his life and he has survived them all. Only one of the Fairy Council's soldiers was ever able to lay a particularly nasty curse on Krad. The curse is still on him—it thankfully limits a bit of his power."

"Why are you telling me this? Madeline and Aysel both assured me I would be fine," I said.

"And you might be. But I want you to be well informed of the situation. Fidem, for all its strength, mostly lurks in darkness. It is not entirely unusual for its leaders to make political statements, but it is rare that they would launch an attack. The magical community is doubtlessly hoping Krad's threats are empty promises."

I sighed. "Great, that's really encouraging. Do you have any other depressing news?"

"Partially. I want to be certain you are not letting the MBRC—or the Moonspell family—enslave you in the future."

That made me sit up straighter. "What?"

"I don't think you realize what a commodity you are. The MBRC is not going to easily let you walk away if you choose to leave the Chicago area."

"You mean they'll wipe my memories?"

"No, I mean they will do everything they can—by bribery or deceit—to keep you as an employee," Devin said.

"Why?" I asked. "I'm not Dr. Creamintin. I can't help magical beings figure out what they have to do to fit in. All I can do is present them with information about every day stuff. If they used Google or Wikipedia even halfway decently they could find way more info than I could ever tell them."

"How many magical beings do you know can use a computer, much less competently use a search engine?" Devin asked.

"More than you would think. Almost all the wizards and enchanters have tablets and laptops. Toby and his hobgoblin friends are all pretty good at using search engines, and I know a few centaur kids who have more technology than me," I said.

"But the wizards have better things to do than to surf the internet, and while Toby might be able to track down data, it doesn't mean he will correctly interpret it. As for the centaurs, their abilities with technology are vast, but it doesn't translate to common human knowledge. They don't know social norms, and they don't know how to interact with humans," Devin said, leaning back, propping himself up with his arms. "Not to mention you are one of only a handful of young humans that know about us."

"What do you mean?"

"It's a well known fact you are the youngest human employed by the MBRC, right?"

"Yeah."

"Only a dozen or so normal humans—not magicians or wizards in training who live separately from human society—under the age of thirty legally know of magical beings. That makes you a product that is in high demand," Devin said. "And it's not like the MBRC can yank another high schooler off the streets to help. The only reason you were allowed to keep your memories is because of my protection. To let a human remain knowledgeable of the magical takes a great deal of political power."

"Alright, I will admit that a bunch of other start-up rehabilitation facilities have been trying to lure me away, but why are you concerned that the MBRC might *enslave* me?"

"You have become a poster child for the MBRC. If you leave, you will take some of their power and prestige with you," Devin said, pulling a paper out of thin air and laying it out on the table.

It was a promotional flyer for the MBRC, highlighting some of their services and specialties. I was shocked to see a picture of me, standing in front of my first Introduction to the American Education System class, featured on the poster.

"Having one human teacher leave can't make the MBRC stumble too badly," I said. "Even if they use me as promo material. They can just as easily brag about Asahi and Kadri—who also teach classes—and the way I mentored them."

"Yes, but you're thinking purely from an education standpoint. Remember, the MBRC is also a money maker. If you leave you *cannot* pretend some of your friends won't go with you."

"Okay, Madeline would tag along with me. So what? She's not even in a coven."

"Madeline would follow you," Devin acknowledged. "As would a number of your cyclops friends."

"...Oh," I said, seeing it in a new light.

The cyclopes are business savvy beings who probably rehabilitated into human society the best out of all magical races. They are also filthy rich and are well known for donating millions to the MBRC.

"Everyone knows you and Hunter Weller are friends. If you choose to attend a college that is anywhere near a goblin branch office they are going to pay their dues and respects to you."

I rolled my eyes. "Hunter is the youngest of all his siblings. They won't…" I trailed off, thinking. During the previous Christmas break, Hunter's family flew into Chicago. I met all of them, lured to Hunter's place by the promise of Cinna's Christmas cookies, and they were all unfailingly nice and pleasant to me—even Hunter's older siblings. They seemed eager, in fact, to promote my friendship with Hunter.

"Having cyclopes in your pocket and goblins watching your back is more than enough to make the MBRC uneasy at the thought of your exit," Devin said. "Unfortunately for you, and fortunately for them, you are in a consultant position, which means you don't have the political clout needed to protect yourself. You were accepted into magical society because of my name, but even if you're attached to me the MBRC can still trick you into signing a shady contract."

"You want me to be careful before committing to anything further?"

"Yes. And if the MBRC offers you a new contract or tries to get you to sign *anything*, have Hunter or Nick—that cyclops friend of yours—read it over first."

"Not you?" I asked as Devin sipped his pint.

"I would love to read your contracts over, but the MBRC's reaction will be worse if they know I'm dabbling with your career. I've already spoken to Nick and Hunter. You can contact them on your MM and they will answer immediately," Devin said.

"Okay."

"I find it odd that they haven't tried to strong arm you into anything yet. Asahi must be crusading for you behind the scenes," Devin said.

"Probably," I said, keeping my face straight. It wasn't a lie. He probably was fighting for me. But there was that time Aysel…

"I heard you're taking your advanced placement class on a field trip."

"Yeah, the Museum of Science and Industry."

"Haven't you been to that one before? I thought you would have hit up all the Chicago museums by now."

"No, I've been avoiding it as it has the highest degree of tech out of all the museums in Chicago. I didn't think my students would get it," I said. "And we've been to lots of places besides museums. We went to a library and a grocery store."

"And Six Flags, I've been told."

I winced. "Yeah. I was stretching them a little for that one."

"I'm surprised you haven't taken them to your high school."

"I was going to take them to a football game, but after Six Flags I decided it was time to take a break. We still might be able to cram in a baseball or soccer game before I graduate," I said.

"If you ask the MBRC, the Center may be willing to foot the bill for a professional American football game in the fall," Devin said.

"Maybe. I'm surprised you know about sports," I said.

Devin grinned. "Only marginally. I'm a rugby fan."

"Funny," I dryly said. "I totally would have pegged you as a swimsuit competition guy."

"A what?"

"Nothing," I said, taking a gulp of my bubble tea. "So what's for dinner?"

"Roasted boar."

"A *what*?"

"You said you trusted me."

"Yeah, that was my mistake."

"You'll love it, I promise. Although the sight of it might be a little off putting."

"Great. I can hardly wait."

Monday morning I shifted in place and stared at the front of the room with a frown. A new semester started the previous week, and I was still getting used to my new class schedule. "How the heck did you talk me into this class again?" I asked Fran.

"Colleges are looking for well rounded individuals," Fran said.

"And *cooking class* will prove that I'm well rounded?" I said.

"It's called culinary arts, remember?" Fran said.

"How could I forget," I said, leaning against my work station.

"Good morning, class!" our teacher said as he waltzed into the room. He had a jiggling potbelly and bright orange hair that was crawling to the back of his head. His name was Dave Smith, and I knew him quite well. He was the vampire that clued me into the whole magical beings bit.

"Good morning, Mr. Smith," my classmates dutifully said.

"Return to your stations, please. Today we're going to tackle the art of omelets," Dave said.

Fran set about prepping our workstation before she headed to the front of the classroom to get three recipe papers.

Each workstation had three students. Fran and I were together, and our third classmate was off flirting with girls as he was one of two males in the class. When he returned with a wolfish smile I said, "I hate you."

My second partner, Frey, gave me a wounded look. "What did I do?"

"You did something weird to Fran to convince her we needed to take a cooking class."

"It's culinary arts, and I did no such thing."

"Then who did?"

Frey hesitated.

"Frey."

"Hunter may or may not have suggested to Fran that culinary arts would be an enjoyable class," Frey said.

"He what?" I said.

"Yeah, he said when you find out I should tell you 'yearbook retaliation.'"

"That little—"

"That little what?" Fran chirped, handing a recipe to Frey and me.

"Nothing. Thanks," I said, taking the yellow sheet.

"Omelet—or as it was originally spelled, omelette—is a French word that became popular in the middle of the sixteenth century," Dave-the-chubby-vampire-turned-teacher said. "However, the dish existed before then."

I shook my head as I watched the rehabilitated vampire discuss the origins of the omelet.

"What?" Frey asked.

"I can't believe the school approved him as the cooking teacher," I said.

Frey shrugged. "It took a little bit of footwork from the MBRC, but you have to admit he's a much better chef than he is a Spanish substitute teacher."

"Yeah," I agreed. "So why am I here?"

"What! Do you really think I was going to suffer through this alone?"

"...variations of omelet including: the Japanese tamagoyaki, the Italian frittata, the Spanish tortilla de patatas, and the Indian tomato omelet—which is **not** a true omelet but is still called one," Dave said, his face scrunching up with the word 'tomato'.

"No," I said.

"There you have it," Frey said.

"You're coming with on the museum field trip, right?"

"Yeah. I thought I would skip it, but Dave put up a big stink about it with one of his teachers. So we're coming," Frey said.

"The most common ingredients used in an omelet are: salt, pepper, mushrooms, cheese, red peppers, green peppers, onions, and tomatoes. I will leave the ingredients up to your individual tastes, but in addition to your eggs you must use at least three of these ingredients," Dave said, waving a hand over the tubs of food piled on his desk.

"I want everything but onions," Fran said, turning to face Frey and I.

"You want nice smelling breath for kissing that Ethan of yours?" Frey asked, innocently batting his eyelashes.

Fran's jaw dropped.

Frey winked before heading for Dave's desk. "I'll get everything but the onions, then."

"I'm sorry I ever thought you should date him," Fran said.

"Yep. But that reminds me, how did your date go?"

"Okay. We went indoor mini-golfing."

I cringed. "Ouch."

"Yeah. When he realized how bad I was he was super apologetic. It was still a lot of fun, though."

"Why?"

"He wasn't much better than me. We lost our balls in all sorts of crazy ways. I almost died laughing when Ethan accidentally shot his golf ball in the mouth of a hollow t-rex statue we were supposed to putt under. By the end of our round we were on a first name basis with the employees."

"I'm glad you enjoyed it," I said, smiling at my friend.

"Yep. He's a nice guy. So did you hang out with Hot Garden Guy after work?"

"A little. We went out to eat. It wasn't like that!" I said when Fran raised an eyebrow.

"Oh really?"

"Yes, really! We talked about work."

Fran hummed. "It might be nice to have an older boyfriend—he can afford to buy all sorts of stuff for you."

"Fran!" I said, shocked.

She shrugged. "I'm just sayin'."

I glared, but was unwilling to comment as Frey returned with a tray filled with dishes of Fran's desired ingredients.

"Alright, ladies. Shall we chop?" he asked.

"Let's," Fran said, taking the red pepper. "You know, Frey. If you're not going to date Morgan, Samantha is single."

Frey, who had just started dicing the green pepper, almost chopped his finger off. "*What*?"

"It's a total code violation to have you floating around school, single. Morgan and I have a lot of nice friends we can set you up with."

Frey sputtered.

I smiled and said with great satisfaction, "I think it's fitting. After all, weren't you worried about suffering *alone*?"

Frey snarled at me as Fran continued on her tirade. "You already know Samantha. She was in second year Spanish with you and Morgan your sophomore year. Do you remember her? Otherwise I can introduce you to Hanna—she's a sweetheart."

4

Mucking with Moonspell

It turns out Devin's warning was very timely. When I strolled into my office on Wednesday afternoon, Baobab had news for me.

"Administrator Moonspell dropped off a new contract for you to sign," Baobab said.

"The Administrator himself? Not one of his minions?" I asked, freezing mid-motion of taking the contract. I rarely interacted with the Administrator—I had only talked to the elf five or six times. Why on earth would he personally deliver a contract?

"Yes," Baobab said. She hesitated before she added, "He said it is a revision of your old contract, but he wants it signed and returned immediately."

I stepped back, peering at the untouched contract as if it were a snake. "Right. I'll…thanks, Baobab," I said, stepping further away from her desk as I dug in my pocket. I pulled out what looked like a smart phone, but instead of having a touch/swipe surface, there was a mirror.

"Magic Mirror, on," I said. The edges of the screen glowed blue as it activated. "Call Nickolas Vontreba."

The mirror stopped reflecting my image and swirled. It cleared, showing a hazy image of Nick, my long time cyclops friend.

"Morgan, it's good to see you," Nick said, peering at me through the mirror surface.

"Hi Nick. Is this a good time?"

"Of course, how can I help you?"

"Administrator Moonspell dropped off a revised contract for me to sign."

"I'm on my way over," Nick said, his face disappearing as he stood up, giving me a view of his tie.

"It's okay. You can take your time, I didn't mean to interrupt you," I said.

Nick's face veered back into view. He had his glamour on, so he had two eyes. "No, Morgan. This is important. I'll be bringing a friend of mine."

"Sandy?" I asked hopefully, naming one of Nick's fellow cyclopes.

"No. A boggart. He's a lawyer."

"Oh," I said.

"We will be at the MBRC in half an hour. Will you be available then?"

"Yeah. I've got to drop by a birthday party Dr. Creamintin is throwing. I'll meet you at my office?"

"Excellent, until then."

"Okay," I said. "Magic Mirror, disconnect." The mirror stopped displaying Nick and my reflection returned. "Magic Mirror, off," I said before slipping the contraption back in my pocket.

"I'll be back in a bit, Baobab. I need to wish Aristotle a happy birthday and give him his present," I said, lifting up a cardboard box that was stuffed with pinecones covered in peanut butter and bird seed. Aristotle was a talking owl, and he had a secret mad passion for generic bird seed.

"Yes, Miss Fae."

The party was a blast. Aristotle loved his present—although his sour temperament wouldn't allow himself to acknowledge that—and I got to hang out with an old friend of mine, a bay colored unicorn named Westfall. Westfall was working in a riding therapy barn—and had been there for a year and a half—so I hadn't seen much of him. Time got away from me as I chatted with the shy unicorn, so I was almost late to the meeting. I slid into my office just as Nick and his boggart friend sat down in chairs in front of my desk.

"Morgan, perfect timing," Nick said. "Miss Baobab has already given us the contract," he said as his boggart friend raised a magnifying glass to his face and stared at my contract. "Morgan, this is Ed. Ed, I am delighted to introduce you to Morgan Fae."

"Huh," the boggart said, pressing his eye to the magnifying glass.

In fairy tales boggarts are depicted as malevolent house spirits who haunt people, bogs, or marshes. In reality, boggarts are just wild partiers, which got them a bad rep with humans.

Nick's boggart friend was fairly typical. He was human shaped but short—almost comically so next to Nick, who is roughly the height of NBA basketball players—and really hairy with big eyes.

"Thanks for coming out here on such short notice," I said. "Krusher, do you want to come in and watch?"

"It's Harrison, Miss Fae," Harrison said, ghosting into the office after me. I imagine he was going to memorize every word that was uttered and would report back to Hunter.

No skin off my nose. Neither Devin nor Hunter would be able to accuse me of being disobedient.

"So how is your work with elementals going?" I asked as I plopped down in a chair across from Nick.

"Quite well. I have successfully negotiated a contract with Magefire Cookies for fire salamanders, which grants them a minimum wage. Ed helped me arrange that," Nick said, smiling.

I once helped the cyclopes bargain with the MBRC to get better eyecare for them. It made me something of a cyclops mascot, and it motivated a few of them—Nick first and foremost—to involve themselves in humanitarian work for other races. Most of them targeted local businesses that were not as kind to their fellow magical beings as they could be, leaving MBRC negotiations up to me.

"Nice job," I said. "Is everything going well with your day job?"

Nick winced. "I dropped my glamour in front of my assistant on accident. He had to be hypnotized, but it seems there is no lasting damage to him, or his memories," Nick said.

"You dropped your disguise? Why?"

"I was in a call with Sandra."

I gave Nick a Cheshire cat smile. "I see."

Nick cleared his throat and tugged on his tie before Ed the boggart shouted, "Got it!"

"What have you found?" Nick asked, peering over his short friend's shoulder.

"It says—and this is assuming you've signed the contract—you 'agree to a non-compete contract, which will ban the signer from signing on with any competitor of the MBRC, for the span of four years,'" Ed said.

"Excellent job, Ed," Nick said.

"That's all?"I asked.

"Isn't that enough to keep you from signing?" Nick asked.

"Yeah, but that's not so bad. It would be disappointing, but all it means is that I would be banned from working at a rehabilitation center for four years. That's not terrible. I'm sure I could find another magical place to work," I said. "The way everyone is acting, I thought Administrator Moonspell might demand my firstborn child or something."

"But that's not all," Ed said.

"There's more?" Nick eagerly asked.

"Yeah," Ed said, setting the magnifying glass aside to pick up a highlighter. "He's extending your contract for two years, and if you quit there's a hefty breach of contract fee."

"What?" I said.

"How much?" Nick asked.

"Ten grand."

"WHAT?!" I said.

Baobab raised her eyebrows and busied herself with work.

Harrison didn't react. (Mostly because Harrison just *doesn't* react.)

The boggart highlighted a line in the contract, marking it vivid pink. "It's right there. If that's not a good enough reason to reject this contract, I don't know what is."

I snatched up the contract and Ed's magnifying glass so I could stare at the portion the boggart highlighted. Sure enough, Moonspell's contract specifically stated that if I left the employment of the MBRC before my two years were over, I would be forced to pay the fine.

"That scumbag," I growled, tossing the magnifying glass aside.

"What are you going to do?" Nick asked.

"I'm going to find Administrator Moonspell, and I'm going to kick him in the shins," I said, storming out of my office.

Nick, Ed, and Harrison were hot my heels.

"Couldn't you just refuse to sign?" Nick asked.

"No, he's gone too far," I said, striding down the hallway.

Ed chuckled as he scurried to keep up with my fast pace and Nick's long stride. "This should be a sight."

"Morgan," Nick said, catching my wrist. "As much as I would like to see you take on Administrator Moonspell, I cannot, in good conscious, allow you to do this. He's a powerful being."

Behind us Harrison cleared his throat and stared at my wrist that Nick held. Nick glanced at the bodyguard and let me go, taking a step back.

I smiled at Nick. "Thanks for your concern, but this guy needs a wakeup call. He has it coming."

"I hope you know what you're doing," Nick said, taking out his cell phone.

"I don't, but I know injustice when I see it, and I'm not about to let it slide," I said as we entered the main MBRC chamber. "Harrison, where is Administrator Moonspell right now?"

"Phoenix floor, heading for the staircase of the main MBRC chamber," Harrison said.

I set off towards the described destination.

Ed trotted with and asked, "How do you know that?"

"Occupational secret," Harrison said.

The phoenix floor was a flight up, so I had to climb some stairs. But when we reached the central chamber, I could spot Administrator Moonspell and his minions at the far side of the room, observing the chamber from behind a railing.

Administrator Moonspell is unfortunately gorgeous, like his sons. He has Asahi's golden sunshine hair, and Aysel's silver eyes. He looks like he's in his early forties, and is probably Aysel's fashion model as he wears robes and stuff, but he's super stiff. He moves so squarely and evenly he resembles a graceful robot.

"I see him. Wish me luck," I said before stalking off.

"Take him to the streets," Ed advised, selecting a good vantage point.

Nick acknowledged my comment with a wave as he called someone on his phone.

Administrator Moonspell didn't acknowledge me until I was a few feet away, but his peons saw me coming halfway across the room, stalking the walkway that snaked around the perimeter of the room.

A few of the minions shrank back, and an elf leaned in to whisper into Moonspell's ear.

"Miss Fae, what part of immediately did you not understand? You arrived at the MBRC well over half an hour ago," Administrator Moonspell said, his voice elegant and careless.

I held the contract up so he could see it. "This was the contract you wanted me to sign, yes?" I asked before I shredded it in half.

The minions gaped at me with slack jaws and horrified expressions. Administrator Moonspell narrowed his eyes—showing me who Aysel inherited his glares from. "You disrespect me?"

"Yes, because this contract is bogus," I said, tossing the two halves to the ground. "Not to mention it's, like, totally illegal."

"You are in the magical community, Miss Fae. Your petty government requirements do not apply here."

"Yeah, but common decency should!"

One of Administrator Moonspell's eyebrows twitched. "Must you *shout* like an unschooled banshee?"

"I'm not shouting," I said with gritted teeth. "And you can be sure I will *not* be working at the MBRC in the future. I might have—before you pulled this stunt. Now you can forget it."

Administrator Moonspell deigned to sigh. "If you mean to threaten me, Miss Fae, it will not work. You have been nothing but a thorn in my side since your arrival—it was not *I* who wanted to keep you employed here. Leave whenever you wish, I care not."

"I will finish my contract! But if you think I was a 'thorn' before?" I chuckled darkly. "Imagine what kind of a pain I can be, with all I know and all the beings I am in contact with now. I promise, you'll be hearing of me soon—and it won't be about any of my classes," I said, turning on my heels and marching away.

My glorious exit was almost ruined when I barely missed walking into Harrison. Harrison edged out of the way in time, avoiding the collision. As I walked away I heard Administrator Moonspell speak to his assistant.

"Evearan," he said.

"Yes, sir?" his elf assistant said.

"You said the Pooka recently returned?"

"I did."

"I can tell," he said, his voice dull and dead before we were out of hearing range.

I stalked back to Nick—who was still on the phone—and Ed.

"Yes, she's still alive," Nick said to the phone. "I think she has as good as resigned once her contract is finished, though."

Ed beamed as he patted me on the back—knocking air out of my lungs. "Good show," he said. "Last time Moonspell scowled like that, a fairy clan was exiled from Chicago."

Still angry and infuriated, the gravity of my actions hadn't yet sunk in. "Someone really needs to put him in his place. What?" I said when Nick held out his phone.

"It's for you," Nicks aid.

I cautiously picked up the phone. "Hello?"

"I love your fire, Morgan. But don't you think you could have reacted a little less impulsively?"

"Devin," I said, recognizing his smooth voice. "Nick called you?"

"He did. I'm glad you took heed of my warning."

I shifted, aware of Nick, Ed, and Harrison, and the way all three stared at me. "You aren't the type to frighten easily. Thanks, by the way."

"You're welcome. Have you given further thought to your future?"

"Devin."

"It was worth a shot. You have your advance placement class shortly, don't you?"

"Yeah."

"Excellent. Run along and attach yourself to Asahi."

"You think the Administrator will retaliate?"

"I don't think, I know. It's only a question of when."

"Why? It's his fault. Besides, I've gotten away with things before."

"Perhaps, but then again you've never called him out in front of the entire MBRC."

"No one noticed," I said, glancing down at the main chamber. It was the usual busy, chaotic mess.

"I beg to differ. No one reacted."

"Whatever. I've gotta go."

"Take care. And try not to pick any additional fights, please."

"Yeah, yeah. Bye, Devin," I said before ending the call. "Thanks," I said, passing the phone back to Nick.

"My pleasure," Nick said. "I'm sorry, but I really should return to my office, if you have no further need of assistance."

"Nah, I'm good. I've got class in about twenty minutes and I need to start preparing for it. Thank you. Both of you," I said, looking to Ed to include him.

"Anytime," Ed grunted.

"Do not hesitate to call if he offers you another contract," Nick said.

"I won't. Thank you, goodbye," I said as we split up and set off in different directions. I glanced over my shoulder. "You okay back there, Krusher?"

"It's Harrison, Miss Fae."

"Yeah. Will you tell Hunter about this… incident for me?"

"Yes, Miss Fae."

"Thanks."

"Of course, Miss Fae."

On Thursday, I was accosted by a dwarf—which was a new experience for me.

I was on my way to my office, edging through the central chamber of the MBRC. I didn't notice anything out of place, but Harrison was hovering.

Normally Harrison stays about ten feet away in crowded places like the MBRC chamber, and about twenty or thirty feet away in empty areas like hallways or streets.

But now he stood so close the sleeve of his expensive suit brushed my arm.

"Is something wrong, Krusher?"

"It's Harrison, Miss Fae," Harrison said, taking his sunglasses off as he looked behind us.

"What is it?" I asked.

Harrison said nothing, but he frowned and placed his arm on my lower back, gently pushing me forward.

"Harrison?" I asked, my heart beating faster. Was Administrator Moonspell about to extract his revenge?

"We're surrounded," he murmured.

I nonchalantly looked around the chamber, my eyes skimming over the crowd. Sure enough, a ring of buff, burly dwarves was closing in on us. "What do we do?"

"I suggest we get to the stairs," Harrison said, still guiding me.

We made it to the base and were about to climb the staircase when a deep, booming voice spoke. "Morgan L. Fae."

I whirled around, and found myself face to face with a dwarf. He had the typical squat, sturdy build of a dwarf, and was plenty hairy. His blonde hair exploded in braids everywhere, but his wore a brilliant crimson tunic, and, oddly enough, sported a gold tuxedo bow tie at his throat.

"Yes?" I said.

Harrison stepped in front of me and crouched into a defensive position as his venom green eyes glowed.

The bow-tie dwarf raised a bushy eyebrow. "Is the guard dog necessary?"

"That depends on what you want."

"We wish to speak with ye."

"About?"

The dwarf's eyes gleamed. "Administrator Moonspell," he said.

I swallowed and took a step up the stairs. "Harrison," I said, my voice tight.

"The princess is in a pinch. I repeat, the princess is in a pinch," Harrison said. (His goblin earpiece must have an ungodly long range.) He then reached out and wrenched a metal pipe from the stair railing, ripping it free with brute strength.

The dwarf blinked. "What? Wait a moment. Settle down, pup. I don't think yer understanding what we desire. I'm from the Silver Heights dwarf clan. Here be my card," he said, passing a business card to Harrison.

Harrison took the card and inspected it. He slid his sunglasses on and flipped it around a few times before handing the card to me.

"It's good to meet you Mr.…Growintork?" I said, trying to pronounce the hazardly spelled name.

"Grogrintork," the stout dwarf gently corrected me.

"Representative of the Silver Heights Clan," I read.

"Aye," the dwarf said. "We be from New Hampshire," he said.

That struck me as a rather odd place to find dwarves, but my years with the MBRC has taught me that magic can be tucked away in the most unexpected places.

"How can I help you, Grogrintork?"

"I was hoping I might talk to you in a more…private location."

I cast my eyes to Harrison. He was no longer standing as if he might throw himself at Grogrintork, but by no means was he relaxed. "Harrison?"

"Your office, Miss Fae," he said before muttering something—probably to his correspondents hooked up to his earpiece.

"This way...gentlemen," I said, glancing at Grogrintork's cronies before taking the lead.

When Grogrintork gestured, three of his companions—who were pretty much walking armories since they were covered in a variety of weapons—separated from the ring and followed us up the stairs. The rest of the dwarves dispersed into the crowd.

We reached my office, thumping in with quite a ruckus since Grogrintork's associates clanked when they walked.

"Miss Fae...," Baobab trailed off, watching the dwarf procession troop past her desk. She hesitated. "Shall I get some coffee for your...guests?" she asked as Grogrintork plopped down in a chair—making it buckle.

"That would be awesome. Thanks, Baobab," I said as Grogrintork's men pushed their way through my office so they could stand behind their leader. One of the weapon covered dwarves would have knocked several pictures off the wall, but Harrison reached out and secured the frames as the dwarves scooted beneath him.

Baobab nodded before she fled, closing the office door behind her.

"Okay. How can I help you, Grogrintork?" I asked, seating myself at my desk. I glanced at Harrison when he silently took a spot at my left elbow.

Grogrintork knitted his leathery hands together. "We're approachin' ye on behalf of the dwarves of the MBRC."

"For?"

"We're officially requestin' yer help."

That was not what I expected. "Oh. Do you need help with rehabilitation—classes, maybe?"

Grogrintork shook his shaggy head. "No. We need representation."

I drummed my fingers on my desk. "Where?"

"In the MBRC."

"I assume you mean places like the MBRC board, and the administrator's staff?" I said—it was a common complaint.

"Sort of."

I held in a sigh. "Grogrintork, I'm afraid to say you aren't alone.

The MBRC board represents only a fraction of the creatures in the MBRC. The trolls, cyclopes, giants, sirens, hobgoblins *or* goblins—none of them have representation on the board. The board has to be small. It *can't* have a member of every magical race or nothing would ever get done," I said.

Grogrintork listened. When I finished he again shook his head, making his gristly hair fly. "We understand that. We have the same problem at clan gatherings. But I wasn't just meanin' the board. There's not a dwarf in a single 'ppointment of power here."

"What do you mean?"

"There's two dwarf janitors and a couple o' tunneling experts. That's it. In the whole MBRC there's less than six hired dwarves."

I leaned back in my chair. "You are not like the cyclopes, who opt not to work at the MBRC?"

"Nope. Our folks have tried fer ages to get hired here. It's near impossible to get in."

My mind buzzed as I tried to recall seeing—or meeting—any dwarf employee. I couldn't, which was pretty odd. Besides Hunter's goblins and the cyclopes, the MBRC hired dozens of every sort of magical being I had ever met. But even though there were no cyclops or goblin employees, there were still liaisons. Harrison was considered a liaison—he even had the paperwork to prove it. "The MBRC won't hire any of you? It's not just excluding a certain, erm, clan?"

"Nope. There's a hirin' freeze on dwarves in general, and we're sufferin' fer it," Grogrintork grimly said.

"How?"

"Without dwarf employees and coordinators, it's wretched hard to get rehabilitation news. We're always behind. Sides the dragons, dinosaurs, 'n chimeras, we're the worst rehabilitated magical being there is."

'There are other rehabilitation centers," I said.

"True, but the MBRC is the biggest, 'n all the other centers are taking their cue from it," Grogrintork said as Baobab returned with a coffee pot and a tray of mugs.

"Thank you, Baobab," I said as she gave me an insulated coffee thermos I kept in my office. I clicked the thermos open and sipped. "They fixed the cappuccino machine, finally?"

"Yes, but the latté machine is dead now," Baobab said in her caramel voice as she poured a mug of coffee for Grogrintork.

The MBRC is…ok at getting their beings used to human food —I mean, they have cookie elves in their ranks. They can out bake and out cook some of the best human chefs on the planet. What I'm referring to is they're so-so at introducing magical beings to ordering and eating in fast food restaurants, Chinese takeout places, bakeries and the like. The one aspect of public human restaurants they have whole heartedly accepted, though, is coffee. Seriously, there's a cult for Starbucks among the hobgoblins.

As magical beings love their coffee, the MBRC cafeteria is fitted with state-of-the-art lattè machines, cappuccino machines, coffee bean grinders, French presses, tea steepers; you name it, they have it.

The downside is that although they can competently run them, MBRC employees are *really* bad at fixing them, so half of the time they're out of order, and the MBRC spends big bucks purchasing new ones more often than necessary.

Baobab looked to Grogrintork's buddies. "Would you care for some coffee?" she asked after a moment of hesitation.

Two of the weapon covered dwarves shook their heads—the motion barely visible thanks to the huge axes strapped to their backs and the cannon balls fixed to their shoulders. The third dwarf, though, clanked as he stared at Baobab.

At first I thought he was nuts for coffee like the rest of the MBRC, but I noticed his eyes—which were the only things besides his large, round nose that was visible in the rat nest of his hair—were hinged on Baobab, and they *glowed*.

Somebody was crushing.

I hid my laugh by sipping my cappuccino as Baobab uneasily shifted.

Grogrintork glanced over his shoulder at his crony. "He's fine," he assured Baobab.

"I'll just go take these back," Baobab said, eager to leave the office.

When the door closed behind her I asked, "Is there a reason *why* you aren't getting hired?"

If dwarves made poor workers I wasn't going to force them on the MBRC, but at least I could see about getting a couple of liaisons in place.

"The high elves," Grogrintork darkly said.

"I'm sorry, what?"

"Dwarves 'n high elves don't rightly get along," Grogrintork said.

I frowned. "You mean that's not just part of the fairy tale we humans made up?"

"Nope," Grogrintork said, resting his hands on his belt. "We're great chums with fire elves, and we get along with the cookie elves 'n wood elves, and most all elf races—even the Beer Brothers! The high elves are the only kind 'o elf we're at real odds with."

"Is there a particular reason for that?"

Grogrintork scratched his chin through his beard. "Might have something to do with all the practical jokes we've played on 'em over the centuries. The gits don't have a sense of humor. But best as I can tell, they just don't like us. We're too different, and now they have it in their silly heads that we're enemies."

"You mean there wasn't a great dwarf-high elf war?" I cautiously asked. "Or the high elves didn't go to war against some great darkness, and the dwarves didn't help them?" I asked, recalling one of my favorite authors—J. R. R. Tolkien.

Grogrintork looked at me like I was crazy. "War? All magical beings work together if there's a war, missy. No questions asked. Nope, last act we made against the elves was back in 1930s. Couple 'o Iron Eye dwarves stuck a whoopee cushion on High Elf Farfwyn's seat in the Fairy Council. They might be right to hold a grudge 'bout that," he grunted.

I stared. "A whoopee cushion."

"Danged funny things," Grogrintork grinned.

I took a sip of my cappuccino for fortification. "Right, so what you're really after is dwarves being able to enter the ranks of the MBRC, and to get rid of this isolation-hiring freeze combo."

"That sounds right."

"Okay. I'm not sure if I can do anything to help you, Mr. Grogrintork, but I can certainly try. Before we go any farther I would like to talk with some of my contacts and associates."

"That's reasonable," Grogrintork said, turning to look behind him when Baobab entered the office.

Baobab tilted her head forward before she seated herself behind the desk.

"Just two more questions," I said. "Why me, and why now."

Grogrintork raised his blonde eyebrows. "Why? The only option is ye, Miss Fae. No one else has the gumption—or cares I suppose—about us lower races. And why now? Well…we weren't sure 'til yesterday afternoon that ye *weren't* in Moonspell's pocket."

I almost dropped my coffee thermos I was so surprised.

"Ye have my card. Contact me when ye wish to talk again," Grogrintork said, hefting himself out of the chair. "Thank ye, Morgan L. Fae," he said, seeing himself out of my office.

His escort followed him, although one of them dawdled in front of Baobab's desk, shyly watching her for a moment before hurrying after his friends.

When the door shut I slumped over my desk. "Whoa."

Harrison stepped away to inspect the area the dwarves had stood in—probably looking for bugs and listening devices or something. (Goblins were just as good with human society and technology as cyclopes were.)

"Well. I think I found my thorn to cram in Administrator Moonspell's side. What do you think, Krusher?" I asked.

"It's Harrison, Miss Fae," Harrison said before straightening the chair Grogrintork sat in.

"Yeah, that's what I think too," I said, thumping my head on my desk.

5

The Museum Field Trip

Saturday morning rolled around, and I was more than prepared for the field trip to the Museum of Science and Industry. I arrived at the MBRC, took roll, and inspected everyone's glamours.

The students going on the field trip were what I consider my core group: Dave, Frey, Frank, Perseus and Athena—his centaur girlfriend—Madeline, a drabby wood elf nicknamed Oak, three drabby fairies—Corn, Sage, and Zinnia—Sacmis the sphinx, and Asahi and his high elf girlfriend Kadri. Esmeralda came with—more to commiserate with me than out of any sort of curiosity—and Harrison, of course, trailed after us.

Perseus, Athena, and Sacmis wore glamours—which served to disguise their less-than-human bodies. Everyone else, though, was disguised mostly by wearing hats, gloves, and jackets. And with good reason.

Because I am occasionally stupid, when we were mapping out the trip everyone begged me to let us walk to the corner of State Street and Jackson Boulevard where we would pick up Bus 10, instead of tacking on CTA bus 7 as well to cover the distance. It was a little over half a mile between Union Station and the bus stop we needed. They reasoned it wouldn't take long, and they badly wanted to people watch as they walked.

They were right. Relatively speaking it was a short walk. But there was just one problem.

IT WAS FREEZING COLD!

"Whose idea was it to walk?" I asked Madeline through clenched teeth, longing to strangle someone.

"Asahi's I think."

"Let's kill him," I said as Madeline huddled closer to me while we waited for the bus.

"Okay," she agreed.

Dave and Madeline fared the worst, being that they're pretty dang cold to start with since their blood wasn't pumping. Poor Sacmis wasn't doing much better than them, but Frank and Frey were disgustingly *chipper* about the whole thing.

Frank tipped his head back to scent the air. "I smell popcorn," he said, his eyes bright. He wore a medium coat, no gloves, no hat, and was *fine*.

"There's a Garret Popcorn Shop back there," I said, tipping my head down Jackson Boulevard, hopping in place to keep my feet warm.

"It smells good," Frank said.

"Yeah," Frey agreed after sniffing the air. "Let's stop and get some on our way back."

"Oohhh no," I said. "You are *not* going to convince me to walk that distance again. No, we're taking bus 7 back."

"Morgan?"

"What?" I said a little more sharply than I meant to as I turned around.

Kadri—dressed in a warm, green colored ski jacket that set off the green of the hazel in her eyes—cringed and took a step back. (Over the past two years her clothing choices, and thus Asahi's, had grown to be more fashionable and sophisticated.)

"Sorry, Kadri. I didn't know it was you. Did you need something?" I asked, making a big effort to sound cheerful in spite of my fingertips that were going to fall off soon.

Kadri scratched at her ears—the glamour used to cloak the pointed tips probably itched. "I was wondering if you have time to meet me for coffee next week."

I blinked. "You want a personal field trip?"

"No-no. I meant coffee at the MBRC. I just, I would like to talk to you," the high elf said, fixing the way her matching scarf covered her neck.

"Sure. Does Tuesday work for you? Say, 4:30?"

Kadri beamed, hitting me with the full force of her high elf beauty. "That would be great. Thank you, Morgan."

"You're welcome," I said, mollified by Kadri's brilliance. I turned just in time to see our bus coming down the street. "Okay, this is it. Everyone have their passes?"

My students got on the bus without gawking too much, and they were pretty well behaved during the ride. In about twenty minutes we were outside the Museum of Science and Industry.

"Into the entry hall. Go, go, go," I said, running into the building. I counted my students as they came in, ticking them off.

"The museum entrance fee is $18—Krusher I already have your ticket. Everyone get your money out. I'm going to put you in a line in pairs," I said, observing the ticket lines. Thankfully it was early enough in the morning that it seemed pretty slow. As long as the ticket sellers weren't in a hurry, my students were advanced enough to buy their own tickets.

"Asahi, Kadri, you go here. Sacmis, Esmeralda, here please. Perseus and Athena, right here. Frank and Madeline—" I paused and squinted at the backpack Madeline carried on her back. It moved as I watched it. "Madeline, what is in your backpack?"

Madeline twisted to face me. "What do you mean?" she asked with false innocence.

I spun Madeline around, ignoring her outraged squawks, and unzipped the largest pocket of her bright pink backpack.

A blue tinted dragon that was a little bigger than a housecat poked its head out of the backpack and held out a cookie to me with one of its front paws.

"Doggy," I said, recognizing the little dragon from my stint at working the information desk of the MBRC. He's a Miniature Doodle—a dragon-poodle, don't ask. Basically he is a pet dragon. His owner is a flamingo pink dragon named Miss Bea who teaches at the MBRC. "What is Doggy doing here?"

"I'm watching him while Miss Bea is visiting relatives in Europe," Madeline said.

"But what is Doggy doing *here*?"

"I couldn't leave him alone," Madeline protested.

"Madeline, you have brought a *dragon* into a human museum!" I said, zipping the backpack up again after Doggy ducked inside.

"Do we need to go back?" Frey asked.

"We might," I said before turning, looking for a student. "Corn, could you come over here, please?" I called to one of the three drabby fairies in my class.

"Yes?" Corn asked.

"There is a Doodle in this backpack. Do you think you can glamour it to look like a service animal?"

"I can try," Corn said, looking around the museum entryway. "Could we go somewhere more private?"

"The bathrooms," I said, dragging Madeline along. When we reached the bathrooms Harrison took up a post outside, looking conspicuously nonchalant for a guy wearing a suit and sunglasses in a museum.

Madeline, Corn, and I claimed the handicap stall—which was big enough to fit all three of us. I unzipped Madeline's backpack, my arms dipping when doggy popped out of the bag and climbed up my arms so he could sit on my shoulder.

Corn cast her magic, and when the glamour was complete I had a furry service animal on my shoulder.

"I'm sorry, I'm not very good with animal glamours," Corn apologized as I skeptically looked Doggy over.

Doggy no longer resembled a dragon, but a fluffy…thing. He had a little blue vest identifying him as a service animal, but it was anyone's guess whether he was a cat or dog. When I pushed back the fur on his face I was mildly repulsed. He had the bulging eyes of a pug, and the nose and muzzle of a slightly squashed faced cat—

although he still had the teeth and lower jaw of one of those toy/purse dogs.

"No one will mistake him for a dragon. And that's the important thing," I said, brightening when I discovered Corn had somehow given Doggy a collar and ID tags. "Madeline, your belt," I said.

"What?" Madeline said.

"Your belt. I need it."

"Why?" Madeline asked, struggling to remove it under her puffy jacket.

"Because even if he's a service animal, Doggy has to be leashed."

"What? Why do we have to use my belt? What's wrong with yours?"

"We're using your belt because *you* are the one who brought Doggy here. Now hand it over," I said.

Madeline grumbled, but eventually fished her belt out from under all her layers. She was wearing a neon pink dress today, but it had a matching, cloth, belt that went around her waist. It was quite long since it was meant to be tied in a bow, which was great because I had to knot it around Doggy and then weave a hand loop for myself. It made a passable leash—it was more convincing than Doggy was, anyway.

"Ok, let's try this," I said, taking a deep breath before shifting Doggy to my arms. "If they ask for certification, we are in so much trouble," I said as we left the bathrooms.

"Why?" Corn asked.

"Because I won't be able to show them any," I said.

"So? Can't Harrison use his goblin powers on them?" Madeline asked, sulking a little as she trailed behind me.

"Oh," I said, pausing. "Krusher, would you do that?" I said, stopping to ask my bodyguard.

"It's Harrison, Miss Fae."

"Thanks, Krusher. You're the best," I said.

Everyone except Corn and Madeline had purchased tickets—I bought Harrison's and mine online the night before—so as one big group we stormed the entrances. (Getting up the escalators went well. Which was lucky, last time we encountered them Perseus almost took a tumble.)

Sure enough, at the actual entrance into the museum—where they look at your tickets and stuff—I was stopped by a museum guard.

"Miss, may I see some certification for your service...animal?" the guard asked.

"Um," I said.

"You don't need to see this animal's certification," Harrison said, his voice smooth and rich like chocolate cheesecake as he took off his sunglasses to look the guard in the eye. "We can move along."

"You know, I don't need to see any papers after all. Enjoy your visit," the guard said with a smile before waving us on."

"Are you a big Star Wars fan?" I asked.

"I beg your pardon, Miss Fae?"

"Hmm. Did George Lucas base Jedi knights off goblins?" I asked, putting Doggy on the ground, but holding tight to his leash.

"I do not know, Miss Fae."

"That's totally a yes. Okay, gang. We're starting with the Coal Mine. It's pretty popular since it's an interactive experience, so we want to go on it now while the line is short. Anyone claustrophobic?" I asked.

Everyone shook their heads.

"Good, this way," I said, leading the way—Doggy trotting at my heels.

We went down through the coal mine—which is actually sort of a mini ride. The wood elf got a little freaked out—turns out yes, he *is* claustrophobic—but everyone else had a great time.

Next we hit up the Great Train Story exhibit—which was a nice, low key exhibit after Oak's episode.

I had Oak stand on the outskirts with me and Doggy to recuperate while the rest of my group pressed around the huge, model train track.

"So it's supposed to represent the path from Chicago to Seattle?" Madeline asked, reading a museum placard.

"Yep," I said, handing Oak a bottle of water.

"Look, it's the Willis Tower. You took us there once," Frank said.

"Yeah," I agreed. The Willis Tower was one of the few locations we visited without any problems or fiascos.

"Is that a cow?" Madeline asked, her voice a little louder than necessary.

Kadri and Asahi approached me, having looped around from the place where the train passed through the Midwest, the plains, the Rockies and the Cascades.

"The workmanship is quite remarkable," Asahi said.

"I appreciate that we can see how trains run," Kadri said, her sincerity shining in her eyes. "The MBRC is built into Union Station, but I have not viewed trains outside an urban area."

"Well, this is a model," I said. "The real train track between Seattle and Chicago goes through way more countryside than could be imposed into one model."

"Morgan," Sage—one of the three fairies—said as she approached me. "There are miniature pink, plastic flamingos in this model. Are they an important part of human culture?"

"Um," I said.

"Can we go to Yesterday's Main Street?" Dave asked.

"What, you want to reminisce?" Frey said, folding his arms across his chest.

"And what if I do?" Dave pouted.

"Ugh, I bet my Dad would love that place," Perseus said, rolling his eyes. The move was a great deal more effeminate than he meant for it to be as he was in his girl glamour—which was considered his normal disguise. "He's always droning on and on about the past and yesterday and how 'memories cannot be made after the moment is gone' and all that weird crap."

"Oohh, there's an ice cream store there. Let's go!" Madeline said.

"It's open seasonally," I said.

"So? Winter is a season."

"I promise it's not open," I said. "Now go play I spy in the Chicago part of the train section. There are lists posted of things to look for."

"Do I get a prize for finding everything?" Madeline slyly asked.

"I'll buy you a cookie."

"Great! Come on, Sage," Madeline said, dragging the fairy with her.

"But, the flamingos," Sage said.

"Who cares about flamingos? Morgan is going to buy us a cookie!" Madeline said.

"I would like to see these pink flamingos. Where are they?" Asahi asked.

"Are they supposed to be bird decoys? Like the ones the hunters use?" Frank asked.

"You know what duck decoys are?" Frey asked.

"A hunter left his out in the woods once," Frank said, scratching his neck. "I sorta figured out what it was when I tried gnawing on it."

"The fact that they didn't smell wasn't a big clue?" Frey said.

"I was hungry," Frank blushed.

I exhaled as the rest of my students drifted back to the model train exhibit. "Are you doing okay, Oak?" I asked as Doggy, the Unidentified Freakish Animal, sniffed a stroller parked near us.

"Better," Oak said, plopping down on a bench.

"Do you need a snack or something?"

Oak held his stomach and looked pained. "No, I don't think so."

"Right, um, do you want to lie down on the bench?" I asked, tugging on Doggy's leash so he returned to my side.

"No. I think if I sit for a few minutes, I'll feel better. Thank you, Morgan," Oak said with a brave smile.

A mother and two kids walked past us—neither of the kids could have been older than five.

"Mommy, what's wrong with that doggy?" one of the kids, a little girl, asked.

Doggy, hearing his name, scampered to the edge of the leash, hovering like a mop brought to life.

"Don't touch it," the mother said, yanking her kids out of range.

"Oh my gawsh, that is the ugliest dog I've ever seen," a teenage girl—probably a cheerleader—two benches over said, pointing in our direction. She was sitting on the lap of a reasonably muscled guy—her football player boyfriend most likely—and two more girls and another guy stood by her.

"I totally bet it's inbred," one of the girls said.

"Look at its teeth!"

"It has alien eyes," one of the boys snickered.

Doggy's head swiveled to look at them. He tilted his head and would have looked very cute if he didn't have the glamour on.

"It's gotta be a service animal, right? I wonder if the sight of it made its owner go blind," the original, hateful girl said.

"What a mutt."

"Who would *want* a dog like that?"

I frowned at them.

"Oh, look. She's mad at us," the probably-a-cheerleader said.

"Why? What we're saying is so true. It's an ugly dog."

It was undeniable that the glamour made Doggy a less than... magnificent looking creature, but there was no reason to make him into a conversation topic open for mockery. A horrified look or a tight comment while passing I could understand, but to sit there and make fun of him? That was mean.

I nonchalantly looked around. At the moment most everyone in the area was pressed in against the train track. "Doggy," I said.

The miniature dragon looked up at me.

"Achoo," I said.

The dragon copied the noise, sneezing up flames.

This made the teenagers scream like harpies. The cheerleader sitting on her boyfriend's lap almost knocked him over as she scrambled to get up.

"Okay guys," I called. "We're going to the next exhibit. Oak, catch up when you feel better," I said, hot footing it out of the area.

"But we were playing I spy," Madeline complained.

"Where are we going next?" Sacmis the sphinx asked.

"Farm Tech," I said.

"So it's about farming?" Corn asked, brightening.

"Yep. But we need to get going. Let's go, go, go," I said, shooing my group out of the hall—Oak was the last to follow after.

I shot a triumphant look over my shoulder at the hysterical teenagers. They had created such a ruckus a museum guard approached them, and looked like he was going to throw them out.

"Who's the ugly one now?" I smirked before I hurried after my group.

The Farm Exhibit was…well I think it was the favorite exhibit for my students, but it was probably my least favorite. Perseus and Athena crammed themselves into a farm tractor—which sounds fine but that's only because you don't understand. Glamours are just illusions. The body is still the same, nothing is transformed. It's just covered up. That's why I had to tie Doggy's leash around him instead of fastening it to his service animal vest.

Perseus' girl disguise—and Athena's—cloaked their horse bodies, but their bodies still existed. I have no idea how they maneuvered themselves up there, but they did it. And then they couldn't get out or down.

A museum employee came and yelled at us before Harrison stepped in because a bunch of little kids wanted to try the tractor and Perseus and Athena couldn't get out.

Then there was the Poop Power station. Oh man, you don't even want to know what happened there. I'm still embarrassed.

We went to a bunch of other exhibits—the chick hatchery, the whispering gallery, toy maker 3000, etc—and decided to finish our tour with the Colleen Moore's Fairy Castle.

I had mixed feelings about this. When I was a kid it was my favorite exhibit in the whole museum. My group insisted on visiting it because they wanted to know what kind of castle humans thought fairies would live in. In general, whenever we view an exhibit that has even a hint of the magical, my students get horribly loud and do their best to obnoxiously point out every mistake.

Thankfully this time they kept their mouths shut because they were awed with the craftsmanship.

"It's so beautiful," Madeline said. "It's like a fairy dollhouse."

"The high elves used to have castles like these—full scale ones," Oak said, lingering in front of the dining room.

"This is Cinderella's drawing room?" Kadri asked. "I see her, in the mural."

"The bathroom is incredible," Athena reported from around the corner of the castle.

"In spite of humans' ingenuity and push for the future, it's nice to see you still have an appreciation for old, beautiful things," Asahi said, smiling at the castle.

"It is," I agreed, standing guard at the exhibit entrance. The Fairy Castle was popular with only a certain demographic—little girls—and as a result it tended to be busy in waves. Thankfully we had arrived at one of the slow times and were the only ones in the room.

"So humans really think us to be pretty and good creatures?" Zinnia—the last drabby fairy—asked.

"For the most part, yeah. Haven't you seen Tinkerbell? I thought you said your aunt lived in Disney World," I asked.

"Yes, but that is just one medium," Zinnia said. "It is gratifying to know others hold that ideal close as well."

"Well, you guys are mostly good," I said. "I mean, there are a few exceptions, but in general magical beings are really kind considering what we humans have done to you."

Oak shook his head, his mouth a grim line. "No, we are not kind at all. Perhaps now, but in the past…" he trailed off.

"You mean history. Like the old stories about fairies leading people off to their deaths and messing with them? You can't blame yourselves for that. Devin's a great example of what I mean. Yeah, he's the Pooka, but he's good. He doesn't do anything harmful—okay, he doesn't *kill* people like some of the previous Pookas did," I said. "Devin isn't responsible for what his ancestors did. You guys aren't responsible either."

"Miss Fae," Harrison said, just outside the room.

"What?"

"Get back," Harrison said.

"Why? What's—" I stopped talking when I looked past him.

Because we were talking and moving like normal in the fairy

castle room, I hadn't noticed anything different. But the exhibits leading up to Colleen Moore's Fairy Castle were graveyard silent.

It wasn't that we were alone. Oh no. There were people still there, in the middle of reading, caught mid sneeze, chasing after their kid or friends, but they were stationary. None of our fellow museum attendees moved. It was like they were replaced with statues.

6

Supervillain Krad Temero

"Time ghosts," Frey called to our group, steering me into the middle of my students. "Use anything you have on hand. Don't worry about blowing our cover—we have to make it through this."

"G-ghosts? Y-you guys said they don't exist," I said as Madeline grimly dug a cast-iron skillet out of her backpack.

"Ghosts—spirits-of-the-dead-ghosts—don't exist," Asahi said, ripping three necklaces from his throat. "Time ghosts are a malevolent kind of fairy."

"What?" I said.

"They use their glamours to look like those deceased, but their real power lies in their ability to stop and slow time," Zinnia said.

"Ever hear of Rip Van Winkle? He played with time ghosts," Frey said before ducking behind the fairy castle. When he reappeared he was a white wolf.

"But the story says he played with ghosts," I protested.

"Yeah, time ghosts," Madeline savagely said.

"Why haven't I seen any of these guys before?"

"They're a rotten bunch. Evil to their very cores. None of them would associate with the MBRC," Oak said.

"Nor would the MBRC have them," Kadri said digging several daggers from under the pant legs of her jeans. "Not even the unseelie court will make an alliance with them. They get their magic from dark sources."

I watched and wondered how my students were able to smuggle so many contraband items through the museum security as Harrison whispered into his mic and listened on his ear piece.

Doggy stirred at my feet. He bristled and starting growling.

"Harrison," I said, my throat tightening when I saw the first time ghost appear.

It was humanoid the way elves and fairies resemble humans. It had the same structure as a human, but it was slightly opaque—as if its physical presence wasn't that strong. Its facial features were smudged—like a watercolor painting—and it wore nondescript, watery-gray robes.

No wonder people mistook them for ghosts.

Six more time ghosts appeared, flickering into view as if they were stepping into this dimension. They made a half circle around the exhibit entrance, ignoring Frank and Frey—who were our first line of defense in their wolf bodies.

The seven time ghosts raised their hands in slow synchronization, and Harrison stepped forward.

"You don't want to do that," he said, his sunglasses off. "You've just realized you can't use your powers here. You want to flee, and you will after you release your time hold on this museum," Harrison said.

The time ghosts paused. They dropped their hands and looked at one another. They turned to look at the frozen humans when someone emerged from the room of statues and clapped.

"Well done. I could recognize that work anywhere. There aren't many goblins who could persuade so many magical beings—much less time ghosts. Harrison the Undaunted, is it?" the emerging person said.

His skin was an ashy gray color and his long but colorless hair was cut at a sharp, jagged angle. His face would have made him a cutie, but he had a puckered scar that tore down through his eyebrow and eye and stopped halfway down his cheek. His eyes were an unnerving black color.

"Dökkàlfar," Sacmis whispered.

"What?" I asked.

"Dark elf," Madeline said, strengthening her grip on her pan. "That is Krad Temero of Fidem."

"Wait...*he's* the bad guy you've all been warning me about?" I said, shell-shocked.

"Yes," Kadri said, shifting so she could better hold her daggers.

"You've got to be kidding. He's, like, ten years old!" I said.

Normally I would say our attacker's unhealthy skin color and black eyes would make him unnerving to behold. There was just one problem. This evil mastermind clearly belonged in elementary school. Seriously, he didn't even come up to my shoulders height wise, and I am not a tall person. His boots were too big for him, and his black jacket had the sleeves rolled up so his thin hands could poke out. He looked like he was playing dress up with his dad's clothes.

The kid glared at me, as if I was a teacher handing out homework. "Silence!" he thundered.

"Shut up, squirt," I said to him over Doggy's growls. "The MBRC is petrified of a snot-nosed brat? Are you kidding me?" I asked Madeline.

"If you recognize the name Krad, can I assume Devin spoke to you about him?" Madeline asked, her voice tight.

"Yeah," I said.

"Squirt?" the dark elf brat said, his high pitched voice loud and piercing. "You speak to me like a *child*?"

"That's because you *are* a child."

"Morgan," Madeline said, her voice artificially light. "Did Devin happen to mention that Krad Temero was cursed?"

I thought for a moment as the snotty elf screamed in anger in the background. "Maybe."

"Did he explain the nature of the curse?"

"No."

"He was cursed to the body of a child."

"So…he's older than he looks?"

"Much older. Krad Temero is an ancient fiend—or he wouldn't be a Fidem captain."

"Oh," I said.

"You," Krad said, pointing to me. His face was twisted in anger. "You will pay for your careless words."

"Timeout. I don't believe you," I said. "He's not old. He has to be a kid."

"What?" Asahi blinked.

Frey growled and snapped at me.

"There's no way an ancient elf would say something like 'you will pay for this'. Clearly this brat has read too many comic books," I said.

In spite of my disbelief, Harrison seemed to take him as a serious threat. His eyes flickered from the dark elf to the time ghosts.

Dave nervously laughed. "Miss Morgan, I don't think you understand what sort of situation we're in," he said.

"I totally understand what's going on. The MBRC is afraid of an elementary schooler," I said.

"ENOUGH!" the dark elf shouted. His scream made some color bloom on his cheeks. When he was finished he smoothed his hair and cleared his throat.

"Someone's touchy about their age—" I got out before Madeline clamped her hand over my mouth.

Krad-the-kid didn't seem to hear my remark. His attention was on Harrison. "I see where you are looking, Harrison the Undaunted. No, you can't keep them under your thumb and try to persuade me as well," the brat said, his features drawn into the same smug little smile my youngest brother uses when he's about to get me in trouble.

Harrison flattened his lips. Instead of attempting to persuade the smart-mouthed snot otherwise, Harrison threw his arms out in front of him and pushed.

A wall of light flashed, rushing forward like a tsunami wave. When it reached the dark elf it exploded, making a screen of smoke and steam. Ahh yes. The so called rudimentary magic of goblins.

I was afraid the smoke would set off the museum fire alarms, but either its magical properties stopped it, or the fact that most of the museum was frozen in time disabled the alarms. When it finally faded the dark elf brat stood there with his hands in his pockets.

"That was a disappointing effort," the dark elf said.

His ability to survive Harrison's magic made me start to rethink my evaluation of him.

"What do you want?" Madeline said, letting go of me and pushing her way to the front of the group.

"Simple. I want the human parasite standing in the middle of your motley crew. Hand her over, and I will leave," the dark elf kid said. "No dirty tricks, no fights."

"Sorry, kid. I don't do the cougar thing," I said, reeling Doggy in so he wouldn't trip anyone.

I yelped when Esmeralda took up Madeline's post and slapped her hand over my mouth.

The dark elf brat narrowed his eyes at me, but the meaning of the term 'cougar' must have escaped him since he didn't throw a temper tantrum.

"I will cease to walk on this earth before I would give Morgan over to the likes of you, Krad Temero," Madeline snarled.

Even though she wore a neon pink dress, Madeline looked, for the first time since I met her, dangerous. Her eyes were narrowed, her pronounced canines poked out from behind her lips, and I felt force and power behind her words.

"I see you treat me with the proper due contempt and respect. I shouldn't have expected less from you, Madeline Stafford. Even so, your answer is unacceptable. If you will not hand the human over, I will be forced to school you foolish whelps."

"So what, now he's British on top of being ten? Yeah, he's also seen too many superhero movies. All the bad guys are British. But it doesn't work anyway. He has an American accent," I said, my voice muffled by Esmeralda's hand.

"Harrison, hold the time ghosts and guard Morgan," Madeline said as Frank and Frey howled and snarled with raised hackles. "Corn, Sage, Zinnia, Oak. Ready?"

"Ready!"

"Go!" Madeline shouted.

Frank and Fray jumped Krad. They bounced off a shadow black shield that surrounded Krad like a fortress, and tumbled head over paws.

Madeline ducked, and the three fairies and wood elf released a charge of their combined magic. It was shaped like a huge, curling vine. It wrapped around Krad's shield and pulled tight, making the shield's surface crackle.

Krad spoke a word that made a noise like a thunderclap boom over our heads before black electricity shot up and down the length of the vine. The vine wilted and eventually turned brown and died, unable to survive the onslaught.

Kadri threw two of her daggers—which hit the shield and stuck there as if they were buried in a wood wall. Asahi took one of the necklaces he tore off himself and threw it at Krad.

It exploded in a ball of white-hot fire that blackened the walls and singed Frey's tail since he was too slow to scramble out of the way.

When I was finally able to see again—the fire ball blinded me for several moments—Krad's shield was still in place, no worse for the wear.

As I watched my students attack Krad and fail, I realized I had underestimated the dark elf. Panic started to build in me as I watched Sacmis—her glamour removed, pounce at Krad with a roar. Though Krad looked like a kid, he had to be incredibly powerful to rebuff *all* my students.

Sacmis didn't even touch Krad's shield. The dark elf raised two fingers, and Sacmis was yanked backwards as if someone dragged her by her lion tail.

Athena and Perseus were huddled together, texting like crazy. Dave crouched next to Madeline. The two vampires spoke in spite of the chaos happening above and around them.

Corn, Sage, Zinnia, and Oak redoubled their efforts, this time circling Krad's shield with red bushes laced with thorns. The bushes groaned as they tightened around the shield, but, just like the vine, when Krad's black lightning hit them they shriveled and died.

Frey and Frank tried jumping Krad's back, but they still bounced off the shield with sharp yips of pain.

"This is what exposure to humanity has done to our great society. It has caused us to grow soft," Krad said, folding his arms across his thin chest.

My heart pounded in my throat as Krad stepped forward, his shield moving with him like his over-sized jacket. "None of you are remotely capable of—" he was cut off when Madeline stepped forward and swung her cast-iron skillet.

Unlike every other thing my students had thrown at the dark elf, the skillet passed through the shield, connecting with Krad's skull with a sickening crunch.

Krad fell backwards, collapsing like a ragdoll.

Madeline wound her skillet up again, preparing to take a swing at Krad like a professional golfer, but Krad shot a bolt of his black electricity at her, sending her flying through the air.

Sacmis tried to catch her, but the force of the bolt slammed both of them into the case that covered the fairy castle.

When Krad stood the circular edge of Madeline's skillet was burned into his skin. He glared, the vehemence of the look made him appear more demonic than childish.

"Are you proud?" he snarled. "Your celebration is too early. I have not even begun to use my powers," Krad said before turning his eyes on me.

He extended his hand and spoke in that booming language. After another thunderclap, I felt hundreds of invisible spiders crawl across my skin, creep up and down my arms and legs, and scurry across the nape of my neck.

I screamed and tried to squash the invisible bugs, violently pounding on my clothing. In my panic I let go of Doggy's leash and almost smacked Esmeralda in the face.

"Morgan, stop. You're feeding him!" Asahi shouted.

Harrison grabbed my arms and helped Esmeralda hold them

behind my back, but the feeling of spiders didn't go away and I hopped in place, a scream tearing from my throat.

Krad chuckled as I yelled. "My power increases with her terror," he said.

"Morgan, listen to me! You are fine," Harrison said, making me look into his venom green eyes.

"No I'm not!" I shouted.

Dave tried to tackle Krad, and was thrown backwards like Madeline.

Corn, Sage, Zinnia, and Oak repeated their vine attack. This time before the vine died the black lightning traveled the plant's length and reached the quartet.

They screamed and howled. Only Oak was able to keep standing. The three fairies dropped, splayed across the floor like dead butterflies.

Krad hit Frank with a club of electricity on his skull, opening up a nasty looking wound that leaked blood—which sent Madeline to the back corner of the room, retching.

Sacmis, Perseus, and Athena went for a combined tackle. Sacmis and Athena bounced off the shield, but Perseus fell at an odd angle and one of his horse legs gave out with a crunch.

"Harrison, you have to use the time ghosts. He's going to slaughter us," Frey said, back in his human form.

"I can't leave her," Harrison—still clamped to me—shouted.

"You have to, or we aren't going to make it out of here," Frey said. "I'll take her."

"Let me go! Make it stop!" I screamed, still plagued by hundreds of little legs crawling across my skin.

"If she's injured I will make you into a fur rug," Harrison warned before he turned and strode towards Krad.

The time ghosts stirred with his arrival. He shouted, his green eyes flashing, and the evil fairies closed in around Krad.

Krad hit them with electricity, bouncing them—and Harrison —backwards.

Past the time ghosts the museum hiccupped. Patrons and attendees moved for half a second.

"Careful!" Kadri shouted.

Harrison grimly beckoned at the time ghosts, who again drew near. The time ghosts held hands and stood in a wide ring around Krad, attempting to freeze him in time.

The museum kept hiccupping, time releasing in half second increments.

Doggy—unfettered—crawled under Krad's shield and launched himself at the brat. He bit down on Krad's thumb, drawing blood and shouts of rage. Krad tried shaking Doggy off his hand, but the little dragon beat his wings and held on with determination.

Doggy's valiance did not go unrewarded. The time ghosts were able to get the upper hand, although the museum kept hiccupping in time.

Just when it appeared that Krad might be bested at the price of blowing open our cover, a squad of twelve magical beings wearing MBRC guard uniforms busted through the back exhibit.

"Target sighted," the wizard human leading the squad said before shooting Krad with a pillar of fire.

"Stabilizing the area," a team of two elves said as they set what looked like an egg timer that was roughly the size of a bowling ball on the ground and started winding it up.

Two war centaurs galloped forward, wielding iron tipped spears. When the wizard pulled back his fire, the centaurs stabbed their weapons through Krad's shield, narrowly missing the childish-looking dark elf.

Krad shouted an oath that was totally inappropriate for his age, and blasted Harrison with electricity, making him lose his already shaky hold on the time ghosts. When the young dark elf snapped his fingers the spider feeling left me, and the time ghosts faded like dispersing smoke.

As clever as ever, Doggy sensed it was time for his exit. He gave Krad one last good chomp and jumped from the dark elf just as Krad took off through the exhibit.

Krad's too-big-for-him jacket flapped behind him like a short cape as he scurried through the motionless humans to keep the wizard from taking another shot at him.

The centaurs, wizard, a war-like fairy, and a hobgoblin ran after him, their faces grim.

"Who needs medical attention?" asked a pinto unicorn, trotting over to my students.

"Start with Frank," Frey said, wading through our friends to pull out Frank—still in wolf form and bleeding from his head wound.

I sat down hard and shook, fear and panic twisting in my stomach.

I was numb with fear.

I couldn't even explain why. It wasn't like seeing Krad had terrified me to my core, but I still felt infected with fright. It was like I had an oppressive cloud of fear wrapped around me. My heart pounded in my throat even though the dark elf was gone.

"Are you okay, sweetie?" a naiad asked me, putting a hand on my shoulder.

I was shaking so bad I couldn't respond.

"Uh-oh. We have a spelled one over here," the naiad said. "Couldn't you persuade her?" she asked Harrison, who was forcing himself to stand dutifully near me.

"She's immune," Harrison said.

"Oh dear," the naiad said. "Whisper, I need you next here when you're finished with the head wound. This one is spelled," the naiad said before wrapping a gauzy blanket around me.

The material was soft and slinky—like fairy wings—but was surprisingly warm. Underneath it I still shivered, mindless terror and panic clawing me.

Harrison talked over his goblin mic, but kept his eyes glued to me even though he was stiff with pain.

I was vaguely aware of the rest of my students taking inventory of their injuries, of Doggy climbing onto my lap, and of the fairies mending and patching the blackened walls and ruined floors.

Light finally pierced my panic when something warm stood in front of me.

"Morgan Fae, isn't it?"

I looked up at the pinto unicorn. She wore a horsey grin, and the black patches splayed over her sparkling white hide gleamed in the fluorescent light.

"This will only take a moment," she said before placing the point of her horn to my heart and pushing.

I screamed in the pain, but after a moment the panic fled, and my mind was flooded with warmth and tranquility.

I slumped backwards, but Harrison caught me to keep my head from cracking on the floor.

The unicorn's pleased smile was the last thing I saw before I drifted off to sleep.

When I woke up I knew I was in the MBRC because of two things. First of all, the decorations in the room were typical for the MBRC —outrageously beautiful and breathtaking. But what really assured me was the high elf sitting in the room: Aysel.

Aysel sat in a chair across from the couch I was laid out on, looking generally unhappy and unpleased. "Finally," he said when he saw I was awake. "I was beginning to think you might sleep all evening."

"What happened?" I asked massaging my temples as a massive headache hit me.

"You were attacked while on an outing with your students," Aysel said.

"The Museum of Science and Industry," I said, my brain restarting.

Aysel nodded. "You were attacked by a Dökkàlfar. Krad Temero, a captain of Fidem."

"Ahh yes, the ten-year-old," I said, closing my eyes as flashes of the fight replayed in my mind. "No one thought to tell me that one of Fidem's masterminds belongs in elementary school."

"Krad's physical appearance does not match his age due to a curse placed upon him by a Fairy Council soldier. He is much older than you, and is quite capable," Aysel said.

"Yeah, I noticed," I said, remembering the way he defended himself against my friends and students.

"Although you were not physically injured, Krad used his powers to enhance and feed off your fear, making his magic more potent."

"He *what*?"

Aysel ignored me and continued with the summary. "As you are immune to goblin persuasion techniques, your bodyguard was unable to abolish your panic. Why no one thought to knock you unconscious is beyond me."

"Wait, back up. This Krad kid uses my fear to make himself more powerful?"

"Yes."

"Can all elves do that?"

"No. That is a trait that runs only in the veins of Dökkàlfar—dark elves. Even still, it is a rare kind of magic among their race. It allows its wielder to use a human's emotions to prey upon them," Aysel said, studying a painting on the wall, as if he was bored with the situation. "The check to the power is that the wielder cannot force a feeling on a human—unlike goblins. It is a reactive power. It can only react to whatever feeling the human displays. Naturally, in such a situation, you were feeling panic," Aysel said, making it clear he found it unforgivable that I had been frightened. "Krad can make you experience things that are not reality, spiking your level of fear."

"So he enhanced it and used it to power himself like a battery," I said.

"Exactly," Aysel said.

"Okay. Did you know he had these powers?"

"To a certain extent. Members in the upper crust of the magical community were aware, but it was thought that those particular powers were sealed when he was cursed. It is…unexpected that he can still access that particular magic skill set," Aysel said. He was extremely blank faced, which is actually his annoyed face. This meant *he* probably hadn't known, although others—most likely his dad—did.

"I'm feeling generous, so I'll buy that. But why are you explaining it to me?" I asked.

Aysel looked bored. "The Pooka wished to explain it to you, but at the moment he is…unsettled."

"He's throwing a fit?"

Aysel scowled. "He broke my office chair."

I winced. "I see. Has anyone told Hunter?"

"I believe your bodyguard passed along the word."

"And there's no news from him?" I asked, perking up in hope.

"None," Aysel said.

I relaxed. "Good. How are my students?"

"Everyone has been cared for and treated. The smaller werewolf suffered a traumatic brain injury. Whispersoft was able close the wound and a team of three unicorns undid the damage. He will make a full recovery," Aysel said.

"Good," I said, slumping back into the couch. "How did you guys know to come?"

"We received several texts from two of your students, and Asahi set off his tracking necklace."

"Tracking necklace?"

"He removed one of his necklaces, which set off the tracking spell attached to it. It led our retrieval team straight to you," Aysel said.

"Wow, that's handy," I said.

"And necessary," Aysel grunted.

"So what now?" I asked.

"You return home. A team of MBRC guards will escort you back."

"And what about Krad?"

Aysel scowled.

"That bad is it?" I asked.

"While the MBRC has guards and fighters at its disposal, it is first and foremost a rehabilitation facility. Our proactive measures are limited. Mostly we must react and mop up after the fight," Aysel said.

"So you're not going after Krad."

"We haven't the man power."

"What about the Fairy Council?"

"They can do very little as well. Krad was already blacklisted before this attack, as was Fidem. The Fairy Council does have troops, but Krad issued warnings to the council as well. Most fear he will attack there next."

"So we're on our own."

"Yes. But additional…measures are being taken," Aysel said.

I sat up on my couch. "He's going to get away with this, isn't he?"

"This?"

"Severely injuring Frank and hitting us with his magic."

"He may evade us for a time, but rest assured. Krad Temero will pay for what he has done," Aysel said, his voice hardening. "In the meantime you must be careful, Morgan."

"Why?"

"Krad did not happen upon you by accident."

"I thought you said everyone thinks he's going to go after the Fairy Council next?"

Aysel drummed his fingers on the wooden arms of his chair. "Perhaps, but he seems to hold the MBRC in uncommonly powerful hatred."

"What would that have to do with me? I'm not the only human in the MBRC," I said.

Aysel studied me with narrowed eyes as he sucked in air. After holding my gaze for a few moments he pulled a pamphlet out of his robe and handed it to me.

It was a promotional pamphlet of the MBRC—similar in style to the poster Devin had shown me. I opened the pamphlet and saw a picture of me. It was another shot of me teaching a class, but it was zoomed in so I could much more easily make out my features.

"The MBRC's PR department used my photo again without my permission. So?" I said.

"You are the only human depicted in the pamphlet."

"Yeah? Well it's not like promotional material represents the MBRC's agenda," I said.

"Krad will not see it that way," Aysel said.

"You're just guessing," I said, on a hunch. "No one else—least of all your father—thinks he's coming after me."

Aysel pinched his lips together.

"What is it? What makes you think he's targeting me?"

"Very few beings knew of your field trip, and it is rare for you to come to the MBRC on a Saturday. Krad was watching the MBRC for you, or he has someone on the inside. Either scenario indicates he was watching specifically for activity from *you.*"

"That can't be true," I pitifully argued.

"He could have attacked you on your way to and from the MBRC. He's doubtlessly been trailing you, but he chose to attack when you had a plethora of magical beings with you. Today was a warning. Next time he won't be so forthcoming," Aysel said.

"So what am I supposed to do?" I asked, my heart beating faster as I thought about Krad following me home.

Aysel stood. "You carry on—without fear. The more you fear Krad the more you empower him."

"And what am I supposed to do about that?" I asked.

"Additional arrangements are being made for your protection—as well as all other non-magical humans employed by the MBRC. You will have a security detail when you are outside of the MBRC."

"I already have a bodyguard," I said.

"Harrison the Undaunted is not an MBRC guard. We take care of our own, Morgan," Aysel said, heading for the door. "You will have additional security guards whether you want it or not," he added before making a quick exit.

I barely had enough time to stand up and fix my twisted jeans before the door popped open again.

"Morgan," Devin said. He was across the room in an instant, his pale, yellow eyes taking careful inventory of me. "You weren't hurt?"

"No," I said. "I'm probably in the best shape out of everyone."

Devin's eyes briefly narrowed. "I doubt that. A Dökkàlfar feeding off you is no easy burden."

"Devin—," before I could finish, Devin swept me up in a hug. "Devin! What are you doing?" I squawked.

Devin didn't answer and squeezed me tighter.

I returned the hug for a few moments before I wriggled out of his tight grasp. "Alright. I'm ready. What restrictions are *you* going to put on me?"

Devin cocked a black eyebrow, his confidence returned. "Restrictions?"

"Aysel has informed me the MBRC will assign guards to follow me around, and I can bet Harrison is going to get some serious backup from Weller Goblin Enterprises. What about you?"

Devin slid a hand under my chin. "Nothing," he said.

Surprised by this unexpected answer, I gaped. "Nothing?"

"Nothing," Devin repeated. "What can you tell me of the battle? What happened when Krad used his powers on you?"

I shivered. "It felt like a million tiny spiders crawling on me."

"How close was he?" Devin asked. When I cocked my head, confused, he added, "I would like to learn as much about his powers as possible. Dökkàlfar powers come in different levels of power. Krad used to be considered a master, but with the curse in effect I'm hoping it dampened his magic, even if it failed to entirely seal it. If we are lucky he now has a low level."

"He was over twenty feet away," I said, running a hand through my messy hair. "He didn't point at me or anything. He just looked."

"He didn't have to touch you?"

"No."

Devin swore under his breath. "That indicates at least a moderate level," he said.

"Great."

Devin folded his arms across his chest and tilted his head to look up at the ceiling as he thought. "I'll reach out to some of my contacts and see if we can find any weaknesses in that brand of magic," he said.

"Thanks."

Devin returned his gaze to me. "Will you be alright this evening?"

"Aysel said I'm getting an escort home."

"That doesn't answer my question."

I smiled fondly at the Pooka. He was a flirt, but whenever I was in trouble, he was the first to cover me. "I'll be fine. I can't wait to get home and see my parents and brothers," I said. "Being home will make me feel better."

Devin bobbed his head like a horse. "I see. Excellent. Until next week, then," he said leaning in to nuzzle me. He laughed when I pushed him away.

"Goodbye, Devin," I said.

Devin winked before he also left.

I shook the wrinkles out of my shirt before I followed him, pushing the door open. I almost tripped over the remains of what looked like an armchair.

Devin, above all, was a terrific liar.

7

Love, Elves, and Dwarves

"Wow, Morgan. You look terrible," Fran said to me Monday morning when she met me at my locker.

"I'm going to add salt and pepper to the banana muffins we make in cooking class today."

"That's culinary arts, and you're welcome," Fran said, yanking her gloves off. "What happened?"

"It was a tough weekend at work," I said. "And I didn't get to sleep enough."

Aysel had assigned the equivalent of a fairy swat team to babysit me Saturday and Sunday since my bodyguard rotation wasn't ironed out quite yet. Unfortunately my youngest brother, Odie, had a cold. Whenever he sneezed at night the fairies busted through my windows, moving in synchronized, flying formations—like colored sparklers. It didn't make for a restful night. "You're grinning like an idiot. I assume you went on another date with Ethan?"

Fran blushed and hugged her backpack to her chest. "Yes."

"Where did you go?"

"We went ice skating."

"That's fun. What ice rink did you go to?"

"We were outside—on the pond over by Dudly's Ice Cream Parlor."

"*Outside*? Is Ethan crazy? It was in the single digits this weekend!" I said.

"Yeah, and the wind was blowing really hard so we couldn't talk while we skated either. Ethan was so bundled up he looked like a marshmallow."

"But you still had fun," I said, studying Fran's face.

Fran reluctantly nodded. "I laughed a lot."

"Hmm," I grunted, not entirely satisfied. "Next time he needs to let you plan the date. When do I get to meet him anyway?"

"Whenever you're free," Fran said.

"Okay," I said, thinking.

"So that will be never. Good morning, Fran," Hunter said just over my shoulder.

I froze in self defense. Hunter's voice was icy cold—apparently Harrison had made a full report.

"Hi, Hunter," Fran said. She hadn't forgotten his name since he served on the yearbook committee, to Hunter's horror—as a goblin he prizes anonymity and uses his powers of persuasion to make people overlook him.

I turned around to face my certain doom. "Heeeeey," I said.

Hunter raised an eyebrow at me.

"How ya doin'?" I added. Harrison alone had trailed my car this morning. Perhaps Hunter wasn't planning to stick more goblins on me?

"I am not pleased," Hunter said.

"Don't blame Krusher. It wasn't his fault," I said.

"Krusher?" Fran asked, putting her hand on her hip.

"I don't blame him, but I am still not pleased."

"I hate to break it to you, but life is not always going to please you," I said.

"She's right, you know," Fran chorused. She was in too good of a mood to be rebuffed by Hunter's brisk disposition. "Life is full of disappointments."

Hunter turned to stare Fran down.

"By the way, the senior student council needs their photo taken for the yearbook. I know you're not on the committee anymore, but you were the only one of the staff photographers who could take a decent photo. Could you come in and take ours again?" Fran hopefully asked.

Hunter narrowed his eyes. "You were speaking of your new boyfriend, yes? Did—," I cut Hunter off, slapping my hands over his mouth.

"Whoa there. What's that, Hunter? You would be *delighted* to take the student council's photo?" I said before leaning in and whispering to Hunter. "Play nice, or else."

"Your threats leave much to be desired," Hunter said, his lips brushing the palm of my hand.

"You wouldn't have said that last year after yearbook class," I said.

"Speaking of which, how are you enjoying home economics?"

"It's culinary arts!"

Fran cocked her head as she watched our discourse. She stuck her tongue out of the corner of her mouth like a painter studying a masterpiece before she said, "So why don't you date Hunter, Morgan?"

My face went stiff like plaster. "What."

"He's hot—even though his wardrobe is a little stiff—he's totally rich, and you guys get along!"

I impersonated a statue, but Hunter backed away from my hand, a suave smile folded on his lips. "I will ignore the wardrobe comment, but otherwise I agree entirely with you, Fran. Unfortunately, Morgan isn't so willing."

"That's too bad. Why not, Morgan?" Fran asked.

"Uhh, why not?" I said, my mind scrambling for an answer. Why didn't I date Hunter? Well the fact that he was a *goblin mob boss* was pretty off putting. But it was more than that.

I was annoyed at Fran for thrusting this upon me. I had scuttled the idea of dating by throwing myself into work, but Hunter always made it clear he was perfectly willing to have a monopoly on me.

Fran was asking a question that was way more loaded than she knew.

"Aren't you two close?" Fran asked.

"Yeah, but," I stammered. "Hunter isn't dating material," I finally blurted out.

Fran gasped, Hunter blinked.

"Ouch," the goblin king said.

"No, you're misunderstanding me," I said. "Hunter is like…my best friend."

"Excuse me," Fran frowned.

I groaned. "You two won't let me finish. How's this: If Hunter had to move halfway across the globe, and ten years from now we met, we could pick up right where we left off and be friends."

"So you're saying I'm convenient?" Hunter said, his voice sarcastic.

"No, I'm saying you're irreplaceable, like Fran," I said.

"So, it's like a bromance. He's like in the fellowship of the ring with you, or he's Ron to your Harry of Harry Potter," Fran said, warming to the idea.

"No way, you're my Ron. He's Hermione," I said.

"I have no idea what you're talking about," Hunter said.

"I'm not marrying him," Fran said.

"That's acceptable," I said before turning to face Hunter, who was still frowning. "But none of those give the right picture. Fran is my best friend, but, Hunter, you're more than a normal friend, you're a companion. We fight together, we work together, we live together."

There were things Hunter knew about me that Fran never would. Hunter and I experienced the magical community together. Yeah, we were with separate factions, but I always knew Hunter would be on my side, and I would be on his. Our friendship was too deep to fracture with romance.

Not to mention he would probably be a totally controlling boyfriend, which is not a trait I find attractive.

"Like Achilles and Patroclus," Hunter said, slamming me with his topaz colored gaze.

"Sure," I said. I had no idea who Patroclus was, but I recognized Achilles as a Greek hero.

Fran looked back and forth between us. She must have sensed there was something we weren't saying, but she didn't mention it.

Hunter sighed. "I've been publically rejected."

I tried laughing it off, but I suspected he was being truthful.

"You're also too controlling for Morgan," Fran said. "Our girl can't be micromanaged, like all your books talk about," Fran said, giving Hunter's backpack a meaningful look.

"So I've learned—and not through lack of trying," Hunter dryly said before eyeing me. "This doesn't mean you're off the hook. There will still be repercussions for this weekend."

"You said you weren't blaming Krusher."

"I'm not."

"Then you're blaming *me*?"

Hunter rolled his eyes. "Why would I blame you for something that is out of your control?"

"I don't know, but you said there would be repercussions."

"I did. I thought it would be a kindness to warn you," Hunter said.

"So, Morgan, is this Krusher guy an option, or what?" Fran whispered, joining our huddle.

Hunter and I hastily backed away from each other.

"It's just a work thing," I said.

"Uh-huh," Fran said, sounding totally unconvinced. "Yeah, whatever. So Hunter, will you take the pictures?"

Hunter sighed. "During our lunch break assemble everyone in the auditorium," he said before turning to me. "We will discuss this later."

"Okay," I meekly said.

Hunter turned and strode up the hallway, flicking his sunglasses back on as he walked.

"Yeah, it's just as well you aren't dating him. I bet he comes with baggage," Fran said, folding her arms across her chest as she watched our classmate leave.

I snorted. "More than you know."

By Wednesday afternoon, Hunter's warned repercussions hadn't kicked in—at least not where I could notice.

Harrison still trailed me as I entered the MBRC's cafeteria and looked for Kadri. In spite of the museum uproar, the high elf asked me to keep our coffee date. I was curious. It was unusual for Kadri to ask to speak to me alone. I had no idea what she wanted to discuss.

"Morgan!" Kadri called. The copper haired beauty was seated at a table for two, a steaming mug of coffee in front of her.

"Hello, Kadri," I said, strolling up to her.

"Thanks for meeting with me. What can I get you?"

"I can grab it, thanks. Is the cappuccino machine still operational?"

"To my knowledge, yes."

"Okay. I'll be right back," I said, strolling over to the machines. I waved my employee ID card at the cookie elf that was adding stacks of scones to a table before selecting two mugs. I filled one with black, decaf coffee, and the other with a French vanilla cappuccino. I placed the decaf coffee on a table two places away from Kadri's and mine before I slid into my chair and took my first sip of the cappuccino.

Mmmm. Heaven!

"So what's up?" I asked Kadri.

Kadri visibly brightened. "I recognize that vocabulary. You mean to ask me what I am doing?"

"Right. But in this case I'm more curious about the reason for this meeting."

"I know you and Asahi are very close. You've been a wonderful mentor to him."

"That's very kind of you to say."

"And I would go so far as to think that you and I, perhaps, share a close bond too?" Kadri asked, looking at me with soulful eyes—like a puppy.

"Of course!" I said, taken in by her cuteness.

"But, would I be overstepping the boundaries of our friendship if I asked for assistance?" Kadri asked, twisting a napkin in her hands.

"Not at all. What do you need help with? Extra tutoring? Career counseling?" I asked before taking a sip of my cappuccino.

Kadri wasted no time in replying. "I was wondering if you would ask Asahi why he won't marry me."

I spat out my drink, spraying the tiled floor. "WHAT?" I said.

Two tables behind me a chair scraped.

I waved a hand, signaling to Harrison all was fine. He returned to his seat and his black coffee.

Kadri leaned across the table and confessed. "Asahi hasn't further pressed our relationship. By this time most elves would have committed or parted. He has done neither."

"So you want me to gang press him into asking you?" I asked, still stunned.

Kadri shook her head. "No,"

"But…what? Sorry, you'll need to start from the top," I said.

"The normal courting period for an elf is…much shorter than the length that Asahi and I have been together."

"So you're taking things at your own speed," I said, tossing a few napkins on the ground and moving them around with my foot to soak up my sprayed cappuccino.

"Perhaps," Kadri said, tapping a finger on the rim of her mug. "But I fear it is something else."

"Like? Is it Aysel? I will totally punch out Aysel for you," I said, quickly warming to the idea. "Or even better, do you think it's his dad? We could jump him."

"No, I do not think his family objects to our relationship. My parents are noble, honorable high elves. There is nothing that makes me undesirable in their eyes—although Administrator Moonspell has mentioned he wishes Asahi and I were not so focused on human knowledge and studied elven arts as arduously."

"So what is it?"

Kadri shook her head. "I am not certain. He seems content enough…but," Kadri hesitated. "I love him."

"You aren't happy just courting him?"

Kadri hesitated. "I've received a job offer from a rehabilitation center in California," she said.

"Wow. Kadri, that's awesome! Congratulations!" I said.

Kadri smiled weakly.

"What's wrong?"

"Asahi will not leave Chicago," she said.

"So he's making you choose between your career and your relationship?" I said, my eyes narrowing in anger. I thought I had taught Asahi to behave better than that. "Frankly, Kadri, it sounds like he's acting like Aysel. In which case I question why you want to marry him."

"No, no. It's not that at all," Kadri said. She thought for a moment, searching for the right words. "When elves marry, it is merging two into one. It brings their souls together. With our extended life and linked souls, it is not unusual for married couples to spend decades apart. The union allows them to be close in spite of the physical distance between the two."

"And you want that," I guessed.

"I have chosen Asahi," Kadri said. "If he does not seek marriage with me, then I must release him and continue with my life, alone for eternity."

Wow, that sounded really depressing and final. But I wasn't that worried, because I knew Asahi was head over heels for Kadri. "I guess that makes sense. But I don't get why you want my help," I said.

"Asahi thinks the world of you," Kadri said, as though this were obvious. (In my defense, Asahi thinks the world of most people.) "I hoped you, perhaps, might speak with him and see if there is a reason for his hesitation."

"That seems logical. So…what do we do next? How am I supposed to talk to him about it?"

"You could ask."

"You mean I should just prance up to him and say 'hey, Asahi. I was wondering why you haven't asked Kadri to marry you yet? She's a great girl and time is a-wasting'?" I said.

Kadri nodded.

"...*seriously*?" I said.

"Many magical beings have asked us why our courtship is so extended," Kadri said.

"Extended? You've been dating for two years! For crying out loud—people should mind their own business and leave you alone to date as long as you want," I said. "So what does Asahi say when people ask him?"

"He laughs."

"That's it?"

"Yes."

"And you think he will react differently to me asking such a blatantly nosy question?"

"I do."

I sighed and leaned back in my chair. "Gosh. Okay. I guess I'll try it. Yenta isn't really in my job description, so this might backfire."

"I am not asking too much?" Kadri asked her eyes large and liquid as she batted her lovely eyelashes at me.

"No, this will be the easiest thing on my to-do list. It's just going to be really awkward," I said. "So I'm supposed to give him what for, and then we'll meet up again and make further plans from there?"

"If it's not too much trouble."

"Nah. I'll catch him after class on Friday. Will that be soon enough?"

"Of course."

"I'm assuming this courtship-questioning was what you wanted to talk about?"

Kadri nodded. "Yes."

"Then is it okay if I head out? I hate to run on you, but I've got an appointment with Doctor Creamintin and a siren," I said, downing the last of my drink.

"Absolutely. Thank you for meeting with me today." Kadri said as she stood and bowed. "I cannot thank you enough, Morgan."

I leaped to my feet. "No, no. The pleasure is all mine. Sorta."

Behind me Harrison cleared his throat.

"Right, I've got to go. Take care, Kadri. I'll be in touch," I said.

"I wish you well," the high elf said.

"Thanks," I said, taking my mug and heading for the counter to drop off my used mug. I waved to Kadri before making my exit from the cafeteria. "I'll need it."

"Thank you for your help, Morgan," Doctor Creamintin said, sinking into his padded office chair with a satisfied sigh. "I tried explaining to her that pop star wasn't a viable career for a rehabilitated siren, but she accused me of having the pop culture knowledge of a minotaur," the good doctor said, his sharp frown accented by his white beard. The man was a shoe-in for Merlin, should he ever hit the streets of Hollywood.

"I can't take much credit," I said. "The photos of drugged up divas seem to be what really changed her mind."

"Indeed. Ah—before I forget," Doctor Creamintin said, spinning his chair to face a filing cabinet. He dug out a thick file and tossed it on his desk. "I looked into the dwarven job status, as you requested."

"Already? Awesome! What did you find?"

"Grogrintork did not lie to you. The MBRC has less than ten dwarf employees. None of them have consultant status; all are considered blue collar workers."

"And the liaisons?"

Doctor Creamintin shook his head. "None. Dwarves are welcomed—somewhat belatedly—to use the MBRC facilities and join classes, but as they have no clan contact or liaison they receive old information. Often they are not told of course offerings and rehabilitation opportunities until the sign up deadlines are over."

I narrowed my eyes. "Do they donate to the center?" I asked.

"They do," Doctor Creamintin said. He adjusted his eyeglasses before ruffling through the papers. "They are not as generous as your cyclops friends, but they manage a tidy sum," he said, handing a paper over to me.

I looked at the amount and whistled. "A tidy sum? That's the cafeteria's operating budget for a year. In what universe is it not generous?"

"The dwarves are wealthy thanks to the natural resources they posses. Many of them are miners and jewelers by trade. Typically they work with human wizards or cyclopes to sell their products in human markets. Additionally, they're one of the few races that can bespell jewelry."

"So dwarves made Aysel's truth spell necklace and Asahi's tracking jewelry?" I asked, unable to keep the wryness out of my voice.

"Elves made Aysel's truth necklace, but yes. The dwarves are responsible for the majority of Asahi's spelled and charmed jewelry."

"Are the dwarves being stingy, then?" I asked, looking to the paper again.

"No, their donation is nice—especially when one considers how little the MBRC aids them," Doctor Creamintin said, folding his hands on top of his belly.

"So you think they deserve a few liaisons?"

"I do. Although I have no idea how you're going to twist the Administrator into accepting them," Doctor Creamintin said.

"It will be a parting gift," I said, smiling darkly at the paper.

"So you do mean to leave then?"

I sighed and dropped the sheet. "Honestly, I don't know. If I was staying in the area I'd consider still working here, but the Administrator is being a pill."

"Take your time in deciding," Doctor Creamintin advised. "Your future is not something to trifle with."

I half smiled. "Thanks. No pressure, right?"

Doctor Creamintin chuckled. "Of course not. How are you holding up? I imagine you are under a substantial amount of pressure—even if one ignores the Administrator."

"I'm surviving. No one has gotten too pushy yet. My parents and school advisors are getting worried, though."

"They don't even know the half of it," Doctor Creamintin said, shaking your head. "You should be proud of yourself, Morgan."

"For deceiving my parents so they think I'm working for a doctor?" I dryly asked.

"No, for taking such responsibility for your future. It is rare to find a teenager who is so aware of the consequences of his or her future education. But worry not."

"Oh?"

"Indeed. I read a periodical that reported most adults change careers four to five times in their life. If you choose the wrong career path to start with you can merely start over—although you will quite possibly lose some of the best years of your life that way."

"Gee, thanks, Doctor Creamintin. I feel really upbeat now," I said, my voice wry.

Doctor Creamintin laughed. "You will choose a fine future, Morgan. Of that I am confident. Now, regarding the dwarves. What will you do? What is your next step?"

"I flashed Devin's name to get access to records from the Fairy Council. I'll look them over and decide what to do next. At a minimum I will get some liaisons in place. If this is a case of the elves excluding the dwarves I would like to see a few of them hired into consulting positions. But I need something they excel at which the MBRC needs," I said.

"You've thought a lot about this," Doctor Creamintin said.

"Not really," I frowned. "Hunter made me watch his stuff whenever he was taking yearbook photos, so I got to read a lot of books about leadership and company politics and stuff."

"Hunter *Weller*?"

"Yeah."

"You do keep high company. It will be a great loss for the magical community if you leave."

I snorted. "You'll find someone to replace me."

"Finding a substitute would not be easy, I fear. You are priceless, my dear—or so I've been told."

"What, did Devin drink too much scotch and got a little tipsy again?"

Doctor Creamintin chuckled. "No, for once it was not your beau. It is merely common opinion."

"I'm not sure how long that will last between this Krad guy and my feud with the Administrator—although that fight is a little one-sided."

"Ah yes. Krad Temero and Fidem. I've gotten an armed escort service to and from the MBRC thanks to them. What measures have they taken for you?"

I clenched my hands and the wryness left my voice. "I've had a fairy swat team since Sunday night. I'm supposed to get the full measures tomorrow. I get the impression I'm going to get more than an escort—which is so not fair."

"But it is. As a wizard I have magical powers at my disposal. You have no such defenses."

"Yeah," I agreed, shoving my hands in my pockets. "But I already have a goblin snapping at my heels like a sheep dog. And if I get many more people following me it's going to be so bizarre and creeper-like, I won't be able to disguise it."

"I'm sure management is aware of the position you are in. They will take the necessary precautions, especially with you being as well connected as you are."

"What do you mean?"

"Administrator Moonspell might not like you much, but he has a vested interest in your welfare. All talks with Weller Goblin Enterprises have gone much smoother since you stepped in as a referee, and Devin—a Fairy Councilmember—visits the center more often than ever. Your presence reassures the MBRC board, and Moonspell wants to keep the trustees happy.

"That's good…I guess," I said, somewhat at a loss for words. Was I supposed to be happy that my value was hinged on knowing a flirt and a mob boss? "Anyway, I report to administration about it tomorrow."

"Good luck. You may need it—the administration department can be a handful."

"I'm hoping I get to speak to Bryna. I haven't seen her in a while."

"She's Administrator Moonspell's assistant, right? A selkie, I believe."

"Yes, she's a selkie, and she *used* to be Moonspell's assistant. Now she's in the upper levels of the administration department."

"I thought you had a show down with her when you first joined the MBRC over the cyclopes' glasses."

"I did, but she's still an awesome person. I'm hoping she'll know if Administrator Moonspell is planning to bother me in the future. But I'll be happy as long as I get anyone but Aysel."

Doctor Creamintin laughed. "I hope your desires are reached."

"Thanks. I'm sorry, but I should head out. I have class in a few minutes," I said, edging towards the door.

"Ahh, that's right. Oh—take this file with you. It's filled with my dwarf findings."

"Awesome, thanks!"

"My pleasure," Doctor Creamintin said, waving me out of his office.

I flipped through the file as I headed for my classroom, idly considering what protective measures might be taken on my behalf. I couldn't keep dragging the fairy swat team with me. They almost busted into my English class when a bird flew into the glass window. These fairies were going to blow their cover wide open soon. Even Harrison didn't follow me around school.

Mostly I wished they weren't necessary and tried not to remember why they were with me.

In any case, I knew I could probably operate on good faith with the administrative department. They would want to see me safe, but not reveal the Center's existence. As long as I didn't get stuck talking to Aysel, everything would be great!

8

Ugly Bling

"This totally sucks," I said, my legs tucked to my chest as I slowly spun in a wheeled office chair. "And by sucks, I mean I really didn't want to deal with *you* today."

I briefly saw Aysel's harassed expression before he spun out of view. "I am not wearing my truth necklace, Morgan."

"I stopped bothering to censor myself around you ages ago," I said.

Aysel huffed in a disappointingly manly manner. "Are you finished pouting?"

"No, I'm not. I want Bryna. I don't want the fairy swat team anymore. And the cafeteria got a frappe machine and it's already broken!"

"Morgan L. Fae. The MBRC has decided on its actions regarding your personal safety," Aysel said.

"How did it even break? They had it for less than a week! One stinky week! What, do you guys use crowbars to change the espresso and coffee filters?"

"To begin with, we are removing the team of specialists that were assigned to you as security detail in the interim," Aysel said.

"Surely *someone* in this place should be able to work those machines. Seriously, you have cookie elves, but not coffee elves?"

"*Will you shut up and listen*?"

I repentantly faced Aysel and, momentarily cowed, was silent.

Aysel glared at me across his desk before he straightened his lord of the rings elf robe and continued. "The first security measure we are putting into practice is this," he said, sliding a box across the desk.

"What is it?" I asked, taking the box.

"A tracking necklace," Aysel said, his forehead wrinkling as he shuffled papers. "If it is removed from you it sends an alert to our defense department. The signal will lead them to you."

Curious, I cracked open the case. I caught a look at the necklace inside and snapped the lid shut. "I can't wear this," I said, my voice tight.

"What?" Aysel said.

"I can't wear this," I repeated.

"What are you talking about? You *have* to wear it."

"You expect me to carry off *this*?" I asked, snapping the box open.

Nestled on a velvet pad was the gaudiest silver necklace I've ever seen. A huge sapphire was mounted into a plate of silver formed by dozens of twisting lines designed to resemble vines. It wouldn't have looked out of place on an Elizabethan or Victorian era BBC show or movie. But on a senior in high school it was going to be hideous. The thing sparkled!

Aysel stared at me. "I don't see the problem."

"Of course *you* wouldn't," I said, casting a dark look at Aysel's clothes.

Irritated, Aysel leaned back in his chair. "It's the highest quality available."

"Don't want it."

"In the name of all things fair, it was forged by the same dwarves who make Asahi's charmed and spelled jewelry!"

"That explains *a lot*," I snorted.

"It's a security measure. You must take it."

"Too bad, I'm not."

"*Morgan.*"

"It's totally outdated! I can't wear that with a t-shirt. Are you nuts?"

"Do you have any idea how much it *costs*?" Aysel said, standing up and smacking his hands on the desk.

"If it cost that much you could have told them to make it a stylish locket or something!" I said.

"A mere locket would not be able to hold such a powerful charm."

"That's too bad. I'll be going without it."

"You don't want the security team, you don't want the necklace. What DO you want, Morgan?"

"I want you to tell me I don't need it," I said, my voice quavering. "I want you to say it's all unnecessary, that I'm not in danger, and this is just your dad being a pain," I said, my voice cracking with emotion. It felt like a giant wrapped his hands around my throat. My tongue was thick and it was hard to swallow as I tried to ignore how scared I was.

Aysel was stone still behind his desk. "Krad Temero is serious," he finally said.

I tipped my head to stare at the ceiling. "I know."

"The necklace will allow us to keep you safe."

"I know," I said in a small voice.

Aysel sighed and sat back down in his office chair—a fraction less graceful than normal. "Tell Devin," he said. "Or Hunter Weller of your fears."

I snorted. "If I tell Hunter he will assign 20 goblins to me."

"Then Devin."

"Maybe…but," I trailed, lost in my thoughts for a moment.

Aysel organized his papers in a neat stack and avoided looking at me.

I cleared my throat and arranged myself so I sat in the chair like a normal person. "So, the rest of my security measures?"

"A pixie will be shadowing you for observational purposes. As far as defensive maneuvers go, she has a few tricks. The major skill she brings is her ability to move about unseen and to cast glamours. She will have no trouble trailing you in the human *and* magical community. If she sees any suspicious activity, she will immediately notify the MBRC. The Center will send out a security team to act as backup."

"Just a pixie?" I asked, my spirits lightening.

"Yes. If you wear the necklace."

I sighed and picked up the jewelry box. "Right. Fine, I'll do it. We have to tell Krusher, though, or he'll knock the pixie out once he figures out she's there."

"Weller Goblin Enterprises and the Pooka have already been informed of our measures. I am certain your bodyguard has been informed."

"Great, is that it?" I asked. I hesitated before I removed the necklace from the box. It was *heavy*.

"Yes," Aysel said.

"When do I meet this pixie?"

"She is being debriefed at the moment. She will be waiting outside your classroom when you finish with your advance placement students. Her name is Sink."

"...What?"

"Her name is Sink."

"*Sink*?"

Aysel's lips flattened in annoyance. "Yes, Sink. Have you become hearing impaired?"

"Her parents named her Sink?"

"It is my understanding that she was named after a famous pixie, but her parents feared an exact copy of the name might bring about the wrath of a corporation."

"....*What*?"

"Tinkerbell, or Tink. She is named after Tinkerbell. Now exit my office at once," Aysel snarled.

"Geez, touchy!" I said, hauling myself out of my chair. "But seriously, Sink? For Tink?"

"Good day, Morgan."

"Right, whatever. Have fun in your little office," I said before making my retreat. I slipped out of the administration department before I realized Harrison was a few feet behind me. "So did you hear about your new buddy, Krusher?"

"It's Harrison, Miss Fae."

"Good. Aysel said she'll hook up with us after I'm done with my classes. Her name is Sink," I said, shaking my head. "I guess I don't hate my parents so much for letting my godmother name me Morgan L. Fae anymore. It could be worse. They could have named me Dishwasher."

Harrison was either unamused by my name comparison, or he didn't care. He said nothing and ghosted along behind me.

I was still thinking about names, so I almost missed it when someone called after me.

"Morgan, Morgan!"

I stopped and listened to the sound before I turned and caught sight of Madeline.

"Hey, Madeline," I said, greeting the blonde vampire as she trotted up to me.

"Hello," Madeline said, briefly wrapping her arms around me in a vise-like hug.

"You've been missing from class since the museum field trip. Is everything okay?"

"Sorry, I was reporting in to some of the vampire Elders. I'm coming to class today, but I wanted to talk to you," Madeline said.

"About what?" I asked, allowing her to thread her arm through mine.

"The field trip."

I stopped for a second, frozen with the memory. "What about it?" I said, recovering my stride.

"I'm certain you have discussed it with various beings, but I want to make sure you feel safe."

Caught completely off guard, I stopped again and stared at Madeline in surprise. I'll be the first to admit I'm prone to underestimating Madeline. With the frilly dresses, her puppy-like demeanor, and her hemophobia, it is difficult to remember she is a vampire that is over a hundred years old.

"What?" I said.

"You have never seen the bitter side of magical beings. The cuckoo ward was as close as you've come to our darkness, and that mostly reveals how petty fairies are. No magical being before has ever *really* attacked you," Madeline said, her eyes hooked on my face. "And while Krad might *look* young, his powers are still great. I have no doubt his magic was a frightening experience. In spite of that, do you feel safe? Are you alright?"

I glanced over my shoulder as I felt tears sting my eyes. Harrison thoughtfully dawdled so he was some thirty feet behind us. I looked back at Madeline and bit my lip to keep from crying.

I shook my head.

"Oh, Morgan," Madeline said before hugging me again, gently this time.

I didn't cry, but I did hug Madeline back.

"Just as there are evil people in the world, there are evil magical beings," Madeline said. "You do so much good for us. It is unfortunate but not surprising that you would become a target for such hateful creatures."

"He's a kid. Just a kid! But the feeling of all those spiders on me, it was terrifying," I whispered when Madeline stepped away.

"I'm sure. Dark elf magic is no small matter. But the more you bottle up your fear, the easier you make it for Krad to prey upon you."

"What do I do?"

"You remember the magical beings you like and love, and you carry a cast-iron skillet."

"A what?"

"A skillet," Madeline said, opening up a small drawstring bag that hung from her arm. "Do you recall how I wielded a cast-iron skillet against Krad?"

"You slammed him in the face. It was pretty hard to miss—even with his magic hacking at me."

"By separating from humans and bathing in darkness, Krad and his minions have given themselves a tremendous weakness: iron and technology," Madeline said.

"I remember old stories that talked about how fairies can't touch iron. After I saw the MBRC I figured that had to be a myth," I said.

"It was reality, once upon a time. As long as elves and fairies hated humanity, they could not embrace the resourcefulness of your race. This showed up mostly in the way iron, and now technology, can cancel out their magic. As you may recall, my iron skillet passed straight through Krad's defensive barrier."

"Yeah."

"It is because Krad and Fidem cling to the old ways. As long as they hate humans, iron and technology will disrupt them."

"You mean I can fight back with that," I said.

"Precisely. Which is why I got you this," Morgan said, pulling a small cast-iron skillet that was just a little bigger than my hand out of her drawstring bag.

"What, did your skillet have babies?" I asked. I almost dropped it when Morgan slapped the thing in my extended hand. It was *heavy*.

"No, I went to about ten estate sales before Perseus found me this one on the internet. Have you heard of eBay? It is a marvelous place."

"It's not a place, really."

"The downside of the skillet is that one must get into close range to use it. But if you're backed in a corner, it is very useful," Madeline chattered, ignoring my correction. "As you have copious amounts of backup in your pocket, the main tactic you should focus on is stalling for time."

The ice was returning to my stomach. "I really don't want to talk about this."

"Morgan."

Madeline's voice was so unusually firm, I couldn't help but look at her. The ageless girl stared at me with unfathomable eyes.

"Just as you are careful when wandering the streets of Chicago, you need to be careful for Krad. I know it is upsetting to think that he is targeting you, but you must be prepared and ready to fight, or things will go worse for you."

I looked away.

"You are strong and proud, Morgan. I know you can do this. You can always picture Devin when you're cracking Krad in the skull," she graciously added.

That got a laugh out of me, easing my tension.

"There you go, you look better now," Madeline said. "Even more so than your skillet, banishing your fear and anger will disarm Krad."

"Yeah, so people have been telling me. But none of you had Krad feed off you," I said, shivering at the memory.

"You are correct," Madeline acknowledged. "But it doesn't change the fact that if you cut Krad off from his source of power—dark emotions—he will be neutered, like a cat."

I stared at Madeline. "Who have you been talking to while you were gone?" I asked.

"I didn't use that phrase right?"

"What phrase? Humans don't say *anything* like that."

"You must be mistaken! A vampire assured me it was a common phrase."

"It's *not*. I should know, I'm human."

"Perhaps it is a phrase said only among adults?"

"It's *not*!"

"Oh dear," Madeline said.

"What?"

"I included that phrase in a formal report I submitted to a number of vampire covens."

"If a vampire told you it was a common human phrase, I don't think you have to worry about other vampires. Only someone as young as Esmeralda would know it's bizarre."

"Speaking of which, she said to tell you she plans to attend class today."

"Class! That's right, I have to go get my notes," I said, jumping into motion. "Are you coming with?"

"Of course!" Madeline said, bouncing after me.

Armed with my cast-iron skillet, we plowed down the hallway, Harrison trailing after us.

"Madeline?"

"Yes?"

"Thanks."

"Anytime, Morgan," Madeline said, her canines flashing when she smiled at me.

Yeah, I definitely didn't give Madeline enough credit.

Friday afternoon I sat in a desk and stared at Asahi. The sunny high elf was animatedly explaining how that afternoon's Introduction to the American Education System went. The advanced placement class was over. Everyone except for Madeline and Frank had cleared out, and they were occupying themselves by trying to find Sink. (In spite of her less than stellar name, Sink is the pixie equivalent of a ninja.)

"—and everyone did great on their tests—from what I saw, that is. We won't know for sure until you correct them and enter the students' scores, but I am quite pleased with their progress," Asahi said, his hair glittering in the dim light.

I was trying to think of subtle ways to ask Asahi about Kadri, but my creativity was failing me. Not like I think there is *any* good way to ask a person why they aren't married yet. Talk about nosey and inappropriate.

"The students seem to comprehend the information I've presented to them, but we'll begin taking a look at middle school education and psychology next week. I was hoping you would teach the first few classes," Asahi said.

I had to ask him. Kadri was counting on me.

"I would especially like for you to describe sports and the prevalent, competitive spirit. I'm afraid I still fail to grasp it," Asahi said.

"Asahi," I said.

"Yes?" Asahi said, looking up from his written out agenda that we were steadily churning through.

"What's up with you and Kadri?"

"What is up?"

I squirmed in my seat under Asahi's golden gaze. "A lot of

people have been telling me your…lengthy courtship with her is pretty unusual. Not that *I* think it's unusual. I think it's healthy. But people—ahh—magical beings, don't seem to share this opinion."

Asahi stared at me.

"What I mean is, uhh. Wow, this really bites. Fine. Why aren't you two married yet?"

Asahi's expression cleared and he smiled. "Oh, is that all?"

"Yeah, that's all," I said, my voice heavy with sarcasm.

I waited expectantly, but Asahi was silent as he organized his papers. (Brother like brother, I guess.)

"Asahi," I said when it didn't seem like I was going to get a reply.

"Yes?"

"So?"

Asahi cocked his head and looked cute. "What?"

I almost groaned. "What's the deal? You don't usually act cagey."

"Cagey?"

"*Asahi*!"

Asahi sighed and leaned back in his chair. "I cannot marry Kadri."

"Cannot? What the—you're totally in love with her!"

"I know," Asahi said.

"So? Why can't you marry her?"

Asahi's shoulders drooped. "Marrying me would be too dangerous for her," he said.

I thought for a moment before exclaiming, "*What*?"

"I am kidnapped on an almost monthly basis. I am a constant target for those who wish to limit the MBRC's power or increase their own. I do not have my brother's wit, nor my father's will. I am the weak target in the family, and I will always be dogged. If Kadri were to marry me, her life would be put in danger."

"Aw come on. You're kidnapped by unions and stuff. People like the Weller goblins. They aren't a basket of kittens, but no one would ever hurt you—or Kadri," I said.

"The Weller goblins are not the only sort who target me," Asahi said. "You are aware how concerned the MBRC is for your welfare due to Krad Temero?"

"Yeah."

"You are aware you are on a high alert watch because of the likelihood that Krad will attack you again?"

"Yes…"

"You and I are on the same level."

"You *are* the Administrator's kid. There's no better way to kick him where it hurts than to get to you or Aysel."

"Aysel is not on the list. He does not even have increased security because Aysel is capable of taking care of himself," Asahi said. For the first time *ever*, the sunshine elf wore a bitter half smile, and I was reminded of his age by the fathomless look in his eyes.

I couldn't reply.

"Before Kadri and I began courting, Kadri never saw combat. Recently she has gotten a tracking necklace and a number of spelled daggers, all because we have been attacked—*she* has been attacked—because of our relationship."

"You can't take the blame for the evil actions of others," I said.

"It is undeniable that Kadri is placed in danger because of me," Asahi said. "If we were married it would only be worse."

"But I'm sure Kadri would be willing to take that risk," I said.

"Perhaps, but I could not live with myself if she were ever hurt because of me," Asahi said. He resembled a wilted flower as his normal vitality drained away.

"I understand you want to protect her. But if she loves you, your decision to let her go will crush her," I said.

"But she will still be alive," Asahi said.

I leaned back in my chair and sadly studied Asahi. I could see I wasn't going to change his mind. After my run in with Krad, I could understand his hesitation—and that was my *first* encounter with someone truly bad. If Kadri felt threatened enough that she needed to have daggers…

"Truthfully, I am surprised you are asking," Asahi said.

"What? Why?"

"Because you are experiencing the same thing, aren't you?"

I stared at Asahi. "What?"

"The Pooka," Asahi said.

"What about him?"

"He flirts and does his best to be seen with a multitude of females in an effort to protect you."

I erupted into snorting laughter. "Are you kidding me? First of all, flirting is not a way to protect a person. Secondly, Devin flirts because he was a born womanizer and will be until the day he dies."

Asahi shook his head. "No, he does it in an effort to downplay his love for you. He is a Fairy Councilmember, *and* the Pooka. If his enemies knew of his affection for you, they would not hesitate to eliminate you."

"You always see the best in people, but I think even you have to agree you're giving Devin waaaaay too much credit," I said.

"But it is true," Asahi insisted.

I fondly smiled at the high elf and shook my head. "Thank you for genuinely answering my question. I'm sorry you feel that way about Kadri," I said, standing up.

"You're welcome, and thank you, Morgan," Asahi said.

I rested a hand on his shoulder. "It will work out," I promised.

"I don't see how," Asahi sadly said.

"It just will. I know it will," I said before turning around and heading for the door. "With a little bit of meddling," I added under my breath.

"Are you all done?" Madeline asked as she adjusted the buckle of Frank's flea collar. The werewolf choked when she tightened it too much.

"Yep, did you two find Sink?" I asked after the collar was fixed.

"No," Frank said, his eyes wide with his choking scare. "I can't even smell her. She has some powerful magic."

"What do you have left to do today?" Madeline asked.

"Not much," I said as I headed for my office. "I need to talk to Baobab and check my schedule."

And help Kadri ask Asahi to marry her.

Life was never dull at the MBRC. That was for sure.

"Oh my gosh. What are you *wearing*?" Fran asked when I took off my winter coat.

It was Saturday morning. We were meeting for a bagel and coffee breakfast before I hit the library to study—I was super behind on my homework and I needed to get some research material.

I looked down at my clothes—my most expensive pair of designer jeans and a cream colored, v-neck sweater—and frowned. "What's wrong with what I'm wearing?"

"The outfit is cute, but what's with the necklace? Talk about costume jewelry."

"It's real," I dryly said, briefly wrapping my fingers around the silver plating of the necklace.

"Whoa, seriously? Is it like, a family heirloom that came over with the Mayflower or something?" Fran asked, eyeballing the sapphire.

"Whatever," I said.

"But why are you wearing it? It must cost a mint, and you said you're just going to the library. Wouldn't your mom scalp you if she realized you're wearing an heirloom outside?"

"It's not a family heirloom. A friend is lending it to me. So why did we have to meet in the morning again? It was my goal to sleep until 11:00, and you have dragged me out of bed and it isn't even 9:00."

"I have a date with Ethan this afternoon," Fran said, ripping wax paper off her bagel. "Mmm, it's still warm from the oven."

"Where are you guys going today?"

"Ethan was thinking of the zoo or getting ice cream."

"Is Ethan stupid?" I asked, still sulking over the criticism of my safety necklace.

"No! Why?"

"Because his date ideas suck. It's freezing outside and the wind-chill is below zero. None of the animals are going to be out, and you'll freeze!"

"We can visit the animals indoors, like the aviary."

"You're allergic to feathers. And ice cream? When we have a blanket of snow outside?" I said, folding my arms across my chest.

"You're just being mean. Ethan's dates are fun," Fran said.

"Uh-huh, right," I said, taking a sip of my hot, spiced apple cider. The warmth of the drink made my toes curl in delight.

"Like you've been on better dates," Fran said.

"I have," I said, popping the lid off my apple cider so I could stir in the puff of whipped cream the barista had plopped on top.

"With who, and where?" Fran demanded.

"Devin has taken me to all sorts of places," I said, biting into my warm, cinnamon sugar bagel. "And he's never let me freeze in a single one of them."

"I thought you and Hot Garden Guy aren't dating," Fran said, frowning.

"We aren't," I assured her. "But he takes me out lots."

"If you aren't dating why does he take you out?"

I stopped chewing for a moment. "I don't know," I said. "But he does."

Fran slyly smiled. "Have any other men taken you out for no apparent reason?"

I took another bite of my bagel and thought about Hunter. I didn't think weekend imprisonment counted, and while I had gone to his place often enough (after making him buy a new building) it was mostly for school, and to trail after his cookie elf chef.

"Nope," I said.

"I knew it. You *are* dating," Fran said, leaning back in her chair and smugly folding her arms across her chest.

"No we aren't."

"You are! You so totally are!"

"No way, he hasn't asked me or anything."

"Maybe he hasn't specifically asked you *out*, but he's taking you on dates. You just admitted that, even if you didn't know it."

"How can I be dating someone and not know?" I scoffed.

"I'm sure you're the only person who doesn't know," Fran said.

"Whatever. Ethan just has you twitterpaited," I snorted. "And my lack of love life has nothing to do with Ethan's terrible planning skills."

Fran gave a love sick sigh and nudged her coffee drink. "He's too adorable. He's totally the smart, serious type, and he gets easily ruffled. It's so cute!"

"Sure it is," I said, going at my bagel again.

Fran rolled her eyes. "You are so unromantic."

"Yeah. So when do I get to meet this Ethan?"

"Do you have any time next week?" Fran asked.

"I have a bunch of stuff due on Monday and Tuesday, but after that I should be over the worst of it, so I could meet up after work."

"In the evening? Don't you get off work at like seven or eight?"

"Yeah, but if I'm just meeting the guy I could drop by your house."

"How about Friday?"

"Sounds good," I said, slurping my cider.

"Awesome! I'm really excited. I hope you like him," Fran said, cupping her hands around her coffee drink.

"If you like him, I'm sure I will too," I said.

"I've told him all about you."

"Please tell me you didn't mention the incident from sixth grade."

"What, when you ate a dog treat on a dare?"

"It was a peanut butter dog cookie, and it tasted great," I argued.

"Sure, you just had dog breath for the rest of the night. And yes, I did happen to mention that."

"Fran," I groaned.

"It's a funny story."

"Whatever. I'm not out to impress this guy. It's his job to impress me," I said, taking a savage bite out of my bagel.

"Totally," Fran agreed as she checked her coat pockets. "Do you have any tissues? My nose is running from the cold."

"Sure, pass over my purse," I said.

"Holy cow! What do you have in there, a brick?" Fran said, nearly dropping my purse before handing it over.

I had forgotten about the cast-iron skillet. Still, I wasn't going anywhere without that thing. I had seen Madeline—undeniably the weakest member of our crew if you excluded me—take out that Krad kid when everyone else failed to. "Just a book," I said as I picked through my purse.

"A book? It must be a freakin' dictionary. Thanks," Fran said, taking the pack of tissues I offered her.

"So how's the college application thing going?" I asked.

"Good. I've got my essay done. My English teacher is going over it for me to look for errors. And you?"

I inhaled deeply. "I would rather not talk about it."

"Why don't you come to Florida with me? We could be roomies and go to Disneyworld over Christmas break," Fran said.

"I'll think about it."

"That means no," Fran said.

"No, it just means I don't know what I want to do," I said.

"Yeah, yeah. So did you know Stephanie and Zach broke up?"

"Again? What was it this time?"

"I'm not sure. Stephanie said she didn't want to talk about it, but she called Zach an unfeeling zombie."

"Ahh, young love."

"Mmmhmm."

9

Krad means Dark

An hour later Fran and I parted. I—stupidly—walked to the library in the freezing cold, while Fran drove off for her date with Ethan.

I shivered, thankful for the buildings that blocked the gusting wind. I turned off Main Street and wound my way up a few streets, taking a shortcut to the library. It wasn't until I crossed a bridge that arched over a wussy river that I realized I didn't hear footsteps behind me.

I whirled around. There was no one there.

I retreated a block and looked up and down the street. Still no one.

"Krusher," I hissed.

I knew he was still assigned to me. He sat three tables away from Fran and me at the bagel place!

"Krusher! Stop fooling around," I said.

Silence.

"...Harrison? This isn't funny. Sink, where is Harrison?"

When the pixie nor the goblin replied I wedged a hand down the front of my jacket, gripping my obnoxious, eye-catching necklace.

"Parasite."

I recognized that youthful voice.

I yanked on my necklace, pulling it free from my neck. It tangled in my sweater, but I knew the alert was tripped, so I left it and reached into my purse as I turned around to face Krad Temero.

"Harrison!" I called.

"Your guard is occupied. I couldn't have him—or the pixie—sweeping in to save you," Krad said, tucking his hands into pockets of his too-big-for-him black jacket.

It was easier to smother my fear than I would have thought. I mean, it was still pretty hard to equate the magic that made me feel hundreds of spiders with the ten-year-old standing in front of me. I didn't really fear Krad so much as I feared he might use his magic.

"Pretty sure I don't need my guard to toss a kid out of my way," I said, tapping my booted foot on the slick sidewalk.

Krad's childish face twisted in anger. "You don't know who you mock, human!"

"No, I totally know who I'm mocking: Krad, the dark elf who is supposedly so scary but is somehow dense enough to get locked in the body of a kid."

"Your stupidity is what gives you such braveness. Even my very name is steeped in darkness!" Krad said.

"I hate to break it to you, but Krad sounds German—which in no way has anything to do with darkness."

"Fool!" Krad scoffed. "Krad is the word dark spelled backwards."

I snorted.

Krad planted his hands on his hips. "What?"

"Hm?"

"You laughed."

"No I didn't."

"Yes you did."

"Well, maybe I did. But that's only because that is the dorkiest naming technique I have ever heard."

"*What?*"

"Also it's dark spelled backwards in English, a human language.

And you are a self professed human hater. Way to go with that one, Einstein."

Krad's jaw dropped and he stared at me, taken aback by the realization.

"You know, you look like a pretty big hypocrite," I continued.

"What?" Krad snarled.

"You yammer about hating humans, and then you wear human clothes?" I said, indicating to his gray scarf and clearly human made jacket.

"Silence! I will not allow you to sully the air with your careless words!" Krad said. He was so mad he didn't notice that I was rummaging through my purse still.

I made a great show of sighing as my hand closed around my baby cast-iron skillet in my purse. "Look, kid—,"

"KID?"

"I can't play with you all day. Just hurry up and tell me what you want," I said, rolling my eyes.

"I am not so stupid as to announce my intentions," Krad said, shoving his nose into the air.

"Really? Because you did that last time we met," I said.

Krad gave me a hateful look, his eyes thinning into angry wedges. He started walking towards me, taking small steps to compensate for the ice and snow. "As long as the Fairy Council focuses on cohabitating with *humans*, the strength of the magical community will never be returned," he sneered. "Moonspell and his ilk fester with weakness. His rehabilitation center is fueled by weak animals—like you."

"Is that what you think?" I asked before I whipped out my cast-iron skill and swung it at Krad.

Krad ducked, but his feet slipped out from underneath him and he fell on his butt, giving me a chance to run.

"It's no use running from me," Krad said, scrambling off the ice and giving chase. "I will take you as my prisoner!"

I was running unfortunately slow thanks to the ice. "I thought I said it earlier. I can't play with you—,"

"I am nearly a hundred years old! I do not play!"

"In that case, PERVERT!"

Krad had nearly caught up with me—for a ten year old he sure was zippy—but my accusation disarmed him. "What?"

"You're a hundred year old man chasing after a fair maiden. There's only one thing you could possibly want," I said before taking another swing at him with my skillet.

"What? I never," Krad said before grabbing my wrist, stopping me midswing. So I dropped skillet, which fell on his arms.

Krad yelped and jumped back. I retrieved the skillet and started running again. "Old man pervert!" I called over my shoulder.

"I am not a pervert!" Krad shouted as he gave chase.

"You're worse than a vampire. At least they're openly perverted. I bet you were happy you got cursed so it gave you a disguise!" I panted, a little short on air.

Yelling and running isn't the most efficient thing to do, but my shout fest was keeping me from being afraid.

"You are infuriating," Krad said.

"Should have thought twice before you attacked the teenage girl, you snot-faced brat. Just try and come at me, bro," I said. "YEEK!"

Krad grabbed my arm by which I held my skillet and yanked.

When I started slipping I reflexively dropped the skillet, which Krad kicked out of range.

I fell, but I yanked Krad down with me. I rolled away when he tried reaching for me, and, for the first time, realized we were running on the unsalted sidewalk of a salted, sanded street.

"Stupid," I grumbled, jumping into the middle of the road—it wasn't like I had seen any traffic since I first started running.

I was shocked when Krad jumped on my back. He slid off, but got a hold of my scarf, which he clung to as he dropped.

Dragged by my throat, I dropped to my knees, coughing. In an act of vengeance I kicked Krad's booted feet. He fell on me, and I had him in a good choke hold when he slapped at my face with his bare hand and activated his magic.

I screamed when the fear I was hiding behind humor overwhelmed me, turning into all consuming, mind shattering terror.

The amplified fear buzzed in my brain. I dropped Krad and

curled over my knees, my heart beating franticly—as if it might burst out of my chest. I couldn't see, I couldn't hear. It was like being dropped in a pitch black cavern filled with water and drowning. My lungs burned with the need for air.

I felt spider legs on my skin, could have sworn the claws of a bear pressed into my back. Even though I was on land I was positive a shark circled me, jaws gaping open and crusted with blood. Then I was sinking in quicksand. Muck filled my mouth and blocked my nose.

Above it all, I could feel darkness looming above me, pushing me down, and holding black magic to my throat.

I screamed in mindless terror.

There was shouting besides my own, and the darkness retreated —although the rest of my fears and terrors still plagued me.

"Morgan!"

I choked on the imaginary quicksand and screamed when the nonexistent shark bit me. Even though I knew these things couldn't be true, I could *feel* them. It felt more real than the stinging January air.

There was more shouting, and suddenly my fears were gone. I was splayed on the sidewalk, my body stiff with cold.

"Morgan!"

I could hear Sink, but I had to blink a few times before I saw her shimmer into view, her angular facial features twisted in concern.

I shuddered with fear and looked up the street. Harrison was standing half a block away, hurling fireballs at Krad.

Unwilling to leave me to pursue Krad, Harrison backed up to stand closer to me. Seconds later an MBRC guard team ran up the street.

"What is it?" the team leader, a hobgoblin, asked.

"Krad, this way," Sink said, popping in and out of visibility as she led the way down the street, chasing after Krad.

"H-h-Harrison," I said, my teeth chattering.

Harrison knelt at my side. "The Princess is secured," Harrison said into his earpiece before he picked me up like a father carrying his child. "Support from the MBRC has arrived. I am taking her back to the Center."

I clung to the massive goblin, my knees too jelly-like to support me. "H-Harrison. I'm s-scared."

Harrison's voice was soft when he said, "It's Krusher, Miss Fae."

I was safe. For the moment.

"Morgan, would you like anything to drink? A tea, a cappuccino, or maybe a frappe?" Corona, a long-time MBRC acquaintance of mine, asked, clasping her paws together.

Corona resembled a large lizard with her reptile-like body and tail and her alligator face and snout. She walked on her hind legs, called most people honey, and was as sweet as could be. I was never more thankful for her comforting presence as I was then, sitting on a sofa and swaddled in blankets.

"I'm fine," I said.

"A hot drink would do you some good, honey. How about hot chocolate? I could send one of the vampires to Starbucks for you," she offered.

Doggy was with Corona, and he jumped up on my lap when I rearranged my blankets, shedding a few blue scales when he rubbed against my arm. "I really don't want anything."

"She will take a lavender or chamomile tea and a few crackers. Thank you, Corona," Doctor Creamintin said as he bustled into the room.

Corona nodded and glided from the room in her swaggering, reptilian gait. Doggy leaped from my lap and scurried after her, flapping his wings in the chase.

"I'm not hungry or thirsty," I said as the door closed behind them.

"I imagine you are not, but your body is incapable of gauging what it needs at this moment. Tea and a snack would do you some good. Tilt your head back please," Doctor Creamintin said before shining a light in my eyes.

"Your entire system is swimming in adrenaline," he said, fixing a stethoscope over his ears and pushing back my blankets to listen to my heart and lungs. "Your heartbeat and breathing are erratic. Lavender or chamomile will help calm your system."

I didn't say anything and fixed my blankets when Doctor Creamintin stepped back.

"Now, how do you feel?" he asked.

"Terrible."

"Were you hurt?"

"No," I said, scrunching my eyes shut. "He was just using his amplifier magic on me. Harrison got to us before he could do anything else."

"Did he say anything to you?" Doctor Creamintin asked, pen poised above a white pad.

"Not really," I said. "We fought a bit. He doesn't seem to appreciate being treated like a kid. He said he wanted to take me prisoner, but that was it."

"I see," Doctor Creamintin said, writing my observations down.

"Where is Harrison?" I asked, twisting in my blanket cocoon.

"He is just outside the room."

"Krusher?"

The door clicked open. "Yes, Miss Fae?"

"Are you okay?"

"Yes, Miss Fae."

"I'm glad. Did you tell Hunter? How did he take it?"

"Yes, Miss Fae."

"Yeah, I didn't think he would take it very well. Thanks, Krusher," I said.

Harrison closed the door as I wriggled deeper into my blankets.

"You two have a unique line of communication," Doctor Creamintin said.

"Has anyone asked to see me?"

"By anyone you mean…?"

"Devin, Asahi, or Madeline?"

"I believe Madeline is waiting for your release with a few other students of yours. Devin…Devin does not know," Doctor Creamintin said, flipping through a few charts. "Now then. I'm giving you a clean bill of health, although you are not cleared to leave. You must drink the tea and snack Corona brings, and remain quiet for an hour. Do you understand?"

"Yeah," I said.

"Good. I will check in with you on Monday," Doctor Creamintin said as he gathered his papers and tools. He paused at the door. "I'm very sorry you had to experience this again, Morgan."

"Yeah, me too," I said, pulling my blankets closer.

"Rest up," Doctor Creamintin said before he left, shutting the door behind him.

When the good doctor was gone I got out my MM—magic mirror—and held it in front of me. "Call Devin, please," I said.

The mirror swirled before Devin's image appeared. He wasn't human, but in his horse form. Based on the way the image rippled, he was probably looking in a pool of water.

"Hi, Devin," I said, sniffing as I fumbled with my MM. "K-Krad attacked me again. I'm okay. Harrison and Sink were with me and fought him off," I said.

Devin blinked his yellow moon eyes at me, and his image was gone.

I exhaled and dropped the MM back in my purse.

The door swung open and Corona walked in. "I used some lavender tea from Orion, and swiped some green tea cookies for you from a Japanese tanuki. Just what the doctor ordered," she said, putting the tray down on a coffee table. She passed the steaming mug to me, which began to thaw my chilled hands.

"Drink up! Lavender is calming," Corona said.

I sipped the hot drink, which—I'm not gonna lie—tasted like weeds and a dash of soap. Still, I didn't think I could get by without drinking it, and it was warming me up, making my belly glow with heat. "Thanks, Corona. For the tea, and for being here," I said.

"Wild unicorns couldn't keep me away," Corona said, passing me a plate of cookies. "Eat one—Doctor Creamintin said so," she reminded me when I stared at the plate.

I took one of the green hued cookies and nibbled on it. It was a strange combination of sweet and bitter. It tasted a little like a sugar cookie, but it had the slight bitterness of green tea mixed in it as well.

"They're good," I said, finishing the cookie before drinking my flowery tea.

Corona nodded. "I'm glad you like them. Now, honey, are you really okay?"

"Yeah. I wish someone would give that Krad brat a good spanking, though," I said, my voice flat.

Corona didn't laugh at my attempt of humor. "It was worse, wasn't it?" she asked.

The second cookie tasted like sawdust in my mouth thanks to Corona's astute observation. I washed it down with tea before nodding in defeat.

"I'm sorry, Morgan," Corona said. "This isn't right."

"What do you mean?"

"You've done so much for us magical beings. You've given up so much. And now you're being targeted and attacked?" Corona shook her head. "It's not fair."

"Life isn't fair," I said without an ounce of conviction.

"That is a terrible saying," Corona said.

"Yeah, but it's true. I mean, usually I've been told it by a teacher who is giving out extra homework, or my mom when she orders me to watch my little brothers. But this…," I paused, unable to continue. Unfair didn't even begin to describe my situation.

Someone knocked on the door.

"Come in," I said, assuming it was Devin.

I assumed wrong. It was Orion and Toby, a centaur and a hobgoblin. Both worked with Corona, and I had worked a bit with Toby before obtaining a tutoring position with Asahi.

"Hi," I said, a little disappointed.

Toby didn't say anything. He walked up to the sofa and frowned deeply at me.

"How are you, Toby?" I asked, pulling a blanket tighter.

"This no good," Toby said. "We find guy who did this to you

and then the minotaurs will play with him real good he won't know what hit him and you'll be safe," Toby said in one breath.

I blinked, trying to process his punctuation-less sentences. "Yeah, I hope so," I said.

Toby grunted and tossed a package of Starbucks coffee—his absolute favorite flavor, which showed what a supreme gift this was —and scurried out of the room.

"You stop by and help me answer questions okay we answer them 1 2 3 fast," Toby said before he closed the door.

"The hobgoblin sees the sputtering light in your soul and wishes to strengthen it," Orion said.

As a centaur, Orion's personal policy was to speak in riddles and metaphors I couldn't understand.

"That's sweet of him," I said when it seemed the centaur expected an answer.

Orion tilted his head and studied me. "To him who is in fear, everything rustles."

I turned to give Corona a pained expression.

The gator patted my shoulder. "We're trying to comfort her, Orion," she reminded the centaur.

Orion bowed. "Minds that are ill at ease are agitated by hope and fear. One must stumble through the fog to see the dawn of the day."

Before Orion could philosophize further, the door slammed open. In stormed Devin—still in his horse form. He whinnied and tossed his head as he pranced to the sofa I was splayed out on.

"Devin," I said when he lowered his horse head to touch my cheek. He blew on my neck and lipped my hair. "What are you doing?"

Corona smiled. "We'll give you two some privacy," she said.

"Please don't," I said.

Corona laughed and slithered out of the room. Orion followed her. "Rest and your soul will no longer be weary," Orion advised me before he gently shut the door.

I put my hands around Devin's nuzzle and pulled his head away from me. "Was that really necessary?" I said.

Devin snorted at me.

"Go change," I said, pointing to a changing screen shoved at the back of the room. "I refuse to have this conversation while you are a horse."

Devin snorted but pranced off, disappearing behind the screen. He squealed—still as a horse—and moments later jogged out from behind the screen, the remaining sparks of his magic leaping from his clothes.

"Are you alright? Did he hurt you?" Devin asked, his eyes scanning me from head to foot.

"Krad only got to use his emotion amplification magic. Harrison and Sink arrived before he could do anything."

"Why weren't they with you?"

"I don't know. Krad said they were being distracted."

"He said that before he attacked you?"

"Before he chased me, yeah."

Devin blinked. "Chased?"

"Yep. I took a swing at him with the cast-iron skillet Madeline bought me before I tried running. I probably could have evaded him if the sidewalks weren't so slick. I'm going to write a letter to Oakdale City Council about that," I scowled. "Anyway, because some people aren't upright citizens and don't salt their sidewalks, he was able to catch up with me and jumped me."

"He what?"

"He jumped on my back. Which was cunning of the little brat. I would have torn a chunk of his hair out, but I couldn't get the angle right."

"Morgan, you are unbelievable," Devin chuckled.

"Thanks," I dryly said.

"To think you nearly evaded him—Krad Temero—because you judge him based on his appearance," Devin shook his head.

"Yeah, I don't think I'll be able to do that again," I said shivering in spite of the warm mug I held in my hands.

I was caught off guard when Devin slid his fingers under my chin and made me look into his pale, yellow eyes. "How bad was the amplification magic?"

"A lot worse," I admitted. "There's no way I'll be able to face him again like I did today," I said, my voice shaking.

"You're safe now," Devin said, using his thumb to brush away the few teardrops that leaked from my eyes. "Krad will not hurt you here. He will not touch you as long as I am with you."

My shoulders shook, and Devin bent over to hug me. I dropped my head onto his shoulder, closing my eyes in relief as the last bits of terror fled with Devin's warmth.

"So, what next?" I asked.

"We'll have to guard you better," Devin said.

"I don't get how he—how Krad—can be so hateful," I said, drinking more tea when Devin released me.

"It's likely that he's been fed a steady diet of hatred and bigotry since he was born."

"But what kind of person would *do* that?"

"It takes dark people to create the darkness that lives in Krad," Devin said. "Also, Dökkàlfar are not known for their parenting skills."

"How can you guard me against such evil?" I whispered.

"With love," Devin said, leaning forward to kiss my forehead. "I'm sure Aysel will have new security measures. He and Hunter Weller seem to take Krad's acts against you as personal affronts," Devin dryly said.

"And you don't?"

Devin cocked an eyebrow at me. "Your safety has nothing to do with my pride, and everything to do with my affection for you."

I rolled my eyes. "If that's true than you must worry over every female on the planet."

"That was hurtful," Devin said.

"It doesn't mean it isn't true."

"Harpy," Devin said. "To reassure myself that you are indeed safe, I'll be staying with you for the rest of the day."

"Devin."

"This is not up for discussion."

"Are you kidding? There's no way this will fly with my parents."

Devin smiled mischievously.

"Devin," I repeated.

Devin retreated to screen. When he popped back into view, he was a black dog that was the size and shape of a German shepherd.

"Oh," I said.

Devin jumped onto the open cushion next to me. He wagged his tail before he tried licking my face with his pink dog tongue.

"Not gonna fly, Devin," I reminded him, pushing against his furry chest to hold him back.

Devin's ears drooped before he popped past my defenses and gave me a great, slimy kiss on the cheek. He then turned around several times before settling into the cushion.

I patted him on the head. "Thanks for coming, Devin."

Devin woofed and thumped his tail on the couch.

Devin placed his head on my thigh, radiating heat as I sipped my tea.

His silent but warm presence was a million times more soothing than the hot tea, and I was grateful he stayed with me.

10

I Receive More Bling

Saturday evening heralded the return of my fairy swat team. One of them actually knocked out Michael—my older brother who was home from college for the weekend—because he didn't recognize him. Thankfully Michael woke up just fine after we dragged his carcass to his room. He thought he passed out in his room due to exhaustion.

Devin stayed with me until the evening, when the swat team was on duty. On Sunday I was banned from leaving the house, but on Monday the fairies informed me I was permitted to go to school and the MBRC.

"Great, so is Sink going to follow me inside school?" I asked the team leader—a surprisingly gruff and buff male fairy—as I fumbled with my car keys in the empty garage.

"Yes. You aren't driving," the fairy said.

"What? Of course I am. How else am I supposed to get to school?"

Outside a car honked its horn.

I popped my head out the side door and saw Hunter leaning against a sleek, black car. Two of his goblins were seated in the front seats, and I spotted at least two other black cars in strategic locations up and down the street.

I darted back into the garage.

"You can't hide, Morgan. I saw you," Hunter called.

I winced and picked up my backpack before locking the side door. I hadn't talked to Hunter since Fran dropped the dating question on us. This ride could be awkward. "This is pointless," I said. "I can drive myself."

"I'm sure you can," Hunter said with one of his falsified, harmless smiles. "But we need to discuss the new security measures."

"The MBRC is going to have its own security implements," I said as Hunter opened the car door for me.

"Yes, but they are working together with Weller Goblin Enterprises," Hunter said, joining me in the leather upholstered car.

"They're what?" I said as the car rolled down the street. As Aysel seemed to be my contact for security measures, I deeply doubted this. He was even less fond of Hunter than he was of me. "You're joking."

"The Pooka is acting as the go between, otherwise I don't think we could do it," Hunter said.

"Why are you doing this, Hunter?" I asked.

"Why wouldn't I?" Hunter asked, his voice innocent.

"I was serious when I explained to Fran why we can't date. It would never work out."

"I do recall that conversation," Hunter said.

"Then why?"

"Because I am Patroclus to your Achilles," Hunter said.

"...What?"

"You said even if we don't date we can still be more than plain friends, right?"

"Of course."

"So twenty years from now when we're married and have our separate lives, we'll still be friends?"

"I am not babysitting your brats if that's where you're going."

"Morgan."

I fondly smiled at Hunter. "Yeah. We'll still be friends."

Hunter exhaled. "Excellent. Then yes, I'm helping you because we are friends. Great friends," He said, his smile was more pleased than he had a reason for it to be.

I was quiet for a moment. "Why do I feel like I was just played?"

"What?"

"You are a little *too* relieved. I don't get it. What's your angle?"

"I have no angle."

"You are made of angles."

Hunter shrugged. "If you must know, all I want is unrestricted access to you. Friendships for goblins are rare. You're more likely to see a dragon in downtown Chicago than find a goblin friend, so the relationship is marked for generations. I didn't want to lose you," he said, sounding slightly embarrassed.

I blinked. "That's why you wanted to date me? Because you were afraid I would eventually cut you out of my life?"

"Maybe," Hunter said.

"How long would you have played along with a romantic relationship?" I said, narrowing my eyes.

"I wasn't sure. I was going to try to find some books about it. Friendship or not, my parents would kill me if I married a human. Nor would I want to, no offense," Hunter said.

My jaw dropped. "What?"

"The idea of having to interact with all your family and friends makes my skin crawl," Hunter said.

"Oh. My. Gosh. I no longer feel sorry for turning you down. In fact, *I'm* the one who has the right to feel hurt and angry. You were totally playing me!"

"It doesn't matter," Hunter said. "You were too skiddish to ever agree to go out with me, so the end result is the same."

"*Yes*, it matters!" I said, glaring at my classmate and friend.

"You said we were going to be lifelong friends. I will hold you to that," Hunter said, reaching for a briefcase. He chuckled when he opened it. "When I do marry, my wife is going to either hate or love you."

"Love, I hope. I'll be the only other female on the planet who will be able to criticize you for being so unromantic," I said, utterly disgusted with myself.

"Perhaps. I'm glad we had this little talk," Hunter said, removing a small box from the briefcase.

"Bully for you," I grunted.

"Here are your new charmed jewelry pieces," Hunter said, ignoring my disapproval and handing me the box.

"I'm glad to see old faithful is back," I said, my lack of enthusiasm obvious when I spotted the obnoxiously large sapphire necklace.

"The MBRC does not comprehend human tact," Hunter said. "Although the new pieces should be more to your liking."

"A bracelet?" I asked, lifting up a black, braided bracelet that had a silver ID tag on it with my name. It looked like it was made out of hair—probably a unicorn's mane or something—but it was surprisingly soft.

"It contains a protection charm," Hunter said as I clipped the bracelet around my wrist.

"What does the ring do?" I asked, picking up a silver ring that had a topaz sticking out of it.

"That was cooked up by some of my people. It's a goblin charm. If you throw it on the ground or a surface it produces a blinding light that lasts for thirty seconds, which should give you ample opportunity to flee or attack your opponent, depending on the situation," Hunter said.

"And this is…?" I asked, picking up what appeared to be a single earring.

Hunter smiled widely. "That was selected by Aysel. It's a truth spell earring."

I clenched the earring—it was a sapphire stud that was unfortunately more suited for Asahi than for me—in my palm and gave Hunter a dreamy look.

"It's single use," Hunter was quick to say. "It only works once before it has to be spelled again, and it lasts about half an hour. The activation word is '*Twit*'."

"Aysel *would* make it that word," I grumbled

"I think he is hoping you will get more information out of Krad if you ever see him again."

"Yeah, because I would totally risk my neck for intelligence gathering purposes."

"You are quite the negative Nancy this morning."

"Gee, I wonder why!"

"Can we continue? We have one more piece of jewelry to look at, and we're almost to school," Hunter said, glancing at a tinted window.

"This thing?" I asked, picking up a small black band—it looked like it was a pinky ring.

"That 'thing' costs nearly as much as a car—*be careful* with it," Hunter said.

"Wow, people are going to think my fashion sense is dead," I said, sliding the pinky ring on before taking out my earrings so I could put the sapphire stud in one ear.

"The ring is a freezing charm. If it hits someone they are frozen —in time and place—for twenty five minutes. It is rechargeable— it's the material, not the spell, that cost a fortune—but you've only got one chance to use the charm. There is no activation word. You just throw it at the enemy."

"What if I miss?" I asked.

"Then you're screwed."

"Can I just touch it against whoever is attacking me?"

"Yes, but the ring must be off your finger to activate."

"Darn," I said.

"It's a last resort," Hunter said as the car rolled up to our high school.

"Hopefully I won't need it," I said, sliding out of the car when the goblin in the seat directly in front of mine got out and opened the door for me. I thanked the goblin before I ran the short distance into the high school. The wind pulled on my jacket and totally ruined my hair. I was restoring order when Hunter joined me inside.

"So is this jewelry the only change to my security?" I asked.

"No. You have an additional three goblins tailing you. Harrison will be the only one to remain in close range. The others will be strategically positioned out of sight," Hunter said.

"Is one of them a girl goblin? I haven't seen any girl goblins besides your mother, sister, and Cinna's wife," I said.

"Two of them are females, and you haven't seen any because female goblins are trained in the art of stealth."

"Like ninjas?"

"Like assassins," Hunter said, casually taking off his jacket in spite of my dropped-jaw reaction. "Sink is still with you. She'll be your only guard during school. She is waiting for you at your locker."

"That's it?"

"Aysel Moonspell wants you to file an accident report, but yes. That's it," Hunter said. "I don't think you get just how powerful your jewelry is."

"Probably. Okay, I'm going to go find Fran—and Sink. Thanks, Hunter," I said, starting down the hallway.

"Morgan."

I turned around to face the young Chicago goblin king.

"Thanks."

"For what?"

"For being my friend."

I wanted to crack a joke about using Hunter for Cinna, his cookie elf chef, but Hunter's eyes were too earnest. I found I could only nod. I was unable to look away until Hunter slid on a pair of sunglasses, shielding his remarkable eyes.

"Morgan, did you finish the math homework? There's two problems I couldn't solve," Samantha, one of my long-time friends, said the second she walked through our school doors.

"Um, yeah," I said, still knocked off my groove from my heart to heart with Hunter.

Hunter smiled mysteriously at us before he strode off.

"Oh, I'm sorry. Did I just totally ruin your conversation?" Samantha asked, her eyes wide.

"Nah, we were done talking," I said. "And I couldn't solve all the problems either. What ones did you get?"

"Alright Baobab, hit me. What's going on today?" I asked, plopping down in my office chair.

"I am happy to report there is nothing on your schedule, Miss Fae," Baobab said, tucking a strand of her earthy brown/green hued hair behind her ear. "No classes, no appointments, nothing."

"Seriously? How?"

"The MBRC has canceled your advance placement class for the week. It will resume its normal schedule the following week, but the teaching department felt you needed the time to recover. Asahi and Kadri have taken over Introduction to the American Education System—including grading papers and assigning homework. Next week the teaching department wants you to touch base with them to see if they require your expertise."

"Ahh yes, Asahi and Kadri," I said, knitting my hands together and staring at the ceiling.

"Pardon?"

"Nothing. Even if I don't have anything on my schedule, I have some things that need to be taken care of. Mainly those two and the dwarves."

"I see," Baobab said, although I could tell by the tone of her voice that no, she totally didn't.

"I'll try calling Kadri," I said. "Class shouldn't have started yet, and she'll be thrilled to receive a phone call. She just got a cell phone for Christmas."

"Of course, Miss Fae."

I smiled wryly at my assistant before I looked for Kadri's contact info in my phone. I found it and dialed her up.

"If you will excuse me, Miss Fae. There is a file I must walk down to the administration department," Baobab said, bowing in my direction.

"Of course," I said, switching my phone from one ear to the other.

Baobab was out of the office by the time Kadri picked up.

"Hello?" the high elf cautiously said.

"Hey, Kadri. It's me, Morgan."

"Morgan!" I could almost hear her light up. "How are you? Asahi and I were so worried after we heard about Saturday's incident! The MBRC blocked all calls to you—they said we were going to overwhelm you."

That certainly explained the lack of contact from my magical friends and students—excluding Devin and Hunter of course. I hadn't seen any of them since Madeline, Frank, Sacmis, and Frey visited me right after I was given approval to go home.

"I'm doing okay," I said. "This attack was much…worse. But hopefully it won't happen again."

"Is there anything I can do to help?"

"Baobab already told me that you and Asahi are doing everything for my intro class this week—including grading. That's more than enough."

"Are you sure?"

"Positive. Actually, Kadri, I was hoping I could help you."

"I'm sorry, what?"

"Are you anywhere near Asahi at the moment?"

"No…"

"Good. I talked to him last week and reached this conclusion: If you want to marry him you'll have to ask him yourself."

"What?" Kadri said, more than a little stunned.

"He's never going to ask you—and not because he doesn't love you. It's actually *because* of his love that he doesn't ask."

"I must confess, I don't understand what you are saying."

"Sorry, I'm going about this in a roundabout way. Asahi isn't going to ask you to marry him because he's afraid if you marry him you'll be a target for bad guys, upset unions, and shady corporations. He says he's the weak link of the family, and he's pretty scared of what would happen to you if you guys got hitched."

"He what?" Kadri said. For the first time since I have met her, there were traces of anger in her voice.

"It's because he loves you, Kadri. He would rather see you alive and unhurt than married to him and in danger."

"…That's selfish," Kadri said.

"Yeah, I gotta admit I thought it was pretty bullheaded of him too. But there is no way I could change his mind. However, the guy totally loves you. If you asked him to marry you, there's no way he could turn you down."

"Do you really think so?" Kadri asked, her voice small with the anger drained away.

"Yeah, I do."

"Okay," Kadri said. "Okay. Will you help me?"

"Yes. I can help you figure out what to say and all that," I said, picking up a pen and clicking it on and off.

"Oh good—will you also go with me when I propose?"

"Wha—um," I said, almost snapping the pen in half. Actually *helping* with the moment of the proposal hadn't really been in my plan. "Er.. are you sure you want me there at such an important moment in your lives?"

"Of course! Why wouldn't we? You are our mentor," Kadri said, sounding bewildered.

I totally should have seen that one coming. "Then, sure. If you think I can help," I said somewhat lamely. (I mean come on, what was I supposed to say, no? Clearly you've never met a sad high elf if you think I could resist Kadri.)

"Thank you, Morgan. Your support means the world to me," Kadri said. The warmth in her voice brought a goofy grin to my lips. "Is there no other way I can aid you?"

"No," I sighed. "Not unless you know how I could get dwarves hired in the MBRC in a position that would give them some respect."

"I am sorry, but I do not. They have a respectable position in the community thanks to their skill with gems, mines, and craftsmanship. I know not how those skills could transfer to human society. It is a shame they are not trained in the repair of kitchen appliances," Kadri said.

I blinked. "What do you mean?"

"Merely that if the dwarves could keep the coffee equipment in the cafeteria running, I'm quite sure even the MBRC board would give their eyeteeth to have them employed."

The thought hit me like a bolt of lightning. "Kadri, you're a GENIUS!"

"I'm actually of average intellect for a high elf—,"

"No way. You are a class A genius. Thank you, thank you, thank you! I've got to go."

"I hope I helped. May I contact you—perhaps next weekend—after I think of how to propose?"

"Absolutely. I'm so in your debt. Thank you, Kadri!"

"Thank you, Morgan," Kadri said.

I ended the call and bolted out of my desk. I had to jump up and down to express my joy.

My office door slammed open to reveal Harrison, who stared at me.

"Krusher—oh my gosh, I think Kadri just solved the whole dwarf workforce thing!" I said, still jumping up and down. (Harrison had seen me in worse positions than acting like an idiot.)

"It's Harrison, Miss Fae."

"Yeah, you're right. We totally need to celebrate! Let's go get coffee!" I said, grabbing my ID card before swooping out of the office. "Coffee for everyone! Inform the other goblins if they want coffee they need to give you their orders, Krusher."

"It's Harrison, Miss Fae."

"This is going to be AWESOME! In your ***face***, Administrator Moonspell!"

"Coffee machines, ye say?" Grogrintork ran a hand through his bushy beard as he considered the idea.

It was Wednesday afternoon. After doing a bunch of research via Google all day Tuesday, I was even more convinced that the dwarves should get involved in the coffee business and called a meeting with Grogrintork to discuss the idea.

I rolled a pen between my fingers. "It's both a luxury and a necessity here," I said, leaning back in my chair. "But the MBRC doesn't have a single race that is able to repair them. Dwarves are already great at detail orientated work."

"Repairing espresso machines is a bit different from settin' a gem or welding gold," Grogrintork said.

"If just a few of your men are trained, I'm certain they could train apprentices and get jobs in any number of rehabilitation centers," I said. "It would take a little work, but I bet you could ask the MBRC board for a contract before dwarves even begin to learn the trade."

"Hmm," Grogrintork said.

I glanced at his walking-armor-closet friends. Two of them stood at attention. The third was making eyes at Baobab, who was doing her best to ignore it.

"Well?" I prodded.

Grogrintork kept stroking his beard.

"You don't like the idea," I guessed.

"It feels like such work is…"

"Beneath you?" I guessed.

Grogrintork shrugged his shoulders.

"Such labor would be highly prized here, and will open up new lines of communication for your people," I said.

Grogrintork said nothing.

Seeing that I wasn't going to get anywhere with him today, I said, "Why don't you think about it and discuss it with the other clans?"

Grogrintork's broad smile returned to his face. "That is a good idea. I will do it. Thank ye for yer time, Miss Fae."

"You're welcome. If you have any questions about the work, feel free to call me," I said, offering my hand to the dwarf representative as I stood up and leaned across my desk.

Grogrintork shook my hand, squeezing my palm so hard I lost feeling in it for a few moments.

"We'll do that," he said, almost to my office door before he realized his third guard was stationed in front of Baobab's desk like a lovesick puppy.

Grogrintork rolled his eyes before he grabbed his guard by the beard and dragged him outside. "Good evening to ye, Miss Fae," Grogrintork said, closing the door behind him.

I barely had enough time to sit down before the door was thrown open and Madeline stormed inside. "So you call Kadri on Monday but you do not bother to contact *me*, your closest friend in the MBRC?"

I blinked. "Hi Madeline."

"Hi? That is all you can say? Hi? I was worried sick about you!" Madeline said.

"Sorry, I thought you would drop by my office if you wanted to talk."

"Contacting you in *any* way was banned by the MBRC until today. And even if I chose to ignore the ban, you had goblins camped out in front of your office. There are some barriers even I will not push though."

"I'm sorry. I didn't know the ban was still in place," I said.

"I had to rely on Kadri for information on your well being. Do you know how embarrassing that was?"

"I'm sure Devin could have gotten you through."

"The Pooka and I are not speaking," Madeline darkly said.

Madeline and Devin had a confusing relationship. It seemed that they were friends—or perhaps frenimies—for a long time. However, I wouldn't put it past them to erupt into fist fights when I'm not around.

"Well?" Madeline said in the silence.

"What?"

"Aren't you sorry for what you've put me through?"

I rolled my eyes. "Yes, Madeline. I am deeply sorry for any worry or anxiety I might have caused you," I said.

Madeline stared at me before she erupted into tears.

Crap. That hadn't happened before.

"Miss Fae…?" Baobab said, half rising from her desk.

"Yeah, I'll take care of it," I said, lunging out of my seat. I hurried around my desk to hug Madeline. The petite vampire cried on my shoulder, making my shirt a snotty mess.

Baobab bowed out of the office as Madeline sobbed.

She was still gone when Madeline's tears slowed to the occasional hiccup.

"So, you wanna tell me what's going on?" I asked, offering Madeline a box of tissues.

Madeline daintily dabbed at her eyes before honking her nose. "I was just frightened. Fidem is ruthless. Before he was cursed, Krad Temero was a fiend. If he managed to catch you.." Madeline shivered. "How bad was the attack?"

"Bad," I said, my voice taut.

"Worse than the previous one?"

"Much," I said. "I nearly took him out with my baby skillet though."

Madeline brightened. "It helped?"

"For sure."

"Good," Madeline hummed. The smile fell from her face. "If you meet again, it's going to be even worse," she said.

"I guessed as much. After the museum fiasco I still hadn't quite chained his magic and his person together as a package deal."

"And you did this time?"

"Yeah."

"That's unfortunate," Madeline said. "Next time you see him and your fear starts to build, it will make him that much more powerful."

"I'm well guarded. There shouldn't be a next time."

"There will be."

I gaped at Madeline. "What?"

"If you were attacked once, he was likely delivering a warning to the MBRC. But twice?" Madeline shook her head. "You are his target. He's coming for you."

"Thanks," I wryly said, my heart pounding in my throat. "Your encouragement is so uplifting."

"I'm not saying it to frighten you, Morgan. I want you to be prepared."

"So I can fight back?"

"Exactly," Madeline said.

I pinched my eyes shut for a moment and rubbed my forehead.

"What are you thinking?"

"That I should leave the MBRC when my current contract is up."

"What? Why? I mean—I know you and Administrator Moonspell are squabbling."

"This isn't worth it," I said. "I love my job and I love you guys, but getting stalked? Being terrified like that, again?" I said, my voice trembling.

"I'm sorry," Madeline said, slinging an arm around my shoulders.

"It's not your fault."

"But I'm still sorry."

"Yeah," I sighed. "Me too."

11

Meeting Ethan

"Okay, so Ethan is gonna pick us up," Fran said, zipping up her jacket.

"And then?" I asked, shouldering my backpack. "I didn't get off work so he could make us prance around outside and freeze our butts off."

Fran rolled her eyes. "We're going to Simply Sweetness."

"The coffee place?"

"Yes."

"That's acceptable," I grumbled.

"I hope you like him—I know you'll like him!" Fran, smiling widely as she clapped her gloved hands together.

"If he stops taking you on stupid dates I'm sure I'd like him a lot more," I dryly said.

"But it's so cute! He's new to the dating scene," Fran said.

"He's a senior in high school, and he's new to dating?" I asked, arching an eyebrow. "What, is he a shut in?"

"As if you could talk," Fran said.

"Hey! We *did* establish that I go on dates!"

"Yeah, yeah," Fran said, leading the way to the front doors of our school. "Let's wait outside."

"Are you just as crazy as him? It's *snowing*," I said.

"Yeah, but he should be here any minute," Fran said, pointing to a clock posted on the wall.

"No way. He's driving from his high school. Classes let out fifteen minutes ago. He can't get over here that fast."

"Yes he can. His school releases earlier than ours."

"That's weird," I said.

"It's convenient. For me anyway," Fran said.

I followed Fran outside, into the blustery wind. I pulled up the hood of my jacket as Fran looked around the entrance.

"There he is," Fran said, pointing to a black Honda idling alongside the road.

Fran and I ran to the car, getting salt from the seriously well cleaned school sidewalks all over our shoes and the cuffs of our jeans.

Fran climbed into the front seat and I threw myself into the back, slamming the door shut behind me to bask in the warmth of the car.

"Ethan, this is my absolute best friend in the whole wide world, Morgan Fae. Morgan, this is Ethan," Fran said over the roar of the heat.

"Nice to meet you," I said.

Ethan struggled momentarily with his seat belt so he could turn to look at me. "It's nice to meet you too, Morgan," he said. "I've heard a lot about you."

Ethan was cute. Not on the level of Devin or Aysel, but he was easily as cute as Frey. His hair was bleach blonde, and he had dark brown eyes. His smile was nice, and he looked like he was an average build.

I looked him over with an extra judgmental eye, being that Fran is my best friend. I found him lacking…but I couldn't put my finger on the how or why.

"Fran says you have this really time-consuming but impressive part-time job," Ethan said, easing his car into the main road.

"It's not that amazing," I said. "I just work with a doctor on research."

"In Chicago, right?" Ethan asked.

"Yes," I said.

"Morgan is a workaholic," Fran said.

"And you aren't little Miss 'I've been in student council every year of my high school career,'" I joked. "Which reminds me, I never asked. Did Hunter take that photo of the student council?"

"Yep, it turned out great," Fran said. "It's a shame he refused to be on the yearbook staff again this year."

"Hunter?" Ethan asked.

"A classmate of ours," Fran said. "Actually, I would say he's a pretty good friend of Morgan's."

"Yeah," I agreed, turning around to look out the back windshield. I could see the dark car with tinted windows that followed a block or two behind us. Good, the goblins were still with me.

"I see," Ethan said. "So, how was your day?"

Fran filled the rest of the short drive to Simply Sweetness with lighthearted chatter. She relayed an amusing story about student council and talked about her teachers.

I was impressed with the way Ethan listened intently. He seemed to recognize by name a lot of the people she mentioned. He was very mindful. But something still bothered me.

We got a great parking spot near Simply Sweetness and piled inside. The place is decorated in a Victorian type style. There are flowers on the wallpaper, the floor is wood, and it's very homey. (Madeline would *love* to come here.)

I ordered a vanilla latte, while Fran and Ethan got some cutesy couple's Valentine drink.

"Where should we sit?" I asked when we got our drinks

"Upstairs?" Ethan suggested.

"Sure. That way we won't disturb anyone," Fran said, glancing at a few college students who were taking advantage of the free Wi Fi.

The upstairs of Simply Sweet was decorated with creaky wooden floors, thick velvet drapes, and framed silhouettes and landscape paintings. We picked a spot that was right under a heat vent, but was also situated next to the front window so we could look out at Oakdale's Main Street.

It was really pretty since the snow was fresh and white and piled everywhere. People were out in large numbers, shoveling and salting sidewalks, shopping, and darting into warm restaurants, bars, and coffee houses for a reprieve from the weather.

Fran took her jacket, gloves, and scarf off, but I stayed bundled up in mine. I wanted to roast a little to warm up first.

Ethan also left his winter gear on, but he removed his scarf and tossed it on top of Fran's. "You two are taking culinary arts together, right?"

"Yes, although Morgan keeps calling it cooking class," Fran said, wrinkling her nose at me.

"That's what it is," I said. "Besides, Dave—Mr. Smith I mean—is not sophisticated enough to warrant calling the class an *art*."

"Don't tell him that," Fran said. "He acts like cooking is his sole passion in life—although he's got some serious hatred for tomatoes."

"So you've noticed that too?" I asked. I would have to tell Dave. Not that most people would assume he's a vampire because he hates tomato juice—which he has to drink to repress his thirst for blood.

"How could you miss it? He turns green whenever he mentions them," Fran said, taking a sip from the stinking huge mug—seriously, it was the size of a cereal bowl.

Ethan took the mug when Fran was finished and also drank from it. "It sounds amusing. Better, at least, than my classes," he said before offering me a smile.

And that's when I realized what was wrong. Although Ethan was mild tempered and smiled almost as much as Fran, the expression never reached his eyes. His brown eyes, in fact, were cold and deep. It was like he wore the smile, but wasn't feeling the emotion at all.

"I don't know. I can't say I really wanted to learn about cooking," I said, my eyes scanning the room. I didn't see Harrison, but that didn't mean he wasn't within hearing range.

"So, Morgan. Have you decided what to do with your life after you graduate?" Ethan asked.

"No. I want to go to college, but I don't know where," I said.

"Ahh, so you're like Fran, then," Ethan said, his lips again forming the shape of a smile as he looked at Fran.

I blinked. "What?"

Fran avoided my eyes.

"You haven't told him?" I asked.

"Told me what?" Ethan asked.

"About—," I cut myself off when Fran kicked me under the table. "Nothing," I said.

Apparently she hadn't told him she had decided on a school in Florida.

I glanced outside when Ethan looked back and forth between Fran and me, and Fran was forced to give an explanation.

"She was just talking about a school thing. I'm hoping to get scholarships," Fran said with a manufactured laugh.

"I already knew about that," Ethan said.

"Yep!" Fran said, her voice forcefully cheerful.

I didn't see any goblin cars outside. I was starting to get uneasy. The lack of backup was weird enough, but Ethan's eyes were so…cold.

"If you'll excuse me for a minute. I'll be right back," I abruptly said, internally swearing when I realized I left my backpack—and purse and cell phone—in Ethan's car.

"Sure," Fran smiled.

"I think not," Ethan said.

My eyes darted to Fran—who was smiling and unmoving—before I took a step away from the table.

"It's useless. I have the building locked down," Ethan said, his cold smile reappearing as a time ghost materialized next to him.

Simply Sweetness was dead silent. Usually you could hear the comforting sounds of hissing coffee and espresso machines, and the murmur of quiet conversations, or the bells above the doors jingling whenever someone entered or exited.

But the only noise I could hear was my breathing.

"You're with Fidem," I said.

"Correct," Ethan said, standing up. "You will come with me. Resist, and your friend will be harmed," he said, glancing at Fran.

I reached for my throat, intending to yank off my tracker necklace.

"Don't," Ethan said, catching my hand. "We know you have a tracking device. Activate it, and your life is forfeit. Do you understand?"

My heart pounded in my throat. "Yes," I said.

Ethan pulled me along with an iron grip, towing me downstairs. Another time ghost stood next to the coffee counter, and a third was waiting outside, by the car.

Ethan shoved me in via the driver's side. I purposely honked the horn, but the area was still frozen in time so it made no difference. When inside Ethan slipped a ring off his finger and dropped it in the car cup holder.

His body shimmered for a moment before his bleach blond hair turned the same colorless shade as Krad's and his skin darkened into that ashy color. His brown eyes didn't change, but they still held no warmth in them. His tapered ears poked out of his short hair.

"You're a dark elf," I said as Ethan started driving.

"Dökkàlfar," Ethan sneered.

I digested this information and reviewed my weapons list. If I dropped the light bomb I would blind both of us. While I couldn't miss him with the freezing ring in this close of quarters, it would be stupid to use it as he was *driving*.

What about the truth earring? My protection charm hadn't done anything yet. Did I need to do something to activate it?

We were still in downtown Oakdale when I recognized that in spite of Ethan's frightening words, I had an advantage. Ethan—or whatever his name was—was a Dökkàlfar. Dökkàlfar's magic was canceled out by technology, and iron. We were sitting in a relatively new model of a Honda. If a car wasn't modern technology, I didn't know what was.

Ethan stopped at a stop sign near a warehouse that was three blocks off Main Street.

I wrenched the car lock open and leaped outside, ripping off my necklace as I moved.

I was already running down the sidewalk when Ethan turned off the car, but he caught up to me with ease.

"Pathetic," Ethan said. "Like a scurrying cockroach," he said before he dragged me along—not back to the car, but to an older warehouse that was for sale.

"Let me go! Help!" I shouted.

Several beings were positioned behind the chain link fence that circled the warehouse. When they saw Ethan approaching—dragging me behind him—they returned to the guardhouse and opened the gate.

Ethan hauled me inside the compound, yanking on my arm when I tried to pull away from him. "Search her," Ethan said to two dark elves guarding the door of the warehouse.

"Help!" I tried screaming again.

"No one will hear you. The perimeter is spelled," Ethan said, his tone bored as he gripped the back of my neck while the dark elves patted me down.

I was deathly afraid that they would take my jewelry, but they either didn't notice the pieces or didn't think I would use them. The only thing they removed from me was my tracker necklace—which was tangled in my sweater.

The dark elf that fished the necklace off me offered it to Ethan and said something in the same booming, foreign language Krad used for his magic.

Ethan replied in the same foreign language—I'm guessing with a few curse words based on the anger in his voice—before he tossed the car keys at the elf and said something bossy sounding.

The elf caught the keys and gave me a disgusted look before he strode away with my tracking necklace.

So much for forfeiting my life—although my guess was that Krad wanted me alive, which wasn't very comforting.

Ethan dragged me into the warehouse, so I wasn't sure where the elf went. I did know, however, that I was in deep trouble when no squads from the MBRC appeared to bust down the fence and retrieve me.

The warehouse was dirty and scummy. It was once a Pepsi

storage facility, but it had been up for sale for at least a year so it was cleared out of all Pepsi products.

"Sit," Ethan said before shoving me into a rickety chair. He held his hand out—palm facing me—and said "Bind."

I shrieked when black chains made of magic looped around my body, strapping me to the chair.

"What do you want?" I said.

"To eradicate humans," Ethan said, giving me another one of his cold smiles. "But we would settle for killing you and crushing the MBRC."

"If you think the MBRC will go down so easily, you're a bigger twit than I thought," I said, lolling my head to the side. It was a good thing I did. My truth earring flashed once to signal it was activated. "How do you plan to bring the MBRC down?"

"We haven't thought that far ahead," Ethan said, totally oblivious to the compelling spell. "Our captain only gave orders to capture you."

"What does he want with me?"

"To kill you, I would say. Though maybe he'll use you to bring about the destruction of the MBRC. Probably not, though. He really hates you," Ethan said, eyeing me. "I wonder what it is about you that raises such hatred in an elf as great as Krad Temero."

"So you started dating Fran to keep tabs on me?"

"Yes."

"That's how Krad knew I would be out last Saturday?"

"Yes," Ethan paused. "Why am I telling you this?" he said before turning to give me another glare.

He swore again in his foreign language. "You're wearing a truth spell," he said.

"What's the language you're speaking?"

"The tongue of the Dökkàlfar," Ethan said, looking furious even as he answered. "Mouth binder," he said, flicking a finger at me.

My mouth snapped shut, and I was unable to speak. But in spite of himself, Ethan was still giving me plenty to think about.

It would be a great relief, to Aysel anyway, that Krad and his cronies had no immediate plans for the MBRC. Actually, it seemed that they were spending most of their resources on attacking me. That seemed stupid and petty to me. I mean, professionally speaking I'm a small fish.

I tried stretching and wriggling to move the dark chains holding me to the chair. They didn't give at all, but I could feel the magic that clamped my mouth shut already weakening.

Clearly Ethan-the-liar was not the best magic user.

I was flexing my jaw and trying to pry my lips open when there was this terrible high pitched squeal.

A dark elf opened a side door and poked his head inside. He said something in the harsh language of dark elves.

Ethan responded in kind, slipping a dagger from the folds of his jacket.

The reporting dark elf replied, twisting to glance behind him.

"*Fran*?" Ethan said, his stance turning slack just as I was able to pop my mouth open.

The peon dark elf shrugged and spoke again, reaching to take the dagger from Ethan.

Ethan held the dagger out of reach before slipping it back in his clothes. He spoke sternly, vigorously shaking his head.

The dark elf guard raised an eyebrow and said something snotty sounding.

I yelped when Ethan grabbed his minion by the throat and pinned him to the wall. He growled at the elf before shoving him outside and closing the door behind him.

With the minion gone, Ethan ran his hands through his hair and looked surprisingly ruffled for a guy that just kidnapped someone.

It seemed my backup had arrived.

"What's going on?" I asked.

"Fran followed us here. *Curses*!" Ethan said, not even noticing that I could talk again.

My heart froze. "What?"

"I don't know how she tracked us here, but she did," Ethan said, pulling his ring out of his jacket pocket before shoving it on. His looks returned to Ethan-the-human, but I wasn't fooled.

"She's not part of this. You have to let her go," I said.

"I can't! She's climbing the blooming fence as we speak!" Ethan said, his face twisted.

"What did you tell your men to do to her?"

Ethan gave me a look that said I was crazy. "To stand down," he said, as if the answer were obvious.

....*What*?

"You can't use her against me," I said, my mind racing as I imagined all the things Ethan might do now that he had no reason to be undercover.

"I don't want to, I just want her safe," Ethan said.

The notion struck me like lightning.

"You want her safe?" I repeated.

"*Yes*!" Ethan shouted in frustration as he looked around the plant, probably searching for a place he could stash me.

The door banged open.

"Ethan Gray," Fran said as she stepped through the door.

I watched Ethan-the-lying-dark-elf transform from a killing machine to a stupid idiot.

"Fran, I can explain," Ethan said.

"My best friend is chained to a chair. No, you cannot," Fran said, marching across the room.

"But, you've just come at a bad time. I was just...getting to know Morgan," Ethan said, glaring at me as if daring me to speak against him.

I stared at him, stupefied by this abrupt change in his personality. Any half-wit would have ordered his men to keep Fran from entering the compound. What the heck was he doing?

"Getting to know her? That's all?" Fran said, pausing long enough to put her hands on her hips and glare at her boyfriend. "You are such a liar. I should have known that the second you told me you loved romantic comedies."

"I do love romantic comedies," Ethan said.

I cleared my throat.

Goaded by my truth spell, Ethan corrected himself. "Actually any movie is ghastly, but I love watching them with you!"

"Yeah, *liar*. You're a best friend stealer!" Fran said, striding in my direction.

"You've got to get out of here and get help," I hissed when Fran knelt next to me.

"Help is already on the way," Fran briskly said, pulling on the chains.

"Not the police!" I begged.

"No, that Madeline girl you introduced me to ages ago said it was being taken care of. I'm just supposed to get you out," Fran said, scowling at the chains. She stood up and turned back to her boyfriend. "Release Morgan."

"But—,"

"RELEASE HER!" Fran shouted.

The chains fell off me.

Fran turned back around to face me. Unaffected by the magical change, she hauled me up. "We're going," she announced, dragging me towards the front door.

"Fran, you have to believe me. I wasn't going to hurt her," Ethan said.

"You weren't?" I asked.

"I wasn't going to hurt her a lot," Ethan said.

"You are unbelievable," Fran said. As we came closer and closer to the door I thought I could hear shouting outside. "We are *over*. If you even so much as text me again I'm going to the police," Fran huffed, opening the door.

Ethan pushed it shut. "We should talk about this," he said.

"No, we're leaving."

"Maybe he's right," I said.

Fran gave me the evil eye. "You can't be on his side. He kidnapped you."

I uneasily laughed, hoping to cover my real fear. I *couldn't* let Fran out that door. In the brief moment the door was open, I saw a squad of shape shifters in army fatigues—the Shadow Shifters. I recognized them because they had saved me before. The weekend I was kidnapped by Hunter, my cyclops friends paid the squad to bust in Hunter's headquarters and grab me.

The Shadow Shifters fought with magic pepper spray laced paint balls, and their magic of shape shifting.

If Fran saw them in action, there would be some serious trouble. (Although I was 98% sure she was going to have to get her memory modified anyway after this ordeal.)

"I'm not on his side. Let's go out the back door. That pops us out in another street," I suggested.

"Fine," Fran said before she stormed back through the plant, still dragging me.

"This isn't what it looks like," Ethan said.

"Dude, your cover is blown," I said.

Ethan gave me a poisonous glare, and Fran whacked him in the arm.

"Rule number one. I will *always* choose Morgan over you. So giving her dirty looks isn't helping you," Fran said.

"But, Fran—," Ethan started.

One of the warehouse windows broke, and I heard the popping noise of paintball guns going off. There was a flash of black electricity and a thundering noise that was going to be extremely hard to get Fran to write off.

"What the—?" Fran said, the rest of her sentence lost in another boom.

Another peal of black electricity crackled. This time it shot in through the open window, heading straight for Fran and I.

"Look out!" I shouted, throwing myself on the dirty ground.

Fran only stared at the oncoming magic, like a deer caught in a car's headlights.

"No!" Ethan yelled, throwing himself in front of Fran.

The electricity hit Ethan right in the chest. I'm sure it hurt worse than a dragon snapping down on him, but Ethan didn't utter a peep. It flared from him, a few sparks and charges diving at me.

I braced myself, but my braided bracelet flared. A see-through, pale yellow shell flickered around me. A horse made of the same yellow vapors intercepted the sparks, killing them on contact. The vaporous animal reared and trumpeted in challenge before fading away—with my yellow shield.

When the black lightning was spent, Ethan slumped to his knees.

"Ethan!" Fran yelled, kneeling next to him.

"You have to get out of here," Ethan said, his clothes smoking.

"But you've been hurt," Fran said, touching his shoulders.

I felt inclined to leave him, but I had a better feeling than Fran for his true nature. "He's right, Fran. We need to go," I said, scraping myself off the ground.

"But—but," Fran stammered, looking back and forth at Ethan and the shattered window.

"Go," Ethan said, pushing her hands away.

"You need medical attention—,"

"GO!" Ethan said, pushing himself into a standing position.

"Fran, come on," I said, pulling my pinky ring off my finger.

"I'll call you," Ethan said, offering Fran a half smile.

"We're still fighting," Fran said.

"*FRAN*," I said.

"Okay," Fran said, scurrying to my side. She cast one more look at Ethan before she slipped outside, into the nippy winter air.

The second she was gone I whipped my ring with the freezing charm in it at Ethan.

The dark elf saw it coming. He could have easily dodged it. Instead he let it hit him, and he stopped moving.

The charm had worked. Ethan the dark elf was frozen in time.

"Morgan!" Fran called from outside.

"Yeah," I said, picking my pinky ring off the floor—Hunter would kill me if I lost it—before busting outside.

"What do we do now?" Fran asked, pulling up her hood.

"I don't know," I said. "Let's head back towards Main Street and see—," I cut myself off when a fast moving car screeched to a stop a few feet away from us.

The window rolled down, and from inside a smooth voice said, "Miss Morgan and companion, get in."

"Vlad?" I said, my eyes practically popping out of my head.

"At your service," Vlad said.

"What are you *doing* here?"

"Madeline said you needed a driver. Now, get in," Vlad said before rolling the window up again.

I bit my lip, wondering if it was really wise to put my life and Fran's in Vlad's hands. Not because I didn't trust him, or he wasn't a good vampire. No, it was because I still *clearly* remembered the night I gave Vlad his first driving lesson in the Best Buy parking lot.

"Do you know this guy?" Fran asked, shivering in the cold air.

"Yeah," I said.

"Do you trust him?"

"With our lives, sure. To drive a car? Not so much."

There was another thunderclap—the kind that typically accompanied the black lightning.

"Into the car," I said, hurrying for the vehicle.

I opened the back seat and threw myself inside. Fran was right behind me.

"Put on your seatbelt. You'll need it," I told Fran as I buckled myself in. "Vlad, what's going on?"

"The MBRC pinpointed your location immediately after you triggered the alert," Vlad said, slamming down on the gas pedal. The car squealed before shooting forward—moving much faster than the 25 miles per hour speed limit. "But the area is clearly urban," Vlad said. "And we knew you were being held against your will."

What he meant was that there were lots of humans around—so the MBRC couldn't exactly bust in, guns blazing—and they had to be careful not to get me killed.

"I see," I said, before I was thrown against the car door when Vlad sped around a corner. "Slow down, you're going to get us pulled over."

"I was under the impression I am a getaway vehicle. Do get away vehicles not get away as swiftly as possible?"

"Just *slow down*!"

"Very well," Vlad sighed. "Where shall I drive you to? The train station?"

"Yes," I said. "But we're going to drop Fran off at her house first," I said, glancing at my friend.

I was surprised when Fran did not protest. "Take a right up here," Fran said, leaning forward to point out the intersection before she was thrown backwards when Vlad gunned it.

"Understood," he said.

We reached Fran's house in a much shorter span of time than we should have. Both Fran and I were a little knock kneed when we climbed out of the car.

"I'll be right back. Put the car gear into park," I said before I shut the car door and followed Fran up the sidewalk to her house.

"So Fran," I said when Fran started rummaging around her coat pockets for her house keys.

"What?" Fran asked.

A fairy briefly flashed in my vision, appearing just long enough to give me an all clear sign. Fran's house was safe.

I smiled my thanks at the fairy before I returned my attention to Fran. "About what happened today."

"It has something to do with your job, right?"

My lips went numb. "What?"

Fran rolled her eyes. "Come on, Morgan. Give me some credit. I've known your job has to be something….weird since the year you started it."

"Something weird?"

"Something that has to do outside the realm of the ordinary," Fran said. "I don't know what it is, and I know you've been trying to keep it from me, so frankly I'm probably better off not knowing," she said, smiling when she finally found her keys.

"You've *known*?" I said, my mouth gaping.

"Well yeah, I'm not stupid," Fran said, unlocking the front door.

Vlad honked on the horn. "The jovial sound is meant to communicate that we should leave post haste," he said after rolling down the window.

I sighed. "We will talk about this later. I promise," I said.

"Yeah we will. In the meantime I have to come to terms with the fact that my boyfriend—or ex-boyfriend I should say—is evil," Fran said.

Recalling the way Ethan threw himself in front of Fran, I shook my head. "I wouldn't be so sure about that."

Vlad honked the horn again.

"I'm coming!" I shouted.

"Go. I probably won't see you for a few days. Will you be visiting your Aunt Erma in Toledo again?" Fran asked.

"Probably," I said, a little disconcerted with my best friend's vast memory and sharp intelligence.

"I'll be waiting for you," Fran said, hugging me.

"Thanks. I'll see you soon!" I said before I hurried down the sidewalk. I waved to Fran before climbing into the front passenger's seat.

"Where to, Miss Morgan?" Vlad asked.

"The Oakdale train station," I said. "And step on it."

12

Questioning a Dark Elf

"What's the situation?" I asked Baobab, who was waiting for me at the employees only door in Union Station.

"The Shadow Shifters attempted to take all Fidem members at the compound captive. Two got away, everyone else was taken."

"Was Ethan collected?" I asked as I pushed the door open.

"Ethan?" Baobab asked.

"The dark elf that kidnapped me. The leader," I said, navigating my way through the boiler room.

"Yes. He was brought back to the MBRC and is being prepped for questioning."

"What happened to my guards?"

"They were attacked enroute to your appointment with your friend."

"Both Sink and Harrison?"

Baobab nodded. "As well as the additional goblin guards."

"Where are they?" I asked.

"Waiting inside the MBRC to meet up with you again. They retrieved your belongings and have brought them here as well," Baobab said.

"Great. Hi, Tiny," I said, greeting a giant seated on a creaking wooden stool.

"Hello there, Morgan. I heard the news—I'm glad to see you're well."

"Thanks," I said. "How's your mother?"

"Couldn't be better," Tiny said as he pulled and pushed gears. "She caused a minor earthquake in California a few days ago with her snoring."

"Please give her my regards," I said.

"Of course. There you go! You two have a great evening," Tiny said, opening the main portal to the MBRC for us.

"Thanks, Tiny," I said before turning back to Baobab. "This is just a guess, but does Aysel want to talk to me?"

"Yes, Miss Fae," Baobab said.

"Tell him he's got to wait. And I need to borrow his spelled truth necklace. Like, now," I said as we walked down a long, dim hallway.

"You wish for me to tell him to *wait*?" Baobab said, shock coloring her voice.

"Yeah. There's something about Ethan that bothers me."

"Who?"

"My kidnapper. Look, could you just tell Aysel and get me the necklace? The truth spell in my earring has run out by now," I said as we reached the end of the tunnel.

"He will not like it," Baobab said.

"Yeah? Well he'll have to build a bridge and get over it," I said, stepping into the central chamber of the MBRC—which was busy as usual.

Baobab blinked. "What?"

"Nothing. Thanks, Baobab. You're worth your weight in pixie powder," I said. "I'll be wherever the MBRC is holding the captives."

Baobab gave me a thin smile. "Yes, Miss Fae," she said before squaring her shoulders and gliding off.

"Miss Fae."

Recognizing the voice, I turned with a big smile. "Krusher, I'm so glad—what happened?" I said, aghast.

Harrison had an arm in a sling, and his suit was ripped and dirty. He wore his sunglasses, but it was obvious a huge bruiser was forming on his left cheek and eye.

"Are you okay? We should get a unicorn up here," I said.

"I'm fine, Miss Fae."

"No, you aren't," I said, my voice thickening as I crossed the distance to pick up my backpack, which was sitting at Harrison's feet. "You are injured. Let me use my MM to call Westfall. He'll be able to recommend a unicorn to me."

"Miss Fae."

"What?"

"I'm fine."

I stopped fussing with my stuff long enough to look up at him. "There must have been a ton of them," I said.

It took a few moments, but Harrison cracked what passed as a goblin smile. "Several dozen," he said most humbly.

On an impulse, I reached out and hugged Harrison's good shoulder. "I'm sorry. Thank you, Krusher," I whispered.

Harrison patted me on the top of my head. "It's Harrison, Miss Fae."

"Is Sink okay?" I asked, releasing my bodyguard.

"She is recovering," Harrison said.

I nodded and wiped my eyes.

"What are you going to do?" Harrison said, asking me a question for the first time in our entire acquaintance.

I half smiled at Harrison. "I'm going to bust a dark elf," I said. "Where are our attackers being held?"

Harrison bowed at the waist before he started through the busy central chamber. I followed him as if I was glued to the sleeve of his good arm. Harrison led the way into a maze of hallways I had never been in. Judging by the zing of magic and the barred doors, it was probably some kind of holding/defense wing.

Harrison stopped next to a barred door and knocked.

A part of the door slid aside to reveal a female centaur's face. "This room is not open to the public."

"I need to talk to one of your captives," I said.

The centaur's gaze flickered to me. "Ahh, Miss Fae. If you seek answers you shall not find them in the darkest pits."

"Are you related to Orion?" I suspiciously asked.

"Who?"

"Nothing. Look, I have to talk to the dark elf that kidnapped me."

"The danger is too encompassing. Those whose fate it is to question shall do so," the centaur said.

I took this to mean they thought Ethan would strangle me, and they would have professionals take care of it.

"Look, I think I might be able to turn him," I said.

The centaur cocked her head. "Turn him?"

"I think I can get him to cooperate with us and abandon Fidem."

The centaur blinked, her mystical air gone. "That cannot be done."

I smiled like a shark. "I think it can."

"But how?"

"By using tools available only to me," I said.

"Your humanity?"

"No, my best friend. Now let me in."

The centaur flattened her lips for a moment before she shut the little window. There was a large thud behind the closed door, followed by the noise of an ancient crank being turned. Then the door swung open on well oiled hinges.

"We will bring him into an interrogation room for you," the centaur said, swishing her flaxen horse tail.

"You guys have interrogation rooms?" I asked, following the centaur down a long, plain hallway with Harrison on my heels.

"The defense department's chief watched many of your detective and crime shows before remodeling this wing for our use," the centaur said.

"Huh. That's actually pretty smart," I said.

"Of course we made adjustments for the magical," the centaur added.

"Naturally," I agreed when we stopped outside a door.

"This is where you will be able to question him," the centaur said. "I will have him brought inside through a different door. I will return when we are ready for you."

"Thank you," I said.

The centaur picked up one foreleg and bowed her head in a centaur bow before she left, her hooves clip-clopping on the flooring.

I took off my jacket and backpack and stretched my arms above my head. "Have you ever broken someone before, Krusher?"

"It's Harrison, Miss Fae."

"Not *that* kind of break. I mean mentally," I said, turning to face the door.

Harrison shifted, a movement unusual for him.

"Yes, I'm angry with him, but more for lying to Fran than attacking me," I said, folding my arms across my chest. "You should have seen it. He totally freaked when Fran arrived."

"Miss Fae?"

I twirled around, breaking into a smile when I saw Baobab. "Perfect timing—what's wrong?" I said when I noticed her frown.

Baobab shook her head. "Aysel is unwilling to lend you his truth necklace."

"He *what*? That little—," I cut myself off with a scowl.

"He said—this is a direct quote—I was to 'inform Morgan the MBRC does not pay her to play detective, and to stop bothering the professionals and get upstairs—the useless twit,'" Baobab said, nervously smoothing her black skirt.

"That-that—UUUGGGHHH," I said meshing my hands together to keep myself from strangling someone—preferably Aysel. After a moment I managed to calm down. "Fine, okay. Krusher, I know you've got to be spent, but can you persuade Ethan to tell the truth?"

Krusher removed his sunglasses, confirming my guess that he would have a black eye soon. Already his left eye was swelled shut, and the skin was red and slightly discolored.

"Holy crap!" I said. "I'm sorry I asked," I said, as Krusher slid his sunglasses back on.

"Alright. Do either of you know of magic—that we can use right now—that will let us know if someone is telling the truth?"

Both Krusher and Baobab nodded.

"Great," I said, unclipping my protection bracelet. "Here's what we're going to do."

Five minutes later, after the centaur told me they were ready, I walked into the interrogation room, and I almost walked right back out. Clearly the defense department chief misunderstood something about the detective shows he watched.

The actual part of the room where the questioning took place was pretty standard. There was a wooden table and several chairs. Ethan sat in one of them, an iron collar encompassing his neck and two minotaur guards posted behind him. What was off was the supposed one-way mirror. Instead of installing the fancy looking glass, there was a giant window that let anyone in the interrogation room see into the observational room.

There were bleachers in the observational room, a popcorn machine, and what looked like a coffee and tea dispenser.

Apparently questioning was considered entertainment in the MBRC.

The bleachers were packed with various magical beings, and I could hear the popcorn popping and a lot of conversations through the glass window.

"I should have expected this," I sighed, seating myself in the chair across from Ethan. "Hey there. We'll get started in a minute. I'm just waiting on something," I said as Krusher took up his position behind me.

Ethan, looking very much worse for the wear, stared at me.

"What?" I said.

Ethan made a derogatory noise in the back of his throat and looked away. I made a show of getting comfortable, and a few moments later the door I entered through opened again.

"I have brought it, Miss Fae," Baobab said, walking into the room.

The audience in the observational room craned their necks to see what she carried.

"Thanks, Baobab," I smiled, holding out my hand so Baobab could give me my braided protection charm. "I'm sure Aysel was a bear to wrestle this from, but I need another truth spell. Mine's tapped out," I sighed.

"My pleasure, Miss Fae," Baobab said before she left the room.

Ethan shifted in his chair. "Take me back to my cell," he said, his voice tight.

"But we haven't even started talking," I said, clipping my bracelet on.

"I have nothing to say."

"I don't believe that," I said.

"I will not betray Fidem," Ethan said, his forehead harrowed.

"You wanna know a secret?" I asked. I leaned forward to whisper, "You already have."

"What?!" Ethan shouted, jumping to his feet. One of the minotaurs laid a meaty hand on his shoulder and tossed him back into the chair.

"Starting about a month ago, you went undercover as the charming human male, Ethan Gray," I said. "Your mission was to ingratiate yourself with my best friend, Fran, so you would have a direct line of information about me," I said. "Am I right?"

Ethan leaned back in his chair, his face scrunched up.

I laid out my arm that had the protection bracelet hanging from my wrist. "Am I right?"

"Yes," Ethan blurted out.

The audience in the observation room cheered.

I glanced back at Krusher. Krusher nodded.

"So you took Fran out on a few dates—some very poorly planned dates might I add—and wooed her, milking her for information until you could arrange a meeting with me and try to kidnap me. Right?"

"Yes," Ethan said, his brown eyes narrowed into angry slits.

"You were a very good operative. Except you totally screwed up in one place."

"What? I did—," Ethan cut himself off, glancing at my bracelet.

I smiled, encouraged that he was totally taken in by my ploy. "You screwed up and committed the worst sin possible for a dark elf in Fidem. You fell in love with your target, a human."

The audience gasped and exploded into whispers.

"But—no!" Ethan said, standing up again.

The other minotaur made him sit down immediately. I was really starting to like those two—they were almost as cool as my female ninja guard goblins.

"You can't lie to a truth spell, Ethan. Face it. You fell in love with Fran. In spite of all your hatred and prejudice, one high school girl managed to wipe it all away, and make herself a place in your heart."

Ethan opened and closed his mouth several times. "To play a role in a mission and be believable you have to take on emotions that aren't really yours," he said.

"Whatever," I said. "You're totally smitten with her. You were turning out to be Krad Temero's golden boy as you were the *only* successful operative. Your comrades were jokes—they were turned back by goblins, beaten and bruised," I said. "But you, you were making it! You were going to get me…except secretly your pristine image was ruined, smeared by your love for Fran," I said.

Ethan tried to reject the idea but his mouth clicked shut and he scowled at my protection bracelet. He instead spoke a booming word and leaped for me, his hands glowing with black electricity.

Our observers shrieked and threw popcorn. Even I was hard pressed to remain stationary and appear unafraid by the display of magic.

The minotaurs, not at all shocked by this turn in events, each grabbed Ethan by his shoulders and hauled him back in the chair, his butt making an audible thump when he was seated.

Ethan muttered in his weird dark elf language and went back to glaring at me.

I smiled like the cat that ate the canary. "Poor Ethan," I said. "Your outburst proves I'm right."

"How?" Ethan snarled.

"You just performed magic, and you're wearing iron," I said, my smile growing so wide I thought it might cut my face in half. "If you really hated humans, all humans, you wouldn't be able to do that."

Ethan froze. His brown eyes were wide, and his breathing was shaky. "Don't tell Fidem!" he said, his words coming in a rush. "If you tell them what I've done they'll kill her! You can do anything you want to me, beat me and imprison me for life, kill me, I don't care. Just don't tell them what happened!"

While the audience in the observational room kicked up a racket with their cheers, I glanced back at Krusher. My goblin guard gave me another nearly imperceptible nod.

"When did it start?" I asked.

"We went ice skating," Ethan said.

"I remember," I said, my voice wry. "Fran mentioned it."

"I kept falling down, and she would try to help me up. Fran is beautiful when she laughs, and she couldn't stop giggling at me," Ethan said, his eyes softening. "I didn't bring a scarf, so when we skated side by side Fran wrapped the end of her scarf around me."

I rolled my eyes and looked off to the side to avoid gagging. I was prepared to have to listen to him yawn on about how special Fran is, but I didn't want a romantic blow by blow of their dates.

"She was so different than what I knew—what I thought I knew about humans. She smiled more, and she wasn't stupid but dangerously clever. She sees the world in such a unique way, and she's *happy*. Her love and devotion are strong and powerful," Ethan said before looking at me. "She would give the world for you—and I hated that," he admitted.

"She would have done the same for you," I said. "But you betrayed her."

Ethan looked down and didn't answer.

"You realize that if we punish you, as you have said, you will never see her again," I said. "Fran doesn't know about magical beings. She can't come here to see you."

Ethan snorted. "She never would anyway. The moment she realized I kidnapped you, it was over," he said, his voice twisted with pain.

"Maybe," I shrugged. "But maybe not. Thing is, if you sit here and rot you'll never know."

Ethan snapped his neck so hard to look at me, I heard the bones crack. "You said if."

I smiled. "I did. If you work with the MBRC and renounce your ties to Fidem, you can see her again. We will rehabilitate you into human society."

There was a painful sounding smack as an elf—one of Administrator Moonspell or Aysel's cronies I bet—plastered himself to the observational window and shook his head.

I gave the elf a friendly wave and returned my attention to Ethan. "It's your choice. Don't talk and rot, or explore your options."

"It wouldn't work," Ethan said.

I was a little disappointed, but maybe I could push him harder. "Why not?"

"She hates me now," Ethan said.

I blinked, surprised at what his objection was. "Right now, yeah. But I think you underestimate the feelings Fran has for you. She'll forgive you—especially if I let her know I forgive you."

Ethan tilted his head. "You would do that?"

"Yes. I would also tell her I think you're a big stinking turd, but she's done worse. Heck, if you reform yourself, kidnapping me is a lesser offense than what Brett Patterson did to her," I snorted.

"Who?" Ethan frowned.

"Her ex. Anyway, the point is I'm *not* going to help you win her back. But I won't stand in your way, and I'm willing to give you another chance," I said.

"Why?" Ethan said. "I said I would kill you—I'm part of an organization that is actively seeking you."

"You *were* a part of Fidem. As to why…," I leaned back in my chair, trying to organize my thoughts. "When we were in the warehouse and the blast of magic hit, you jumped in front of Fran."

"So?"

"It wasn't something you did as part of your mission or fake character. You were terrified she was going to be hurt. That's why," I said.

Ethan stared at the table for a few moments before he nodded.

"Although," I added. "If you ever put her in jeopardy or make her cry, I will put you in agonies worse than anything the MBRC could muster," I said, my voice dark as I glared at the dark elf. I murderously held his gaze for a few moments before smiling. "That's all I have to say. Start spilling your guts, and I'll get to work on your release."

"Do you think you can really get me freed and rehabilitated?" Ethan asked.

"Yes," I said, sliding out of my chair. "It might take a while, but it will happen."

"Then I'll do it," Ethan said.

Our audience erupted in chaos. Different beings scrambled every which way as they tried to prepare themselves for the tsunami of information they could get off Ethan.

"I can give you headquarter locations and layouts, member names, and operation plans," Ethan said. "But we'll need some paper, writing utensils, and a cream colored pony."

"That's a bizarre request, but whatever. They'll get on it right away. I'll be in touch," I said, opening the door and stepping into the hallway.

"Morgan."

I stopped to turn back to the dark elf. "Hm?"

The dark elf looked like he was warring with himself before he finally spat out, "Thank you."

I smiled. "You're welcome," I said before Harrison closed the door.

"That was good of you, Miss Fae," Baobab said.

"You're giving me too much credit. I wouldn't have bothered if I didn't see how happy that pointy eared rat made Fran these past few weeks. Thank you for pretending to deliver the truth spell, by the way."

"It worked," Harrison said, sounding surprised as he passed a glowing ball of magic—it was both the reason why Harrison had to stand behind me, and why Harrison knew if Ethan was lying or not. It was a Pixie-tell, a magical glass globe that glowed different colors depending on whether or not the person speaking was telling the truth or lying.

"After all we've been through, we deserve an easy win," I groaned. "Where's my stuff?"

"I had it sent to your room," Baobab said.

"My office?"

"No, your room."

I frowned. "What room?"

"The room you will be staying in for the foreseeable future," said a cold, snobby voice I unfortunately recognized.

"Aysel," I said. "What do you want?"

"It is not a matter of what I want so much as you have unnecessarily inflicted yourself on the defense department and have, once again, managed to muddy the waters," Aysel said as he continued down the hallway, two hobgoblins tagging along with him, carrying blocks of paper.

"Are you referring to how I just turned one of Fidem's agents into an MBRC hopeful?" I asked when he stopped next to me.

Aysel frowned. "You do not have the clearance required to make such bargains, Morgan."

"You're just jealous because I was able to make him crack without your precious necklace," I said.

Aysel narrowed his silver eyes at me. "I do not experience an emotion as low as jealousy."

"Do too."

"I do *not*."

"Totally do."

"I DO NOT, WOMAN!" Aysel thundered. He took a moment to get himself under control. "While you dealt…admirably with the captive, such bargaining and promises of rehabilitation can only be made by professionals."

"Come on! I'm sure one of the teachers or guys I know would be glad to take him on," I said.

"Perhaps, if he was released under your name and your protection, but he can't be."

"What do you mean?"

"You made it perfectly clear to my father that you will not further pursue employment with the MBRC when your contract is up."

I hesitated.

"And you do not deny it," Aysel said, cocking an eyebrow at me.

"I still don't know what I want to do, and after this mess with Fidem…," I trailed off.

"I am not attempting to beguile you into staying, Morgan," Aysel said, some of the fight leaving him. "You must do what you need to do. However, you cannot keep your superstar status if you leave. We cannot release the dark elf for rehabilitation without serious collaboration between the defense and teaching department."

"Will you at least try?" I asked.

Aysel pinched the bridge of his nose, as if my presence gave him a headache. "I will attempt it—although I am not optimistic of my success."

"Thanks, Aysel," I said.

Feeling that the conversation was done, I turned to ask Harrison a question, but Aysel interrupted me.

"Here is the key to your room."

"Did you change the locks to my office or something?" I asked.

"No, it's for your new living quarters."

"My *what*?"

"It is too dangerous for you to live off the MBRC's grounds. You have been attacked once a week for the past three weeks. That is unacceptable. Until Krad Temero is stopped or caught, arrangements have been made for you to live in the MBRC."

"But, you can't just, what will my parents say?" I said.

"They are under the impression you are staying with a friend for a week."

"In the middle of the school year?!"

Aysel was mute.

"You used magic on them to make them agree, didn't you? Gosh! It's going to be a pain in the butt to get to school in the morning. Do you have any idea how cramped the train cars will be?"

"You will not attend school, either."

"Aysel, it's my senior year in high school. I can't just stop going. I need to graduate!"

"Hunter Weller is taking care of your absence. Dave Smith and Frey Christenson will gather your schoolwork for you and deliver it to you every evening."

"Aysel!" I whined.

"This is not negotiable, Morgan," Aysel said. "Since you were held in the warehouse you are perhaps not aware just how difficult the fight was to retrieve you. If Madeline had not used your human friend to distract the leader, we might not have completed the retrieval. The MBRC cannot allow your life to be put in further danger. That is final," Aysel said, his voice just as icy and bossy as his father's.

I bit my lip. "Couldn't I stay at Hunter's place?" I asked.

Hunter had all the newest gaming systems, memberships to a ton of streaming movie services, and HD TV. At the MBRC the most I could do is try to surf the internet on my iPod.

Aysel glared at me.

"What?" I said. "It was worth a try."

"If you attempt to leave, Harrison the Undaunted will notify the defense department, who will forcibly bring you back," Aysel said. "If you do decide to leave, please inform me. It would warm my heart to watch the minotaurs drag you back, kicking and screaming."

"Where's my room?" I asked, glaring at Aysel.

"Harrison and Miss Baobab have been informed of its location," Aysel said.

Harrison bowed in acknowledgement when I gave him an accusing look.

"Fine," I said, my upper lip curling with distaste. "Good luck questioning the other captives."

"Hmph," Aysel said.

"Miss Fae," Baobab said, placing a gentle hand on my elbow. "Perhaps you would feel better after washing and changing?"

My shoulders slumped in defeat. "I would," I admitted.

"This way," Baobab said, leading me away from Aysel.

I glared at the high elf one last time before I followed my secretary, Harrison trailing behind me.

13

Elf Proposals

I almost died on the way to my room because it was on the *TOP* floor of the MBRC, and the center never bothered to install elevators for public use. We actually had to take a break halfway up I was so out of breath.

The top floor was decorated in a marine theme. There were wall paintings of mermaids sitting on rock formations that overlooked a frothy ocean. Even though the decoration was a painting, the picture moved. Mermaids flipped their tails and braided their thick, beautiful hair, and waves crested and rolled in the ocean expanse. On the far side of the floor were water nymphs, playing in mountain streams.

Baobab led me down a small hallway that was perhaps the most detailed in decoration I had ever seen. Every scrap of the wall was painted. The left wall was a solid forest, and the ceiling was an expanse of the sky, which was colored purple with the hint of night. The right wall depicted a glassy lake. A hand was stretched out of the lake, clutching a shining sword.

"Is that…?" I gawked.

"This is your room," Baobab said, stopping at a door.

I jolted out of my reverie. "Right. Um, thanks, Baobab," I said, unlocking the door with the key Aysel gave me.

Harrison very nicely cut in front of me to get into the room first, to my bemusement. He disappeared inside, but I remained slack jawed at the entrance.

"Whoa," I said, feeling the first prickles of guilt for my irritation with Aysel.

In spite of his sneering, he had hooked me up with a seriously sweet place.

The room was decorated in shades of blue and gray. The door opened up directly into a small library filled with a lot of books that I probably couldn't read based on the scripts emblazed on the spines. Past the library was a bedroom.

A circular bed—no joke, the mattress was circular—hung in the air, fastened to the ceiling and the trunks of two huge trees that grew all the way to the ceiling. The branches were spread across the ceiling like vines, spreading their silver blue leaves through the room.

There was a beautiful dressing table and armoire that were stained a deep brown color and had trees carved into the sides. The library shelves and chairs in the library and the dressing table and the armoire were beautifully polished, but when I touched them my fingertips buzzed with the feeling of magic. They were probably as old as Chicago itself, if not older than America.

Still full of wonder, I popped into the bathroom—where Harrison was doing his final checks for…booby traps and stuff I guess.

The bathroom was worthy of a mermaid. It was a sea of marble with two sinks, and a giant mirror ornately framed by wood carved and colored to resemble seaweed. The bathtub was twice the size of my family's dining room table, and it was practically deep enough to swim in.

"Does the MBRC run a hotel up here?" I asked.

"The MBRC houses many visiting dignitaries and leaders who visit Chicago," Baobab said. "This room is typically used by water nymphs or naiads in positions of high leadership in the seelie court, or the Fairy Council.

"Wow," I said, again feeling a little guilty for my complaints. I was still going to be bored out of my skull, but at least they weren't shoving me into an empty office with a cot. (Which I would not put past Aysel as his first choice for me.)

"The room is clean," Harrison announced.

"Thanks," I said, taking inventory of the bath salts and oils lined up next to the enormous tub.

"If you will excuse me, Miss Fae. I must set about obtaining additional clothing for you," Baobab said.

"Thanks, Baobab. You're the best," I said.

Baobab left after bowing her head, leaving Harrison and I in the bathroom.

Harrison did his best to stand in his usual stiff stance, but with his arm in a sling it was pretty tough. As curious as I was about the various bottles—there was *essence of sea pearl* in there—standing in the bathroom with my bodyguard was more than a little awkward. So I made a retreat to the bedroom under the pretext of wanting my stuff.

"Do you know where they put my stuff, Krusher?"

"It's Harrison, Miss Fae."

"You're right. The armoire is the likeliest place," I said, heading for the beautiful furniture piece. I paused when I heard a knock on the door.

When I turned towards the library Harrison ghosted out in front of me. I followed him to the door, which he opened a crack and blocked my view of it with his body.

After a moment he stepped aside and swung the door open, making way for Madeline and Frank.

"Madeline, Frank, hey," I said, smiling at my friends and students.

Madeline didn't say anything, she just threw herself at me. I caught her, my ribs protesting as she squeezed me tight. I pushed her blonde hair out of my face before looking to Frank for an explanation. The sweet werewolf had his head hunched into his shoulders. His eyes were soulful and upturned as he looked at me like a puppy longing to be petted.

I reached out with my free arm and patted the werewolf on the head.

"What has you two looking so downcast?" I asked.

"You have no idea how terrifying it was when we realized you were taken," Madeline said into my shoulder.

"Really? I thought it was a lot scarier when Krad used his magic on me," I said.

"That's because you have no sense of urgency," Madeline said. She gave me one last squeeze before releasing me.

"I wasn't hurt at all," I pointed out.

Madeline gave me a sour look. "Only because we got lucky when we sent Fran in."

"Yeah, that reminds me. I don't appreciate you using Fran as bait. You should have wiped her memory and sent her home. Oh, come on in," I said, backing up.

I plopped down on this overstuffed settee that forced me to sit up in perfect posture. Madeline plopped down next to me, and Frank sat in a wooden chair that was probably a lot more comfortable.

"But we had to use tact," Frank said. "Fidem picked their hideout in the middle of your town. We had to get past the warehouse gates—which were spelled—before we could start using our actual magic."

"Could we start from the beginning? Like, how did you find me? Last I saw my tracker necklace, a dark elf was carrying it off."

"As soon as you set off the charm, the MBRC pinpointed your location. A team used magic gates to get to your location instantly. Using magic, they were able to confirm your presence in the warehouse and the absence of your guards," Madeline said. "When they realized they couldn't get through the gates without potent magic, they called for specialized backup. That's when Fran stumbled on them—apparently she recognized her boyfriend's car on the street."

"She's smart," Frank chirped. "Most of the MBRC soldiers were hidden. There was just one who was out in the open a street up from the warehouse. She approached him and asked about you."

"Being that MBRC soldiers are fighters and not rehabilitated, he panicked and called for additional help. Since Frank and I were available, and it is well known that I have been introduced to some of your friends and family, we were asked to come and speak with Fran," Madeline said.

"Ahhh. Didn't they know about your hemophobia? No offense, but you aren't the first person I would choose to take on a mission that might involve fighting and bloodshed," I said.

"They were aware," Madeline said.

"Not like she could hide it," Frank added.

Madeline scowled at him before continuing with her story. "The Shadow Shifters have been under contract with the MBRC since Krad Temero made his threats, so they were dispatched to take care of the situation. It was Fran who suggested she should be the one to climb over the gates."

"But why did Shadow Shifters let her do that? There's no way she knew or understood that her boyfriend was a dangerous member of an anti human, magical organization!" I said.

"Well, she didn't ask anyone from the Shadow Shifters," Madeline said.

"So it was *you* who told her to go ahead?"

"Um," Madeline said.

"A soldier tried climbing the fence first and got a flesh wound," Frank helpfully put in. "Madeline was on the verge of passing out. I think she agreed cuz of that."

Madeline scowled at Frank. "Was it really necessary to share that?"

Frank gave Madeline his shy puppy smile, making the vampire roll her eyes. "Okay, yes I was a little groggy. But I knew that if Fidem set up headquarters in the middle of a human town and no one realized it, it must mean they were being careful not to bother humans. They were in a warehouse, right? I remember you telling me how teenagers occasionally break and enter into such areas. I figured they wouldn't be as guarded against Fran, so I agreed to the idea. I did tell her that her only objective was to get you out."

"Madeline," I started.

"I don't regret it," Madeline said, tucking her head like a stubborn donkey. "We were desperate to get you out, Morgan. I don't think you understand how bad it was. If Fran hadn't appeared, I don't know what the Shadow Shifters would have done to get you out."

"How did Fran entering the compound make such a difference?" I asked.

"We think the dark elf in charge gave his men orders to hold their fire and let her come in. But even though they didn't stop her, the guards were watching her. So some of the Shadow Shifters changed and attacked while they were distracted," Frank said. "Once we were in the warehouse perimeter we were safe to use magic thanks to the charms and spells they had on the place. It worked out great. It kept humans from seeing all the flashy magic."

"Was Vlad your idea too?" I asked Madeline.

"He was in the area, and he so wanted his new skills to be put to use," Madeline said with a charming smile.

"Yeah, next time you ask him to play chauffer, you get to ride with too," I said.

"I will pass, please," Madeline said.

"So it was a pretty smooth operation," I said.

"Hardly. Letting Fran stay with us could have easily botched it," Madeline admitted.

"But it worked out great. I was captive for like, less than an hour."

"You shouldn't have been kidnapped at all!" Madeline said.

"Yeah, but an hour is great when you compare it to my weekend of captivity with Weller Goblin Enterprises," I said. "Although I have to admit that wasn't captivity so much as it was a forced retreat."

"Weller held you against your will. It was captivity," Madeline dryly said.

"So what happens now?" Frank asked.

"I live here until the MBRC thinks the threat is over, I guess," I shrugged.

"Are you going to start the advanced placement class back up?" Madeline asked.

"Maybe."

"What do you mean maybe? You'll be sitting around all day… unless," Madeline said, her eyes lighting up. "We could accompany—excuse me—I mean hang out! We could go to the cafeteria and get food, and I could show you the MBRC stables and library."

"I'm sure I'll have plenty of time to do that," I said, interrupting Madeline before she could really get on a roll. "But I also have a few things I need to finish."

Frank blinked. "Like?"

"Schoolwork for starters. And I would like to see if Grogrintork has talked to any of the dwarf clans yet about my idea for a few dwarves to study the mechanics of coffee machine repairing. And there's the small matter of Kadri and Asahi," I said.

"Their teaching skills?" Frank asked, tilting his head.

"No," Madeline said, studying me. "I think not. If I might guess, I would say you are aiding Kadri?"

"Yeah."

"Good luck. You shall need it," Madeline said.

"Thanks," I said.

Frank's stomach growled like a hungry bear. Madeline slowly turned and stared at the scruffy werewolf, making him blush. "Sorry," he said, looking down at his feet.

I laughed. "Actually, food sounds like a good idea, although I would really love to get cleaned up first," I said.

Although my clothes hadn't gotten too dirty or gross, I still wanted to shed the memory of that afternoon.

"Great," Madeline said, hopping off the settee. "The kitchen staff just came out with this new tomato soup I've been dying to try! You take your time refreshing yourself. Frank and I will wait for you in the cafeteria."

"Thanks, guys," I said, accompanying them to the door.

"Absolutely! I'm sorry you were kidnapped, but it's going to be so fun to have you at the MBRC all day!" Madeline said, clapping her hands.

Frank nodded, his eyes soulful and serious.

"Yeah, it will be interesting. I'll see you soon," I said as the duo exited my rooms.

"Yep, at dinner," Madeline said before she swung the door shut behind her.

"Did you hear our plans, Krusher?" I asked.

"It's Harrison, Miss Fae."

"Good. Think about what you want—I'll pay tonight."

There was silence before Harrison ventured to speak his second question ever. "Doesn't the MBRC cover your meal tab?"

"They do," I said with an evil grin. "So order all you want! Aysel, I am going to make you gnash your teeth by the time this is over!"

"This is really how high elves propose?" I asked, clutching the oddly shaped guitar Kadri had thrust in my hands.

"It is," Kadri said, wringing her hands.

It was Tuesday, day four of my forced stay at the MBRC. On Monday I nearly died of boredom, so I called up Kadri to discuss proposal tactics. I was shocked to learn she had been preparing ever since my last chat with her, and she was ready to propose to Asahi whenever I was available. (At least she claimed she was ready. Mentally she didn't seem to accept it yet.)

"I've said I can't play this thing, right?" I said.

"Several times," Kadri said, pacing back and forth in front of me.

I plucked a string and watched the nervous high elf, realizing my pessimistic estimation of my musical skills was not abating her nerves. "Don't worry, this will go great. Asahi is going to say yes," I said, attempting to pluck out the three chords Kadri had taught me. I had to roll up the sleeve of the elf robes I was drowning in to be able to reach the instrument without getting a ton of cloth wedged between the instrument and my arm.

"I don't know. This is crazy, what am I doing? What if he doesn't want to marry me?" Kadri asked.

"He does," I said with confidence, wincing when I played an off key note. "And if he doesn't I'll break my guitar over his head."

"It's a lute."

"Whatever. It will still work."

Kadri nervously chuckled, which sounded more mechanical than genuine. She peeked past the shelves of the MBRC library, spying on Asahi in his study nook.

Of all the places to propose to Asahi, Kadri had chosen the MBRC library. I suppose the two of them being such human fanatics and researchers it was probably appropriate.

"Are you ready?" I asked, adjusting my grasp of the lute.

A yeti with an armful of books slowly trod past us, his eyes going between Kadri and myself.

"Hey," I said to him, again striking an off key note on the lute-guitar-thing.

The yeti hurried out of my eyesight.

I couldn't blame him.

Kadri was beautiful in cream and bronze colored robes with a tiara made of white metal placed on the crown of her head. She carried a ring with her that she would offer to Asahi as a token of her proposal. That part was surprisingly normal. However, my lack of understanding of magical customs was not entirely disappointed, because Kadri also carried a big-ass jewel—the thing was the size of a coffee mug—which she would give to Asahi as a symbol of her family/house. Or so she said.

Even weirder, Kadri asked me to be her 'marriage trustee' (which I took to mean best man). My role as marriage trustee was to play the lute so she could *sing* her proposal, and to drag several carts of food and drink. Apparently, whenever elves proposed there was a lot of celebrating that instantaneously brewed up.

As her marriage trustee—because elves were supposed to know proposals were coming—I was also in charge of hauling whatever booty Asahi offered up when he accepted her. Kadri said it was unlikely he would have anything on hand, so I wouldn't have to do it today, but later at their marriage ceremony—if Asahi accepted. I just hoped he wasn't going to give her a goat or cow.

If it wasn't the carts of fully prepared foods (a lot of fish, some fancy looking breads, fresh fruits, and enough kale to kill a hippie) that made the yeti run off, it was probably my clothes.

As Kadri's marriage trustee, she asked me to dress appropriately. I thought this meant I would get to wear some lord of the rings robes and prance around with my hair braided.

Nope.

Not even close.

I wore robes, yes, but because elves love symbolism, I had a magic burning lamp that hung from my back—it was supposed to resemble their burning love or bright future, I don't remember which—and a crown of grape leaves on my head—for the wine? I don't know—and my over robe was a tapestry of Asahi and Kadri standing together.

Yeah, I was about as tacky as you can get, not to mention majorly sweaty. (Having a burning lamp hang against your back is no joke.)

I shook my head. "Are you ready, Kadri?" I repeated.

"I don't know if I can do this," Kadri whispered, leaning against a bookshelf.

I had to waddle to her side since the lamp swung on my back and the lute hung from my neck. "Hey, you got this," I said. "Remember, the only reason Asahi hasn't asked is because he's terrified you will be hurt. He loves you, Kadri. He would be an idiot not to," I said.

Kadri narrowed her eyes. "He's making the decision for both of us with his stubbornness."

"Yeah, he totally is," I said, nodding to encourage her. "And he's being selfish because he's not willing to let you go, either."

"He is, isn't he?" Kadri said, ire growing in her voice. "But if he did break up our courtship I would be alone, forever," she added, her voice mournful again.

"Kadri!" I said, slapping a palm on my lute. "Do you want to marry this man—erm, elf?"

"Yes," Kadri said.

"Do you want to spend the rest of your life with him?"

"I do!"

"Is he worth the risk?"

"He is!" Kadri said.

"Good! Then we're gonna go out there, and we're gonna knock his weird, pointy shoes off with the best, freakin' proposal song that has ever been sung!" I said. I strummed the lute to make my point but I probably shouldn't have because I made one of the strings break.

Kadri was so fired up, she thankfully didn't notice. "We will," she said, straightening her shoulders and correcting her posture. "I am about to propose to the love of my life. This is what I have dreamed of."

"Yeah!" I said in my best supportive-coach voice.

"Thank you, Morgan."

"That's what marriage trustees are for!"

Kadri nodded decisively. "Right. Let us sing," she said before sweeping out past our hiding area.

As she approached Asahi's study nook, I followed after, dragging the two carts of food and drink. This, let me tell you, was no picnic to move.

Asahi didn't even look up, in spite of the massive rumbling the carts made and the weird looks the few people studying in the same area gave us.

"Asahi," Kadri said, stopping directly in front of Asahi's desk.

Asahi looked up and a sunny smile bloomed on his face. "Kadri!" he said in genuine delight. "What brings you to the library? I thought you finished your Human Ethics paper?"

Kadri kept her pose stiff. "I have something to say to you."

Asahi's smile dimmed. "What?" he said.

Kadri turned around to nod at me after I got the carts in place. I fixed my robes and adjusted where the stupid lamp fell before I started playing the three note, ever repeating song Kadri spent the morning teaching me.

I totally thought Kadri was going to sing in elvish, but she shocked me by proposing in English.

"I love you with a timeless passion,

One as old as the stars,
Asahi, my morning light, you brighten my days and illuminate my nights,
You are precious to me, you are my hero,

I would give my life to be with you,
I would sacrifice all I have to see you,
I fear neither death nor darkness,
For your love is worth fighting for,

I have waited all my life for you, the love of my heart and soul,
So I ask for the greatest gift you could give,
I ask for eternity,
I ask for your life and your love, and I seal it with mine
Asahi, will you pledge yourself to me?"

Normally I wouldn't share such an intimate moment, but Kadri's proposal had a profound effect on me. It made me realize how weak and pale we humans define and describe love. We use the same term for describing our fondness for chocolate, our one week dating relationships, and our affection in marriage.

Human love is wretched when you compare it to elf love. It's bland and one dimensional.

Just like my relationship with Hunter or Fran or Madeline couldn't be summarized by saying they're my friends, Kadri's proposal made me realize that there is infinitely more to romantic love than Hollywood's romantic comedies would have you know.

Asahi dropped the pencil he was holding and stared at Kadri.

The beautiful high elf clasped her hands. She looked at him from under her long eyelashes. "What do you say?" she asked when the silence became unbearable.

Asahi swallowed sharply, his eyes still hinged on Kadri. "You will be hurt because of my name."

"I'm willing to take the risk," Kadri said, her voice as soft and caressing as silk.

Asahi's golden eyes filled with unshed tears. "What if they kill you?"

"And what if it is *you* who are killed?" Kadri asked. She took several steps forward, bridging the gap between them when she crouched down in front of Asahi. "My love will not die, Asahi. Even if my body dies, you shall posses my love for eternity," she said, placing a hand on Asahi's cheek. "No matter if you say yes or no, you will feel my love for you each day when the morning sun warms your skin, and in the stillness of the night."

Asahi and Kadri were both crying by this point, but they smiled at each other through their tears, their eyes burned with a kind of love that I didn't understand.

Asahi asked Kadri a question in elvish. Kadri replied in kind with a joyous laugh before Asahi stood, picked her up, and whirled her around.

"Did he say yes?" I asked.

"Yes!" Kadri and Asahi said, clinging to each other.

Asahi set Kadri down and gazed into her eyes before he rested his forehead against hers. When he started to kiss her I turned my back to them to struggle with my stupid lute. By the time I fished it off my neck, removed the danged-hot lamp from my back, and poured two goblets of wine the pair was back to staring into each others' eyes.

"Congratulations!" I said, smacking down the goblets of wine on Asahi's desk. "Eat, drink, and call your friends! I have a whole smoked salmon in one of those carts, and I'm not going to have dragged it down here for nothing," I said.

"Morgan is your marriage trustee, Kadri?" Asahi asked as I dusted my fingers off on their stitched faces in my tapestry robe.

"She is," Kadri said, accenting her response with a giggle.

"Morgan, we cannot thank you enough," Asahi said, disengaging one hand from Kadri to extend it to me.

"Yes, Morgan," Kadri echoed, also holding out her hand.

"It was my honor—*ack*," I said when the pair yanked me into quite possibly the most awkward hug of my life.

"Wow," I said, sandwiched between the two. "This is…special," I said as they chattered to each other in elvish above my head. "So Kadri, did you give him the ring?"

There was a moment of silence before Kadri sprang away. "Oh, I almost forgot," she said before pulling the ring out of her robe.

I made my silent retreat and scuttled to the side to watch. Over the course of the hugging, we had somehow gained an audience of roughly twenty. Most of them were beings that I recognized who also knew Asahi and Kadri. Corn—one of the three fairies in my advanced placement group—was present, so I elbowed my way through the crowd so I could stand with her.

"Asahi Moonspell, will you take this ring as a token of my love for you? If you take it, you seal our marriage contract, which even death cannot break," Kadri said, holding a plain, gold ring.

"I will take it, and receive it with the love I will shower upon you for all the years of our lives," Asahi said, taking the ring.

I cheered, and Corn was quick to follow my example. Soon the small crowd was cheering, whistling, and clapping to the embarrassment and delight of the couple.

"Thank you, everyone," Asahi said when Kadri hid her face in his shoulder. "Thank you for being present during this special moment of our lives. Let us celebrate!" he said, indicating to the carts of food.

I felt too giddy to eat, but no one else seemed to have my scruples. A couple fairies, dryads, selkies, a centaur, and two leprechauns broke into the refreshments.

"To Kadri and Asahi!" a leprechaun shouted before taking his first swig of wine.

"To Kadri and Asahi!" the centaur echoed, taking an apple.

"To Kadri and Asahi!" a selkie said as she cut into the salmon.

Everyone, before taking their first bite or drink of the celebration banquet, said "To Kadri and Asahi!" as more gawkers from the library moved in on our location.

They must have been able to recognize it as an elf engagement celebration, because the new arrivals also toasted Kadri and Asahi before snagging refreshments.

People—people Asahi and Kadri didn't even *know*—lined up to congratulate and compliment the engaged couple.

"Is this a success?" I asked Corn, who was nibbling on kale.

"By elf engagement celebrations? Certainly. They will have a second one with their family, likely sometime next week," Corn said.

"Oh," I said.

"During that celebration they will reenact the proposal so all members of the family may witness it," Corn said.

"That's pretty cool," I said. "Wait, does that mean I have to dress up like this again?"

"And carry some of the food into the feast, yes," Corn said.

I scrunched up my face. "Goodie," I said.

"You'll only have to do it once a year. Once they are married the celebrations will be condensed into one feast per year," Corn said, drinking some of the cider I had also brought.

"What do you mean, per year?" I suspiciously asked.

"Aren't you Kadri's marriage trustee?"

"Yes."

"Did she not explain it? As marriage trustee you are the sole witness and pillar to their marriage. Whenever they celebrate it, your presence will be desired and exalted."

"It's that special of a position?" I asked.

Corn nodded. "When you stand as marriage trustee you essentially make a public statement that you believe in their love, and you will stand witness to it as long as you survive."

"Oh," I said. It was pretty hard not to feel even more honored after that. Out of everyone they knew, Kadri wanted *me* to stand up for them. "Well, they're good kids," I said.

"I would be prepared for that as well," Corn advised before starting for the happy couple.

"Yeah," I agreed before the advice sunk into my skull. "WHAT?"

Corn was too far away to hear my question. She approached Asahi and Kadri and bowed to them before speaking.

They listened to her with beaming smiles before they looked at each other and nodded.

The exchange took away my apprehension for the future. I peeled back my tapestry robe and watched the pair embrace.

Asahi and Kadri looked at each other with…with so much more than just *love.* Their eyes expressed hope for the future, unending loyalty, and fathomless endearment. Their love was more than just an emotion, it was something you could feel when you saw them. They weren't going to let anyone get between them.

Although I was filled with joy and well wishes for them, a small part of me wondered if anyone would ever look at me the way they looked at each other.

Day six of my MBRC imprisonment I spent catching up on homework. Someone had a desk hauled into the library in my room, so I had my books piled up there and various snacks and treats from the MBRC cafeteria sitting on an end table within arm's reach.

I was just finishing my pre-calculus homework when there was a knock on my door. "It's open," I said, glancing at the clock.

Harrison—fully healed since I had all but made him seek unicorn medical attention on Monday—stuck his head into my room.

"It's the Pooka, Miss Fae."

"Oh," I said, a little surprised. "Send him in."

Harrison disappeared, and the door swung open to admit Devin.

"Hello," Devin said.

"Hey. Welcome to captivity," I joked as I reached for a bear claw. "Want a donut? The cafeteria staff feel really bad for me so they whipped up a fresh batch this afternoon."

"I'm fine, thanks," Devin said, plopping down in an armchair next to me.

"M'kay. Do you want…well I have a cappuccino, but I could send down for coffee or tea if you want. They do room service.'

"I'm fine," Devin repeated, propping his feet up on a footstool. "You seem like you are holding up."

I brushed sugar from my bear claw off my face. "It's not so bad here. There are lots of different places I can visit, and the food is good. I get bored at night when there's nothing to do, but during the day I can hang out with my friends. I actually worked at the help desk with Toby for a few hours today."

"How many questions did you average?"

"One every minute."

"That's unusually long for Toby."

"Yeah, we were catching up too. Did you know his sister had her fifth baby?"

"No, I can't say I did. What a fortuitous event."

"Yep," I said, sipping my cappuccino. "Devin, what are you doing here?" I finally asked when the Pooka sat there like a lump.

"I'm assuring myself you are well. You look better than last time," he said.

I shrugged. "It wasn't as scary. In fact the whole episode felt a little ridiculous, probably because I didn't see the fighting."

"Perhaps," Devin said. He studied my face, as if looking for something. "I have an invitation for you," Devin said, withdrawing a letter from inside his black shirt.

"For what?"

"A private meeting of MBRC staff," Devin said. "They're finally going on the offense against Krad Temero."

"Why? I thought all he's done is terrorize me?"

"He does seem to have a special hatred for you, but his men destroyed a mermaid stronghold in Lake Michigan this week. Earlier today he collapsed an underground tunnel system the MBRC uses for shipping purposes. He's becoming more of a problem than a pest," Devin said.

"In other words, Moonspell decided it's finally worth his time and effort to do something."

Devin smiled—the first one he gave me since entering the room. "Yes."

"Good," I said.

"We can have the meeting because of the cooperation of that dark elf you negotiated with."

"Ethan?"

"I believe that is the name he is using, yes. He has given a lot of useful information."

"Awesome. Although I can't take too much credit. Fran—my best friend, you've met her before—is the one who changed him."

"I hear you want to get him released and rehabilitated."

"I do."

"That won't happen unless you stay at the MBRC," Devin said.

"Aysel told me as much, but I'm hoping Asahi will take him on after I go."

"It's too dangerous to have the MBRC Administrator's offspring in charge of a deserter dark elf," Devin said.

"I hadn't thought of it that way," I admitted, sliding away from my desk. "I'll be glad when this is all over."

"So you're going to go with a normal life, then?" Devin asked.

"I don't know. Probably," I said, rubbing my eyes. "You don't mind?"

Devin shrugged. "Just because you don't work at the MBRC doesn't mean I cannot barge in on your life."

I laughed, but Devin frowned and dug his MM out of the pocket of his jeans. "What?" he said when he answered it.

I could hear a male voice speak, but the volume was too low for me to understand what was being said.

"Now?" Devin asked.

The caller responded.

"Fine. I'll be there soon," he said before swiping the MM off and returning it to his pocket.

"The Fairy Council?" I guessed.

"Yes," Devin said, rocking to his feet. "They are the biggest bunch of worriers I have ever run across. They think the world is on the brink of destruction every day," he said, groaning as he stretched his arms and shoulders. "They're holding a conference call with the Administrator, and require my presence."

"Good luck," I said, watching the handsome fairy shifter as he brushed his clothes off. Sometimes I still found it unbelievable that *Devin*—the most flirtatious guy in the MBRC community—was given a seat on the powerful and highly honored Fairy Council.

"Thanks," Devin said. He walked over to my chair and leaned down so he could kiss me on the top of my head. "I'm glad you are safe, Morgan," he said, curving one arm around my shoulders and using his other hand to tuck a strand of my hair out of my face.

"Yeah," I said, finding it suddenly hard to swallow. "Thanks. You better go get to work."

"You enjoy killing moments and dreams, don't you," he said, his voice playful as he tugged on my hair. "Why can't you just accept my affection quietly without ruining it?"

"Because I can't be bought off like other females," I grinned.

"Morgan, when was the last time you ever saw me kiss someone on their head?" Devin said.

I was silent, thinking about it. "Well, I haven't, but it doesn't matter. I've seen you hanging on lots of other females."

Devin scrunched his eyes shut and briefly hugged me just as tightly as Madeline does. "It's a good thing you're adorable," he said. "Or I might take offense to that."

"You're supposed to take offense to it. That was the general idea of the comment."

"Take care. I'll swing by to escort you to Moonspell's precious meeting tomorrow," Devin said, kissing my forehead before he backed away so I couldn't take a swing at him.

"Don't bother. Harrison and I can find it on our own," I called after the flirt.

"Until then, I will suffer without your presence," Devin said, winking at me.

"You're ridiculous!" I called after him when he slipped out the door.

"As are you, my darling," Devin said, firmly shutting the door.

"Flirt," I grumbled under my breath before reaching for another donut. "Who needs him anyway?"

14

Forming a Plan

"This emergency meeting has been called for the express purpose of discussing Krad Temero and his actions," Administrator Moonspell said. "It is a closed door meeting with invitations extended only to those who are directly involved in the matter, and those who are responsible for running the MBRC."

The Administrator's voice echoed in the large room—we were in the biggest board room available to accommodate Blood Binder—the dragon who represented magical creatures on the board. He was quite big, even for a dragon. Normally he was about the size of an airplane, but today he let Dante—the wizard representative—put a shrinking spell on him so he was only as big as a greyhound bus.

"In what way are the Chicago goblins directly involved in the matter?" Luka Farka, the vampire representative, said as he studied Hunter with narrowed eyes.

"It's well known that Morgan Fae is a dear friend and close associate of mine. Of course her security is a top priority for Weller Goblin Enterprises," Hunter said, knitting his hands together. He was the picture of innocence as he leaned across the square table formation we were seated around to address Luka.

"The Chicago goblins are the main users of the MBRC tunnel that collapsed," I guessed.

"That too," Hunter agreed.

"If the investigation is over, may we begin?" Elros Gloriath, one of two elf representatives, said, rolling his eyes at Luka.

"Krad Temero must be captured or taken care of," Blood Binder said. He heated the room with his breath when he spoke, and his deep baritone voice made the floor rumble. "Or it appears he will set up a permanent headquarters in Chicago."

"How could we ever hope to beat him?" the fairy representative asked, worriedly brushing her dragonfly wings with her spindly fingers. "Our defense department is competent, but we've been forced to hire mercenary groups for additional protection and Krad has *still* attacked us."

"Capturing him would be difficult, if not impossible, if we attempt it when he is already attacking us," Ranulf, the werewolf representative, said.

"You insinuate that we must attack him if we wish to be successful," said the second elf representative, a pretty female named Gywndyn.

"Yes," Ranulf said.

"We would need more troops," Dante said, wringing his hands. "We can recruit volunteers of course, but we can't afford to hire more mercenaries."

"Why not?" the dryad representative asked.

"Because the Shadow Shifters are the best, and they're already bleeding us dry," Ranulf said.

Dante nodded in agreement.

"It seems unfortunate that we should be forced to drain our savings to rid the magical community of a problem that has plagued many besides us for decades," Luka said, tracing the rim of his glass of tomato juice with his pointer finger.

Administrator Moonspell sat with Aysel at his elbow. Aysel whispered something into his father's ear, and the Administrator nodded. "I agree," he said, dragging his eyes to Devin—who wasn't sitting at all but was strolling around in the shadowy perimeter of the room.

"If we have a day and hour for a planned strike, could the Fairy Council lend us troops?"

The MBRC board members turned to stare at Devin.

The Pooka shrugged. "They might."

"Would you bring our request forward to the council if we write it up?" Administrator Moonspell asked.

"Sure. But it's not numbers or even skill that is going to bag Krad."

Administrator Moonspell raised his eyebrows. "How, then, do you suggest we attack if you find our chance of success so low?"

"Bait him," Devin said, tipping his head so his full moon eyes almost glowed in the dark. "The curse that was placed on him is more effective than it would seem."

"Its purpose was to limit his power," Aysel said, unable to keep his mouth shut at the chance to be a know-it-all. "We have firsthand accounts that prove he still has most of his magic," he said, glancing at me.

"Yes," Devin agreed. "But I wasn't thinking of his magic when I said the curse works. If Krad keeps his head on his shoulders he will be impossible to beat. But if he loses his cool, we can more easily handle him."

Blood Binder shifted, his scales scratching the stone floor. "You mean he can be goaded into throwing a temper tantrum?"

"Exactly," Devin said.

"With all due respect, Councilman, that is impossible," Elros scoffed. "Krad Temero is a mad genius. Curse or not, he would *never* behave so, so childishly!"

"But he already has," Hunter said.

"What?" Elros said.

Hunter studied me for a moment before he smiled at Devin. "Why don't you tell them, Councilmember? You are the one who shared the intelligence with me."

Devin briefly frowned at the Chicago Goblin King. "Krad has shown us he is perfectly willing to be involved in a screaming match with Morgan—something he wouldn't have done before he was imprisoned in a child's body," he said.

"A screaming match?" Luka repeated as he swiveled to face me. "How did that happen?"

I squirmed uncomfortably in my chair.

"Morgan," Aysel said.

"I insulted his name," I said.

"…you what," Luka said.

"And I told him he was a pervert."

"Was that before or after you nearly hit him with the cast-iron skillet?" Hunter asked, his shoulders shaking with silent laughter.

"After, I think," I said.

The MBRC board stared at me.

Feeling the need to defend myself, I added, "I would have gotten away if the brat hadn't jumped on my back."

"I apologize for my private doubts, Councilman," Luka said to Devin. "It appears the curse has indeed inhibited him."

"Aye," Ranulf said.

"Devin always has such good points," the fairy giggled. "Ouch," she said when the dryad representative kicked her under the table.

"Remember your cousin and the way he dumped her," the dryad advised the frowning fairy.

"Very well. Krad Temero can be goaded. How do we achieve the state?" Elros said.

"Perhaps we could have our soldiers employ a mocking method?" Dante said.

"If they fail to rouse his temper, you can be certain we will never find an opening to attack Krad again," Ranulf said.

"Which brings up another point—how do we attack Krad? We have the location of several of his bases thanks to the dark elf informant, but do not know which one he will be in at any given time," Luka said.

"We could have pixies follow him," the dryad said.

"Pixies are already assigned to him," Gywndyn said, her lips creased unhappily. "He evades them with great cunning."

"Then perhaps we should assign someone better suited to tracking to him," Luka said.

The fairy representative narrowed her eyes at him. "The pixies are the best we have."

"I think not," Elros said. "Or they wouldn't *lose* him so consistently."

"Take that back!" the fairy representative said, standing up from her chair.

"I would consider it if they showed any skill at all in their assigned task," Elros said.

"Why you—,"

"Enough!" Blood Binder said. "Fighting gets us nowhere. Our enemy is Krad, not each other. If you cannot say anything constructive, *think*."

The board was silent.

Administrator Moonspell drummed his fingers on the table and frowned at me. "The easiest solution is to dangle Morgan Fae before him," he finally said.

I opened my mouth to tell Moonspell what he could do with his idea, but Hunter beat me to it.

"Absolutely not," Hunter said.

"Why not? Clearly Krad has her shadowed. He will undoubtedly make an appearance if we use her," Administrator Moonspell said.

"This is true," Ranulf said, tilting his head as he considered the matter.

"He seems to follow her movements closely," Gywndyn said.

"Morgan has already encountered Krad and his men more than she should. She has gotten information for you and turned a black hearted Dökkàlfar who has given us more intelligence than any of your scouts. She has done more than enough," Devin said, coming to stand behind me. He planted his hands on the back of my chair and leaned over my head. I couldn't see his face, but based on the various guilty expressions the board members were showing, he probably looked scary.

"Additionally, you cannot make her," Hunter said.

"She is an MBRC employee," Administrator Moonspell said.

"Perhaps, but there is a clause in her contract that makes provisions for her safety. Telling her to face Krad Temero is most certainly a breach of that clause," Hunter said.

"And how do *you* know the contents of her contract, Hunter Weller?" Administrator Moonspell asked.

Hunter narrowed his eyes and said nothing.

I shrugged, not surprised. Harrison had probably gotten a good look at it. Naturally he would report back to his leader.

"Hunter Weller is correct," Aysel said after a few moments of silence. "Morgan Fae cannot be forced to face Krad Temero according to her MBRC contract."

"Plus there's the matter of her humanity," the dryad said.

"What does her race have anything to do with this beyond the fact that it has earned her Krad's eternal hatred?" Luka asked, rolling his eyes.

The dryad flushed angrily. "If Krad doesn't get upset and he uses his magic on her, she'll be used to charge him beyond what we can handle. We would essentially be sending him a tool to use against us."

Everyone turned to stare at the dryad.

"What?" she said. "I am not completely vapid!"

"I never thought I would utter this, but Privet is right," Elros said, looking deeply perplexed.

"I forgot about Krad's magic," Dante admitted

"So what do we do?" the fairy representative asked.

Devin finally stood upright. "We could always call the Beer—,"

"NO!" everyone shouted.

"We just got rid of them a year ago," Administrator Moonspell said. "I will not invite those ruffians back."

"They *ruined* the skytop gardens the month before they left," the fairy representative said.

"Then what do we do? We have limited options," Devin said.

The board fell silent again. Each board member's face was twisted in their particular thinking pose.

I spoke for the first time since the meeting started. "I'll go."

"You'll what?" Luka asked.

"I'll confront Krad. Privet is right. I can power him, but I'm confident I can get him into a good screaming temper tantrum before he thinks to use his powers. You'll have a short time to snatch him," I said.

"Don't be stupid, Morgan," Hunter ruthlessly said. "It's too dangerous."

"I can't spend the rest of my life cooped up in the MBRC," I said. "It's been a week and I'm about ready to lose it. Plus, spelled or not, pretty soon my parents are going to realize I haven't been going to school."

"If you gave our fighters even a minute, I'm certain it would be enough to take out Krad," Dante said, a smile splitting his face.

"We would send the Shadow Shifters to be sure—it's about time they earn their paycheck—but whom else?" Elros asked.

"Weller Goblin Enterprises will lend some security personnel," Hunter said.

"At what cost?" Blood Binder dryly asked.

"A reduced price, I promise," Hunter purred.

"Morgan," Devin said, pulling on my chair so I faced him. "Are you sure about this?"

"Yeah," I said.

"Last time you saw him you were terrified," Devin said, his voice quiet. "You don't have to do this."

"I know," I said. "And I still might be terrified when I see him… but I can't keep cowering in safety."

Devin slowly nodded. "I will go with Morgan," he announced, circling the table to take his place in an empty chair near Administrator Moonspell.

"You're just as stupid as she is," Hunter said without hesitation.

"We can't send her in alone," Devin said. "Krad will see straight through that. We need to make him think it is his idea to attack us, or he will not show."

"You are a councilmember *and* the Pooka! It's too dangerous," the fairy argued.

"It is my choice to accompany Morgan. None of you have the rank needed to stop me," Devin said.

"You have no heir—you cannot risk it," Blood Binder said.

"Then you'll just have to be careful to actually *get* Krad, which I would hope you do anyway as Morgan is risking her neck for you," Devin said with a frosty smile that didn't reach his eyes.

"Morgan, I need to speak to you," Aysel said, ghosting up to me.

I almost jumped out of my skin in fright. "Okay," I said, when my heart recovered.

"Outside," he said, tipping his head to the door.

"Is that okay?" I whispered, glancing at the board. Most of the members were still trying to convince Devin to stay out of it.

"It will take the Pooka some time to win them over. We will not miss anything. Come," Aysel said.

I followed him, slipping out of the meeting room and past the two minotaurs and four elf guards posted by the door.

We strolled down the empty, undecorated hallway. Aysel led us all the way to a small inlet that was just one intersection from the main MBRC chamber. It was part of the hallway, but there were chairs, a fish tank, and two coffee shop tables.

"So, what did you want to talk about?" I asked as we sat down at one of the tables.

"Are you positive you want to face Krad?" Aysel asked. He was not concerned like Devin was, but he was very serious.

"Yes. No one is forcing me. I just see how tough it will be to bait him properly without me. Besides, I already have such great practice," I wryly said.

"You are certain?"

"Yes."

Aysel nodded. "Very well. I am sure you will be informed in how you should handle yourself should Krad use his magic on you again, but I want to remind you that it is your emotions Krad's magic depend on."

"Yeah, my fear charges him. I got that."

"It is not just your fear. If you express love, Krad will be flooded and powered by that emotion. It will swamp him the same way your fear does."

"I think you told me that when I first talked to you about his magic."

"I did, however, even I had not realized how easily his powers can be turned against him," Aysel said.

"What do you mean?"

"The dark elf defector—Ethan. His opinion of humans changed because of the affection one human girl had for him—and he doesn't have a scrap of the dark magic Krad has."

"So you're thinking if Fran had such a profound effect on Ethan without magic, if I radiate love I should have an even bigger impact on Krad?" I asked.

"Exactly," Aysel said, his eyes glowing with excitement.

"Why tell me this separately? This is great news," I said.

"My father does not believe Ethan is truly changed."

"He thinks Ethan is lying?"

"No. We know he is not thanks to our spells and charms. He believes Ethan never hated humans as much as Krad, and was already weakened by the time he went undercover."

"You've got to be kidding me. Those dark elves sound like a bunch of bigots. There's no way Ethan would be less prejudiced."

"I agree," Aysel said.

"Well, thanks for the tip," I said. "I hadn't made the connection. Maybe you're right. Maybe dark elves hate humans just because they haven't ever been loved by us."

Aysel shrugged. "It is certainly worth knowing—although I hope such knowledge proves to be unnecessary during the attack."

"Yeah, but still. Thanks, Aysel," I said, surprised that we were able to have a half decent conversation together.

Before Aysel could respond, Asahi popped into the hall. "Oh, hello!" he said with his usual sunny grin. "Is the meeting over?"

"No," Aysel said, standing. "I was discussing the mechanics of Krad's magic with Morgan. We will return shortly."

"Already?" Asahi said. "I think it's good you two share some guardian-ward time."

"*Shut up*," Aysel hissed at the exact same moment I said,

"*What*?"

"Bonding time. I thought that was a common practice with humans," Asahi said.

"It is. But what was the guardian-ward thing?" I asked.

Aysel actually groaned and shielded his eyes. "Asahi," he said.

Asahi glanced back and forth between Aysel and me. "It is you two?" he said carefully.

"What are you talking about?" I said.

"You never told her?" Asahi asked his twin.

"I was trying to avoid it lest she take advantage of it, as I would not put it past her to do," Aysel sourly said. "But since you've already spilled the secret you may as well explain it."

"Sorry," Asahi said before turning to me. "Don't you remember? Aysel claimed you the weekend you were held ransom by the Chicago Goblin King."

I remembered Aysel shouting that he would claim me if his father didn't. "Yeah, so?" I said.

"That was when he officially claimed you as his ward," Asahi said.

"Wait. I'm, like, Aysel's *kid*?"

"NO!" Aysel said.

Asahi shook his head. "Not at all. More like he accepted you as his responsibility to watch and guide until you marry and align yourself with another family. His name offers you protection that Devin's name cannot give you when he is gone to the Fairy Council. It's a great honor. The ward title hasn't been used by the Moonspell family on a human for at least four or five centuries. Aysel really cares about you to bestow it upon you."

"Were you ever going to tell me this?" I asked Aysel.

"No," Aysel said, still glaring at his twin.

"Sorry," Asahi guiltily said.

"Wait, does this mean you're my uncle even though I'm your fiancée's marriage trustee?" I asked, feeling a headache coming on.

"It is a little confusing," Asahi admitted. "That's why it's such fun to have a human in the family."

"She's *not* in the family!" Aysel thundered.

"Of course she is! She's your ward. And even when she gets married she'll still be Kadri's marriage trustee," Asahi said before smiling at me. "You will get to come to our family feasts. It is such fun—Great Aunt Florawyn speaks freely after a few glasses of moon wine."

"My head hurts," I said.

"Good," Aysel bluntly said.

"Aysel, that is no way to treat your ward," Asahi scolded.

"You said I fall under the protection of Aysel's name?" I said after a few moments.

"Yes," Asahi chirped.

"You don't have to confirm it," Aysel hissed.

"Why not?" Asahi asked.

An evil smile crawled across my lips.

"Because of that," Aysel said, brandishing a finger at my smile.

"Sorry," Asahi said.

Aysel pushed his dark colored hair over his shoulder. "If you'll excuse me, I must return to the meeting."

"Oh Aysel," I said in a sing song voice. "I didn't know you cared so deeply for me."

"I don't," Aysel said, gliding back in the direction we had come from.

"Then why did you take me on as your ward? Bye, Asahi," I called over my shoulder as I hurried after Aysel.

"It was merely that your permanent captivity would have been a hassle for the MBRC. We would have had to wipe the memories of all your family and friends and classmates—it was safer to accept you as my ward."

"Uh-huh, sure."

"It is true," Aysel said.

"So does this mean I get to call you dad?"

Aysel actually shivered in horror. I'm not even kidding! He looked totally offended. "If you call me by that title, I shall rip your wagging tongue out of your mouth," he said.

"Child abuse, wow. You're a stellar guardian, did you know that?"

Aysel ignored me and marched on.

"Is this why you always pick fights with me? You're attempting to—how did Asahi put it—guide me?"

"I will not respond to foolish questions," Aysel said, his voice taut like a violin string.

"This opens up *so many* possibilities," I said, practically skipping next to Aysel.

"I suggest you put those possibilities behind you and focus on your future: Krad Temero."

"Killjoy."

"Yes."

15

Fear and Love

My heart thumped as though it was going to break out of my chest and run down the street. If it did it was obviously smarter than I was, but no. I was the one stupid enough to offer to be bait.

"Morgan? Did you decide where we should eat?" Devin asked, encircling my waist with an arm so he could pull me closer. "If you are frightened already, Krad will know something is off," he whispered in my ear, his breath warming my neck.

"I know," I said.

"Interference!" Madeline said chopping down on Devin's arm with her hand.

Devin sighed. "Was it really necessary to bring the...pink knight?" Devin said, sparing Madeline in her pink winter jacket a look of disgust.

"I didn't invite her," I said, slipping from his grip.

"But you should have. I've missed you," Madeline said, throwing her arms around me in a bear hug as she gave Devin the evil eye.

"So this is what a small town looks like?" Frank asked, staring at the streets of Oakdale like the stores were made of gold.

"Selfie!" Athena said, holding her cell phone out in front of her to take a picture of herself and the female-disguise-wearing Perseus.

"Speaking of invites, did you really have to bring your entire *class*?" Devin asked. "It was supposed to be a date."

"There is strength in numbers. Besides, I trust these guys. Oak, DO NOT stick that in your mouth," I called to the downtrodden elf who had just liberated an icicle from a storefront.

"Drink your tomato juice, Dave, or I'll make you order tomato soup for lunch," Frey said.

"Considering you have never partaken in the foul drink, you are awfully bossy in administering it," Dave complained as he unscrewed a thermos.

"I will admit your students keep the mood from being too somber," Devin said.

What he meant was instead of being scared off when I explained what I was doing, all of my students insisted on coming with. They were behaving beautifully, as if we were really on a field trip instead of attempting to lure Krad into a trap involving the fifty or so soldiers and a dozen wizards that were following us.

"Sacmis, are you warm enough?" I asked the disguised sphinx, who was wrapped in about five coats and ten scarves.

"Yes, thank you," Sacmis said, barely audible through her scarves.

I stopped to look over my shoulder for reassurance. Harrison was there—wearing a trench coat over his suit, and his sunglasses. He nodded at me in reassurance. I gave my goblin guard a shaky smile.

"How long do you think it will take?" I asked.

"Long enough for him to figure out we're going to the park. He'll have to get time ghosts into place, or some kind of magic to mask the confrontation from the general public," Devin said, covering his words with a wide smile.

"Morgan, which way do we go?" Madeline called from the front of the group.

"Left," I said. "Follow the signs for Independence Park."

"We're going to a park?" Corn asked, clapping her gloved hands.

"It won't be that exciting," I said. "But there is a steep hill. If we ask nicely we could borrow some sleds from the kids already there and go sledding."

"We're going to see kids?" Sage said, brightening a little too much so I saw her wings briefly flicker into existence behind her.

"Yeah. It's a Saturday and we've got snow, so it's pretty much expected that there will be sledding at Independence Park," I said.

"I have not had the chance to go sledding before," Kadri said, all smiles and cheer as she walked, hand in hand, with Asahi. (I was 99% sure Administrator Moonspell didn't know they were with us, and I was 99% sure Aysel would kill me when he found out.)

"I went once with a few elves on glaciers in Canada," Asahi said. "I'm not certain we did it right."

"It's easy. You just sit in the sled and have someone push you down. The hard part is walking back up the hill," I said. "But you'll have to be careful. The sledding hill ends at the tennis courts, which are surrounded by chain link fence to keep the balls in. It's pretty easy to get enough momentum going so you'll fly into the fence. You need to bail out if it looks like you're going to hit it."

"Bail out?" Frank asked, fascinated.

"Jump out," Frey said.

"That sounds much less exciting," Zinnia said.

"Believe me, when you jump out of a zooming sled it's *plenty* exciting," Frey said.

"Will we eat after that?" Devin asked.

"What is up with you and eating?" I asked.

"It is an event I greatly enjoy."

"Uh-huh. There's a few small restaurants near the park we could eat at," I said.

Devin again curled an arm around my shoulders. "What are the chances of you sending your students home after sledding?" he asked, briefly nuzzling the top of my head.

"Not happening," I said, trying to squirm away from him.

"Krad's been sighted," Devin whispered. "He hasn't noticed our following friends."

"Okay," I said before Devin released me.

"I say, are we almost there? These boots are *heavy*," Dave said, dragging his feet.

"It's right there," I said, pointing to a cluster of evergreens that marked the park border.

"Sledding!" Madeline cheered. She stopped to look both ways before hurrying across the street like a giant, pink puffball. Frank bounded after her, but the rest of my students were slower to follow.

Oak frowned as he made an inspection of the trees. "This is an Austrian Pine. It isn't native to this area, and it is sick and inflicted with moths," he said, squirming through the branches to get a better look at the trunk. "If they don't act quickly, the moths will attack other trees."

"Where is this sledding hill?" Kadri asked.

"My feet hurt," Dave said.

"May I take a soil sample?" Zinnia asked.

"Hashtag: Yolo," Perseus said, throwing a snowball at Athena.

"Remind me to never have kids," I said to Devin.

The Pooka chuckled. "I hardly think any children of ours will act so oddly."

"Mine, Devin. If I have kids they will be mine, not yours," I said.

"So my part of the parentage will be ignored?"

"You will not be part of the parentage," I said as Frank came bounding up to me.

"Madeline fell and thumped her head on the ice," the werewolf said.

"Is there any blood?" I asked.

"No."

"Then she'll be fine."

"Okay," Frank said before he ran off, heading for the bright pink blotch on the snowy horizon.

"He's moving in," Devin said, looking down at his feet.

"Great," I said, rolling my shoulders back.

I was surprised when Devin took my hand and squeezed it. "There's nothing to fear," he said. "You're not alone."

I offered him a weak smile. "Thanks."

"Miss Fae," Harrison said, moving to my left.

"What is it, Krusher?" I asked.

"Isn't this disgusting? It's the inferior human with her weakling *friends*," Krad said, appearing just past Harrison. As was his custom, he was clothed in all black in a jacket and pants that were much too big for him. He wasn't wearing a scarf today, but he had black gloves.

Devin squeezed my hand again. "You're up," he whispered before making a show of whipping out his MM.

"You still haven't learned any good insults, have you, Krad? You obviously got that straight from a comic book."

"I did not!" Krad said.

"Uh-huh, right. So what are you going to do this time? Start a snowball fight?"

"Today is the day I rid the world of your festering presence," Krad said as several time ghosts crawled into view.

"I'm so afraid, I have no other choice but to call the babysitters' club," I said.

"This park is under *my* control," Krad snarled before nodding to the time ghosts, who froze the world.

Trees stopped swaying in the breeze. I couldn't hear the excited shouts of the kids on the sledding hill, and the traffic noise from Main Street died.

"You use the time ghosts waaaay too much," I said, rolling my eyes as my students rallied behind me.

"What?" Krad stiffened.

"It's like, all you do. You appear and use time ghosts to stop time so you can recite clichéd villain lines. I know it's probably supposed to be your modus operandi or something, but I hope you at least pay them overtime. Do you guys have a union? Because if you don't you really should at least bargain for higher wages together," I said to the time ghosts.

"It isn't all I do," Krad said, his childish face scrunched with anger.

"It is, pervo," I said.

"My name is *Krad*!" Krad shouted.

"Yeah, I know. There's no way I could forget your lame-ass name," I said, folding my arms across my chest.

"What?" Krad said, his jaw dropping. "Like your name is anything to be proud of!"

"Hey, at least I'm named after a legendary sorceress," I said. "You sound like a badly titled super villain."

"I *am* a villain!"

"Maybe, but you certainly aren't super."

"You!" Krad said clenching his hands into fists with such emotion that they shook.

"There is a problem," Devin said, his voice was very low as he stood next to me. He turned his back to Krad, so the brat wouldn't be able to see him talk.

"What's wrong?" I said, ignoring Krad as he shouted his fury in the language of dark elves.

"Our reinforcements have been intercepted."

My blood turned into ice in my veins. "What?"

"Troops from Fidem intercepted them. They're taking care of them, but they might not reach us in time," Devin said.

If I strained my ears I could hear the faint pop of the Shadow Shifters' paintball guns, and the thunderclaps that accompanied dark magic.

"So he's told you," Krad said, standing on his tip toes. "I found out about your little trap. Your help isn't coming."

My heart thundered in my ears, and panic sank claws into my chest.

"Don't," Devin said. "Don't give him any fear to feed on."

"What do we do?" Perseus asked.

"Everyone circle up. We can't be drawn away from each other," Devin said.

"Those with shielding magic move to the perimeter," Madeline said, having recovered from her head bump. "Morgan is in the center."

"No," I said.

"You're a liability if you make yourself an easy target. Get to the center," Frey said, pushing me into the middle of our small circle.

Harrison ignored our pow-wow and took out what appeared to be a battery operated nail gun. I watched as he loaded it with nails, flicked it on, and turned to face Krad.

Krad raised an eyebrow at him. "Human guns are mere toys to me," he said.

Harrison shot a stream of nails at him.

Krad's shield flared to life, and the nails passed straight through it. They barely missed Krad. One nail actually got close enough to slice his cheek.

Krad collapsed to his knees in shock—and perhaps a little terror—and Harrison grunted in irritation as he looked down at his weapon. "Aim is off," he announced.

My students and I stared at the goblin in shock.

"What is that?" I finally said.

"Iron nails," Harrison said, reloading his unusual weapon.

"That's pure genius," Dave said, eyeing the nail gun in jealousy.

"Shields up!" Devin called, pushing his way to the front of our group just as black lightning cracked over our heads. Devin raised his hand and said something in some kind of old Gaelic or Celtic. A yellow shield the same color as his full moon eyes briefly formed around us, absorbing the lightning.

Thunder boomed, and my ears rang. A piece of our vaporous shield broke off in the shape of a shadowy horse and reared.

Well. I now knew where my protective charm bracelet came from.

I felt the first brush of spider legs against me and screamed.

"He's reaching for Morgan," Sacmis, who stood next to me, shouted.

"Break his concentration!" Devin said.

Harrison shot nails at him, driving the pint-sized villain behind a bush.

Oak, Sage, Corn, and Zinnia—who were all holding hands —grinned.

"Excellent!" Oak said as the roots of the giant bush burst out of the ground, *inside* Krad's protective shield. The roots wrapped around the dark elf's thin legs and crawled upwards.

Krad shouted in dark elvish and used black lightning to fry the roots off him. He left the safety of the bush and ran for a park sign that wasn't far away.

Harrison shot at him, but all the nails fell short. "Out of range," he said.

"Great," Devin sighed, flexing his arms.

Krad peeked out from behind the sign. He must have realized he was safe, because he emerged. "Are you done playing yet?"

"That's funny considering *you're* the one running around like a kid," I said, my voice shaking in spite of my false bravado.

"Krad," Madeline shouted. "If you don't get lost I'm going to call the Beer Brothers."

"The who?" I asked.

"Wow, Madeline is tough," Asahi said.

"You wouldn't dare," Krad said, his eyes narrowed.

"Don't test me," Madeline said, holding a pink cell phone up in the air. "Leave."

Krad scowled. He shouted in dark elf to the time ghosts and pointed at Madeline. Eight ghosts peeled off from the park perimeter, gliding towards us.

Madeline hit a speed dial number. "Hello. It's Madeline. I've got drinks and a Dökkàlfar that's being a pain in the butt. We're at Independence Park in Oakdale, Illinois. Goodle it."

"Google," I said.

"Google it," Madeline repeated before she hung up.

"Administrator Moonspell is going to kill you," Perseus said.

"At least I'll be alive for him *to* strangle. Incoming!"

"We can take one," Asahi said as he and Kadri slipped out of the circle. "Don't you think, Kadri?"

"Yes," Kadri said, tossing one of her wicked-looking daggers at their selected time ghost. Instead of going straight through the ghastly fairy—as I thought it would—the dagger pinned the time ghost's wraith-like robe to the snow covered ground.

Asahi punched the time ghost in the face—no, I'm not kidding. He clocked it right in the jaw—and the fairy sagged to the ground. Asahi grabbed it and shook it like a dog shakes a toy.

Zinnia, Sage, Corn, and Oak took on three time ghosts. Using the park bushes and trees, they kept the time ghosts occupied. The Austrian Pine Oak previously held disdain for actually *burrowed* through the ground and snow and wrapped a time ghost in its branches. The fairies and elf used a benign looking, snow covered bush to devour the second time ghost before their last time ghost smartened up and tried running away from them.

Frey, Frank, Perseus, and Athena worked together as wolves and undisguised centaurs to occupy two time ghosts, leaving Harrison to deal with the last two.

"I don't like this," I said to Sacmis, Dave, and Madeline—the only three besides myself not involved in combat.

"I'm sure," Madeline dryly said.

"We just have to sit tight and trust in Devin to protect us until Madeline's backup arrives," Dave said seconds before black electricity tried to encase us.

Devin activated his protective shield again, which absorbed the blow.

"You've already tried that. It's still not going to work, squirt," Devin said, adopting a superior tone as he spoke to the cursed dark elf.

Krad glared at Devin before his eyes popped wide open and he darted back behind his sign, barely missing a spray of pepper infused paintballs.

Shadow Shifters dressed in fatigues and MBRC guards in their uniforms pushed through the park perimeter. I didn't see any MBRC wizards—they were probably being guarded by the goblins Hunter was lending the MBRC—but I did see bubbles of water and tongues of white hot fire through the trees.

Unfortunately, they weren't alone. Dark elves, ghouls, skeleton soldiers, and some dark fairies oozed out of the shadows to engage our allies in combat.

I almost shrieked when there was a thud behind me. I whirled around to face a cute guy in army fatigues. I recognized him, although I couldn't tell you what his shifter shape was.

"Shadow Shifters are in play. We are still engaged in combat, enemy is pursuing us," the cutie said into his radio before he turned and jumped on me. "Get down!"

A black ball of fire was popped off at us from one of the pursing Fidem members, but Devin's shield held against it.

"Harrison, can you grab all the time ghosts in the immediate area?" Devin asked.

"Yes, Sir," Harrison said. Already six of the eight time ghosts that attacked us were trailing after him like ducklings as he made the rounds to persuade the remaining two—which were held in place by Oak and the fairies.

The shifter peeled off me. "The Princess is as safe as she can get. This is Black leader, initiating shift," he said, after offering me a hand up.

He crouched down, and his gear—his fatigues, paintball gun, and radio—condensed into his skin as his body twisted, shrinking down to the body of a fruit bat.

"Wow, he's actually kinda cute," I said, momentarily distracted by the shifter's big eyes and triangular head.

"He can't take off from the ground," Devin said.

"What?" I asked, looking up as the Pooka held off another blast of black fire.

"Not all bats can fly from the ground, pick him up and toss him in the air," Madeline said before throwing a rock and clocking a dark elf in the back of the head.

I eyed the shifted mercenary, who looked up at me with his somewhat-cute-but-still-creepy eyes.

"Throw him, Morgan. He's not going to bite you, and he doesn't have rabies," Devin said, grinding his teeth as he held his shield against a three pronged attack made by dark fairies.

"Shadow Shifters get their yearly shots," Madeline added.

"Get ready to fly," I told the mercenary before I picked him up and threw him as high as I could when the onslaught against us paused.

The bat shifter flipped in the air before he got his wings under him and flapped off.

"We need to condense. If we're a smaller target Devin can strengthen his shield," Madeline said, pulling me closer to Dave and herself.

"I'm going to engage the enemy," Sacmis said, ripping off her scarves.

"Will you be okay in this temperature?" I asked.

Sacmis gave me a wide smile before she removed her glamour, reclaiming her lion body. "I doubt I'll notice it in the heat of battle," she said before she roared loud enough to make my chest throb. She twitched her tail and jumped out of the safety of the shield, pouncing on a ghoul like he was a hapless mouse.

Just past Sacmis, Frank and Frey were pulling a skeleton soldier to pieces. Frank, in his scrawny wolf body, gave an extra good chomp on the bones after the soldier fell apart. Frey had to headbutt him to get him to stop chewing.

A Shadow Shifter was trying to force Asahi and Kadri to the safety of Devin's shield, and the sick Austrian Pine took out a row of dark elves before it was shucked like an ear of corn.

I watched a Shadow Shifter mow down six fairies with pepper laced paintballs before her partner—a lion shifter—attacked them with his claws and teeth.

Perseus, Athena, and four MBRC minotaurs chased down a pack of skeleton soldiers, stampeding over them and splintering them as if they were made of matchsticks.

An MBRC elf soldier teamed up with two pixies to stun and take down three dark elves. Unfortunately a dozen ghouls noticed the activity and raced to the dark elves' rescue.

The MBRC forces were winning the fights, but Fidem kept a steady supply of reinforcements piling into the park through the shadows. The problem was that our wizards were tied up in a battle past the park borders—I could hear the earth rumbling and could still see the sparkle of magic between the trees—and couldn't cut off whatever magic Fidem's soldiers were using to get in.

A Shadow Shifter in the shape of a small fox with huge ears was almost caught by a dark elf that slithered out of the shadows, leading more forces from whatever gateway magic Fidem had set up.

Skeleton soldiers newly arrived to the scene pulled at Frank and Frey, hacking at them with blunted weapons.

The Shadow Shifters took turns firing at the hoards of enemies so they could reload in safety, but sooner or later they were going to run out of paintballs.

"We need to cut Fidem off," I said as Madeline hugged me to her with a stranglehold.

"No, we need more help," Madeline said just as Asahi and Kadri were forced into the shielded area with us.

As if on cue a car—a Ford Focus actually—jumped up over the curve, ran over a bush, and skid out on a patch of ice about a dozen feet away.

The driver's door opened, and my brain almost ceased functioning.

The driver was a dark elf—at least I *think* he was a dark elf. He had the same dark, ashy colored skin as Krad and his pals, but his hair was bleached platinum silver and covered with a baseball cap turned backwards. He wore a university hoodie and stonewashed jeans that were sagging so his boxers were showing.

This frat-boy/dark elf combed the fight with his eyes—which were the typical black for a dark elf. When he looked in my direction he lit up. "Maddy! I got your call," he said before thumping the roof of his car with his fist. "This is the place, boys. Everyone out!" he said, kicking his door shut.

Three other elves popped out of car. One had on huge, oversized headphones and a beanie. Another wore a leather motorcycle jacket and man boots, and the last had a puffy jacket that was open to reveal his polo shirt—the collar of which was popped.

"Text Boxy, would ya? He got lost four turns back. If Shale

misses out on the fun she is going to be *epic* angry," the driver said to the headphones elf.

"Already did. They're walkin' in," headphones reported.

An MBRC fairy guard turned around and paled when he spotted the unusual foursome. "Oh *no*," she groaned.

"Administrator Moonspell will have our head!" another MBRC elf said.

"Then toughen up and push Fidem back!" a Shadow Shifter barked as another five of the dark elf frat boys—although two of them were girls, I could see—climbed into the park via the hole the Ford made with its unusual parking spot.

These five elves were dressed like the original four—in college fashion. In *human* fashion.

"You really called them?" Krad angrily shouted to Madeline. "Are you *mad*?"

"Whoa, it's Krad! Hey Krad," the hoodie driver shouted, waving to Krad.

"What *happened* to you?" said motorcycle jacket as he and his buddies drew closer. "You're a little dude."

"Silence!" Krad shouted, shooting a bolt of black lightning at him.

To my shock, motorcycle jacket brushed the attack off like it was a snowball.

"Someone's got a complex," one of the elf frat—or sorority I guess—girls said, rolling her eyes.

"I'm not surprised. He totally always acted superior because he's a *captain*, or whatever," the second girl said.

"I can't blame him. He was pretty superior," the driver said. "But now he's a little dude!" he added in sheer delight.

"Maddy, where've you been, girl?" popped polo shirt asked, stomping through Devin's shield so he could hug Madeline.

"I've been around. The drinks are in back with our wizards. They're fighting with warlocks right now though, so be careful on your way back there," Madeline said.

"No prob, bra!" the driver said, walking in between a giant dark elf strike force that was attempting to create a black, tarry wave of fire. The frat elf's presence interrupted the spell, and he ruined the whole thing when he walked through the center of it. "Sorry, dudes," he said when he realized what he did.

"Did you get us Sprecher or A&W?" headphones asked.

"Both," Madeline lied.

"You're the best, Maddy!" headphones said, running to catch up with the driver—who was now involved in a slug fest. "Kerrick, what the heck are you doing? The warlocks are further back," he shouted before jumping on a dark elf.

"...Root beer?" I said. "I thought you called them the Beer Brothers?"

"Yeah, they came up with their own title and they wanted the alliteration instead of Root Beer Brothers. They don't drink alcohol *at all*, actually. They're terrified of getting a DUI because it took them forever to get their licenses," Madeline said.

"Oh my gosh, they have a hive gate here. That is so bad for the environment! Shale, help me close this," one of the girl elves shouted.

"They're pretty weird, but they're ex-Fidem members. They rehabilitated themselves into human society, although I'm not sure how successful they are," Madeline said with a raised eyebrow.

"More successful than you would think," I said, watching one of the elves from the second car bludgeon a band of skeleton soldiers with a golf club.

"I'll be back. Stay here with Dave, Asahi, and Kadri," Madeline said, shaking a finger at me before she ran to stand with the sorority elf girls, who were doing magic in one of the shadowy areas Fidem soldiers kept crawling out of.

I looked to Asahi and Kadri, who both gave me sweet smiles before they shot out of the protective space of Devin's shield and jumped into the thick of the fight.

Dave was chugging his tomato juice with admirable gusto. He stopped drinking long enough to scrunch up his face and say, "Watch out for Krad," before he resumed chugging.

Devin wasn't paying much attention to us. He still had his shield up and going, but he was helping out random MBRC forces in the fight, covering them with a shield if it looked like they were about to be hit.

I pulled my coat tight. I was sweating from adrenaline despite the cold temperatures, and it was making me even colder. I twirled, trying to get a good feel of the battle and searching for Krad.

The pint-sized villain was still standing by his sign—which was covered in a layer of paint balls. When I looked at him, our gazes locked.

"Crap," I said as he smiled at me.

Instantly I heard the terrifying rattle of a rattle snake, and I could feel snake scales on my feet—even though they were safely tucked in boots.

Mucky water filled my mouth and nose. The winter wind stung my arms as if I was stumbling around in a t-shirt instead of my winter jacket, and I heard and felt the bones in my left hand crack and my skin split as if an animal was biting me.

"No!" I screamed.

"Morgan, he's got Morgan," I heard Madeline shout over the noise of battle.

"Morgan, stay calm. You need to—," before Devin could finish he was shot by a ball of black fire that caught him unguarded. He went flying out of my eyesight and into the snow.

My heart beat faster and faster as I wrenched the glove off the hand I could *feel* an animal mauling.

Krad laughed as he absorbed my fear and used it to take out a squad of MBRC soldiers.

He was using me.

I was *helping* him.

I screamed, drowning in invisible water as Krad wrapped his magic around me, cutting me like fishing wire.

I remembered Aysel's words. I had to stop this! But the fear paralyzed me, and I screamed as magic spiked my nerves, making me feel pain from sources that weren't real.

I looked at my bare hand and saw the simple silver band with the topaz gem. I laboriously pulled it from my finger. It took me a few moments to fight the feeling of a snake wrapping around me before I could throw the ring at Krad.

It fell short, but the brilliant light it exploded into created a wall between us, and his magic lessened.

I started crawling across the snow, moving in Krad's direction.

"WHAT are you doing, moron?" Frey said, flinging the insult at me as he grabbed me by my belt and hauled me to my feet.

"I'm going to end this," I panted, still weak kneed.

"How? By giving Krad what he wants?"

"Just, trust me," I said. "I have to get closer to Krad."

Frey squinted at me. "How close?"

"Close enough to touch him."

Frey swore and scratched his head. "You are crazy, do you know that? Come on," he said sliding his arm around my back. He held me upright and dragged me through the snow, heading for the blinding light—that was quickly fading.

"Good luck," Frey said, tossing me at Krad when the light disappeared.

I yelped and crashed into Krad before I fell to the icy ground with a splat.

"Humans really are stupid," Krad said, placing his bare hand on my neck.

I howled as I felt nameless terrors claw and scratch at my back. Teeth grazed my face, spiders crawled across my skin, and fire burned my fingertips. Hands tightened around my neck—squeezing air from my body—a sword plunged into my gut, and a wolf howled in my ear.

The terror was enough to make my heart stop. I was crying in fright and pain, but I clung to Aysel's words as I reached above my head and shakily placed my bare hand on Krad's jacket.

Then, in spite of the phantoms pressing down and the illusions that were choking me, I thought of Aysel.

His scowling face was enough to make me steel myself. I thought of how we fought and insulted each other, and how that was an expression of our twisted but close relationship.

It made the fear in me buckle.

Elated, I turned my thoughts to Harrison. My goblin guard was as emotional as plumbing, but he was stable and solid in the turmoil of the last month. More than once I knew I was really lucky and grateful to have the stoic goblin with me.

With this revelation, I felt a small splinter of fear flake off.

Buoyed by the change, I thought about Asahi and Kadri. Their adorable relationship warmed my heart, and their insistence in including me in their lives was touching. I didn't deserve their love, but they were intent on slathering me with it.

I chipped away at the wall, thinking of my students—one after another. Frank, Sacmis, Perseus, Athena, Oak, Corn, Sage, and Zinnia—and my coworkers—Baobab, Corona, Orion, Toby, Doggy, and Dr. Creamintin.

Above me Krad grunted and adjusted his grip on my neck as he increased the power and potency of his phantoms.

I scrabbled in my thoughts for someone I really loved as I felt my panic bubble, and I remembered Madeline. Her bright smiles, warm hugs, and open affection were enough to punch through the wall of fright that surrounded me. I thought about how much I liked her, how she was goofy just when I needed to laugh, and that she did the weirdest things that both frustrated and amazed me. I thought about how comforting it was to have her with me to face Krad Temero.

Krad hissed, as if my warm affection for the vampire stung. "What are you doing?" he asked.

I forced myself to my knees and grabbed the collar of Krad's coat with my hand as I thought about my cyclops friends—Nick, Sandy, and Ralph.

"Stop it," Krad said. "Let go!"

Next I thought of Hunter. He was infuriatingly bossy, and he liked to move me like I was a chess piece, but he made sure he didn't sacrifice me. Hunter could tell my moods like I wore a mood ring, and he spoiled me rotten with treats from his cookie chef. If Aysel was my Frenemy/work partner and Madeline was my second best friend, Hunter was my closest ally.

The fear phantoms dissipated further. Soon I could feel only the faintest flicker of claws on my back and fire in my fingers.

"NO! What are you *thinking* of? Stop it!" Krad screamed as the murky black smog that covered his fingertips turned a warm champagne color.

"No," I said before I reach out, hugged him, and thought of Devin.

As soon as my thoughts turned to the mischievous Pooka, Krad screamed as if I shot him. He collapsed into me, and I sat back on my butt, the brat splayed across my lap. The phantom fears he pushed on me were gone. He was too weak to do anything.

My hands were soft as I ran them through Krad's hair and thought about stupid, *stupid* Devin. The Pooka had the loyalty of a pigeon. He was a notorious flirt, had a flair for drama, and was fiendishly mischievous, but I could always count on him to save me. He was the one who cared enough about me to break through the enchantment that kept me from remembering the MBRC two years ago. He had my employee contracts checked, kept the MBRC Board from making me their slave-liaison through his name alone, and he bankrolled my MM and probably my charmed jewelry based on my protective bracelet.

"N-no," Krad whimpered, limp and shocked.

I briefly shut my eyes and steeled my resolve. I hauled Krad upright and wrapped my arms around him as I laid the most powerful blow on him that I could.

I showered him with love.

Instead of dwelling on the terror and fright he ruled with, and the damage he wreaked against those he hated, I thought about how adorable Krad looked, and how cute he was when he protested his age. I remembered how happy and pleased he was over the dorkiest statements, and I decided all his hate was really a scream to feel love.

Krad glowed like a star going super nova before the light that surrounded him exploded in a spectacular burst, washing over Independence Park like an ocean of fizzing champagne.

The skeleton soldiers went down. Whatever magic was making them move was cut. I could hear the wizards and the Beer Brothers shout past the trees as some of the dark warlocks had spells malfunction and explode in their faces instead of striking the enemy.

The ghouls howled and covered their faces, shielding their eyes from the warm light that soaked the snow and sky.

The Shadow Shifters and MBRC forces were easily able to subdue the remaining dark elves and fairies since the female Beer Brothers shut the gates.

And me? I gawked at the drop dead gorgeous dark elf splayed across my lap instead of the pint-sized Krad.

He looked a few years older than Devin—he was maybe pushing 30—and with his long eyelashes, perfect hair, and beautiful features he easily trounced Aysel as the hottest elf I knew.

"Who. Is. This," I said, staring down at the elf.

The dark elf barely opened his eyes. He murmured something in a different language and extended a hand, barely brushing my cheek before four shifters pounced on us—scooping me away from him.

They clapped iron shackles on the dark elf, but it didn't matter. He was clearly unconscious and wouldn't be waking up anytime soon.

"Dang. That was great, Morgan, but did you have to break his curse?" Frey said, wiping blood from a tear in his shirt before he twisted into his jacket.

"What?" I said, my brain and limbs numb. "Who?"

"That is Krad Temero," Frey said, pointing a finger at the hot elf. "And *you*," he said, shifting to prod me with the accusing finger. "Just broke his curse."

"…That was KRAD?" I said when I was finally able to process again.

"Yeah. The Administrator is going to give birth to dwarves when he hears what you've done," Frank said.

"And here's Morgan! She just defeated the final boss—Krad Temero," Athena said, prancing up to Frank and me with her cell phone extended. "How do you feel, Morgan?"

I thought for a few moments before turning to Athena. "I

thought Krad was old."

"He is," Athena said.

"Like, I thought he was a grandpa."

"No way," Madeline said, joining us. She turned green and looked away when she caught sight of Frey's various scratches. "Dark elves live longer than even high elves. All that hate keeps 'em rotting longer. Urph," she said, before covering her mouth with a hand.

Frey eyed Athena. "What are you planning to do with that video?"

"I'll combine it with Perseus' video—he's scouting out the wizards and warlocks—and we'll post it on YouTube. It might go viral!"

"Athena, you can't post something like this on YouTube," Frey groaned.

"Why not?"

"If you barf on me I am going to cut ties with you," I warned the ill-looking Madeline.

"Madeline?"

Madeline and I turned to Frank, who had already covered his scratches with bandaids and first aid tape. "Are you okay?" he asked.

Madeline threw herself at Frank, practically sandwiching her head in his jacket. "You don't smell like blood—YES! I love you, Frank," Madeline said, her voice muffled in Frank's jacket.

Frank turned pink and shyly scratched his head as I observed the unlikely couple.

Maybe, just maybe, a weirdo vampire and a scruffy werewolf could form the most unlikely relationship known to the magical community *and* Hollywood and urban fantasy novels.

"Morgan," Devin said, his voice tight.

"Yes—WHAT?"

Devin scooped me up and tossed me over his shoulder.

"You're getting checked over by unicorns. *Now*," Devin said.

"But I'm not even hurt. I can walk, put me down!"

"No. You're lucky I don't tie you up and drag you like luggage after that trick you pulled," Devin said.

"Hey, that 'trick' worked! I beat Krad," I said.

"You didn't beat him. You fried his mind with love, I'm guessing?"

"Yep."

"Not bad. But you also broke his curse, which I don't think anyone will be happy about except for him," Devin said.

"I think we should focus on the positives instead of the negatives —ouch," I said when Devin threw me higher over his shoulder. "He's in the MBRC's custody now. His reign of terror is over."

"Perhaps," Devin said, setting me down in the relief unit that was being built. "Krad used his magic on her. I want a complete medical checkup," Devin said, resting his hands on my shoulders as he turned me to face the unicorns.

I was going to complain. I wanted to complain. But even through the thick fabric of my jacket I could feel that Devin's hands were shaking. So I didn't resist when a unicorn—the pinto who went over me at the museum—turned to face me.

"Morgan, wasn't it? I have the perfect volunteer who will see to you," the pinto said, her muzzle wrinkling in the horse version of a smile.

She stepped aside to reveal a bay colored unicorn.

"Westfall," I said, my hesitations draining away as I smiled at the shy unicorn, who happened to be the first magical being I ever helped to rehabilitate.

"Hello, Morgan," Westfall said, nuzzling my temple. "You're chilled, and you have an increased heartbeat. Let's sit down out of the way," he suggested.

I didn't answer—I couldn't. Snot and tears clogged my throat. I sagged into Westfall's warm neck and grabbed a fistful of his warm mane.

"You're safe now, Morgan," Westfall said, tucking his head against my back in the horse version of a hug. "You've done well. You can rest now."

I barely got to sit down on a puffy toadstool a fairy grew just for the occasion because it radiated heat before I passed out, exhausted and sapped.

16

My Decision

"The Magical Beings' Rehabilitation Center would also like to thank Miss Morgan Fae. Miss Fae worked with the Center's defense department to extract information about Krad Temero's plans, and she played an integral role in his subdual and capture," Administrator Moonspell read.

I fidgeted on the stage, uncomfortable in the high heeled boots I was borrowing from Fran for this very public appearance in the magical community.

"The Center is very blessed and lucky to have such a *talented* instructor in its ranks. Thank you, Miss Fae, for all you have done," Administrator Moonspell said, giving me a withering glance even though his voice was pleasant.

I shifted, being careful not to move too much so I wouldn't pitch head first off the creaky stage they had raised in the middle of the MBRC central chamber for the presentation.

The MBRC board was lined up in front of the stage, watching with various sizes of grins—or in Elros and Luka's case, pained smiles.

A captain from the Shadow Shifters, an MBRC guard, and one of the wizards who fought with us stood on the podium with Devin and me. Moonspell had gone down the line, lauding and praising us to the gathered crowd for about an hour. I was ready for this ceremony to be over.

"Windbag," I muttered.

Devin gave me a lopsided grin. "He's almost done," he whispered.

"I don't believe it."

"…Center of course extends its thanks to all involved in the takedown and capture of Krad," Moonspell went on, but his speech was interrupted by a Beer Brother.

"Yeah! Way to go, bra!" the frat elf said—I think it was the Ford Focus driver.

Administrator Moonspell gripped the podium he stood behind until his knuckles turned white. If Madeline were here, he would have ripped her head off. But the blonde vampire had wisely made herself scarce the past few days since it became apparent that the Beer Brothers were back, and they weren't intending to leave for a while.

"This concludes our presentation. Thank you," Administrator Moonspell said, his voice stiff with fury.

"Freedom," I said, heading for the stairs. I wanted to join the gigantic crowd as soon as possible.

"Afraid Moonspell will yell at you again if he catches you?" Devin asked.

"Yep," I said. Administrator Moonspell only had a few minutes to lay into me for breaking Krad's curse when our war party dragged our sorry butts back to the MBRC the previous day. I didn't want to give him the opportunity to revisit the topic since the first time was enough to make him spit in fury. (To his credit, he found out Asahi and Kadri went with me, the Beer Brothers were back, and Krad's curse was broken all at once.)

Devin helped me down the stairs, where Harrison was waiting.

"Thanks," I said to the Pooka before I turned to my bodyguard. "You look pretty sharp, Krusher."

The stony goblin had eschewed his usual suit for a tuxedo that looked awesome on him. "It's Harrison, Miss Fae."

"Devin, could we speak to you?" a high elf I didn't recognize asked Devin. He was with a lady that had huge, feathered wings tucked against her back.

"Valan, Qwark, certainly. Just give me a moment," Devin said before turning to me. "I'll be around," Devin he said, hugging me. I tried to squirm out of his grip until he said, "Ten seconds."

"Five," I said.

"Deal," Devin said, renewing his embrace. He hugged me tightly for five seconds, and I bore it without a complaint or accusation. "Steer clear from Moonspell—and his eldest brat. Harrison, I'm counting on you," Devin said before kissing me on the top of my head and slipping away with his associates.

"Hey—you! Grr," I said, narrowing my eyes at his retreating back.

"Don't you look happy? Here," Hunter said, passing me a champagne flute that was filled with something purple and fizzy. "It's sparkling grape juice," he said after I sniffed at it.

"Thank you," I said before taking a cautious sip. The bubbles popped on my tongue, mimicking a burning feeling, although it tasted great.

"You looked thirsty, and when the Beer Brothers find out there are refreshments they'll clear the place out," Hunter said.

"I don't understand how I never met them before," I said.

"I'm not surprised. There are less than a dozen of them, and the center rarely holds big receptions that are open for all to attend," Hunter said, gesturing to the packed room.

"It's an occasion to celebrate, I guess," I said.

"You guess? You stopped an international, magic-fueled terrorist."

"Yeah," I said.

Hunter rolled his eyes. "You are impressed with the oddest things. A cookie elf could play you like an instrument, but the capture of a dangerous fugitive is minor to you."

"I didn't say that," I said. "But that does remind me. Krusher and I are great pals and everything now—,"

"It's Harrison, Miss Fae."

"But the threat is gone. Like, totally gone. I don't think I need a bodyguard anymore. How much longer am I going to be guarded?"

Hunter looked thoughtful. "I don't know. Do you have any idea, Harrison?"

"...Wait, what?" I blinked.

"I forgot, we never told you," Hunter said.

"Never told me what?"

"About a month ago the Center started to complain about having a non-MBRC guard assigned to you—one of its staff members. Really it was just that Moonspell had his robes twisted in a knot because I received that pixie powder distribution license for *Firefly*," Hunter said, pausing to drink his sparkling grape juice. "So I asked the Pooka if he would provide paperwork that would say Harrison is *his* employee. Devin is considered a dignitary since he's a Councilmember, so he's allowed to have bodyguards and assign them to whomever he wants."

"So isn't it name only, then?" I asked.

"That was my plan, but the Pooka took him on. He's been bankrolling him for the past month. Our agreement was that we would share information, and Harrison could call for goblin backup and assistance and remain plugged into my network."

My brain buzzed as I processed this information. Hunter seemed to expect a reply or something, but all I could do was sip my drink and stare at him.

"The extra goblin guards were fully mine. We could get away with it because the MBRC board was embarrassed how easily Krad was able to attack you," Hunter said.

"Oh," I said.

"I think you misunderstand him most of the time," Hunter said.

"Who, Krusher?"

"No. Devin."

I gave Hunter a look, and he shrugged. "Or maybe you don't. I don't care. It would suit me just fine if I was number one in your heart."

"Fran is number one. Madeline is number two. You and Aysel *might* tie for third place."

"The best friend isn't a surprise, but really? A vampire?" Hunter shook his head. "You are slipping, Morgan. There's no way you will leave the magical community."

"Watch me," I said.

"I will," Hunter smiled, his topaz eyes glittering.

"If you will excuse my interruption, I would like to speak to Miss Fae. I believe the MBRC board owes her a great debt of gratitude," Blood Binder said, carefully standing behind Hunter in his shrunken/greyhound bus-sized body.

"Of course," Hunter said. "I'll see you in school tomorrow."

"Yes," I said, relief drenching the word.

Hunter laughed. "Until then, take care. Harrison, if you would continue the reports?"

"Yes, Sir," Harrison said.

"Great. Enjoy," Hunter said, disappearing in the packed crowd.

"Miss Fae, we are so thankful for your help and assistance in capturing Krad Temero," the fairy board member said, taking my hand and squeezing it.

"I don't think our troops could have done it without you," the dryad added.

"If there is anything we can do for you, please do not hesitate to ask," Blood Binder said.

"Actually, there is something," I said, biting my lip.

Elros raised an eyebrow at me. "That was swift."

"Elros," Dante, the wizard, scolded.

"I would like the dark elf and ex-Fidem member Ethan to be put in a rehabilitation program. It doesn't have to be now. I understand if you want to wait to make sure he's not just pretending he's changed."

Ranulf, the werewolf board member, seemed to hear my request as he and Luka joined Elros. "That's a tough request, Morgan."

"I know, but I don't think it will happen unless someone from upper management intervenes," I said.

"Ethan-the-nameless has committed crimes. He must be punished for them," Luka said.

"Yeah, I totally agree," I said. "But that doesn't mean he should be imprisoned for life. The guy helped us when we *really* needed it. That should count for something," I said.

Blood Binder sighed. "What we have refrained from saying, Miss Fae, is that frankly our rehabilitation staff are terrified of him. Dark elves have not been kind to our society since we hid. Distrust and dislike has been forced into us."

"If you give us a few months, we might be able to release him into your custody," Ranulf said, folding his arms across his massive chest as he pondered the idea. "You have high enough clearance, and the knowhow. Although I'm aware you don't usually handle rehabilitation cases."

"That is a stupendous idea!" the fairy representative said.

"It won't work," I said. "I'm planning to leave the MBRC after the school year is over. It will take longer than a few months to get Ethan into human society. He fared well on his own before, but now that he's going through the MBRC he'll have to take classes and tests."

"Oh," the dryad said, drooping.

"We will try," Blood Binder said.

"I will ask my staff to look at it, but I would not hold much hope," Elros said. "Aysel Moonspell was requesting the same thing earlier. He was refused."

"Thank you," I said. "Even if you just try, I would be very grateful."

"We will miss you when you leave," the fairy representative said.

"I heard as much from Madeline, but I hoped you would reconsider," Luka said.

I shook my head. "Krad, the whole Fidem mess," I shivered. "I can't," I said.

"I won't pretend to understand, but we always knew we couldn't depend on you forever. Thank you for your service, Morgan," said Blood Binder. "It's been our pleasure."

"Thank you," I said. "And I'll still be around for a few more months."

"Oh good," Dante said in relief. "Weller Goblin Enterprises has another export contract renewal coming up in two months."

"Dante," the fairy hissed.

"What? He behaves so much better when she is there," Dante said.

"I am sure there are many people who would like to thank you and recognize your sacrifices today. We won't take up anymore of your time," Blood Binder said.

"Thank you," I said. "I'm glad that—,"

"Morgan! Morgan, Esmeralda said I should come get you," Perseus said, squeezing his horse body between Blood Binder and Dante. "Dave is talking a troll into showing him some wrestling moves."

"So?"

"They're getting started—here and now!"

"Igottagobye," I said, shoving my empty glass in the fairy's hands before I hurried after Perseus, stumbling in my skirt and borrowed boots. "Where did you leave them?"

"Over—," there was a deafening crash on the left side of the room. "…there," Perseus said.

"Fantastic. Let's go—before anything else is ruined."

"Okay. Can I record this for an Instagram video?"

"NO!"

It was a full week before I returned to the MBRC to work. I had to catch up with my homework, get all my notes in order, and make up with my parents who were *not* happy with me for being gone so long. (You think the MBRC would have gotten Hunter or his goons to persuade them to accept it, but noooo they didn't have *clearance* for that!)

My first day back, a Monday afternoon, I actually snuck inside —with Harrison's help. I didn't want the dozens of interruptions I was sure to have because I was still trying to file paperwork for Ethan's release and rehabilitation.

Since no one was supposed to know I was in—besides Baobab and Harrison anyway—I was shocked when the door to my office was slammed open. "Mornin'," Grogrintork said, shuffling into my office with his three bodyguards.

The bodyguard that was infatuated with Baobab stopped to give her a deep bow before one of his companions grabbed a chunk of his hair and dragged him along.

"Grogrintork, what a pleasant surprise," I said with a genuine smile. "What can I do for you?"

"I wanted to make sure ye were alive 'n' kickin'," Grogrintork said. "I heard 'bout you takin' on Krad of Fidem. You're a brave gal!"

"I wasn't alone, and I did the least fighting," I said as Grogrintork plopped down in a chair in front of my desk.

"Still. Tis a great thing," Grogrintork said. "Dark elves be no joke. I heard the MBRC's got custody of Krad?"

"Yes."

"They plannin' to charge him with anything?"

I hesitated. "I don't know," I finally said. "When the MBRC took him captive his curse was broken and…I think he's changing."

"That'd be a miracle," Grogrintork grunted.

"Yeah," I said. "Now, what are you really here for?"

"What? Ye don't believe me?" Grogrintork said, puffing up like a marshmallow melted in a microwave.

"It's not that I don't believe you, I just doubt you hauled your bodyguards and yourself all the way to my office on a day no one knows I'm here to ask how I'm doing," I said.

Grogrintork nodded his head. "I talked it over with some of the other clans. They didn't take too kindly to the idea of learnin' to service coffee machinery," he finally said.

At the dwarf representatives words I leaned back in my chair. "I see," I said, unable to keep the disappointment out of my voice. I was counting on that being the solution to the dwarf problem.

"We're a proud race, see? The idea of servin' others like that, doing low labor, didn't sit right," Grogrintork continued. "We decided we'd rather get desk 'n office jobs."

I tried to keep back a sigh. They were turning into the nightmare I had originally thought they were.

Coffee machine repair work was necessary to the MBRC, and they thought it would be belittling? They obviously had higher expectations than I was prepared to deliver—there was no way I could launch them high up in department positions.

Perhaps their lack of jobs wasn't just because of the elves. Maybe it was that they were unwilling to do what they viewed as crappy work to make the sacrifice for the future.

I sat there, thinking and staring at Grogrintork. "Then I don't think I can help you anymore," I finally said. "I can't get you office work. The MBRC does a lot of internal promotions. Office jobs are snapped up almost immediately by internal personnel, unless it's something specialized—like teaching human psychology," I said.

"So ye won't help us," Grogrintork said, frowning slightly.

"No, you just aren't willing to accept the help I can give you," I said.

"You mentioned liaisons," Grogrintork protested. "We deserve liaisons 'least!"

"Not if you aren't willing to work in the MBRC," I said, starting to feel a shred of sympathy for Administrator Moonspell. No wonder he was a sourpuss.

"If ye find us acceptable work we would," Grogrintork argued.

I massaged my eyes. The dwarves were good natured—I could see it in Grogrintork and his guards. If only I could make him see…"

I straightened up and smiled. "If you would come with me—all of you. Baobab, would you come as well? We need to step outside for a few minutes."

"Certainly, Miss Fae," Baobab said, although her curiosity was clearly piqued as she, Grogrintork, and his men trooped for the door.

I led them outside—the smitten dwarf was close at Baobab's heels—and down the teaching department's hallway. After a bit of walking we reached the main chamber of the MBRC—the center of the web.

I led them down flights of stairs until we were just two stories above the main floor.

The chamber, as usual, was crowded with magical beings.

Two Japanese kirin were being escorted by a British hobgoblin. A giant stepped over a hippogriff, who had stopped to snap at a manticore. A phoenix flew out of the administrative wing and dove down to the bottom floor, shedding sparks and spreading the scent of ash as she flew. An ice dragon lowered its head to avoid her, although it didn't stop talking with the high elf, dryad, and naiad that were conversing with it.

A small group of four, big eyed selkie kids were being led towards the MBRC help desk, where Corona beckoned to them and smiled in welcome.

Sacmis was down on the main floor with Frank, Frey, and Madeline. All four of them were deep in conversation, and Frank kept suspiciously scratching himself.

Fairies of all sizes buzzed, walked, and glided through the chamber. One fairy barely bigger than my hand flew past Baobab and her dwarf admirer, carrying a message for another magical being. Another fairy, one that was about as tall as a high elf, wore a leaf crown on her head and extended her hand to a minotaur, who knelt before her and pressed his bull forehead to her palm.

A hobgoblin was shouted at for bouncing on a genie, and a griffon from our floor jumped onto the railing before throwing itself in the air and spiraling up towards an upper floor, his beautiful black wings pumping to push him up.

"You see all of this?" I asked, gesturing widely to the mind boggling assortment of legendary creatures before us. "They're working together to merge their magical society with the human world. They're doing things they've never done before to reach that goal."

"Unicorns are having their horns removed and joining therapy riding barns," I continued. "Goblins pump goods and produce into the center like grocery stores. Naiads are being hired out as gardeners, and lots of dryads work in boating companies or give lake and river tours. The Michigan mermaids run an *aquarium*, and fairies do everything from running smoothie stands to working in the fashion industry. Some elves are architects, others are home economics teachers."

"What are you tryin' to say?" Grogrintork asked.

"I'm saying that no work is beneath you, if you do it with all your heart. If it helps your people be rehabilitated, there is no shame in it. The center needs espresso machine repairmen, just as it needs CEO cyclopes to donate, and fairies to run messages. The center *needs* you."

Grogrintork rested his hands on the railing as he peered out over the central chamber with me.

"Being rehabilitated does not mean doing the same thing, only with humans. It means changing and adapting to another way of life," I said, watching a vampire coven skirt the edges of the chamber. "To be rehabilitated, to join the MBRC, you've got to be willing to set aside the old ways and to change. It's not less enjoyable. It's just different."

"You have a choice, Grogrintork," I said, waving when Madeline caught sight of me. "You can change with this world, doing things your kind has never done before and breaking everything you thought was absolute, or you can be left out."

Grogrintork eyed me. "Ye really believe in this place. Dontcha?"

I thought for a moment. "I do."

"What about politics? What about beings who do wrong—like Krad Temero?" Grogrintork wanted to know.

"The MBRC isn't perfect," I acknowledged, observing a three headed hydra being led to the stables by a werewolf. "But it's still beautiful. It messes up and makes mistakes, and sometimes—a lot of times even—things are overly political. But you have to look at the *good* it does for people. Dave—a vampire I know—has gone from being a total weirdo, to acceptably unusual and employed in a position he *enjoys*. Entire packs of werewolves have united to help preserve forests and parks. There are so many cases, I can't list them all. *That's* why I teach at the MBRC. That's why I'm here. I believe in what they're doing, and I see the joy it brings," I said.

I was quiet after that. It was a revelation to me that I really loved the MBRC that much.

It also made me realize, in that instant, that I couldn't leave. I couldn't follow Fran to Florida, or go to the UK with Devin.

I belonged in the Chicago Magical Being's Rehabilitation Center.

"All right, Miss Fae. You've sold me," Grogrintork said, slapping me on my lower back.

"What?" I said, slightly shocked.

"We want to be a part of this MBRC of yers too," Grogrintork said with a big smile. "And if being coffee machine repairmen is what it takes to get us in…well…blades raised to coffee!"

Grogrintork's three guards each raised no less than five assorted weapons in the air to attest to his statement.

"You won't regret it, Grogrintork," I said. "Sometimes you'll want to pull out your hair and kick Administrator Moonspell in the face, but every day is rewarding."

"Amen," Grogrintork said, holding out his giant hand.

I hesitated before offering him my hand. He shook it vigorously. "Ye've got spirit, Miss Fae. I wouldn't be surprised if ye ran this joint one day. Now, how do we begin?"

I was unable to keep the beaming smile off my face. "Let's go back to my office and discuss your options."

"Aye."

I found Madeline, Frank, and Frey in the cafeteria later that evening. They were trying to get the cappuccino machine to work without much luck.

"Morgan," Madeline said, pulling on Frank's shirt to get his attention. "See, I told you I saw her."

"Morgan, what's up with the—," Frey started.

"I'm staying," I blurted out, unable to keep the news to myself.

The vampire and werewolves blinked.

"What?" Frey asked.

"I changed my mind. I'm staying in the area—in Chicago—because I want to stay with the MBRC," I said.

"That's great news! Morgan is staying!" Madeline said, giving me a bear hug.

"What are you going to do about college?" Frey asked.

"I don't know. I might take a year off, or do online courses. I want to take some Dale Carnegie classes, and I think I would like to visit the Fairy Council in Britain before I declare a major," I said, laughing and hugging Madeline back.

"That sounds serious," Frank said, his eyes wide.

"It is," I said, backing away from Madeline when I noticed Frank's bare neck. I needed to get him another flea collar. He probably already had fleas, and Madeline hung out with him way too much to avoid contracting them. "If I'm staying at the MBRC I'm not content to just skate along. I want to move up in departments."

Behind me Harrison cleared his throat, momentarily checking my enthusiasm.

"Father is going to be so disappointed."

I slowly turned on my heels to find Aysel standing behind me, dressed in his lofty high elf robes. "Oh, hey, Aysel," I said.

"So you are going to stay," Aysel said.

"Yep. If your dad offers me another contract," I said.

Aysel snorted. "If he doesn't the MBRC board will," he said, studying me with his unnerving, silver eyes. "I...look forward to a continued working relationship."

"Me too," I said, the smallest excuse of a smile flashing on my lips.

Aysel gave me a look of disgust. "You desire one of those infernal human signs of affection, don't you?"

"It would be the guardian thing to do, guardian," I said.

Aysel gave me a sour look. "Don't call me that," he said before opening his arms wide.

I gave the stiff elf a passable version of a Madeline hug. He patted me on the back three times before giving in and squeezing me once.

"Stop that," he said, brushing me away when I started laughing.

"I can't help it. I'm just so *happy*, finally! I've got to tell my class —I've got to tell Asahi and Kadri!"

"Tell Perseus and Athena," Madeline said. "They'll love passing the word along. They've been campaigning to try and get everyone in our class an emailbox."

"It's just email," Frey said.

"Yes," Madeline said.

Aysel straightened his robes. "I suppose I could inform the administration department," he said.

"Morgan should totally be the one to tell the MBRC board, though," Frey said. "I bet the fairy and dryad will cry. Any takers?"

"I'm glad you're staying, Morgan," Frank said, shyly hunching his shoulders as he looked at me.

"So am I. I love you guys!"

"It just took a Fidem captain and a bunch of dwarves to make you realize it," Madeline said in a sing-song voice as she grabbed Frank's hands and started twirling in an impromptu dance.

I laughed when the pair almost bowled Aysel over.

"Morgan," Frey said.

"Hm?"

"Welcome home."

17

Devin the Flirt?

"So your parents *finally* let you out of the house, huh?" Fran asked me two days later. I skipped out of work to hang out with her, mostly because we haven't had a real conversation since Ethan attempted to kidnap me.

"Yeah. They've gotten over it since my grades didn't slide or anything," I said, hunkering down in the couch.

As Fran's family was gone for the evening—I think they were seeing a movie—we had opted to hang out at her place.

"That's stupid. I would have thought your work could have pulled out one of those Men In Black gadgets and made them forget you were ever gone," Fran said.

I nodded my head at the casual remark and ate a handful of popcorn to buy myself a few seconds. "Speaking of my job—,"

"We don't have to talk about it. It fact, we shouldn't," Fran said, wrapping a fuzzy blanket around herself.

I stared at her. "What?"

"Isn't it, like, top secret?"

"I don't work on a secret government project."

"Heck no! They would have pulled you from school for good if they realized you were worth something. No, I know you have something to do with things that aren't…human."

"How long have you known?" I asked.

"Since I met Madeline and Hot Garden Guy. So which movie do you want to watch? I'm feeling like it's a Pixar night"

"What? You can't gloss this over like that! You met them over two years ago. Why didn't you say anything?"

"Because you were still willing to make us work," Fran said, "If you started to drop our friendship, or developed, like, a nervous twitch or something I would have asked."

I couldn't say anything. I was shocked by the revelation Fran had even an *inkling* that my part-time job wasn't what it seemed. "That's why you would accept work excuses so easily, wasn't it? Man, I thought Hunter just had you persuaded!"

"Had me what?" Fran asked with narrowed eyes. "Wait, no. I don't want to know. It's better if I *don't* know."

"Why?"

"I'm very happy the way my life is. I like the world. It's dirty and humans fight too much, but I suspect whatever or whoever you work for would blow my mind. Besides, I don't want to find out that my ex-boyfriend is, like, an alien or something."

"Oh yeah, I wanted to talk to you about Ethan," I said. "And for the record—no, he's not an extra terrestrial."

"Good," Fran said, sharply exhaling. "I was starting to think he had kidnapped you to…probe you or something."

"No. Totally not. Anyway, he doesn't have to be your ex-boyfriend. He's being released in a month or so by my employer."

"That's fabulous for him, but I will not take him back."

"Why not?"

"The dirty rat *kidnapped* you, in case you forgot."

"Yeah, well he's sorry about that," I said, scratching my neck.

"Sorry doesn't cut it. If anyone messes with you they're on my blacklist—boyfriend or not," Fran snorted.

"I think you should give him a second chance," I said.

"And why would I do that?"

"Because you genuinely like him. And I think you miss him," I said. I considered telling her how Ethan pined for her in the MBRC holding cells, but I felt that would be more than a little mean to the reformed dark elf.

"Nope, I don't. He just proves that my taste in men sucks. First *that guy*, and then Ethan-the-kidnapper. Wow, I'm on a roll."

"Look, I liked Brett Patterson too. I actually liked him before you did," I said, ignoring the hiss Fran gave when I uttered his name. "But I think the whole kidnapping thing gave you the wrong idea about Ethan. You really need to give him a second chance. He made you happy, Fran," I said.

Fran sighed. "You're too understanding."

"Hah! As if," I said. Really it was that I felt guilty for leading the dark elf to think I could reunite him with Fran if he spat out enough information.

"I'll meet up with him again, but I *won't* date him," Fran said.

I sagged with relief. "Great," I said. If I gave Ethan the chance to make up with Fran, that would be more than enough. He would totally win her back over.

"I mean it, Morgan!"

"Sure you do," I said.

"I'm serious," Fran said. "I was going to break up with him in June anyway."

I froze. "What?"

"Well I'm going to Florida for college," Fran said.

"So? Haven't you heard of long distance relationships?"

"Morgan you are too old fashioned. I'm going to be a freshman in college in *Florida*. I *want* to be single then!"

"But you can't!" I said.

"Why not?" Fran asked, arching an eye.

I clamped my mouth shut, glaring at Fran. I had pulled serious strings and embarked on a journey of paperwork to get Ethan sponsored and to pump him to an early release. I did not do *all* that work so Fran could dump the poor elf!

"You better change your mind," I muttered.

"Like you can talk. You're permanently single!" Fran said, stretching her arms above her head.

The reminder drew a sigh from me. "I know."

Fran froze mid-stretch. "What was that?"

"What was what?" I asked.

Fran practically quivered with excitement as she rearranged her blanket and turned so she could perfectly face me. "You sighed and, for once, sounded sad about your lack of relationships."

"I did not."

"You *totally* did!"

"I didn't mean anything deep by sighing."

"You can't fool me, Morgan. I have been your friend longer than your little brothers have been around. Spill!"

I rolled my eyes, this was going to be embarrassing. "You know how sometimes you think a guy, or maybe even a couple guys might like you?"

"Yeah."

"And then you find out that *none* of them do?" I said.

My pride had taken a bit of a beating to learn that Hunter was only interested in being my permanent friend, and if I was being totally honest I thought maybe, just maybe, Aysel found me even a little bit…I dunno, alluring? Yeah, the guardian/ward thing totally killed off that thought.

"Oh yeah, that sucks," Fran said, leaning back in her couch. "It always shocks me how books and movies pull off love triangles when they don't happen a lot in real life. Our freshman year I deluded myself into thinking Michael Hoffman, Jake Anderson, and Clint Kegian liked me."

"You never told me that!"

"Yeah it's a good thing I didn't, because *none* of them were interested. Anyway, you do have a guy that likes you, so you can't be embarrassed."

"Who?"

"Hot Garden Guy."

I rolled my eyes. "Devin doesn't count. He likes *all* women."

"No way," Fran said, shaking her head. "He has got a thing for you. He's so smitten it's ridiculous."

"How could you know? You only met him a few times!"

"And that's enough for me to know he likes you. When he met me he acted like a guy trying to present his best side to the parents of the girl he wanted to date. If he were a flirt he would have behaved differently."

"Devin is a slick operator," I said.

"Then explain the dates."

"..."

"Does he give you gifts?"

"Maybe," I said, glancing at my protection charm bracelet. It was the only piece of magical jewelry that I still wore. "But Hunter does too and he made it perfectly clear that friendship is the ideal role for him."

"And you're complaining? You were the one that suggested it in the first place. Anyway, Hunter just brings you food, doesn't he?"

"Yes," I slowly admitted.

"Look. I just think it's pretty messed up that you're embarrassed you thought guys liked you when they don't, and you have Devin all lined up, and perfectly willing to do whatever you ask him to."

"He's a flirt."

"Then tell him to *stop* flirting!" Fran said, throwing a couch pillow at me. "If he agrees to, you know he's interested. If he doesn't then he's a flirt and I'll admit I was wrong and take you out for ice cream to console you."

"It's February. It's too cold for ice crea—,"

"Then I'll take you out for coffee, or donuts, or something! Just *ask* him! Jeez!" Fran huffed.

"Thanks Fran."

"No problem. Somebody has to be relationship minded here."

"No. I mean, for everything."

"Me too," Fran said, smiling at me.

"I'm sorry I can't tell you more about my job."

"Hey, like I said. I don't think I *want* to know about your job. I'm happy with a normal life. Or I will be happy as soon as you talk to Hot Garden Guy."

"Okay, okay. I'll talk to him tomorrow. So, what are we going to watch?"

"I was thinking a Pixar movie, but now I'm almost in the mood for something with superheroes," Fran said sliding off her couch to look at her family's DVD collection. "Wait," she said, freezing mid stride. "Please don't tell me you work for like…the Avengers or the Justice League."

"Fran. Batman and Ironman are made up."

"I know *that.* I mean, you don't work for superheroes, do you?"

"No."

"Good," Fran said. "I didn't want to be stupid girl who fell in love with the supervillain."

"Don't worry. Ethan wasn't leveled high enough in his organization to be considered the top villain," I said.

Fran glared at me. "I didn't hear that! I'm going to pretend I didn't hear that. I am *not* a villain's minion girlfriend!"

"Well he's not a minion anymore."

"YOU AREN'T HELPING, Morgan."

"At this point I'm not really trying to."

"I CAN TELL."

I laughed as my childhood friend grumbled under her breath and savagely picked out a DVD for us to watch. No matter what happened with Devin, I was happy. I had my friends, and I would keep working at a place I loved.

Life was perfect.

"Are you certain you want to do this, Miss Fae?" an MBRC minotaur from the defense department asked.

"I am," I said, my voice strong. "I *need* to face him."

"Very well. We will bring him in shortly," the minotaur said before leaving the questioning room, his hooves clip-clopping on the tiled floor.

The glass window into the observation room let me see that no one would be watching us, but I knew there were going to be at least four guards in the room besides Harrison.

The MBRC wasn't taking any chances with him, and I couldn't blame them. Krad Temero had been a pain to catch.

"Harrison, we need to talk," I announced.

Harrison shifted, probably shocked by my usage of his real name. "Yes, Miss Fae?"

"This isn't really the ideal place to do it, though, so we can wait."

"Miss Fae."

I turned to study my bodyguard. Even though I didn't meant to say anything, I couldn't help asking, "Are you happy?"

Harrison gave no response. He didn't move, I couldn't even tell if he blinked since he was wearing his sunglasses.

"What I mean is, do you *want* to keep guarding me? I know your radio goes directly to Hunter's guys, but are you okay with the fact that you aren't his employee anymore?"

"What do you mean, Miss Fae?"

"I've just been thinking. It's really unusual for a goblin to be employed outside of the goblin community, and technically as my bodyguard you report to Devin." I took a deep breath before I said, "If you want to quit and go back to working for Hunter, I would totally understand. I would miss you tons, but you are a goblin and goblins, what I'm trying to say is…oh gosh. I've botched this terribly."

"Miss Fae."

"Yeah?" I said, miserably looking up at my guard.

"I will stay."

"You'll be my bodyguard?"

"Yes."

"Even though you'll be working for the Pooka and guarding a human?"

"Yes."

"…Is Hunter making you stay?"

"No."

"Then why?"

"Goblins only work for goblins because loyalty is at our core," Harrison said.

"You mean…" I trailed off. I couldn't say it. I couldn't ask Harrison if his loyalties now stood with me.

Harrison nodded.

"Aw, Krusher! You're going to make me cry," I sniffed.

I was emotional for a minute or two while Harrison was… Harrison I guess.

When the minotaurs brought Krad in, he was shackled in enough iron to attract a car sized magnet. He was still jaw-dropping beautiful—which I found surprising, the Beer Brothers and Ethan didn't even come close to Krad's hotness level—but his face was wane and he was clearly not in his element.

"So you *have* come," Krad said when he was forced to sit in a chair that the minotaurs chained him to. "I thought you would."

"I what?" I asked, seated in a chair across from Krad.

"You have come for restitution. To take your pound of flesh for all the misery I put you through," Krad said.

"Oh," I said, studying the proud dark elf.

I knew I should be gleeful to see him restrained. But it was sad to see him weighed down in chains. Not that I wanted to see him prancing around unfettered, but I could see his soul in his eyes and he still ached for love.

"Nope. Not really," I said, grabbing my backpack.

"Then you have come to shout at me. To scream at me," Krad said.

"No," I said, still digging in my backpack. "I'm pretty sure Administrator Moonspell could do that way better than I could anyway."

"You fear that I will escape and you wish to assure yourself I am safely captive," Krad said, leaning forward. "You are right to be afraid. I will slither my way out of the MBRC and I will—" he was cut off when one of the minotaurs jerked one of his chains, slamming him back in his seat.

Krad winced.

"Still love those comic book lines and telling me your great plans, huh?" I said, placing a baggie of cookies in front of him.

Krad raised an eyebrow. "Foolish human, I will not eat what you give me. Clearly you wish to poison me."

"They're not poisoned," I said, putting my backpack down. "I made them in cooking class."

Harrison cleared his throat and I rolled my eyes. "I mean, *culinary arts*," I said, opening the baggy to snag two of the cookies. I passed one back to Harrison and ate the second one while I watched Krad stare at the baggie.

The dark elf stared at the baggie of cookies like it was an alien or unknown creature.

"They're peanut butter oatmeal cookies. They're quite good—provided you're not gluten intolerant and you don't have a peanut allergy."

"I won't be bribed," Krad said.

"I'm not trying to bribe you," I said, finishing my cookie.

Krad made a noise of disbelief and looked away.

"The villain act isn't necessary right now. Do you think you could ditch it?" I said.

Krad laid me with a dark glare saturated with hatred. "It is not an *act*, Morgan Fae. I hate you and dream of your demise—" he was cut off again by a minotaur.

I brushed off my fingers before I stood and walked around the table.

Krad, Harrison, and the minotaurs all stiffened when I stopped directly next to Krad's chair.

"Maybe it's true. Maybe you do dream about killing me. But your soul isn't as black as it used to be," I said to Krad before I placed my bare hand on his cheek and dimly reflected on my love of the MBRC.

Krad leaped out of his chair as if my touch burned. The chains wouldn't let him get very far, though, and both he and the chair fell to the ground with a clatter.

Oh yeah. As much as he pretended to hate me, there was no way I could mistake the way he tried to touch me back at the park. I was going to win the war!

As the minotaurs fished Krad back into a sitting position and put his chair upright, I returned to my side of the table.

"Why are you doing this?" Krad asked.

I threw my backpack over my shoulder. "I don't know," I lied.

"You mean to torture me."

"Nope," I said. "I want something that you would probably consider even worse."

"What?" Krad asked.

I laid my sweetest smile on the dark elf. "I want to change you," I said, heading for the door. "Enjoy your cookies. I've got work to do," I said, heading for the door. "See you later," I said.

"Wait—later?" Krad said, but Harrison and I were already out of the room.

"You intend to return?" Harrison asked, shutting the door to the questioning room.

"Yeah. I think so," I said.

Harrison grunted.

"You don't approve, Krusher?" I asked.

"It's Harrison, Miss Fae."

"Good. I thought you might understand my reasoning. Where is Devin?"

"Your office."

"Perfect. To my office, then," I said, leading the way.

When I arrived Baobab was mysteriously missing. (Grogrintork's guard was making a serious campaign for her. I wouldn't be surprised if the two started dating in a few weeks. Baobab was a tough cookie to crack, but he was making pretty good work of it.)

Devin was seated in my desk chair, his body stretched out.

"What are you doing?" I asked, somewhat surprised when Harrison closed the door behind me instead of following me inside.

"Isn't it obvious? I'm wasting away while I wait for you to arrive," Devin said.

"Poor you."

"Does being poor make me even more handsome and dashing?" Devin asked, flashing me a white smile.

"No. It makes you pitiful."

"That wasn't quite the emotion I was looking for," Devin

chuckled as he sat up but did not get out of my chair. "So. You are staying."

"Yes," I said. "Who told you?"

"The snot-nosed elder Moonspell brat got to me five minutes before Madeline did," Devin said. "I'm hurt you didn't think to tell me yourself."

"I didn't think I would be able to reach you before Madeline. Aysel's strike comes as a surprise, though," I said.

"Not really," Devin said with a wry expression. "He wanted to wave your future contract in my face. Madeline mentioned you might come visit the Fairy Council, though," Devin said, his dashing smile returning.

"Yeah. I think I want to get a better feel for my options before I decide on what to major in," I said.

"That's wise," Devin said.

"Thanks."

"Will your parents be okay with it?"

"I was thinking about asking Doctor Creamintin to meet with them, so they would know I'm not throwing my life away on a no-good job. I think he'll be a calming influence. Or at the very least he'll remind them that my college will cost quite a bit so it's better that I go into the experience *knowing* what I want instead of jumping around."

"You've thought this out, haven't you?" Devin asked.

"Yep," I said. "Are you going to get out of my chair anytime soon?"

"No. You could sit on my lap," Devin mildly suggested.

"Devin," I rolled my eyes, making the Pooka laugh. I studied the dark haired shifter and thought about my conversation with Fran. Encouraged by my success with Harrison, I blurted out, "Would you stop flirting with other girls?"

"…What?" Devin said.

"Would you stop flirting with other girls? With other females?" I said, correcting myself.

Devin twitched two fingers at me in a 'come here' gesture. I scowled at the order but drew closer.

I was shocked when Devin reached out and cradled my hands in his. He looked up in my eyes, studying me as intently—if not more so—as I had studied Krad and Harrison minutes ago. "Okay," he said, kissing my hands.

My jaw almost dropped. "What?"

"Okay," he agreed. "You only had to ask," he added, as if it were my fault he was such a flirt in the first place.

"You make my head hurt," I grumbled.

"I would say that's fair compared to what you do to me," Devin dryly said. He stood up and wrapped his arms around me. "You're not even complaining. My, my! Who had a talk with you?"

"Fran," I said into Devin's shoulder.

"Does this mean if I confess my eternal love for you, you won't give me one of your dirty looks and call me a flirt?" Devin asked.

"You can't have eternal love for me. Since the day I met you in human form you've been perfectly honest that I am temporary."

"Come on. That was before I *knew* you. I thought me dragging you from the depths of ignorance so you would remember the MBRC proved my love," Devin said.

"And then you ignored me for several months."

"Only because I was worried you would be targeted if my affection was publically identified," Devin said, stroking my hair.

"Whatever."

Devin paused. "You mean you don't really know?"

"What should I know?"

"Morgan, I flirted with all those extra females for *you*."

I gave Devin a flat look.

The Pooka shook his head, a disturbingly serious look pasted on his face. "You don't get it. Morgan, I love you. As soon as that goes public you're going to be put in danger."

"Why? Because you're a Fairy Councilman?"

"No, because I'm the Pooka."

"So?"

"Of course you would see nothing special over that," Devin sighed. "There is only one Pooka at a time, and the title is passed from father to son. It's a powerful position."

"Yeah, I know. What does that have to do with me?"

"An adult Pooka is extremely difficult to kill. Between our shape shifting skills and magic wielding abilities, we have the survivability of a cockroach. So what would be the easiest way to kill off the Pooka line?"

"By murdering the Pooka's children before one has a chance to inherit the title," I slowly said.

"Exactly. It's a strategy some have tried for centuries, but obviously it hasn't worked. I'm here, after all. Well, in the past two generations, my family's enemies have grown even more ruthless," Devin said.

"Oh?"

"Yes. They've switched from targeting children, to targeting the Pooka's chosen wife."

I was silent.

The explanation filled in a lot of Devin's weird behavior—like the fact that most of his relationships hadn't lasted more than a week or two, and the erratic way he paraded around with other females but was a constant, solid presence in my life.

I look up at Devin with pursed lips. "I should punch you in the face for hiding all of this from me."

A warm smile teased across Devin's face. "Is that acceptance I hear? And in my defense, I thought you knew."

"You owe me a big apology for all the flirting."

"I do. I am sorry, much more so than you know."

I exhaled. "You couldn't have been more obvious that you like me?"

"Sweetheart, I told you just about every time we met."

"How was I supposed to take you seriously when you flirted with so many other females?"

"I haven't been that much of a flirt since you arrived in my life," Devin said. "I *am* loyal. Even if it takes the rest of our lives, I will prove it. And I promise you I will never love another woman besides you."

When I hugged Devin back and his warmth surrounded me, it felt incredibly good. His touch was soft and his embrace smashed all my doubts and worries to pieces. But when I looked up at Devin I had to gulp. His eyes held something warm, and powerful, and *big*.

Something that looked terrifyingly close to the way Asahi and Kadri look at each other.

"I don't think I'm ready for this," I said. "At least, I'm not ready to be as serious as you might be. As I think you might be."

"That's okay," Devin said, kissing my temple. "We have to take it slow anyway. Madeline said she would cut off my family jewels if I laid a finger on you before you had a career launched. She would do it, too."

I stiffly laughed.

"Morgan," Devin said, stepping back so he could place his hands on my shoulders and look me in the eyes. "Your future is what consumes you right now, and I understand that. It's okay. I've waited two years without any trouble. I can wait a few years more—as long as I get open access to you. And more hugs with less complaints," he said, winking.

"Deal," I said, something bubbling in my chest. "Thank you, Devin."

"You're welcome, sweetheart," Devin said, hugging me again.

We embraced for a few seconds before Devin added, "This might be awkward timing to bring it up, but I need to make sure that you want kids, right?"

"Yeah. A few—I don't want a pack, though."

"Good," Devin said. "We just need a few."

"Yeah…the Pooka thing," I said. "Is that brat going to drive me crazy?"

"Possibly. If it's any consolation, historically Pookas adore their mothers. It's their Pooka fathers they can't stand."

"Oh really?" I said, brightening. "That's not so bad."

"I thought you might take comfort in that," Devin dryly said.

"I do. Thanks," I said, squirming out of Devin's hug. "Okay, I have one last condition."

"What?"

"You have to meet my parents. I hide so much about my work

from them already. I don't want to hide our relationship—our extremely *casual* and not serious relationship—from them."

"Deal, but only if I can meet with your student council friend—Fran, you said?—beforehand."

I eyed the mischievous shape shifter. "Why?"

"Because I'm going to need all the help I can get with impressing your parents. Fran will help me. She seems like a good soul companion."

"Deal," I agreed. "You know...This is a lot less romantic than I thought it would be."

Devin laughed. "Morgan, I have a lifetime to shower all my love and affection on you. Just *wait.* I haven't even started yet."

"Is that a promise?"

"That's a guarantee," Devin said before kissing me square on the lips.

I was shocked by the sudden gesture, and I was even more shocked by how *right* it felt.

Man, was Fran going to give me one heck-of-an '*I told you so.*'

I will **not** end my story saying we lived happily ever after. Devin and I have an understanding—or as he would call it, a bond of love—but life isn't smooth sailing after you find your significant other.

I graduated high school with Fran. Fran headed off to Florida. It took Ethan four months of busting his butt to complete classes and get a special license, but he arrived in Florida only a month after Fran started college.

Yes, they are in a serious dating relationship.

Asahi and Kadri got married during a three-day-three-night party. Let me tell you *that* was a real circus. They had enough food to feed an army, and we had to reenact their engagement no less than eight times. (Let me go on record to say that I still *hate* the lute.)

None of my other students are in a serious romantic relationship, but I do suspect Frank will soon work up the guts to ask out Madeline. The two have been a pair since I first met Madeline. I'm pretty sure the only reason Madeline doesn't see it coming is that it hasn't occurred to her that it *isn't* coming.

Aysel is now in some pandering position that reports directly to the MBRC board. He's the one who drew up my employee contract, and he never lets me forget it. Since he knows I'm staying at the MBRC we've started getting along slightly better. (Don't tell anyone, but we are forming secret plans for MBRC domination.)

Hunter is still Hunter. He's suave, flirtatious, and sends me baked goods whenever he needs a good word put in at the MBRC for him. He and Aysel are actually starting to get along better—which is probably better for the MBRC's future.

Fidem is still out there. Losing Krad did cripple them a little, but I have no doubt they will be back, just as anti-human as before. Krad still snarls at me whenever I come to visit him, but the minotaurs told me that he eats whatever snacks I bring him when he is put back in his cell.

I think there's hope for him. I don't think I'll be the one to make him totally change his mind, but I would at least like to soften the ground for whoever that is.

Which brings us back to Devin and me. I can't say I ever really pictured marrying a famous shape shifter—I have already been attacked three times by various factions since we reached our… understanding—but I'm starting to look forward to it. It's still a long ways off, but Devin has been a dream since our talk. I am deliriously happy with my future, and I'm so glad it's Devin that I'll be spending it with.

So Dave…if you're reading this I owe you an apology and my thanks. If you hadn't blown my world open, I never would have met any of these people, and I love them all. Thank you, Dave, for being a bald, fat, vampire.

THE END

A Special Note From the Author

This sequel was made because of the votes of readers and fans. In April 2014 I held a poll to see which book readers most wanted to see a sequel to. Vampires Drink Tomato Juice *won!*

Additionally, after a cut-throat contest, three readers/champions were given the chance to name three characters in this book. I would like to thank Tricia *for her goblin name, Harrison;* Celia *for her fairy name, Baobab; and* Erin *for her dwarf name, Grogrintork.*

I also want to extend a special thanks to all the Honorable Mentions. These guys came up with some incredible names, I wish I could have used them all. Thanks again to: Lindsay, Chotley, Kelly, Lorelei, Nicole S., Joan, Nicole K., Jean, *and* Lesslie.

An author's greatest asset is her readers, and I am so blessed to have such a great crew. Thank you to everyone who participated!

The Lost Files of the Magical Beings' Rehabilitation Center

AN MBRC SHORT STORY ANTHOLOGY

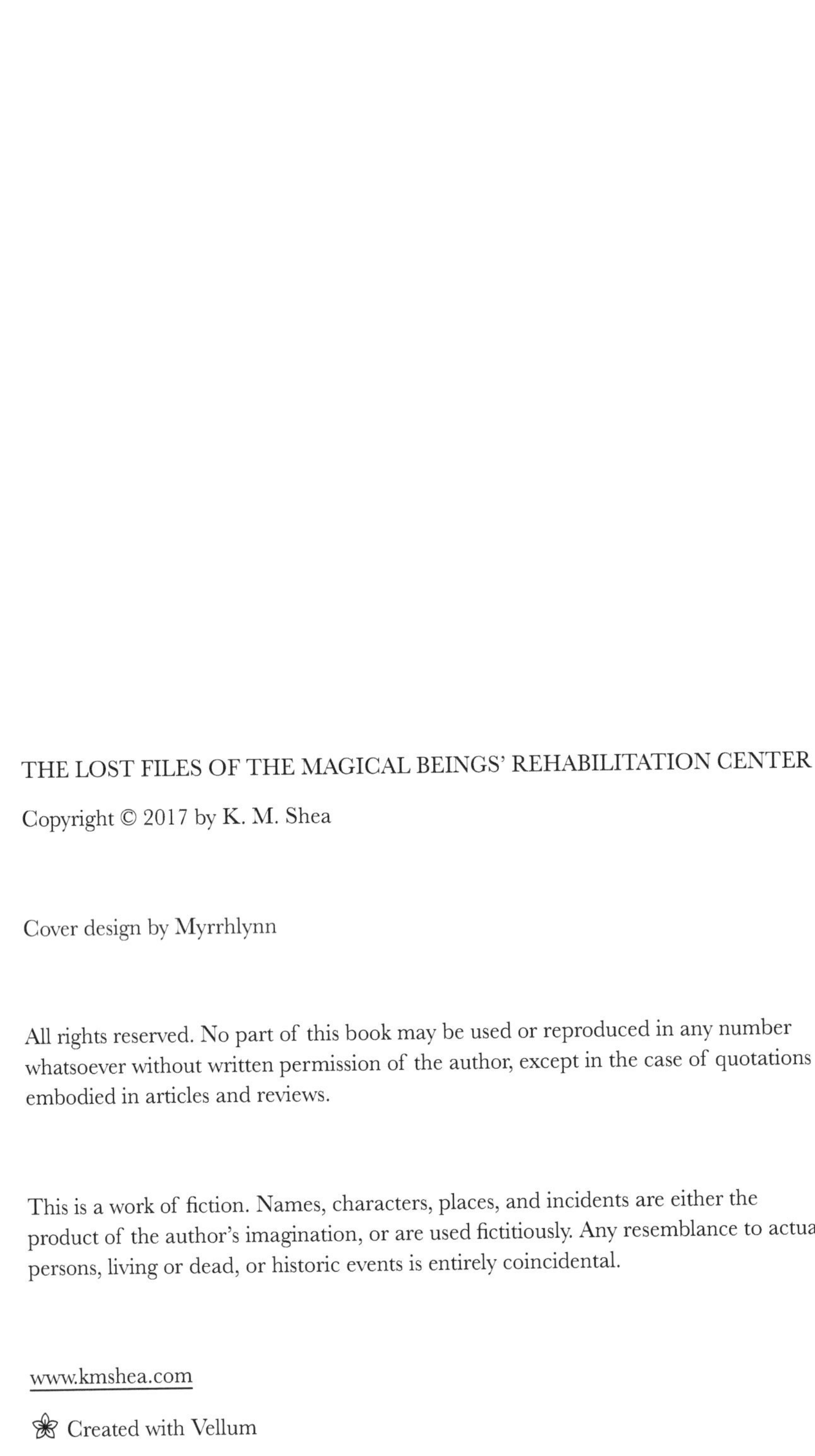

THE LOST FILES OF THE MAGICAL BEINGS' REHABILITATION CENTER

Cover design by Myrrhlynn

www.kmshea.com

Created with Vellum

1

A Magical Birthday

(AGE 21)

I wasn't planning anything special for my twenty-first birthday. I had some MBRC work piled up, and I hadn't finished all my college homework. I couldn't even think about celebrating with all my group assignments pushing down on me. But Madeline wouldn't leave me alone.

"Kerrick says a human's twenty-first birthday is a rite of passage," Madeline said, her arms folded across her chest.

"Cha. Sure is, bra," Kerrick—a so called "Beer Brother," a dark elf, and an ex-member of the hateful Fidem organization—snorted. He was wearing a football jersey and sunglasses, even though it was already after sunset.

I rubbed my eyes. "It's kind of a thing, but I have too much work."

"Too bad. You only turn twenty-one once," Madeline said, smoothing the skirts of her hot pink dress.

"It doesn't matter. I have responsibilities—"

"Okay, we gotta go. Now," Frey said, barging into my bedroom.

"What are *you* doing here?" I asked.

"I'm part of your celebration escort," Frey said.

"My what?"

"Doesn't matter, we gotta get going. Your little brother tried talking to Frank, and he started hyperventilating."

"What, and you think a night in town will ease his delicate nerves?" I asked.

"Out. Now," Frey decreed, jabbing a finger at me.

"Fine," I groaned.

"Boxy and I are driving," Kerrick said, jingling the car keys of his Ford Focus.

"What? No!" I said, leaping from my desk chair.

Frey rolled his eyes. "Come on, Morgan. He's not as bad as Vlad."

"You can sit in front." Madeline patted my hand.

"M-Madeline?" Frank called from downstairs. His voice was strained.

"Coming!" Madeline said, mercilessly yanking me from my room and down the stairs.

"Um, guys, are you sure about this? This place seems pretty exclusive," I said, trotting behind Boxy—another Beer Brother. There was a long line leading down the sidewalk, which Boxy ignored.

"Totally," Shale—one of two female Beer Brothers—said. She swiped a manicured hand through the air. "We go way back with the owner."

"Wait, is it owned by a magical being?" I asked. I was turning around, trying to see Harrison, but my goblin guard must have decided to lurk farther back than usual, as I didn't see him.

"Yep," Boxy said, flipping up the collar of his polo as he led the way around a corner. "Here we go—awesome! Sky Screech is the bouncer tonight. Dude! Sky! What's up, man?"

"You've got to be kidding me," I said, staring at the club's name—which was lit up with bright lights.

"What?" Madeline asked, tugging Frank along behind her.

"I know, right?" Frey nodded at me.

The magic-owned club was named *Dragon's Den*. And judging by the bouncer's name, it was probably run by dragons.

"Sky! Wicked glamour, bra," Kerrick said, flicking down his sunglasses so he could study the troll-sized bouncer.

The bouncer lifted a hand to inspect it and shrugged. "The Boss made a deal with a couple of fairies from France. Our old charms kept dropping at…inopportune moments. You want in?" his voice was deep and vibrated in my bones. He was easy to hear above the chatter of the line.

"Totally," Boxy said, rocking back on his heels. "Everyone here?"

"Hunter isn't," Madeline said.

"Hunter is coming?" I asked, brightening at the mention of my long-time friend. I saw him frequently—he was in half of my college classes—but it would still be great if he joined my impromptu party. He was fun to hang with, but he also had the magical ability to persuade people, bending them to his will. If something went wrong—and with the company I was keeping, it was likely—he would help Harrison and me clean it up.

"He said he would meet us here," Frank said, edging away from the humans waiting in line. Some of them were starting to watch us with curiosity.

"Hunter Weller is twenty and is not of the legal age necessary to enter *Dragon's Den*," Sky Screech said, his brows lowering over his craggy nose.

"Come on, Sky. We're not gonna drink," Shale said, adjusting her perky pony-tail.

"Of that, I am aware," the dragon-bouncer rumbled.

"We're celebrating Morgan Fae's birthday," Madeline said. "You can't celebrate Morgan's birthday without the overbearing Hunter skulking around."

"Yeah," Frey chimed in. "Who else would bankroll our drinks?"

"Our non-alcoholic drinks," Kerrick added.

"*Dragon's Den* will not test the law—human or magical. No one underage is allowed inside," Sky Screech firmly said. "Now are you entering, or not?"

"What do you think, dudes?" Kerrick asked.

"We can text Hunter inside," Frey said.

"Yeah, and *Dragon's Den* is only number one on the list, right? Maybe we can link up with him somewhere else," Madeline said.

"Wait, there's a *list*?" I asked.

"Yeah, twenty-one clubs for twenty-one years—some of them Hunter *owns*. He'll totally be able to get into those," Boxy said, pulling a piece of paper from the pocket of his polo.

"If I get a drink at each club, I will be more than intoxicated; I'll probably be comatose from alcohol poisoning," I said.

"Don't worry; you're not getting alcoholic drinks either," Kerrick said, patting my shoulder.

"Then why on earth are we going *clubbing*?" I asked and was ignored.

"Alright, we're ready. Could you let us in, Sky?" Shale asked, propping a hand on her hip.

Sky Screech moved aside, letting us through the door. "Happy Birthday, Morgan Fae," he said as I slipped past him. "Enjoy your evening."

"Thank you," I said, following my friends inside, gaping at the innards of *Dragon's Den*.

I hadn't been inside a club before—not only do I believe in following laws, but I also didn't have the time or inclination to prance around in one alone, as the only one likely to join me (my best human friend, Fran), went to school states away—but *Dragon's Den* not only exceeded my expectations, but it set an impossibly high bar.

Dragons Den didn't have any of the regular pulsing, seizure-inducing lights you see in a normal club. Instead, the ceiling and the walls were decorated with hundreds of tiny lights that winked and sparkled like stars. The floor was smooth rock that looked like the ground of a cave, and the few tables and chairs that bordered the club were large and chunky—built to withstand a lot of weight. The air was surprisingly cool in spite of all the bodies smashed into the club, and there was a distinct *wind* that blew through the place.

"What do you think?" Frey asked, shouting over the music.

"It's totally awesome! I love the ceiling."

"It's 'posed to make you feel like you're flying," Boxy said.

"That must be why they have the breeze. It's really refreshing, but I do *not* want to know what their air conditioning bill is," I said.

"It can't be too high," Shale said, rocking back and forth with the music. "The air temperature is regulated by the staff. A few frost fairies and ice dragons are on the payroll. Kerrick, let's go get Morgan her first drink!"

"I'm coming, too," Madeline said, slipping after the two dark elves.

Frank moved to follow Madeline but chose to slip into my shadow when he saw how she had to push through the crowds to approach the bar. "It's loud," he said, pulling his shoulders up so his neck almost disappeared.

"Yeah, there's a reason most humans are stone-deaf when they get old," Frey said, rubbing his ears.

I felt my phone buzz in my clutch, alerting me to a text message from Hunter.

Sky Screech is a wingless worm.

"Hunter's here, and Sky still isn't letting him inside," I reported, interpreting the message.

"Tell the little bro to chill. We'll only be ten minutes," Boxy said, looking at his wristwatch. "Gotta keep a tight schedule if we want to hit all twenty-one clubs."

I was typing out the reply and almost dropped my phone when Kerrick presented me with my drink. It was smoldering, had a lit sparkler poking out of it, and was a pearly white color.

"Ta-da! One non-alcoholic Dragon's Breath!" Kerrick said. "They whipped it up special for you—normally it's got enough booze in it to tip a cow."

"Happy twenty-first birthday, Morgan Fae!" Shale said,

bumping her glass against mine. After she and Madeline distributed the drinks—varying flavors of soda—we waited until the sparkler died before I took a swig.

My drink was smooth—like a shake—though not as thick, and it tasted like a perfectly toasted marshmallow with a hint of burnt sugar.

"Only take a few sips. You gotta have room for twenty more drinks," Kerrick told me as he chewed on an ice cube.

My phone buzzed again.

I'm having my car pulled around—and at least one of my clubs better be on that stupid list.

"Hunter's ready for us," I said.

"Great, we're out of time anyway. Next club!" Shale said, plucking my drink from my hand.

"This is really good. Why don't we have this stuff in the MBRC?" Madeline asked, downing her cup of Mountain Dew.

"Getting it stocked would be a pain," I said.

"Come on, let's move, people. Next club!" Kerrick declared.

"Make sure Hunter can get into this one," Frey said, slapping cash into Boxy's hand.

"Onward!" Madeline declared, pointing to the door. "Let us find more mountains of dew!"

"Thanks for coming, Hunter," I said as I walked arm-in-arm with him. "Everything might go okay since we're only staying in each club for less than twenty minutes, but you can never tell."

"No. You must proceed with caution if you continue to let your vampire and scruffy werewolf friends run loose," Hunter said.

"So where are we going now?" Madeline asked, skipping past Hunter and me.

"The *Tea Room,*" Kerrick said, flicking up his sunglasses so he could read a street sign.

"Is it owned by a magical being?" I asked.

"No, but it's managed by one, and all the staff are magical. Up this way," Shale said, her pony tail bobbing as she led the way up a set of stairs.

This club didn't have a line, but men in crisp suits and women wearing beautiful, flowing dresses entered ahead of us. Before they were let inside, they had to present cards—which explained the lack of a line.

I gulped. The place had to be really exclusive if it was members only.

There were two bouncers by this club's ornate, wooden door. They had pasty white complexions, were neatly and meticulous dressed, and even I could smell the heavy dosing of cologne they wore.

"Vampires?" I asked.

"Acquaintances of Madeline's, I think," Hunter said.

My vampire friend skipped to the front of the line, her hot-pink dress glowing in the streetlights. "Hello Victor, Bromwell," Madeline said.

"Good evening, Miss Madeline. Your table is prepared," one of the bouncers said. "You may enter."

"Except for the honorable Hunter Weller. We regret to inform you that as you are under the legal drinking age, we cannot allow you into our establishment," the second bouncer said.

"You've got to be kidding me," Hunter said.

"Oh, but we're not gonna drink," Kerrick said, giving the bouncers a thumbs up.

"So Miss Madeline claimed. Unfortunately, the law is the law," the bouncer said, unmoved.

Hunter growled and dropped my arm. "Harrison, are you feeling generous enough to help me?"

My massive goblin bodyguard—who was employed by my boyfriend, Devin, rumbled, "Miss Fae?"

"It would be nice," I said.

Harrison nodded, his bald head shining in the dim light. "Yes, Miss Fae."

"Great, thanks," Hunter said before turning to Frey. "Watch her. Harrison and I will be in shortly."

"Sure thing," Frey said, rubbing his fingers together in the international gesture for money.

Hunter rolled his topaz-colored eyes and slapped a crisp one hundred dollar bill in Frey's hands. "Use it—if I find out you hoarded it, I will kill you and hang your pelt in my office," Hunter warned before he retreated a few steps to speak with Harrison.

"Come on, Morgan. You'll *love* this place. It's so pretty," Madeline said, impatiently pushing the doors open before the bouncers could stop her.

The bouncers frowned and stepped back to open the doors for me. "Happy Birthday, Miss Fae," they said in unison.

"Thank you," I said, smiling at them.

The *Tea Room* was nothing like a club. It was more of a lounge, and it had beautiful antique furniture arranged in separated spaces, chandeliers, gold candlesticks, and patterned, pale pink, Victorian wallpaper.

"Wow," I said, feeling shabby and underdressed in my best pair of jeans, black boots, and black blouse.

"Party for Miss Fae? This way, please," said an elegant hostess. Judging by her pronounced canines that flashed when she smiled, she was a vampire, too. She led us to a private inlet. I sat on a white, velvet sofa. Madeline plopped down next to me, but everyone else seated themselves in polished armchairs.

"Glad you had contacts here, Maddy. We've never been in here," Kerrick, said, straining his neck so he could look at the rest of the club.

Madeline clapped her hands in excitement. "I ordered ahead, so our drinks should arrive soon."

"Great, I'll go pay off our tab," Frey said, shaking the bill Hunter gave him.

"Hunter?" I said, cocking my head as the blond-haired business tycoon strode towards us, Harrison at his shoulder. "You used your persuasion magic?"

"How else did you think I was going to get in? Bribery?" Hunter scoffed, seating himself on my other side.

"I'm just impressed you made it at all," I said.

"Just because *you're* immune to my powers of persuasion does not mean I am weak," Hunter said, his voice tight.

"Oohh, our drinks! Woah, what did you get us, Maddy?" Shale asked.

"Tea. The *Tea Room* only serves brandy and some wines. But they're renowned for their tea, so I ordered some for us! Morgan, you have the rooibos vanilla honeybush."

The teas were served in delicate, china cups painted with flowers and rimmed with gold.

I took several sips of my drink—which had a soft, sweet flavor sprinkled with brown sugar and earthy undertones. "It's really good," I said.

Madeline hugged me, almost sloshing my cup. "I'm glad you like it! Happy birthday!"

"Where's the bathroom?" Frank whispered.

Madeline released me and jumped from the sofa. "I'll show you."

As she and Frank made their exit, Frey returned to the group. "Our tab is paid. How much time do we have left?"

"Eight minutes," Kerrick said. In spite of his sunglasses and football jersey, he held his delicate china cup with elegance and assurance—his posture straight as he primly sipped his cup of tea.

Our hostess glided by. She stopped and looked at Hunter with narrowed eyes. "Mr. Weller," she said, frowning in displeasure.

"Don't mind me," Hunter said, smiling at her. His topaz-colored eyes glittered in the shimmering chandelier light.

"I beg your pardon, but I must insist that you leave the premise of this building, Mr. Weller, as you have not yet reached the age required by American laws to drink."

Hunter leaned forward, his eyes fixed on the hostess. "You needn't worry. I won't drink. You can go about your work."

"The issue has nothing to do with worry and everything to do with your age," the hostess said dryly as she signaled a male attendant. "And your persuasive techniques shant do you any good."

"Come along, Mr. Weller," the male vampire said.

Hunter stood with a growl and looked to Harrison.

The goblin guard shrugged. "They aren't bothering Miss Fae."

"Your loyalty is astounding," Hunter said, giving his ex-employee a withering glare.

"We'll see you shortly," Boxy said, daintily stirring his tea with a silver spoon.

As soon as the attendant began escorting Hunter out, Madeline and Frey scurried through the lounge.

"We have leave—*now*," Madeline said, a smile plastered on her face.

I set my tea aside and bolted up. "What did you do?"

"Nothing, nothing at all. Right, Frank?"

"Right," Frank said, nodding emphatically.

There was a boom at the back of the club.

"*You*!" I hissed.

"Later!" Frey said, hauling me towards the door. "You can yell at her later. Our first priority is to get out of here!"

"Rad tea. We'll have to rate this place on Yelp," Kerrick said, setting his tea aside and following us.

"Totally," Shale said. "We'll have to become members. Maddy, can you hook us up?" she asked as we exited the *Tea Room* in a herd.

"Of course," Madeline said as the door closed behind her.

There was a second boom, this one so loud it shook the building.

"I told you that you shouldn't have adjusted the display case," Frank said, tugging on his black necklace—which was really a flea collar.

"It was a ring! How was I supposed to know touching would activate it?" Madeline whined.

"Hunter, get your car pulled around, STAT!" Frey yelled.

"Enjoy your birthday evening, Miss Fae," the vampire bouncers said.

"Thanks," I said. "I'll try."

"Stop dawdling, Morgan, and come on!" Frey barked.

"Yeah, I'm coming," I said. The building rumbled again, and I scowled at Madeline.

"What?" she asked, fluttering her eyes at me.

"I can't take you anywhere."

"That's hurtful!"

"Then don't ruin places!"

"The car is here. Come on," Boxy said.

"Seriously," Shale said, rolling her eyes. "Vampires are the worst when you ruin their stuff."

"Stop talking and get in the car!" Frey yelled.

"Happy birthday, indeed," I muttered.

By bar number twelve, my bladder was ready to explode.

"What club are we going to now?" Madeline asked, fluffing her hair and ignoring the long line of hopeful club attendees that we walked past.

"*Carousel*," Boxy said, looking at the list.

"You'll love this one," Shale promised. "They have a huge carousel built in the center of the place—it's where the bars are—and you can sit on carousel horses instead of chairs."

"That's really great, but I'm mostly concerned with locating the nearest bathroom," I said, feeling the squeeze. After consuming so many drinks—even though I only took a few sips of each—I needed to use the bathroom, *badly*.

"That's cool. Boxy's bra is the bouncer here. Get us in, Boxman," Kerrick said.

"Gotcha," Boxy said, waving to the tall bouncer—who was a troll if I ever saw one.

"If I'm not allowed in this club either, I'm going to purchase every club that has denied me service," Hunter scowled.

"You couldn't afford to—they've *all* denied you service," Frey hooted.

"That reminds me, Morgan. I saw some of your cyclops friends yesterday. They said to tell you happy birthday," Madeline said, jumping in place next to me.

"That's wonderful," I said, shifting uncomfortably, wishing for the bathroom. Harrison stood just behind me, an impressively tall and reassuring black shadow.

"Kay, guys. We can go in!" Boxy said, gesturing for us to follow him inside.

"Except for the younger goblin," the troll grunted.

"What? How do *you* know I'm not twenty-one?" Hunter stormed.

"Should we go in?" Frank asked, his eyes flicking worriedly from Hunter to the door.

"Yeah. By the time he finally talks his way in—*if* he talks his way in, it will be time for us to leave," I said, my desire for a bathroom making me ruthless.

"I dunno. When that female bouncer at *Stardust* tazed him, it was worth sticking around to see," Frey said.

"We're going in!" I said, hurrying to catch up with Boxy.

"Morgan?"

I spun around to see two girls with three guys standing at the front of the line. I recognized them all from my school, and I had classes with one of the guys and both girls. They were in one of the few classes I did *not* have with Hunter, and they were also in one of my group projects but had so far resisted doing any of the work.

"Oh…hi, Tad, Lindsey," I said.

Lindsey was chewing gum, which she chewed loudly as she raised her sculpted eyebrows at me. "There's a line," she said.

"She's with us," Frey said, throwing an arm over my shoulder and tugging me away.

"Come on," Kerrick shouted, standing in the doorway. "We've only got thirteen minutes left here."

As I turned to follow my magical friends, I heard Tad snort.

"Stuck up brat thinks she's better than us. She's gotta be bangin' one of those guys to get in."

I rolled my eyes, intending to ignore his childish words, but then someone screamed.

I whipped around to find Harrison standing next to Tad with one of his big hands wrapped around the college student's throat. "You will refrain from insulting Miss Fae."

"Harrison, stop!" I shouted.

"And in we go," Frey said, yanking along.

"We have to stop him! Violence isn't the answer…unless it's against Aysel," I said.

"Maybe, but I'm not going to try separating a goblin from his target. Plus that punk needs to be taught a lesson. Didn't you have to go to the bathroom?"

"But—"

"Well done, Harrison. Indeed, if I hear of you slandering Morgan Fae again, frat-boy, I will have you sued for slander and underwater in debt before you can blink." Hunter said, squatting down in front of Tad, who was now kneeling on the ground.

"Aren't you going to stop him?" I asked the bouncer.

"Nah," the troll said.

Before I could further protest, Frey pulled me inside and helped me find a restroom. As soon as I left the bathroom, Shale shoved a drink in my hand. "Get sipping, girl! We've got nine more bars left to visit!"

"You've got to be joking," Hunter said, his face folded in a storm cloud.

"I'm afraid not, sir. As you have not yet turned twenty-one, we cannot allow you inside," the bouncer—a tall, muscled female —said.

"I *own* this place!" Hunter yelled, pointing at the glowing *Firefly* sign hung above the club.

"And you told us to follow human laws to the letter," the female bouncer—one of the rarely spotted female goblins—said, as she studied her nails.

"I would never say something so stupid," Hunter declared.

"I wanna go home," I groaned, leaning into Harrison's arm for support.

"Come on, Morgan. It's the last club! You can do this!" Madeline said, pumping her arm.

"I want to *sleep*!" I growled.

"If you do not allow me inside, I will have you fired," Hunter threatened his employee.

"That's fine, sir. You have a lovely severance package, and your older brother has made me several lucrative job offers already," the female bouncer said.

"What?" Hunter stiffened.

"That's rough, bra," Kerrick said, flicking up his sunglasses to give Hunter a look of sympathy.

"Harrison," I said.

"Yes, Miss Fae?"

"Please take care of this and get us inside—*all* of us," I said.

"Yes, Miss Fae," Harrison said. He leaned me up against a building and strode up to the female bouncer, murmuring to her in lowered tones.

"That's a pretty tall order, Morgan. Harrison hasn't worked with Weller Goblin Enterprises since you were in high school," Frey said, watching my bodyguard.

"Doesn't matter. Krusher can solve any problem," I said, my faith absolute.

"We can go in, Miss Fae," Harrison announced.

"Hunter, too?"

"Yes, Miss Fae."

"You're the greatest, Krusher," I said leading the way inside since everyone else seemed content to linger outside. "That's why you're—why is it dark in here?"

"SURPRISE!"

I shrieked as all the lights in the club were flicked on, revealing a huge crowd that had gathered. Nick, Sandy, Ralph, and a number of my other cyclops friends were present, as were Perseus and his emo equine friends, his father Orion, Corona and Toby from the helpdesk, Dr. Creamintin, a number of my old students—including

Esmeralda, a sphinx, three fairies, a wood elf, Asahi and his wife Kadri—and a bunch of MBRC employees, like Aysel, Grogrintork, Baobab, and more.

I placed a hand over my heart and stared at the huge assembly.

"Happy birthday!" Esmeralda shouted.

"May it be a blessed year," Dr. Creamintin said.

"Happy Birthday!"

"Felicitations on another year!"

"Happy birthday—on behalf of the Silver Heights Dwarf Clan!"

"May the stars shine down upon you and illuminate the depths of your innermost."

"Congratulations!

Above the clamor of well wishes, I heard a voice as smooth as chocolate say, "Happy birthday, Sweetheart." Out of the crowd stepped my charming boyfriend, Devin the Pooka, who had told me he was going to be stuck in Britain with the Fairy Council for my birthday.

"Devin!" I beamed, launching myself at him. He kissed my cheek as everyone laughed and gave awws of approval.

"What's going on?" I asked, peeking out at the guests.

"It's a surprise party—for you!" Nick said with a beaming smile.

"But I, how?" I stammered.

"Madeline and Devin did most of the organizing, but they enlisted Hunter and the Beer Brothers so they could really pull one on you," Esmeralda said, gesturing at the crowd with her soda can.

"I brought you a gift," Devin said, turning me so I faced a different wall.

"Happy Birthday, Morgan," Fran, my human BFF, said, her smile as bright as the sun as she stood with her dark elf boyfriend, Ethan.

"Fran!" I yelped, abandoning my boyfriend for my best friend. "Oh, my gosh, you're here!"

"Yep! For the weekend—and I'm taking off school on Monday, too! You, Madeline, and me are gonna go shopping! Your lovely boyfriend is paying, of course," Fran said, her smile turning mischievous.

"You have no idea how much legwork I had to perform to get her legally invited to an MBRC-sponsored party," Devin said dryly as Fran and I squealed and embraced again.

"Thank you, Devin," I said, stepping away from Fran long enough to grab Devin by the front of his dress shirt and drag him down an inch or two so I could kiss him.

Devin smiled down at me after I pulled away. "It was well worth it, if it makes you this happy."

"Awesome party, bra!" Kerrick said, giving me a thumbs up.

"Madeline, Frank, Frey, Hunter, Harrison, Kerrick, Shale, and Boxy—*thank you*," I said, tears of joy stinging my eyes. "Thank you for hauling me out of my room and bringing me here."

"Is it a night you'll remember?" Madeline asked, eagerly wriggling like a puppy.

I laughed. "Absolutely. This is the best birthday, ever!"

THE END

2

Swindlers

(AGE 25 & AGE 23)

"Morgan! You look fantastic, chicka! Married life certainly suits you."

I choked when Esmeralda squeezed me in a hug so tight my breathing was restricted. "Good to see you, too, Esmeralda," I said, patting her on the back. Although I hadn't seen her since my wedding—and only briefly then—she hadn't aged a day. It was a "perk" of being a vampire.

"Do you have your bags?" I asked.

"Yep, I only brought this," Esmeralda said, kicking a black, rolling suitcase.

"Awesome. Let's go. I parked in the hourly parking garage across the street, and they really take you to town with parking fees," I said, leading the way out of the airport.

"Thanks for coming to pick me up," Esmeralda grunted as she dragged her suitcase behind her. "With the vampire conference starting today, just about all safe transportation services are booked up."

"It's my pleasure."

"No, seriously. I feel kinda bad, asking an MBRC Department Head to pick *me* up."

"We're friends, Esmeralda. I don't mind. Besides, it's in my best interest that the conference runs smoothly, and I want you there to keep Madeline on a tight leash," I confided.

"Gotcha," Esmeralda laughed. "Congrats, by the way. The Public Relations department is way lucky to have you. Didn't Aysel get promoted at the same time, too? What's his title now?"

"He's working his way up the Administration Department."

"I bet he's aiming for Administrator. Everyone knows Administrator Moonspell is totally trying to bag a seat with the Fairy Council," Esmeralda said.

"Yeah," I acknowledged as we entered the parking garage, the click of my high heels echoing loudly in the barren structure. "But Administrator Moonspell won't snag a seat for at least another year or two, thankfully," I said, leading the way to my car.

"Nice ride," Esmeralda whistled as I popped the trunk and helped her heave her suitcase inside.

"Thanks," I grunted.

On an extreme whim, I had bought a Lexus sedan—which the MBRC had considerably subsidized for me as I was one of a few department heads/persons of influence who could drive. This meant I frequently had to chauffeur high-profile guests around.

"Okay, we haven't had time for girl talk in *ages*, so you have to spill," Esmeralda said as we climbed into my car.

I paused to wave at Harrison as he glided out of our shadow and slipped into his car. The stone-faced goblin was parked directly behind me, probably pouting because I wouldn't let him drive Esmeralda and me.

"Spill about what?" I asked, twisting in my seat and looking suspiciously around the parking garage for crazies who might hit my precious car as I backed up.

"How Devin got you to marry him," Esmeralda said. "I mean, Madeline totally called that you two were going to get married when you were still in high school, but neither of us thought he would actually wear you down until you were like…thirty. I thought you wouldn't be engaged at least until *after* you were out of college."

"Oh. Yeah. That's what I was planning," I acknowledged as I backed up. "But Devin swindled me into it."

"He *what?*"

"It's a long story."

"I've got the rest of the drive."

I was in my first semester of my senior year at college when Devin made his move. I was already twenty-three—I took a year off to work with the MBRC and the Fairy Council before entering college. I was eager to snap through the university system, so I had stupidly filled my schedule, cramming the usual four-year program into three. (It helped that the summer I spent with the Fairy Council counted as an internship and gained me a hefty number of college credits.)

As a result of this ambition, my semesters were quite full, and finals were always an…*interesting* experience.

"Morgan, are you really certain you need *all* these books?" Devin asked, swiveling a stack of textbooks so he could study the titles.

"Yes. Thanks, Krusher," I said, taking an armload of books from Harrison and dropping them on my desk. We were in my office at the MBRC—with the door locked to avoid any interruptions during my study session. "Is this everything? I think this is everything. No, I forgot my drinks!"

"The cases of Red Bull in your trunk, right?" Devin asked, slipping his hand into my jean pocket to snag my keys. "I'll bring them here."

"Could you bring my coffee thermos, too?" I asked.

"Red Bull doesn't contain enough caffeine for you?"

"Never!" I said.

"Even though it's probably the cause of your eyebrow twitch?" Devin asked.

I self-consciously slapped a hand over my left eyebrow—which had started jumping up and down the week before when I began gearing up for finals.

Devin chuckled. "You don't have to hide it. ***I*** think it's adorable," he said. He tried kissing me on the lips, but I moved at the last moment, so he got my cheek.

"One day, Morgan, I will get you," Devin promised.

"Mmm, I need my Red Bull."

Devin rolled his eyes as he slipped on a black coat. "Sometimes I think you confuse the title of boyfriend with butler."

"Thanks, Devin," I said as the Pooka walked to the door.

Devin winked. "I will miss you as I miss air when I hold my breath," he said before ducking out of the room to avoid the pencil bag I chucked at his head.

"Krusher, I think I have questionable taste in boyfriends," I said.

"Yes, Miss Fae," Harrison said, drawing a grin from me.

Devin and I had what could very loosely be considered a relationship. Between my crazy school schedule and his position as a Councilmember with the Fairy Council, both of us were incredibly busy and saw each other infrequently.

I trusted Devin not to wander—since we started "dating" when I was still a senior in high school, he had cut off all dalliances and appeared to be fine—if not thriving—in his new monogamous status. However, I never considered the two of us "serious," as we hardly saw each other.

My finals were the first time I was seeing Devin since the semester started—although we conversed through Magic Mirrors once or twice a week. We were just…low-key. I didn't mind the lack of pressure; I enjoyed it, even.

That was how Devin was so easily able to swindle me.

But I'm getting off track here.

While Devin retrieved my energy drinks, I set up my work station. I piled my textbooks in the order I would need them, dug up my notes, and had just started going through them when my door flew open.

I looked up to see who had managed to open my *locked* door, and my lip curled up in disgust. "What do *you* want?" I snarled.

"It is beyond me how the bulk of the MBRC board finds you 'charming,'" Aysel said, looking at me like I was a bug he found in his food.

"I'm busy. I don't have time to play with you today," I said.

Aysel looked repulsed. "I did not come here to *play*; I came to make an offer."

"A what?"

Aysel took a stack of study guides off a chair positioned in front of my desk and placed them on the floor. "You will graduate next semester, so it is time you thought about procuring a job."

"The MBRC has already offered me a fulltime job in the teaching department," I said.

"So I heard. I want you to reject it."

"And *why* should I play to *your* whims?"

"Because I have a better offer to make."

I guiltily glanced at my textbooks before I leaned back in my chair. "I'm listening."

"The MBRC hasn't expanded since it was initially built, even though every year we receive more requests to hold conferences, to expand our available curriculum, and requests from magical beings looking to enter our rehabilitation program."

"So?"

"I believe it is time for the MBRC to facilitate new programs and enter into new revenue streams. It is Chicago—not New York or LA—that is becoming the magical center of America. If the MBRC is to remain the number one rehabilitation center in the world, we must change to match the growing interest of the magical community. There have been *some* changes in the most recent years, most of them sparked by you. In that light, I would like to ask you to enter a business partnership with me."

I almost fell out of my chair in surprise. Aysel—the resident know-it-all—was asking *me* to partner with him? "Why?" I said when I finally got my mouth working.

Aysel scowled. "Although I clearly have superior Administration capabilities, I would be remiss if I did not admit your abilities to spark change and move people are perhaps…greater than my own."

I stared at Aysel, my brain silent with shock. "My head is filled with studying schedules right now, Aysel, so I need you to be upfront. What is your end-goal?"

"I wish for us to be Co-Administrators of the MBRC."

"*Co*-Administrators?" I echoed, shocked to the core. Everyone knew Aysel was ruthlessly pushing his way up to the top of the MBRC. But it was **not** his personality type to drag a person with him.

Aysel's face warred between a scowl and a glare before he sighed. "You are skilled, Morgan. You understand people—humans *and* magical beings—in ways I don't. I need that to make the MBRC better."

"You don't share power, Aysel. You don't share *anything*. What could you possibly get out of our partnership that would inspire you to suggest it?" I said.

Aysel straightened his robes. "After a considerable amount of pondering, I decided I would rather share power and run the finest Rehabilitation Center in the world than to solely rule one that is merely great."

"If you want me to be your partner, why should I reject the position in the teaching department?"

"Because there will be a position in the Public Relations Department that will soon open up, and that one will more swiftly pose you for a climb to be a department head," Aysel said.

"You have this all planned out, don't you?"

Aysel sniffed. "Of course."

I groaned and massaged my forehead. "Let me get through finals first. After that, we can talk."

"You are interested?" Aysel asked.

I gave the high elf a half smile. "Yeah, I am. Now beat it; I have to study."

"You are quite unlikeable."

"And you are soooo charming. Scram," I said, making a shooing motion at the high elf.

"Think on it," Aysel said before he slipped out of my office.

"That was weird," I said.

"Yes, Miss Fae," Harrison said.

"And totally *bizarre*."

"Yes, Miss Fae."

"That was real, right? It wasn't a hallucination from all the Red Bull I've been drinking?"

"It was real, Miss Fae."

"Weird," I repeated before returning my attention to my books.

"Ready for a break?" Devin asked, easing his weight on the edge of my desk before he temptingly offered me slices of banana and apple.

"Yes," I groaned, pushing aside my textbook for my entrepreneurship class.

"How is the studying?" Devin asked. After dropping off two cases of Red Bull and attempting to steal a kiss, he had left to attend a meeting with the MBRC board. I hadn't even heard him enter my office.

"Good," I said, eating an apple slice and sipping on my Red Bull. "Had the weirdest thing happen, though."

"Oh?" Devin asked, moving to stand behind me so he could massage my tight shoulders.

"Yeah—That feels wonderful, thanks. Aysel asked me to partner up with him…I *think* so we can take over the MBRC and rule the rehabilitation world."

Devin abruptly stopped massaging my shoulders. "He what?"

"Yeah, that was my reaction, too," I said, pushing a banana chunk around the plate before nibbling it and wishing Devin would start massaging me again.

"How late do you plan to study tonight?" Devin asked.

"Pretty late. Why? What's up?"

"Nothing. I just realized I forgot something in my room. What did you tell Aysel?"

"That we could talk about it after finals," I said.

"Wise idea," Devin said.

"What do you think about it?"

"About his offer? There are worse things than to be offered a free ride on his coattails. He'll get you up in administration much faster than you could hope for. He's been working at it much longer. Of course, you would be partnering with *Aysel*. That alone could be considered a downside," Devin said as he started rubbing my shoulders again.

I laughed.

"So, you really are committed to the MBRC, then?" Devin asked.

"Yeah. Why, you were cheering for me to switch to the Fairy Council?"

"A man can hope," Devin chuckled, his voice rich and throaty.

"Thanks for the food...and the massage," I said, eating another apple slice.

"Time to get back to studying?"

"Yeah," I sighed.

Devin bent to kiss me on the top of my head. "Good luck. I'll leave you to it for a bit. I need to go pick up something," he said, pausing to open another Red Bull for me.

"Thanks," I said, stretching my arms above my head before I attacked my notes with renewed vigor. "Let's do this!"

"Morgan, are you sure this is healthy?" Madeline asked me with a frown as I chugged another Red Bull late that night.

"Of course I'm sure I can't shut my eyes this is so awesome," I laughed.

"You sound like Toby," Madeline said, referring to a caffeine-addicted hobgoblin I've worked with before.

"My heart is beating sooooo fast," I said, a Red Bull in one hand, my coffee thermos in the other.

"And cramming like this will actually help you perform well on your tests?" Madeline asked, her voice seeped in doubt.

"Studying!" I cheered.

"You aren't even making sense anymore."

"Did you know that moms represent the biggest market share most marketing teams for mainstream products worry about?" I asked.

"That's it. I'm calling Westfall," Madeline said, rising out of her chair.

"Tell him I say hi," I said, highlighting a portion of my notes.

"Morgan, this isn't okay."

"It's called a caffeine rush. College students live off 'em," I said, my hand holding the highlighter was shaking so bad I highlighted the wrong thing.

"That doesn't make it *right.*"

"I'm back. Thanks for watching her, Madeline," Devin said, appearing behind my vampire friend.

"You need to stop her from doing this," Madeline insisted.

"After tonight, she will never binge on caffeine again," Devin said. "I promise."

Madeline gave him a look that said she didn't believe him and then hugged me. "See you later, Morgan." She skipped out of the room. I vaguely noticed that Harrison followed her out and stood guard outside.

"Studying!" I cheered again.

Devin grinned as he pulled a chair up to mine. "Think it's time to call it quits? You need to sleep."

"No way it's an all-nighter tonight I can feel my heart beat in my wrists," I said, turning a page in my notebook.

Devin opened a small, white box and removed a sparkling ring. One of the bands—there were two of them—was made of platinum; the other was studded with small diamonds. There were three bigger diamonds in the center: two smaller ones that were a pale yellow like the moon and placed on either side of the large one that glowed like it was on fire.

"Pretty," I said, sipping my Red Bull.

"Will you marry me?" Devin asked with a smile that I noticed was oddly crafty.

"Totally! Will you get me more coffee?" I asked.

"Sorry, but no. I think you've had enough," Devin said, slipping the ring on my ring finger.

"But I have to study," I complained.

Devin ran a hand through my hair. "I'm sure you'll do fine. What are you studying?"

"Marketing!"

The following morning, I woke up at my desk with a dry mouth and the awful taste of stale Red Bull, a throbbing headache, and a stiff neck.

"I'm getting too old to pull all-nighters," I said, clutching my temple before rubbing the back of my neck. I paused when I felt my hair snag on something. I held both of my hands in front of me, fingers spread wide, and froze when I noticed the gorgeous engagement ring on my finger. The night's events came back to me in hazy details.

I tried pulling the ring off. It wouldn't budge—it wouldn't even twist.

"DEVIN!" I screamed, shooting out of my desk. "I'M GOING TO KILL YOU!"

"So he got you to agree by waiting until you were too hyped up on caffeine to keep your head straight?" Esmeralda asked.

"Yeah," I said, changing lanes. "He purposely made himself scarce the whole next morning."

"I imagine so. You would have killed him if you found him."

"Probably," I agreed.

"So what happened after?"

"What do you mean?"

"Obviously, he must have officially proposed, or you would have kicked his butt to the curb. Or did he say 'no take backs' or something?"

I laughed. "He convinced me quite well when I found him later that afternoon."

"How?"

"DEVIN!" I growled as I kicked open the door to Devin's suite in the MBRC that afternoon.

The Pooka was there, dressed in a black dress shirt and nice jeans, holding a rose. Behind him was a table piled with gifts, but I didn't see that. I was still so enraged, I was practically seeing red.

"What is *this*?!" I demanded, pointing to the ring on my finger.

"Your engagement ring," Devin said with a charming smile.

"Harrison, if I kill him, do you think you could make it look like an accident?" I asked my bodyguard as I rubbed my hands together.

"Yes, Miss Fae."

"Hold up; just wait a moment. You can't be that mad—you're still wearing the ring."

"I'm still wearing it because it is MAGIKED ONTO MY FINGER," I roared.

"Harrison, could you give us a minute?" Devin asked.

"Are you sure that is wise, sir?"

"I think I can handle her."

"I'm going to rip your pretty-boy hair out!" I said, stalking across the room.

"If you say so, sir." Harrison stepped out and closed the door behind him.

Devin caught my hands when I launched myself at him. "Morgan, you are right. The ring is charmed."

"I knew it!" I said, starting to get a hold of myself. "You better—,"

"It's charmed so that as long as you love me, it won't come off," Devin said, interrupting me.

I blinked. "It what?"

"It's what the magical community calls an Evermore. It will stay with you as long as your love for me lasts," Devin said, bringing my hand with the ring up to his lips so he could kiss my fingers.

I frowned at the beautiful ring. "You didn't have to trick me into marrying you. I was planning to, eventually."

Devin chuckled and scooped me closer. "I know, but I wanted to stake an obvious claim before anyone got any…ideas."

"I thought you promised your proposal would be romantic. This was not romantic," I complained.

"I said nothing about my proposal; I only said I would shower you with love for the rest of your life. It's important to make promises I know I can keep," Devin teased me. "And the first part of my proposal wasn't romantic, but we haven't reached the second part yet."

"Second part?" I asked, perking with interest.

Devin pulled me forward by my hand, leading me to the table of gifts.

"This one first," Devin said, passing me a knobby bundle wrapped in white and gold paper. I cautiously opened it, my forehead wrinkling. "A…horse brush?" I asked, picking up the brush to study it.

I jumped when Devin's room faded like smoke, and I suddenly found myself standing in the middle of a stable.

Devin laughed and slid his arms around me, moving me to face a stall.

To my shock and surprise, I saw *myself* walk down the stable aisle. "Good afternoon, Westfall," my twin said as Westfall—a bay-colored unicorn—retreated to a hay pile. My twin turned on her heels and looked back and forth between a white horse and a black horse. "And which one of you is the kelpie I'm supposed to brush?" my twin asked.

The white horse sniffed contemptuously, but the black horse released a friendly nicker.

Devin tilted his head against mine as he watched the image play out. "When I first saw you, I was captivated instantly—intrigued by your willingness to interact with the magical community. I actually heard about you and purposely planted myself there," Devin said, kissing my cheek. "Poor Westfall tried to tell you what I was. I don't think I ever apologized," he admitted.

My twin complained about Frey as the black horse—Devin—brushed her cheek with a velvet muzzle. Once or twice, Westfall tried to speak to me, but whenever I turned to face him, horse-Devin would leer murderously over my shoulder.

After a few minutes, the scene faded away, returning Devin and me to his room.

"Is there one I need to open next?" I asked, my eyes sifting over the huge pile of presents.

"Nope, I just wanted to start with that one," Devin said.

I selected a package wrapped in lilac purple paper. When I ripped it open, a Monarch butterfly made of sparkling, paper-thin metal fell into my hand, and I found myself standing in a field in early spring.

I recognized where we were this time—it was my first date with Devin since we had become "official." He had taken me to some private land a buddy of his owned in southern Illinois, and we had a picnic lunch. He had transformed into a horse to give me rides, spoiled me with all my favorite foods, and waited on me hand and foot, but the butterfly had plopped us down at my favorite moment of the day.

"Ready for something spectacular?" Memory-Devin asked.

"As your first penance for flirting? This better be good," Memory-me laughed, splayed out on the ground, my head resting on Devin's calf.

"It will steal your breath away," Devin promised me. He checked his watch and glanced up at the sky before dropping a seed on the grassy knoll we were sitting on. When the seed touched the ground, it unfolded into a monarch butterfly, which took flight—but it wasn't just one. Hundreds, perhaps even thousands of butterflies launched into the air, their brilliant wings adding so much color that Memory-Me—that *right now* me—started to choke up at the sight.

"This was when I realized that waiting several more years for you was going to be a trial," Devin said, tangling his hands in mine.

"The butterfly glamour was pretty hard to get crafted, but it was worth it. You are *stunning* when you laugh."

After a few moments, the scene faded, and we were back in Devin's room.

Many of the gifts were small items with memories attached. In each moment, Devin had a side comment to add—something he loved about me, or an explanation about what he felt at that moment.

We visited our first kiss, the time when Devin moved the entire MBRC to get my memories back for me shortly after I first met him, our two-year anniversary, and more.

Some of the gifts were actual gifts with nothing attached—there was a platinum necklace with a horse pendant, three dozen yellow and white roses, and—what touched me the most—a collection of framed photos. Some were of me at work; there were a few family photos; and a bunch were of me and my friends—magical and normal alike. Most of the photos had Devin in them, with me. The frames were a glossy black, but when I touched them, they made the noises and sounds associated with the picture.

"Devin, this is *amazing*," I said, rubbing a picture of Fran and me posing at Disney World during spring break the previous year.

"I hoped it would make you rethink your reaction," Devin said.

When I turned to face him, the Pooka was down on a knee, holding an open white box that contained two gold bands with a few swirls etched into the surfaces.

"Devin?" I said uncertainly.

"I lied about the engagement ring. There is a charm to take it off—although it's a bugger to complete. But these are true Evermores."

"What are they?"

"Wedding bands, one for you and one for me. My band is charmed so it will stay on my finger as long as you love me."

"And my band?"

Devin smiled. "Your band is charmed so it will stay on forever."

"Why forever? That seems impractical."

"Because that's how long I will love you," Devin said.

I had to bite my lip to keep from crying.

"Marry me, Morgan. I am not a great man, but I will do everything in my power to make you happy, and to show you every day just how much I love and treasure you."

I was so touched, I could only nod, my eyes misty with tears of joy. Devin snapped the box shut before he stood and planted a passionate kiss on my lips.

I clung to him and buried my head in his chest when he pulled away. "But you're right about one thing," I said.

"What's that?" Devin asked, his hands sliding around me.

"I will **never** binge on caffeine again. Who knows what you would do next time?"

"That is so cute!" Esmeralda cooed. "I didn't think the Pooka had it in him to be so attentive, but you have that boy trained!"

"I can't take credit," I dryly said as I pulled into the underground MBRC parking lot. "If we had followed *my* life plan, we wouldn't be married for another year or two."

"I'm glad you two got married sooner. You're both very happy."

"We are," I agreed, parking and turning off my car.

"Are you ready for the next adventure?"

"Adventure?" I asked, getting out of my car as Harrison pulled in behind us.

"Having a brat. You gotta give birth to the next Pooka, you know," Esmeralda said, dragging her suitcase out of the trunk.

I wrinkled my nose at the beautiful vampire. "I think I'll wait a little longer for that one, thanks."

"Right. We'll see how that goes," Esmeralda said, rolling her eyes. "Thanks for the ride!"

"Of course. If we go in through the entrance, there should be a siren waiting to show you where to store your luggage for the rest of the day," I said.

"Thanks, Morgan. Take care. I'll see you for dinner tonight," Esmeralda said, hurrying to the parking garage door.

"Yes, see you then," I said before I turned to talk to Harrison about my plans for the day. I didn't get a chance to speak to my tall bodyguard, though, because my Magic Mirror rang.

"Hey, Devin. What's up?" I asked, looking at the small, phone-shaped mirror.

"Nothing, just missing you terribly," Devin said. The mirror showed him propping his chin up on his hand. "The Councilmen are having a hard time adjusting to our new council location."

"I thought the Fairy Council found a beautiful place. South Korea is amazing," I said.

"Come visit me, then?"

"No way. You'll be back home in a week; we can suffer until then," I laughed.

Devin fondly smiled.

"What?" I asked.

"Nothing. I just love you," Devin said.

"I know," I said, holding up my hand so Devin could see my wedding band. "Me, too."

"Thankfully," the Pooka wryly said, studying his wedding band.

"Come home soon, okay?" I asked.

"What happened to 'we can suffer through'?"

"Devin," I said, wrinkling my nose at him.

Devin laughed. "As soon as I can escape, I'm all yours."

"Yes, you are."

THE END

3

The Marriage Trustee

(AGE 19, AGE 22, & AGE 25)

"Well, I'm glad that's over," I said, setting my lute and the stupid magical lamp on the table before slumping into my chair.

"For now," Hunter said. He was seated in the chair next to mine, wearing a flawless suit that gave him a James Bond look, even though he wasn't yet nineteen.

"You're right," I groaned, stretching my legs out. "They always want an encore or two around midnight."

Hunter rested an arm on the back of my chair and platonically patted my shoulder. "You'll get better at playing the song every year. At least, you can't get any worse."

"Your support is heart-warming."

"Be grateful I agreed to sit in for Devin, or you'd be enduring this alone," he said, looking around the room with an amused expression.

"You're benefiting from this situation, or you wouldn't have come," I scoffed.

"That's a mean thing to say," Hunter said, eyeing Asahi's Great Aunt Florawyn. On an average day, Florawyn was unusually animated for a high elf, but tonight—with several glasses of moon wine churning in her—she was downright vivacious.

"But I'm right, aren't I?" I asked.

"Maybe."

"I knew it! There are too many powerful people here for you to pass up a chance of possibly charming someone."

"That's certainly one of the benefits, but it's also a treat to watch you perform the proposal song with Kadri. I have never before seen you look so uncomfortable."

"*Thanks.*"

Hunter gave me a handsome grin. "I'm surprised the Pooka didn't forcibly rearrange his schedule for tonight. Aren't you two officially dating?"

"Sorta, but not quite. We have an understanding," I said. "Devin would push for a serious relationship, but he knows I'm still trying to get my future figured out and is willing to wait."

"Aren't you visiting him in Britain?"

"Yeah, that's why he couldn't come tonight. The Fairy Council has him chained like a dog since the MBRC is lending me to them for a month."

"Is your internship over after that, then?"

"Hardly. I'll go to Britain in the spring, but I intend to work up until college starts. If things go well in the UK, I'll spend two months there instead of one, and after that Nick—a cyclops pal of mine—was going to pull a few strings and get me a temp job in his corporation," I said, watching Kadri and Asahi lead some of their relatives in an elaborate elf dance that involved swishing robes and perfectly-timed claps. "I was hoping to take a week or two off to visit Fran and Ethan in Florida, too."

"And you want to work in a corporation, temporarily?"

"Yes. I think the MBRC could be even more successful if it operated like a business. It can't be run like one—the MBRC doesn't make any money—but there are some things businesses do that are far more efficient that I feel the MBRC could copy."

"You could work in Weller Goblin Enterprises for a few weeks, if you like."

"Would you actually let me *go* after the weeks were up?"

"Possibly."

I grunted. "What about you? Are you going to start college in the fall, or are you going to keep on working?"

Hunter, like me, hadn't gone straight to college, but instead concentrated on re-branding the Chicago branch of Weller Goblin Enterprises.

"As soon as your internship ends and you decide where you're going to college, I'll enroll as well," Hunter said, watching Aysel glare daggers at the beautiful high elf female one of his relatives shoved at him.

I smiled, delighted with Hunter's declaration. "I'm glad we're still friends," I said, leaning into him.

"Of course," Hunter said, resting his topaz eyes on me so I could see how serious he was. "A goblin friendship is a lifelong commitment. Although I have to say, this party has reminded me just how glad I am we aren't romantically involved."

"Oh?"

"Yeah. If I had to attend this party every year, I would probably lose my mind. Everyone is so…*cheerful.*"

I laughed. "It's not the cheer that messes with you as much as it is the loud and bubbly atmosphere, I think."

"Whatever it is, it's enough to make me sick," Hunter shivered.

"Morgan, come! Dance with us!" Corn—one of my long-time students who also happened to be present at Kadri's initial proposal—shouted to me. She stood with her fellow fairies—Sage and Zinnia—and Oak, a wood elf. (Most of my students from Asahi's class were present.)

"See?" Hunter said.

I stood and stretched. "I think it's fun. Want to join me?"

"Not for my life."

"Suit yourself!"

"Why do I have to do this every time?" I grunted, straining to drag a cart of food into the giant hall Asahi and Kadri rented for their annual marriage celebration. I would have thought being a junior in college—and hauling around my laptop and textbooks—would have prepped me for this, but I was beginning to think Kadri had put half a cow in the cart! It didn't help that the magic lamp was hot on my back, making me sweaty even though the air was nippy from the freezing outside temperatures.

Kadri said something in elvish to the crowd—which was awash with whispers of anticipation. Asahi added a few additional lines, again in elvish, before he and Kadri held out their arms to me.

I smiled at them, yelping when they yanked me into our traditional-but-still-somewhat-awkward, three-person hug. It really was touching that they treasured my role in their relationship, but I hadn't managed to shake my embarrassment of the public affair. This was—if one counted their actual marriage ceremony—my fifth year of taking part of the celebration, and I was still self-conscious whenever we had to reenact the song proposal.

"To Kadri and Asahi," I shouted.

"To Kadri and Asahi!" the celebrators yelled, shaking the floor of the hall.

As the crowd surged forward to the food—in addition to the cart I had brought in, there was a veritable banquet set out—I ditched my magic lamp and stood on my tip toes, looking for my boyfriend.

"You look hot," Devin said, his velvety voice caressing my ear.

I whirled around to face him. "I am. My under-robe is moist with sweat."

He chuckled. "I meant you looked attractive, but I suppose dragging a cart and having a fire on your back would make you uncomfortable."

"No kidding. If we get married, do we have to do anything like this?" I asked, eyeing the crowd.

"No, not really. We'll have to have a party every year, but that's more because of my work—*our* work—than what I am. Our ceremony and reception can be in human tradition."

"Good," I said. "Because this is a lot of work. This year, Asahi is giving Kadri a *car* as a token of his acceptance. How am I supposed to get a *car* in here?"

"I don't know. I'm still a little worried that you said *if* we get married."

I rolled my eyes. "I'm still in college, Devin. I don't want to have this conversation until I've graduated."

"Hmm," Devin frowned, his eyes narrowing.

"Hey kids, what's up? Wow, Morgan, that robe is tacky," Frey said, sauntering up to us. (As Asahi and Kadri's friend, he snagged an invite every year.)

"Thanks," I said, looking down at my robe—which was a tapestry of Asahi and Kadri's faces—with a grimace.

"It's been awhile, mutt," Devin said. In spite of his words, he smiled, and his voice held a note of friendship. "How's your pack?"

"Good. We've had a few more join. They were assigned to us by the MBRC since they are certified and released for public interaction. It's exciting. How about you two?"

"Sweaty, but good," I said.

"I'm excellent," Devin said, curling an arm around my waist and flashing Frey a smile.

"Did the Fairy Council give you some time off or something?" Frey asked, raising an eyebrow.

"Finally, yes. Those old gasbags were nearly impossible to escape this time."

As I knew and respected some of those "gasbags," I decided it would be best to switch topics. "How's work?" I asked the skinny werewolf.

"Good. Dad's letting me go solo on some jobs."

I shook my head. "A werewolf electrician. I've been a part of the magical community for a long time, and I *still* question that."

"It's a good job—although my Dad's puns about electricity and light are enough to make me shift," Frey added.

"Speaking of which, Frank looks about ready to change from fright," Devin said, indicating the frightened werewolf, who was being cornered by three of Kadri's cooing, beautiful high elf cousins.

"Where's Madeline? She usually keeps him out of these situations," Frey said.

"Unless she was the one who got him into the situation," I wryly said.

"True. Better go save him. I'll see you two around," Frey called over his shoulder.

"Bye," I called.

Devin kissed my temple. "Are you sure you don't want to get married until you're out of college?"

"Positive."

"I could try changing your mind," Devin suggested, pulling me a step closer.

"I never pegged you to be wedding crazed."

"I'm not. I'm just crazy for you."

"That line would work better if I wasn't drenched in sweat and wearing Kadri and Asahi's faces."

"You're gorgeous no matter what you're in."

"You are a smart man."

"See? Don't you want to put a ring on it?"

"Not particularly, no."

"I'll catch you, someday," Devin chuckled. He kissed me on the lips before he stepped away. "I think your lute recital is about to begin, though, so for today you are allowed to evade me."

"Thanks. I'll see you after the proposal song."

"I'll be waiting at our spots."

I smiled as I left my boyfriend and went to collect my lute—which was looking more and more battered the longer it had to put up with my accidental abuse. I really did love Devin. We had an unusual relationship, but then again there was nothing "usual" about my life. He was a perfect fit for me.

"I am finally rocking this stupid thing!" I declared, brandishing my lute like a sword.

"Just in time to learn the Song of Birth for your godchild," Aysel said.

"There's a *birth* song? Does this mean I have to be present for the delivery?" I asked, almost dropping the instrument.

"Yes."

"Dang it!" I flopped down in a chair near Aysel's. "But if that's the case, you better brush up on your lute skills, too. There's a fifty percent chance *you'll* be the godparent."

"I think not," Aysel said.

Asahi and Kadri told Aysel and me when they first announced Kadri was pregnant, that they wanted us to be their children's godparents—Aysel because he was Asahi's twin, and me because I was Kadri's marriage trustee. However, they couldn't decide who should get the first child—because apparently it's a big thing to be the godparent of the eldest child—so they decided if they had a girl, I would be the godparent, and if they had a boy, it would be Aysel.

As Aysel was borderline disgusted with all the cheer and emotional warmth that entailed being connected to Asahi and Kadri, he was particularly adamant that they should have a girl.

"No way. I've had to play a lute at these celebrations for five years. The least you could do is join me in my misery."

"I've been meaning to speak to you about that."

"My mad lute skills?"

"No. Your upcoming nuptials."

I scowled and put the lute on the ground. "Marrying Devin is *not* going to make me miserable."

"Perhaps not," Aysel acknowledged. "Instead it will merely drive you crazy. Time will tell—though I hope it does not negatively impact our plans."

Aysel and I were co-conspirators, and if we played our cards right, we were just a short ways away from becoming the co-administrators of the MBRC.

"You better get me a *really* nice wedding gift," I complained.

Aysel frowned. "I already gave you a nice gift."

"Yeah, for my wedding shower—and you so owe me for letting you get out of attending that party."

"The gift was a bribe so I wouldn't have to," Aysel said.

"Whatever. So what about my wedding? You can't squirm out of attending now. I already handed in your RSVP. You're in the head-count for the reception."

"About that, I was wondering if it was too late for me to add an additional RSVP."

I stared at the high elf. "An additional one? Why?"

Aysel audibly ground his teeth. "Because I have a date."

My jaw dropped. "You're serious?"

"Perfectly."

"You hoodwinked someone into *liking you*?" I asked, baffled by the idea. Aysel and I were friends for life, but the guy has the personality of a rabid wolverine and the exterior of a porcupine.

Aysel glared at me, his silver eyes gleaming in the dim lighting of the hall. While his glares weren't unusual, I couldn't miss the vulnerable set of his mouth. I was probably the first person he was telling about his...date. (I had to be, or the MBRC would be whistling with gossip!)

"When did you meet her?" I asked, settling down a little. "Does your dad approve—I bet he only cares about how pure her family lines are," I said, thinking of the conceited MBRC Director.

"She's human."

"She's *what*?" I shrieked, rocketing out of my chair.

"There you two are! How sweet—the guardian and his ward!" Aysel's great aunt Tiranthyn cooed as she sauntered up to us. Though she had to be centuries old, she looked younger than Aysel's dad.

"We will discuss this later," Aysel hissed. He raised his voice to address his relative. "Not for much longer, aunt."

I lifted my hand so my engagement ring sparkled in the night. "I'm getting married in a few months."

"Nonsense. Once a Moonspell, always a Moonspell. Someone should tell that to your father, Athel. I think such a thought might kill him. Rivers—his face would be a delight to behold!"

"It's Aysel."

"Of course it is, Abel. You did a wonderful job with the song, Morgan. You are much improved this year."

"Thank you," I said, smiling out of respect and delight. Tiranthyn was *such* fun to watch. She was even more personally affronted by Administrator Moonspell's haughty demeanor than I was!

"It is good timing," Tiranthyn said, looking to Kadri. "I do believe they'll have a little girl—my sympathies; the delivery will not be as delightful to witness as their proposal—and something tells me I'll be seeing you play the lute even more often in the years to come," she said, giving Aysel the eye.

Aysel stiffened, but Tiranthyn didn't seem to notice. "There's your sourpuss father, Angel. I had better go pay my *respects*. Enjoy your bonding time," Tiranthyn said as she danced away.

"I do love your relatives," I reverently said. "So…your date?"

"I would rather not discuss it in such an unsecured location, or half of the magical community will know by the morning."

"So true."

"Morgan!" Madeline shouted. She was standing with Devin halfway across the room. "Devin says Kadri hired out one of Hunter's cookie elf chefs, and they made turtle cheesecake. He says you have to try it!"

"Coming!" I said, peeling myself from the chair. I glanced back at Aysel. "You'll tell me tomorrow?"

He nodded.

I walked away without saying goodbye—he and Devin would likely be my only company when the party would start to wind down just before dawn—and navigated my way through the crowd, aiming for my fiancé and close friend.

As I walked, I dwelled upon Aysel's request. "Dang it!" I shouted.

"What?" Devin asked, kissing me and then handing me a plate of cheesecake. "Did Aysel do something?"

"No. Not yet, anyway," I said.

In the back of my mind a nagging voice whispered that I might also soon be playing the lute for Aysel, in addition to playing for Asahi and Kadri's marriage and serving as their first child's godparent (Tiranthyn had an uncanny knack to call stuff like that). "Impossible," I muttered. "Aysel would ask Asahi…right?" I frowned and tried to picture it before giving up with a shiver. Bright Asahi as the sour-tempered Aysel's Marriage Trustee would be a disaster waiting to happen.

"It doesn't matter. It just shows that Tiranthyn was right," I sighed. "Once a Moonspell, always a Moonspell."

THE END

4

Release the Kraken

(AGE 25)

"When I told Grogrintork to teach his people how to fix coffee machinery, it really was a stroke of genius," I hummed as I sipped on my Turtle Frappe—which was practically heaven in a cup.

"Have you finished congratulating yourself?"

"Seriously, you should try one of these, Aysel," I said, folding the whipped cream into my drink. "I think you would be 10% less grouchy as a result."

"Food does not affect one's mood," Aysel scoffed.

"I dunno. I was pretty impressed you wanted to meet up for lunch. Most days you disappear around lunch and come back looking insufferably smug and happy. I would call that mood-changing," I said, keeping my voice speculative. I had been trying to worm Aysel's lunch location out of him for months but had nothing to show for it. I had a hunch it had something to do with his date for my wedding, but I couldn't confirm it.

"We needed to discuss our business and partnership goals, and this was the soonest you could meet." Aysel scowled as he swiped a screen of a tablet—his birthday gift from Devin and myself. I was getting the snobby elf accustomed to technology whether he wanted me to or not. Surprisingly, over the past few months, he had grown quite open to the learning process. He probably thought it would help him improve the MBRC or something—which was good, as most of the MBRC computers were still operating on ancient systems and software programs from the late 90s and early 2000s.

"Yeah, okay. Wait, is that an *agenda*?" I asked, choking on a crushed pecan from my drink when Aysel set his tablet up with a list opened on the screen.

"Naturally. That is the easiest way to organize such a meeting as ours," he said.

I covered my eyes with my hands. "Why am I working with you again?"

"Because you enjoy power just as much as I do. Our main order of business pertains to an assignment you will soon receive from management," Aysel said, pausing to sip a flowery-smelling drink.

"How do you know what assignment I'm going to get? You're in the Administration Department, not the Public Relations Department, like me," I suspiciously asked as I took a forkful of my crispy cranberry pecan salad.

"It's a big event that requires the cooperation of several departments. As I am on the committee, I was able to assure this particular part of the event was assigned to you."

"Great. What is it?"

"The Kraken is visiting the MBRC. It will be your job to greet and guide him."

"The who?"

"The Kraken—an aquatic magical being."

"Wait, you mean the kraken as in a *giant squid*?" I said, dropping my plastic fork in shock.

"I believe you less-intelligent humans picture him as such, though now his presence is mostly met with disbelief."

"A giant *squid* is coming to the MBRC? How on earth is that going to work?"

"He's not a giant squid; he's a kraken—*the* Kraken. And he won't arrive in his aquatic body; he has a human form he uses to interact with mortals," Aysel said, wiping a smudge off his tablet. "It is quite an honor that he's visiting. He's very reluctant to travel, and when the rare event occurs, he almost never visits a location that is not near the sea. We are very lucky Lake Michigan is so large, or he might not agree to it."

"Wow, he sounds like *fun*," I said.

"He has a right to feel entitled. He is one of the oldest magical beings in the world."

"Entitled? That doesn't sound like a great recommendation," I said, taking a sip of my Turtle Frappe to console myself.

"It's not. The Kraken is an old, fussy, mule-headed individual. He used to live in the Greenland Sea, but he's been in California for the past few years."

Awesome. If *Aysel* thought a magical individual of importance was a pain-in-the-butt, that meant they had to be a nightmare. He was willing to suck up to just about anyone if it would further his career.

"And why did you volunteer me to guide this fussy, mule-headed guy around?" I asked.

Aysel prodded his toasted crescent roll. "Because as dislikeable as he is, he is extremely influential. If he wished it, he could have a permanent seat on the Fairy Council—like your fiancé. In fact, he would likely be a top leader. The Kraken, however, has refrained from entering politics. Even so, if you impress him it is likely he would become a supporter of the MBRC, making us the first rehabilitation center to gain the support of a globally powerful being."

"So if I make him happy, that will make MBRC management happy, which will lead to an eventual promotion, I imagine?" I asked, waving to Perseus and his friends as they clip-clopped past.

"Yes."

I finished my turtle frappe and set the drink aside. "I gotta tell you, Aysel, you have awful timing. Did you forget my schedule is so packed because I'm marrying Devin in a month?"

"Which is why it is so important you impress him *now*. Marrying the Pooka is a wonderful career decision, but before you attach your name to his, it would be best if you proved yourself to the MBRC staff, so all know you are progressing forward as a result of your own merits instead of the Pooka's power," Aysel said.

"I'm marrying Devin because I happen to *love* him, not for your plans of MBRC world domination," I reminded him.

"Perhaps. It is still a good investment," Aysel shrugged, unbothered.

"Whatever. So do you have any inside information on how I'm supposed to impress this guy?" I asked, drumming my fingers on the tabletop. I got along really well with most of the magical community, but I usually bristled at the upper class—like Administrator Moonspell. By the sounds of it, this Kraken guy was going to be even worse than him. Yay me.

"No," Aysel said.

"What?"

"He's something of a recluse and has strange moods. None of my colleagues have been able to successfully understand his personality," Aysel said.

"And you want someone like that to support the MBRC?"

"He's quite rich."

"Ah."

"You will be lucky in your interactions with him. All you must do is take him from location to location. You will not have to grovel or beg for financial backing," Aysel said, his eyebrow twitching. I could tell it irked him to have to pander to someone—even if that someone was an ancient, mythical being who was uber powerful. Aysel is conceited like that.

"Right, well, thanks for the warning. What else is on your *agenda*?" I asked, returning to my salad.

"Next, there is the matter of—"

"Aww, look at you two! Are you having a guardian-ward lunch date?" a bright, sunny voice asked.

Recognizing the voice, I said, "Hello, Asahi," before I even looked up to smile at the dazzling elf—who was also Aysel's younger twin. "I'm afraid it is strictly business right now. No bonding whatsoever."

"I cannot wait until you are married, and I no longer have to deal with that stupid vow," Aysel muttered.

"Business?" Asahi asked, tilting his head.

"Yeah. How are your students? Have they finally grasped the concept of phones?"

"I believe so. Thank you for coming in for that wonderful demonstration," Asahi said. "Oh, I nearly forgot. Kadri said she has secured the veil of the summer queen for you to use in your marriage ceremony."

"Wow, thank you. That sounds like a big honor," I said.

Asahi nodded. "It is, as you would say, a big deal. The summer queen is an elf, and it isn't often elf artifacts are lent to a human. But it makes sense as you are our marriage trustee and Aysel's ward."

"Only for another month," Aysel reminded his twin.

"Perhaps, but you two are 'totes besties,'" Asahi said.

Aysel's face morphed into a look of offense, his eyes narrowing as his chin went up with chilly disdain.

I choked on the lettuce leaf I was munching on. "We're *what*?"

"Totes besties. Did I say it wrong? I thought that phrase communicates that you are fully best friends," Asahi said, his handsome face creasing with distress.

"No, you used it right. It's just, uh, I wouldn't call us that," I said, glancing at Aysel.

The dark-haired and silver-eyed elf was scowling so forebodingly that I had no doubts if Asahi wasn't his brother—no, if Asahi wasn't his *twin*—Aysel would have murdered him. There would be no recovering him from this kind of snit. The safest route was to retreat.

"Wow, look at the time. I really should get back to the office. Why don't you come with me, Asahi?" I asked intending to drag the sunshine elf with me so I could be assured he wouldn't accidentally get himself killed with more naive words.

"I would, but I must speak to Aysel," Asahi said.

I scrambled to gather my things. "No, I insist. You *must* come with me. We'll have another chat again soon, right, Aysel?"

Aysel gripped his plastic cup containing his flowery drink so hard the plastic cracked.

"Yeah, wonderful. See you then!" I said, dragging Asahi off, leaving the elf to stew alone.

A week later, I stood next to a stretched limo, leaning against its crystal-clean side as I chatted via magic mirror with my fiancé, Devin the Pooka. "So you don't have anything on this guy?" I asked.

"I've never met the Kraken—although my father did. He rarely surfaces, and when he does, he doesn't often choose to immerse himself in the community elite," Devin said, his lips folded in a slight frown. "You're sure you're okay greeting him alone? I could ride in with you—I'm attending the same meetings as he is anyway."

"I know, and no, I'm fine. But thank you. Aysel has made it abundantly clear that I have to do this without your help, or everyone will think I can't pull my own weight," I said, glancing up from the phone-sized mirror to look at the crowd that swarmed around the limo.

I was waiting at the Chicago O'Hare airport to pick up the Kraken. It was a strange location to meet the magical. A few beings fly on airplanes—mostly vampires who had been turned in the last fifty years—but most don't, especially not those belonging to the upper-crust of the magical community. They usually arrived via dragons or flying carpets.

"Plus, the PR Department Head herself gave me a day's worth of sensitivity training about this guy," I said, watching the crowd for a grizzled, old man. So far, no such figure had shown, but it was pretty hard to see around the blond-haired surfer dude who was standing ten feet away from me and holding a massive surf board. "This guy must be a total jerk the way everyone trembles at the mention of him. Administrator Moonspell certainly holds no love for him."

"That's not necessarily a problem. Administrator Moonspell *hates* you," Devin chuckled, his velvety voice easing my tension.

"Maybe, but a lot of the MBRC board members were less than

thrilled with the prospect of interacting with this guy. Aysel said he's ancient, though, so maybe he has a right to be grouchy. If I was that old, I would be grouchy too," I said, brushing off my black slacks. I craned to try and look around the blond surfer guy. Not only was he a roadblock, but he was starting to make me a little uncomfortable. He wore sunglasses, but it felt like he was staring at me.

"Magical beings with pure blood tend to be stuffy," Devin said.

"How did you escape that? You're a straight descendant—and you're on the Fairy Council."

"My entire bloodline tends to miss it. As we live roughly as long as humans, we've learned not to take ourselves too seriously," Devin said.

"Good to know. I should probably go. He's going to arrive any minute," I said. "I love you."

"I know," Devin smugly said.

I rolled my eyes. "Cute. See ya soon."

"I love you, too, Morgan. Good luck," Devin said before he disconnected, and my magic mirror went dark.

I slipped the phone in a pocket of my slacks—it was why they were my favorite pair—just as the surfer dude took a few steps towards me. "Excuse me," I said, flashing a professional smile when he placed a tanned hand on the door handle of the limo. "I apologize, but this vehicle is reserved."

"Tubular, thanks for picking me up!"

"No, I'm afraid you don't understand. This limo is reserved for…" I hesitated. As far as I knew, the Kraken didn't have a name besides Kraken, but it probably wasn't a good idea to flash that name around, as it was sure to garner me some strange looks.

To my shock, the frizzy-haired surfer smiled, flashing white teeth at me. "Kraken, right?"

My body stiffened. "What?"

"And you're Morgan, huh? Took me a while to figure out it was you—I didn't know for sure until you mentioned the Fairy Council," the surfer said, leaning his surfboard against the limo. He sported a five o'clock shadow, orange shorts adorned with a white orchid pattern, sandals, and a white tank top.

"Wait, *you're* the Kraken?" I asked, my voice cracking with disbelief.

"Yep," the surfer said, flicking his sunglasses on top his head. He was tan, but apparently he wore his sunglasses a lot because he had a perfect white outline spanning his eyes, the bridge of his nose, and a little line on the side of the head.

He was so ridiculous, I couldn't help the rude and loud goose honk "HAH!" that ripped out of my throat. I slapped my hands over my face and stared at the Kraken with stricken eyes.

I had laughed at one of the oldest magical beings in the world and mocked him while he stood ten feet away.

I was so screwed.

"It was *awful*, Krad," I moaned into my arms.

"You've said that four times already," Krad said, flipping a page of his Captain America comic book.

"Because it was that bad! When Aysel hears about it, he is going to kill me. Who laughs in the face of an ancient and powerful magical being?"

"That would be you. All the time," Krad said, snatching a fudge brownie from the plate I brought him. "It's amazing no one has successfully offed you, yet. No, it's embarrassing, actually."

I sat up. "This is not the time to go on a villain monologue."

"No, apparently it's time to have a pity party like you're the heroine of a romantic comedy movie," Krad said, swapping the Captain America issue for a Superman comic.

"How do you know what a rom-com is?" I suspiciously asked.

Krad froze. "Wednesday human trivia nights?" he said, his answer sounding suspiciously like a question.

"You're going to that?"

"Do you have a problem with that?"

"No, I just didn't think you seemed the type," I said, studying the dark elf with new eyes. As it was roughly seven or six years ago that the MBRC took Krad into custody, he had changed quite a bit.

"So you didn't learn it from—" I started.

"Triva night," Krad said, shoving his face in the comic book to cut off the conversation.

I grinned, bingo! That explained it. Krad totally learned the term from his mentor. Supposedly, a human girl—the college-aged daughter of an MBRC-employed sorceress—had been fulfilling a community service quota from her mom by mentoring Krad in an effort to get him ready for the rehabilitation program. Come to think of it, she must be the one who gave him the comic books, too. I certainly hadn't brought them. When I tried giving him a comic book four years ago, he almost mauled my face off until Harrison swatted at him with a set of iron knuckles.

"Right," I said. I glanced at my cell phone and groaned. "I have to get to work."

"Good. Leave, mortal," Krad said, though I wasn't fooled.

"Aww, you'll miss me."

"I will not!" he sputtered.

"Even if you're big now, you're still cute," I said, reaching over to ruffle his hair.

Krad rolled his comic book up and used it to smack my hands. "Stop saying that! You saw me only a few times when I was chained to a child's form, and you have known me for years in my true body."

"Yes, but you were adorable! When you weren't trying to kill me, anyway."

Krad snorted. "Get out of here and go about your business."

"Yeah, yeah," I said, standing up and slipping my purse strap over my shoulder with a sigh.

"And next time , bring peanut butter cookies," he said as I left his dorm-style room through the open door and joined Harrison in the hallway.

"Let's go, Krusher," I said, making a face. "Aysel has probably found out by now."

"It wasn't that bad, Miss Fae."

"Thanks for kind thought, but I'm afraid you're wrong this time," I said, dragging myself out of the residence wing. "I know you were there, but even if the Kraken didn't *act* mad, you can't say an ancient magical being like him could take all the accidental insults I spouted off with a smile."

Harrison was quiet as we climbed the stairs.

"Morgan, hey, Morgan. Sup?"

I spun around, trying to identify who was speaking to me. I was shocked to see the Kraken—still wearing his sandals, beach shorts, and tank top—trotting after me.

"C-can I help you?" I stammered.

"You're a real Chicago res, right?" the Kraken asked, giving Harrison a smile and saying, "Hey, dude," before turning his attention back to me.

"I live in a suburb, but I know Chicago well," I cautiously said, glancing at the suit- and dress-clad officials who scurried up the stairs after us.

"Awesome. Do you think you could take me to the Navy Pier? I need to see some water, dude. I'm starting to dry out."

"Um, Navy Pier is on the water, but it doesn't have lake access," I said. When I glanced at the officials—one of them was my boss, the head of the PR Department—they wildly gestured for me to go ahead and take him out, so I was quick to add, "It's got a ferris wheel, though."

The Kraken looked crestfallen. "No beach?"

"No," I said, weighing out my words carefully. "But there are several beaches and piers in and around Chicago that I could take you to."

The Kraken flashed me a smile full of white teeth. "That'd be wicked cool! Can we go now?"

"Of course, Mr. Kraken," I said.

"Call me K—or Crazy K, if you like. This is gonna be awesome!" he said, pumping his fist in the air before he turned and clattered down the stairs, plowing through the stiffs behind him. "I'm gonna go borrow a boogie board from a Michigan merman I met earlier. Be right back," he said before disappearing down a hallway.

Harrison cleared his throat—which is as close to an "I told you so" as he ever got.

"That was bizarre," I muttered.

"Miss Fae, we are depending upon you," my department head said, clasping my hands. "Please, give him the most favorable experience of Chicago—and Lake Michigan—possible."

"I'll do my best," I said, feeling bewildered. When my phone buzzed, I looked down to see I had received a text message from Aysel.

"*Don't mess this up.*"

"No pressure, huh?" I muttered.

"This is *sweet*," the Kraken declared, his nose slathered with suntan lotion that hadn't been rubbed in yet.

"I'm glad you like it," I said, avoiding a swarm of kids building a sandcastle.

"Not many waves, but the water's got *depth*. It's totally chill." The Kraken pulled a red cooler on wheels behind him.

"Great." I followed him to an empty patch of beach with Harrison on my heels.

"Here is our spot," the Kraken declared. I gaped in shock as he pulled a giant umbrella, three lawn chairs, and a pile of beach towels from his cooler—which was way too small to hold any of that. In minutes, he had the umbrella pitched and angled towards the lake, and the beach towels folded and displayed like it was an ad for a *Better Homes & Gardens* magazine.

"I gotta go greet the water. You guys chilax!" the Kraken said, marching towards the lake.

I held my hair down, fighting the fishy-smelling breeze. "Chilax?" I said. I looked to Harrison, who looked super out of place with his pale—faintly purple-hued—skin, shining bald head, and spotless suit.

"Well, I can't say I ever thought I would be the assigned lake-monitor for an ancient and powerful magical being, but there are worse gigs. Unless he brought me here with the intension of dragging me underwater and drowning me for insulting him," I said, sitting down in the middle lawn chair.

"Not likely," Harrison said.

"You think he's not the drowning type?" I asked.

"No, there are too many people here to make a clean kill."

"Fabulous. Thank you, Krusher, for that moment of gentle comfort."

"You're welcome, Miss Fae."

For an hour, I watched the Kraken splash and play in the waves. He was really competent at interacting with humans. He tossed wayward beach balls back to children, chatted with the on-duty lifeguard, and admired sand castles—almost like my annoyingly friendly older brother, Michael, would.

I was surprised when he sauntered up to Harrison and me and threw himself into the open lawn chair.

"How was the water?" I asked.

"Rad! A little warm—I like my water cold—but it's a keelin' lake," the Kraken said as he rubbed his head with a towel, making his sun-bleached hair fluffy.

"I'm glad you like it?" I said, unsure if he was happy or not.

"Totally! Although—you got a problem with Asian Carp, but it's those Zebra Mussels that are churning out all that algae. Sick, man. Why are the mer-clans putting up with it? The California mermaids wouldn't use a zebra mussel for shark chum."

"I don't know why they allow it," I neutrally said. "I'm sorry; I'm not really versed with merpeople policies and…lake activism."

The Kraken refolded his towel. "I bet. I heard you've got plenty of waves you're riding already." He offered me a friendly grin and opened the cooler again.

He pulled out two hollowed halves of a small watermelon, poured a fizzy liquid from a bottle into an ice-packed thermos, shook the crap out of it, poured the drink into the watermelon halves, and finished it with colored bendy straws.

"Woah! Almost forgot." He reached into his magical cooler and pulled out two paper umbrellas, which he stabbed into the watermelon rinds before handing Harrison and me each a "drink."

"Thank you," I said, awkwardly accepting the gift. "What do you call it?"

"Crazy K's chill wave!" the Kraken proudly said, setting about to make one for himself. "It's got mangos and papayas—which, I gotta tell you, it's wicked hard to find organic mangos and papayas here."

I watched Harrison start his before I took my first sip—I wasn't taking any chances that the Kraken was a poison guy instead of a drowning guy. It was tangy, refreshing, and fizzled in my mouth. "It's really tasty!" I said, blinking at my straw in surprise.

"Awesome!" the Kraken said.

"Thank you for making it; it's perfect for the beach," I said.

"Yeah, that's what I told old-man Moonspell when I made one for him. Pretty sure he'd shrivel up and dissolve if he came out here, though, so I told him he better stay on land."

I almost inhaled my fizzy drink in mirth at his adept description.

"Woah, what's wrong?" he asked, leaning out of his chair to peer at me with worry.

I coughed. "I'm fine," I wheezed before my phone beeped at me. I dug through my purse and swiped the screen to see I had a message from Aysel—probably another warning not to mess up.

"Sweet, you have a cell phone? Can I get your number? It was way hard contacting officials for this trip," the Kraken said, sliding a smart phone out from underneath the pile of towels.

"You have a smart phone?" I asked, surprised. Only a few magical beings at the MBRC had one. Aysel was probably the most influential cell-toting member, and he had one only so he could track me down.

"Cha! Gotta check my weather apps and text my buddies so I know when we're gonna catch some waves," the Kraken said, his eyebrows furrowed in slight disapproval at my disbelief.

"I'm sorry, it's just…erm…not many magical beings at the MBRC have cell phones, so I was surprised," I stammered.

"I don't doubt that," the Kraken snorted. "They call me reclusive, but they're relying on ancient spells to make contact. Way out of touch."

I kept my mouth shut to avoid inserting my foot into it.

"Just shows how different we are, I guess," he continued.

"Why do you say that?" I asked.

The Kraken shrugged. "A lotta magical beings love hanging out together—like schools of fish. The fairy council, and the officials at the MBRC, they're part of a world that's long gone."

"Is that why you don't interact with others?" I meekly asked.

"Hm? Oh, I interact tons—just with humans. Snotty elves in robes and fairies dressed in silk don't float my boat. The merpeople, them I like. But these business types—like old-man Moonspell? They bring to mind the few dragons who refused to go into hiding because they wouldn't leave their treasure hoards behind. Every last one of them was slain because they wouldn't change and release their old lives," the Kraken said. Much of the California beach bum accent left him, and the light in his eyes made him seem older than I could possibly fathom.

"But that's what the MBRC is for," I said. "It's supposed to help magical beings so they can be launched into human society—so they *won't* be killed."

The Kraken turned his ancient eyes onto me. "Do you really think that?" he asked. "The fairy council and the upper-crust of magical beings stay in realms of the purely magical. It's the little guys they're shoving towards human society, not the high elves and the like."

I swallowed. This was a serious question from a prospective investor. I had to answer this well. "I'm not saying there's not a certain level of politics and selfishness in the Fairy Council—or the MBRC. But change is scary. It takes *time* for an entire society to change."

"I've given them centuries, and they're just as far away from humans as they always were," the Kraken said, his normally laid back tone was laced with hints of anger.

"No, they're not," I blurted out.

The Kraken raised his eyebrows at me.

"They're not," I insisted. "Kadri Moonspell—Administrator Moonspell's daughter-in-law—currently works part-time in a public school. You haven't met her yet—she's in California right now—but her husband, Asahi, is finishing some online classes through a human college so he can join her. Hunter Weller, one of the heirs of Weller Goblin Enterprises, is going to college with me—a *human* college. Nick and Sandy—two cyclops friends of mine—are helping some dwarves launch a small coffee machine repair business. Devin—the Pooka—is *marrying* me."

"But you work for the MBRC," the Kraken said.

"Yeah, and I don't have a speck of magic in me. I'm totally human. There is nothing unusual or magical about me. But I'm rising up through the ranks of the PR department and marrying the equivalent of a fairy celebrity. If this was *all* political, that wouldn't be possible."

The Kraken didn't say anything.

"They're trying. All you need to do is look at Aysel Moonspell, and you'll know that," I said.

"What about Aysel Moonspell?" the Kraken asked, zeroing in on the thought.

"W-what?"

"What about him proves that the elite of the magical society are changing?"

"Well, uh, he's got a cell phone," I said. I thought it was a really lame and dumb point, but the Kraken drew back, as if I had just delivered the most astonishing verbal blow.

"Seriously?" he asked.

"Yeah, he's been sending me texts ever since we left," I said, opening up my texting thread so the Kraken could see. The most recent entry was an exchange of insults between the two of us, so I did not hesitate to let him see that I openly called Aysel a "pucker-faced prude," and he referred to me as an "embarrassing tangle of poor manners and a broken volume control."

"Devin texts me, too, though we usually use a magic mirror to talk," I added as the Kraken stared at the cell phone screen.

"Right. Guess I gotta admit it, M. You're right. The MBRC is tighter than I thought." He handed me my phone and reclined in his chair. "Guess I'll hafta be more serious 'bout this."

I blinked. "M?"

"Short for Morgan. You're one of my buds now," the Kraken said, giving me a white smile.

"Does this mean you'll be funding the MBRC?" I asked.

"Sure," he said, flicking his sunglasses down so they covered his eyes again. "I'll have to jet around for a bit and find some sunken ships. Won't be too hard."

"…what?"

"Yeah, it's how I pay for my California beach house. I find treasure on the bottom of the ocean other creatures can't reach. Getting it out is the trickiest part. I'm way massive when in my real form. Makes it hard to look in tight spaces," he complained.

"Wow," I said. "So you have serious funds?"

"Yep."

"How do you feel about using that to bring about more change?"

I watched in smug satisfaction as the Kraken signed a contract with several officials—including Administrator Moonspell.

"I should have known better than to arrange for you to have time alone with a prospective investor," Aysel grouched at my side.

"Why? He signed on the dotted line and is supporting the center, isn't he?" I asked, waving to the Kraken when he glanced in my direction.

"He is. But with all the budget changes he demanded—which is due to *your* influence, you can't tell me *he* knew about the Cuckoo Ward and the budget cuts threatening the unicorn riding-therapy program—and the requirements he has tacked on to allow us to actually *use* his funds, it's almost not worth the hassle," Aysel growled.

"I notice you said almost."

"He is making a generous donation to begin the partnership,"

Aysel admitted. "But, I by no means enjoy his company. He has worse manners than the Beer Brothers," he shivered.

"That's a shame."

"Why?"

"I was going to put him at your table for my wedding reception. I guess I'll just have to find some other high-ranking MBRC official to play nice with him," I sighed.

"No," Aysel said, on the issue like a vampire on a paper cut. "I can accept his presence for an evening."

"It's no trouble," I said. "I mean, you just said you don't like the guy. Surely there're lots of people invited to my wedding who would be honored to chat with *the* Kraken. Of course, this means I'll have to kick you off the table—which also has several influential members from the Fairy Council sitting there—Devin's coworkers, you know."

"You are *not* threatening me," Aysel said, his eyes narrowing.

"Oh, no. I'm just concerned about your happiness," I said, doing my best to give him a charming smile.

"You word-twisting mortal," he started. "You are my ward. Until the moment you marry that romance-spouting Pooka, you are at my mercy in magical society."

I smirked. "That's the funny thing about receptions. They take place *after* the wedding."

Aysel growled as his twin strolled up to us.

"You two really are totes besties," Asahi said, patting his brother on the shoulder.

"Maybe we are," I said. "So are you gonna tell me where you run off to during lunch, *bestie*?"

"No!"

THE END

5

My Career at the Magical Beings' Rehabilitation Center

AN EXTRA CHAPTER BY K. M. SHEA

"All three of your brats are in school now? Wow, I feel aged. It seems like just yesterday you were waddling like a hippo, pregnant with your youngest," I said, adjusting my earpiece as I walked down the Chinese dragon hallway of the MBRC. (How an underground facility managed to get perfect cell reception still boggled me.)

"Ashley is only in preschool; it's hardly anything to wail about. And thank you for giving me a boost to my confidence," Fran said from the other end of the line. "I will be sure to go to you the next time I want to know how I look."

"I will not be faulted for this. Ashley was a *massive* baby. You looked ready to pop by your second trimester," I said.

"I did resemble a whale," Fran admitted.

"A whale with very stylish hair."

"Thanks!"

"Of course," I said, glancing down at my phone when my ear piece beeped. "I'm sorry Fran, but I've got another call coming in that I have to take."

"Work or personal?"

"Both."

"Oh, if that's the case, tell Hunter I say hello, and thank his wife for my birthday card for me, would you?"

"Sure. I'll talk to you tonight?"

"Yeah, until then!"

I smiled even though Fran couldn't see me as I accepted Hunter's call. "Hello, Hunter. What's wrong? Did Cecelia kick you out of the bedroom again?"

"Considering you're supposed to be *my* friend, you should side with me more often than with her," Hunter said. The fact that he was complaining and his voice wasn't its usual throaty, "I'm-handsome-and-I-know-it" tone meant that I was right on with my guess.

"Give me some credit, Hunter. I side with whoever is right," I said, reaching the main chamber of the MBRC. I smiled and nodded to those who stopped to bow or salute me as I climbed the stairs with expert dexterity in spite of the three-inch heels I was wearing. (Training in high heels significantly helped my lifespan. I could outrun some of the members of my security team in them!)

"You side with her every time!"

"That's because she's always right. The sooner you realize this, the happier you will be," I said.

"Just for that, I think I'm going to pull out the massive, magical retail unit I was going to launch in Chicago."

"A retail unit? You're going to build a magical *mall*?" I said, delight filling my voice. "You have to get some cookie elves to open a restaurant in it!"

My newest guard—a nervous-looking dark elf—glanced at me in wonder as we broke off from the stairs and started down the phoenix hallway.

"I was considering funding several cookie elf restaurants, seeing how much you love them, but now I don't think I will."

"Several? Hey, if you can staff it, do you think you could open a cookie elf stand in the MBRC? I keep making a motion for it, but Aysel blocks me every time, the rat. Anyway, I'm sure there would be a significant profit from it."

"Perhaps, but speaking of your partner, I need you to do something."

"Oh, how the tables have turned."

"I just submitted a request for a larger pixie powder distribution license and emailed it to your personal email address. Could you look it over? Whenever I submit it to your work account your dear *partner* deletes it."

"Certainly," I said. "You do know I have a boggart lawyer in my staff, right?"

"I could never forget my run-ins with Ed," Hunter dryly said.

"Right. I've got to go. I'm almost at my office. Fran says hello, and thank you to Cecelia for the birthday card. Also, could you ask Cecelia to give me a call later this week? I need help shopping for my next business suit. A troll threw up on my old one, and I haven't been able to get the stink out."

"I'm sure it will delight her to help. Take care, Morgan."

"You, too. Good luck groveling."

"*Thanks*," Hunter said, his voice full of sarcasm before I hung up.

I removed my ear-bud and slid it in a secret pocket in my black slacks. "Krusher?" I called, looking over my shoulder.

My goblin shadow was there, discreetly directing the dark elf and minotaur that were following me as part of the day's security team.

"Yes, Miss Fae," Harrison said, his fingers briefly resting on the battery-operated nail gun attached to his belt.

I smiled at the affectionate title. Even though I was married and had a kid, Harrison still called me Miss Fae. "I heard an MBRC guard got injured breaking up a fight between a chimera and a manticore this morning. Is he okay?"

"He has already made a full recovery and has returned to active duty," Harrison said.

"And the fight?"

"Yes, Miss Fae."

"Wonderful. Thanks for taking care of it, Krusher," I said, fondly smiling as I stopped outside a set of beautiful wooden doors that towered tall enough to give entrance to a small dragon.

There was a golden plaque on each door. The one on the left

read, "*MBRC Co-Administrator Moonspell.*" The right one said, "*MBRC Co-Administrator Fae.*"

My plaque had sticky residue on it where Devin kept trying to stick a post-it-note with his last name on it, but Aysel seemed determined that my plaque should stay with my maiden name.

Steeling myself, I pushed the door open. "Aysel, if you keep deleting Hunter's license renewals, the MBRC Board will take our cafeteria privileges again. I'm pretty hooked to my iced frappes—did you know the Bronze Fist dwarf clan adjusted the frappe machine so it will add chocolate chips to your drink?—so I recommend you stop it immediately."

"You're late," Aysel said. He was sequestered behind his massive wooden desk that was arranged directly across the room from, and facing my modern, glass desk.

"I am not," I said, brushing off my slacks before plopping down in my office chair. I looked around my desk. "I miss Baobab."

"She hasn't been on staff for three years," Aysel dryly said as one of our three joint secretaries—a shy little leprechaun—scurried between our desks.

"I still miss her. She always left me little notes, warning me when you were in a snit," I sighed. My wonderful secretary was off, living in beautiful New Hampshire with her dwarf husband. She still sent me Christmas cards, which I loved. They have the best pictures every year.

"Did you finish looking over the notes from last night's board meeting?"

"Yes. I'm surprised they got Elros to agree to add a gnome representative to the board," I said, crossing my ankles.

"Never underestimate gnomes," Aysel advised.

"Are you going to Harmoni's birthday party next week?" I asked.

"What does my niece have to do with gnomes?"

"She doesn't. I just want to know if you're coming."

Aysel sighed and rolled his eyes. "I suppose I will. Why?"

"Would you go in on a gift with Devin and me for her?"

"I suppose, provided I only lend funds and am not required to take part in the selection."

"Deal," I said, picking up the framed picture my god-daughter had given me a few months ago. It depicted an extremely unhappy-looking stick person and a smiling stick person sitting behind desks. My name was printed under the smiling stick person; can you guess who the frowner was?

Behind me, Harrison stirred.

"What is it, Krusher?"

"There is a visitor—,"

The doors banged open, and in walked my husband—unusually ruffled and mussed as he was dragged forward by our four-year-old daughter.

"Mommy!" Lindy, my precious daughter, said as she tried to launch herself in my direction.

Devin yanked her back by the pink princess backpack on her back. "Lindy, what have I said about running in the office?"

Lindy squirmed out of her backpack and walked as quickly as possible in my direction. Devin smiled and set the backpack by the door.

"Mommy!" Lindy said, giving me a gap-toothed smile. Her pale yellow eyes—the same shade as Devin's—sparkled with love and laughter.

"Hello, Baby," I said, hugging Lindy when she climbed up on my lap. "What are you doing here?"

"Daddy thaid his heart is empty and the light in his thoul has gone out because he mithes you tho much," Lindy said, a slight lisp to her words thanks to her two missing teeth.

"Really?" I said, grinning at my husband. "And I haven't even been gone for three hours. That must be a new record."

"Lindy," Devin hissed. "Daddy told you *not* to tell Mommy that!"

Lindy gave Devin a look of disgust.

"Thank you for visiting, Baby, but I do need to talk to Daddy," I said.

Lindy sighed dramatically. "Yeth, Mommy," she said, pitching her voice so she sounded heartbroken.

Behind us, Harrison shifted, distracting my pint-sized daughter.

"Kruther!" Lindy said, flinging herself off my lap. She scrambled up to the tall goblin who stooped to pick her up. When she was nestled into his chest, Lindy removed Harrison's sunglasses and cooed over his "Pretty eyeth."

"Good timing, Devin. I wanted to ask you when your next business trip to the Fairy Council would be. I know you said next month, but I forgot Aysel and I are going to a conference, and I need to make sure the dates don't coincide," I said, standing and joining my husband in the middle of our office.

"Right, I'll call my assistant in Korea and get the dates. Good morning, Love," Devin said, kissing my temple.

"Funny, with all your powers of charming females, I would have thought you would manage to get your own daughter to like you at least a little," Aysel said as he ambled up to us.

Devin looked down on my co-administrator. "It's just a phase she's going through," he said.

"A phase that has lasted all four years of her life," Aysel dryly said. "I would say she inherited it from her mother, but she most strongly bears a resemblance to you."

"Morgan, are you *certain* you wish to remain here? Couldn't you open up your own rehabilitation business at the new Fairy Council location?"

"We're not moving to Korea. My mother would kill me," I said.

"You're obligated by contract to remain co-administrator for two years," Aysel said.

"Sometimes I wonder what you had to give your wife to bribe her into marrying you," Devin said.

Aysel scowled. "Leave her out of this."

"Aysel, give Devin a break. He was up all night on a video conference with the Seelie Queen, convincing her that Chicago is a good location for a winter-vacation home," I said.

Aysel raised his eyebrows. "You succeeded?"

"Yes," Devin said, rubbing his neck.

"Well done."

"Thank you."

"Guardian Aythel, Guardian Aythel," Lindy said, tugging on the hem of Aysel's lord of the rings elf robe.

"I wish you hadn't taught her that," Aysel grumbled. "What is it, street urchin?" he said to my daughter.

"I have a joke. Do you want to hear it?"

"Must I?"

"You look tired. It mutht be becauthe you've been running through my mind all day!" Lindy said, giving Aysel her sweetest smile.

Aysel stared at my daughter as everyone in the room was silent in shock. Aysel lifted his gaze to bore holes into Devin's skull.

"I did *not* teach her that," Devin said.

"I have another! Do you want to hear it?" Lindy asked.

"NO!" Devin and I shouted.

Lindy shrugged and thumped past Aysel.

"I wonder," Aysel said, narrowing his eyes.

"Devin, who have you been talking to that Lindy heard that pick-up line?" I asked.

"No one. I would never stoop to saying something so cheesy. My flirtation is of a much higher caliber, as you know," Devin said, winking at me as he slipped his arm around my lower back. "You look beautiful today," he added, kissing me on the corner of my mouth.

"Thank you," I said, watching Aysel chase Lindy. "I should be home early today. What do you want for dinner?"

"Mmm, you," Devin said, briefly kissing me.

"Devin!" I said.

Devin chuckled, making my spin shiver. "How about seafood?"

I narrowed my eyes. "If you try to give me oysters as an attempted aphrodisiac again, there will be consequences."

"I learned my lesson the first time with that one," Devin said, kissing me on my nose.

"Stop that," I fussed as Lindy—Aysel lagging behind her—ran past.

"Why?"

"I'm at *work*, in case you haven't noticed."

"So? I wouldn't care if you wanted to make out in front of the entire Fairy Council," Devin said.

I rolled my eyes. "We can't all live as fearlessly as you. Which reminds me, Madeline and Frank are coming to dinner tomorrow."

"Why?"

"Because we're friends."

Devin sighed.

"You're friends with Madeline, too," I said.

"Only in the weakest sense of the term. Did you buy a flea bomb for when they leave?" Devin asked, stopping Lindy long enough to fix her pigtails. He let her go when Aysel just strolled within an arm's length of her.

The speedy four-year-old zipped off, and Aysel gave Devin a dirty look before he trailed our daughter in a controlled but stubborn stroll.

"Yes, although I don't think it will be necessary. Ever since I bought the flea shampoo for Frank, his outbreaks have been much less frequent."

"Really?"

"Yes. I'll have to call Frey and tell him thanks—he's the one that told me about it," I said.

"I have caught you," Aysel said to Lindy.

"Guardian Aythel, you have caught *many* women," Lindy said.

Aysel stared at the four-year-old. "I beg your pardon," he said.

"Can we take next week off from social engagements?" Devin asked.

"No. It's Harmoni's birthday. As her godparent, I really need to be there."

"You just don't want to send a refusal to Asahi and Kadri."

"Do you?"

Devin sighed. "No, I suppose not. How about the week after that?"

"We're entertaining Councilman Vincent for two nights. Remember, he's coming from Korea to work out the trade agreement between the dwarf clans from Wales and the Dutch mermaids," I said.

"How could I forget. The week after that?"

"I think that will work."

"Good. Block off your schedule. We can take Lindy to your parents for a few days," Devin said.

"The universe must be joking," Aysel said.

Devin and I turned our attention to the rather peeved high elf, who was holding Lindy so she dangled by the collar of her shirt.

"On second thought, probably not. It's most likely your fault, Morgan," Aysel said, scowling.

"What is my fault?" I asked.

Aysel's hands glowed with magic as he jabbed a finger at Lindy. "Of course *you* would see fit to give birth to the first female Pooka, *ever*," he said.

When his magic-covered fingers grew close enough, a patch of a pale yellow shield sprouted between Aysel and Lindy. When Aysel withdrew his fingers, the vapor formed into a tiny horse the size of a quarter that reared before dissipating entirely.

My jaw dropped.

Devin's jaw dropped.

"Which begs the question, of course, can you give birth to more than one Pooka?" Aysel said, cocking his head as he studied Devin and me like we were scientific specimens.

"H-Harrison," I called in a small voice.

Harrison stepped forward and took Lindy from Aysel. My beautiful daughter giggled and snuggled into Harrison's shoulder as Harrison whispered into his radio.

"I'm not sure how I feel about you asking another man for help after the stunner we just received," Devin said.

"It's only because it's Harrison that I called for him," I said, retreating to my desk.

Harrison picked up the princess backpack and looped it over his free arm.

"I should tell my father about this new development," Aysel said.

"No, you shouldn't!" I said.

Aysel gave me a smile that was surprisingly smug and childish for Aysel.

"If you break the news to *anyone* before we do, I will have you hauled in front of the Fairy Council *and* I will tell your wife!" Devin said, brandishing a finger at Aysel.

"Come along, Sir," Harrison said, nudging Devin towards the door like a border collie herding sheep.

"Morgan, we need to talk about this," Devin said over Harrison's shoulder.

"Later," I said, waving to my husband and daughter.

"Bye-bye, Mommy," Lindy said.

"Morgan!"

My shared office was quiet when Harrison shut the door, cutting off Devin's protests.

I leaned back in my chair and tried to process what happened. Of course, Aysel couldn't let me have my peace and had to be an insufferable know-it-all.

"You have no respect for tradition, do you? My father might have been right when he said partnering with you would bring this facility to its knees."

"Aysel," I groaned.

"I wonder if I could call him," Aysel said, looking at his wristwatch.

"Don't even *think* about it," I hissed, angrily eyeing Aysel across the room. "Besides, it's night-time in Korea right now."

"He's not in Korea. Because he has junior status as a Councilman, he was sent—by your *dear* husband—to Russia to settle a dispute with Baba Yaga."

"How sad for him," I said, pushing a pencil across my desk.

Aysel shuffled papers for a moment. "Are you alright?"

"Aysel, I just learned my daughter is the future Pooka. Do you think I'm alright?"

"I was just trying to be sensitive."

"So some of the information from that *Sensitivity in the Workplace* seminar we hosted last month actually sank through your pretty head?"

"My head is not pretty; it is handsome."

"Whatever. You and Devin could have started a boy-band if you dressed right," I sighed.

Something on Aysel's desk beeped. Aysel dug out his cell phone and frowned. "I'll be out for the rest of the day," he said, abruptly standing.

"Hm? Why, is your favorite store having a blow-out sale of last season's elf robes?" I asked.

Aysel shot me a look and he flipped his dark, glossy hair over his shoulder. "Call me when the ophthalmological branch sends us its projected budget."

"Right-o."

Aysel left our office, his robes swirling behind him. He was gone about thirty seconds before the door opened again, this time to reveal my handsome husband.

"Didn't you leave?" I asked.

Devin arched an eyebrow at me, looking as good as a magazine model as he sauntered across my office. "I would never go without a proper farewell," he said, leaning across my desk to kiss me on my lips.

"How did you get Aysel out of here?" I asked as my various secretaries and staff members attempted to disappear and blend in with the office furniture.

"I sent him an email from one of his peon's accounts stating that they saw someone hitting on his wife."

"Sometimes I forget how deviously clever you are," I said.

Devin chuckled, a sound as rich as a chocolate truffle. "Why of course," he said, his eyes flashing before he leaned in to kiss me again. "Although, I want a promise from you that we will talk about Lindy."

"We will," I said. "Tonight, after I get off work."

"Must it be tonight? I thought we established I was going to have you for dinner?"

"*Devin!*"

Devin snatched one last kiss before he leaned back to avoid me when I swatted at him. "Have a wonderful day, Love."

"Thanks. You, too," I said.

"I will think of you until you are home, in my arms," Devin said with a sly wink.

I rolled my eyes. "Goodbye, Devin."

After another peal of chocolate-rich laughter, Devin was gone.

I leaned back in my chair and rubbed my eyes as a faun approached my desk.

"There's a rehabilitation certification for you to sign off on, Madame Administrator," the faun said, sliding a folder on my desk.

"Now? Typically rehabilitated beings aren't graduated at this time of the year." I stopped talking when I read the name on the certificate.

I smiled and reached for the fancy feather pen Fran had given me for Christmas two years ago. I signed it with as much style as I could, adding a personal note below my signature. "Flicka, could you make a copy of this certificate and have it framed?" I asked.

"Of course, Madame Administrator," the faun said. "You have a right to be proud," she added.

"Thank you. I can't take much credit though," I said, stamping the MBRC seal in a gob of wax on the certificate.

"Of course you can, Madame Administrator," the faun firmly said. "If it weren't for you, he never would have started the rehabilitation process."

"Maybe. Either way, his graduation of the program is something that should be remembered."

"Yes, Madame Administrator," the faun said, holding out her hand for the certificate.

I took one last glance at the paper before passing it over with a smile.

We, Co-Administrator Morgan Fae and Co-Administrator Aysel Moonspell, commend Krad Temero for his completion of the MBRC rehabilitation certification.

Well done—little pervert—and welcome to the melding of the magical and mundane.

THE END

Other books by K. M. Shea

The Snow Queen:

Heart of Ice

Sacrifice

Snowflakes: A Snow Queen Short Story Collection

Timeless Fairy Tales:

Beauty and the Beast

The Wild Swans

Cinderella and the Colonel

Rumpelstiltskin

The Little Selkie

Puss in Boots

Swan Lake

Sleeping Beauty

Frog Prince

12 Dancing Princesses

Snow White

Three pack (Beauty and the Beast, The Wild Swans, Cinderella and the Colonel)

The Fairy Tale Enchantress:

Apprentice of Magic

Curse of Magic

The Elves of Lessa:

Red Rope of Fate

Royal Magic

King Arthur and Her Knights:

Enthroned

Enchanted

Embittered

Embark

Enlighten

Endeavor

Endings

Three pack 1 (Enthroned, Enchanted, Embittered)

Three pack 2 (Embark, Enlighten, Endeavor)

Robyn Hood:

A Girl's Tale

Fight for Freedom

The Magical Beings' Rehabilitation Center:

Vampires Drink Tomato Juice

Goblins Wear Suits

The Lost Files of the MBRC

Other Novels

Life Reader

<u>*Princess Ahira*</u>

<u>*A Goose Girl*</u>

<u>Second Age of Retha: Written under pen name A. M. Sohma</u>

<u>*The Luckless*</u>

<u>*The Desperate Quest*</u>

<u>*The Revived*</u>

About the Author

K. M. Shea is a fantasy-romance author who never quite grew out of adventure books or fairy tales, and still searches closets in hopes of stumbling into Narnia. She is addicted to sweet romances, witty characters, and happy endings. She also writes LitRPG and GameLit under the pen name, A. M. Sohma.

Printed in Great Britain
by Amazon

50489882R00366